HELL IN A HANDBASKET

TIMOTHY J AMERINE

Olympus Story House

Table of Contents

Preface

Beaver. Yes, beaver from the headwaters of the Missouri, the Musseleshell River in Colorado, the Powder and the Wind River in Montana are what Lewis and Clark brought back when they ended their whirlwind adventures to the Pacific in 1804.

Years later the *St. Louis Gazette* and *Public Advertiser* ran an advertisement for William Ashley and Andrew Henry in 1822; "Enterprising young men to ascend the Missouri to its source, there to be employed for one, two, or three years." This was to become the Rocky Mountain Fur Company. Answering the call were such names as Jedediah Smith, Etienne Provost, young Jim Bridger, Thomas "Broken Hand" Fitzpatrick, Hugh Glass and the untold numbers of men that were camp workers and muleskinners.

Seeing this was an opportunity for making money, many a young man ran away from the farms and clerk jobs for the lure of adventure. The part of the story that wasn't told was the dangers of trapping in the wilderness. How a spring leg trap could break a hand and sever fingers, how bears the size of wagons could devoir a man while he fought for his life. The dangers of the wilderness itself. The snow that could blind a man, the frost-bite that could cause the loss of fingers and toes, narrow ledges that a horse could fall off, ice storms that would soak the paltry wool clothes of the new trapper, the never-ending rain that could drown a man in a moment's notice, but the worst danger of all was kept from them. The American Indian.

These lords of the mountain and plains were the death of many a trapper, the Blackfoot, the territorial Crow, and the treacherous Ree. The Great Plains had the Pawnee, the Dakota, the Cheyenne, and the Osage. They weren't told that the Flathead and the Nez Perce could be a safe haven in times of peril. That the Absaroka would help the trappers in a time of desperation. None of this vital information was noted on the advertisement.

While the trappers were making their mark in history, the stern wheel paddleboats were making their mark on the rivers, the Missouri and the Mississippi. These ships provided a needed service to the returning adventurer, a way to get the plews from the fur company' to the eastern hat makers. Yes, the beaver hat was the rage, and everybody that could afford them wanted one. Thick bear coats and, fox and wolf decoration on wool coats perpetuated the fur business's existence. The small crafts worked for a penance of the large up-scale boats in any attempt to get their share of the fur market. If it meant using slave labor and young boys and girls to achieve this, then so be it. This is the story of such a couple. A young blond boy of twenty-one years and his newly formed partnership with the beautiful redheaded girl from Nauvoo, Illinois.

List of Characters

Billy White's Family
Ells Emery White, his mother
Matthew White, his father
David White, his grandfather

Dallas City
Sash Blue, saloon owner
Ruben Stillwater, Justice of the Peace
Ms. Marcia Blankenship, owner Perishing Dry Goods Store

Stiffer Farm
Hiram Stiffer father
Ester, wife
Kelly Ann Stiffer, daughter
Kathleen, daughter

Slaves and River People
Ells (White) Emery, Billy's mother
Beulah, Mary Jane's adoptive mother
Mary Jane, runaway
Ivory, runaway slave

Niota
Ashley, barkeep

Flatboat
Ike, captain
Aarnel, rower
Markus, rower
Justin, gauger

Foxes Village

He Who Walks Quietly, chief of the Kaskaskia.
Black Tail, head warrior
Blue Bird, warrior
Brave Dog; warrior
Brings Water, Brave Dog's girlfriend
Crooked Arm, warrior
Crushed Hand, warrior
Morning Dove, Black Tail's wife
Red Fish, He Who Walks Quietly's wife
Runs Like Water, He Who Walks Quietly's wife
Small Otter, warrior
Sparrow Woman, He Who Walks Quietly's wife

Crew of the Alice May

The White Man (a.k.a. William White) Billy, runt, adventurer
Rebecca Alma Magnuson, adventurer, Billy's wife
Sun "Slim" Chung, laundry worker onboard the *Alice May*
James Dugan, party guest
Josh, navigation officer on the *Alice May*
Matthew Harris, first mate on the *Alice May*
Thabo Mbekiuki, a.k.a. Jonah, Louis, fire stoker on the *Alice May*
Michael, dining room worker onboard the *Alice May*
Captain Ezekiel Meyers, captain of the *Alice May*
Muhammad "Hamhead", maître d' on the *Alice May*
René, galley worker onboard the *Alice May*
Roy, gambler
Sheila, worker onboard the *Alice May*
Thomas, fire stoker onboard the *Alice May*
Katherine Trip, party guest
Ming Yao, head laundryman onboard the *Alice May*

Bushwhackers

Rene Baker
Russell Kincaid
Joseph Roushe
Louis Osborne

Fur Trappers
William Ashley, leader of the trapping brigade
Murray Aston, trapper
Talbot Barnett, trapper
Silas Becton, trapper
Dirty Bill, trapper
Jean Bouchard, Hudson Bay trapper
Mel Bridges, trapper
Joseph Champeau, camp worker for Bill Sublette
Johnny Cottone, trapper
Ben Harris, trapper
Davey Jackson, trapper
Shannon Leif, trapper
Two Thumbs McReady, trapper
Clay Meyers, trapper and brother of Captain Meyers
Daniel Rose, trapper
Luis Sanchez, Hudson Bay trapper
Jedediah Smith, trapper
Alison Staily, trapper
Micah St. Clair, trapper
Bill Sublette, trader
Bud Warner, trapper
Isaiah Weatherspoon, trapper

Arapahoe Warriors
Cut by the Eye, warrior
Fat Belly, warrior
Soft Belly, warrior

Flat Lance, warrior
Heavy Hawk, warrior
Owl, warrior
Old Bull, Shaman
Running Bird, warrior
Sings Well, warrior
Slips in the Night, warrior
Sharpen's Knife, warrior
Talks Allot, warrior
Gray Wolf, Arapaho chief
Two Wolves, warrior
Two Toes, warrior
Wounded Bear, warrior

Crow
Iron Hand, Crow chief
Great Owl, shaman

Grand Pawnee Warriors
Blue Nose, warrior
Bright Horse, chief Grand Pawnee
Cut Finger, young warrior
Red Blanket, young warrior
Running Dog, warrior
Two Sticks, trader
White Moon, the White Man's wife

Sioux Warriors
Badger, warrior
Great Horn, shaman
Long Bow, lead warrior
Red Calf, warrior
Stands Tall, warrior

White Bird warrior
Wolf Killer, warrior

Raiders
Simon Breaker
Billy Gaines
Luke Finnegan
Frank Lisa

Riverfront People
Elijah, greeter
McFearson, constable
Melissa, whore
Mike, barkeep
Red Bow, mystery Indian
Sally, whore

Beck Farm
Ann, daughter
Beck, father
Mary Beth, daughter

Fort Mason
Janie, storekeep
Mr. Basting, storekeep
Samuel Jenkins, blacksmith

Town of Franklin
Olof Andersen, storekeep
Samuel Blevins, saloon owner
Eva Low, constable's wife
Frank Low, constable
Markus Low, constable's brother

The Journey Begins

CHAPTER 1

Billy pulled Joe the mule around for his father so they could plow another row in the crisp early morning June air. There was just enough chill in the air to get a slight shiver out of him as he laid the reins over the back of the big black mule; then he looked west. He had been consumed by the thoughts of leaving the fertile farming community of Illinois ever since he'd read about the adventures of Lewis and Clark in one of the county newspapers. He could barely contain himself as he longed for the day when he would bid Hancock County adieu.

Billy was sure he didn't want to visit the town of La Harpe again and very sure he wanted to leave the loamy dirt farm east of the Mississippi River. Pulling the reins over the plow's long handles as he watched as Matthew nodded in approval. Billy was unaware the amount of money Matthew had spent on the cast-iron plow that Billy took for granted.

Rumors around the township of a plow made out of cast iron had wetted Matthew's interest enough to see John Deere, a blacksmith, about his creation. Matthew took the wagon trip to the town of Moline, Illinois, and purchased the plow with hard currency to assure him of one of the first ones in the county. He looked at the shiny metal, gleaming from being pulled row after row. He smiled no more having to wait on wood to be repaired that would stem his productivity at a whim of a rock or root. *Nope, just line up and go,* Matthew pondered as he looked at his son. Billy could see Matthew was smiling.

"What got into you Matthew?"

"Just happy to be out here with my son that's all. Get up Joe!" as he started another row. The Whites weren't like the rest of the farmers in Hancock County; Matthew was a handsome thick man weighing in a tad more than two hundred pounds complimenting his six foot frame with close-cropped coal-black hair and dark complexion made his green eyes ever so striking, and his father David had left the fertile fields of Virginia to find more land to farm. They had sold the tobacco plantation on the Santee to move here, arriving very wealthy. They had the luxury of getting the best of whatever they wished. David had become accustomed to using slaves for his labor, but his son Matthew had been independent to a fault. He refused the offer to buy slaves; he'd rather he and his son do the work in the fields. On the other hand his uncle Lewis had scores of them in Virginia. Lewis had decided to stay on the east side of the Appalachian Mountains; there were no savages in Virginia except a few cranky Mohawks and Cherokees.

So now here was Matthew with his new three-piece plow. The chance to make a small fortune was sure to be had this year. He and young Billy could plow his land and then hire themselves out to the neighboring farms as well. Matthew was pleased that it would slice through the dirt cleanly, making it easier on his mule as well.

"Pappy, I want to go west." Billy called out from behind his father's neatly carved row. Now here was his son, who wanted no part of the new tool.

"Son, you belong here, with your mother and I. We're farmers. Your grandfather's a farmer as was his father back in Virginia. So you'll be. You've got a good education now. Use it to our best here. You and I can continue to work this land. I know you son. Just have some patience." But young Billy White had no patience.

"No Matthew I want to go west." He had become accustomed to calling his father by his common name. It bothered Matthew, but he knew Billy was already a man by western standards. But it was happening too soon; here was his son, strong, a little on the wiry side, but a hard worker that wouldn't quit. He needed his son.

"Look Billy, next year. After next year's crop you'll be twenty-two. Then you can go west. Just one more season."

"Pappy you said that three seasons ago. Will you give your leave or am I gonna leave on a bad note?" Billy persisted.

"Is your mind made up?" Matthew sighed knowing he'd kept his son longer than he'd already promised.

"Mind's made up." He answered firmly. Matthew pulled Joe to a halt.

"Will you consider working for the rest of the planting?" he asked as he dangled the smooth brown leather reins in his fingers, hoping young Billy would help until at least to late June. Young Billy looked out at the field. It was late May. A few more weeks wouldn't make a difference as he started his frequent daydreaming.

"Sure Matthew a few weeks. But as soon as the last kernel of corn is in I'm heading off." Billy answered, but his mind was on his neighbors, Kelly Ann and Katherine Stiffer. At nineteen Kelly Ann had been adamant about not giving her favors away. Marriage first then kids. No compromising. No favors. She had a grand plan of being the proud farmer's wife. Bearing children and raising crops. Being the wife of Billy White one of the most sought-after young farmers in Hancock County, she'd be the richest young wife; and the air of wealth appealed to her greatly. True she would have to put up with the copulations that went along with marriage, but that would be it.

"'Sex is so you can have children' is what my mother told me. 'All else is just lust and carnal thoughts,'" she had preached to Billy. Kelly Ann had put off the young man too many times for him to continue to pursue her any further, but her sister Katie? Now that was a completely different story. He and the younger sister had been together many times.

Billy's thoughts were of Katie, who was more than anxious to get in the loft or a meadow with the wiry young man. Billy's mind wandered to the time he and the seventeen-year-old walked home from the La Harpe School on a unusually hot early May afternoon. It was like it was the day all over again as Bill's inner eye watched it all.

"Come on Kate, let's head over to the La Moine. It's too hot to do anything else but to go fer a dip." Billy asked his blonde schoolmate.

"I'll go. But you gotta promise me that we'll do more than swim around. Promise now. I won't go unless you promise to poke me proper." She pouted as her big blonde curls fell around her face. Billy liked this girl as she was direct. He had shown her the ways of adulthood and she wanted it more than anything else in the world. Billy had proven to her over and over he could go three times in a row, and for that she couldn't get enough.

"Oh all right. I reckon I'll fork you if that's what you want?" he teased her.

"You know that's what I want. Come, let's hurry. The sooner we strip the sooner you can slip that big carrot of yours in me." She ran ahead of him on the path that led them to the slow-moving brown water of the river.

"You best hurry. I don't want to wait." She was gone, running like a two-year-old doe. Soon she was out of sight leaving Billy to walk on his own.

"Oh I'll be there. You can count on that Katie. You can count on that." Bill's mind wandered on.

Matthew stepped over grasping his son's hand shaking it firmly bringing the glassy-eyed youngster back to reality.

"Okay. Deal. Last kernel and you're a free man." He shook it firmly. "Damn you've got a hard grip." his father commented as he massaged his hand. Now that agreement was over Matthew called Joe to move out as they continued the plowing and planting. Billy followed his father dropping seed after seed in the ground as his mind returned to the river and Katie.

He came around the bend in the path to see her lying naked on her dress, her hands on her ankles pulling her legs up to expose the garden for her secret beau.

"Don't you want this?" She looked around her leg to him. He was amazed on how nimble she was. Pulling her legs up was as easy as spreading jam on a chunk of warm bread.

"Sure thing Katie." Pulling his shirt over his head as he closed the distance he dropped to the ground before her, pulling off his worn brown leather shoes. Then came the wool breeches. Now completely naked, he crawled to her awaiting invitation.

"Go ahead. Lick me like you did before." she requested. He stopped inches before her musky crotch, admiring the soft blonde hair before him. He put his tongue to the soft lips, forcing them open and buried his face in her as he began.

"Um, that's it, right there. Okay. Now, up a little. Down. Yes. Right there, now not too rough." she instructed him as she waited for his expert tongue to do its job.

"Okay, here I come." she whispered to Billy. He barely heard her, but he felt her legs encircle his head as she softly squeezed him. Then she let out a sigh.

"Okay, now I'm ready for you to stick me." the naked lad crawled in between her legs as he slipped into the wet canal.

"The first one, make it really fast. But I want you to squirt on my titties. Can you do that for me?" she asked as the young man began to perform as he'd done before. Quickly as a buck in the rut, he slammed into her.

"Here you go." He called as he pulled out, showering her with sticky white semen.

"Oh, that's very good." she answered, rubbing it all over her small white breasts. Then she pushed him back as she sat up.

"Now, I'm gonna get me a taste." She giggled and bent down as her legs were straight before her. She lowered herself to the young man's stiffening pod.

"Good thing you can go more than once." she whispered as she placed the semen-covered pod in her mouth. Bill watched her head bob up and down as she brought forth another load down her slim throat. The young girl didn't gag or miss a beat as she sat up looking at him.

"Okay. Now, I want the last one to stay in me." she requested.

"Uh, you won't get pregnant?" he asked concerned.

"Nope. I'll be starting my bleeding tomorrow or the next day. So, there's no way I can get pregnant." she said matter-of-factly.

"How are you so sure? Who told you that?" he asked as his pecker stiffened again.

"I asked Kelly Ann." She paused, "She told me how to become a woman after I'm married." I never told her I wanted to do this before I'm married. She's such a prude. She wants you worse than Parson Daniels wants coins for preaching. I never told her you were giving me favors. She'd shit, such a prude. Come, do me again." the girl requested. Billy, not one to miss a chance, quickly slipped in again for the third time. Stoking slowly, he relished the feeling of this girl as he came closer and closer to pleasing her.

"Okay. Here you go." He pushed in and waited as he filled her with his remaining seed.

"Very good young master White. Very good." She closed her eyes as Billy withdrew slowly to be sure to leave as much in as he could.

Billy came back from his daydream as he dropped the last few kernels in the row finishing out the day behind his father. They finished the field that day, Matthew driving the plow, Billy dropping kernels in and covering them up as they worked steadily. The sun dropped into the western fields as they called it a day. He began unbuckling the mule while his father began wrapping the reins on top of the harness.

"We did good today, you and I. We'll be done before June's over." He stopped looking at the vast acreage that had been already plowed and planted.

"I figure maybe the end of next week and we'll be ready to hire out for more work. Well, me anyhow, since you'll be heading out for your own life." Matthew went on, "You know, we have a friend over in Dallas City. She owns a store on the river, Marcia Blankenship. She owns Pershing's Dry Goods. I'll give you a letter of credit to stay there while you figure out what you want to do."

"Thanks Pappy. Do you think Mother will take it hard, me leaving an' all?" he asked, genuinely concerned.

"Your mother's a strong one, she's most likely figured it out already. Her an I've spoke of you leaving a few times, so I don't expect her to be too surprised."

They walked in silence back to the large white house of Matthew and Billy's grandfather, David, with a veranda front porch that elegantly wrapped around the house. It's wide broad steps leading up to the glass front door. Rockers and hardback chairs sat all around it as well as a three-place swing on the western side. With two stories, it had fifteen hundred square feet and four big bedrooms; Billy's mother stayed busy, keeping the rooms clean, and it offered plenty of storage for her crafts.

A gifted woman that hailed from New Orleans, Ells had met Matthew in Virginia when her parents had moved there in a quest for farming property. They were not wealthy like the Whites, so when Matthew asked for her hand in marriage, Dobbs Emery quickly accepted. Happy to have one less mouth to feed.

She and Matthew had been married and quickly started her family. She had a difficult labor, almost dying in the process. The doctor spoke solemnly to Matthew after Billy had been given to his mother to nurse.

"Matthew, your wife, she can't have any more children. This little one is lucky but frail." He looked into Matthew's eyes. Seeing moisture welling up, he continued, "Her insides are hurt. Her uterus got damaged with the young lad coming out somehow. She'll never be able to have children again. If your son makes it through the next month, well, he'll be fine. I'm not going to call him a runt, but he's small." The doctor wiped his hands on a bloody towel as he looked away.

That had been twenty-one years ago. Young Billy had been a slow grower. His spirit was strong though. He didn't take to harassment from his schoolmates in the township of La Harpe as he was always coming home with black eyes or knots on his skull from fighting. Many times the large boys would press Billy into a fight. Sometimes he won, but mostly he lost.

His father always told him, "Son, don't take, no guff from them boys. They're not any better than you. Stand up and fight. You'll get beat, but you'll earn their respect an' respect they can't take from you."

True to his father's words, he did get beaten. Often. But Billy fought back. He'd given his share of black eyes to the other farm boys. The big redheaded Irish boys were the toughest on Billy. At times they'd gang up on him to assure themselves of a victory, beating the lad severely.

Billy, a toe-head blond, knew how to pick his fights. He'd wait until one of the Irish boys was alone then make his move, punching and kicking the boy until his sobbing was uncontrollable.

"You tell them others they'll get the same if they come after me again. You hear me!" his face inches from the bloody youngsters.

"All right Billy, jest don't hit me no more."

So Billy got beaten less and less. He made friends easily with the other children playing pirate-and-soldier games in the fields and woods in Hancock County. The boys, as well as a few girls, found Billy to be easygoing and friendly; he found his classmates were admirable in their devotion to his friendship, eventually helping in the backyard brawls with the Irish kids. Because of this, the Irish lads kept away from him, giving him much-earned latitude.

Bill worked hard with his father in the fields and through his years in school; learning quickly Bill matured into a fine young man. Unlike his classmates that quit school when they reached twelve or thirteen, Bill stayed on until he'd finished with his last grade. The teacher commented to his mother often, "Billy has a good head on his shoulders. He's smart and ambitious. I know you're proud of him." That was the last time Billy had been in school. Now he was leaving. Maybe not today or tonight, but his time had come.

Matthew's house had an inside pump for water, three fireplaces, and a servants' room downstairs that was used as a storage room for his mother's jams, preserves, and canned vegetables. Ells took great pride in keeping the floor swept and hot food on the table. She watched them, father and son, through the kitchen's wavy pane glass window. Her heart swelled seeing her men. *My, my, our Billy's a man fer sure. He'll be a wantin' his leave soon. Matty's not goin' to like it one bit either.* She pumped out a pitcher of fresh water for them when they came in. *Nope, he ain't gonna cotton to it one iota.* She smiled to herself.

The pair went into the large barn as Billy took the mule to his stall. He called to his father over his shoulder, "You go on in Pappy. I'll take care of Joe." His father nodded in approval and headed to the house, leaving Bill to his chore of hanging up the harness, collar and reins.

"Well Joe, you and me are gonna be splittin' up here purty soon. You'll not have me to bite on. What do ya think of that?" Bill slipped into his much-practiced western drawl as he picked up the curry brush.

"Nope you's gonna get taken care of by some niggers sooner than you'll want. Maybe so they'll treat you good. Matthew says they's hard workers, that's if ya feed 'em good." He brushed the mule, thinking of where he'd go or what he'd do. *I wonder, should I get on at a store over in Dallas City? Maybe I can get real lucky an' land a job working on a steamship. Grandfather says that they travel up an' down the Mississippi like they was tied nose to tail.*

Whores. Pappy never spoke of whores. I wonder if he's seen 'em. I know Grandfather did 'cause he said he fancied them after Grandmother passed after the war. Maybe so, I can get me a whore with Pappy's line of credit. Nah, that wouldn't seem right. I'll have to get me a job. Maybe I can get into some of them store clerks' britches. He stopped briefly looking at the ebony creature in front of him. *Well, one thing first. Get the goddamned mule brushed an' some supper. I hope Mother ain't got no mutton. I like some venison from the cellar. That's what I can do. I'll be a hunter for some paddleboat. Living free an' hunting fer a living.* He looked at the three horses in the other stalls. Jed, the white-speckled Arabian stallion, and the two brood mares his father had brought from Virginia. Both were sleek and strong and as black as coal. Last spring the mares, Bridget and Fanny, had brought forth two foals each that had made Matthew a great deal of money. There were many folks that wanted high-quality livestock, and they were willing to pay for it as well. But to get an Arabian from Virginia, for bragging rights, that would be a feather in the cap of any of the people in the county So they were sought after for the local racing competition. But here were three of the finest around. He finished up with the mule. As he closed the gate, he looked around once more. *Everything's in its place,* he thought.

"G'night critters." He called to them as he latched the big door; then Bill began walking up the stone-covered path as he headed for the house.

Ells watched her husband walking alone to the house. *Billy must be finishing up in the barn.* Then she pulled the pitcher away and put it on the cotton tablecloth next to the mutton stew. Ells kept a garden where she raised carrots, potatoes, onions, and green beans that she used in her stews as well as boiled in the dishes she had brought from the east. Ever so the cook, she used whatever she had to feed her men, making her home a place of refuge after a hard day's work.

That evening at the meal, Matthew looked to his father and to his wife and then started with the news, "Billy's going to be leaving us Ells. He wants to start his life out west. So after we finish planting, I'll honor my promise to him. He'll be free to go." Ells looked at Billy through her deep-blue eyes.

"You'll do fine, son." she said, brushing her long blonde hair from her face.

"You'll do fine." she spoke steadily to her son with her strong Louisianan accent.

"Billy, I knew you'd be a leaving. Jest couldn't figure out when."

"Goddamned kid, what the hell you leaving fer? Shit. You're ol' man needs you something fierce. Now yer gonna jest up an' run off like a hound with a hard-on?" his grandfather cussed often and colorfully.

"Lookie here, you sawed-off runt, you stay on an' work with yer pappy. Hell, marry that slut over on the Stiffer farm. She's a fine stout girl. She'd bear you a passel of young un's to help with this here goddamned farm. You know me an' your pappy. We built this farm with our own two hands, pulling stumps an' rocks in order to give you a heritage. Now you're gonna up an' run off. Humph!" he spat the words out, throwing his dinner napkin on his plate, and fumed off to his chair on the porch.

"Don't worry about Grandfather, son. We'll just buy a few niggers to work this place. He's wishing he could go with you as well but knows he can't." Matthew smiled at his son. They ate quietly until Ells spoke again, "We've got a friend over in" Billy broke in, "Dallas City. Pershing's, right? Matthew's already told me about them. He said he'd give me a paper with credit to them."

"You're ahead of me Matthew." she smiled. "Thank you."

"No worries Ells. I'm sad to see him go, but I don't want anything to happen to him." Matthew spoke as he slipped his hand into hers. She lifted it, kissing it tenderly, then she lowered her face to it and hugged the weathered hand. "Billy, would you mind cleaning up for me? I've a notion to use your father here." She had a twinkle in her eye as she spoke to Matthew, causing him to blush.

"Sure thing Mother." Billy blushed as well. His mother didn't beat around the bush. When she wanted loving, she was straight to the point. They left Billy to do the dishes and put the food into the cellar that was off the kitchen for keeping. He heard his grandfather come in the front door.

"Where'd they go?" David asked quietly.

"Mother had a notion to use Matthew." He called over his shoulder as he scraped the food into the pig's bucket.

"You really gonna split off?" David asked.

"Yeppers. Soon as the last kernel is in the ground, I aim to pack up and leave." He spoke to the water in the copper apron sink.

"You know anything about living on yer own boy?" Grandfather asked, sitting in the hard-backed chair reserved for him,

"Fix us some coffee, that would do me fine this evening." It was quiet, and then he continued, "I like you too much to have you to run off. There ain't nobody else to tell my stories to." Billy could hear his fingers drumming on the table.

"You'll have to watch out fer them goddamned Miamis or the shithead Peorias. I heard they's causing a ruckus up north ways."

"Sure thing, Davey, sure thing." Billy answered, not seeing David's head slumped onto his chest.

"I'll fix us a good cup of coffee, right?" The drumming had stopped as there was no sound from behind him.

"Grandfather?" Billy turned to see his grandfathers' head on his chest.

"You don't be falling asleep on me. You said you wanted some coffee." Still no response. Bill turned and walked the few paces to his grandfather's side, his hands dripping water onto the hardwood floor. He shook his hands off and dried them on his shirt. Slowly he placed his hand on the deeply oiled walnut dinner table. He leaned down to his grandfather's side, "Davey? Grandfather?" he asked. Billy felt a strange feeling running up his spine.

"Shit." He pulled a chair around and sat down, reaching over to his grandfather's hand. It was cold. *Too cold to be sleeping.*

"Shit." He felt his eyes welling up in tears. The house was quiet except for the wispy evening breeze coming through the open kitchen window. He heard his parents coming down the stairs laughing and sassing each other.

"You get them dishes done 'fore you sit around listening to Grandfather's stories." Ells commented on Billy's absence from the sink.

"No more stories Mother." He spoke to her with tears running down his cheeks. She saw what had happened. She kneeled down next to her father-in-law, looking at his ashen face.

"Did he have any last words?" she asked, holding his now-graying hand.

"Yeah, he wanted a cup of coffee and fer me to watch out for the goddamned Miamis an' the Peorias. Said they were causing a ruckus up north." Billy took a deep breath. *I'm not going to die out here on a farm. I want some adventure 'fore I take up the rockin' chair.*

She spoke in a whisper, "He's fighter. I reckon he was just tired, and stop yer cussing."

"Shit, he's like seventy some odd years old. I'd be tired too!" Billy exclaimed and continued to cuss anyway.

"Stop your cussing, and he's seventy-four. Let's take him to his room so your mother can clean him up. I'll go to the town and get Parson Daniels tomorrow. I know he'll say some good things over him." He looked at his son, seeing the sadness in Billy's eyes.

Ells broke in, "He'd hate that Matthew. He hated that preacher worser than cold nights. Let's tell the folks he passed on but no preacher." She knew Davey well better than her husband had ever known him. She and David had many spirited conversations some that ended up in yelling. Others had happy endings of laughing and knee slapping.

"Are you sure we shouldn't have a preacher?" Matthew couldn't get past that part.

"No preacher Father. You know he didn't care for religion or preachers and their hellfire sermons. Called it bullshit and lies to scare us into giving more money to the offering plate." Billy interrupted.

"Billy, stop yer cussing. You know I don't like to hear that." she spoke sternly.

"Nobody else is cussin' around here. Might as well take up where Davey here left off." He patted his grandfather's shoulder.

"All right then. You go ahead an' carry on, but folks won't respect a foul mouth." she chided him. He looked to his father.

"You ready?"

"Yeah, let's do it." He sighed.

So Matthew and his son carried David up the wide stairs to his room. They invaded the dark room as they laid him on his quarter sawn oak bed. It creaked quietly as his weight compressed the soft feathers and the hemp rope that held up the mattress.

"Hold on." Billy spoke softly as he turned up the oil lamp.

"He liked this quilt that mother made for him. Let's cover him with it." Billy brought up the patchwork quilt from the foot of the bed. David's short-cropped white hair looked so out of place.

"Mother's gonna have her hands full getting his cow lick to lie down, eh, Father?"

"Yeah, he couldn't get it to lay down, so I expect your mother won't either." He sighed.

"Let's go on now. We've got a full day tomorrow." Matthew turned and left the room.

Well, Grandfather, you're on a new adventure now. Don't save a space fer me 'cause it'll be a long time 'fore I sit with you to drinkin' coffee. He leaned down, kissing his forehead.

"See you tomorrow afternoon." Then Billy put the lamp out and left the room.

CHAPTER 2

In the morning the house had a somber atmosphere. At the breakfast table Ells made her men eggs and biscuits with a pot of fresh coffee. Matthew held his biscuit up, admiring it slowly, then swabbed his eggs.

"Good food, Ells." As he ate, he barely acknowledged Billy's presence. Unlike him, Billy was jubilant as he entered the kitchen; after all, he was one day closer to leaving.

"Billy, you eatin' this morning?" Ells questioned her son.

"Yeppers, I surely am. I'm sad that Grandfather pass'd on, but shit, "

Ells broke in, "Billy, watch your language!" He smiled at her.

"Okay, Mother, you know he's happier where's at. Not having to be cold or hot. Not having to battle them skeeters too."

"You don't know that son. He may be in a place of uncomfortable heat." his father interjected.

"Now why do you say that, Father? Jus' 'cause he cussed?" Bill asked over his coffee.

"No, I know he cussed, but he was in the French Indian War. He did things that were not right by God. He told me stories when he returned from the war. At first he was arrogant about killing the Indians and the French. But later he spoke of how they butchered people, did unthinkable things for that he was ashamed. He'd weep, saying he was sorry to have killed so many people."

"Grandfather said they were rascals. They killed the British folks too. That's what he said." Billy defended David.

"Yes, he said that. I'll grant that to him." Matthew answered as he laid his napkin next to his plate.

"You best remember these things he's told you as you'll be meeting them Peorias or maybe even those Miamis when you leave here. We've been very lucky, living out here on the edge of the wilderness, not to have any run-ins with them."

"You really think them Indians would pester us?" Ells asked as she sat across from her husband, her coffee steaming, listening to the conversation.

"We've got some prime land here. Kicked them off we did. So I don't really know why they haven't come around asking for gifts. I heard they did that exact thing over on the Coopers' farm. Thomas Cooper wouldn't give them anything. They stole his daughter for it too." Matthew stood up and walked over to the sink with his plate and cup. He laid them down as he looked out at his land.

"It could happen to us just as well." He turned his back to the window and looked at Billy and Ells.

"It surely could."

"Don't go getting all melancholy. Your pappy done pass'd away, so you'll have to run the show here. You's gonna have to buy a bunch of niggers. You know that, don'cha?" Ells spoke evenly, putting out the fact her best friend lay in his bed above them as she spoke.

"You don't have to tell me, Ells. I quite know my father's gone." He looked at Billy with his wispy blond hair then back to his wife, admiring his wife, then back to Billy. The narrow face and blond hair and those blue eyes. Yeah, he's his mother's son.

"Come on son, we have a grave to dig."

"Yes sir. Mother, thank you for the good coffee." Rising, he reached out to put his hand on her shoulder.

"Coming, Pappy." Then they walked out, the outside door closing quietly behind them.

CHAPTER 3

Gonna have to take care of Davey. Cain't wait too much longer. The ol'boy's gonna get ripe being this warm. Ells put her dishes in the sink with her husband's as she watched the men walk to the barn.

She went to her pantry taking a few towels down. She paused looking at each of them, each towel had hand-embroidered flowers and hearts. *Gotta get on with this.* Ells took a large copper pan to the hand pump, pulling the handle several times until cool clear water rushed into it.

Matthew reached the barn first, pulling the ten-foot door open, letting Billy latched it. Billy walked to the tool wall to get a shovel but was called back by his father.

"Billy, get Joe ready first. Then we'll dig."

He turned and walked toward the mule, "Hey, ol'Joe, you ready fer another day pullin' the plow, you ol'nail?" Billy called to the mule. The big black mule turned its head to the voice of the young man and then went back to chewing on the stall rail.

"Now come on Joe, you know it ain't that goddamned bad." He looked over to see Matthew frown. "Matthew's got you a new sharp plow, so you won't get so wore out an' cranky." He chuckled as he opened the chewed-up gate.

"You've been gnawing again. Hey, ol'Joe done chew'd up another rail." He called back to Matthew as he walked in.

"Dern mule, he's just bored." Matthew answered. Billy pulled on the lead rope, turning the big mule to lead him out. Joe had taken two steps out of his stall when a four-foot kingsnake slithered by. Joe was scared of snakes, any snake. He quickly whirled to kick at the slithering creature.The snake was long gone but not Billy's leg. The iron-shod hoof grazed his thigh, knocking him across the aisle way.

"Jesus Christ Joe!" Billy cried out as he sat up rubbing his leg.

"That's enough, son. I've put up with your cussing long enough. That's the last straw. I won't tolerate anymore of your blasphemy." Matthew face was red as his hand came up to slap his only son, but he stopped, quivering, "You gather your things. You're not needed here." He regained his composure.

"Have your mother get your things together and I'll give you the credit I promised. When you can speak without cussing, you'll be welcome at our home. Do you understand? This is, is, is a very bad thing you've done. Do you understand?" His eyes were still fiery.

"I just cussed a bit. Besides, what about burying Grandfather?" he asked.

"Your Mother and I will do just fine. Gone on now. Get your things and be about your leave." He spoke, grabbing the mule, leading it over to the harness.

"That's it. Jus' go on an' git, like some cur dog? Father?" Bill questioned his father, not accepting the decision.

"You made your choice. You're not Grandfather. He cussed his whole life, and he's burning in hell for it. He was my father, and I loved him. You'll understand when you've got a son of your own." He turned his back to Billy, ending the conversation.

Billy limped past his father; there was no more talk to be had. He was dismissed. Billy set his eyes on the house as he limped away from his father.

Ells was upstairs with David, cleaning him, putting his clean shirt on, and brushing his silver hair. *I remember when we met, your hair was as blonde as mine. Now its plum white. Yer blue eyes took my breath away.*

"Damnit. Your hair jest won't lay down. I reckon it never will neither." she cussed under breath. She looked over her shoulder to make sure Matthew had not heard her. She liked to hear David tell his stories. She very much enjoyed the colorful language. But she had to be strict around her son as he was too impressionable as she'd already noticed. Pulling his dirty britches off, she saw the long handles she repaired time after time. Reaching out, she touched the soft fiber.

"Oh, David, why did you have to die?" She began to sob as she placed her head upon his thigh. "You were the one I wanted. Your son just was the only way I could get you." she spoke as she wiped the tears from her eyes.

"Goddamn!" she screamed as she pummeled the dead man. "Why did you have to die?" She stopped crying as she stood up. She walked next to the bed. She slid in next to the dead man, resting her back against the headboard, pulling him into her arms. *I'll never get to use that stick of yours again. You were good. I'll say that fer ya, three in a row. Matthew could never do that. Pop his cork once an' it's sleep fer him. I wonder if Billy will get your forkin' skill. That's something I'll ask him when we're having a quiet chat away from his father.* She heard the door slam shut in the front room. *Matthew? Billy? What they doin' back? They musta forgot something.* She slid off the bed, laying David down slowly. *See you in a while, Davey.* Turning, she walked out pulling the door shut. She headed for the stairs to see why one or both of her men was here.

CHAPTER 4

Ells floated down the stairs quietly, her hand gliding along the polished mahogany banister, not intentionally quiet but she was smooth as a cat and as quiet as a coon stealing pastries.

"Billy? What are you doing here? I thought you were with your father digging David's grave?" she questioned looking at Billy then out the window to see Matthew leading the black mule to the hitching rail next to the barn.

"Matthew don't cotton none to me cussing. A kingsnake spooked Ol'Joe, an' that sumbitch kicked the shit right outta me. Look." He pointed to the hoof mark on his leg.

"Son why must you cuss so? You know I don't care for it." she lied. The hypocrisy of her words caught up with her. The loss of her lover and friend came to a head.

"That ain't right." she said as she slumped into her hard-back chair folding her legs behind the foot rungs.

"You talk the way you want, son. I ain't got no right to tell you how to talk. You're your grandfather's son." she whispered.

"Grandfather's son? What do you mean? Matthew ain't my father?" he asked, confused.

"That's right." She crossed her forearms on the table then hid her face in them.

"You an' Davey—you an' him were—" he stammered.

She broke in, "It was like this." She began to weave the tale for her son, what had happened twenty-one years ago. "When we moved into Charleston, your grandfather an' I hit it off. Hit it off real good." She raised her head to look to her son's eyes, seeing shock, hatred, confusion, and sadness. "Now 'fore you get all pissy, wait till you hear me out."

"All right, I'll let you finish." He sat down opposite of her.

"See, what happened was, Davey was sweet on me. He was a slick talker an' smoother than Kentucky whiskey. Me an' him had a fling one afternoon, the same night your father asked me to marry him. I knew Matthew was strong an' would be a good husband. So I said yes, and we were married the next morning. So I got a good provider an' I got a good lover in one I do'. We moved here, an' the rest is history. So now you know all about it." She asked, her red eyes showing relief from the secret that had hung on to her for such a long time, "Do you hate me, son?"

"No, I don't hate you. I'm pleased that Davey was my real father. He talked a good story, an' I don't believe he's in hell for his ways." He looked out the front door seeing Matthew already four feet deep in David's grave.

"Pappy just kicked me out. Says that my blasphemy was the final straw. See, when that black mule kicked me, I yelled Jesus Christ, an', well, that was more than Pappy could take. Shit, he jest about slapped me too. So I figure he's right. I should just git." He turned to his mother.

"You said that? Well, son, I'll tell you, he's lit into me a few times fer bad language as well. I had to keep on you as I knew you were a curser an' it would rub him wrong. Jest didn't know how wrong. Reckon you'll be needing some food and the credit then." She stood up quickly, wiping her hands on her cotton dress.

"Billy, I gotta ask you something. Something real personal. Now don't be thinkin' me a tramp or whore, but I gotta know something." She turned away so he couldn't look into her eyes.

"Mother? What is it?" He stood walking over to her; he put his hands on her shoulders, feeling her trembling. Leaning down to her ear he whispered into her blonde hair. "What is it?"

She turned to look into his blue eyes, looking at his wispy blond hair. He was her son that's for sure.

"Billy, when you get favors from the Stiffer girls, " She stopped and pulled away from his grip. Leaning over the sink, her arms out with her head looking down between them, she blurted out, "Can you go three times?" Relief washed over her. *There, it's out, but I had to know.*

"Why? Why do you ask this?" He knew he could as he had known this since he was in his early teens. That's one of the reasons that Katie didn't care where or when. She just wanted sex all the time. She watched Matthew climb out of the grave, brushing himself off and begin his walk to the house.

"Tell me. I have to know. Tell me before your father comes in. Tell me!" She was almost hysterical.

"Yes, I can go three in a row. Hell once Katie got four outta me. That's what you wanted to know? That make you happy?" he asked as he noticed his father closing the distance. "Why are you so goddamned concerned?"

"David could. He's the only man I've ever heard of that could. I've asked around too, you an' him. That's it. Don't you see? Your heritage isn't this fucking farm. It's you. Your heritage is you." She ran over wrapping her arms around him, crying and hugging him strongly.

"Yes, now I understand. Here comes Father. It's to be our secret, Mother." He wrapped his arm around her as Matthew walked in the front door.

Seeing Ells's eyes swollen from crying, he knew he had been too abrupt with his decision making.

"Son, look, I'm sorry to be so quick, but I can't tolerate that cussing especially taking the Lord Jesus' name in vain. You must understand it's more than I can tolerate."

"I know now. I'm not changing, so I reckon this is my good-bye then." He released his mother. "I'll get my ruck from my room. Be back in a few shakes."

Billy walked away to the stairs. The first step up the maple tread hurt as he strained the hurt leg. The next ones were easier as his young muscles loosened up. He heard his parents quarreling as he turned midway up, listening.

"Why? Why must you be so religious? You've done drove off our son? Do you know that? You've drove off my son as well. My son! He was starting to get interesting, an' you threw him out. Goddamned you, Matthew White! I hate you at times!" She was screaming now. Then he heard it. The crack of skin on skin. He jumped halfway down the stairs. Graceful he wasn't. Missing a step, he fell down the rest of the flight. He heard another whack. He got to his feet and hobbled to the kitchen in time to see his father on the floor, his mother standing over his father. with a cast-iron skillet.

"Go on. Me and your father were just finishing, right, Matthew?" she spoke evenly, but Billy could see her reddening cheek. He looked down to see a black eye coming on his father's right eye.

"Yes, we're finished. Ells, you best pack your bags as well. I won't have a hellcat as you under my roof. I'm the lord and master of this house, and I won't tolerate a blasphemy-speaking woman." He spoke with his rage barely contained.

"Oh, I see. Well then, I'll be on my way. Come on, we won't need this man where we're going." She threw the skillet on the floor it, bounced and slid to a stop next to Matthews foot. She grabbed his arm as they left the red-faced farmer in the kitchen to nurse his black eye and swollen cheek. When they were upstairs he asked her, "What are you gonna do? You gotta stay here."

"No, I don't. I have half of everything here. I know I can count on the Justice of the Peace over in Dallas City to get things straightened too." she said as they parted for separate rooms.

Billy took but a few minutes to wrap up his clothes and grab a warm wool coat. He left his room and walked into his parents' room seeing her bustle about like a carefree lark, humming a song as she threw her clothes into a large carpetbag. She looked over to see Billy standing there.

"You done already?" She asked.

"Hell, I only have a few things. You gonna get the credit to stay in Dallas City too?" he asked as she hefted the bag.

"I won't be going there. I'm heading back to Virginia, back to where my kin is. I don't worry about money. I've got means too." She smiled, leaning forward, showing the ample cleavage. Then she shook her breasts, sending them swaying under the cotton dress.

"Mother? You ain't gonna do that, are you?" he asked, quite shocked.

"If I want to, I can. It's not something I haven't done before." She smiled, shaking her breasts again, watching Billy's jaw drop open. She heard Matthew coming up the porch stairs.

"Our secret, right?" She winked.

"Yeppers. Ours alone." He spoke as he turned to see Matthew take the last step up the stairs. He was walking like the weight of the world had come crashing down on his shoulders. His steps were a shuffle as he closed the distance to the pair. He walked past the two to his roll top desk, lifting the accordion like cover he quickly wrote a note of credit at the Blankenship store. He pulled the drawer out where he kept his currency's. He quickly counted out $200 for Ells. Closing the drawer and he rolled the top down and turned to his family.

"I'll give this to you now." He handed Billy a paper saying that Matthew would pay the tab accrued by Billy. "And this's for you." He handed Ells a stack of American currency.

"This is it? How much are we splitting?"

"I gave you $200. That's more than fair." He turned and walked away.

"I want Fanny. Billy wants Bridget." she called after him.

"I'll give neither of them to you. You've a considerable amount of money there, Ells. You best be leaving." He turned his back to them assuring the conversations ended. As the head of the house, Matthew determined when there was no more to be said.

"I want $1000, Matthew!" She said in a gravelly voice.

"No" he spoke over his shoulder to her.

"I made this a home, loving and taking care of you, clean clothes, hot food and I want $1000!" She was almost yelling.

"Alright! If that's what it'll take to get you out of my life then." He fumed back to the sectarian and all but ripped the roll top off, "Here! Leave now!" He slammed $800 in her hand. His face was red and the blood vessels were bulging on his temples.

"Billy? You ready?" she asked.

"Yeppers. Let's git." He answered as they walked past Matthew. He didn't turn when Ells walked past. Neither one spoke a word. So down the steps, mother and son walked arm in arm and out the front door, leaving it wide open. They had walked to the edge of the barn when she stopped and turned to look at the house he had built her. The white wash was fading, and the weeds were starting up again.

"I won't miss pulling them." she spoke, looking at the house.

"What? What won't you miss?" Billy asked, looking at the big house that was to be his heritage.

"Weeds. Matthew will let this place fall down on him, and he won't buy any niggers. Nope, he's a proud an' stubborn man. He can't cook, he'll let himself fall apart in a few months, an' he'll die." she spoke solemnly as she turned her back on her home.

"You sound sure of yourself." Billy turned, putting his arm around his mother's shoulder.

"I know him. Without me to help him along, he'll just die. We'll never know unless someone sends news. Now where shall we go?" Her arm wove around his waist as they set off to the west.

CHAPTER 5

Matthew didn't live as long as Ells thought he would. The day his wife and son left, Matthew was feeding Joe in the evening when the mule saw the kingsnake again. This time, though, it wasn't a grazing kick but a full hoof in the back of the head. Matthew White died instantly. Matthew never missed a church service in the small parish of Parson Daniels; the little congregation took notice that the farmer hadn't shown up and immediately sent over Luke and Marcia Bigaloe to investigate. They found the mule had walked out and was grazing on the grass near the front of the house. With no Ells or Billy to tell the tale, they set out for a search to find out what had happened. They found Matthew in the barn on the dirt floor; his head caved in by the hoof of the mule and his prize Arabian horses in their stalls. On with the investigation. They knocked on the front door waiting to hear David cussing them to leave as he had become accustomed to doing, but silence greeted them as they called to Ells or Billy. No answer quelled their curiosity; so they entered the house, calling again, hoping to hear Ells coming done the stairs to greet them coolly as she'd done before. No voices. Then the smell caught their attention.

"Someone's dead. You don't figure Mr. White done killed his wife, do you?" Marcia asked Luke.

"No. You stay here. I'll go look." Then Luke slowly climbed the stairs waiting to see a body hacked up, but he only found David in his bed. The smell was too much for Luke, so he returned to Marcia.

"It's Mr. Whites father. He's been dead for a few days. We should go. Let Parson Daniels come back and bury these folks." They closed the door and left the house. They would tell the local constable of the findings. The property would be sold and the money sent to Matthew's brother in Virginia. So the legacy ended.

CHAPTER 6

Billy and his mother set out for Dallas City, traveling as a carefree pair. Arm in arm they walked through the summer wheat fields.

"Billy, when did you start getting favors from the Stiffer girls?" she asked candidly. Billy found it strange that soon as they left the farm he had considered Ells as a woman, not his birth mother. She was a looker even at thirty-seven, with her long blonde hair she kept pulled back, her brown skin from the days in the wind and sun, and her blue eyes. She had her cotton dress unbuttoned, showing great amounts of her cleavage to her son as they strolled through the fields of wheat.

"I reckon I was fourteen 'er so. I tried to get a poke with Kelly Ann, but she'd have no part of me unless we got married. I didn't want to get hitched, Mother, " She broke in, "Call me Ells, would you? I like it when you call me Ells."

Billy looked at her as she turned to meet his eyes. The twinkle was there like when she had a use for his stepfather.

"Sure thing. If that's what you want, then that's what I call you. Anyway, Kelly Ann's a prude. I figure she'll dry up soon as she's popped a coupla kids out. But her sister, now she's a mink. That goddamned girl, shit, she wants it all the time. See, one time, her an' me were out behind her pappy's barn. We was kissing, an' I had both of titties out, " He stopped talking for a moment. "You know, I feel like I can tell you anything Ells, anything." He looked away from her to the western horizon.

"Well? What happened? Tell me what happened." She pulled on his arm. Bringing his face to her, she kissed him on his cheeks. Not a peck. No, she stayed there a brief moment too long. Billy found himself tingling.

He found himself thinking thoughts that had never been there before. "Well, she pulled my bean out. Usually she just lets me play with her tits, but this time she pulled it right out." He stopped weaving his tale as walking a few steps in silence, he found he liked to make her anxious to hear the story, so he started teasing her with bits.

"Billy, don't stop now. You're a little shit. Keep telling me what the little slut did." She squeezed his arm.

"All right." He pulled his arm free and whacked her rump through the thin cotton dress. She jumped forward.

"Billy White. You stop that." She giggled.

"Well then, after she had my pod out, she started jacking me off. You sure you wanna hear about this?" He cocked his head looking at her.

"In the worst way. Tell me everything. Forget who I was. I'm not her anymore. She's gone forever. That woman is dead back there at the farm, she's never coming out again. So Billy now, I'm just a woman with a handsome young man, walking through a beautiful field of wheat. That's what I want, every last detail. Every drop of your story, every breath she took, every time she touched your pecker. I wanna hear it all." She smiled at him.

"Okay, you're sure?" he quizzed her, knowing full well she wanted to hear it all.

"Goddamn, you little fucker. Tell me what happened!" She turned and jumped on him, knocking him down onto the ground. She was on top of him. His arms were free, but she sat on his waist.

"Tell me what happened!" She cocked her head sideways and seductively smiled. Billy brought his hands behind his head as he looked up at her. Her breasts were heaving slowly, almost ready to fall out. He found himself harder that a fence post, seeing this woman on top of him. He blocked out she had given birth to him, suckled him, and washed his balls off when he shit himself. No, now she was just a woman that wanted to hear his story.

"Well, where was I?" he asked, making her tell him.

"She was jacking you off. She was pulling on your bean. She was pumping your piss'r. That's where you left off!" she spoke as she slid back positioning herself over his groin.

"Feels like you have something going on under me." She turned her head slightly.

"Yeppers, you want the story or what?" He smiled up to her.

"Go on." She closed her eyes, sitting up. "Go on."

"Well, she was pulling on me real good, an' 'fore you know it, I popped. She wasn't none too happy about it either. She said if that's all I got, then she was gonna find someone else. I told her to try again. So she looked down at all the spooge on her hand. Then she licked it off. Well, I got hard right now. Shit, Ells, I had never ever heard of a girl doing that." Ells rolled her head back as she wiggled herself on Billy.

"Hold on." She stood over Billy as she raised her dress. "Won't need these." She pulled her underwear off right in front of Billy. He could see her dark triangle of hair as she stepped out of them.

"There, that's better." She lifted her dress, rubbing herself slowly. "Go on. Tell me how she sucked your dick." she spoke in a whisper.

"She said I tasted good, and she bent down slow like an' sucked me off. She was good, Ells, shit. I popped again. She sucked it up too." The sight above him mesmerized Billy as she had her hand rubbing on the mound of hair as Billy spoke.

"That's two. You said you could go three?" she spoke looking down at him, her hand still rubbing herself.

"Yeppers I did. Well, after she got done sucking me off, she said she wanted me to slip it in her. I was already hard, so she hiked up her dress like you are right now, and then she sat right down on me. Yep, she rocked back an' forth, leaned forward a few times, kissed me a bunch, and then I filled her up but good." Ells looked down at Billy.

"She sat on you, like this?" She lowered herself onto Billy's britches, grinding slowly as she leaned forward.

"Then she pulled her tits out. Like this?" She took one hand and pulled both white breasts out before Billy.

"Then she wiggled them like this?" Ells made her white breasts inches from Billy's face. The red nipples were standing up like prairie dogs, inches from his lips.

"Yeppers she did, but they didn't look as good as these." At that instant Billy's life changed forever. He wanted sex. All the time, anyway, with anyone. This woman wasn't his mother anymore. She said it. Now he believed it.

"This ain't gonna do." He reached up, pulling a nipple into his mouth. The commitment was made. His teeth raked the hard nipple; he pulled and teased them viciously as he felt the woman above him shudder.

"You're right. This ain't gonna do." She stood up and took two steps back. Looking down at Billy's britches, she could see his pod struggling against the wool cloth.

"Nope. This ain't gonna do one bit." She sat down on his shins as her fingers were a blur opening up his buttons. Out came Billy's pod, standing straight and tall.

"Nope. Ain't gonna do." She leaned down, putting his pod in her mouth. She sucked and jerked him as Katie had done. Billy reached down to hold her head firmly as he released himself into her. When he was finished, he released her head as she sat back up.

"Yep, you're David's son. Taste jest like him too. You got some more boy?" She pulled her dress over her head, leaving her shoes on. She looked down on Billy, smiling. Billy looked at the shape of her breasts, the narrow waist, the dark hair covering her privates.

"Let's get to business Billy. I know you got two more, maybe three if I play it right." She reached down to pull his wool britches down to his ankles. Then she pulled his shoes off and finished pulling his pants off. He sat up and pulled his shirt over his head.

Using it for a pillow, he lay back down.

"You's ready, ain't you?" She smiled.

"Yeppers, I surely am. Stick it in woman." He ordered her. Ells slid forward as Billy could feel himself against her warm flesh of her stomach, then the coarse hair, and finally he let himself touch her innermost part.

"You gonna wait forever or you wanna it in?" He looked into her eyes.

"I want it in the worst way." She reached down with her hand and guided him into her. Billy felt the warmth of her as she sat up.

"There, that's what I want." Then she lifted a nipple to her own mouth, flicking her tongue to it.

"Fill me up, fill me up. Don't hold back on me. Fuck me as hard as you can." She released her breast and leaned back over Billy, letting them sway before him. Not one to miss a chance, he rammed into her. He went harder and harder with each stroke, her knees were almost coming off the soft wheat as he buried himself with each stroke. "You're hurting. Me. You're hurting me. Don't stop! Make me beg!" Billy was confused but kept ramming her as hard as he could.

"Here. I. Come. Slut!" Billy raised himself into her, holding his position as he filled Ells up with his seed.

"Oh Christ. Oh Christ. Oh Christ. You fucked me. You really fucked me, oh Christ." She rolled off the young man, touching herself gingerly. "Oh Christ, oh Christ." She turned her face to Billy's.

"You hurt me."

"Hell, you said to." Billy answered, confused.

"No. Not bad. Good hurt, very good hurt. Let me get this ready again. Oh Christ, you hurt me so good." she whispered as she pulled around to get Billy's pod hard again. He felt her lips, and then he could feel himself getting hard again.

"You're ready? Oh my fucking god, you're already hard!" She sat back in dismay. "You're rock hard already? Jesus fucking

Christ. Fucking hard." Billy was shocked hearing the swearing, but it didn't matter. Here was a woman that wanted him and was willing to give herself to get to him. She went back down on him, pushing his pod deep into her throat over and over.

"Hold on, woman. Here it comes again." He spoke in a soft voice. She was up and over him like a flash of lightning. She buried it deep into her as she sat straight up.

"Let me have it. Let me have it." She moaned, her head falling from side to side. Billy obeyed, releasing himself into her again.

"Good. So good." She stood up and took a step forward, letting the seed drop onto Billy's hairless stomach. She stood there watching the drip. She stepped off and picked up her underwear and began wiping herself off.

Billy lay there watching her, the breasts, the rump, and her blonde hair now hanging about her shoulders.

"Don't move young man. I'm not done with you." she spoke as she put her finger in herself. Pulling out the semen, she continued to wipe herself off.

"Not too many men like their own taste. I figure you ain't no different." She looked down on him.

"I ain't never tried it. Might like it if it was in your pussy."

"Well then, let's see?" She stepped over him, squatting slowly.

"Lick it up good then." Billy could smell his seed, but her musky odor was too much for him. Lifting his face into her, he sucked and bit the delicate lips. She was right. He didn't like it.

"Run your tongue up till you find my button." Billy brought his tongue up until he found her clitoris. "Suck it, bite it, hurt me there." she asked. Billy did. He could feel her oozing down his chin as he worked on her. Closer and closer she was getting to climax.

"Oh! Billy suck it. Suck it. Oh Billy!" She was tossing her head to and fro now as she climaxed.

"Let's see what we have here." She leaned down to his stiff pod. Into her mouth it went. Billy could see she wanted to continue, so he obliged her as he started again on her clitoris. He felt her lower herself more until she had her stomach on his chest. But she kept on his root, bringing him closer to popping.

"Here I come!" he spoke into her.

"Me, too!" She flooded Billy with her honey as Billy filled her stomach with his seed. She scooted back until her face was over his. Then she held his face as she kissed him, letting his seed into his mouth along with her tongue as she kept kissing him. Billy didn't pull away, but he didn't want it. He returned her kiss until she came up for air and sat back. Opening her legs, she touched herself slowly.

"My, my, you're full of surprises." she commented as Billy spit out his seed.

"Come here." He asked.

"More?"

"Nah, I want your pussy juice to get the taste out of my mouth." He answered.

"Well, by all means, taste away." She crawled over him again. Billy buried his tongue deep, pulling her honey into his mouth. He pushed her forward as he sat up looking at her butt. He leaned forward and kissed her there.

"What? Are you still frisky?" She turned to him.

"Nope, just kissing you." He answered. She stood up stretching.

"My, we had a good time, didn't we Billy White?"

"Yes, we did, Ells White. Yes, we did." he answered as he pulled his shirt on.

"Ells Emery. My name is Ells Emery. Ells White isn't alive anymore." she spoke as she stepped into her worn out drawers. *Not sure I even need these.*

"You're quite a lover, you runt, quite a lover."

"Yeppers, you're a handful too, you sleazy slut." He smiled at her as he pulled his wool britches on.

"Yes, and don't you ever forget this. Ever." she spoke as she pulled her dress over her head.

"Oh, I won't 'cause as soon as we find something to eat, I'm gonna want to be eating you." He smiled as he pulled each shoe on and began lacing them snuggly.

"Oh? Well, I've some news fer you. It won't be anytime soon." she answered, as she rummaged in her bag until she found a hair tie.

"What?" He stopped, looking at her his mouth agape. "No more?"

"No," pulling her hair back into a ponytail. "This is where we part company. I got what I wanted. We'll have this memory forever." She paused stretching her back.

"Jes' to let you know, I've never been fucked like that. Ever. It was truly the best I've ever had. Good-bye Billy."

She picked up her carpetbag, turned, and walked away into the wheat field, leaving Billy standing alone, letting it all sink in. *Gone. She's gone, jus' like that, huh? I might as well get use to his, being alone. I'll head over to the Stiffers' an' see if Katie wants to fork,* he thought as he picked up his jacket and his meager ruck, heading for the farm miles away.

CHAPTER 7

The blue sky of an Illinois spring was shining on Billy as he walked closer to the Stiffers' farm. The plowed fields were making it hard to walk for the runt, the dirt continually falling into the top of his shoes.

"Walk with the row, not again them. That's what Grandfather would say." Billy spoke aloud. He turned walking to the end of the field. Then he turned and walked the edge until it led back to the Stiffer's farm.

"I'll be glad when I'm out of this an' into a town. Yeppers, Dallas City, here I come." he spoke as he saw the barn of the Stiffers on the horizon.

"Oh, Katie, you yellow-haired slut. Come suck my pod." he spoke aloud.

"She's in for a surprise today." He continued to talk to himself more often now that he was alone. *I wonder where she's at? In the barn milking that derned cow, picking up eggs?*

He closed the distance coming on the corral side of the farm; he could see Mr. Stiffer working on a broken part of the fence.

"Hallo, Mr. Stiffer." Billy called

Hiram stopped, stood, and shaded his eyes.

"That you Billy White?" he answered back.

"Yes sir, it surely is. Is Katie about?"

"No. And neither are you." Billy was a bit confused over the last part of the conversation.

"Why's that, Mr. Stiffer?"

"You've been ruining my daughter, an' I'll have no more of it." he spoke, dropping the wood moving closer to the fence post. Billy couldn't see the Derringer flintlock rifle standing in the shadows.

Billy closed the distance as he felt the hair stand up on the back of his neck. Something was going wrong, but he didn't know what it would be. He froze in his footsteps.

"You and the tramp runn'd off on Mr. White. Matthew was a good friend to me an' mine. Good Christian man he was." Hiram continued speaking, drawing Billy closer as the farmer neared his gun.

"What you mean was?" Billy had stopped walking; he was twenty yards away from the farmer now. The sun was in Stiffer's eyes, so he wasn't too sure on the distance, but Stiffer felt he could get a shot off at the runt if he held still.

"What happened to Matthew?" he asked watching the old man moving closer to the fence post. *Something ain't right. Something jus' ain't right.*

"You don't know? Your father's dead. The black mule done kicked him in the head an' kilt him, just like I'm gonna do to you!" Stiffer had made it to the gun at last. Hefting up the long slender gun, he brought to aim but Billy wasn't there. He lowered the Derringer a bit, trying to find his target. Then he saw Billy had made it to the side of the barn. Bringing the gun up in one fluid motion just as he had during the War of 1812, he pulled the trigger and felt the gun ram against his shoulder. He looked through the smoke only to see the runt was gone as was a chunk of his barn.

"Damnit!" He seldom swore, *I want that runt dead an' if that slut of a mother was here, I'd shoot her as well.*

Billy dropped his jacket and ruck and was hotfooting it away from the barn as fast as his feet would carry him, putting distanced between himself from the angry father.

"Damn, Pappy got kilt by Joe." He was panting now as he had been sprinting for almost the complete width of the plowed field. *Good thing the credit is in my pocket. I can find more clothes.* He slowed a bit when he heard a zing by his ear. He turned his head to see Mr. Stiffer on the side of his barn loading for another shot. *Goddamned, that ol' bean's a good shot!* Billy had no idea of zig zagging to make himself a poor target. He tripped and fell flat on his stomach in the freshly plowed field, which just saved his life. He saw the puff of dirt four feet ahead of him. *That woulda been through my heart!* he thought.

Back on his feet Billy headed for the nearest rise he could see. It was off to his right not more than twenty-five more yards away. Then he felt his shirt tug as the bullet ripped through the linen material. *Good god, I gotta git outta range or I'm dead!* his mind screamed.

That last shot had been 125 yards, not the farthest Stiffer had killed a man at; but he was rusty, not having to shoot for such a long time. That's what saved Billy's life. He dove over the crest of the hill and rolled to the side. Not looking up, he crawled quickly for a narrow rain ditch at the edge of the field. He heard another zing. A small sapling just inches from his head fell over, cut in two. He fell into the ditch and began crawling when he saw a clump of brush not more than twenty feet away.

"Won't stop a bullet, but he won't be able to see me." Billy spoke through a trembling voice.

Another zing, and the dirt right next to his face spurted up in a geyser. He stood up and took off at a full run as he made the brush. Ripping his way through the wild roses and blackberry bushes, he stumbled and fell down into a rotten log. Lying there, he waited. Another lead ball went harmlessly over his head, hitting a tree five feet to his left.

"Cain't see me no more. He's just trying to get lucky." He panted. As he waited, the rotten log was hit by another lead ball.

"Christ!" he screamed and took off crawling for the back side of a large walnut tree, putting his back to it. He panted, waiting for his heart to slow down. Billy ventured a quick look around the tree. *Nothing, that's good.*

"Whew. That ol'bean's sure is pissed." Then he saw a chunk of bark fly off the tree right next to his hiding spot.

"Good god!" He was up and running again to the next tree that would afford him safety. Another lead ball hit it.

He's on the run fer me! I can outrun that ol'knot! Billy scrambled to his feet. Looking down he found a deer trail that led away from Mr Stiffer. He ran like a man possessed, his feet didn't fail him this time. The distance increased as the trail was twisting through the woods, dipping and turning quickly. Another ball hit the tree right in front of Billy. It was high though. Billy ducked to the right and the left as he ran for his life. Up ahead he saw a large ditch, *must be a crick. Shit, if I get stuck, he'll shoot me like a rabid dog. Gotta jump it!* He was running as fast as he could to jump the ten-foot gulley. The next bullet went through the heel of his right shoe, knocking it off. With only one shoe, he continued around the next bend that led around a large hill.

"He cain't shoot around a corner." He panted. Looking around, he decided to climb the hill, the hardest way out; but if he was on the high ground, he could see where Stiffer was. On all fours he climbed like a treed coon. As he crested the hill, he stayed on his hands and knees. Crawling slowly he looked to his right. Below him was Stiffer and a pair of speckled dogs. *Looks to be pointers,* he thought. *Gotta find some water. Gotta get shut of my scent.* Back to his feet he ran for the open field again, but with Stiffer below, he had a better chance of outrunning him.

So he ran, not stopping for anything. Then he came upon his savior; a dead deer. *This has to help. Them hounds won't be able to tell me from this here dead critter.* He grabbed a hunk of rotting leg and rubbed his feet with it and then smeared it on his legs and finally on his hands and face. *Christ, this stinks. Hope it works. Might as well bring it in case* as he heard the distant baying of the hounds. He took off running again. *Damn, he sure is a vengeful ol'nut. Hope he gives up soon. I'm running outta ideas.*

He changed direction, heading west again. *Dallas City is only a day away, and at this pace maybe sooner,* he thought. He kept running, and they kept coming. *Shit, no wonder they can follow me. I'm leaving a shoe print an' a footprint. Even a blind man can follow that.* He was slowing again, kicking off the remaining shoe. *Git your ass back to running Billy boy, or that ol'bird will have your guts for supper.* So his pace increased. Running along the field in the soft dirt, he saw something that would give him the edge. A road. *I can lose them fer sure on this. With so many tracks on it an'me stinkin'like a rotten critter, they'll have to stop.*

He finally reached the road to Dallas City. As he stepped onto it, he heard the faint baying of the dogs. Turning to the west, he took off, hoping to find a wagon or someone walking to mask his scent and hide his footprints. He began to jog. It wasn't too bad as the wagons and carts had kept it smooth and mostly rock free. Tiring, he saw something in the horizon, a cart? His wait was rewarded as he came up to a slow-moving hoop-covered oxcart. Throwing the deer leg into the weeds, he slowly approached the cart. He saw the man and woman on the seat looking forward. He slowly walked up listening for a child or dog to warn the owners, but no noise came to him other than the creaking of the cart. He approached it and closed in on the driver's blind side as he looked into the cart. Luck smiled down on him for once. There hanging from a hook on the back hoop was a pair of shoes, black and used but they were a pair. He slowly reached up and lifted them off and stopped, watching the cart pull away. Happy with his theft, he stepped off the road to a small stump where he sat down and tried the shoes on. *A tad big but only a tad.* Pulling the laces slowly, he tied them and returned to the road as the hounds baying came to his ears.

"He won't be able shoot me if there's a bunch of people 'round." he spoke aloud. "You don't sound so sure of yourself Billy boy." He laughed. "I ain't." The runt answered himself as he walked quickly to catch back up to the cart.

Once again he slowly approached the cart, looking carefully inside while he stayed out of sight. He saw a black no-script wool coat and a small-brimmed dark-blue wool hat. Carefully he picked the hat up and placed it on his head, a perfect fit. Next came the coat. Once again luck held out for him as he retrieved it in the same manner. *Must be a kid's coat an' hat 'cause they fit perfectly,* he thought as he once again stopped watching the cart pull away.

"Let's loose them dogs." he spoke aloud as he stepped off the road. *Hmm? Those look inviting.* He peered at a small patch of oak trees not more than a hundred yards from the road.

"I'll just move to Dallas City this way." he chatted aloud as he turned to hear the dogs getting louder. The blond lad did a quick sprint to the trees, quickly darting behind a larger oak to await the hunter. His wait wasn't long as the man and his two pointer dogs found his only shoe. Then they were lost. They couldn't find the scent. Around and around they went, howling and barking but not finding where he had stepped into the gray-and-green sanctuary. Watching from a hundred yards away he watched Hiram Stiffer toss the shoe to the ground and turn, looking up and down the road. He didn't move. Billy was panting as he waited.

Stiffer brought his dogs closer. Picking up the shoe again, he let them smell it one more time, hoping for any chance the scent would put them back on the trail of the defiler of his daughter. Both dogs sat down and panted, going nowhere. He tossed the shoe once again and turned to leave, but he stopped dead in his tracks looking directly at the oaks where Billy was holed up. Billy watched him for his hiding place. Bringing up his Derringer, he shot the tree that hid him. Bark shattered, but he didn't run. He stayed right where he was. Another shot but at a different tree this time. Six shots were fired and all at different trees.

"That ol' man's trying to spook me into running." he whispered. He slowly snuck a look around the tree to see the old man walking back toward his farm.

I'll just stay right here till I'm sure he's gone. No since taking any chances. He looked up at the sky through the canopy of the oak tree. *Only have a few hours till nighttime anyway.* Then he noticed the limbs above him. *I bet I can climb right up there an' watch Stiffer leave fer sure.* So he climbed carefully up the tree until he could see where Stiffer was. *Good thing I didn't run off directly.* He saw the revengeful old man sitting on a stump watching the oak trees where Billy was hiding

"Can you believe that? He's just sitting, watching." He whispered to the tree that was hiding him.

Stiffer got up and began walking to the oaks where Billy was hiding, slowly at first. Then he picked up the pace until he and the dogs were running flat out, but Billy didn't move. He just hugged closer to the trees using the foliage to conceal himself as he watched the tracker closing the distance. Soon he could see the spots on the dogs and the scowl on Stiffer's face, but the farmer had no idea he was within a stone's throw. The dogs milled about, but the mixed scent was confusing them. He heard a snapping branch off to his right as Stiffer brought up his gun and fired like he had been born with it. he looked fifty yards away, and a large doe went down thrashing and then she was quiet. *He came over for a deer? Well shit my pants.*

"Well, too bad, we lost the boy's scent. Bet he's over in Dallas City by now." he spoke as he reloaded his smoothbore flintlock.

"That's okay. We'll get him in a while." He kneeled down, caressing his dogs.

"That's right, girls. We'll let him get all comfy, and then I'll slit his throat and bring you his liver." The dogs yipped and turned in circles with the softness of his voice. He treated his dogs well, and his touch reflected that he was a kind man to them.

"Let's git 'fore we have them cussed Miamis come over and steal our meat. Come on, girls. Come on." Billy watched from his tree limb as Stiffer began to carve off a leg. Then he backed up under Billy's sanctuary. The he stood quietly and the old man of many a skirmishes lifted his gun to fire, but an arrow went through his eye and out the back of his head. He was dead before he hit the ground. The dogs sat down. Without a command, they had been trained to sit and wait. It was their downfall as they too became pincushions.

It all happened quietly, no shots, no barking. Just silent death. He still didn't move as the Miamis, or at least he thought that was who they were, came over to retrieve the gun, possible bag and arrows. The brightly painted roach-cropped warriors spoke in a hushed voice as they began cutting the man and dogs into pieces as they waited for the others to get the deer. When the deer was secure, they faded away into the forest. *No sounds. They made no sounds. I think I'll wait till it's dark. Then I'm gettin' the hell outta here. Christ, that was close, twice. I'll have to 'member that. They made no sounds whatsoever. Damn.*

Finally the sun started to fall into the western tree lines and darkness hid him as he climbed down from his tree. Then he felt around to see if the Indians left anything, hoping for a scrap of food or a pocketknife; but nothing had been left as his fingers found the gaping wounds, the severed head, the cold guts, along with the torso. *Ughhh!* He vomited into the ground next to the corpse, so he had escaped death twice in one day.

He headed for the road but stopped and waited in the tree line. He would be open game if he went out now. If there were more Miamis in the area, he'd be gutted for sure.

Billy watched it all from his secret hiding place. Thankfully he'd not been found out. *All right, git!* He told himself as he headed down to the dirt road that led to Dallas City and his new sanctuary. On the road he picked up the pace and began to run to the faraway city on the great river. The Mississippi waited for him.

CHAPTER 8

Billy walked and ran most of the night. By the false dawn of his second day of travel, he was on the tiny outskirts of Dallas City. It was hardly a large town; all told, there was a small two-story wooden inn, a tent saloon, and the wooden building of Pershing Dry Goods Establishment.

"There's where I'm sittin' my ass down fer a while." He spoke in a soft voice. The town was as quiet as a graveyard as he slowly walked in; the sun had started to peek over the eastern tree line when all that changed. The local roosters began crowing long and loud, enough to make someone in the inn yell at them to shut up.

"Ah, here we go. I'll just sit right here an' have me a wait." Billy plopped himself on one of the tall back chairs on the walkway in front of the dry good store rocking it back against the front of the store.

"Yep, wait 'till they show up." Billy pushed the small-brimmed hat to the back of his head while he watched the town come to life. Soon he could smell meat cooking through opened windows. *Gonna be a fine day, now that I ain't gotta be lookin' over my shoulder for ol' man Stiffer,* he remarked to himself once again. *Damn, the Injuns were quiet.*

The sunlight came over the east side of town and began to bathe young Billy with warm rays. *Hmm, this feels just about right. If I had me some biscuits and coffee, well, that would be perfect.* Billy closed his eyes for a moment when he heard the dirt being crunched from someone walking towards him.

"What are you doing? I'd like to know what you're doing loitering about?" the voice called to him. Billy opened his eyes to see a short stout red-faced woman looking at him with stern eyes over her pointy nose.

"I was waiting fer the owner." He calmly pulled his hat down and answered back, *No sense getting all riled up. Yet.*

"Oh. I see you meaning Mr. Pershing?" she asked, trying to see what the drifter knew.

"Nah, I'm waiting fer Marcia Blankenship. She's the owner."

"You ever met her? This Blankenship woman?" she interrogated further.

"Nope, never had. My father, Matthew White, said I was to give her a letter of credit 'till I could get on my feet." he spoke calmly.

"You Matthew White's son Billy? Heard you and your mother ran out on him. Parson Daniels says so." she spoke, not moving to open the doors.

"Why should I tell you my private business unless you be Marcia?" He looked up and down the street to see if anyone else was making tracks toward the store.

"I'm Ms. Blankenship. Now answer my question." Her eyes narrowed to thin slits of fire.

"I can tell a much better story if I had some coffee an' a few biscuits." he sassed her, lifting the bill of the hat up. Before Billy knew what had hit him, she was up the two steps and had him on the wooden walkway with her knee on his throat.

"You best think your words out very carefully boy. Very carefully." she spoke, barely able to contain her contempt for a snotty brat.

"Sure thing. Let me up, an' I'll tell you as much as I know. No bullshit." He stopped mid sentence.

"You ain't down on cussing are ya?"

"Tell me. Now." she spoke thin lipped to Billy.

"Let me up an' act civilized an' I'll tell you." Billy sassed back.

"Fair enough." She released Billy as she stepped back and fanned her nose.

"You stink. Don't you ever bathe?" She commented.

"Not fer a few days now." He answered.

Her hand dove into her apron pocket, producing a large skeleton key; she stepped over Billy and pulled open the double doors to enter her store.

"Come in and don't try to steal anything because I'll be watching you." she spoke as she vanished into the dimly lit store.

"I got a line of credit you know." Billy spoke as he got to his feet, grabbing his hat. Walking in he pulled his hat back on as he was surprised at the goods she carried. Guns, hoes, cloth, canned fruit, candy in big jars, cigars, umbrella, and hats.

Marcia came back to face Billy. "Spit it out!" her face inches from his.

"Well, it happened like this." He leaned back against the chest-high countertop, his elbows resting comfortably on it.

"Me and Matthew had come up with an agreement of me leaving. He gave me a line of credit. But the morning before last, I was fixin' to leave."

She broke in, "Where's this leading to?"

"Marcia, it's how things happen."

She broke in again, "That's Ms. Blankenship to you!"

"All right then, Ms. Blankenship, it's the way it happened." He defended his story to her.

"Is that so? Well, get to the point then."

"I was leading Joe the mule out when a kingsnake startled him. He kicked me, I cussed, and Matthew sent me away. He and mother got into a quarrel, he slapped her a few times, and she hit him with a skillet. He kicked us both out. I just found out from Mr. Stiffer yesterday that Matthew had died."

"Where's your mother? She should be there taking care of the place until she finds a new husband. What about your grandfather? He can still run the farm?" she lashed out with her words, throwing her attitude of dominance at Billy.

"Mother's gone back to Virginia. Matthew gave her some cash money to leave, an' she did. For all I know, she could be in Kentucky by now." He said the words, but he wondered of his mother, as he had recently found out, Ells wouldn't be too far from men. That means she's heading for Hannibal, not Kentucky.

"David died two days ago. Matthew threw us out before we could bury him proper like." Billy felt the sadness all over again.

"Your mother? Where's she off to? I told everyone she was a, " Marcia stopped as she was very close to telling how she really felt. But she went ahead. She didn't like this runt or his mother.

"Tramp, she was a tramp. I hope she comes to her senses and goes back to that farm. Your grandfather and Matthew worked hard to get it to where it was."

"You don't seem to understand. She wanted the horses but no part of the farm, or the house. My father threw her out. Just a few dollars to get on with. That's it. Now you tell me, Ms. Blankenship, would you go back to that?" Billy put her on the defensive.

"It's her responsibility to carry on. Men will do that kinda thing. They have to be stern and rule. They have to be stern." She stepped back and began wringing her hands.

"That line of credit? Since you are his son, it's up to you what's to be done. Go speak with the Justice of the Peace. He can sell the place for you. Then you won't need a credit." She turned, leaving Billy standing there hungry and thinking. *I could sell everything an' be rich, find Mother, an' her and I could be together. That's what I'll do.* He headed for the door.

"Good day Marcia." Billy called to her as he walked out. Just before he closed the door, he remembered Mr. Stiffer and his pointer dogs. He opened the door, sticking his head in.

"Oh yeah, I almost forgot. Mr. Stiffer? He's dead along with his pointer dogs. Miamis got him a few miles out of here toward his farm. Carved him up bad too." *That'll keep her thinkin' fer a bit.* Billy chuckled as he closed the door and stood on the steps looking up and down the street. *Money, I'm gonna be rich, rich, rich,* he thought. He looked at the inn across the street; right next to the sign was a star and a sign saying Justice of the Peace.

"Here we go." he spoke aloud.

CHAPTER 9

He opened the door as a small bell tinkled at his arrival. A pudgy older man in his sixties with a round red face and small round glasses rose to meet Billy.

"What may I do for you sir?" he spoke clearly and politely.

"I'm looking for the justice of the Peace." Billy asked as politely as possible as he pulled his hat off.

"That's me, Ruben Stillwater. What may I do for you Mr. White?" He asked, but he already knew, as the whole town did of what had happened, as gossip traveled faster than a hungry fox.

"Well, a coupla things. I wanna sell my father's property." Billy claimed to the impish-looking man.

"Lock, stock, and barrel?" Ruben asked. He could already see dollar signs floating in his head.

"Yeppers. The whole shootin' match." Billy said as he looked at the balding man.

"How soon? How soon do you need the money?" Ruben already had a plan formulated.

"Soon as possible." Billy fell into the snare as easily as a quail in a box.

"I can get to look at the property this morning and have a number by this afternoon. How would that be?" Ruben pulled a tad tighter, bringing the trap to play.

"That would be fine. Could I get a cash advance 'till it clears? I had a line of credit but Marcia won't honor it."

"You'll be fine, I'll speak to her. Let's go right now." Ruben got up leading Billy to the door, he opened it allowing Billy to leave first. The young lad squinted from the bright light and quickly replaced his hat. He turned to see Ruben flip the Closed sign over as the door clicked shut. Ruben walked in front, "Let's go." he spoke to him like a puppy dog. Bill's mind raced, *out of the frying pan an' back inta the fire. Damnit I hope this goes good.* They crossed the street to the door of the woman who had been such a hard-liner to him.

Ruben pulled the door open as he called to her, "Good morning. I believe you've already met this young man." he spoke as he stepped closer to her. "Marcia, you be whiter than a sheet. Are you all right?" Stillwater rushed over to the woman as she sat on a small chair, which could barely contain her ample bottom.

"Yes, we had a brief conversation." she said as she spoke slowly.

"Did he tell you about Hiram?" the woman asked with tears welling up in her eyes.

"What's this about?" He turned and rushed to Billy, grabbing him by the arm and shaking him like a badger would a mouse.

"What about Hiram? Speak up damn you! What have you done?" He was at a panic now.

"I've done nothin' to that ol' goat. Goddamned Miamis kilt him dead. That's what happened." Ruben released him as he turned resting his arms on the on the polished countertop. Burying his face in them, he began to weep. *Well, tan my ass an' send me to bed,* he thought. *Hmm?* He looked at the woman her eyes wet with tears as well. Ruben regained his composure as he went to Marcia.

"Here, Marcia, let me help you." He folded his arms around her as she laid her head on his fat belly, weeping openly now.

Billy was absorbing the whole scene in front of him. *Maybe this here woman had her a thing going on with ol' man Stiffer. That has to be it. But why's this goddamned Justice of the Peace so derned interested?*

Ruben looked at him with hatred in his eyes, his face turning red; he released the plump woman and began walking towards him, each step a deliberate move.

"Boy, you best be telling me everything. I have a notion to hang you right now, I mean this instant, so you best choose your words carefully." He spoke, his lips pursed almost shut. Ruben could barely contain himself from the anger and grief this runt had bestowed on his small river town.

"Hold on now. I didn't do nothin'. I saw Stiffer kill a doe. Then them cuss'ed injuns made him and his pointer dogs pincushions. I didn't get a chance to help. There was too many of 'em. Shit. Stiffer didn't even get a shot off. They were so quick an' quiet." He defended his actions and left out the part about being chased down like a wounded wolf.

"Why were you with Hiram? He hated you with all his heart for what you've been doing to his daughter." He stepped closer to Billy. The blond runt knew at this point he was in a world of shit and it wasn't going to get any better. *Gotta think of something quick like, but Christ, what can I say to change this here fella's mind? Think! Think!*

"We were hunting together, yep, then the Miamis surprised us, and I got away, but they got ol'man Stiffer." Billy lied as best as he could.

Billy's lips had barely closed before Stillwater was on him, his hands on his throat, throttling him as hard as he could. The runt tried to pull the hands away, but Ruben's rage was more than he could handle. His eyes bulged as his face turned blue. Years of fist fighting came into play instantly as he brought his knee into Ruben's groin as hard as he could. Ruben's grasp lightened as Billy rammed his knee again, feeling relief in his neck. The runt reached up, pulling the hands from his neck, watching Ruben's eyes in shock as Billy began to overcome his weight and strength. Once more Billy kneed him. The last one caused Ruben to fall to the floor, his hands going to his groin as he rolled into a ball moaning.

"Goddamned you! What the hell you doing? You just lay there!" he yelled at the prone man as he rubbed his neck.

"I don't give a rat's ass what you three had cooked up. You can't go around trying to kill people." He looked at the surprised woman and the prone man.

"Shit. Yeah, me an' Katie had a fling, but it weren't nothin' to go an' try to kill me over. Christ." Billy stepped closer to the door as Stillwater rolled to his knees then slowly rose. Bill could see the pain in his eyes as he stood straight.

"You're a son of a bitch, and you're going to die for the pain and suffering you've caused! That girl is Marcia's daughter, you dumbshit. Hiram was my brother!" Billy's mind was reeling. *I thought Katie was Stiffer's daughter? How in the hell? Wait, he's Stiffer's brother and she's her daughter? This's too crazy.* He froze as he saw Ruben lean over the top of the counter, *I gotta git going before he gets a gun. I can see it. He's gonna shoot me. Gotta git quick.* Ruben's fingers searching for Marcia's flintlock pistol. His search was rewarded as he brought it up and began to train it on where Billy had been.

Billy was right to leave when he did. When Ruben had gone to the counter, he bolted out the open door, running as fast as his feet would carry him.

"Hurry Ruben, he's getting away!" Marcia screamed as the surprised man aimed at where Billy had been. Seeing his prey gone, he rushed to follow the blond runt.

Billy had been shot at before and he didn't care for it one bit. As soon as he was clear of the doorway he veered to the right then ducked behind the store running to the woods not far behind the small town.

"Shit!" was all he could muster up as he ran for his life. Ruben ran out expecting to see the runt running down the center of the small town. He saw Marcia out of the corner of his eye; she had grabbed another pistol from her display case.

"You go right. I'll go left. He couldn't have got far." he spoke to he as they began the search.

"Hey Ruben, what's goin' on over there?" the owner of the tent saloon called from the front of his flap door. Sash Blue had already heard of the money to be made from Matthew's death. He wasn't going to be left out of the deal either.

"Sash, White's runt tried to rob Marcia. Get your gun. We gotta get him 'fore he gets too far!" Ruben lied as his eyes searched the dirt road for any sign of the runt.

Billy had no idea of what had transpired. I'm looking for the Justice of the Peace as he was a mile award before the small town had got organized.

Running. Shit. I'm on the run again. Bill's mind raced for ideas. *The river, there has to be something on the river. Work. Place to hide. Something?* he thought as he continued to run.

CHAPTER 10

The small town had no clue of where the runt had gone. Just as well though. They were going to get the whole farm and horses to split up now. With no one to contest it, they were going to be rich.

"Well he's gone." Sash came back from behind the store where he'd lost Billy's trail. The six-foot man wiped the sweat from his bald head. At 250 pounds, he sweated a lot. Running was one of the things he hated the most too.

"You okay Marcia?" he asked, wanting to assure his partner was up to snuff.

"I'm fine." she answered, slipping the gun into her dress pocket. She turned to Ruben.

"Hiram. My sweet Hiram." She then wept.

"Come on now, Marcia. Come on." He helped her up back to the store.

"He's gone now. Let's go find Hiram and bury him and the dogs proper."

"What about Hiram?" Sash asked if Hiram was out of the picture. That would be another cut to be split up.

"The runt said the Miamis killed him outside of town." Ruben spoke over his shoulder as he walked Marcia back to her store.

"Too bad. Hiram was a good man." was all that Sash could come up with at the time, but he was already counting the purse they'd be getting.

CHAPTER 11

The runt continued running looking over his shoulder occasionally in fear that they'd gotten horses to chase him down. He watched the sun begin to sink into the western tree line. He noticed the hills and hollers of the east had given way to marsh and standing water. He cautiously approached the tree line of the sagging debris-covered weeping willows.

There were a few trees that been broken down in the last flood that got Billy's attention.

"That musta been some kinda flood. Shit, if the water line's plum up there on that tree", he paused looking back over from where'd come from.

"Shit, I bet Dallas City's was swimmin' fer sure." He climbed up on one of the fallen trees and he stared at the Mississippi before him.

"I cain't believe how big it is." he spoke in a slow whistle. *I need to find a place to hole up fer the night.* His stomach growled. "And some food." he spoke quietly to the tame-appearing river before him.

"I ain't had a good meal since Grandfather passed on." He rubbed his stomach, thinking about all the things that had happened in a few days. Climbing down the tree, he found a game trail that led to the edge of the muddy river.

"Goddamn, it's huge!" he spoke as he looked up and down the river. *Well, I guess I'll head south. I heard Matthew say the riverboats stop at Hannibal, so I'll go there. I wonder how I'm gonna get across this thing. Maybe it'll stop on this side over at Bluffs? It's a fer piece, or at least that's what Matthew said the last time he went over to it.*

Bill looked for a place to lay his head as dusk was rushing to him. *This place looks good as any I reckon,* he thought, looking at a few limbs that had fallen over on a downed tree, giving it a crude lean-to appearance. Crawling under them, he inspected his new temporary home. *Yeah, I'll do okay right here.*

Bill sat looking out through the branches as he saw a paddleboat slapping the waters as it went south in the dimming afternoon light, its lamps giving the ship the appearance of fireflies hovering about as the ship passed out of sight. He felt a tickling on his arm. Looking down in the remaining light, he saw a small deer tick climbing up his arm.

"Damn. Now what? Ticks. I hate ticks." He plucked it off and crushed it between his fingernails. His mind drifted back to the day's events. *I wonder about the sumbitches that chased me out of Dallas City. Cain't do nothin' about the money from the farm, though I know Ells woulda loved to get her hands on to it. I wonder where's she's at.* Bill's mind began to drift as the darkness increased. Soon his eyes closed as he thought of his mother and the pleasure she had brought to him. He drifted into a light sleep when it clouded up and started to rain. The heavy drops woke Bill up as he became soaked to the bone in just minutes; he sat in his little hovel of sanctuary as the summer storm washed over him. In the time it took to start, it stopped, bringing the moon out in all its brilliance.

Staring up at it, he decided it was time to move. *Might as well walk as sit in the mud here. Ain't doin' no good now how. Gotta find some grub.* He crawled out on his hands and knees, the rich black mud squishing up between his fingers. He could feel the mud soaking through his knees of his wool britches. Pulling his coat tight, he stood in the moonlight. He looked north and then south.

"Well, might as well get." he spoke in a low melancholy voice. "Sure would like to find something to eat." He stepped south and headed inland to drier ground.

CHAPTER 12

Bill began to walk through the waist-high grass in the light of the moon, keeping the river on his right as he ambled south. Bill began to walk through the waist-high grass in the light of the moon, keeping the river on his right as he ambled south. The moonlight made travel quite easy as the game trail stuck out like a black ribbon against the tan grass.

"Shit. I bet if I found me a farm, I could talk my way into some work. Get some food anyway." he spoke aloud, trying to bring his spirits up.

The young lad walked through the night, not seeing anything other than the moon. Occasionally he heard a coyote yap or a hoot owl challenge, but for the most part it was just a quiet walk in the dark. Bill was beginning to feel the lack of food and sleep as he stumbled.

Gotta find a place fer a nap. Or I'll fall down right here. He looked for a clump of trees or a thicket of hedge to crawl into as he continued to walk. The false dawn began to creep into the field where he walked as he stumbled again. This time he wasn't able to catch himself as he fell headfirst into the trail.

"Shit. That's far enough." He moaned as he got back to his feet.

"I'm just gonna walk over here and lay down fer a minute." The lad stepped a few paces off the trail and fell into the soft grass. Sleep overcame him quickly as the morning sun rose over the eastern tree line.

Something woke Bill. It was voices, and he wasn't alone. *Who'd be talkin' out here?* His mind raced for any recognition of a familiar voice, but no one came to mind. He lay still trying to figure his predicament.

"Beulah, what do you think? Is he dead?" the voice asked with a thick Irish accent.

"No. He be a sleepin'." Another female Irish voice answered.

"You gonna rob him?" the first female voice asked. Bill still made no movement to open his eyes or flinch a muscle.

"No, I already searched him. Shit. Poorer than us." Beulah spoke back, but it sounded to Bill as her voice was fading. Then Bill felt a sharp kick in his shin.

"Hey, you! Wake up!" Bill's eye sprang open from the pain.

"Ow! Why'd you go and kick me?" Bill sat up quickly, his hands rushing to his shin. But before his hands could reach the violated appendage, there was a knife at his throat.

"Don't go moving too quickly now laddie." came the sultry female voice. Bill's eyes moved toward the voice, his body staying rigid with a knife to his throat.

There before him crouched a redheaded woman. Bill's eyes took in her clothes and face as he waited for them to make the next move. She had on a ragged coat that was unbuttoned, showing her very low-cut dress. The white breasts were all but falling out. His eyes went to her cherub-like face. It was young full and round, and her teeth were straight and her eyes blue. *What the hell you doin'? You're about to be turtle food, and you're eyeballing this here woman with a knife to your windpipe.* Bill's mind raced.

"Well now, Mary Jane, let's see what we have here." Beulah asked as Mary Jane pulled the knifed hand away.

Beulah asked. "Who are ye? And where are ye bound to?" As Mary Jane lowered her knife.

"I was on my way to Hannibal. I just took a nap fer a bit." Bill spoke as he picked up his hat. Slipping it on casually, he watched Beulah take it all in.

The one called Beulah had hair that was as orange as a spaniel's, her eyes were green as moss, but she looked noticeably bigger. thicker. With no coat on, she had her dress unbuttoned all the way down to her waist, assuring Bill a full view of her large breasts adorned with the largest nipples Bill had ever seen. *I bet they're as big as a tea saucer plate.* His mind raced to the shape and fullness.

"You like what you see?" Beulah asked Billy, lifting them up for his inspection. She appeared to be about his mother's age.

"Yeah, shit, who wouldn't? I mean, any woman with titties as nice as yours can pull a knife on me any." he never got his sentence finished when Mary Jane was on top of him, forcing him to his back the knife on his throat.

"Listen here, ya little speck of fly shit, that be me mother ye be talking about. So ye best be watchin' ye tongue or I'll be havin' it for a snack. Ye be unnerstanin' me, runt?"

"Yes." was all Bill could say as he was afraid if he breathed the knife would cut his throat. *I jus' wanna to be out of here.* His mind raced for an option for something to throw things in his favor. Nothing came apparent. Yet.

"Now, now, Mary Jane, let's be giving the young lad a moment." came Beulah's smooth, silky voice. The redhead released her hold on Bill. She stood over Billy looking down at him, smiling.

"No offense runt. Ye just be careful of how ye speak about me mother." Then she winked at him. Bill couldn't figure this girl and mother out. One moment he was enjoying a good view. The next he was close to being slit from ear to ear.

"All right boy, be tellin' us straight now. Where, when, an' why?" Beulah asked.

"You ain't gonna hump me with that knife again, are ya? I mean, your mother's got a extrafine set of titties," Bill paused, waiting for Mary Jane to come back at him. But she just smiled as she sat next to her mother.

"Nice as these?" Beulah asked as she reached over to her daughter's dress, pulling one out at a time. Bill was in heaven as the breasts were large with nipples the size of his thumb tip. *I've done died an' gone to heaven.*

"I'd have to hold 'em to be sure. I'd hate to make a rash decision." Bill laughed aloud, knowing there was something more than them showing him their breasts.

"No. You'll not be doing that small one. Now, where are ye headed an' why? Best be truthful or Mary here with slit ye wide open, and I guarantee she can do it." Beulah's beautiful smile faded into a stern frown

"I'm on my way to Hannibal to hire on a paddle wheeler." Bill spoke as he crossed his legs, not being aware that Indians sat cross-legged.

"Look, Beulah." Mary pointed to Bill's sitting position.

"Boy, you be a half breed?" she asked, her eyes going to thin slits.

"What if I am? Will you both slip them clothes off an' let me hump the hell outta you?" Bill sassed, testing the water. *I wanna see what these women want. If I can get them laughing an' giggling, then there's a chance I can get that knife an' get the hell outta here 'fore I get skewered.*

"Lad, ye best not be joking about that. Are ye a half breed?" Beulah asked, pulling a knife of her own.

Bill understood the severity of his next few words, so he began slowly as he uncrossed his legs.

"Lookie here, I just sat here, but I ain't no half breed. I'm from a farm over by La Harpe. I'm on my way to get work on the river. That's all." The little blond runt watched his captures carefully.

"Ye haven't finished yet there, runt me boy. Why? Why ye be leaving a good farm? Why ye ain't got nary a cent? Hell, ye ain't even got a knife. Ye have to be the sorriest shit I've seen recent like." Beulah laughed as she nudged her daughter. Both women laughed, their breasts back into their dress now.

"Aye. Very sorry." Mary Jane chimed in.

"Look, I've told ya enough. If you're gonna put my lights out, then get on with it. I don't like being threatened. I don't give a shit if you got the best tits in the county." Bill spoke, his eyes going wild. He stood up watching for Mary to make her move.

"So get on with it or get the hell away from me." His wait was rewarded as she stood quickly, taking a lunge toward Bill.

The blond runt from Hancock County had never been in a bona fide knife fight, but he'd defended himself before. Bill was waiting for her to make her move; and when she thrust the knife toward his heart, he turned to the side, grabbed her arm, and pulled her past him, twisting her arm as she went by, causing the knife to drop. As the blade was falling, he dropped to a knee, catching it handle first as he spun to see Beulah rising to her feet.

"Well now, I see we have a sly little one here. What else do you know blondie?" Beulah asked as Mary regained her footing behind Billy.

"I know enough that two hussies like yourselves will make short work of me. I know you've done this a few times before. I know that one or both of you might die this morning." Bill backed away so both women were in front of him.

"Is that right? Why don't you give Mary Jane back her knife, and we'll take you to our fort? Give you some grub and a cup of coffee." Beulah spoke as she tossed the knife from left to right. Then faked a jab.

"What you say there blondie, or do you want to play?" She reached down pulling her dress up, sticking it into her belt so as not to stumble on it, as she was preparing for the fight. Bill's eyes went to her unveiled crotch. A thick mound of red hair hid the ground he held sacred.

"Oh, I see. You like pussy. Drop the knife, and ye can slip into my pussy. Yep lad, me an' Mary will let ye slip right in. Just drop the knife. Yer pod will be no use to us if ye be dead. Go on. Just lay it down, and we'll have some fun, me an me daughter here. What ye say?" She began to circle him.

He weighed his options; food sounded good as did sex. He knew nowhere to get either of them. Killing these two women wasn't something he wanted to do as he's never killed anyone, let alone a knife fight with an experienced fighter.

"All right. You got a deal." He flipped the knife and offered the knife to Beulah handle first. *If I'm wrong, I hope she does it quick.*

"Ye be shitting me? Ye think I'd be offering ye a poke an' food? Shit, I can carve ye liver an' be back to the fort in time for a poke before the sun sets." Beulah dropped her guard as she took the knife.

"Here Mary Jane." She tossed the knife to the redhead.

"All right laddie, follow us."

"Beulah, ye ain't really gonna take him back to the fort, are ye?" she asked as she sheathed her knife.

"Aye, he coulda killed you right out. Hell, he might even stuck me a time 'er two 'fore I cut his gizzard out. But he be honest." Beulah spoke over her shoulder as she set out for the mystery camp. *Well now, this is a change. Hopefully she was honest, or I'll be the treat for the evenin',* Bill thought as he watched her sashay down the trail. It was midmorning now, and the sun was already starting to bake the grass and dirt.

"He'll be fun won't he, Beulah? He'll be fun." Mary Jane called to the leader.

"Aye, he'll be fun." She laughed.

CHAPTER 13

Bill followed the tall woman ahead of him, watching her rump rock from side to side as they walked south into a large forest of hardwood trees.

He was reminded of his hiding place when the Miamis were killing ol'man Stiffer. *Damn, here I am again. Hopefully there ain't no goddamned Miamis around.* Bill's mind raced as the forest closed in on them.

"Beulah, ye think Ivory will cotton to us bringing another mouth to be feeding?" Mary Jane asked.

"No more than when ye walked into my life, daughter of mine." she replied, not turning her head.

"Well, if Ivory lets him stay, then I aim to use him first." Mary Jane promised her mother.

"Ye have to get past me an' Judith. Judith will say she's hers as ye've had the last two to yourself." Beulah sassed her daughter.

Bill was listening to the banter and felt he had most likely made the right choice. *Gettin' used by these here women makes more sense than fightin'.* The only thing he wasn't sure of what he was being used for. *Hopefully it'll be like when Ells pulled on my pod.* He smiled to her back. Mary Jane closed the distance, speaking into Bill's ear, "Ye be on ye best behavior boy. Ivory's a good man, but he don't take to slackers or thieves."

"That so? We'll see then." Bill sassed her back, not letting their intimidation get the best of him. Then he saw the vertical logs of the fort. The gate, an old barn door, slowly swung open as a tall shirtless muscular black man appeared in the doorway. His bald head was reflecting the sunlight, making it look like a shiny brass doorknob. *Good god, that's a huge nigger!* Bill's mind raced of an escape route as he scanned the small fort. Nothing materialized.

"Oh, what have you brought home today, Beulah? I see he's small and white, not like your usual catch. Or is this MJ's choice?" The big man smiled at the women as Mary Jane gave Bill a push, causing him to miss a step and fall.

"What the hell?" He spat as he rolled over, seeing the crowd encompass him.

"Just wanted ye where I can keep an eye on ye." she answered as Bill looked at the faces around him. Bill sat up as he watched the door being closed. Bill looked up at the crowd around him; blondes, redheads, niggers, old and young, fat and skinny. *What've I gotten into?* raced through his mind.

"Get him cleaned up to meet her." the big black man spoke. Then he turned and walked into the crowd.

"Well, ye heard Ivory. Get your ass up boy. Sounds like Ivory wants you to meet her. I don't know how you rate to meet her on your first day. But she must have a reason." Mary Jane helped him up and pushed him towards the stone well in the courtyard of the fort.

"Go on. Do your toilets." she sassed Bill, "ye smells pretty bad too." as she leaned on the edge of the stacked rock well as the afternoon sun began to sink. The crowd vanished as quickly as they had assembled. Bill scanned his new surroundings; a few young men were in the corral working a colt, a few women were sitting with a quilt across their laps, but for the most part, the place looked deserted. *Where'd they run off to?* he wondered.

"Hey, what's your name?" she asked.

"Why? You gonna suck my pecker if I tell ya?" he sassed her back. Bill saw the hand coming and swiftly ducked. Dropping down and spinning around, he swept her legs out from under her, causing her to fall to the ground.

"You look better down there." He stood up, reaching for the bucket full of water. He splashed the water on his face, ignoring the woman on the ground. Mary Jane wasn't sure what had happened. But she was sure she was sitting on the ground and this runt was the cause.

"How'd ye do that? I mean I was standing here. Then I was on the ground. How's that ye know how to fight so quick like?" She stood up leaning against the well once mor

"Learned in school. Being a runt I had to fight a lot, so I learned a few things." He pulled off his coat then his hat and finally his linen shirt showing his white skin.

"Well, look at ye, not a scar to be seen. I figured ye woulda been all tore up. But ye ain't a runaway, so I figure ye be telling the truth about ye being a farmer." She reached over with her hand, running along his shoulder.

"Not much meat. I guess ye've been starving, ain't ye?" She smiled as her beautiful face lit up like an angel.

"Yeppers, been hungry fer a spell." Bill splashed some more water on his chest, wiping himself down with his shirt as he looked around the small fort.

"Who's this I'm gonna be meetin' anyway?" he interrogated the Irish lass before him. Immediately Mary Jane hand retracted.

"She's the queen of us. Ye'll be a seeing her soon. Look over there. See how folks are leaving to their tents. The queen says she wants to be alone with all the newcomers. That be ye, so I bid you adieu, runt." Mary Jane bowed out and vanished to the tent nearest the corral. He stood looking around, not a soul to be seen.

Bill stood next to the well as he got a chill from the atmosphere. He barely noticed the wet shirt on his back as he looked for the queen.

I cain't see a real queen being here, so this here lady musta got these folks bamboozled by something. Hell, maybe she's a wizard or a witch an' turns people into toads. Hey, what a gag, getting turned into a toad. Then with my luck, a damned cat would eat me, he continued to reconnoiter the small fort. *Looks to be mostly tents inside the walls, one, two, three doors into small cabins, a corral, looks like a garden. Nope that's two gardens, but don't see no jail. The far door opened, and the queen appeared. Well, here we go.*

Slaves and River People

CHAPTER 14

Bill strained his eyes in the dimming light, looking at the woman walking into the courtyard. She was dressed in a cotton dress with a bright-red shawl draped over her head and around her shoulders even though it was uncomfortably warm. Something was familiar; the walk, the way she carried herself. The blonde hair fluttering from beneath her shawl in the afternoon breeze. *Hell, if I didn't know better, I'd say that was Ells, but she's in Hannibal.* He stared as she closed the distance. *Yep, it's her. Luck finally smiled at me.*

As Ells closed the distance, she too recognized the runt before her. *It's my son! What? Well, he said he was going west,* "Billy?" Her eyes went wide as her expression told Bill he was in high cotton.

"What are you doing here? Never mind that. Come here!" She opened her arms as Bill quickly walked into them.

"Goddamn, it's good to see you, Ells. Do I call you queen?" he asked.

"Oh, never mind that. My god, I didn't think I'd ever see you again. What're you doing here?" She held him close, feeling his embrace, smelling his hair, reminding her of the field of summer wheat field. *I missed my son. He's been so good for me.*

"Good to see you, Ells. Can you tell me what's going on here?" He spoke into her ear as she continued to hug him.

"Later son." she whispered to him. "Later."

With her arm around him, she looked at her small dynasty she had taken over.

She called out in a loud voice, "People of the River, come out!" The blond runt watched the doors open as the people filtered into the courtyard.

"This lad's to be honored. None of ya better harm a hair on his head, ya'all understand?" she spoke with her usual Louisiana accent as she looked at the twenty-some people that filled up the courtyard.

"Well, I ain't talkin' to hear myself rattle on here." She looked at her people nodding and smiled.

"Beulah, take the runt here and get him cleaned up. See if you can do something with his clothes. When he's all cleaned up purty like, bring him to me in my room. You good with that? Or do I need to get someone a little younger?" She smiled at her longtime lover and friend.

"No worries, My Queen, I'll be getting the runt all gussied up fer ye. Come laddie, let's get ye ready." Beulah said as she pulled the runt over to her, an arm wrapping around his shoulder.

"Let me get my coat an' hat." He pulled away from her as he grabbed them from the well's lip.

"All right, Beulah, lead the way."

Bill and Beulah walked away as he heard Ells speaking to the crowd, "How're we doing on supplies, Ivory?" He never heard the answer as he and Beulah entered into a tent near the corral.

"How's it you know the Queen?" Beulah asked as she led him to a small stool in the corner of the old tent.

"Oh, I just know her from over in Hancock County. How 'bout you? When did you meet her?" Bill pried, trying to find out what this little village was about.

"With some luck, we'll get them rags of yours cleaned up. Strip 'em off, lad. All the way down, socks too if ye have any on."

Bill laid his coat an hat down as he began to pull his now-dry shirt off. Looking around the tent, he saw an old steamer trunk near the front and a pile of blankets on the other side. There was a small cot with a large quilt that hung off the sides on to the dirt floor and a single lantern that was hung by the hook off the center pole. *Kinda cozy.*

"This is nice in here. Is it yours?" Bill asked as he pulled his shoes off.

"It's Mary Jane's." She skirted Bill's questioning.

"See she just walked in an' took charge, made life here worth living. Gave us all hope she did." Beulah spoke as she waited for Bill to continue with his disrobing.

"She jus' walked in, an' that was that?" Bill quizzed the redhead before him.

"Aye, that was that." She stood with her hand out. "Come on, laddie, get them britches off."

He pulled them off and handed them to her. He stood naked before her. As his hand went to his pecker, he stretched it. Then he pulled the foreskin back, exposing the head. "Damn. Feels good to skin 'er back."

He met her eyes as she glanced at the lad's pod.

"It ain't as small as I figured it to be, but I suppose it will do the job. You just sit there. I'll be back in a kick of a turd." Then she walked out, leaving Bill to his own demise. *Well, this is something I hadn't counted on.* His hand pulled on his pod, bringing him to an erection. *Might as well take me a nap as long as I ain't doin' nuthin'.* Bill walked over to the quilt-covered cot to lie down; with one leg hanging off the side, he put both hands behind his head as he drifted off to sleep.

The runt was awakened when he felt someone touching him. He didn't flinch or jump up. He just opened an eye to see Beulah with a pan of water and washcloth, wiping his legs clean.

"I see yer awake, runt. Ye clothes be here from the mend as well as being scrubbed up. From the dirt on ye, it appears ye don't see too much of the water." She dipped the rag back into the pan of water.

"Nope, I didn't get a chance to bring my tailor with me neither." He smiled at the woman performing the chore.

"You suppose to do my pod as well? It ain't to particular who handles it." He smiled at the redhead.

"Yer a sassy runt. The queen wants ye this evening. Don't want ye tooting right off the get-go, so I'm going to make sure ye don't go squirting yer squirt too soon." She put the rag back in the water.

"Yep, she wants to use ye for a spell I imagine." Out came the rag going for his pod and balls. "Ye best hold off on squirting at me. I'll give you a chance in a bit, laddie." She pulled his balls up, wiping them slowly.

"Don't be squirting." The rag went back in the water.

"Just a bit more." Out came the rag to do his hairless white chest and armpits.

"Ye be something special. Aye, I saw it right off when the queen first saw ye standin' there. Most of the newcomers just get some food an' a place to sleep overnight. We don't have a lot of food, but when we do, we share." The rag returned to its place in the pan.

"There, ye be as clean as I can get ye. Now about ye squirting? I'm gonna get you to toot, an' it'll be quick like. So don't go a thinking you're gonna slip your carrot into me. Not tonight anyway." Her hand went to Bill's piss'r as she skinned it down. Slowly she began pumping the lad.

"I don't mind if you stick it in yer mouth and suck on it, Beulah. I don't mind a bit." Bill smiled at the woman working his pod.

"Nope, ain't gonna get no such thing. Ye just toot, and I'll be on my way." She went about her business like she was milking a goat.

"Hey Beulah yer goin' about this kinda rough there woman. Ain't gonna squirt thata way." Bill mentioned as he was quite enjoying the attention.

"Oh, I think you'll be squirting in no time a'tall." She readjusted her legs under herself as it was plain to see it was taking longer than she had planned. *He's as hard as a hickory stick. He should be a squirting. He's not making faces holding back. Hmm?* She was perplexed at the young lad.

"You're gonna have to suck on it, woman, I ain't jerked off since I was seven 'er eight. All I get anymore is sucked off an' pokes. So you might as well get on with it. Sides you already washed the ol'boy off." Bill tried again to get her to pleasure him with her mouth.

"Nope, ye best be a squirtin'." She increased her tempo. Bill watched her hand; it looked like a snake shaking a rat. But he held back, not giving in to the redhead's request. He could see her slowing for the exertion. Finally she stopped. Bill's pod was so hard she couldn't believe it hadn't popped.

"Lookie here. I'm real close. Why don'cha just give a quick suck, an I'm sure to pop quick like." He led her on.

"Fine. Ye best not pop in me mouth, ye hear me? Ye be a pullin' out." She lowered her face to his pod as she began to pleasure the runt.

"Sure thing. I'll pull it out after I pop." He murmured.

Her wait wasn't long; Bill timed it perfectly. As his pod was at the back of her throat, he released his seed. She swallowed by reflex. Her head came up without a drop on her lips.

"Boy, ye just squirted. Damn you, I said not to." she said swallowing over and over but not tasting the semen.

"I don't taste it, though. You're clever ain't ye?" She smiled at the runt; he smiled, his limp pod growing hard again.

"Sure am." He bragged.

"I told ye not to do that, huh? Ye be hard again?" She stared at the boy's pod as it stood up again.

"Ye be ready again? It's not so. This isn't supposed to happen. Nary a man can do this, not Ivory or any man. But here ye lay, butt naked with a hard-on." She leaned over to inspect his pod to assure herself it wasn't a trick, her fingers touching it gingerly.

"Ye be hard. How many times can ye do that runt?" she asked, staring at the penis.

"Three, sometimes four if it's the right women." He smiled.

"Women? You do more than one at a time? Does the queen know of this?" she asked, waiting.

"Yeppers. She does that for a fact." Bill reached down, pushing his pod straight up.

"You want to sit on it?" he teased her.

"Later, after the queen get's through with ye. I should go. Ye best be a gettin dressed an' meet the queen at here room." She stood up quickly. Bill could see her trembling.

"Don't run off now." He stood his pod sticking out like a tree limb.

"Walk over with me." He pulled his britches on, pulling his pod in as he buttoned them up.

"Her room is at the end of the fort, the only door with flowers next to it." The woman turned and bolted away, leaving Bill to finish alone. *Goddamnest thing I've seen in a spell, woman getting all shook up over sucking a pecker. Now Katie she could suck the bark off a tree. Yeppers, that girl has some talent.* Bill slipped his shoes on and grabbed his hat, pulled it on, and then slipped his coat on. *Okay, here I come, Ells.*

CHAPTER 15

He walked out of the dirty canvas tent into the black of the night, taking in the fort's atmosphere. *Walls are high enough to keep varmints out and livestock in and a few lamps lit. Makes the fort pretty peaceful.* As he started his walk to the door where his mother was to be, something whizzed next to his ear. *What the hell?* Then he heard whatever it was, clang against the wall of the fort. A few steps more into the darkness of the courtyard when another arrow flew at him. The cherry-wood arrow knocked his cap off, barely missing his scalp. *Goddamn! Shit! What the hell?* Luck was with the runt as another arrow glanced off his shoulder.

"We're being attacked! We're being attacked! Git yer asses up! We're being attacked!" he screamed as he dropped to the ground. No response from the fort.

"Hey goddamnit! Goddamn Indians are attacking!" Bill screamed again. He saw the lights brightening as fort folks readied themselves for battle. Another arrow skipped inches from his face, showering him with dirt.

"Gotta get some cover!" he spoke aloud as he looked for the safest place. *The well! That's it!* Bill crawled like a scared skunk to the well. He put his back against the cool rocks. *Hope them damned arrows can't hit me here.* From the security of his newfound hiding place, he watched as torches were being lit, and the fort came to life. Then he saw Mary Jane coming out of her tent with a lantern she held high, making her a perfect target. In the bright light of the oil lantern, he watched her become a pincushion just as old man Stiffer had become.

There were so many arrows hitting her body that he lost count. As the lantern fell to the ground, landing upright, it cast an eerie light across the courtyard, giving him a front-row seat of the horrors of death.

"Mary Jane! Don't move!" He screamed out to her. His mind raced. *She might be dead, might not be. Just lay still.* Bill thought about scurrying over to her but decided she was dead or would be soon. *No, I gotta help her.* So leaving the security of the well, he scampered over to her, the onyx-tipped shafts of death whizzed past him as he closed the distance to the prone woman. He reached her as two more arrows found her limp body with one through her arm, pinning it to her waist, and two more in her torso. Placing his hand on her limp body, he realized his risk was in vain. *Shit, she's a goner,* he realized.

Not giving up on her, he whispered, "You're gonna be okay. Just don't make any noise." In the bright lights of the numerous lanterns that had come to life, he saw the big black man come out of one of the wooden doors carrying a long Pennsylvania rifle.

"You men get close to the walls. Don't give them a target. Move! Damn you! Move!" he bellowed to the defenders as the fort became alive now. People began scurrying about like roaches in the light.

Still the arrows flew with propensity of a sleet storm, showering the humans with flying death. Then a musket fired and another. The sounds ripped through the night as screams of the wounded warriors pierced the black night, causing the hailstorm of arrows to slow.

"Get those wounded to the queen's cabin! Move quickly! Move!" the deep voice of the ex-slave boomed in the courtyard as Ivory and Ells pushed over a small oxcart to give them a small sanctuary from the malevolence of the attack. Seeing they had a small recluse from the attack, Bill tried to pick up Mary Jane to take to the cart but she was too heavy for him.

"Can you walk? We gotta get you to a safe place. Mary Jane?" Bill yelled at her, trying to arouse her. But the redhead had been dead since the first volley of arrows. He had no idea the first arrow had punctured her lung, and she had drowned in her own blood.

"Shit. Gotta git." He laid her down. As he heard arrows whizzing past his head, two more struck the dead girl with a sickening 'thunk'. The bright light of the lantern illuminated the battle as he could see them flying into the tent and around him, striking the ground.

The three tribes of the Illini Confederation knew how to stage an offensive. They who were doing the attack had their differences, but the thought of killing the white people on their land made them put their squabbles aside.

The Peorias started the next level of the attack with flaming arrows while the Miamis concentrated on getting over the eight-foot walls. The Kaskaskia were hammering on the thick front gate with great mallets as the orchestrated attack proceeded into the night. Bill watched the flaming arrows flutter through the black night like venomous fireflies as the thundering hammers echoed with each blow against the wooden door.

This is looking pretty bad. Bill's mind raced on how to help or at least fight, but there was nothing he could do. *Shit, I ain't even got a knife.* More guns were being fired now, and he started hearing the cries of the attackers as the few shooters that were picking them off had the cover of barrels or overturned tables.

"Runt! Are you hit?" Beulah's voice sounded like a clap of thunder.

"No. Mary Jane's dead." He called back as arrows accurately pinpointed his voice. Bill tried to make himself as small as he could while he waited for her reply.

"Damn." she responded.

"I don't have a gun or knife to fight with. You got anything I can use?" he called to her.

"No, get Mary Jane's. It might be in the tent." she called back to him.

The runt patted down the dead girl, finding nothing except blood and arrows. *Might as well look in there.* He looked at the dark tent. Picking up the lantern, he headed into her tent. Another arrow came through the canvas wall, burying into the cot he'd just been on.

Ducking down to the floor, he searched frantically for the knife when his hand found the handle sticking out from under one of her rolled-up dresses. Finally. *Got to get outta here 'fore I get skewer'd as well* was all he could think about as he threw the lantern out, watching it bounce and break open, overspilling into a puddle of flames the arrows showered all around. The archers had the range down. *Gotta get over to the rest of 'em,* the runt thought as another arrow came in through the flap of the tent, sticking in the steamer trunk.

"Shit!" he screamed as he used her knife to cut a door on the side of the tent. Pausing for a brief moment, he prepared himself for the sprint to where Beulah's voice had been.

"Beulah! Here I come, woman!" Leaving the tent, he sprinted into the lit-up courtyard. But no voice replied. He skittered to a sliding halt on his butt next to the overturned table where she had been. Bill looked down to see an arrow in her forehead.

"Shit!" He waited. Another arrow hit the table with a clack.

"Hey, nigger? You there?" Bill asked as a shot sounded from across the courtyard followed by a scream.

"Yes, I'm here with Ells." came back the deep bass voice. Ells's voice pierced the night air. "Son, get yer ass ovah herah! Don't get stuck, boy. I still have a use fer ya!"

Bill felt the ground where Beulah had been hiding. *Ah, here it is.* He found her knife. *Ready, set, go!* Bill crawled like a scalded dog to the oxcart they had over turned.

"Here, runt." Ivory handed Bill a horse pistol, "You know how to shoot, right?"

"Goddamned right I do. How you doin', Ells?" Another arrow hit the wheel.

"Christ!" He pulled himself closer to the bed of the cart.

"You got a plan, nigger? Ells?" Bill asked as he watched the river people were being systemically killed.

"We got one chance. In my room there's a tunnel leading out of here that me and Ivory built it the last time we were attacked."

"Last time? Good God woman, how many times? How many times has this happened?" Bill asked hysterically. Before an answer came out, Ivory shot the first Kaskaskia that came through the broken front gate.

"Counting this time? Two." She leaned over, bringing her short flintlock frontier gun up as she fired into the mass of attackers. Bill took her lead, leveling his pistol on the nearest roach-cropped attacker, and fired. The man rolled back, grasping his knee.

"You're a bad shot, runt." Ivory scolded him.

"Maybe, but he'll be hurting too much to fight." Bill reached for the powder horn and shot. Pouring powder in the barrel, he dropped a ball in and quickly rammed it home. Looking around the cart, he saw Peorias coming over the wall. The fire arrows had several of the tents flaming as well as the main structure of Ells's cabin.

"Shit. We gotta get Ells. Your cabin's a fire." Bill's rattled voice sent urgency to Ells. He primed the pan, flipped the frizzen down, and took aim at the nearest man. The warrior had a large roach with a multitude of feathers adorning it. He fired and waited for the smoke to clear to see the man lying flat on his back.

The siege stopped. The Peorias looked at the dead man, and then Ivory's musket sounded off, hitting the man closest to the dead warrior. Ells got another one in the head.

"They's not sure what to do. The runt must have got the leader." Ells called to Ivory as Bill was priming. Then it got quiet; he leaned out to fire again but found no targets. The fallen man was gone as were the others they had shot.

"Huh? What the hell?" Bill asked as he sat back with his back to the bed of the cart, panting from the excitement.

"Ells? Ivory? What's happened?" he asked again.

"You've killed the leader. Without him, they cain't figure out what to do. So they pick up their dead and vanish." Ivory answered the small blond that had fought next to him.

"I'm not a nigger. I'm a free man. Don't you understand boy? I'm free. Not a nigger or a slave." Ivory stood up looking over the wheel into the fire-lit courtyard.

"Well, kiss my ass. A free black man, huh? Damnedest thing I've heard of other than being attacked by a bunch of painted-up sumbitches. Who were they? Any clue?" he asked.

"Most likely Peorias. Coulda been Miamis." He paused looking down to where He was seated. "I recognized the one you shot, damned Kaskaskia. They get them others all riled up. They's the ones that usually organize these attacks." Ivory answered, "We'll just wait here until sunrise. Don't go walking around. We've seen them come back after they regroup. Ells, looks like we're the only ones left." He spoke quietly as he reloaded.

"You primed?" he asked the small blond man next to him.

"Yeah." He responded, "Ells, you primed?" He asked.

"Got the gun ready, an' I'm ready to fight, you little turd. I cain't believe you're here with me, fighting these goddamned Injuns." She smiled into the night as they sat quietly waiting for the sunrise.

When sunlight finally broke over the eastern wall, they slowly rose to see what was left of their fort.

CHAPTER 16

The fires had all but burnt out as the sunlight of another day washed over him. Somberly he walked through the fort, seeing the bodies of the people he had just met; many of them had died slowly, bleeding to death. Arrows marked by crimson stains showed the trauma of death as he walked to Mary Jane, counting nine arrows in her body.

"Jesus, girl, I barely got to know ya." He reached down, touching her cold gray forehead. Bill stood up and walked into her tent, retrieving a blanket, and solemnly laid it over the body the best he could; but with all the arrows in her, it kept the blanket from covering her.

"Shit." He pulled the blanket off, laying it next to her. He began the grizzly chore of pulling out the arrows. When the last one was stacked, he placed the blanket over her, covering her head and torso.

"Where'd they come from?" he called to Ells that was doing the same thing to Beulah.

"Should we go after 'em?"

"With what? There ain't but three of us. Look around son. Three lone souls. We had twenty-three people here. Now we have three." She looked around at the corpses that littered the courtyard.

"We won't be staying here. We'll put them folks in what's left of my cabin an' burn this place down." she said, shaking her head, "I'm heading for Hannibal. At least we won't get shot up by a bunch of fuckin' Miamis." she spoke as she covered a child.

"You're right there. What about your nig, I mean Ivory?" Bill caught himself halfway through his word.

"I'll be with Ells. I'm a freeman, but it doesn't hurt to travel as a slave. Keeps questions to a minimum." He smiled as he hefted a large round man over his shoulder. The arrows that had killed the man gave him the appearance of a sickly flower.

"You don't worry about this man. Me an' him? We'll be fine. You know what I think we're gonna do? Head back to Dallas City an' rile them folks up." She smiled to him.

"Go on back to the farm. Get them Arab horses. Sell the place, an' me an Ivory will get out of Illinois an' go on down to Louisiana fer a while. What say you, Ivory?"

"Sounds good, Ells. I like New Orleans quite a bit. I had some friends down that way as well." He smiled through the early morning light.

"Well then, this is it. Until the next time, Ells." Bill leaned over to kiss his mother's cheek.

"What? You think ya gonna get away with jest a peck on the cheek?" She reached over, bringing him to her. Wrapping her arms around the lad, she hugged him.

"You know you an' me? We had some fun, didn't we? Maybe so I'll see you again. Maybe not. But you'll always got a sweet place in my heart." she said, her cheeks flushed. Bill walked to the oxcart to retrieve the pistol he had used during the skirmish.

"I'm gonna keep this here pistol, and I'll be takin' some powder an' shot. Never can tell who I'll be meetin' out in the wilderness." Bill stuffed the pistol under his belt next to the knives as he looked to see the two of them staring at him.

"I'll be heading for the Bluffs. Gotta find some work an' a place to ride out the winter." he spoke as he turned to leave the fort.

"Son, why don't you come back with me an' Ivory? You can have ol'Joe. He'd be a good mule, an' you already know him." Ells asked, trying to sway him.

"Nope. That derned mule killed Matthew. I don't want nuthin' to do with it. He reminded himself of the work he went through harnessing the mule, the cantankerous moods it went into. The fear of snakes that caused the problem in the first place, nuthin' from that place neither." He stood fast on his decision.

"Lookie here. You come with us, we'll sell the mule. We got three good horses, an' you an' me an' Ivory we can travel down to the Natchez Trace to New Orleans, the three of us. You an' Ivory can entertain me when we need a distraction from the trail. Plus, three of us would keep them pirates away. What say you, son? Will you come with us?" she asked her hand, reaching up to his soft wispy blond hair, her fingers going through it combing to a rest behind his right ear. Delicately she slid it off, letting her finger caress his lobe as she let it fall.

He looked around at the work they had before them, the death that had encompassed the three of them in a blink of an eye. He knew the work that was going to take to clean the place up to leave. Here they stood, dead bodies around them, and she was aroused by the lad.

"All right. I'll go with you." Bill had changed his mind.

"After we take care of these folks." He was not sure of the Bluffs, and having Ells offer him entertainment was too much to pass up.

"It's settled. Come on, Ivory, let's get them taken care of." Ells wrapped her arm inside the big black man's arm as they walked to the still-smoldering cabin, leaving him alone. *Well, it's better to get a poke than to starve out here trying to winter up with folks I don't know. That big nigger will scare off most pirates an', shit, a lot of the goddamned injuns too. Yeppers, he surely will.* His mind raced as he leaned over to pick up a child. He looked at the horror on her little round face. *God, this be hard.* But he toted her to the pile that Ivory had started.

"You gonna get anything from in here?" He asked as he laid the child on a half-naked woman that Ivory had just placed. He stared at her lying there, blouse ripped open, her white breasts lying open like a pair of dinner plates, her chest caved in from a tomahawk. She was sure purty as he stared at her face, once. He turned to retrieve another and another until the small cabin was a heap of Ell's people.

"Come on runt, we need to stack wood." Ivory called to Bill as he pulled pieces of the broken fort apart.

"Shouldn't take too much. There's still a lot of her cabin left."

"Bill, we're gonna be okay once we're away from this place of death. You'll see." she spoke, dragging a piece of the corral to the burned cabin.

"I know." He answered back as he leaned against the well, watching Ell's shoulder carry the wood up to the pile. *Shit, one minute I'm on the way fer a poke. Then next thing you know, everybody's' dead. sheeit.* He let out a long sigh.

"You ready?" Ells asked Ivory.

"Almost. Let's gather up as many pistols, powder, shot, and muskets as we can carry. Be sure to get every last scrap of food as we'll need as much as you can find." the big black man ordered as he stuck several pistols into his belt.

Bill walked over to the nearest musket, looking down as he read the manufacture's name, Andrews Brothers, SC fifty four caliber. *Hmm? Never heard of them, but it's a fine rifle. Purty too.* Bill admired the maple tiger striped half stock. The wood stock went half way up the octagonal barrel and the smooth dark-grained leather sling added to a perfect thought out weapon. He didn't care if it was an American manufacturer from South Carolina. *Not bad, a nice rifle, a pistol an' two nice butcher knives.*

"I'm done. Ells? Runt?" the ex-slave asked.

"Sure, let's be on our way." He answered as he wicked up the fire in a lantern, watching the flames grow. Then he leaned back and threw it onto the wood, causing the lantern to smash open and spill oil onto the stacked wood and bodies. In moments it burst into an inferno.

"That didn't take much." The fire spread quickly as they went out the broken gate. Bill turned to see the small fort, now completely engulfed in fire.

"Shit, not long a'tall" Bill spoke as he turned to watch Ells wrap her arm into Ivory's.

"Nope. Not long."

CHAPTER 17

Bill followed Ivory as they walked the same trail he had come to the fort on. The narrow black line leading away reminded him of Beulah and her spaniel hair. He thought of the way she tossed the knife back and forth with the effort of combing her hair. *She'd been fun.* Bills mind jumped to Ivory's back. *Cain't believe how big he is. Gonna take a shitload of grub to fill his gut sack up too.*

"So what happen'd in Dallas City?" Ivory called over his shoulder.

"Yeah, tell us." Ells chimed in.

"Well, I looked up Marcia Blankenship. She didn't like me right from the git-go." He began to tell tale.

"Nope. Hey, I got some terrible news, Ells." he spoke to her back.

"Bad news." She stopped, turning around to look into Bill's eyes.

"What bad news?" she asked only inches from Bill's face.

"It's about Matthew." he spoke quietly.

"What? Matthew already got him a woman?" She smiled.

"Naw, nuthin' like that. The day after we left, ol' Joe got spooked an' kicked Matthew in the head. Kilt him dead. I figure it was a snake that got Joe riled up as he didn't care for them. Anyway the church folks found him and David. They were a bit upset that you split the blanket with 'em. They was a figuring that you'd be goin' back to run the farm with a new husband." Bill looked at her blue eyes, her blonde hair blowing wild in the wind.

"I told 'em Matthew done kicked me an' you out. We had no idea that he'd been kilt. Blankenship an' the Justice of the Peace had something going as they were quick to get me gone."

He watched her go from sadness to rage.

"Well, them uppity church goers! They'll get nuthin'!" she fumed as she spun around, putting her back to Bill.

"No. No. That's not true. They'll get the farm. That Ruben, he's a slick one. We'll have to be wary of that polecat. He's got something up his sleeve. Him and that Stiffer, they's tight. I know Marcia's in with 'em. She's a weasel with a slit she is. That's fer certain an' fer true, my son. We'll have to be shrewd to get cash money for the farm, though. We might be too late. Hopefully we get them Arabs, though." She spun back to Bill.

"What else? Is there more?" she asked.

"Yeppers, there's more." He paused, looking at her smooth skin, her hair gently lying over the side of her face.

"Stiffer's dead. Got kilt by some Miamis chasing me. 'Member I'd been getting favors from Katie? Well, he was madder than a cat dipped in turpentine. He got his dogs an' was chasing me down. I hid in a tree, an' the Miamis kilt him an' his pointer dogs. Did you know that his girls was Blankenship's daughters?" Bill paused looking at his mother's expression.

There was a thin smile. Bill continued, "Yep. Anyway, when they found out ol' Stiffer was done for, they wanted to string me up on the spot. I barely got away with my neck in one piece. That's God's own truth." Bill watched her now. He could see her mind working.

"Well, it's as plain as a broke jar. You cain't be going into the town. Let me think on this." She turned, leaving Bill and Ivory standing there as she began the walk to Dallas City.

"Runt, you know how to get her riled up. I'll say that for you." Ivory spoke to Bill as he walked by the small man.

"Shit, I was jus' tellin' her which ways up. That's all." he called to the back of the black man.

CHAPTER 18

The June sun had been out, showering them with warm rays as they closed the distance to the small town of Dallas City. The trio chatted as they strolled along, barely making ten miles the first day.

The afternoon wildlife had become to show itself as they crested a small hill not but five miles from Dallas City. A small herd of white-tailed deer grazed on the hill not more than a dozen yards from the refugees, so content with the sweet grass they never noticed Ivory split off from the group. He had become good at hunting as his former master had taught him well. Slowly he crept up in a small gully downwind of the animals. Lifting up the long Pennsylvania rifle, he brought the front-sight pin on the small doe's heart. Then his finger gently pulled the trigger, and with a poof of the frizzen powder a .36-caliber ball rushed toward the doe. She didn't fall down or rush off; she flinched when the ball hit her but shook it off as she began to bleed to death. Then the circle of life came to an end, and she finally lay down and died. The others looked at her not with fear but with an almost casual glance as they wandered off to the nearest scrub of maple trees.

Ivory reloaded quickly as the other deer walked away. Up from his hiding place, he approached her cautiously, the rifle ready for another shot. It wasn't needed as she lay there dead, her eyes lifeless and dull. The big man quickly cut off her scent gland patches and field dressed her. Then picking her up like a small rag doll, he walked quickly to his newly formed band of travelers.

The small camp was in a clump of maple and oak trees just off the trail, surrounded by blackberry and cloudberry bushes with a smattering of raspberries briars, making entry almost impossible, except where she had laid a few logs on top of them, giving them an easy doorway. He watched Ells set up camp like she had done it many times before. She had a nice fire going, and a few deadfall logs were dragged into a crude circle, forming a ring around the fire to provide the troop with a comfortable place to lounge as the evening rushed to meet them.

"Son, why don't you get the guns an' powder counted up fer us? We'll be needin' 'em come time we get to Dallas City." she called to him as she skinned down a few saplings to hang the meat off.

"Sure thing, Ells." Pulling the pistol out of his belt, he removed the powder horn off his shoulder. He looked at its shape. The long, smooth, and nice bulb-shaped stopper gave it the shape of an over-sized penis. He held it up to Ells, waiting for her to notice.

"I see you have something on yer mind?" The blonde woman smiled.

"Looks like an interestin' shape, don't it?" He answered back with a grin.

"You just take care of the guns. We'll take care of the rest of the other things soon 'nuff." She tossed a few more sticks on the fire, which had simmered down to a radiant glow, providing a good bed of coals for cooking as well as a decent heat source for the evening and the up-and-coming activities.

Ivory returned with the doe under his arm. "Here we are. Supper."

"Good shooting, nigger." He complimented the big man. Ivory scowled at him for the remark but held his tongue as he laid his favorite rifle against one of the logs.

"I'll cut this up. Give him yer guns an' powder." She nodded to her son. "He be tallying it up fer our Dallas City run." She spoke over her shoulder as she quickly sliced up the venison for the evening meal.

"Here, runt." Waiting for him to stand up to get them, he held out the two pistols.

"I want these two back, understand?" he spoke to Bill, holding his rage back from the slanderous remarks he was so freely saying.

"Where the hell do ya think I'm goin'? Ivory, I swear you ain't all there at times." Bill insulted the man.

Listening to the banter Ells smiled to herself, seeing a fight coming. She swiftly used the knife until she was satisfied with her cuts. *I'll jest hang these here.* She hung the meat from the sapling spits, watching the meat to ensure they would cook without burning. *I wonder how I'm gonna to approach Ruben about the sale of the farm.* Ells watched the fire thinking about how much things had changed in the short time she'd left the farm; her husband dead, her son becoming her lover, and the black man at her side. She cut a small piece of venison, watching Bill stare into the fire.

"What's on yer mind?" she asked.

"Just figuring how to get this farm thing to our favor. You and the nigger here." He was interrupted by Ivory.

"I told you! Stop calling me that!" The big black man was off his small log he had been perched on, making strides toward the small blond man.

"Sorry, just a habit." Bill never moved a muscle as the big man stopped inches from him, his fist balled ready to give him a solid thrashing. "I'll work on it." Bill smiled at Ivory.

"Next time you call me that, you'll get no warning. I'll just punch you in the face. You understand? I'll whop you a good one." Ivory turned back to his log.

"Ells, your nigger's testy, ain't he?" Billy smiled at her, seeing her eyes twinkling. She knew Bill would poke a stick at a wounded badger just to see what would happen, and this was no different. She knew Bill and Ivory had to get the pecking order established. *Might as well get it over with now rather than later. Hope he don't whop the boy too bad. I won't mind getting a poke before I close my eyes tonight.* She smiled as she watched the large man spin around, leaping for Bill, hands out in a fit of rage, ready to tear Bill's head off.

The small blond man didn't know about Ivory's short-fused temper. But here was the huge man flying through the air like a tree squirrel covering the distance to Bill before he could move. Ivory landed on him like a barrel of nails, knocking the wind out of the small man. Ivory quickly swiveled around on the lad's body, bringing a head lock to play.

"I told you I'd thump you for your nasty mouth." the big man spoke, barely containing his rage. He looked up to meet Ells's eyes. Even in the dim light of the fire, he could see her leaning forward, noticeably excited by the roughhousing. The ex-slave brought his fist to play as he smashed Billy's face several times.

"You had enough runt?" he asked, looking down at Billy's bloody nose and lips.

"Okay. I've had 'nuff." muffled Billy in a choked voice.

"No more insults?" Ivory persisted. He waited before releasing the lad.

"Nary a one." the runt answered back.

The black man released him and sat back down next to Billy. The runt paused, wiggling his jaw delicately.

"Honest, nigger, I'll call you no more names." Billy coughed through the blood, filling his mouth. Bill never saw the fist coming; and once again it slammed his face, knocking Billy over backward and unconscious.

"How about now?" Ivory asked. But there was no response as Billy was out cold from the last blow. Ivory stood looking down at the small man on the leaf-covered floor of the camp.

"Shit, you whumped him good." Ells smiled, watching the man straighten his shirt.

"I gave him more than a fair warning." Ivory immediately felt remorse for beating the blond man. Ells chimed in, "Billy's like that. When he comes to, you'll get no relief from his mouth. The boys fought too many times to quit just 'cause, a nigger as yourself, thrashed him."

"Ells, you know I don't like to be called that. Why do you still do it?" he asked as he cut another piece of venison. Sitting with a solid thump, he reached out and shook Billy's foot.

The small man moved slowly. "Uh, christ, Ivory, you just about caved my face in." Billy came to slowly, rolling over to his side.

"Shit, nigger, I can hardly open my mouth now." Billy muttered, spitting out more blood. He looked up in time to see the back hand of Ivory coming, but he couldn't bring a hand up to defend himself, so the back of Ivory's hand struck him hard, knocking him into the briars behind him.

"I told you don't call me that." Ivory took a bite, looking at Ells. She had a hand over her mouth, hiding her laughing.

"I told you." She lowered her hand, trying not to laugh at her son's stubbornness. The lad pulled himself up through the bramble standing on his weaving legs.

"You about done eating? I want to suck on a piece of that. I don't figure I can chew fer a bit yet." Billy spoke through swollen lips, blood running out his nose and lips.

"There's plenty here. I think you best quit while you's ahead." Ells said as she cut a chunk off for her son.

"Here." She tossed it to him. Bill barely caught it as he was still dizzy from the beating. Stumbling, he sat down close to Ivory.

"You know, nigger, you hit like a girl." Bill waited for the next blow, but it never came.

"I can't hit you no more, runt. Any man that take that kinda beating and still pokes at me, well, I'd say you're either dumber than a pile rocks or got some sand. I'm leaning toward the rocks." He smiled at Billy, admiring the spunk the kid had. Not too many men had been able to take a beating from him and still harass him. But here sat the runt, still taunting him.

"You still hit like a girl, a big mean girl I might add." He smiled through his swollen lips.

"You's gonna be useless to me tonight." Ells spoke to Billy as he put the meat to his lips, sucking the juices slowly.

"My pod's still good. Just cain't eat no pussy." Billy spoke through the bloody lips.

"You got that right. I won't have a bloody mouth on my pussy. I have to put up with it coming once a month already. Ivory, get that horse cock of yours out. I aim to use it." She stood up, walking toward him.

Ells kneeled before the black man in the dim light of the fire. Billy watched the huge man produce a thick black penis.

"Good god, nigger! That's the biggest cock I've ever seen, not that I look at peckers all the time, but I've seen a few of my friends jerking off. That's big as a horse dick." Billy spoke, spitting out more blood. Thankfully his lips had stopped bleeding.

"Now you understand why we get along." She reached up, pulling the foreskin down, exposing the big black head. Billy stared at the man's pod. It looked as big as a newborn's arm.

"I swear, Ivory, this thing looks bigger every time I see it." she commented as she placed it to her lips. Opening her mouth, she engulfed the black pod, her lips stretching around it as she began bobbing her head. Billy watched the man's pod swelling even more as Ells worked on it. Soon it was at full length.

"Holy shit!" Billy exclaimed as Ells bobbed away. She lifted her face from the chore.

"He's only got one pop, and it's a big one." She stood up, pulling her dress over her head, showing she had nothing on under it, save her shoes.

"Come on, nigger. Use that thing." she sassed Ivory as she lay down on her dress. The big man didn't pull his wool britches down. He just stood over her. He pulled her legs apart, revealing her thick dark-brown matted triangle. He looked at Bill. Then he reached down, opened her lips, and dribbled a long string of spittle into her. Onto his knee he went, guiding himself into her.

She leaned up onto her elbows as to watch the massive root that was to begin pounding on her. The man went like a rabbit at first, slamming her hard, ramming his pod half way in.

"Oh. Oh." whimpered Ells as her vagina was being abused by the huge man on top of her. Bill watched, getting aroused, feeling his pod stiffing under his wool-buttoned britches.

"Hold on, nigger." Billy called to the shiny-headed black man.

"Roll over on yer side, Ells." he instructed. Ivory pulled out as the woman brought her right leg over so she was on her side.

"Okay, go ahead an' slip in again, but don't go poppin' yer load yet." Billy instructed through his swollen lips.

"What's on yer mind pup?" Ells asked as she felt the huge pod stretch her again, her eyes following Billy to the powder horn.

"No Billy. I'm not, " Billy cut her sentence off.

"It'll hurt. A lot." he answered as he spit on it.

"Hold on, nigger." Bill instructed. Ivory stopped, leaving his penis buried deep in the white woman. He watched as Bill leaned over, separating her ass hair, dribbling spit on her anus.

"Just relax, Ells." He gently slipped a finger into her.

"Relax, Ells." He felt her loosen up her grip on his finger. Slowly he stroked her feeling her relax even more. Then he pulled his finger out and inspected it. *No shit, that's good. Okay, now two.* Bill leaned over, spitting once more on her butthole. One finger, then two.

"Okay, Ivory, stroke her good." he ordered the black man. Ivory obeyed as he watched Billy using the two fingers, feeling them through the thin wall of the woman's birth canal. Ells had been quiet, not moving except to breathe. Bill went to three fingers and immediately felt her cringe.

"You gotta relax, Ells." he called to her as he watched the huge man pummel her. He felt her go limp again. With all the commotion going on, he reached down for the powder horn. Spitting on it, he pulled his fingers out, putting the bulbous stopper against her butt. She was in ecstasy by now, feeling the huge man using her briskly; she never tightened as Bill pushed the stopper in and out. Soon he was matching every other stroke with Ivory. The quicker Ivory went, the faster Billy went.

"Get. Ready. Ells." the black man warned.

"Stick it up my ass. Hurry! Hurry!" she pleaded. Her hand went down to the swollen button as she rubbed it in a blur.

"Now! Now! Up my ass now!" she demanded. Ivory and Billy timed it perfectly. Out came the powder horn. In went the huge penis stretching her even more.

"Waugh! Christ, oh gawd. Oh gawd, hurry! Hurry!" She was in tears as the big man pushed it in all the way and stopped, filling up her with his seed. She squeezed her sphincter as she climaxed, her back arching, legs sticking straight out, knocking the man over in the process. Ivory's pod came out followed by a thick stream of white semen.

"Oh my gawd, oh my gawd." She brought her legs up into the fetal position as she cried.

Billy looked at Ivory. The smile was gone, replaced by a look of concern. They both looked down to Ells as she cried. Billy pointed to her butt. A small stream of blood was running down her cheek onto the dress.

"Oh, my butt. Oh, my butt." She rolled back and forth between the sides, crying loudly, pleading for any kind of relief.

"You ever do that before?" Billy leaned over, whispering into the man's ear. The big man shook his head.

"No, the most I've ever done was one finger. And she swore never again." He reached out, placing his huge hand on her thigh.

"Don't touch me! Neither one of ya!" she screamed as her hand went back to her butt. Gently she touched herself. Feeling the moisture of blood, she brought it to her face in the dim light of the campfire.

"I'm bleeding? How bad? Tell me how bad." she requested, her demeanor changing.

"Please son, see how bad I'm hurt." she asked quietly, accepting her injury.

"I'm gonna scoot ya over to the fire so I can see." Billy gently pulled her over to inspect the damage.

"Not too bad. It's stopped bleeding. You got a small cut going to your pussy, but it ain't hardly bleeding. Now." Billy answered.

"You fuckers will not do that again, you understand? Never. That's off-limits." she scolded.

Billy nodded. "Here, have some venison." He carved off a chunk of the dripping meat.

"Not right now, christ, Ivory, I ain't gonna shit right fer a week." Out came a burbling fart. Her hand quickly retracted from the sound. She placed it over her mouth, hiding her laugh.

"Gonna have me some runny farts fer a while. I like it better when you don't fill me up, Ivory. Damn. Man's got him a bucketful of spunk too. I'll say that fer him." She rolled over to her hands and knees, turning her butt toward the big black man; she arched her back, sticking her butt in the air, causing another sloppy fart out, spraying Ivory with his own semen.

"Shit, Ells! Damnit, you! Got spunk all over me!" he complained wiping his face and chest off. Billy was out of range as he watched their antics.

"I might as well get dressed fer the skeeters chew up my pussy. At least it didn't get tore up by your big dick." She waved her finger at the bald man that had abused her anus.

"Your niggers got him a horse cock. I'll say that fer him, Ells. He been forkin' ya regular like?" Billy leaned back against a log, picking up the nearest pistol, admiring it in the glow of the fire.

"Yep, he's fucked me ever since we met up, before the river fort. He's good too. Minds well, cleans up after himself, which is more than I say fer you late stepfather." She paused as she slipped the dress over her head, hiding her striking figure from the two men.

"Speaking of such, we gotta get to town first light an' get them horses an' such things. Billy, you're gonna have to hide out in the woods till we figure out how things are gonna pan out." she causally spoke, pulling her hair back into a ponytail.

"What did we end up with shot an powder?" Ivory interrupted, pointing to the task before Billy.

"Got two rifles, three pistols four powder horns." he laid them in a row, the hammers up, sparkling from the evening fire light.

"Ells, how about wrapping your lips around this here root? Nigger man there popped his nut. You creamed yourself, an' I didn't get shit." *I figure cain't hurt to ask,* he thought.

"Sure thing. Ivory, put some wood on the fire will ya while get his lad to squirt." She walked to Billy.

"Get it skinned back, Bill. I wanna get a nap in 'fore the morning."

"Sure thing." Billy leaned back, unbuttoning his breeches and pulling out his semi-erect pod.

"Don't fret none. I'll pop the cork quick like." He pulled on his penis, making it stand tall.

"Your pecker ain't very big. Looks like a dogs, so small and all." Ivory commented as he watched his lover walking toward her task.

"Nope. It ain't big like the root of yours, but I bet I can slip 'er in her butt." he pointed to his mother, "an she won't be bleedin' from it." Billy defended his penile size.

"You ain't stickin' anything up my butt, so you can jest ferget that right now." She kneeled down in front of Billy, her slim hand gently grasping his pod. She pulled the foreskin down as her mouth engulfed the man's penis. Billy lay back against a log. Closing his eyes, he relished the moment. *Never can tell when I'll get nother one of these. As long as I'm with the nigger an' Ells, should be regular like.*

Ells wanted to get some sleep, so she went quick as a bat on a summer night to bring Billy to a quick end, which wasn't long at all. The lad lifted his head to warn her, but she already knew the boy was coming by feeling the quivering in his flesh. Her wait was rewarded as Billy filled her mouth with his semen.

"Thanks ye, Ells." Billy said as he pushed his wet pod into his breeches. She nodded as she stood up. Then she surprised Billy as she turned and jumped on the sitting black man, knocking him back as she grabbed his cheeks, forcing his mouth open. Pressing her lips to his, she spat the whole load into his mouth. The black man pushed her back, but it was too late. He went to spit, but Ells was on him again, jumping on his belly. She knocked a bit of wind out of him, gasping for air. He tried to spit but swallowed instead.

"Ahh." He drew in a breath.

"Damn, why did you go and do that?" he said as he wiped his mouth off, making a terrible face.

"That's fer tearing my asshole up." She stood up and walked back to the fire with burbling farts every other step.

"Shit, woman." He made more faces as he reached for a knife to cut some of the meat from the doe. She smiled and winked at Billy, knowing she'd got her vengeance on her partner.

"That's just wrong for a man to take another man's spunk. Just wrong." he said as he chewed the tender meat.

"We only have a few hours 'till dawn. How far to Dallas City?" She paused, delicately wiping the corner of her mouth off.

"What five miles? We should get there just after breakfast, so everybody is full and relaxed. Then we'll see where our horses are or who's stole 'em" Ells spoke as she plopped next to Bill. She rolled over to one cheek letting another gurgling fart out.

"Damn. I better wipe that one off." She chuckled as she rolled to her left side. She pulled her dress up, revealing her butt with the man's spunk on her cheek. Nonchalantly she scooped up the residue of semen and fecal matter with her right hand. Then she wiped it on the leaves next to her. Not satisfied with her toilets, she moved the leaves over until she found soft green grass. Ripping a handful, she gently finished her personal business.

"Christ, Ells, I figured ya stepped over to the trees to do that. Now this place is gonna stink like ass." Bill spoke as she straightened her dress.

"Ya did that once. Ain't gonna happen a'gin." Billy boasted. The taste came to him instantly as he thought of the lovemaking they had had the first day together.

CHAPTER 19

The night was gone in a flash of a fallen star. The daylight crested over the eastern tree line, bathing the group with the promise of a fresh day.

"Gawddamned, shame, I ain't got no coffee," Ells spoke as she yawned, stretching her arms up, bringing her full bust up and almost out her cotton dress.

Billy sat up, seeing Ivory still sleeping, his mother stretching. Then he immediately became aroused seeing her breasts near to falling out.

"Damn, Ells, yer titties want out somethin' fierce. Why don't you bring them over here fer me to nibble on?" the young lad asked anxiously.

"Oh, jest like that? Come hear'h an' let me play with yer titties? Simple as that?" she asked the lad, not bothering to adjust herself for modesty.

"Yeppers. Simple as that." He paused for a moment.

"Tell ya what. Ya suck my pecker, an' I'll pop a load up yer butt again. How's that sound?" he pressed on.

"You ain't stickin' nuthin' up my butt. That's fer certain an' true," she spoke, pointing her finger at him.

"But figure it like this, get useta it an it'll get to the point where ya be likin' it regular. Then you can have me in the back an' the nigger there in the front." He smiled through his swollen lips, pointing at the still sleeping man on the other side of the smoldering fire.

"Jest as simple as that? Me bend over an' get another buncha juicy farts? Me walking inta Dallas City farting jism?" she asked, her head cocked to the right.

"Yeppers. Think of how it'll be. Standin' there jawing with Megan—" She interrupted Billy, "Marcia. Her name's Marcia."

"Marcia then, an' rip a gurgly ol' spooge fart." He laughed, slapping his knee. Ells stared at Billy, thinking the scenario out. *His pecker ain't big like the niggers. Disgusting those fuckers will be worth it too.*

"All right, boy, you gotta eat me first, if you think you got the guts," she answered back, her smile coming to her sensuous lips.

"Sure thing. I know's you be tasting good as the nigger didn't pop a cork in yer honey pot." Billy stood and unbuttoned his breeches. '

"Come suck me off first." He held his pod to her. Ells pulled her dress over her head as she had done the evening before. She closed the distance to her son.

"You already hard? Christ. You're David's son fer sure. Ain't no two way 'bout it." She dropped to her knees before Billy pushed his hand away to allow good access to his pod.

"Pop quick. I wanna be getting outta here soon" was the last thing she said as she lowered her mouth to bring the lad to eruption. *Damn, she's good. Didn't take no time a'tall.* "Here I come," he called in a few short minutes as she swallowed quickly.

"Lay back an' I'll squat over ya." She turned around, revealing her rump to Billy.

"I thought ya wanted to eat yer puss?" he questioned Ells.

"Naw, just stick my asshole," she answered as she spread her cheeks to allow Bill easy access.

"It ain't gonna work thata way. Jest get on yer hands an' knees an' I'll poke ya quick like." He pushed her away gently.

"Humph. Alright. I wonder how long the nigger's gonna sleep," she asked as she did as Bill requested.

"Not too long. After I fork yer butt, I'm gonna kick him awake an' tell him I done got to fork yer rump. That'll teach him to be a sleep in." Bill smiled as he approached Ells with an already-stiff penis.

"I'm gonna spit on yer butt. Then I'll slip a finger er two an' get ya warmed up. Rub yerself like ya did last time."

"All right" was her only response as he began. Slowly he slipped in a fingertip, then the whole finger as he felt her tense up. She didn't say anything. *She'll have to learn how to relax.* Then two fingers as he spit on her again.

"I'm slippin' 'er in. Rub it good." He placed his pod on her anus as he pressed slowly. He popped in with no resistance. Stroking slowly, she made no other movements other than her hand rubbing herself.

"Right there. Make it go right there," she instructed Billy. So he obliged as she had requested.

"Oh christ! Faster, right there, faster!" He felt her tense up.

"Squirt yer squirt! Now!" she requested in a husky voice, so Billy pushed all the way in as he released himself.

"Oh shit!" she called over her shoulder. "That was good, but pull it out slow." She leaned forward as he slipped out.

"I didn't figure it would be that good. It didn't even hurt. Once again you've surprised me, Bill." She got to her feet, walking to her dress. As she bent over to pick it up, he heard her fart, but it wasn't like when Ivory filled her up. "That was a little toot. I'll be careful to save the rest to later. Wake up Ivory so we can get," she said as the dress settled itself on her slim shoulders.

"Hey, nigger, get up." Billy kicked Ivory's large booted foot.

"I've been awake. You think I could sleep through that? If you do, you're dumber than I thought." He sat up, rubbing his eyes.

"Let's get." Bill kicked dirt on the smoldering fire as Ivory picked up his brace of pistols and powder horns.

"Here, Ivory." Ells handed him his squirrel rifle. Looking into his eyes, she smiled seductively, "It hurt, but I liked it." Then she picked up her ruck and led the way out of her now-defunct camp.

CHAPTER 20

They walked into the morning without seeing another soul as the destination came into view."

"You find a place on the other side of town, like you was going to the farm. Me and Ivory we'll see where our stock is. If we ain't out of there by dark, you get to wherever you need to be. Don't come in looking fer us as we'll be in a pickle an' you're scrawny ass won't be able to help. Say you understand, Bill. Tell me you'll do as I asked." She held he hands in hers, looking into this blue eyes.

"Tell me, you ass-fucking, jism-squirting three-shooter." She smiled at him.

"Nope. I won't do no such thing. If you ain't out by dark, I'll find ya, by hook

er crook. We'll be together tomorrow night. You got my word on it, Ells." Bill smiled.

"You cum-guzzling gutter slut of a whore?"

"You've remembered some of David's catchy cussing. Good, that's good. All right, Ivory. Let's go." She wrapped her arm around the big man's waist as they strolled out of sight to the small

town. They were not even out of sight before Bill followed their steps. *I'll goddamned to sit around an' wait. I'll see what's going on. That's fer certain an' fer true.*

The young man swiftly closed the distance to the back of Marcia Blankenship's store as he peeked around the back corner. Satisfied he was undiscovered, he turned to the back door of the store and quietly approached. He was listening intensely with every step; hearing no conversation, he came to the open door and carefully stepped on the first of the three steps leading into the back of the store. Then he heard it—voices—but it wasn't Ells's or Ivory's.

Hell, I bet Ivory don't say two words in there. They'd be figurin' he's a smart nigger an' steal him.

The next step was as quite as the first as Bill's worn black shoe went closer to the voices—still no sound other than inside. He looked back over his shoulder. Seeing nothing, he continued up the last one as he stopped. Straining, he listened. *It's that damned Marcia. She got someone with her. Sounds like that barkeep.*

Bill stepped inside to the dimly lit back room. Looking around, he saw the small storage area of Marcia's: bolts of cloth, shovels, rakes, picks, rolls of rope, hanging coats, and a barrel of nails. But what got his attention was the long rifle. Hooked around the barrel was the possible bag and powder horn. *Damn, I'll be takin' that on the way out.* He crept on unnoticed. As he came to the curtain that separated the front from the back, he heard her speaking.

"Look Sash, if you want me to suck you, wipe your cock off," she spoke in a whisper. Bill pulled the edge of the curtain back a smidgen as he looked for the voice. He saw the bald head of Sash with Marcia in front of him, her hand on the man's penis. Admiring it, she placed it in her mouth and began bobbing her head.

"That's good, Marcia, real good. Okay, get ready. Here I come," he said as he placed a hand on her head and the other on the oak countertop, Bill saw Marcia stop as she looked up at the man, "You ready?" she spoke with her mouth full of semen.

"Yep, come here." He reached down, placing his hands on her face as he lifted her to his mouth where they passionately kissed. Bill knew what that was about and was surprised to see a man requesting such a thing.

She pulled away, her hand coming to her lips.

"Sure better than me swallowing it. You'll not see me swallowing very often. I'll do it once in a while, but as long as you like it, you can have all you want."

She turned, walking back to where Bill was hidden. Billy looked around for a hiding place but failed to see any place that would hide him in the short notice. She was just reaching for the curtain when the front door swung open and Ells and Ivory walked in. Marcia turned immediately from the curtain to Bill's relief. He peered back as Sash got off the counter and turned to face Ells and Ivory, his penis still hanging out but hidden from view.

Sick bastard that one, Bill thought.

"Well, look who's back. The whore. I see you got yourself a nigger. You're too late to get that farm." Marcia spouted as she walked around the countertop

"Good day to you too, you fat cow. My son says you nice Christian folks run him outta town. That so?" she asked in her Louisiana drawl.

"Yep. Heathen lad, that son of yours." she snapped back. That stung Bill's ears, making him hate her even more.

"My son's no such thing. I ain't here to argue about my kid. You said I'm too late?" she asked as she picked up a roll of calico cloth unrolling it on the floor. Marcia made no move to stop her. Bill watched from his concealment. He wanted to see how far Ells would go. He thought if he were to show himself, she might stop on the interrogation.

"Why should I buy what's already mine?"

"You were gone, your bastard son run away, husband killed, as is his daddy. So we got together and wrote up a deed. The place is all ours. All final too. Nice Arabians. That mule's bit testy, but Sash here got a way with mules."

"He's got a way with a cow as well I see." Ells snapped back. "You'll be tearing that deed up and returning my stock then." Ells spoke as her fingers found an axe handle sticking out of a barrel, "Or I'll be breaking Sash's legs there."

"Go right ahead. Won't do you no good. Them horses are safe, and you'll never find them. As for you hurting Sash here."

Before she could say any more, Sash came around the counter in a fury, forgetting his penis hanging out. Bill leaned back, avoiding being noticed as the curtain ruffled from the man's swift movement.

"Stay there, barkeep. You ferget something." Ells pointed to his crotch. That stopped Sash dead in his track as he looked down. His fingers went to work putting his penis away. Bad thing for him, he didn't see Ells take a step toward him; and before Marcia could warn him, she swung the axe handle swiftly connecting solidly with the side of his head. The barkeep dropped like a bag of flour, his pod still out for all to see. Billy's jawed dropped as he watched from his secret place.

"Now, Marcia, where's my horses? Or do you want to finish your life hobbling around on a broken knee the rest of yer life?" Ells asked smoothly.

Marcia dropped to her knees, her hand resting on Sash's neck. She looked up to Ells, "You killed him!"

"No. I didn't kill him. Just knocked him stupid. Where's my horses?" She stepped closer, swinging the handle like she was using a scythe.

"I'll not tell you, and you can't make me." Marcia stood up, folding her arms over her ample bosom in defiance.

The axe handle swished in the air, barely missing her but hitting a huge glass jar of pickles. The broken glass and pickles sprayed Marcia as well as splattering the nearest bolt of calico cloth.

"You won't get them. You can tear my place up, but I'll not tell you where they are!" Marcia took a step closer to Ells.

"I think you will." Ells swung again; but instead of aiming for the large woman, she spun around, connecting a solid blow on Sash's outstretched arm. A sickening thunk and a following crack reverberated throughout the store as Sash's elbow shattered. He was still unconscious and made no movements as he was tormented.

"So where's my stock?" Ells asked politely.

"Never." she answered meekly. Ells lifted the handle again. It was like slow motion watching the axe handle floating toward Sash's kneecap.

"No. Stop! I'll tell you!" she cried out too late as the handle hit Sash's knee, breaking the cap into shards. The last blow twisted Sash's leg into a contorted position as his knee became inverted.

"Please no more, no more. They're right over in the corral next to Sash's tent bar." She dropped to her hands and knees, crawling to her broken lover.

"Oh, Sash. I'm so sorry. So sorry." She wept as she cradled his head against her chest.

"Take the horses and leave. You'll not get the property." she spat out.

Bill stepped through the curtain, "Sorry Ells, had to watch yer back."

"Ivory, hand me yer skinning knife. I think his pod's big 'nuff to feed to some cur dog."

She held out her hand, not taking her eyes from Marcia as she felt the handle of the big-bladed stag-horned knife as it touched her palm.

"You'd not do that. No. I'll not let you." She fell over Sash's still-uncovered pod. Ells grabbed her by the hair and threw her back against the counter where she crashed, knocking several hoes and rakes over. Bill watched her hand find a handle as she began to right herself. Ells wasn't watching her.

She reached out to find Sash's penis.

"Where's my deed?" Ells laid the axe handle behind her as she rested on her knees. Then she lifted the knife and, gently lifting the man's limp penis, placed her knife under the foreskin.

"Drop that hoe, or I'll feed you Sash's pecker." Marcia dropped the hoe and folded her hands to pray.

"Please, I beg you. Please don't do this." she wept, tears running down her cheeks.

"The deed's over in Ruben's safe. He'll give it to you. Just don't cut Sash. Please don't." Marcia begged.

"All right, you saved him." She flicked the knife, cutting a piece of Sash's foreskin. It actually flipped in the air, landing on the wooden floor next to his head. The man quickly began bleeding. Billy stepped back and grabbed the rifle and possible bag. Marcia swiftly applied a handkerchief to Sash's crotch.

"You're sick. All of you are sick." Marcia spit at Bill and his mother. Billy didn't hesitate for an instant when he swung his black shoe and connected with her arm.

"You'd best leash yer tongue woman. I don't see a problem cutting it out." Ells said and turned, looking at her. The sitting woman sucked her lip in trying not to admit the pain Billy had just administered.

"Let's get our deed an' horses and get." Billy said as he stepped around the store keep.

"Yeppers. Let's git. Come on nigger." she called to Ivory. He nodded, knowing it was all just a show for the white people.

"Yes'm. I be coming." he answered with his practiced ignorant voice. The three of them left the store and made the short walk to Ruben Stillwater's Justice of the Peace office.

"Billy, take Ivory and get the horses saddled. We'll be getting as quick as we can." she spoke as the door loomed ahead of them.

"Watch yer ass, Ells." he called to her.

"I will." She jumped up the two steps and had her hand on the knob as Bill and Ivory rounded the corner to see the three horses. They looked no worse for wear as they scented Bill. Jed, the white-speckled Arabian stallion, immediately pranced to Billy's outstretched hand. The two brood mares slowly began walking to where the stud was, hoping for the snacks Billy always provided.

"These horses are magnificent. I've seen these when I was a small boy in Africa, simply beautiful."

"Bridget and Fanny are those. This one here? He's Jed. The boss horse, I don't see ol' Joe." He scratched the stud behind his ears as the small stallion bowed his head, remembering the attention he had become accustomed to.

Ells entered the office in a bolt, throwing Ruben off balance. He knew they had made out like the bandits they were. But now here stood the owner of the horses and property, and she didn't look like she was on a social call.

"Ells? I was told you had moved away. Well, we've kept your horses here, and the deed's right here in my drawer." He reached for the tall right drawer in his office desk. He didn't see her move, but she was across the desk like a wisp of smoke of a blustery day, her hand covering his, stopping the drawer from opening.

"No. You push your chair on back Stillwater." she commanded the fat man. He obeyed slowly as his right hand crept behind him as he slid away from the desk. Ells didn't see the sledge hammer handle he had in the corner behind him. As she opened the drawer, he grabbed the handle and swung it at Ells. She had been looking into the drawer and saw the pistol.

"Ah? Now what do we have here?" Her hand went into the drawer and never saw the handle coming at her at full speed. Ruben was lucky as the handle hit her behind her left ear. The crack was as loud as it had been when she had busted up Sash, but this time it wasn't her luck. Her head snapped to the side as she started to fall to the floor. Ruben watched it all as she careened to the floor. She died as her brain ruptured and never felt the wooden floor.

Ruben stared at the beautiful woman on the floor as blood oozed from her ear, forming a puddle on the floor before him.

"Oh no." He sighed as he slumped in his chair. He had no idea that Bill and Ivory were with the horses.

"Where is she?" Ivory asked, concerned.

"Hell, how would I know, nigger? I've been sitting here with you." Bill sassed the big black man.

"You stay here. I'll go check." Ivory dismounted, handing his reins as well as Ells's to him. Billy watched him disappear around to the front of the store. *Better get this gate open an get ready to skedaddle soon as they get back,* he thought. He nudged Jed to the latched gate as he pulled the rail back, allowing the horse to step through.

Ivory walked to the door and opened it slowly, looking inside as he stepped into the room. It smelled of urine and death.

"Where is she?" he asked. He looked around. Seeing the fat man and the gun, he brought up the barrel on his squirrel rifle.

Ruben looked up. Seeing the big black man with a gun entering his sanctuary, he panicked. His hand found the pistol as he brought it up leveling at Ivory's chest.

"You killed her?" the black man asked as the pistol fired. Ruben had never been a good shot but this time was different. He lifted and fired without aiming, and bad luck was with Ivory as the bullet went straight into his heart. He tried to bring the rifle up for one last shot, but he was dying too quickly. One last shuffle and he fell to the floor dead.

"Goddamned nigger." Ruben almost spit the words out as he opened the drawer to retrieve the loading supplies.

"If she's here, so is the runt. Might as well finish this." He was shaking now as he rammed the ball home.

"Damned kid will be looking for his whore of a mother. I'll send him to meet her as well." he spoke as he poured powder into the frizzen and flipped it shut.

"Yeah, that takes care of the whole family." he spoke as he stepped over the dead bodies to the door. He looked back and smiled. *Yeah, send them all to hell.*

CHAPTER 21

Bill had heard the gunshot and knew something wasn't right. His mother or Ivory hadn't come back. *It's not right. Something jest ain't right,* he thought.

That's when he saw Ruben round the corner, bringing the gun up aiming at Billy.

"Shit!" cried Bill. He dropped the reins for the two mares and kicked Jed hard in the ribs just as Ruben fired. The bullet missed Bill by a mile but not Jed. It had struck the Arabian just behind the front leg, a good lung shot. Jed was high-spirited though. As he was urged to go, he did just that leaping off so quickly Billy almost fell off, dropping both of the rifles and possibles bag in the process. Down the middle of the town they went at a full gallop, but the horse was bleeding to death as they left the town.

"Go, Jed, go!" Billy kicked harder as the horse stumbled.

"Come on, boy, let's get!" he urged the wounded horse on. Jed made it another mile away from the town until it stumbled one last time. It dropped to the ground, throwing Billy over the front.

"What?" Bill called as he hit the ground, rolling several times ahead of the dead horse.

"What the hell?" He got up and walked back to see the belly of the horse covered in blood and the hole.

"Damn!" he exclaimed.

"Damn!" he said once more. He sat down on the animal, wondering what to do next. *Well, I got me sometime 'fore them rotten bastard come fer me. But then again maybe they ain't got no gumption to finish it. They's got the horses an' the deed to the farm. Shit, I'm just a pain in the ass now. No worries unless I go back.*

He spoke to the dead horse, "Sorry I gotcha kilt, Jed. You did fine 'cept I got ya killed. Damned piece of bad luck, huh?" He stood and began the walk south toward the Bluffs. He turned once more to look at the road behind him. Seeing no pursuit, he turned and left the only family he had known.

CHAPTER 22

Ruben cussed himself for his poor marksmanship as Billy left the town at a full gallop. So consumed with his poor accuracy he failed to see a movement to his right. Spinning to meet the new threat, he pointed the empty gun at Marcia. He froze seeing her dress covered in blood.

"Are you all right, Marcia? What happened in there?" he asked, unsure of himself at this point.

"The whore busted up Sash bad, broke his arm, knee, and just about cut his cock off." she answered, wiping her hands.

"I heard gunshots. Did you get her?"

"I caved her head in with an axe handle and killed the nigger with this pistol." He held it up for her to see.

"Ruben, you couldn't hit your foot if the gun was tied to it. You say you shot the nigger dead?" she asked, looking at her partner.

"I shot at the runt as well, but I don't know if I got him or not. He was going too damned fast." Ruben confessed. Then he pointed to his office.

"She's in there along with the nigger." Then he noticed the pile of supplies and the guns on the dirt road.

"Look, the runt dropped his guns."

"That was Sash's. I doubt he'll ever get a chance to use it again as he's busted real bad. Might have to take his arm and leg off." She looked back at her store.

"Christ, Marcia, that's bad. He may not live through the saw bones." Ruben shook his head.

"I know, but there's not much else we can do. I'm telling you she whooped him bad. Shit, his cock got a slice on it as well. But his leg's going the wrong way as is his elbow. Makes me queasy seeing him that way." She shook her head.

"Maybe we should do Sash a favor?" Ruben asked, looking at the dirt road.

"No." she answered quickly. Then they both heard it, the scream of a wounded man. The ear-piercing screams of a man in excruciating pain. Marcia covered her ears.

"You're right. He'll never live with those breaks. You go do it." she asked, tears streaming down her face. So Ruben walked away to his office and ultimately to Marcia's store. Then a gunshot and it was silence. Ruben came out to see Marcia's eyes meet his.

"Fucking whore." he whispered as he took her in his arms. The small town was deserted except for them.

CHAPTER 23

Bill walked through the rest of the day, seeing no one on the lonely road that turned into a deer trail too soon. He was already missing his mother and Ivory. Keeping the river on the right, he walked solemnly south. Occasionally he saw deer, but with only a pistol and no shot and powder, he would just stare at them as he kept his nose pointed south.

"I really don't know how far it is to the Bluffs. I hope I can make it a week 'er so." he spoke aloud as depression seeped into his soul. By midafternoon his stomach was rumbling loudly in protest of not being fed since the day before. *I gotta find some grub of some kind. Maybe so I can find a farm an' talk them outta of some grub.* He stopped in his tracks. Turning around, he looked to where he'd been. *I ain't walking no more. There's two fine horses an' plenty of food back there, an' I aim to get both.* Billy had formulated a quick plan as he started walking back to the town he had just escaped from.

Past the dead horse, he kept walking, and by dark he began to see the lights of Marcia's store. A small light in the store shone dimly through the wavy glass window. *I don't recall seeing nobody else in the whole town. I mean, nary a soul the whole time we was there,* Bill remembered as he found where the mares were in the corral. He walked to the spit-railed corral and called to them quietly.

"Hey, come here girls. Come on, Bridget." he called softly to the pair of horses. He whistled softly to the horse. Finally the nearest one walked over, waiting for a treat.

"That's a good girl." Bill rubbed her muzzle, letting her sniff his hands and coat.

"Let's see if we can find a saddle an' bridle." he cooed to her. The runt stepped through the rails as he headed to where he'd found the saddle earlier in the day. Reaching out slowly, he found the saddle that Ivory had used. *This's gonna be just fine.* He hefted the saddle and blanket; feeling his shoulders strain as he picked them up, bringing to his chest, he walked slowly to Bridget.

"Ho girl. Good horse." he called as the saddle blanket and saddle rested gently on her back. He turned to see if he was still alone. Satisfied he pulled the latigo strap tight as he reached for the breast strap. Pulling it tight, he buckled it quietly.

"Good, girl. That's a good girl." he whispered to her. He turned to go back to get a bridle, his fingers touching the leather of the other saddle and finally resting on the hackamore bridle.

"That's what I'm looking fer." he said as he touched the bridle. He returned to finish up with her. Satisfied he led her out of the corral, making sure he left the gate open knowing that Bridget and Fanny wouldn't go anywhere without each other. He walked around out of sight where he tied her snuggly.

"I'll be back in a minute. Then we can get." he spoke softly to the horse. Bill turned to go to the back of the store. He knew his way around there now, and he was hoping Marcia hadn't bolted the door shut. His hand found the latch as he lifted it slowly waiting to hear a creak or groan, but nothing alerted the inhabitants of Bill's entry. He strained listening as the door swung open.

"So far so good." he whispered. Then he heard the voices. He brought the door closed as he stepped to the familiar curtain. Pulling it aside an inch, he looked into the dim light seeing Marcia sitting on her countertop, her dress pulled around her waist, her heels resting on the edge. Bill couldn't see who was in front of her but knew it had to be Ruben as it seemed that there was no one else in the whole town. Satisfied they were occupied, he left the back room, closing the door as he latched it quietly.

"I bet the ol'boy's got some grub an' I know he's got my gun.

Hell, he most likely got Ivory's squirrel gun an' pistols." Bill spoke quietly as he crossed the street; he stopped looking back to the store where he could see Ruben's head in between Marcia's legs.

"He'll be there fer a bit."

Bill skipped to the front door of Ruben's office. Placing his hand on the knob, he turned it slowly. It didn't move. He turned with more force. Still no movement. He put his shoulder against it and pushed as he turned the knob. Still no movement.

"Shit. I wonder if he's got a back door." he spoke aloud, "Hell, might as well check." He left the front door as he quickly walked to the back of the small building. He found the flat-hinged door but no knob. *Shit. I'm gonna have to break a window. Hope it won't sound too loud.* He quickly walked back to the front. Using his elbow, he moved it forward to get a decent ram on the pane glass. But before he broke the glass, he noticed something catching the light from Marcia's store. Something twinkled. *What do we have here?* Taking a step forward, he reached out, finding a skeleton key dangling from a nail from the sway-backed awning. *This's better than breaking the glass.*

The runt quickly inserted the key and turned the knob and pushed the door open slowly as he remembered the tinkling bell as the door slowly swung open. There was the odor of urine and feces in the room. *I wonder what they did with Ells an' Ivory? Figured they drug the bodies outside of town for the critters.*

Bill quickly walked to the corner where the case held them. Reaching out, he found the rifles and gently lifted one out. It stopped as the chain through the trigger guard became taut.

"Christ. Now what?" He exhaled a breath in frustration. *Gotta be a key as well. Must be in the desk drawer.* So Billy quickly moved in the dark to the three-drawer desk and began opening the drawers. He found a pistol. He had no idea that one had killed Ivory. Pushing it into his waistband, he rummaged until he found a small powder flask. He stuck it into his coat pocket; still his hand went back into the drawer where he found a small leather pouch with the balls. Into the opposite coat pocket, it went as his fingers searched for the key. *Shit. Maybe the middle one?* He went to open it but found it locked. *Ugh! Goddamnit!* He reached on top of the desk. Finding a letter opener, he quickly broke it, trying to open the drawer. *Shit.* He went to the third drawer and opened it, his hand searching. He found a key. Which one? He quickly tried it on the drawer. No luck. He almost ran to the chain holding the guns, quickly sliding his fingers along the chain until he found the lock. *Please open.* In went the key. He turned it as the lock clicked open.

"Thank you very much." he whispered as he hefted the curly maple-stocked fifty four caliber gun out. Straining his eyes, he looked for more guns but only found Sash's possible bag.

"It'll have to do." he whispered. He quickly turned to leave when he noticed Marcia's light get brighter. *Maybe the fat fart's gonna spend the night* he thought as he went to the door. Slowly he stepped into the cool air of the night. He watched across the street to the open window. There he saw Marcia standing naked, her thick triangle of hair and her saggy pancake breasts. He watched as she reached up to let her hair down. It cascaded down over her shoulders in a great wave of gray and brown. Curiosity got the best of Bill. He crept across the street, staying out of the light as he peered around the window frame. There was Stillwater lying on the blanketed floor, his fat pod pointing to his bulbous stomach.

"What in tarnations is goin' on here?" Bill whispered aloud.

"I'm gonna get them sons of bitches fer killing Ells and Ivory." He quickly left them and went to the horses. He had been right about Fanny. She stood next to Bridget, the left hind leg up, resting.

"Good girls." he spoke soothingly to them, rubbing their necks one at a time. Then he stood the rifle and possibles against the corral rail.

"You girls just wait a bit." he spoke soothingly to them as he left them to exact his revenge. He ran to the back of the store where he opened the door once again. Creeping in quietly, he approached the curtain, listening to the lovemaking in the front of the store. He looked around in the lantern-lit room. *There. That's what I'm looking for,* he thought.

"One, two, three." he mouthed the words out.

He busted through the curtain, taking the couple by surprise. Marcia rolled off, leaving Ruben's erection quivering in the well-lit room.

"You!" She looked to Ruben.

"You said you shot him!" she blasted away the man as he sat up, his pod being hidden beneath his belly.

"I thought I got him. Looks like I missed." Ruben spit the words at Billy. That's when they both saw the pistol leveled at them.

"Well now we've got that out of the way, you, Marcia, on your belly. Fat boy, you stay right there." Billy commanded.

"I'll do no such thing." She folded her arms on top of her breasts, making no motion to cover up.

"Get down! Now!" Bill screamed as he approached her. She saw the hammer back and the frizzen closed. Not knowing if the gun was primed or just cocked, she slowly decided to fight another day and lie down.

Billy quickly slipped the pistol back in his waistband as he looked for the roll of hemp rope he had seen earlier. Working quickly, he got it down and began to unroll it; he stopped, pulled out Mary Jane's knife, and quickly cut two three-foot sections and approached the pair.

"Put yer hands behind yer back." he asked somewhat politely. Her hands came back as she rested on her breasts.

"You'll not get away with this. We'll hunt you down and make sure you swing from the gallows." she threatened.

"I'm sure you will but not today or 'morrow fer that fact." He admired his knot tying. Satisfied he moved to the Justice of the Peace.

"Same to you. Hand behind yer back." he called to the fat man before him.

"Just 'cause you tie us up naked won't do you no good. Folks will forget this soon, and all they'll know is what we'll tell 'em." He laughed.

"Sure thing." Bill answered as he rolled the fat man onto his stomach.

"Hmm, this ain't gonna work." He rolled the man back over.

"Make your mind up runt. You know that's same pistol I killed the nigger with.

"No doubt." Bill retied Ruben's hands in front of him. Ruben looked to Marcia in question.

"You think 'cause you killed Ivory with this here pistol that I'm gonna beat you or kill you? No chance." he said as he quickly unrolled about twenty feet more of rope. He looked to the middle of the store to the front door. Nodding approvingly, he cut the rope. He quickly tied the rope to Ruben's hands, making several extra circles.

"That oughta do it." He quickly walked to the counter where he tied the rope to the boot rail, pulling it tight as Ruben's arms were pulled over his head. Billy actually began pulling Ruben toward the counter.

"Augh. My shoulders! Stop! You're hurting my shoulders!" Ruben cried out almost in tears as his arms were pulled taut.

"Good. Very good." Billy spoke quietly.

"What are you going to do? You're hurting him." Marcia pleaded.

"Damn right." Bill picked up more rope and walked to the door. He quickly tied a knot around the knob and opened the door out. He nodded. By now Ruben had lifted his head to see what was going on. Bill quickly walked to the counter and found a chalk stick and a small blackboard. He wrote in large letters; "DOOR STUCK PULL HARD." He admired his handiwork and began walking to the front door where he put it under the curtain.

"That'll help." He laughed a bit. Marcia looked at her lover as it all began to fit together.

"No. No. Don't do it, Bill. Don't." she was pleading her face, looking up from the blanket.

"You're quicker than that fat fart." Bill nodded to Ruben.

"What's he doing? I can't see." Ruben begged now.

"Oh, we're gonna pull a tooth." Bill answered. Then it all clicked into place.

"You'll be hunted down and killed. I'll see to it personally." he spit out the words as he held his face up through his arms.

"You'll bleed to death and not get that pleasure." Bill spoke as he approached the prone man. Ruben pulled his legs together, trying to hide his penis. It did little good as Bill pried his legs open and tied the rope around Ruben's scrotum and penis. Then he pulled them tight as the skin stretched out. Bill pulled more until they were stretched tight. He cut another section of rope and tied the fat man's legs together, watching the rope cut into the soft flesh of the man's ankles.

"Let's see how that's gonna work." He walked to the door and began to open it as he watched Ruben's genitals stretch.

"Yep, that oughta hurt just fine." He looked at Marcia.

"Now fer you, my fat cow."

"No, please, don't. I'll do whatever you want. Please don't." she wept.

"Nope, you saw fit to take all my family had. Not very Christian-like now, was it?"

Bill squatted behind her, her face turning to see what he was up to. Bill stared at the fat rump, the dimples, and the black hair growing out of her ass crack.

"Okay, Marcia." Bill walked to her and untied her hands, then rolled her over so her head was next to Ruben's feet.

She began to cry uncontrollably. Bill tied the rope around her hands as he pulled them toward her black thick triangles hair.

"Please don't do this. We'll give you anything you want. Please don't." she begged, weeping in deep breaths.

"A little too late fer that." he answered as he rolled her over pulling the rope into her crotch.

"Ah, you're tearing my puss!" she yelled, her crying stopping instantly.

"Yeppers." Bill answered as he rolled her onto her stomach, the rope coming out her ass crack. He pulled it hard as she yelped. Her hands were being pulled towards her crotch.

"There. Step one." Rolling her over onto her back he took the rope to her breasts next. Roughly he pulled each massive breast out so they're on top of her arms. Then he tied the rope under them, pulling tight. The rope through her crotch were now linked to her breasts.

"There." He repeated the steps to the opposite knob on the door. Returning to her feet, he tied her feet together and then went back to the boot rail, pulling the rope as he'd done for Ruben. He watched her breasts being pulled up covering her head, but the rope stayed around them as he secured it. He walked over to inspect his work, her vulva hiding the rope as it was buried deep into her person.

"One more thing before I head off to Cincinnati." he lied. Billy found two handkerchiefs.

"Gotta keep you quiet while you wait for your next customers." He bent down to muffle her when he saw the daggers staring at him.

"My, I do believe you're pissed." He chuckled.

"You can go in shit, peckerwood!" Then she spat him.

"Hmm, okay, that's the way you want it." he stood up, pulling the knives and pistols out. He dropped his wool breeches. Taking the kerchief, he wiped his butt. He looked and saw the brown stain.

"That oughta do just fine." Bill hiked up his breeches. Securing them he, smoothly replaced his weapons as he moved to Marcia's head. He held her head as he tied the stained section so it gagged her mouth. He knotted it tight as she grunted insults.

"No. No, there's no need to thank me." He smiled as he turned to Ruben.

"Now for yours." Bill began to lift Ruben's head, expecting insults, but Ruben eyes were closed. He made no noise as Billy secured the handkerchief.

"You're a bit smarted than the cow. I'll give you that." Bill finished walking to the doors. Once more he slowly pulled one at a time, inspecting the work, watching the genital being stretched.

"That's it. If you folks get to Cincinnati, look me up." He turned and walked out the way he came in.

He stopped seeing jerky, apples and rock candy. *Hum I don't mind if I do.* He emptied the jerky jar into his coat pocket. Next he opened the candy jar filling his pocket as well. Retracing his steps he went to the curtain and out the back door closing and latching it. He stepped into the false dawn. *Should be sunup in a bit. I'll be long gone by then.* He quickly made his way to the horses and grabbed his gun and possibles as he mounted and began his journey too Bluffs.

Bill rode through the early morning, making good time as he passed Jed.

"Not to worry, Jed, I got your girls here." he called to the dead horse as he passed the bloating Arabian. "Come on, Bridge, let's get." He kicked the horse to a canter as he left the soon-to-be memory of the fine horse.

Bill and the two horses made good time as they put the miles behind them. Soon the Big Muddy was before him. He reined her to the left. *Damn sure better than walking, I say that fer sure.* Bill looked over his right shoulder. Seeing the river through the trees, he smiled.

"Keep it on the right, an' I'll be in Niota in no time." he spoke to the quickly moving horse. He turned to see Fanny right behind Bridget, keeping up with no worries.

"Yep, real quick like." he continued on with his narrative.

"It's gonna be a fine day. Yeppers, a fine day." he spoke to the horses as they quickly made their way down to the next town. Bill thought he was on the way to Bluffs, but in fact, he was on a direct course to newly formed town of Hannibal, Missouri.

CHAPTER 24

Bill had no idea what was going to transpire at Marcia's store. He knew there'd be bloodshed. That's if all went as he planned.

In the morning a lone wagon pulled into town. Katie, Kelly Ann, and their mother, Ester, had come in for the supplies. Since her husband had been killed, they had been doing all the work on the farm. Both of the girls were haggard and worn as Ester pulled up the mule in front of Marcia's store.

"You girls get the nails, a new hoe, and you can each get a piece of hard candy. I'm going to see Mr. Stillwater."

"Are you going to marry him or that bald man Sash? We need a man, and they're the only ones around these parts unattached." Katie called goading her mother.

"You hush. No, I'm not going to do that. I want to see about selling our farm and moving to St. Louis. Now you girls go on like I told you." Ester turned and began her walk to the Justice of the Peace's office.

"Momma needs to get a man under her skirt. She's been a bitch ever since Daddy got killed." Katie whispered to her sister.

"Oh, shut up. It wouldn't be like this if you hadn't been slutty with that Billy White. He's no good." She looked around the quiet town.

"He's a bad person. I wouldn't give him any favors. That's for sure." Kelly Ann boasted to her sister.

Before Katie could stop herself, she snapped back at her prude sister, "He's not bad. He's very good." Her hand went to her mouth as she slipped her secret. Kelly Ann whirled around.

"What do you mean he's very good?" Her expression was confused and angry.

"Oh, well, if you must know me and Billy I have been doing it all the time. You know he can squirt three times in a row?"

"You! You're not old enough to having sex. You're what? Sixteen? You've ruined yourself for marriage now. No man will want a slut." she spat as she recovered her composure.

"Oh fuck you!" Katie snapped. "I'm seventeen."

Kelly Ann's jaw dropped open. She'd only heard that word from the boys at school.

"We'll not speak of this anymore in public. But you can be sure that we're on the way home, Momma will hear it all." Kelly Ann spit the words to her sister.

"Fine. You tell Momma about me, and I'll tell about you and the goat." Katie whispered back.

"What? I've done nothing with a goat!" Kelly Ann answered back flabbergasted.

"Oh? We'll see." Katie answered as she stepped to the door of Marcia's store

"You coming?"

"Yes." Kelly Ann jumped up the two steps as her hand went to the doorknob.

"Hey, I bet I open it faster than you." Kelly Ann challenged her sister.

"Oh? Okay, let's see." Katie answered back.

"Ready. On three. One. Two. Three." she called out as they swung the door open to be greeted by horrific muffled screams.

Flatboats and Arrows

CHAPTER 25

Bill reined the lathered mare to a slow walk just short of the water's edge; the black horse was panting as it had been a hard ride since leaving the Dallas City mess.

"I ain't gonna get ambushed this time. You hear that, Bridge? We're going all the way to St. Louis if we have to. But ya know, I've heard that Nauvoo had some fine prospects." He kicked her gently as she lurched off at a canter to the south.

"Come on, let's get." Young Bill rode through the first day until Bridget wouldn't go any more than a walk.

"You played out girl? I thought you Arabians could go forever." He watched the black horse slow more and more with each step.

"I reckon I'll give you a break and take Fanny fer a bit."

Bill reined up under large oak tree while he changed to Fanny. He looked out into the sunset, trying to figure out if he wanted to rest here or find a better place to camp.

"I didn't get a chance to shoot no supper." he spoke as he threw a leg over the saddle. "But I've got that jerky, that'll have to do."

"Well, we might as well keep going an' stop where it'll be safe an' find you some water an' grass."

He called to Bridget, "Come on girl, let's get." Bill adjusted the pistols in his waistband as he pulled her halter rope, leading her into the darkness. The thought of Nauvoo in the distance made him want to ride into the night, wishing for the small-town lanterns to show themselves in the late night.

Hours passed as the young man pushed the inky black horses farther into exhaustion, but then he saw it. The small town in front of him was Niota, not Nauvoo like he had thought. The town had a small glimmer of light sparkling in the dark night.

"Fanny ol' girl, looks like we get to sleep under a roof tonight." He patted her neck.

"Let's go." They closed the distance quickly as he counted four houses and two tall front buildings in the darkness of the late-summer night.

"Here we go. Ready?" Fanny stepped off into the darkness.

He pulled up behind the last house in the row on one side of the dirt street. *No dogs to be a barking. That be good.* He quickly slid off the sweaty horse, tying her to the small fence behind the house. Grabbing his rifle from the horn, he quietly walked to the front until he could look through the glass window. There he saw a man about Matthew's age sitting at a table, reading a book by lantern light. Bill looked slowly around the room. There he saw what he figured was the wife. The large plump woman sat across from the man, her Bible in front of her. Bill looked closely at her pale skin that seemed to glow in the lantern light; her hair pulled into a bun with her nightgown buttoned up to her double chin. He stared into the room, listening to the night around him. Then he heard a voice of young girl from inside the small home.

"Papa, all my friends have boyfriends. Why can't I have one?" the voice asked, but he couldn't see her.

Bill thought, *This is gonna be good, a roof over my head and a girl. Yeppers. Very good.*

"I told you, Lira, when you turn nineteen, you may take a caller. But until then, it remains no. There be no more talk on this." the father spoke, not looking up from his book.

Bill pondered, *Hmm, well, I might as well look around to see what else this town has to offer.* He walked away from the home. As he approached the next house, he heard no movement as it was dark inside. *That leaves two more.* He closed the distance quickly to the third house in the row of homes. He heard voices from one of the tall buildings.

The crackling voice called out in a beggar's whine, "Ashley come on, sweetie. I'll give you a silver dollar for just fer a few minutes alone with you upstairs." the voice pleaded.

"Samuel, go on home to your wife. Give her the dollar an' see what she does with it. Go on. I'm closing up." The nineteen-year-old barkeep helped the drunken man to his feet as she guided him toward the door. Bill stepped into the darkness as the drunk wobbled to the dark house Bill had just left. Watching he saw the door open and close. No lights ever brightened as the man vanished. *Hmm? Might as well see how my luck goes inside.*

Bill stepped around the corner on to the porch and looked into the room as the woman was putting the chairs upside down on top of the tables.

He put his hand on the knob and turned slowly as he pushed the door open. A bell above made a slight tingle.

"We're closed for the night." she spoke but never turned around.

"You have a room I can rent?" Bill asked as he watched her turn to see to whom she was speaking with.

"Well, I've a room upstairs. Not for rent, though." She lifted another chair up, quickly flipping it upside down she placed it carefully on the table.

"You're new, ain't you? You look familiar. Aren't you from over in La Harpe? You the one whose daddy got kicked by a mule?" She asked, a chair in hand, as she looked upon Billy.

"How's it you know of me?" he asked, shocked that his family's business was second nature to this person.

"We all heard of the Whites. Not much happens that we don't hear about. I heard you maw done ran off to Kentucky or some nonsense. That true?" She put the chair on the table and walked behind the oak plank bar, pulling out a bottle of amber liquid.

"You wanna drink?" she asked.

"I need some company. Old Sam he wanted under my skirt. His wife would have my liver if I ever gave in. Sahara's good old nigger, an' she loves Sam like an old hound. We don't care if she's black. She cook up the best meat pies this side of the Mississippi. So, Mr. Billy White, how's Katie?" She smiled as she poured the whiskey. She stopped when it's half full. She pushed it to Bill as she poured one for herself.

"How? How is it you know of her too?" Bill asked as he stood his rifle up against the plank bar. He picked up the whiskey, holding it up to the light.

"You seem to know a lot of me, an' yet I know nuthin' of ya." he asked as he sipped the whiskey, feeling it burn as he pretended to flinch. Playing it up, he gave a small cough. Billy and his pals had been sneaking booze to drink when ever they could.

"Don't drink much?" she asked as she tossed hers back like it was sweet tea.

"No." He coughed again.

"No not much." He exhaled as he sipped another taste. This time he didn't cough but made a winching face as the burning liquid seeped into his gut.

"I know Katie. She's talked a lot of you. She described you to me one time. You look just as she said. Blond. Thin." She poured herself another drink and paused.

"An' cute."

Bill smiled at the woman before him.

"But she told me other things as well. Are they true?" she asked keenly.

"Like what other things?" Billy played her game, sipping slowly out of the glass.

"Oh, like what you were like in the bed. She says you have a gift. You can please women three times in a row. That's what Katie says. Three in a row?" Ashley asked point-blank to Bill.

It was late; he and she were the only ones in the town awake. Morning was but a few hours away, and it was plain to Bill this was going to be a sleepless night.

"I can show you. If you'd like?" He tossed his drink back, faking a cough again.

"I hope you screw better than you drink." She poured another.

"Come on, drink up. I don't want you to toot too soon. Hurry up farm boy. This place is closed anyway." She walked over, pulling the dead bolt in place, and then she pulled the shade down on the door.

She looked back at Bill. "Room's upstairs."

She pulled the window shades down as well.

"Go on up. I'll lock the back up an' join you in a minute." She walked past Bill as he headed for the narrow stairs that led up to the second floor.

"Wait. I left my horses tied up behind the house across the street. I'll fetch 'em an' be back in a shake." He turned to go out the front door.

"Never mind them. Goldstein will put 'em in the corral behind his store in the morning. You can get them then." She left Bill as he heard the bolts on the back door.

"He won't try to steal 'em?" Bill asked, concerned.

"No, he won't try to steal them. He's a good Jew. He'll feed and brush 'em down. Just like I want to brush you down. Come on Billy." She wrapped her arm around his waist leading to the stairs; on the way past the bar, he grabbed his rifle with his free hand as she led him up the stairs that went to her room.

"Goddamned Ashley the booze is workin' quick on me. You best hurry up an' drop that dress. I think my peckers gonna split my breeches." Bill lied. He felt himself hardening as he looked at the brown-haired girl before him. She had round cheeks, soft pouty lips, small pointy nose, and the greenest eyes Bill could remember seeing.

"Well, aren't you the quick one?" She stepped on the first of the many steps leading up. "I cain't wait that long, girl. Drop yer drawers." His breath was coming in short quick gasps.

"Right here, huh? Just pull up my skirt?" she asked, her head cocked to the side.

"Either that or just wrap yer lips around my pod. Either way I'm popping one off 'fore we get up there." Bill moved the pistols to the side as he opened his breeches, his pod sticking out like a spigot on a barrel.

The girl looked down to see his pecker stiff and ready for attention. Shit, she wasn't joking when she said he was a randy sum bitch.

"I'll just drop these." Her hands went under her dress, pulling her much-used drawers off, letting them rest on her ankle-high shoes.

"How's that White Man?" She pulled her dress up, revealing her dark triangle of hair.

"Just fine. Just fine." Bill laid his musket on the steps. It slid down to the floor, but he made no movement to retrieve it, kneeling between her legs as he slipped into her.

"My, my, seems you be wetter than the dew girl." Bill commented as he began rutting on the stairs.

"It don't take much for me to get slippery. Especially when I see a hard cock." she spoke, her eyes closed as Bill pumped quickly. He knew he'd be quick since he hadn't got anything since he had been with Katie. "Don't squirt in me. Squirt it on the steps. I don't wanna be dripping all night." she responded. *Damned if he ain't quick. Good thing he can go three times as I didn't even come close to getting mine. I hope he takes longer next coupla times.*

"You best be letting me have mine or you'll be out on the street, three times or not." she sassed him as he stood before her, pod quivering like a broken back cat.

"Oh? You'll get yours. Don't you fret none. I had to get one off quick like. That's all." He reached back and grabbed his rifle as he stood up looking as the mess on the steps, not bothering to put his pod away.

"Christ! You left a puddle like a cup of spilled milk! Good thing you didn't leave it in me, or I'd be a douching all night to get rid of you. Come on, I want mine." She picked up her drawers then turned to lead Bill up the steps.

Bill followed her up the stairs like a calf to a cow as she led him to the lantern-lit room of hers. He entered behind her, taking a look at the room as he closed the door behind him. There against the wall was a small dark dresser with an oval mirror, another dress hanging on the corner of the bedpost.

She tossed her drawers on the floor and pulled her dress over her head. Bill had not taken two steps into the room when Ashley hopped up on the poster bed and lay back on the worn quilt, her head resting on the tick-filled pillow. She reached for a post on either side of the headboard with her hands, leaving her shoes on.

"Don't wait. Get to it." she spoke, her legs opening and closing quickly. Bill turned and stood his gun in the corner; then dropped his pistols, knives, and breeches; and kicked off his shoes.

In the excitement he almost ripped his shirt as he pulled it over his head. Walking around to her, he reached for a nipple and gently rolled it between his fingers.

"Stop with that. Suck my pussy. I can rub my tits anytime I want." she demanded.

Bill stood back. It was the first time the foreplay wasn't requested or even wanted.

"Just like that?" he asked. "What about yer shoes?"

"You ain't fucking my feet. Would you get to it?" she asked in a quick short voice.

"Sure thing." Bill answered as he crawled onto the bed, pulling her legs apart, placing each heeled shoe at his elbow.

Bill neared her musky crotch and lost himself in her aroma. The young lad buried his tongue into her as he felt her relax. Then Bill lifted his mouth to the button of life and sucked it like a calf on a teat.

Ashley lifted her head to look down onto the blond man at

her groin. Never before had a man done this. She felt a climax coming. She arched her back as she oozed onto Bill's chin, but the lad never stopped. He raked, bit, and sucked on the red swollen clitoris as she came again and again. Finally, when she was in pain from his abuse, she relinquished her grasp on the bed and pushed his head away.

She propped herself up on her elbows as she looked upon his shiny face.

"No more. I musta came six or seven times, maybe more, I can't recall, but you've worn it out. Shit. Katie never said anything about your tongue."

"So." he looked over her slender stomach past her soft white breasts to see he eyes half closed, "you happy?"

"Oh yeah. Christ, you've done more than I ever could. You can have your other two now. I'm not gonna hold you back one bit." She slumped her head back to the pillow.

"Christ." was all she could muster.

Bill crawled forward, lifting her legs up to on top of his shoulder as he placed his pod to the saturated hole. No effort was needed as he quickly thrashed away at her.

"You can leave it in as a reward." she spoke without lifting her head. Bill had other plans. He felt the familiar tingling as he neared eruption, but instead of filling her up, he pulled out and shot on the outside of her swollen vulva, watching it slime down to her butt.

"You get too excited, did you? That ain't the first time a man's done that. Pulled out too quick and missed the hole." She went to bring her leg over Bill's head to get up, but he stopped her.

"I ain't done." He pulled her leg back to his shoulder.

"You ready to go again?" she asked, surprised.

"Yeppers." He smiled. Bill put his stiff piss'r into the goo as she laid her head back onto the pillow.

"Well, you go ahead and get your last one. It'll be light in an hour or so, and I still have to open up."

Bill knew what he wanted to do, and he made things would go well. He pumped a few times as he reached down to gently rub her sore button. Instead of pushing away, she relaxed and rubbed her breasts as Bill worked his magic. Satisfied with its progress, he pulled out and lifted her legs forward, and then he slipped his pod to her anus.

"No you don't!" She arched her back, trying to prevent Bill from entering her private hole.

"Relax, Ashley. Relax." he spoke soothingly.

"No. Not my asshole." She fought harder, "Stop it! I don't want to be farting spunk all day."

"You like what I just did, didn't you?" He paused, the head of his penis resting on the rim of her butt.

"Of course but not my asshole." She quickly pulled her legs away from his shoulders.

"I'll do anything but that. You can pop yer cork in my mouth or pussy fuck me again. Whatever. Not my butt. You clear on that?" She sat up, arms straight out locked behind her.

"All right. But you've missed out on one of the greatest squirts you'll ever have." Bill sat back and rested on his legs, not giving up.

"Better than the eating you did?" Her curiosity wetted.

"Better." he said as he stroked himself.

"No. I'm satisfied." She leaned over, placing his pod in her mouth, and quickly bobbed her head. It took Bill little time until he filled her mouth. Unlike the other women he'd had the pleasure of, she sat up and spit into her hand, then got up, and left Bill to his own accord. She picked up the dress on the floor and wiped her hand clean.

"It'll be daylight in a half hour or so. You be gone when it is. I don't want no trouble from anyone 'cause of you." She pulled her drawers on, "You clear on that?" She kicked the soiled dress into the corner.

"Gone." She reached over and took the other dress, slipping

it over her head.

"I got work to do. You come down and get." She turned and left the room to Bill.

I ain't never had this before. Might as well get I reckon. He dressed himself quickly, grabbing his pistols and knives, placing them in the familiar places. He retrieved his musket and left the room. He made his way down the steps to see her already into a glass of whiskey.

"You're good. I'll say that for you, but you best be getting." She poured another glass full and pushed it to him.

"No hard feelings?" She nodded to the glass.

"Nary a one." He picked it up and threw it back without the least bit of a cough or choke. He winked at her and headed for the door. Just as he closed the paned glass door, he heard her yell, and the drinking glass hit the doorjamb.

"Fucker!" was all he heard as Bill walked to where the mares were tied. They nickered as he approached them in the darkness.

"Hey, girls, we gotta get." He hung the rifle on the horn as he seated himself on the saddle.

"Come on, Bridget. Get Fanny. Come on." Bill nudged Fanny out of the small town as the sun peeked over the eastern tree line. He headed south closer to Hannibal.

CHAPTER 26

Bill watched Bridget stumble again just like Jed had done. She went down pulling the halter rope as she crumpled to the dirt path, her sides heaving as she died.

"Shit, it's you an' me Fanny." He tossed the halter rope onto the dying horse. Then he spoke to the heaving horse he was sitting on, "Come on let's get 'fore them red bastard catch us." He nickered her quietly as he gently touched her ribs. She walked off, but her head was hanging down. Bill watched her, knowing her time was soon. The last of the Indians were miles behind him, and his horse had played herself out, avoiding capture or certain death.

When Bill had left Niota, he had headed south in the early light of another day as he neared the river. He had failed to notice the moccasin tracks covering the worn trail as he and the two horses plodded toward what Bill thought was Hannibal.

The young traveler had no idea the Kaskaskia had set up an ambush for the solitary rider. Bill had been daydreaming about the night he had had with Ashley. He had made mistakes that could be fatal. Mistakes that weren't tolerated by wilderness life. Even though the town of Niota was only twenty miles behind him, he was still very much in the wilderness.

Bill had been watching the river through the willows and moss-covered oaks when the first arrow went through the sleeve of his linen shirt. If he moved a fraction more forward, the arrow would hit him squarely in the lungs as the Kaskaskia archer had misjudged Bill's pace. Bill kicked Fanny hard as another arrow zinged by his head.

"Get! Get! Yaw! Go, Fanny, go!" He tried to make himself small as the Arabian shot off like an arrow. She had had a good night's rest back at Niota and was anxious to run. Bill eased up on the reins as he hunched over, watching for movement ahead of him. His watch was rewarded as a half-dozen brightly painted warriors stepped from behind the trees and showered him with arrows.

Bill and Fanny's luck held but not Bridget's. Two arrows found their mark as she became a pincushion. Bill pulled the pistol and aimed for the nearest warrior as the man knocked another arrow to send Bill's way. He never got to release it as Bill fired at point-blank into the painted face. The fifty four-caliber ball ripped the man's head apart. Fanny jumped over the slumped man on the ground as they broke through the gauntlet of warriors.

"Go!" he screamed as Fanny set a blistering pace. So fast was she that Bill had never got the pistol put away but instead hung on to the horn with the reins with one hand and the pistol in the other as the black mare increased the distance between them and the ambush.

Bill let the mares run as fast as they wanted as they distanced themselves from the ambush. He noticed the lead rope being pulled back as Bridget stumbled and collapsed to the ground, her lung punctured by two arrows. Dropping the rope, he spoke to his mount, "Shit, it's you an' me, you Fanny."

Into the early afternoon they traveled as he kept an ever-constant lookout for a sign of an ambush or trap. When the sun began to drop into the western bank, he heard voices, American-speaking voices.

"Looks like we finally found someone to hole up with." He paused, looking toward the voices.

"What you say, girl? Go meet up with 'em? Yeah, I think that'll be fine." he spoke as he patted her neck, heading into the dusk and to the river's edge.

Pulling up short of the voices, he called to them, hoping for a warm reception.

"Hello the camp!" He turned his head, listening for a reply.

"Who's there?" a deep billowing voice answered.

"Bill White of La Harpe. Can I come in?" Bill answered, hoping to hear a friendly response.

"You all by yer lonesome?" came a different voice, one that had a Spanish accent.

"Yeppers. Jus' me an' my horse." Bill waited.

"Shit, we may have made a mistake, Fanny." he spoke quietly to the mare as he gently pulled back on the reins, nudging her back from the voices, not wanting to get into another mess.

"Come on in boy." a deep voice answered back.

"Well, here we go, Fanny." he whispered to her as he nudged her forward through the wall of broken branches and dead trees. His eyes came to rest on the wide flat boat tied to a stump. Four men looked at him. All had guns trained on him as he pulled up at the water's edge.

River men, Bill thought. He knew nothing except they'd be better than the Indians that had tried to kill him several times since he'd left his home a lifetime ago.

"Howdy fellers. I heard yer voices from back yonder." He pointed behind him.

"Anyway I've been getting deviled by the goddamned Injuns since I left Dallas City an' figured it would be a helluva lot safer traveling with folks than getting skewered on my lonesome."

"You want a pup lazing about on yer boat, Ike?" Aarnel smiled at Bill, by far the largest of the crew. His salt-and-pepper beard hung well below the opening of his sleeveless calico shirt. Bill stared in awe of this huge man. His long blond shoulder-length hair fluffing the early-evening breeze reminded Bill of mother. The look on his face convinced Bill he had a good heart, if that could be true of a river man.

"I ain't yet too sure if I want him aboard. What say you, Markus?" Ike asked as he sized up Bill. Bill turned his attention to the pilot. His black waistcoat opened, revealing a once-white shirt. His small brimmed river hat cantered to the right, revealing his gray hair that was cut close to his ears. The eyes caught Billy's attention; they looked to be smiling at Billy as he spoke. *This is what a river-man should look like,* Bill thought as Fanny leaned down to munch the fresh grass at the water's edge.

Bill's attention turned to the man called Markus. The runt looked to the man with the greasy black beard. his stomach looked like he'd swallowed a watermelon. It was so round and full. His once-white and navy-blue striped shirt was ripped beyond repair. The tan stomach hung out below the shirt's hem; the rope belt hung loosely almost to his knee-high pants where he saw the huge bare dirt-covered feet from days of no care.

"Yeah, I could stand a new face on the boat. He looks like he can be a hard worker. You a hard worker boy?" Markus asked as he looked Bill up and down like a slab of meat.

Bill looked into Markus's face, and he saw lust, no two ways about it. The man wanted Bill all to himself. Bill gazed to the last crew member. The quiet one sat on a keg, his musket resting across the top of his legs. He stared at Bill with no interest other than another man to man.

The one called Ike spoke at last to Bill.

"What would you do with that horse you be a sitting on if we were to let you aboard?" Ike asked as he admired the fine horse flesh Billy sat on.

"I reckon I'd cut her loose. Let her be on her own hook. I could stash the saddle an' gear onboard if there's room." Bill leaned down, patting the mare's neck. *I may have made the wrong decision here,* he thought as he went waiting for a vote.

"I say let him aboard." the one called Ike broke the silence as he looked at Billy seriously.

"What you say men?"

"Let him on." the biggest one spoke, lowering his gun and stepping aside to show a path onto the large freight hauler.

"Markus? Justin?" Ike asked again.

"I'd like to have him. I surely would. I mean I'd like to see him come aboard." Markus smiled. Billy caught the slip as the man smiled through his beard, showing his gray teeth at Billy.

"Justin? It's your call. What say ye?" Aarnel asked over his shoulder to the last man.

"I hope you can defend yourself." He stood up straight, showing Billy his true height, at least six feet if he was an inch. The quiet one was dressed as Ike, with the black coat and white shirt, his buckle shoes showing from under the long trousers.

"You say you're Bill White? Well, Mr. White, you'll have painted men after you as well as that turtle fucker there." Justin pointed to Markus. Justin didn't like Markus, but he was a crew member just as he was.

"Shut up, Justin, or I'll punch your face in!" Markus turned as he whipped out a large broad-bladed knife.

"Stop it you two. You can draw your wages if you want to fight." Ike laid the fight to an instant halt.

"Ike, you know that Markus will have that lad strapped over a barrel trying to hide his cock in the lad's rump in the time it takes a bass to jump fer a skeeter." He looked to Billy.

"Mr. White, you best be careful if you come aboard." Justin spoke as he kept his hand on the slender musket, resting in the crook of his arm.

"Come on boy, if you're comin'. Don't want none of them filthy red niggers catchin' us tied up here." Ike spoke as he walked back to the stern of the boat.

Billy quickly slid of Fanny. He rushed pulling the hackamore and saddle off her. The men on the boat made no effort to help.

"All right, Fanny. Get. Yaw! Get!" he yelled at the black horse. Fanny had other plans, though. She'd known no other life than Billy and the brood. She had been around Billy too long; she walked to Bill and grabbed his shirt, pulling him back off his feet. The crew laughed as Billy and the saddle landed on the broken limbs of the bank, snapping with a loud crack. Before Billy could right himself, she brought her muzzle to his face and proceeded to rub him vigorously.

"Boy, looks like your horse will have none of you leaving her!" the biggest man roared as they all had a good laugh on Billy. The lad quickly rolled over and continued to put his gear on the flat boat all the while having Fanny harass him. Bill threw his saddle and tack onto the front of the boat as Fanny backed away from the water's edge. Last, Bill laid his musket across the saddle as he jumped on. Fanny watched it all. She began to prance watching the young man leave her.

"Shove off, Aarnel. Man your poles, you scurvy river rats. Get me out into the currents. Heave to!" Ike yelled as the men quietly went to their assigned post of labor. Billy watched the black horse tramp to and fro, trying to make her mind up of what to do. Seeing Bill drift away, she turned and faded into the green of the river's edge.

"You had a good horse boy." Markus spoke as he walked forward to pole the water.

"I had three to start with." Bill looked at the man that had spoken to him, wondering if it was true what the quiet man had spoken of.

"Three horses? You a rich boy? You got some coins to pay for the boat ride?" Ike asked from the rudder.

"No, sir. The horses were my pappy's. Fanny there was the last one. I don't have anything to pay with unless you wanna take my saddle an' tack fer payment." Bill suddenly felt alone.

"We'll see later. You good with that rifle?" the quiet one asked from the front of the craft.

"Yeah, I've kept myself fed with it." he lied.

"Good. Then this evening when we tie up fer the night, you can get us some grub then." Ike spoke as he steered them down away from where Billy's life had been. The crew became silent as they floated down the Mississippi, bringing Billy closer to Hannibal where he figured his life would really get interesting.

Into the late afternoon they traveled, Bill was amazed at how fast the landscape floated by. *It woulda taken me days to get this far. I bet we're not far from Hannibal,* he thought as he watched as steam-powered stern-wheeled paddleboat went past them as it splashed north. Not bothered by currents, the ship was out of sight in no time, leaving Billy in a state of awe.

"Sumbitches move right along, huh?" he asked Aarnel, watching the big man, pulled on the long oar.

"Yep. They'll put us outta business too soon. Think you could get a fat doe for supper, lad?" he asked as he lifted the oar out of the water and started the ritual of oaring again.

"Sure thing." Billy answered as he watched the western shoreline for any sign of life, be it man or animal. His watch was rewarded as a herd of white tail deer ran into view. They scattered as Billy watched. Painted men materialized from the foliage and systematically killed them.

"You see that? That's why we don't wanna be tied up too long. You jest got to find us at the right time boy. Jest yer good luck." Markus called to Billy as he rowed in sync with Aarnel.

"Looks like I'm really beholden to you fellers. I'd be in the stew pot before nightfall. That's fer certain and fer true." Bill spoke as he watched the painted men fade from sight as soon as they had gotten their prey. He leaned back against a barrel and propped his elbows on the edge as he looked back to where Ike piloted the large floating freighter. Ike brought his finger up to the side of his nose and then flipped it forward to acknowledge Bill's attention.

The pilot had seen many a young lad come across the deck of his boat. Many had moved on to greener pastures, but a few had met their watery graves on either side of his boat. The river was quick to take her ounce of flesh from unaware travelers. It mattered not to the Big Muddy if it was an experienced river man or a wet-nursed farm boy. If the river needed an ounce of flesh, it found a way to get it. Anything from a snag to jolt the boat to a sudden stop throwing the men off the decks to an underwater eddy could flip a freighter over like a snapping turtle. Ike had been piloting flatboats for near to three years and not lost a crew member, though a few interim travelers like the lad on the front of his boat now had been killed.

He nodded to Billy. Seeing the determination in Bill's expression, Ike hoped he'd back up his words of delivering food and defense when the call came. As for now, they were just on the river, and Hannibal would be the next stop tomorrow or the next day, but tonight they would stop for food. Ike looked at the oarsmen on the starboard side then to the port, both men pulling their share. Justin near the front, ready to man the gouger, or front rudder, at a moment's notice. Ike depended on Justin heavily for the river travel. Justin was ever bit as good of a pilot as Ike; he'd been there to save the day more than he could count as peril loomed at every bend in the river.

Justin don't mince words, Ike thought; every time a young man came aboard, Markus would try every ploy he could to get the man's breeches down to his ankle so he could sodomize them. Justin had fought Markus at every grog shop they pulled into. Knife play had come quickly, but the men were equals with the blade. Ike needed both of them, and they needed each other if they were to get to New Orleans to collect another journey's wage. Justin spoke freely to the newest travelers to warn them of the man that pulled the starboard oar.

Billy didn't know the history of the boat and he had no interest to learn it. He wanted to get to Hannibal in one piece, and if it meant riding with that man, then so be it. Bill looked to the west as the sun began it's race to the tree line. *Won't be long 'till we pull in for the night.* His mind raced from the mooring to the time when he'd lay foot on the Missouri soil for the first time.

Bill's wait was rewarded. Ike called out to head for the nearest grove of willows on the western bank that would offer them a place of sanctuary for the night. Billy watched the well-oiled crew to steer the boat out of the main channel toward what looked to be a poor place of mooring. The trees came right down to the edge, offering the chance of an ambush to the river men.

"Not tellin' you yer business, but that place yonder don't look too good fer a tie-down place." Bill called over to Aarnel as the big man started to reverse his stroke to bring the boat to Ike's request.

"Pull in there, Aarnel! Justin, be ready to tie us quick. Markus, steady as she goes." Ike called as the boat slowly edged its way to the shore. Bill watched as Justin prepared his ropes as the boat slipped into the nearest tree.

"Markus pull now! Grab that limb Aarnel!" Ike instructed the crew as the large boat came to a stop.

"All right, lads, look sharp." Ike called as he held the boat steady.

"Get your ass out there and snag us some meat. Don't come back here. We're gonna move down to the next grove of trees. Maybe a half mile down. You come find us. You got it? You come to find us." Ike spoke as he looked into the trees outside of Justin's grasp.

It didn't take too long for Billy to figure out what the plan was. If any Indians watched them come to shore, there'd be no ambush. For if they went to where the boat was supposed to be, all they'd find would be where they had been.

"I understand. See you later then." He quickly grabbed his possible bag and rifle as he jumped into the mud on the bank, sinking up to his ankles immediately. A few quick steps and he was hidden from view of the freighter.

"Gotta be quick. Can't mess around here or them Injuns will be eatin' my liver." he whispered to the foliage around him. Three more steps and the river was completely out of sight. *Gotta find a game trail. Then I can find where them critters are watering up fer the night,* he thought as he quickened his pace in the waning night. He came upon a trail. A well-used one too.

"Shit." He looked up through the canopy of the forest to see what little of the early evening sun was left.

"Still 'nuff light to hunt by." The lad stepped off to the south at a light jog. He was running as quietly as he could, hoping to bump into a deer, coon, or opossum. The light was fading as fast as he was running now; his bag softly bouncing off his hip, he stopped at a fallen tree that was blocking the trail, when movement caught his attention ahead of him. He skidded to a stop and leaned behind a large maple tree. Peeking a look around the tree, he saw red men coming his way. *They're going to where the boat had been!* he thought as he straightened against the tree, waiting for them to close the distance.

They ain't seen me. I'll let them go by and beat feet fer the boat. Maybe I can still snag a critter on the way, Bill planned as the men ran past his hiding place. *One, two, three,* he counted, *six, seven, eight. Too many to fight. Gotta outrun 'em. No time to hunt. Jus' stayin' alive will be hard enough.* Bill counted to three after the last warrior had gone past. He looked around the tree just to make sure he'd not bump into a back marker. *Nothing. Gotta go!* He came around the tree and started his sprint to where he hoped the boat would be. Billy had no idea there were two more Foxes were on a collision course with him. They had stopped to get a rock out of one of their moccasin and were hotfooting it to catch up with the raiding party when a small white man bowled into them, knocking them both back onto the trail they had just run on.

Billy had seen them before they had seen him. *No chance to hide. Gotta hit them hard and keep running.* He did just that. Using his shoulder as a battering ram, he hit the first one hard, knocking him back into the trailing man. Bill leapt over the second one, not missing a step.

He heard them jabbering and making a commotion to alert the others. Now he was running in almost-complete darkness when luck smiled at him; a small doe walking ahead of him. She didn't hear the runt as she was watching the trail ahead of her, listening and stepping carefully. Bill didn't miss the chance; he fired from the hip as he neared her. The round ball smashed into the back of her head, dropping her to the ground almost immediately.

The runt slid to a halt and turned to look behind him. *Can't see a derned thing. That means they can't see me neither.* That's when he heard them; the boat crew. *Not being too secretive,* he thought as he hefted the deer over his slim shoulder. It promptly fell off. Once more he tried. This time he pulled the front legs down so they dangled on his left side. Picking up his rifle, he began to lope toward the noise.

"Hey boys!" he called out.

"Come on an' help me! I got a doe, but there a shitload of Injuns on my heels!" he called again, "Hey, goddamned it! Get over here!" and the deer began to slow his steps as he heard the Foxes behind him getting louder.

"Where are ya, runt?" It was Aarnel.

"Over here. Hurry, they're right behind me!" Billy yelled in a panic.

"I'm right here." Then out of the darkness the mountain of the man grabbed the deer like a toy and turned to lead Billy back to the boat.

"We figured you'd been killed when you didn't show up right away." Aarnel called over his shoulder.

"Jes about didn't make it. They're catching up. We gotta hurry." Bill called to the man ahead of him.

"Don't worry none. Ike's got him an' the boys lined up ready to back us up as soon as we're onboard." Aarnel spoke without turning his head. Then they were there. A few lanterns lit the boat up as Billy and Aarnel came closer.

"Hey there Billy. I see ya got us some supper." Markus called as he offered a hand to the small man.

"Yeah, I got us a doe. We gotta get. They's hot on my heels."

He felt himself being lifted onto the deck, and he heard a thump of the deer hitting next to him. Then he heard the wrong noise.

"Augh! My back!" Aarnel called.

"Help me!"

"Hurry, boys! Grab him!" Ike called as the remaining three hefted him aboard. Arrows began to shower the freighter in the dimming light.

"Shove off, Justin. Markus, Billy, man Aarnel's oar. Be about it quickly now." Ike called as an arrow plunged into the prone man on the deck. The man made no sound, though. Billy had only watched the oarsman before, but he had enough adrenaline in his system to make up for any shortcomings concerning the chore.

The boat slowly backed into the current as the arrows kept landing all over the boat, hitting no one. The craft caught the current, and soon the skirmish was over.

"You reckon they'll chase us down?" Billy asked.

"Maybe so. We'll have to post a guard soon as we pull in. I've heard of them chasin' rivermen down. They come in on logs and by them skin boats. We gotta pull in somewhere. Can't be out here at night. We gotta look after Aarnel too." Billy noticed the concern in Ike's voice. In the front of the boat, Bill heard Justin, "He's gone, Ike. They done killed Aarnel Gustavo."

"You sure? Maybe he's just passed out from the pain." Ike asked.

"The arrow went in his back and came out the front. He was dead 'fore he hit the deck." Justin answered from the blackness of the front of the boat.

"He weren't worth no deer." Markus spoke quietly as he pulled the oar slowly.

"Nope. Not anywhere close." Justin whispered loud enough for Billy to hear.

"Not anywhere close." Billy answered back.

CHAPTER 27

The two seasoned freighters gently poled the large boat to the water's edge as it slowed to the bank. Markus spoke in a harsh voice to the young soon-to-be-river rat, "Ye get the first watch, boy. Don't be sleepin' or I'll be the one cutting yer throat. You readin' me?"

"I hear you, Markus. I'll be doing my shift just fine." Bill hefted the rifle onto his lap as he began the chore of guarding against further attacks. Billy looked to where the man was covered with the blanket, next to the deer that cost him his life. It was then he realized he'd never reloaded the long rifle, the same gun that had protected him since the small town of Dallas City. He quickly pulled his possible bag up to load a fresh charge. He finished with the prime on the long gun when he remembered shooting the man with one of the pistols. That man had killed Bridget but had died for his deed. Now both of the pistols he carried at his waist were charge and primed. Satisfied with his charges, he stood and walked along the perimeter of the flat boat as the nightlife on the river increased in crescendo. Listening to the night, he became aware of the noises and tried to pick them out as he heard them.

"Them frogs." he whispered aloud. Straining he listened for more animals. A screech owl hooted its loud calls as the crickets and river insects began their melodies. Hours passed with nothing more than hoot or a distant coyote. Then Bill heard a whip-poor-will. Answered by another one on the other side of the boat.

"Hmm? They sounded different." he spoke loud enough to hear himself.

"What's that?" Justin asked from under the cover of his blanket.

"Somethin' ain't right. Get up quick like." he whispered to

the tall thin crew member that had warned him about Markus. In a few heartbeats the whole crew was up and crouched behind barrels of trade goods.

"You sure kid? Or you just scarit of the dark?" Markus whispered to Billy for getting him out of his bedroll.

"If I'm wrong, then you can laugh at me later." That's when Bill saw the shape materialize in the aft of the boat. Not waiting to find out who it was, he pulled the trigger, sending a ball and flames to the intruder. A scream sounded. The man fell into the water. Then havoc ensued as the sides of the boat became alive with Foxes as the orchestrated attack unraveled. Bill had no idea he had killed the raider's leader just as he had killed the leader back at Ells's river fort. The attacked went bad for the Foxes. Two more shots as two more painted men fell into the river.

"That makes three! Load quick, boys!" Ike called out as he too busied himself pouring powder. In the dark he was hoping to get most of it down the barrel. That's when Billy saw the fourth man materialize right in front of him. He went to pull one of the pistols, but the older warrior knocked it to the deck. Bill heard a splash as it bounced into the water. Turning his attention back to the man in front of him, he saw the shape of a tomahawk coming for his head.

"Shit!" Billy screamed and dropped his long gun and lunged for the shape before the tomahawk could find its mark. The two men crashed into the black muddy water. *Gotta hold him under. He's gonna whack me if I let him get a swing at me.* Billy swam down under the man as he grabbed his slick buckskin moccasin from below. The man began kicking Billy in the face repeatedly, but the lad was determined as a wounded badger. Pulling hard Billy kicked deeper as the man gave up on kicking and bent over to grab the runt's hand to make him release his grasp.

Not gonna let you kill me, you red nigger. I'll drown first. The man was frantic now, thrashing in terror of drowning. The warrior had no idea Billy was on the verge of blacking out and drowning. All the man knew was this small white man was pulling him deeper with each kick. Billy had the blackness invade his brain as he kicked deeper. His ears hurt from the depth, and his lungs ached for fresh air. He began to lose consciousness as he longed for his mother's embrace. To hold Katie again or even to sit on the black horse, Fanny. Then he noticed the man had quit moving and was sinking toward him. The white runt let go and swam past the dead man on his way to the surface. *Cain't see the surface! Gotta swim! Kick! Kick, you runt, kick!* Billy screamed to himself as he realized he was going to live. He broke through the surface twenty-five feet aft of the flat boat and being pulled away from the boat as muddy water splashed into his mouth before he could call out.

One more hard kick to bring his face clear of the river, and he called out, "Ike! Ike! Ike! I'm over here! Ike! Justin! Help!"

"Thar he be Ike!" Markus called to the pilot.

"Justin, shove off quick 'fore he goes under. Man your pole, Markus." Ike pulled on his rudder.

"Good eyes, sir. Good eyes. Now heave to you son of a bang-tailed whore." Ike was pulling hard on the rudder as the heavy boat responded slowly.

"Aye, Ike. We'll get him. That little fucker's like an otter. Water ain't gonna bother him no how." Justin called out as he strained his strong back on the front gouger to get the boat into the current.

"See him kill that fucker. Shot one dead and drown the other. Ike, you gotta get him to hire on. That boy knows how to fight." Justin beamed in the darkness as he pulled hard on the front rudder. He was proud of Billy, not because of his keenness to survive but because of the fact that the butt-bandit Markus wouldn't get to ruin him. That itself was a glorious thing.

"He got a place on my boat if he wants it." Ike called as the boat floated to where Billy had been.

"Billy White! Where ye be?" Markus called out, *Gotta find him.*

He's more than I could ever ask fer. A fighter! Ain't none of them ever been fighters. He licked his lips, thinking about having Billy tied down, his pants torn off, his butt cheeks bleeding from the beating. Markus felt himself hardening as he dreamed of sticking his pod up Bill's ass.

"Over here! Toss me a rope. The waters too strong to swim again ." Bill was relieved to see the shape of the flat boat bearing down on him.

"Don't run me over, Ike. Jes' get a rope!" Bill bobbed in the muddy water as the dark shape of the boat began to pass him. Then out of the darkness, a hemp rope splashed a few feet from him. Tired and exhausted, the blond runt swam; but a few small strokes until he reached it, he grabbed the rope as relief flooded him. Quickly he curled the rope around his wrist, and he pulled as hard as he'd ever pulled in his life. The shape of the silhouette flatboat materialized, but as he closed the distance, an undertow pulled him down. The runt pulled once again on the rope to try to get the Mississippi to release its grasp on him. Finally breaking the surface, he was only a few feet from Ike's rudder.

"Ike, you wanna give me a tug?" the runt called out to the pilot.

Ike quickly pulled on the rope, bringing the man closer until he could make out his shape on the river. He grabbed the small man's worn linen shirt and pulled him over the transom.

Bill lay on the deck, panting like a catfish out of the water; he rolled over to look up at the lantern-lit faces that were peering down at him.

"Good to see you boys. I wasn't sure you heard me, but yer here, so ya did." Bill sat up, spitting out the taste of the muddy water.

"Damn! That was close. Damned undertow just about got me."

"Undertow? You killed two of them fuckers, Mr. White. Hand to hand? Shit, I ain't never heard of a runt killing like you did." Justin spoke as he held a lantern up to show Bill his beaming face.

"Ye are welcome at our table anytime, Billy White. Anytime." Ike laid a soiled blanket over Bill's shoulders. Bill had already begun to shiver in the cool night. The soaking hadn't helped him any as the water had sapped his body heat quickly.

"Thanks, Ike." Bill pulled the blanket tighter around his shoulders.

"We got to pull back in. Justin, find us a place to wait the night out 'fore we hit a snag and all drown." Ike called to his partner.

"Aye." Justin went back and pulled the rudder as the boat slipped out of the main stream and began to head for shore once more.

"Markus, man the oar."

"Leave him be pilot. Steer us in!" Markus called out jealously.

"Mind yer tongue Markus. I know my job. Ye pull ye bean-skinned bandit. Pull!" Ike relieved Justin on the rudder and steered them into a quiet glade of black walnut trees. Bill heard the boat grind on the hidden stumps as it came to a slow halt.

"We'll wait out the night here. Markus, you finish up the watch. Justin, get the boat ready for the morning.

"Aye, Ike." Then it was quiet like it had been before the ill-planned raid.

CHAPTER 28

In the morning Justin began the grisly chore of carving up the doe that had cost his friend's life.

Bill watched the man work as he emptied out his possible bag to dry as well as wiped down the only pistol he had left. He lifted his powder horn, too damn heavy. Powders turned into mud.

"Can you boys spare some dry powder? Mine's ruin't from my swimming last night." Bill asked as he dumped out the black powder into the water. He had already cleaned the knives, and most of his clothes had dried.

"Yeah Markus, pour out some from the larder for the lad." Ike called as he looked into the shoreline. *Never can tell who's out there,* he thought.

"We need to find a safe spot to bury Aarnel 'fore he starts stinking up the boat." Markus called out as he watched Justin perform the dressing of the doe. The lanky man kicked the gut pile over the side. A sliver of the sun creeped into view over the eastern tree line as he called Markus.

"Markus, stoke up that fire, and we'll have some venison for breakfast. Ike, I liked Aarnel just fine, but the river was his home, and the river is where he'll be buried." Justin spoke to the pilot in a firm voice.

"Aye." Ike answered back.

"Markus, Billy, come over here." He stepped closer to the covered body.

"Aarnel was a good man and never shirked a duty. We'll miss him. May the good Lord watch over him and keep him safe from the devil. Amen. Go on. Push him over." Ike spoke as he pulled his hat over his chest. The crew members heaved to rolling the huge man over the side. A small splash was all that was heard of their friend.

"River gives, and the river takes?" Billy asked.

"Aye. That it does. Get that doe on the fire." Ike ordered. Markus soon had the sandpit fire crackling with bright yellow flames.

"That's gonna hit the spot, boys. Me gut has thought my throat's been cut. I got take me a piss." Ike got up and left the company of his crew walking aft on the craft.

"I'm plum starved. Tonight I'll get us another deer. How's that sound, fellers?" Bill asked as he rolled up the blanket he'd slept on. The night had been short, but the rest felt good. The wet clothes and hard deck hadn't bothered him as he was exhausted from the day of cheating out death.

Ike returned to the men, his penis still hanging out for all to see.

"Markus, them boys you been ruining ain't got no cock this big. I'll lay wages on that." Ike shook the fat stubby appendage at the Mexican.

"How would you know? You been with boys before?" Markus sassed back.

"No! It's them boys ain't grow'd up like me with a good-sized cock." Ike answered back, his hand pulling back the foreskin exposing the head of his pod to the crew.

"So you real judge of cockery, are ye? You been lookin' at cocks, have you, measuring them up to yer own self?" Markus spoke, not looking at the pilot's penis. He threw a few more pieces of wood on the fire.

"Hand me a few strips, Justin. We'll get this going 'fore we get bushwhacked sitting here." Bill spoke as he approached the thin man.

They ate until the venison was gone and the fire put out. Bill was thrilled to have such a meal under his belt.

He'd cheated death again. *Yeah, cost a man's life, but there's no telling the future out here. Could be in a heartbeat or years from now. Yeppers. Never can tell.* The runt wiped his mouth on his dirty shirt as he felt the hair on the back of his neck prick up. He looked up to see Markus staring at him. Then Markus winked and licked his mustache with his red tongue. The sight took Billy by surprise; he looked to see if anyone else had caught the man in the vulgar act. *Justin? Nope, he's pulling in the front mooring line.* He craned his neck to see where Ike was; near the aft, checking the strapping lines. When he looked back, Markus had his back to Billy, tending to his oaring station.

Son of a bitch, I hope I don't have to kill this ol'coot. Ike an' Justin need him bad if they wanna get his load to Orleans. Bill stood up and prepared himself for the day of hard rowing.

"Heave too, lads. Let's get her out of her an' on the river where we belong." Ike called as the crew manned the poles to push the boat out of the shallows. Bill stuck the long pole in and used every ounce of his weight and strength to push the boat out into the currents.

From the seclusion of the forest, the new leader of the Foxes raiding party, Black Tail, watched the boat pull away. This time the fighting crew of white men had surprised them. They had usually killed the crew and stole all the goods. Then they'd go down the river and barter with the Winnebagos or the thieving Chickasaw, but this time the raid had gone poorly. One of his best friends and the leader of the raiding party had been killed by what looked like the same white man that had drowned the boy and killed his oldest nephew. There would be no way to get revenge. Not yet anyway. With four killed, he would have a difficult time explaining to He Who Walks Quietly how they were defeated by the white river men. They nodded to one another and vanished, waiting for another opportunity to exact their vengeance on the crew of the freighter.

CHAPTER 29

The river's current caught the freighter quickly, and it began the journey once more for New Orleans. The freighters carried the river trader of the early west; these men of never-ending work, drinking, and grog houses. Many had short lives. Knife fights often left them cut and dying behind a whorehouse or facedown in one of the many tributaries of the Mississippi.

Ike and this crew were good at their trade. They had traveled three times down the river, never losing a man. That was until the runt appeared the fateful day on the shore, on his splendid black horse. That ill-fated day had changed the crew. On the bad side his friend had died. However, here was a young man that would give the sodomizer a run for his money. Although he was never caught in the act, they knew he preferred young men and were sure Markus reveled in the fact he'd been able to ruin many a young man.

The boat slipped from current to current as the pilot placed the boat where he felt the Big Muddy would do the best for them. Ike had seldom made mistakes concerning the river. Justin and Markus trusted him beyond reproach. They'd always made it down the river in a quick time, considering the amount of time they spent hauling one another out the riverfront dram shops. Many a time Justin had to drag Aarnel from under a painted woman as the boat was making ready before he was done.

Ike watched the young white man pull the oar. He saw the boy meant well but didn't have the weight to pull hard enough to match Markus's steady smooth pulls. Ike would be very choosy finding a replacement for Aarnel. He liked the runt, but he wanted a large man to pull with the crew. His gaze drifted to Markus. The man was smooth when it came to making the boat perform for Ike. The only reason Ike kept him onboard was that fact. Aarnel and Markus were like a matched pair of Belgian horses. Billy was working to match Markus's strokes but coming up short with every pull of the long oar.

Markus felt the boat pull to the leeward side. He turned to Billy, spitting a taunt, "Come on, ye runt, pull! You gotta match my strokes."

Justin returned to the front where he kept watch for snags, sandbars, or submerged logs.

"All right. Keep in time with the Mexican over there, an' you'll do fine." he called to Billy.

"I ain't a Mexican. I'm Spanish. My kin came from Spain. Ain't no greaser. You hear that runt? Spanish, not Mex." Markus called from his side of the freighter.

Justin called from the front, "All the better to watch where you drop ye britches, Mr. White."

"I'll be watching." he answered back as he strained his shoulders pulling the long oar into the black water. *I've heard of these men, corn holing other men. I hope I don't have to fight Markus. He appears to be a solid fighter, not to mention stronger than an ox.* Now it was on Billy to keep up.

"I'm getting the knack of it. A few more hours and I'll be keeping up. You'll see." Billy shot back as he struggled to pull the heavy oak oar.

"You're doing fine, young Mr. White. Just fine. Don't let that Mexican bother you none. Me an' Ike will keep this flatboat going where it needs to be." Justin pushed the gouger to compensate for Bill's effort, quickly giving Markus a dagger stare.

Markus knew he and Justin would cross blades again. Not soon. But in New Orleans. He's leave Justin to die in his own blood for his sharp tongue. This was Markus's last trip with this crew; he knew the place he wanted to be. It was on the steamships that ripped the water as they traveled up and down the great brown river. However, for now he'd have to put up with the rail-thin man at the front of the boat. *I wonder, as he drowns in his own blood, would he still fight as I ripped his asshole apart? That would be the ultimate insult. Fucking him as he dies.* Markus pulled the oar as he stared at Justin's back, wishing the man could read his mind.

This is how Bill watched the day drift by; the man on the front insulted the man across from him. With each pull, Bill saw the sun begin its journey to the western tree line. One step closer to Hannibal as he pulled again.

"Justin, make for the inlet there." Ike pointed the area to the west where a tributary dumped into the river, revealing a shoreline. The crew once again lined the boat up for a mooring, slipping next the submerged stumps the crew aimed for the designated point.

"Remember last time? Same thing except don't bring back no Injuns. Okay, lad. Don't bring none back. We've less than ten miles from Hannibal, so we'll get there tomorrow morning or midday. You hurry. We'll wait a spell, and if you ain't here soon, we'll meet you down river like last time. You understand? Like last time." Ike spoke as he rested his weathered hand on Bill's bony shoulder.

"Yeppers. I won't be long. Just don't leave me. I'll meet you." Bill got his coat and hat and pulled his belt outside of his coat, then slid the pistol in one side, then Mary Jane's knife in one side, and Beulah's in the back. He slid the possible bag and powder horn over his shoulder, then grabbed the now-familiar SC musket, and hopped off into the evening.

Before Bill was even out of sight, Markus chimed in, "So find us some fresh meat, boy, like that doe you got us yesterday. Maybe you can get us a fat opossum too. Don't be gone long neither, or we'll just keep all you gear an' shove off. You understand, boy? Leave you to the damned Chickasaw or whatever thievin' red fuckers live about here." Markus had his hands on his hips, staring menacingly at the young man's back.

"Leave him be, Markus. He's to have you for a snack. He'll find us a fresh deer or a grouse or two. Ain't that right, Mr. White?" Justin spoke to where to Billy had been. Ever since the night Billy had helped defend the small boat, Justin had been there to defend him. He spoke as he watched Billy nimbly land on the nettle-covered bank. The third boatman, Ike, listened without saying a word.

Ike missed his chum. *Damned red bushwhackers killed a good man. The boy's all right, but he'll not make it unless he toughens up.*

"I'll be back soon. Don't you worry none about it." Bill boasted as he faded into the bank of vegetation. As soon as he was in the thick of trees and plants, Bill stopped moving, listening to the forest around him. Any noise or smell that would alert him to danger or game that was so prominent. He leaned against a black walnut tree, feeling the coarse bark going through the wool coat as he began to ponder his current position.

The night quickly darkened, and Bill hadn't returned. "I say we shove off, Ike. Little fucker's gone and left us high and dry like we just hit a sandbar." Markus spoke as he shook his head looking at the bank.

"He's right, Ike. If he ain't back by now, he ain't coming back." Justin agreed with his unsavory partner, even though he liked Bill.

"We can't stay here. Injuns mighta marked us."

"Push off, Markus. Maybe we'll bump into him at Hannibal." Markus and Justin prepared to pole the heavy ship back as Ike pulled on the rudder. The boat hit one of the stumps, stopping them dead in the water.

"Markus, what say ye lad? Is it bad?" Ike asked.

"Nah, we'll just pull from over yonder." Markus pointed to a black tree silhouetted in the dusk.

"We'll be out quicker than popping a girly cherry." They all turned their attention to getting the boat out unaware that the same Foxes that had attacked them earlier were stalking them.

Black Tail spoke to Brave Dog and Crushed Hand, "We must be quick. No shots missed. I'll take the one on the back. Crushed Hand, you take the thin one. Brave Dog, you get the fat one as he comes to shore. We mustn't miss. It will be glory for us to bring in this freighter, considering our friends that have died."

The freighters had no idea they were to be ambushed again; they carried on as if they were moored up at Hannibal's new dock.

Markus spoke up as he prepared to hop on the shore with the winching rope, *I'd like to have a go with him. I bet he'd fight like a cat with its tail on fire.* Markus was in midair when an arrow went into his chest. He landed on the shore with a great thud as the arrows began raining on the crew like a firestorm, killing Justin instantly but only wounding Ike. The arrow in Ike's lung made him drop the winch rope. Trying as hard as he could, he couldn't get his hand to work on the gun that was standing not more than inches from his grasp.

As soon as it started, it was over, not a musket shot fired. Crushed Hand was on Justin as the thin man pitched over the side into the inky-black water of the Mississippi. The young Fox warrior pulled the dead man to shore and began cutting his arms and legs off as he screamed, "This is for my cousin! This is for his widowed wife. Eyeee!" The tomahawk flew in a fury as he mutilated the thin man until there was nothing left but a bloody torso.

"Bring the heads, arms, and legs! We'll show that we've killed these whites like the spineless worms they are!" Black Tail called as he watched Ike stare at him.

Brave Dog threw Markus's legs and arms onboard as he kicked over the lantern, causing the ship to catch fire. Crushed Hand held up an arm and screamed into Ike's face, "You'll die slowly white face." Then he got very close to Ike's face and spit in his eye. Ike was so weak from blood loss he knew he'd never make it very far, or at least he hoped. He could feel the blood filling up his lung. *I gotta drown myself.* With a deep breath, he exhaled, blowing all the air out of his working lung. *It hurts so bad. Gotta finish it out.* He drew in a breath as the blood began to fill out the lung, crushing against the heart and filling up the sternum. Once more, he exhaled a bloody froth. Ike fought the urge to cough, and blood went down his good lung in a gush as he inhaled one last time. Then he suffocated.

Black Tail saw the boat was burning too much, so he ended the triumph over these puny whites and called to put the fire out.

"Brave Dog, put out the fire. Crushed Hand, help him then get a rope to the tree and let's get our bounty out of here!" Black Tail called as he pulled on the rudder. He watched so many white men do it before. Brave Dog was over the side and back before Crushed Hand had the fire out. Crushed Hand and Brave Dog pulled with all their might. Slowly the big craft unseated itself from the stump, and they were away.

"This is getting too easy." Brave Dog called back as he pulled on the big oar, which was too big for him.

"Yes, but this one cost us too many of our kinsmen. Hopefully, when He Who Walks Quietly sees these gifts, we'll be honored." He pulled on the rudder. They were but hollow words and would never replace the men that died.

Bill thought on, *Nothing says I got to go back. Derned Markus, I seen the way he was eyeballing me. Rascal's out to get my rump. That fer certain an' fer true.*

Waiting and listening, Bill still didn't move from his tree. Soon squirrels were barking and making a ruckus as he watched a fat coon come out the den hole on the big maple tree across from him. *Hmm? Do I plug this old boy or wait for something else? I say take what I can get and look for more later.* He slowly brought up the SC musket in the dim of the evening light and pulled the trigger. The gun kicked into his shoulder as the round ball went swiftly through he coon's lungs, killing it before it hit the fern-covered ground. Bill didn't move except to reload the rifle, still listening.

Well, looks to be quiet. Might as well get it. The hairs stood up on his neck like they had did the night of the attack, so he froze like a pillar of salt.

Something's coming. He sniffed the air; a rank odor came wafting through the early-evening air. Then he heard the low groan, almost a growl. Still Bill didn't move. Then he heard the brush and deadfall break as something large began homing in on the scent of blood. *Goddamn, that sounds big. Hope it don't find me, whatever it is.* Bill was facing west, the coon was to his right, and the noise was coming from the west, putting Bill almost directly in the path of the oncoming danger. *I might as well slip behind this here tree. No sense gets 'et by what's coming.* Smoothly he rolled his back around the tree hiding from the noisemaker.

The smell was incredibly bad, like rotten meat. He took a chance and looked around the tree to see the black bear moving toward the coon. The bear had no idea where Bill was, but twenty feet from it as it continually tested the air for anything objectionable. *Shit, that'll feed us fer days, not to mention the hide. Gonna plug that ol'boy. Yeppers.* Leaning around the left side of the tree to hide himself, Bill shouldered the gun to his left as he sighted in on the monster. Still, it had no idea death was looming seconds away as it waddled toward the coon. Bill had no idea how many shots it would take to kill the three-hundred-pound bear. *Gotta be quick reloading, maybe even do it running, most likely take a bunch of shots. Maybe so it would be better to go hungry then get 'et by this black critter. No. Go on, shoot.* His brain agreed on. *I could drop my gun or stumble an' fall then get ate.*

The musket went off, surprising him. He'd been pulling the trigger the whole time he was arguing with himself. He quickly slid back behind the tree and began loading as quickly as he could; powder, ball, frizzen, cock, his mind raced. He leaned back to face the bear again. To his surprise, the bear lay on the ground, pawing at the pain at its side. Moaning the bear threw its massive head from side to side, making Bill to be quicker to finish the job. He waited until the bear looked away and fired. The ball went in behind the right ear and exited through the left eye, killing it instantly.

"Huh? It's dead, just like that?" he spoke aloud.

"Well, I'll be shucked fer an' ear. I done got a coon an' a bear." *Best be getting some help on this one.* His mind began to race. Bill quickly raced down river to where the boat should be. It wasn't there.

He quickly backtracked upriver to where he'd last seen the boat, moving as quickly as possible in case some unwanted company might be there about. As he neared the river, he saw a glow from where the boat was. Then the voices came across the night air. *Injuns, oh no!* He panicked for a second, then caught himself, and began to slip up on the freighter from downriver.

There was the flatboat ablaze with painted men shaking body parts in the flame's light. He heard the biggest one of the raiders speak in the grunts and barks. He pointed to the fire, and two of the warriors quickly put it out with blankets and a few buckets of water.

Bill silently backed away, leaving everything he owned on the boat. The crew had broken one of their own rules, staying moored to a site too long after dark. It cost them their lives too. *Not mine. I'm off to Hannibal. Too bad about them fellers. I like two of 'em. The third got what he had coming.* He shook his head, the shoulder-length blond hair tossing about under his brimmed hat. *Not true. Markus only looked at me, never laid a hand on me, so it's too bad fer all of 'em.*

Bill put the river on his left side as he looked for a place to hole up for the night. *Might as well go back fer that coon come sunup, no sense leaving all that meat to rot. That bear might be a challenge, though. Too bad I don't know nuthin' about tanning hides. That skin would be good come winter, but that's a long way off yet.* The lad argued with himself like he'd done earlier. He found a black section of bushes and climbed under it.

Pulling his collar up and his hat down, he fell asleep as soon as his eyes closed.

CHAPTER 30

Bill awoke with the sun shining through the canopy of willow limbs. He didn't move, though, just lay there, letting his eyes wander about the forest to assess any danger. The squirrels were barking and running about on the floor of the forest not more than a few feet from where Bill had slept.

That's a good sign. I'm all by my lonesome. Might as well head back fer that coon. He crawled from under the black bushes he had found sanctuary in the night. The squirrels quickly ran up the trees, and the jays and forest birds started giving him hell for ending their morning feed. Pulling his rifle out, he arranged his pistol and knives and looked back at his hiding place. He couldn't find a better place if he'd searched. The oak that had fallen was stopped against an old willow; the willow's branches provided a natural door to conceal him from sight.

"Shit, lookie there, Mr. Squirrel, you didn't even see me. What do you to think of that?" Then he hefted his rifle up and sighted in on the small tormentor of sound.

"Bang, yer dead, Mr. Squirrel. Ha-ha. Not today you rascal."

He turned to leave and looked for a familiar piece of landscape to bring him back in case he needed to stay here another night. There, three willows with the middle one having two forks. He spoke to himself for the memory of the location. He turned and walked back to where his friends had died, which ended up being farther than he remembered. He found the coon and the big bear where they had fallen. Walking past them, he shook his head for the amount of work to getting meat from either one of them.

He slowed and began to walk and listen as he neared where the boat had been. The smell of dead met him before he saw the remains of the crew. On the left, at the water's edge, was Markus's remains. His arms and legs were gone, half of his head was gone, his belly was opened up like a trout, his guts was ripped out and covering the bloody scene on the shoreline. Bill stared, not being able to move. Crawdads quickly scurried away when they became aware of an interloper to their dining. His eyes moved to the right. There he saw the thin man, Justin. Well, it was Justin's once-white shirt. There was no head or appendages. Just the torso, opened like Markus. Bill slowly scanned for Ike. He was gone as was the freighter. Bill remembered back to the night before. The big Indian had been commanding the others. *That one I gotta watch out fer. I still got ten miles to got to get to a place to whole up fer the winter. Sorry, boys, no burial fer ya. I got git in case there's another bunch of them goddamned raiders here about.*

He stopped and carved off a chunk of the bear's haunch and the rear legs of the coon. *That should do it fer a coupla days.* Bill quickly put distance between himself and where the flat boat that had given him safe passage had been. Ahead of him was the town of Hannibal. It wasn't more than a day's walk now, and Bill quickly forgot the men on the boat that had been waiting for him. He found his trail back to the willows. He quickly entered his newfound home and listened to the forest around him. *Quiet. That be good. That be real fine.* He brought up the bear meat to his lips but couldn't bring himself to eat it raw. *Nope, gotta cook this.*

He brought up the possible bag that had belonged to Sash the barkeep and flipped the smooth leather flap to allow him to rummage inside. He paused and looked through the willow branches, thinking back to the night where they'd frolicked in the small campfire's light. *Damn, she's gone. Hard to believe it's gone like a snowflake in the spring.* He continued with the contents in the fringed bag. A small sharpe awe, a ball puller, a long pick for cleaning out the touch hole, a handful of balls, a few extra flints, and then his fingers found what he was looking for; the steel ring that was used for making fire.

"This should be just fine." He whispered to himself.

"What about the smell and smoke?" he continued to argue.

"I wonder if them red niggers is about. No matter, I gotta eat." he once again spoke aloud to himself for no other reason than just to hear a voice. He pulled the bag out off to the side and positioned his rifle out of the way. He hunched over, gathering the deadfall from inside his little impromptu home, preparing to light the smallest of the leaves and twigs. He quickly got out the powder flask, dribbling a little bit on the kindling he flicked, the flint with the steel, and little sparks jumped out into the most delicate gunpowder to ignite them, causing a small flame to burst out.

"There we go." He blew on the bottom as the fire began to grow. Slowly he added a few more twigs as it crackled and grew. Bill dusted off the area around his little fire to ensure it wouldn't grow any bigger as he continued to add sticks until it was burning evenly. Pulling Mary Jane's knife out, he sharpened a stick for his cook tool. *This oughta be just about long 'nuff,* he thought as he pulled the bear meat over and rammed a stick through it. Billy held it over his meager fire as he watched it begin to cook. Slowly he moved it from side to side as he continued to add fuel. The smell came to him as the wind shifted.

This is gonna taste purty good, yes siree. Purty good. Bill licked his lips as the meat sizzled and dripped into the fire, causing it to jump in bright yellow flames. He continued turning his meat as he added twigs for the most part of an hour as he thought of the food before him. *Still got them coon legs if this don't fill me up, yeppers. Eating good today.* The meat was browning quickly as he watched it, mesmerized by the brilliant flames that were brought about by the fat dripping into the fire. Finally about midmorning he pulled the meat back and cut a chunk off. Carefully he raised it to his mouth, smelling the fresh scent of cooked meat. At first the taste was strange, almost revolting for such a good smell. "Good lord!" he spoke aloud as he continued chewing. The blond man kept cooking and eating well into the afternoon. Then when the bear was gone, he smothered the fire and curled up in his new home, drifting off to sleep quickly.

Bill slept fitfully into the evening. The meat, though filling him up, caused him to have mind-tweaking dreams. All he could see in his dream was his mother being ravaged by the big Indian that had killed his friends, and then his mind raced back to the big mule that had kicked him at the farm. It stood up and walked like a man, swatting men like they were flies. Then it spoke,

"How do like that, human? Do you like to be whipped?" Then the mule turned into Ivory and produced his long penis, which grew into a sword. Then Ivory wielded it like a buccaneer would slashing at his mother, cutting her into pieces. Ivory swung it toward Bill and approached with a wicked gleam in his eyes. Billy awoke with a start, sweating under his coat as he remembered where he was. *Only a dream, Billy boy,* he reassured himself.

"I gotta get from here. Might as well travel now. At least the red niggers won't be able to see me." he whispered aloud as he crawled out of his sanctuary, pointing his nose south. *Jest keep the river on the left. Yeppers. Hannibal, here I come.* He calmed himself as he slung the rifle over his shoulder and set off into the black night.

CHAPTER 31

Billy traveled into the night, occasionally hearing a lone screech owl or distant coyote.

"Them real ones?" he spoke aloud into the darkness. He continued on the pale ribbon of a trail that led south through the willows and water damaged oaks. Then he heard a coyote again but closer. A quick bark followed by a whippoorwill. He remembered the same sound that had come before the attack.

Ain't no whippoorwill out at night, them's morning birds. He froze in his steps as he listened to the nightlife more intensely. Another quick coyote bark followed by a hoot owl. *That's too much of a coincidence,* he slowly moved to the nearest black tree as he listened to the night.

Leaning against the coarse bark, he strained his eyes to see any movement. Minutes passed with no noise coming through the forest, Bill began to think his paranoia was overcoming his common sense.

Ain't nuthin but animals. I reckon it's better safe than dead I guess. I'll jest wait a bit more, jest to be on the safe side. Then he heard it; a voice, a lower-uttering barking noise like the Fox raider had used on the freighter. This time it was right next to the tree Bill had been leaning on. He remained as stiff as a walnut door. Only moving his eyes to try to see anything that would alert him of the position of the voice.

The fragrance of an unkempt body came floating to his nose. *It smells like Markus. How can that be? Markus's dead. Unless these Injuns are wearing Markus's clothes.*

He heard the low whispers clearly, not knowing what they were saying. He understood they were within an arm's reach of him. *Hope they don't smell me.* Still Bill didn't move. Then it was quiet again. *That was too close. Them rascals is still lookin' fer me. They'll find the campfire come morning and be on my trail faster than a hog on snake eggs.*

Bill waited a few more precious minutes then stepped back onto the pale path he'd been on. *Maybe I'm farther from Hannibal than I figured. Best not lallygag around here.* In a few steps Bill had increased his stride to a quick trot, holding the possible bag down with one hand and the slung rifle with the other, trying to put the distance between himself and the Foxes.

The three Foxes had tied the freighter up and had backtracked to find the small man that killed two of their companions. Using animal calls, they covered a hundred-yard swath of the river bottom as they crept back to the ambush scene.

"You smelled the meat as I did, so he has to be somewhere close." Black Tail spoke as he leaned on the opposite side of the tree Bill was against.

"Yes, I smelled the smoke as well. Only a white man would cook this close to the river. He's not far. You know it was a bad idea to wear that fat one's coat. It smells like a white man. He probably has lice living in it." Crushed Hand commented to Brave Dog.

"You are right. I will have Morning Dove clean it when we get back." Brave Dog commented as they traveled on the same path Bill had been on.

"I can smell the burned wood now. It's very strong right around here." Black Tail told him,

"You can forget my wife cleaning it. She will not touch a white man's coat. Owl says that she can't touch a white man or his belongings, or she'll never bear us children."

"You really think Owl knows such things?" Crushed Hand answered back. He had been fooled by the old shaman a few times already. He sniffed for the smell of burned wood as he got down on his hands and knees and crawled toward the willow tree Bill had hid under.

"I found it." Crushed Hand lifted up the black curtain of willows as he entered where Bill had found sanctuary.

"He cooked a bear here. He must be a very good hunter to kill a bear." He placed his hand on the cold coals of where the fire had been.

"Cold. He cooked here today before sunset." The warrior crawled out from under the tree and spoke to the shapes of his friends.

"Let's find the bear." Brave Dog spoke his stomach growling.

"No. We wait until morning then we can find where he went." Black Tail spoke.

"I'm going to look anyway. I'm hungry, and the meat will not be bad, only one day old."

Brave Dog turned to go back to where the ambush had been.

"I'll join you." Crushed Hand called after the younger man.

"Fine. We'll all go." Black Tail fell in behind the younger raiders.

The three said no more until they smelled the stench of the gut pile.

"Not much for skinning. He cut into the stomach." Brave Dog commented as he found the bear by smell.

"Over here. He got a raccoon also. Only the back legs are gone. This one is traveling light. He seems to be smarter than our average white man." Black Tail commented as he looked east to the false dawn of another day on the Mississippi River bottom.

"This one has proven to be more than any of us had thought of. He's killed two of our friends, killed a raccoon and a bear, and cooked right under our noses. When we get this one, we will make sure he lives a long time. No quick death for him."

Bill was making good time as the early dawn of a new day lit up the path, enabling him to put a fair lead on the Fox warriors. He slow to a walk, trying to catch his breath, when something caught his attention on the river.

Huh? It looks like Ike's boat. He took a few steps toward it, forgetting that there could have been more raiders about; so he froze, listening for any sign of guards. Then he stepped through the willows and deadfall from the past storms to the stinky black bank of the river to make sure it wasn't his imagination, and there it was. Ike's freighter. *I wonder if I can move it,* he quickly formulated a plan to get the boat out on the river.

Hopping up on the gunwale, he found Markus's long pole and slipped it in the water quickly and began to pull with all his might to move the boat. *Shit. I cain't budge it.* He quickly surveyed the position of the boat. *I ain't moving it.* He saw his saddle and gear on the deck where he'd left it. *I'll be taking this.* He threw his blanket on the bank, *Now I'll make sure them thievin' niggers don't get nuthin'.*

Billy quickly went to the sandpit where the doe had been cooked. As he blew lightly, the fire jumped up on the coals. He quickly fed it with scattered remnants of some clothes that were in the corner by the pit. As he pulled more cloth to the fire, it began to build in size. Bill stood up and looked around for anything that would burn. Into the flames went the poles, the oars, and all the bales of raw wool. He searched frantically until finally he found the small keg that had been by Ike's sleeping mat.

"Gunpowder." He exhaled a deep breath of relief as the fire was raging now. It had consumed all he put in and was burning the roof of the cabin near the aft of the boat, sending a black column of smoke up in the early morning. Picking up the ten-pound keg, he turned and ran past the flames until he was at the front of the boat. Pulling out Beulah's knife, he stabbed the bung repeatedly until he could pry it out. Pouring the powder onto the deck into a great pile, he backed up to the shore. Leaving a trail of black powder, he hopped off to the bank. Bill picked up his bedroll in one arm and the powder keg in the other. He backed away until he was out of sight of the boat. Lifting up the keg to stop the flow of powder, he sat it down.

Gonna give them niggers something to think about. Yes sir. Boom! He chuckled. Bill poured more powder out and walked into the nearest pile of driftwood and broken trees. The powder on the boat caught fire in a great whoosh. It sent gray smoke up like a great cloud. Bill stopped to hear the boat burning, crackling like a wildfire. He knew there'd be nothing left for the pirates that were behind him

Satisfied with the trail of powder, he returned and laid the keg on its side with a puddle of powder on the ground. He laid a few willow branches over it. Breathing heavily from the excitement of getting caught plus the anxiety of surprising the Indians, he ran back to the cover he had found and got himself situated for his stand.

"Gotta get me a fire going here. Shit, I shoulda just brought something burning from Ike's boat. Never mind, I'll have something going before them Injuns show up." he spoke aloud as if he was telling a companion. Quickly he brought out his flint and steel, and after a few well-aimed sparks, he had a meager fire started.

"Not too big now. Just 'nuff to light the fuse." he cautioned himself. Bill looked behind him for a way out.

There. Through those trees and up that hill, that oughta buy me some time. If I can get up there, I'll be able to pop off them rascals if they come after me. Yeppers just like old man Stiffer did to me. He brought back the memory of almost getting killed by the irate father.

Bill's wait wasn't long until the Fox raiders caught up to the fire. They ran right past the hidden keg in hopes to salvage the boat. They had no idea of the level of damage Bill had caused. From his hiding place, Bill waited. *Gotta wait from them to come back the trail, 'er, almost back. They'll be cussing an' pointing fingers to why they lost the prize. Then I'll blow them up. Yeppers. Boom!*

Bill's wait was rewarded as the painted men came back from the burning boat and stopped at where he'd hidden the gunpowder. He stared at these men that were so infatuated with stealing and killing. The tall one, obviously the leader, was adorned with a broad belt that held a tomahawk and large knife in a bead-covered scabbard. In his hand he carried a bow that was at least four feet long. Over his right shoulder was a quiver full of arrows that was hidden by his long black hair. The striking features of his face, his square jaw, and the black paint covering his cheeks.

"Holy shit. He's a mean-looking rascal." Bill whispered aloud. He looked to the others. They were dressed in the same manner but not nearly as large. The one on the right seemed to be pissed about the turn of events, and he pointed repeatedly at the large man as he kicked a branch near the powder.

"Here we go." Bill touched the powder with a burning twig and grabbed his gear and fell back to his sniping position. The warriors were so intent on blaming one another it wasn't till the smoke of the burning powder was only a few feet from them did they realize the danger and dove for cover.

The keg exploded, sending red and yellow fire shooting up in a great fire cloud. The explosion wasn't as dramatic as Bill had hoped for, but it made a lasting impression on the men that had hunted him. Burning debris rained down on the prone men like a bad hailstorm as the long-haired men scurried away like roaches caught in the light.

Bill hefted his rifle to his shoulder and laid it across a log that was providing a steady rest as well as cover. The scene below him was that of confusion and fear. After the smoke blew away and the fire simmered down, he watched the men begin to stand with wobbly legs. Bill watched the ensuing argument from his vantage point as each one brushed off the leaves and twigs that had been blown all over the floor of the small forest clearing.

Brave Dog threw his hands in the air as he shouted to Black Tail, "We must go to the south and catch this thorn in our side. He's made a fool of us!" Black Tail shook his head.

"If this thorn has done this to scare us, then I'd bet he's got us in his gun sights even as we stand here. Now is not the time to track him. Later, we can find him." He pointed inland.

"We must go inland for a while, let him think we've given up. Then we'll come back and track him down and bring him back for torture." Then he folded his arms across his well-defined chest, indicating he was done arguing with his nephew.

Still Brave Dog pointed south. He wanted to continue the hunt for Bill. The big one shook his head and turned to leave the area.

Bill watched almost laughing aloud at the comical sight he was beholding.

"No! We are to go south. I'm not afraid!" Brave Dog grabbed his arm and pulled Black Tail around to face him. Brave Dog never got a hand up to protect himself from the blow that was to follow. Black Tail had had enough of this argument, and when he felt his nephews hand, he knew that Brave Dog had gone too far. It was time to make sure he knew who led this raid. He backhanded Brave Dog like a disobedient wife, sending him careening back almost to the ground.

"We will speak no more on this. We will find this thorn soon. Do you understand?" Black Tail wanted to be sure that Brave Dog understood he was the leader.

That was too much for Brave Dog. His hand went for his knife; but before he could pull it out, Crushed Hand was on him, holding his hand down to prevent him from pulling his knife.

"Don't do it, Brave Dog. You'll be the one bleeding if you do this." Crushed Hand pleaded.

"You listen to Crushed Hand. He's right. You'll be dead before you hit the ground. Now go. We'll speak no more of this." Black Tail pointed inland once again. Brave Dog thought hard about this. *If I kill him, I'll be banished from the village. If I wound him, he'll be a martyr. I'll wait until the time is right. Then Black Tail will beg for his life.*

These two men were vying for leadership, all because of Billy was one step ahead of them. They walked past the leader. The small one strutted past Black Tail spitting on the ground in front of the leader.

"Well, I'll be 'et fer a tatter. They're leaving. I needed a break, and it worked." Bill relaxed as the men faded into the forest below him.

CHAPTER 32

Billy gathered up his blanket, tying it into a roll, and slung it over his back, and then he shouldered his musket and set off for Hannibal. Billy knew he couldn't be that far from the town he'd heard so much about.

"I better put some distance on them rascals 'cause they ain't given up. They just want me to think they have. They'll be on my trail as soon as they know I've forgotten an' let up on my guard. Yessiree. I ain't fallen fer that." he spoke aloud as he prepared to make some time on the vengeful Foxes. He pulled on the front of the sling to tighten the musket to his back as he started to run. Not a formidable runner by any straw but he could go for quite some time without stopping. He ran well into the late morning as he distanced himself from the Fox warriors.

The afternoon came quickly as he was still five miles from the nearest house, and he decided to enter the town in the morning. The young man walked over to the nearest log that looked to be comfortable and plopped down. *Damned Injuns, I bet they ain't far behind me.* Then he saw a large keelboat floating down the river. *I bet they'll be tying up an' be drunk 'fore I even get close to town.*

He looked over his shoulder, expecting to see the large painted man coming to kill him. *Now I gotta look over my shoulder. Shit. Well, I got them coon legs to cook up. Might as well do that and find a place to hole up fer the night.*

He walked back into the bottom, looking for another fallen tree or even a decent willow that he could seek shelter in as the sun began its ever-present race for the western skyline.

"This ain't too bad." he spoke as he found a large den dug under a fallen oak tree. *This should be fine even if they were lookin' fer me. Gotta find some way to hide the cooking smoke.* He looked about. *Put some of these willow branches over here.* He laid them carefully over the makeshift chimney. *Yeppers, this should work jes' fine.*

He cooked his meager supper of coon legs, careful to keep the smoke to a minimum as he thought about the next day. The town didn't know anything about the Whites or how his family had been torn apart. His mind drifted back to Ells, Katie, Ashley, Aarnel, Justin, and his stepfather with his fire-and-brimstone lectures. He remembered the stories of his real father, the cussing that had driven the family apart. With the sun barely into the western trees, Bill pulled his hat down. He drifted to sleep as he thought about Dallas City, with Marcia and Stillwater, the fat Justice of the Peace, and Sash the barkeep with the shattered bones. Then back to Ells and Beulah and the wonderful sex he'd shared with them, and then he remembered Mary Jane. The spaniel red hair. He fell into a deep sleep, not hearing the night animals or the insects of the night filling the area with the racket of the woods.

In the very early morning Bill awoke warmer than usual.

"Goddamned it's getting hot down in these bottoms." He crawled out as he could feel sweat already dripping down his back. *Damn, it's gonna be a hot summer.* He had a severe urge to take a piss. He crawled out, pulling the rifle and bedroll with him. He saturated the nearest ferns as he looked around in the false dawn, admiring a new day. *Too bad I ain't got a woman to suck this pod of mine. Damn, I got used to that.* He buttoned up his breeches, looking at his surroundings.

Might as well get going. He shouldered his rifle and blanket and stepped off to the south and the sanctuary from the vengeful Foxes.

A Short Stay

CHAPTER 33

He was relieved to see the first house, and then another, and finally he saw the first of a few small buildings in the newly forming town of Hannibal.

The summer did an early assault on the river valley. He could feel the heat already seeping in as he closed the distance to the store. Looking up, he read the name on the wavy window; Bates Mercantile.

"Damn. Getting too hot too soon." he spoke as the humid air seemed to hang in the midday air. Opening the door, he stepped in, feeling the cool air of the store.

"Howdy." He looked to see Jonathan Fleming behind the counter. It reminded him all too much of the Blankenship store with the same wall full of goods and tools. He scanned the shelves looking for the hemp rope he had used at Marcia's store, looking carefully until he spotted the spool on the floor by another cast-iron plow. It brought back the memories of a day of revenge, and he hadn't looked back since.

"My father had one of those." he blurted. *Shit, I shouldn't said nuthin'.*

"What's that?" the clerk asked, looking up from a tally sheet that he was working on.

"I was saying my father sure could use one of those." Bill quickly backtracked, hoping the clerk hadn't heard for sure. Looking over his small round spectacles, he frowned at Bill as if he had just ruined his whole day by entering the store.

"What can I do for you today?" Jonathan asked, placing his hands on the counter and leaning over to see Bill in all his glory.

That's when the runt noticed the disfigurement of the man's hand.

"I'm new to town, and I'm looking for work." Bill stood as straight as he could. Looking at the man behind the counter. A tall thin man with shiny dark hair plastered down and cropped close. His long pointy nose reminded Billy of a witch from a story book. Bill looked into the sunken eyes behind the small round spectacles with the pock marked complexion and he saw meanness.

"That a fact. You know ciphering?" Jonathan asked as he leaned back against the wall of cloth, making no move to hide his hand or the fact he was in charge.

"Yes sir, I do." Bill shifted his weight from one foot to the other, trying not to look nervous, but he'd not done any math in some time.

"We're not really needing any help this late in the year." He paused and looked to the rear of the store where one of the several other employees was working.

"Joseph, we needing any help?" he called to the employee that was rolling a large barrel to the back of the store.

"Yes sir, we can always use the help Mr. Fleming." Joseph McCorley answered. He didn't care for Jonathan as he considered him a bully and a scalawag. Ever since Jonathan had lost his fingers, he had a chip on his shoulder and felt the world owed him a living.

"You hear that? We really don't need any help." He snipped at Bill, but his mind was racing. Kinda scrawny. We really don't need no help, but if I can get him to do inventory, I can get in some extra work over at the mine. Lord knows Bates pays better at the mine than he does here. Bill turned to leave the store, but Jonathan called to him as he neared the door.

"Can you read? And write?" Jonathan asked, playing out his plan.

"Yes sir, I can." Billy answered and returned, and looked directly into the man's eyes.

"All right. We'll do a little test. Read this and add up these five things." Jonathan pushed out a small book and four items marked with paper tags.

"Read."

"Sure thing." He picked up the book and opened it to the middle, turned a few pages forward, and then went back to one.

He began, "In the spring I'll love you. In the fall I'll worship you like the flowers of the field until the sun that rakes the boroughs of the meadows of the newly formed day. I beseech you. Come to me when times breezes the last breath of love. I do beg you to come to me, early father of time. How's that?" He laid it down to see the keep's jaws hanging slack.

"Now let's see here; two bits plus two dollars and forty five cents. That would be two and seventy plus two bits. Bring it up to two dollars and ninety five cents, and then this here." He was interrupted by Jonathan.

"If this calico is a dollar fifty a yard, how much would two yards be?"

"It's three dollars. You want the other stuff too? That would be five dollars and ninety five cents. Bill adjusted his pistol in his waistband as the clerk stood there looking at the man across from him.

Jonathan's mind raced. *Ain't that sumpthin? He never even wrote the numbers down, did them all in his head, he reads as well as my wife or daughter.*

"I can rent you a room upstairs for two dollars a month." Bill's employ was the furthest thing from Jonathan's mind; he was already calculating how much he would make at the Galena lead mine.

"Sounds good. I'll go store my ruck an' be back in a shake. You say it's upstairs?" Bill smiled, looking about to see where the stairs were.

Jonathan was watching Bill scan for the stairs.

"They're out back. The doors open. Don't lallygag either. Hey, what's your name anyway?" he called to Bill as he headed toward the rear of the store.

Bill froze thinking quickly of a name. "Name's White Man." Billy answered as he neared the rear of the store.

"Hold on boy." Jonathan called to him.

Oh shit, now what? Billy's mind raced. Had Blankenship already got word   here?

"What's your Christian name?" Jonathan persisted.

"I just go by White Man." Bill answered, his hand on the back-door latch.

"Hold on. Come back here." Jonathan's interest had been sparked. "You tell me your full name, or you'll be out on your ear." Jonathan pressed on.

"Look here, Mr.."

"Mister Fleming. Mister Jonathan Fleming." Jonathan informed Bill.

"Mr. Fleming, I go by White Man. If that's not good 'nuff, then I'll get the hell outta here."

He rested his hand on the pistol butt. The other he hooked on the SC rifle sling. Joseph had stopped working and stood to watch the scene at the front of the store. *Finally someone's going to stand up to Fleming. Or at least try.*

"Not good enough. I don't want some trouble later. You're in trouble, ain't you? That's why you won't use your given name. Ain't that right?" Jonathan pressed.

"Let's say that if White Man ain't good 'nuff, I'll bid you a good day Jonnie." He all but insulted the storekeep. Joseph put his hand over his mouth to contain the laugh that was on his lips. He knew that Fleming hated it when anybody called him Jonnie or anything common.

"Jonnie? You got some sand I'll say that for you. I ain't been called Jonnie since I was draggin' on the teat. All right White Man. You got a job 'till your past finds you. Then I'll be the one to put the shackles on you if you got it coming. One other thing. You ever steal from this store, they'll not be enough left of you to put in a mason jar. You read me? No threat. Just facts. I'm hiring you 'cause you can read and cipher, not because were friends." Jonathan wanted to intimidate the young lad.

"Mr. Fleming, I don't want to work for you. I was being honest with you, an' now you're trying to bully me. I'd rather sleep in a cave with a panther than work for you." He turned around and headed for the door. His hand was on the knob, and still no words came to him. He turned the glass knob and stepped into the muggy afternoon air. *Well, shit. I was hoping to be in a nice bed tonight. There's other stores.* His eyes swept the few buildings.

Stepping out on the dirt lane that he'd come in on, he looked at the meager places that might offer him sanctuary from the onslaught of the rising heat. Noting nothing other than the storefronts and no people, he began to think it was going to be like Dallas City. A ghost town.

He walked to the south looking from side to side for another opportunity when an attractive girl about his own age stepped out of her cabin, giving Bill the once-over.

"Good day there sir." she called to him. He looked at the woman, her black dress pulled tight and her dark bonnet letting out her auburn hair in the front. Not thinking too much more of the greeting, he answered back, "Howdy."

He walked to her as he noticed the other members of the community returning to the stores to finish off the afternoon workday.

Bill's mind raced quickly. *No wonder I didn't seen nobody. They was all eating* .

"I'm Maria. I help cook for the settlement, and you look like you could use a meal. Won't you come in and enjoy the cool of our cabin and some hot food?" she asked as she folded her arms under her breasts, making them stand tall.

"I hate to be a bother. I've just arrived here and I'm looking for work to pay for my meals and keep."

"Never mind that for now. Come on in and cool off while you

can. Besides, you probably want to get some food in your stomach. We can find you work soon enough. Come on." She turned and opened the door, allowing Bill access to the cabin.

He walked in and looked around, seeing three men sitting at the tabled eating, not even taking notice of the small blond man entering in.

"Nice place you have here. Anything I can do to help?" he spoke as he stood his rifle up in the corner and hung his hat on the hat stand. Looking at the other patrons, he noticed none had stopped from eating.

"Nope. Just sit down, and I'll bring you some pork soup. We have Mr. Masterson to thank for the hog that gives us vitals. Now you just sit yer butt right down." Her hand rested on his shoulder a moment too long. "And I'll have something for you in a shake."

He sat down at the long dining table, and she quickly returned to the big stew pot hanging over the fire and began dishing out a large portion to his bowl, his mind raced about her hand lingering. *Did she do that on purpose?*

"Here's some fresh bread Mrs. Masterson made. Mrs. Masterson, my mother, and I do all the cooking here." She laid the bread down next to Bill's hand as her hand smoothly touched the top of his. She put the steaming bowl of soup in front of him with the other.

"Thank you." Bill sat down and began to eat looking at nothing more than the food in front of him.

"Say lad, where do you hail from?" One of the other patrons took notice of the small man eating down the table from him. Bill didn't want them to know he had been involved with the trouble with Marcia and Ruben.

"Oh, here an' there. Just trying to find work through the summer. I'm looking for work to pay for my keep." he answered, shoveling the metal spoon into his mouth. *Purty damned good pig,* he thought as he savored the salty taste.

"Do you have a trade? Blacksmithing? Carpentry? Hunting perhaps?" the man asked.

Bill quickly thought about his answer. "I'm good with numbers and can read an' write." He tore a chunk off the bread and soaked it in the soup.

"That so? You could ask Jonathan. He's always looking for help since he got crippled up an' all." the man answered Bill.

"Nah, he don't like me none. Tried to bully me." Bill looked at the man that had addressed him.

"I won't be bullied."

"That so." the man continued to pry, working on Billy's history to see if he would fit into the town.

"Yeppers. Who are you? If you don't mind me asking." Bill stopped eating, looking at the bearded man sitting down from him. He appeared to be a small man, black beard trimmed well, slightly gray on the tips, but he wasn't much different than Bill, just a lot older.

"Name's Henry. James Henry. You care to show me you're education? I believe I can get you a job in one of the Bates stores." James spoke as he looked into Bill's eyes.

"I can, but why do you wanna help me? Hell, you jes' met me." Bill asked as he pushed his empty bowl away. He had barely laid the spoon down before one of the black slaves came over and scooped it up.

"If I can do anything to be a thorn in Fleming's side, well, I'm there. You know the words I'm speaking of, lad?" James smiled, showing straight teeth and a sparkle in his eye.

"At times, some folks do become a bit of a burr under the saddle. I know horses, did some farm-work this year too." Bill spilled out more than he wanted to. *Damnit I shouldn't said all that.*

"Is that so?" another patron spoke from around James.

"Justice of the Peace Zachariah G. Draper. At your service. Where exactly did you farm, and workhorses? If I ain't prying too much." Zachariah asked. Bill's mind went frantic. *Shit! Shit! Shit!*

"Over by La Harpe, Illinois." Bill's hand crept under the table to the pistol in his belt.

"Illinois? You're a traveling man I see." he commented. "I know a few folks over in Dallas City, Illinois. You ever been there?" Zachariah asked.

"Oh, been there a few times. Know Ruben Stillwater?" He jumped ahead, taking the offensive.

"Name's familiar." he answered.

"How about Marcia Blankenship?" Billy pushed it all out in the open.

"Nope. I did know a barkeep. Sash Blue. You know him, a barkeep?" Zachariah asked. Bill knew it would only be a matter of days before the news spread of the debacle at Dallas City. *Shit, Niota knew about then. There's no reason to think this town wouldn't hear about it as well.*

"I knew him. Last time I saw him, he was with a broke leg an' arm." Bill slowly began to pull the pistol out, his thumb gently pulling back the hammer.

"Ol' Sash was a rough customer. I'm surprised he's still alive. Saw him kill more than a few folks at the back of his bar. Good riddance I say. How'd he get all busted up son? You know how it happened?" Zachariah picked up a mug and sipped it, not looking at Bill.

Don't fall into it. Just give them a tad.

"I sure do. My mother did it." She dropped a pan, causing James to jump. He shot an angry look at her.

"Mister?" Billy had already forgotten the man's name.

"Draper. Zach if you want." The Justice turned his face from Bill.

"Mr. Draper. If I tell you all the facts, what's to become of me? It was in Illinois, an' we're in Missouri territory." Bill watched the side of the man's face for a sign.

"Tell me the truth now 'fore I hear what someone else wants to tell me. And put that pistol back. We don't use guns here unless we're chasing off the Injuns." Zach turned to look into Billy's eyes.

"You, my fine lad, you're a killer. I can see it in your eyes. Saw it back in the war. Them that are survivors have that look to go all the way. Ain't that so." Zach spoke, turning away from Bill again.

"Yeppers, I go all the way." Bill kept his hand on the gun.

"Come on, lad, what's your name?" Zach pried gently.

"I go by White Man." Bill answered looking toward the doors. *Shit, I shouldna done that.*

"Won't do no good to run unless you don't plan on living with the Sacs or the Foxes. Then you'll be dead before the Fourth of July. So you might as well tell us what's the real story." Zach slowly turned to look into Bill's eyes again. This time Zach saw the hollow stare of a man that was on the edge, ready to meet his maker if it came to it.

"Why? What does it matter? Let it be. Jes' let me work an' ride out the summer. I'll stay outta trouble here. You got my word." Bill spoke slow and steady; he was, in fact, ready to fight his way out if he had to. He just wanted a place to work and live until he could figure where to go next.

"James, do you want this mystery man working around you? How about you, Isham?" he spoke to a distant man at the far end of the table.

"He's pissed off Fleming. That's enough for me." James smiled at Billy.

"Ables?" Zach continued.

"Damn, I don't know. Boy, you really a killer or just at the wrong place at the wrong time?" Isham asked, looking at the blond man down the table from him.

"It was just like that." Bill eased his hand off the butt. The man called Isham Ables nodded in approval.

"Then you're welcome to stay and work. By us anyway." Zach said as he slowly stood.

"Welcome to Hannibal, White Man." They filed out of the cabin one after the other, each nodding to her as they left.

She waited until she and Bill were alone, "There's an empty cabin that used to belong to Sam Thompson, and you're welcome to stay in it as long as you need." Bill stayed seated, watching it all unfold so quickly.

This has turned out jus' fine. I was hoping to stay put fer a bit.

"Thank ya kindly for your hospitality." Bill rested his elbows on the table. He exhaled a deep breath of relief.

"Come on White Man I'll show you where you can store your ruck and get settled." She grabbed her ankle-long coat and slipped it on effortlessly. *Too damned hot for a long coat. Too damned hot* Billy thought.

CHAPTER 33

Bill picked up his rifle and followed the woman out of the cabin and down the road to a small cabin at the edge of town. It wasn't much bigger than two of the stalls he'd cleaned out back in Illinois a few glass windows in front and a thick door with a simple iron-latch opening.

"This was Sam Thompson's place." She held the door open as Bill stepped through. She closed the door behind her and Bill.

"What happened to him? This here Sam Thompson?" Bill asked as he stood the rifle in the corner.

"He was sent off to St. Louis for trial. He killed a Sac Indian a while back. It was a bad thing for all involved if you ask me." She picked up some of the firewood and carefully laid it in the hearth. Bill watched as he sat on the rope bed against the nearest wall.

"See he was down by Masterson's hogs one day. That's the woman's husband that made the bread. Well they have hogs. So one day these Sac Injuns sick'd their hounds on one of Mr. Masterson's hogs. Kind of making sport of it. Well Sam shot and killed one to stop them from killing the hogs. The Injuns took off and came back with Mr. Campbell. He's got a place over on the bay. He's trades with 'em and speaks Sacs, so they all got it settled that Sam and the Injun that shot Jonathan to go to St. Louis to stand trial."

"Hold on. You say a Sac Injun shot Fleming's fingers off?" Bill interrupted her.

"Kinda eye-for-an-eye thing?" he asked, trying to put everything together.

She was bent over, making the fire as she spoke to Bill.

"Yes, Mr. Fleming was down cutting wood, and the Sacs came to get revenge for killing one of theirs. They shot Mr. Fleming.

When he got back here, we had to barricade ourselves in until till help arrived. That was old man Campbell. They made a deal that would take the Injun that shot Mr. Fleming and Sam for shooting the Sac Injun to trial, like I was saying. That's why we have this cabin empty. Mr. Thompson never came back." He watched her work, thinking she had told him a lot in just a small time. *Most likely ain't got nobody else around to hear the telling of the story*

"Maria, you said you an' your mother are cooks for the town also?" he questioned her in an attempt to keep her longer inside the cool cabin. She stood up as the fire started burning on its own.

"Yes, she does. Like I said before, she, Mrs. Masterson, an' me do all the cooking. Why?" She looked into Bill's eyes her brain racing, *He's no killer. Not this one. He's got love on his mind. This is good. There hasn't been anybody here close to my age for quite some time.* Her mind stepped back of the last beau that came courting, *Now he's over at galena in the lead mine, but this man has his emotions on his sleeve.*

"I was just wondering what I could do to add to the town. Bates Mercantile seems to be all but dead as long as Jonnie boy is there. I didn't see much of any horses here either. No farmer buggies. Just a few freight wagons." He stood up and stretched. Now the flames had warmed up the room quickly, and Bill began feeling more comfortable with the woman in front of him.

Pushing his hat back, he asked, "What do they do, them freighters?" He leaned down to put another piece of firewood in the hearth.

"I see you like it warm. Those wagons? They carry salt from the mines to the keelboats. You know, we have riverboats coming to town now." She now felt very warm from the fire but also from this man. He was intoxicating. Just him speaking to her as an equal was more than she had bargained for.

"Well, I have to get back. Nice to have you around. I'll see you tonight. I mean at the cabin for supper." She stuck out her hand to shake Bill's. He was pleased to touch her slender hand and made sure he held it longer than necessary.

"Sure thing. See you at supper. That would be at dark? Or is there a bell?" he answered, not releasing her hand.

"Just when you feel like it. We keep food going pretty much all day. Well then, good-bye for now." He released her grip, and he watched the door close as she left.

Damn, this can be good. Maybe I'll go out and snag a few rabbits or coons to pay for the hospitality. Sacs and others are about, though. Hell if them others ain't been able to catch me, I doubt these will be able to either. He turned to stare into the fire. *Them others. I bet they ain't too far from here. Better get out while it's still light.* He grabbed the rifle, possible bag, and powder horn and walked out, pulling his door shut as he surveyed the town. With rows of houses and a few stores, he looked to the river, seeing a pier jutting out. *Must be for the riverboats. I wonder. Maybe I could get hired on.*

CHAPTER 35

Well, first things first. He walked around the cabin and faded into the forest around him.

Bill walked casually in the forest, pulling himself through the thick pea vines as he began to notice the squirrels barking and jumping about like circus animals. *Not you. I need something bigger. I'll get you when I'm bored.*

The heat radiated as he stepped farther from the town. He started to feel relaxed. *I feel like I can do this all day, being in the woods. This is where I belong. Maybe I can go west like the men I've heard about from the folks in La Harpe. The Mountain Men.* He froze as he heard a snap of a branch, or he thought it was a snap. It could have been a deer stepping on a branch or a man being careless.

He leaned against the nearest tree and waited. *No smell yet.* Then came the smell of wood smoke. *That smells like someone's been next to a cooking fire.* Still he made no movement other than his eyes slowly scanning for the noise. Then he saw the movement; a man walking clumsily through the woods. Bill made no attempt to meet the man. He just watched him from his vantage point.

When the man was close to Bill, he finally called to him, "You from around here?"

The man froze; he looked about, trying to see where the voice was coming from. Bill looked at him now that he was close. He looked like any white man; long unkempt black beard, a sharp nose, black brimmed hat cocked on the back of his head, his black coat and trousers stained of mud from falling in the woods. But the man was looking for the voice with those close-set eyes. Bill saw he was noticeably shaken by the way his eyes were darting about.

"Over here." Bill called as he stepped from behind the tree.

"I'm the White Man. Who are you?"

"I'm Jospeh Décarboné. But the people here call me Joe the Frenchman. You, I don't see you before." The man stuck his hand out for Billy to shake. Bill could see his face now as he smiled.

"Whatcha doin' out here without a gun?" Bill spoke quietly as he looked about as they made their greetings.

"My dog Pete, he's run away. I thought I could find him before the darkness. But I've not. You are a hunter for the town, yes? Maybe you can find my dog. He's a good dog, long ears and very friendly. He likes to chase the raccoon. Sometimes he brings one to me. He's a good dog, a black and tan." He stepped away and stumbled again, making a terrible ruckus as he fell. Righting himself, he called over his shoulder, "I must be going. If you find him, please bring him to supper tonight. Je evous en remercie."

Then the man was gone, leaving Billy alone. *Well, if that don't beat all, a coon dog. That oughta help get me some grub. Now to get back to hunting.* He slowly stepped farther into the woods; the ferns and briars quickly hid his trail as he went deeper into the woods. Bill walked and listened for anything that seemed to be out of the ordinary. The canopy hit the meager sunlight, casting shadows on the forest floor as he walked farther from the town. Stopping and listening, he thought he heard something. There, that's a dog barking. He listened, turning his head so he might be able to hear a bit better. *Yep, that's a dog. Sounds like he got something treed. Might as well go see what it is.* He walked slowly toward the noise, carefully stepping toward the baying hound. The sound got louder as he closed the distance. Then he heard voices, not American-speaking voices. *Now what?* He stepped from tree to tree, slowly closing the distance until he could see the men that were speaking. Three of them. Not all painted up though. Looked to be trying to get a shot at the critter in the tree. He looked around for any others. *Nope just the three. I bet Joe's dog done made them some grub, I wonder.*

He stayed hidden, but he called out, "Hello." He peered around the tree, only showing an eye or so. He watched two of them pull their bows back and the third one level his gun toward Bill's voice.

"Who's there?" the American voice echoed in the woods.

"Show yourself, and there will be no trouble." the voice called to him.

"I see you got Joe the Frenchman's dog there. I was wanting to take it back to him." Still he made no move to reveal himself.

"Come out an' we'll see about it." the voice answered back.

"We'll not harm you. We just don't like being snuck up on. It's our job to be sneakin'."

The voice laughed.

Bill stepped from around the tree, his rifle in the crook of his arm, the pistol easily in reach.

He saw them clearly now. *Two of 'em be Injuns but the third's definitely be a white man.*

"Hell, you're just a pup. Who are ye lad?" The man speaking stood his rifle up on its butt and leaned on the barrel in total relaxation. His face was clean shaved with a blue and red headband around his sandy blond hair that laid on his white frocked shirt. All three men had on buckskin legging's adorned with pony beads and silver tubes. The two Indians took the tension off their bows as they too relaxed on the example of their friend.

"I'm new to the town. I go by the White Man." He pointed to the dog with a hemp rope around its neck.

"That's Joe's dog."

CHAPTER 36

"So you're the White Man? Jimmy Henry said you might be out here about. He also said you an' that threes-fingers Fleming had a go at it already." he spoke casually to the other buckskinned hunters.

"Don't got a Christian name?" The buckskinned man spoke calmly, looking Bill over slowly.

"Hey Crossed Lance, this pup has his own handle, and he's still wet behind the ears." The older man laughed, his attention turned away from Billy.

"Oh I got one, just don't wanna use it. Who be you?" Bill asked, keeping his hand close to his pistol butt.

"Well now, we can talk 'bout that later. You know Joe the Frenchman?" The man wagged his head as he busted a big smile across his face.

"Shit, he couldn't find water if'n he was standin' in it. We heard him stomping around an hour ago. Ol'Petey here is better off with us anyhow. The ol'Frenchy feeds him table scraps, ruins a good coon dog is what that does. But I have to admit, boy, you did put the sneak on us. Hell, didn't even smell ya. So I reckon you've been on yer own hook 'fore. Not some local town folk looking for a squirrel or rabbit. Am I reading yer signs right boy?" the man asked.

"I've been around. So who are you?" Bill asked again.

"I'm Micah Bohen. I've been here since the Sacs kicked the Foxes' ass outta here. You ever hear'd of me boy?" Micah asked.

"Nope, sure ain't. Like I said, I'm new to these parts. Did bump into a few awhile back. Hope they ain't with your partners here." Bill confessed.

"Bumped into. That means you left 'em where they fell?" the man asked, looking steadily at Bill.

"Drown one." The other had a hole the size of yer hand in his gut. Is that what you mean?"

Bill wasn't sure about telling this man all the past, but he wanted to be sure he didn't have to look over his shoulder during his stay in Hannibal.

"Put some folks under did ya? Where might have this happened as we've not heard any of our folks get killed, except by that damned Sam Thompson. May he rot in hell wherever he is." Ice came from the voice of Micah.

"Over in Illinois I had a few bump into me and my mother. The Kaskaskias, some Peoria's, and Miamis hit the fort I was staying in. Killed twenty-three white folks and a few niggers. Three of us made it through." Bill felt he could speak to this frontiersman with no worry of judgment.

"My, they's a wild bunch them Kaskaskias. I've heard they did that kinda thing." Micah acknowledged.

"Well, the ones I shot were on this side of the river. Big ol'boy. Him and two of his friends just about got blow to hell." Bill laughed.

"Oh? Was they dressed like these bucks?" He pointed to his two companions

"Yeppers. 'Cept his hair was all dolled up fancy. Had a blacked face too." Bill watched the faces of the others as he told the story.

"This man. You say he big. This big?" the one called Crossed Lance spoke, holding his arm up to show the height of the imaginary warrior.

"Crossed Lance, you know who's he's talking about?" Micah asked.

"Yes. I've escaped his knife before. He's Black Tail of the Foxes. A fierce black-hearted man. He's taken the lives of Sacs and whites all up and down the big river. How is it you did not get killed small one? Black Tail is one of the best trackers in the Missouri Territory."

"It's a long story, and I gotta get some food for the folks in town." Bill started to leave, but Crossed Lance and his friend quickly brought back his bow to full pull.

"I believe you ain't goin' nowhere." At that moment Micah's rifle jumped up into his hands like a new puppy.

"What?" Bill pulled the pistol in one fluid movement and had it leveled straight at Micah's face.

"You ain't with them Foxes are you?"

"You'll be making a mistake son. You'll be dead 'fore you hit the ground. Now let's all just rethink this. Crossed Lance, the boy ain't goin' nowhere. He's staying right down in town. We can talk with him later." Micah spoke, but his rifle stayed trained on Bill's midsection.

"How we know he not spy? Make up story?" Crossed Lance sneered.

"You ain't no spy are ye lad? Jus' out huntin' up some grub and trying find ol'Pete here. Ain't that right? Look, Crossed Lance, Jimmy said he was a good lad. We can hear his story when it ain't so late. 'Sides I'm getting awful hungry, and Mr. Coon up there is getting to look mighty good." Micah lowered his rifle and slowly put his hand on Crossed Lance's bow, lowering it slowly.

"We need to hear all that you have to tell us about them cussed Foxes." He turned to his buckskinned friend.

"Crossed Lance?" Micah spoke soothingly to the man beside him. The whole time the third man had not spoken a word but had taken key from the other Sac hunter with his bow pulled taunt.

"Hey boy, look, we ain't gonna get but this one coon. Why not come on back with me and my Sac friends? We'll have us a good meal. Two Bows's wife cooks up a mean coon, and you can tell us more of yer past." Micah was getting to like the lad after just a few minutes with him.

"Nah, I'm gonna be headin' back to the town. I'll just tell the Frenchman I didn't see his dog. I was hoping to take a coon or something back as a gift for the hospitality those folks show'd me so far." Bill looked up into the canopy, seeing the frightened animal staring down at the humans.

"I'll snag a rabbit or two over on the meadows by the river then." Bill spoke as he slipped the pistol under his belt.

"Well, till we meet again then Micah." Bill turned and began his walk back to where he figured to get a few plump rabbits.

"Hold on there White Man." Micah called to him, "You can have this one. We got a nice doe this morning. Crossed Lance, what say you?" he asked as the night began its attack on the daylight.

"Yes, he can have coon." Then in one fluid movement, he pulled back the bow and released the ash arrow into the animal in the tree. Bill figured it to be a good thirty feet in the air. The arrow found its mark, and the ring-tailed animal fell backward to the ground, the shaft sticking through it. Bill watched Two Bows quickly walk to the dead animal where he pulled out the arrow and picked up the critter by its hind legs.

"You remember. Crossed Lance and Two Bows. No shoot us." Two Bows stepped around the tree and recovered the thirty-pound animal.

"No shoot us. We friend to the whites, like Micah. Friends, no shoot."

"Sounds good Two Bows. I won't shoot you, an' you remember me, right?" Bill offered up his hand to shake. The Sac warrior reached for it, but instead of palm to palm, his hand slid up to Bill's forearm as he tightened his grip. Bill responded equally.

"Deal?" the man asked.

"Deal." the runt responded as he looked into the slender face of the man before him, the almost-black dark eyes; the smooth complexion with the high cheekbones, the hairless face, the thin lips, and the coal-black hair that gently blew across his face. *I hope the rest of these her Sacs are this friendly as these here two.* Bill's mind raced.

He looked over to see that Crossed Lanced had already turned to leave, with Micah not far behind him. Then Two Bows quickly followed them into the forest. *Not much for talkin' when they wanna get. Might as well get this critter skinned out.*

He picked up the coon and pulled out Mary Jane's knife and quickly cut through the back leg to give him a slit between the two bones. Bill looked about until he found a maple tree that had a good fork. Then he slit the other rear leg and walked to the tree. Sheathing her knife, he pulled Beulah's large knife and trimmed the two limbs to give him a fork the he could hang the animal freely. Satisfied he pulled Mary Jane's knife again and cut around each leg and slid the back legs over the forks so the animal would hang securely. *That oughta do just fine. Now a cut here, now a cut here.* He cut along the back of the legs to the ringed tail.

"Now where's me a coupla sticks?" he asked aloud, looking at the ground of the forest.

"Ah, here we go." He slid the sticks into the tail and sandwiched them and pulled quickly as the rat-like tail came out of the ringed fur.

"Now the hard part." he spoke as he began to pull the pelt off the coon, stopping occasionally to slit here and there. Soon all he had to do was cut around each front leg and then trim the ears and the muzzle as the pelt fell free.

Never gets any easier, I'll say that. He let outa breath from the exertion. He quickly slit the belly open and removed the intestines. *Damn, I hope them folks don't want the guts.* He reached in, pulling the rest of the organs out. *They oughta be glad to be getting' fresh meat.* He slid the pelt on top of his possible bag and picked up the coon. *Here we go.* And he began the walk back to the cabin he could call home.

CHAPTER 37

Bill entered the warm cabin as he felt relief to have a roof over his head.

No sense wasting about, nothing to eat here. He threw another piece of firewood in the hearth and headed out to the Bobbs' cabin. As he walked down to the cabin, the dark had a quieting effect on Billy. No more having to look over his shoulder for a Fox arrow or fancy man trying to get him bent over a barrel. *Yep, gonna be good this winter.*

Bill neared the cabin where he could see light and folks inside at the tables. *Yep, gonna be a fine winter.* He lifted the latch and stepped into the lamp-lit room, only to see the table full of people eating and carrying on brisk lively conversations with Fleming at the head spot at the table.

"Well well, if it ain't the White Man." Fleming sneered.

"Hello there Jonnie boy. I surprised you could fit through the door?" The cabin went quiet as Bill insulted the head storekeep.

"With you being so full of yerself an' all." He looked to see her mouth hanging open with shock that anyone would speak against the Bates man.

"Here you go. I brought some fresh meat." He walked to her, handing the animal to her feet first.

"Why thank you White Man. You didn't have to do that. But thank you. I'll make a fine stew for tomorrow." She blushed.

"You find the critter dead and brought it with you? I'm surprised you didn't get lost being new to our community." the man continued to insult Bill.

Bill looked around the cabin to see Jimmy Henry, Zach, and Joseph McCorley from the store and two new women including Mrs. Bobb and Mrs. Masterson.

"Nah, one of the local Sacs killed it fer me, said he had a nice doe." He looked around to see the faces looking away from his glances.

"Yep, them and Micah was right hospitable to me unlike someone else in this here room. Say there, Jonnie boy, you bring anything, or are you just mooching off these folks?" Bill turned and stood his rifle in the corner, his back to Fleming. He knew the man was egging for a verbal spat, and he really didn't want to get into an insulting duel with the man.

Fleming jumped out of his chair, sending it crashing back against the floor.

"Mind your tongue boy! Or you'll be eating soup all winter!" Fleming yelled to Bill's back. Bill slowly turned to the man, his face red. Even in the light of the room, Bill could see he was teething for a fight, verbally or physically.

"Oh sit down Jonnie boy. I ain't gonna fight you tonight, not tomorrow neither. Go on now. Sit back down and relax a smidgen 'fore you pop out an eyeball or something. Go on now. Sit back down and finish yer supper." Bill spoke casually to the man as if they just finished a nice game of horseshoes.

"Who do you think you are to be ordering me? You. You. You runt!" he spat the words to Bill.

"Hell, didn't you know?" Bill pulled an empty chair out and slowly sat down, not even looking at Fleming.

"I'm the White Man. Lover, fighter and wild horse rider." He laughed, seeing the relief on Zach's face for not getting pulled into the storekeep's harassment.

"How ya doing Zach? The food good tonight?" he deliberately ignored the Bates man.

"Well now, it's a good stew. You say you met some Sacs? Micah too? Good man Micah, keeps the locals friendly." he spoke, ignoring Fleming that was still looking for a fight.

"You're on thin ice, Zachariah. You side with this outlaw, and you'll be out of a job before the first snowfall! I'll see to it personally!" Jonathan was speaking slowly and menacing, giving the threat and meaning every word of it.

"Jonathan, please sit down." The woman nearest to him gently pulled on his arm.

"No. Let me go Louise!" He wrenched his arm away from his wife.

"Zachariah, what'll it be? You best be thinking about your woman." he continued his assault on the Justice of the Peace.

"All right Mr. Fleming." He looked whipped to Bill as he whispered, "Sorry young man."

Then he turned his face from Bill. Billy looked up at the man at the end of the table, seeing he was not going to let a sleeping dog lay. Their eyes met, and Bill knew that his days at Hannibal would be numbered. Either his history would catch up, or he'd be on the run for beating the shit out of the man at the end of the table.

"There's a steamship coming in tomorrow, the Alice Mae. You be on it or these people will be out of work and freezing this winter. You understand boy? You be on that ship." He stood now with his arms folded over his chest, fuming with authority.

"Why, I'd say you got a chip on your shoulder big enough to fuel your idiocy fer quite a spell. Too bad, as I like this town, save one pig-sodomizing, goat-sucking, three-fingered, egg-sucking varmint." Bill rocked back on his chair.

"Zachariah, arrest that man. Make no mistake White Man or whoever you are. You'll be gone tomorrow! Or I'll see you dead! Now get out!" Jonathan Fleming was very sure of himself on the matter and made sure that if the Justice of the Peace didn't follow his orders to the letter the winter would be long and cold.

"All right, Mr. Fleming. White Man, let's go. You'll be in your cabin 'till the ship comes tomorrow." Zach stood up waiting for Bill.

Bill's hand was inching close to the pistol on his waistband, but James Henry spoke before Bill's hand finished its journey.

"Don't do it son. You may get him, but there's more to follow him for sure, and they'll string you up for it." James spoke calmly to the runt across from him.

"Zach, I'll do as you say. I don't want nuthin' to come down on you folks. Too bad you got a three-fingered bully pullin' yer strings. Yep." He stood up and walked to his rifle.

"Yep, too bad." Bill reached for the door and turned to see the people that had no chance to right the wrong that was happening to them.

He pulled the door when she blurted out, "I'll cook this coon and bring some over to you when it's finished", she shot an angry look at Fleming, "since you brought it in an' all." The head storekeep wanted to say something, but Bill was gone before he could.

The small cabin was silent as Fleming sat back down, his chest still pumped from his show of the mock superiority.

"Mrs. Bobb, bring me some of your fine mutton stew would you please. I've a good appetite tonight." He picked the wooden spoon, waiting for his service.

"Yes sir." she spoke in a hushed voice. Mrs. Bobb thought of the events that had come to play in one day. Her life had been fine, but this blond man had turned it into turmoil. No, it wasn't the White Man. No, it's been like a boil waiting to pop ever since this man ran into the Sacs and lost his fingers. Yes, that was what did it, not to mention him and Mr. Bates being so close. I wonder what Mr. Bates would say to all this. Well, I hope she gets a son or daughter from the White Man. She's so ready for a young one, but no. She can't, or it'll be a bastard. I'm so upset. Damn him! She ladled another spoonful into the bowl as she stared at the fingers on the man's hand. Mutilated and scarred. The woman snapped and swung the spoon in the air to smack Fleming, but James saw it all happening and quickly stood to sliding his arm around her quickly, pointing her to his bowl.

"I'll take a bit more, Mrs. Bobb." She met his eyes, wishing her husband was here instead of being in the Bates lead mine.

"Sure James. Sure." She exhaled, realizing she had been holding her breath. Fleming had no clue he had been close to a good clean frap. She looked around to see if the other folks had taken notice, if they had, they made no move to indicate it.

"Mother, I'll fix this up for the White Man. Excuse me." She turned away from the table and took the carcass to the back of the tiny kitchen to begin preparing it for Billy.

"Now Maria, be sure you give me the best cuts now. Don't want to wasting it on that drifter now, do we?" Jonathan called over his shoulder to the woman in the back. Her mother's mouth fell open. *I'll pay to have those Indians finish the job, and whatever it takes, I'll pay!* Her eyes met James, and he gently shook his head as if he'd read her mind.

"Yes sir, only the best for you, sir." But she had no intention of giving any to the man.

CHAPTER 38

Bill walked to his cabin with Zach behind him, Zach's hands in his coat pockets, making no attempt to protect himself if Bill decided to fight.

Zach felt that Bill would leave when the *Alice Mae* docked. He knew the frustration the town felt. His mind raced, *but with Fleming having Bates's ear, there wasn't much we can do until we have a better voice to speak for us. That's it! We'll hold an election and get a mayor and set up a town council and make sure Fleming doesn't have a hand in any decision making!*

"White Man!" he called to Bill's back in the dark walk to his cabin.

He stopped and faced the man in the darkness, not knowing what to expect next. *I'll not take another word. I'll leave tonight and never return after I beat the dog shit outta of Fleming.* But to his surprise, Zach found his hand and pumped it vigorously.

"You're a Godsend!" Zachariah spoke to him in the darkness.

"Huh? What are you talking about?" he questioned the man in the dark.

"We'll vote. We'll vote and make a mayor and town council members and make sure Fleming has no word in our decision making. We can be a township of our own. Bates can pull his puppet strings all he wants, but we'll not need him anymore." Zach wrapped his arm around Bill's shoulder as they walked to his small cabin.

"Now why is that?" Bill's curiosity had been piqued.

"The same punishment that he's dealing you? It'll be our savior. The steamship will bring commerce to our town. We'll prosper, and Fleming or Bates will have nothing to do with it. We can build our own destiny." They neared his cabin by now.

"Have a good night." He let go of Bill and turned to leave but hesitated and he turned to Billy.

"Maria's cooking? Makes my mouth water, her cooking up that coon. She's a fine woman." he hesitated.

"Too bad you're in a pinch. She'd be mighty comforting on a cold night. This is it until tomorrow, White Man." He had gotten a few steps when he turned to see Bill in the doorway, his shape silhouetted by the meager light from inside the cabin.

"I'd like to know." he called to the man in the light.

"What?" He answered back, having an inkling he was going to ask his Christian name.

"Your name. Your real name." he called to Bill.

"William White." Bill closed the door and began to think of his next move.

There were no more questions now; it was just Bill and his small fire. His mind quickly raced to the events that would transpire in the morning. *Well, I guess I'll just see someone about work. I imagine someone will come ashore and do business with the stores. I'll just ask them about getting hired. I can do just about anything.* He pulled another chunk of wood off the small stack and placed it in the hearth. As he watched it burn, his mind went blank. Then another and another until the room was hot enough to make him start sweating. He pulled off his coat and hat lying on the cot. *I'll need more wood before the night's over.* Giving it no more thought, he opened the door and walked into the cool evening to a stack of oak wood against the south side of the cabin. Hefting an armload, he returned to the room only to find Maria and an iron pot greeting him

"Your door was open, and I brought that meat I promised you." she spoke, setting it down on the small table in center of the room. She pulled off her coat.

"My, you keep a warm cabin. I guess with you leaving in the morning, you're not going to worry about having wood for tomorrow night." She laid the long coat on the bed against the wall.

"I was bored, so I jus' kept adding wood. I didn't think about how warm it was. You want the door open?" he asked as he piled the wood next to the mantel.

"No, I like it warm. So what's next for you? Riverboat life or are you going to go west? I doubt it'll be riverboat life for very long. I can see you've a strong will and most likely not do well with someone barking orders to you. Am I right?" She undid the top button of her dress, fanning herself.

"Lookie here, I can open the door if yer getting too hot." Bill got up to open the door.

"Please don't. I really don't mind. Aren't you warm?" Bill wasn't sure what was happening, but he knew what an open proposal was. The last time he'd been with a woman was the barkeep Ashley, and that seemed like months ago. He quickly thought back of the barmaid, her refusal of his advances, and the quick coupling on the stairs and his hasty retreat in the darkness. But there was no retreating here, just a woman wanting some intimate attention, and he was sure to give it to her.

"Hold on, I'll lay our coats down." He fetched their coats from the cot and laid them down.

"We can have a little picnic." He sat down next to her, his coat barely big enough to cover very much of the floor.

"You're funny. A picnic inside? Sure why not? Let me get some of that meat for you."

She went to get up, but Billy stopped her.

"I ain't hungry fer no coon. There something else right in front of me that would taste far better than a greasy old coon." He gently pulled back a loose strand of her auburn hair, his hand lingering on her face.

She looked into his blue eyes, and her mind raced. *Oh my, He's really going to do it. I thought he might be too shy to follow my lead, but here he is, ready to make love right now. He doesn't care of my age or if I'm,* her mind went blank as Bill brought his hand behind her head and guided her face to his. *Oh my!* Bill's lips met hers as she opened her mouth, feeling his tongue quickly shoot in her mouth.

Oh my. She felt flushed to her groin. Her breasts heaved as this new man began to arouse her unlike what she'd experienced. Bill pulled back, looking into her eyes.

"You didn't come up here to bring me some meat, did you?" His eyes covered every inch of her face.

"No." She shook her head a little, "No, I—I—." She leaned back to the coats. Bill leaned with her. His lips met hers as she opened her mouth. Bill responded by exploring her mouth once again. This time her tongue met his as she lay back on their coats.

He raised himself up.

"Hold on. Let's do this right. No sense acting like a pair of school kids. I'll cover the windows with that old blanket, and you get undressed. We'll do this right, me and you. We're going to enjoy this all night."

"Huh? But I thought we're going to make love?" she asked, confused. It was all so strange to her. That last time she had been with a man he had simply pulled her dress up and fumbled around, leaving her with a messy set of bloomers. Now this man wanted her to undress. Be naked.

"Yeah, we're gonna make love. But it ain't gonna be a slam-bam-thankie-mam. No sir'ree bob." He chuckled at his little joke. He pulled the blanket off the meager cot. He measured out half and pulled Mary Jane's knife and split it in two. He scanned the window, looking for a nail or something to hang the blanket by. His eyes were rewarded by an iron nail on both sides of each window. Both windows musta had some kind of window covering at one time. Bill walked to the windows and hung the blanket halves up. Stepping back, he admired his work.

"That oughta keep prying eyes from seeing us." He turned her and watched her pull her dress over her hips. Not narrow like his mother but not big either. Then came off her slip, and then she looked up at him.

"Aren't you going to get undressed too?" She stopped her arms folded across her breasts like she had done earlier.

"Hell yeah. It won't take me but a shake 'er two be down to nuthin'. You just keep a going." He undid his belt, letting the pistol and knives clank to the floor. She continued on. Her bloomers came off and finally her under shirt. There she was naked and standing next to the fire. The light bounced from her hips and breasts as she watched the young man before her. *I've never seen a man really naked. I've seen Mrs. Masterson's son Michael before but never a grown man.* She sat back down on her coat, her arms around her knees, her long hair cascading around her shoulders, revealing nothing to Bill. He had watched her and saw she was a bit timid about her nakedness.

"You're beautiful. Too bad none of these folks can see that." He kicked off his shoes and dropped his breeches. He quickly pulled his thin shirt off and stood before her as naked as her. His pod quickly grew with the anticipation of sex.

"You thingy is getting bigger." She watched Bill pod getting stiff.

"Yeppers, it don't take much to set it off too." He paused, looking down at her.

"I take it you've never done this, I mean being naked an all." He stepped closer to her, so his penis was level to her head now. She lifted her head until she was staring at the end of his pod.

"No. I've never had a man, this close." Then she looked up, and her eyes met his.

"No sweat pretty maiden. We'll do it upright tonight. So the next time a caller comes to you, you'll be the one in charge." He spoke, his hand reaching for his pod.

"Now, I want you to put your mouth on this an' suck on this like a piece of rock candy. Think you could do that?" he spoke soothingly to her.

"Why? Aren't you going to just stick it in me?" she asked, leaning back, locking her arm behind her, exposing her smooth breasts but her legs closed, not playing into Bill's idea.

"A few women I've been with like the taste of spunk. I figured you might be one of.

His hand was at the base of his pod, pointing to where her head had been.

"Are you sure? Will I choke?" she asked, still away from Bill's small appendage.

"Pretty sure you won't." He stopped and wanted to make sure it was her idea to go further.

"All right, I'll try." She rolled over to get on her knees before Bill, her hand reaching for his pod. Bill watched her hesitate as her hand touched his penis.

"I just suck on it?" she asked, not sure of the procedure.

"When are you going to squirt? I mean, do I swallow it or spit it out? What do real women do?" she asked, genuinely concerned.

"Most of them stick it down their throat and breathe through their nose and swaller it. A few hold it their mouth and spit it out, like the." he stopped talking as she brought her mouth to his pod and placed it in, waiting for him to spew. He slowly slid it in and out until she got the idea. Then her head began to bob like a chicken in the pen. She went at it in such fury he felt himself tingling quickly.

"Here it comes." He steadied himself with one hand on her head, and he released into her mouth. She didn't gag or spit; she just pulled his pod out and looked up to him, then opened her mouth to show that great gob of semen on her tongue. To Bill's surprise, she swallowed it in one large gulp.

"It didn't taste bad. I kind of liked it. Can we do it again?" She placed her hand on his quickly hardening pod.

"Or can you stick it in me?" She had no clue Bill could go twice more. She thought it was normal for men to keep going.

"Sure thing. Go ahead and do it again." His hand guided his quivering pod to her mouth. She went at it with the same fervor as before, but as Bill began to tingle, he pulled his pod out and spoke to her, "Lay back."

She did as he requested, expecting to be mounted; but to her surprise, Bill opened her legs and got on his stomach and placed his face to her awaiting crotch. Her musty fragrance startled him. *She smells a bunch differ than them other girls.* He used his tongue to open her up as he found her wet as a bowl of soup. He stuck his tongue deep in her as he felt her tense up. *She's in for a good night,* his mind raced. He lifted his tongue to her swollen clitoris and touched it as she froze. He kept at it licking and sucking on it until she cried out,

"Oh my god!" Her legs came together as she squeezed hard on his head for a moment, then her legs opened slowly as she began to breathe again.

"I didn't know I had that place down there. Oh my god, that was the best thing that's ever happened to me. Can you do it again?" she asked, holding her head up, looking at Bill's shiny face.

"Sure thing." Bill went back at it as she came quicker this time. But instead of squeezing her legs, she let them flop open. Bill was surprised when she asked again. He obliged again until she finally pushed his head away after the fifth time.

"You want to stick it in?" she asked.

"Yeppers." he answered as he crawled in between her legs. She was so wet from him, Bill just about popped his cork. He slid in and out, slowly letting her get the feeling of intercourse.

"Oh my. I like that too." She lifted up to meet his strokes. Bill was stroking away on her like a butter churn.

"You want it in, or you wanna suck it?" he asked in ragged breath.

"I want it in my mouth again." she spoke without lifting her head.

"Okay. Get. Ready. Here I come!" He pulled out and leaned back. She sat up and leaned over, placing the honey-dipped pod in her mouth and swallowed again.

"I like the taste. That other taste is my own ' stuff'? I like it too. Very smooth, like a thin honey. Can you do it again?" she asked, wiping her mouth on the back of her arm.

"Yeppers. Lay back down." She did as Bill requested. Bill lifted her legs apart as he went back to her honey pot. He continued to lick and suck until he could feel himself hardening again. *I'll give her something different.* He reached up and slipped his fingers in then slowly rubbed her anus with her wetness. She didn't resist. She had no reason to stop him. It had all been so new to her. *Why stop now?* Bill went back to the honey pot until her butt was equally slippery. Then he slipped in a finger and lifted up to touch her inside. Her anus squeezed as she came instantly.

"Do it again. Just like that. Do it again." she spoke without lifting her head. *My god, I've got a hellcat on my hands!* Bill slipped another finger in her and kept at it as he slid it in and out quickly. She started to meet his strokes as she had done earlier, but Bill pulled out his fingers and lifted her legs as he guided his pod into her honey pot and then pulled out and aimed it to her butt. She didn't resist or fuss. Bill pushed against her hole, and then he went in as cleanly as he had earlier.

"Go faster! Go faster! Rub me like you did before. Rub me and, " She stopped in mid-sentence as Bill felt her come again. But he didn't stop with is actions.

"Don't squirt it in me. I want to eat it again." she called out as Bill neared popping.

"Okay." He felt himself getting closer.

"Here. You. Go." He pulled out as she once again sat up reaching for his pod. Not caring about where it had been, she slid into her mouth as Bill released himself. She fell onto her back as she swallowed again, licking her lips.

"Can you do it again? Can you stick it up my butt again?" she asked.

"I don't think I can, not fer a bit anyway." He looked at her lying naked before him; her breasts had been neglected the whole time, so he leaned over to them, placing a nipple in his mouth, and sucked on it then the other. Back and forth he went as he waited for himself to harden again. But alas he was played out.

"Lick me again. Like you did before and use your fingers on my butt. Do it all over." she requested without lifting her head. *My god! What have I created?* he thought as he went back to her mound of dark hair. He did as she requested until she came again and again. Still his pod refused to come to life.

"Can you make it hard for me?" he asked when he sat up for a breath of fresh air.

"Yes, I can." She sat up and pushed him back on the wooden floor. On her hands and knees, she went until she was over his pod. She lifted the limp penis up and placed in it her mouth and did as he had taught her, but his member refused to come to life.

"I'm played out. Let me put some more wood on the fire. Maybe it'll come back to life." He got up and walked over to the hearth where he put a few more logs on the all but out fire. Slowly the fire licked up in yellow flames as it began to heat up the small room once again.

"You want some of this coon?" He lifted the cover and pulled out a morsel of meat out.

"No, I'm only hungry for more of you. When can you do it again?" she asked as her hand explored her intimate anatomy.

"Not fer a bit yet, little guy has to get some rest." He walked over to the blanketed window and pulled it open to see the eastern sky begin to lighten up.

"It's almost morning." He spoke without looking at her. Had he, he would have seen she was asleep. One hand on her breast the other on her mound of hair. The fire began to warm the cabin up quickly as he looked at her. *My god, how many times did she come last night? Hell, I lost count after four.* He peered out the window as the heat radiated on his rump and back. *I'd never had guessed she would be like that.*

"White Man, can you do it once more before you leave?" She was awake now.

"Sure I can do it once more for you." He turned from the window and walked toward her. Seeing her before him, ready to do whatever he requested, he felt himself coming to life again.

"You're gonna have to work on it." he spoke as he neared her.

"Oh, I hope so." She got up on her knees as he approached her.

"Let me." She pulled him to her. Into her mouth went the semi-erect pod of Bill. She wrapped her tongue around it as it slid her mouth up and down, trying to arouse the blond runt one last time. *He'll be gone soon, and I'll only have his taste to remind me of this past night. Unless I can get him to leave me something else.* She felt him slowly hardening as she continued to work on him.

"Stick it in me." she asked as she lay back on her rumpled coat.

"I'll give it a try. It's getting there." Bill put his almost-erect penis to her honey pot and slid it in. The feeling was as good as ever, but he had to close his eyes and concentrate on staying hard. The runt increased his tempo until he was pumping savagely, breathing hard in quick short breaths as he worked feverishly to accommodate the woman below him. Then he felt the familiar tingling as he neared his fourth time.

"Here you go. You want it like before?" He was almost ready to pull out, but she stopped him.

"No, leave it in." Her hand came around to his butt as she wrapped her legs around him and squeezed, ensuring that he couldn't pull out. Bill felt his last squirt leave him. His knees gave out as he fell over.

"That's it. I got no more left." He was panting now.

"That's fine." was all she said as she felt the warmth inside her. *I hope it takes. I want to remember this always.*

"I imagine Zach will be here soon. When does the steamship come in?" he asked as he sat up and reached for his clothes.

"Usually first thing in the morning. I suppose you could see it coming in if you were to go looking for it." She made no effort to dress. She lay naked as she had the whole evening. Bill pulled on his shoes as he reached for his belt.

"You're amazing. Simply amazing." He slid the knives where they belonged and slipped the pistol across the front. Standing up, he reached down for his shirt and slipped it over his head, looking at the woman on the floor across the room from him. She had worn him out. *Not had that fer a spell. That's fer certain and fer sure,* he thought. *Damn.*

"Will I ever see you again?" she asked as she sat up, her hand going to her honey pot. She rubbed her clitoris slowly then she increased the tempo, arching her back a second and slowly lowered her self to the floor. In went her fingers and brought them out to inspect them. She rubbed them onto her nipples.

"Can all men do as you've done? All night lovers?" she asked as she reached for her undershirt, slid it over her head adjusting it precisely.

"Nope. I'm the only one." He leaned over to get his coat.

She stood up and pulled on her bloomers and slip. She stood to look at Bill and finally pulled her dress up to her waist and slid an arm through the straps.

"And you're getting run out of town by a bully. That's not right." She leaned down to pick up the coat off the floor when she noticed a puddle forming by her foot of the semen that had missed her bloomers. *Oh, well there goes the chance of having the White Man's baby.* Bill saw her looking at the dropping.

"That's all that's left of me." he commented as he reached for his rifle, "that puddle on the floor."

"I wanted to get pregnant. I wanted something to remember you by forever. My first lover, not just a young man that was quick and rough. Now my chances are gone." she spoke quietly as she leaned down placing her fingers on the wet wood, "gone forever." She sighed.

This took him by surprise; he'd never even considering pregnancy in all his couplings. He quickly thought back to all the women he'd been with in the last few days, and not once had he considered any of them wanting to have his child. Now here was a woman wanting this.

"It wouldn't be good, Fleming for sure would make it hard on any child that came into the world." Bill looked at her in the morning light. She was still a handsome woman, not some young farm girl infatuated with a neighbor boy. This woman was one of the most mature women he'd met.

"Nothing says I'd be raising our child here. There are many towns up and down the river where questions aren't asked. Dallas City over in Illinois and the there's St. Louis. The French are very good to us Americans." She walked over to the coon stew and picked it up, looking at the lid hiding the meal they never had a chance to eat. Then she looked up to see his blue eyes and the blond hair tumbling from under his hat.

"Let's go before I make you go three or four more times." She walked past him to the door and opened it, letting the cool river air to invade the small house.

Well, that's that. Riverboat life for me now. He pulled the door shut, stepping into another adventure.

The Death Boat

CHAPTER 39

He and Maria headed down to the Bobbs' cabin, but before he got close to the door, Zachariah intercepted him.

"The steamship's already pulled in. I saw the first mate over at Bates store putting up and advertisement for work hands. Best you be going." He stuck out his hand to shake Bill's.

He took it immediately and shook it firmly.

"It coulda been different. Ya know that. It coulda been different."

"That's a fact, Wil." He stopped before finishing out the words.

"White Man. Yes, it could have been different." He released it and stepped aside, allowing him a straight passage to the store that the bully ruled, as he neared the store he saw Fleming and a man dressed in a dark jacket and river man's hat shake hands. *Shit. I bet he's the hiring man, an' no doubt Fleming already spoke to him about me. Damnit!* he thought as he neared the porch of the store. He walked up to the pair and read the advertisement tacked up on the store wall. It read;

WANTED;

Working men looking for adventure on the river
For information see, Mr. Harris, First Mate
Or apply on the steamship *Alice Mae.*

"Hello there. You from the riverboat?" He asked the obvious and felt he'd just made a terrible error. *I shoulda run off with Micah. Damnit!*

The man nodded to Fleming and addressed Bill straightforward.

"Yes, Mr. Matthew Harris. First mate on the Alice Mae. You looking to sign on?" Matthew asked, relying on what Fleming had spoken to him about. If he hired on the runt, Fleming would see that Harris would get free whiskey and the girl at the Bobbs' house on the next trip. Matthew had seen the woman on the last trip and immediately wanted to get her alone.

"Yes sir. I'd like to sign on." He stepped forward and extended his hand to shake a greeting

The man took his hand and firmly shook it.

"Very well. You'll not be needing those." He pointed to Bill's guns.

"Mr. Fleming will hold them and the knives as well until you decide to return. No guns aboard except by guests or officers." He watched Bill's expression for anything that resembled defiance.

"Sure thing Matt, here you go Jonnie boy. Take good care of these for me." Bill made one last insult to Fleming. He knew it would be the last time he would ever see his most prized possessions.

"Not that either." He pointed to Beulah's knife. "Okay." Bill handed Fleming the knives as well.

"No worries runt. They'll be here if you return." Then he slid the rifle over his shoulder and put the pistol in his apron pocket, then stuck the knives in the doorjamb.

"Let's go." Harris spoke to Bill as he led the way, as he followed Billy was thinking he'd was in for an honest employ.

"What's your name boy?" Harris asked to Bill as they closed the distance to the paddleboat.

"I go by White Man sir." Bill answered, trying to keep up.

"Very well." he acknowledged not saying anything else. They neared the ship as Bill watched the black men loading the trade goods up the narrow plank. He followed Harris on to the first deck and down one of the many passageways.

"Here's your quarters. Any bunk open is yours. Go to the ships laundry, they'll give you the uniforms you are to wear for your duties. Stow the uniforms in your foot locker. Go to the galley when your finished."

He turned to leave but stopped in mid-step. He turned to Bill and addressed him, "Mr. Harris is my name. You ever address me common again, and I'll make you wish you were never born. You understand?" he threatened Bill.

"Sure thing sir. Where's the ships laundry?" he asked.

"Aft, near the engine room." He turned and instantly vanished.

CHAPTER 40

Bill stowed his meager possessions, basically his possible bag, coat, and hat in his foot locker. *I might as well go find the laundry room and get the show on the road. He said the same near the engine room, shouldn't be that hard to find.*

Bill left the small crew's quarters and walked out to the riverside of the boat. It was as he'd imagined it. Watching the brown water, he looked to the Illinois side for anything, but the shoreline was empty of life. *Well, here we go,* he walked back towards the aft of the ship, and began his search for the laundry room at a leisurely pace.

As he turned inboard, he heard the voice of Harris.

"Get to the laundry room, you lazy, cockless river rat!" screamed the first mate as he tried to kick the young white lad. Bill swiftly sidestepped the flying stub-toed boot as he hustle to the back of the ship. The first mate yelled after Bill as the runty young man scurried away, "You no count, sorry-assed, shit-for-brains! Get your stinkin' ass to the laundry room before I kick your ass up to your ears!"

On the balmy July morning the paddleboat *Alice Mae* pulled away from Hannibal as it began its journey south on the Mississippi River. The craft was smaller by standards, and it wasn't as fast as the bigger one. Its paddle wheel would slap the water noisily as it sliced through the swift current, making sleep for the crew difficult as the quarters were located not far from the enormous stern paddle wheel. The vessel traveled up and down the Big Muddy, its small crew working feverishly to keep its whitewashed bulkheads spotless and the decks clean of debris as it went on regular runs between the newly formed town of Hannibal Missouri, and the booming town New Orleans Louisiana.

The boilers were punished to an overload condition as she struggled against the swift current going up the river. The huge iron boilers were constantly in need of repair, many times from a faulty gauge or a despondent fireman that would be neglectful in their maintenance, causing the ignored boiler to explode.

Their were stories of the boilers blowing up and sending the whole ship to hell. They were whispered through the ship's crew like smoke in a light breeze on a hot night. Bill found the laundry room. The Chinese workers all wore black baggy clothes that hung from there bodies like scarecrows. He approached a gleaming polished wood counter and waited untill one of the frail looking men came to the counter.

"What you want?" Ming Yao demanded, he knew this was a new hire. *Another white urchin to get his uniforms*, he surmised.

"I'm here to get my uniform." Billy stated.

"Wait." Ming Yao tapped his long finger nail on the counter.

"Where'd ya think I'd be goin'?" Billy snapped back to Ming Yao who was trying to bully the small white man. The laundryman turned and waved his hand to wait to the new hire.

Billy looked around the room, *not very big to clean all the clothes on this old boat. What do I care anyway, get this here uniform and then get to the galley.*

Ming Yao reappeared with a stack of clothes. A pair of white tunic's, a pair of black trousers, five under shirt, five pair of underwear, and five pair of socks. He looked at the white linen jacket with silver buttons that ran up each side of the tunic. *Damn, these are 'rite purty.* Next he inspected the black trousers with the razor sharpe crease in the front of each leg, they had thirteen buttons on the front flap. Next were the shoes, shiny ankle high lace ups.

Then Ming Yao seemed to vanish right in front of him. A different man materialized.

"Put mark." His long frail finger nail pointed to a section on the trousers and then to the tunic's. Billy complied, sketching his initials, WM.

"You drop in shoot, get clean, all clothes." Sun Chung instructed Billy pointing to a rectangle box with a pile of soiled clothes in a push cart.

"All right Slim." Bill nick named him. Sun Chung had very little time to argue with the small man so he quickly turned and vanished into the vast rack of hanging clothes.

The small white man picked up his newly acquired clothes, his mind was jumping like a flea on a hot skillet, *nuthin' else to do here, might as well get to the crew's berthing,* so he headed forward. It took him than a few miss steps but he found it and stashed his new belonging.

"Now, to find the galley." he mumbled aloud. He hadn't taken more than a few steps when out of another passageway a small man stepped out. He was wearing the uniform. He turned to see Billy.

"You are new, no?" He asked in his French accent, "You should put your uniform on, that will give Mr. Harris one less reason to kick you."

"Thanks," he replied as he quickly shed his personal clothes and slipped into his uniform." He skipped underwear and socks.

"Wait." René stopped him. "Put on the underclothes. I've seen Mr. Harris beat a man severely for not wearing everything, even the socks."

"Huh? No shit?" He asked his new French friend.

"Oui. Mr. Harris will beat you, never the face, as customers will see it. To your stomach or your legs." René warned Bill.

"There. How's that?" He asked René.

"Good. I was trying to find the galley." Billy confided.

"Come with me, I'll show you zee way, no since having Mr. Harris trying to kick you in the bottom."

"I'm the White Man." He waited for an explanation but there was none to be made.

"Oui."

They found they galley quickly and entered to find two new faces to Billy, Rebecca and Shiela. Rebecca was a very attractive red headed white girl. She had on a white dress and black apron. The very handsome, very big black woman, she had a dress similar to Rebecca's but had on a black tunic that barely cover her very ample bosom was Sheila.

Matthew Harris said, "This's Sheila. She'll will teach you your responsibilities while your on board, you backtalk her and she'll make sure you won't do it again." He then walked out into the passageway and was gone.

"My my, what have we here? A little scrawny but a cutie. You know how to work hard or work just hard enough?" She quizzed him.

"I reckon a bit a both. So, what's my job?"

"You's a bit sassy, I like that. The But only a bit."

"Okay, this's Rebecca, she'll be workin' with ya. But one thing, she's mine. You try to fuck her or anything else without my permission an' I'll beat you. Beat you real bad. You got that?"

"Yeppers I surely do?" Bill acknowledged. *Whoa, she's gorgeous!* His mind raced with thoughts that would get him busted up.

"You already met René. You wear your uniform all the times, you get one mess'd up an' use the other'n. You keep using 'em like that, one set after the other. You'll wear 'em whenever your out side the crew's quarter's.

The days jumped by Bill as he became comfortable with his new surroundings, not enjoying the work but he'd made a few friends. Bill slinked about the dark passages, avoiding Harris at every chance he could as the paddleboat headed south.

As he looked up at the duel smoke stacks, the tops looked like an emperor's Crown. Bill watched the ebony vaporous fumes pouring from them into the air as the craft splashed into the early evening; he was in awe every time he watched them dissipating into the early afternoon.

The young lad snuck into the fire room to sit and watch the once-proud Africans as they shoveled coal or wood into the boilers.

He entered through the open oak plank door as a light rain started, turning the decks into hardwood mirrors; he looked over his shoulder, seeing the distant bank disappear in the rain.

"Goddamned rain." he muttered, turning a water bucket upside down as he sat down in one fluid movement.

"You niggers work your ass's off night an' day. Kinda makes me squeamish when I think 'bout it, havin' to work that hard." the young lad spoke aloud to the backs of the rail-thin ebony-skinned slaves as they shoveled load after load into the devil's belly, their bare skin twinkling from the sweat that gathered on their backs as they shoveled in four man teams, two stoking the dragon's belly, two of them bringing coal or wood. Bill liked to watch them work; they would stop briefly, giving the runt a sharp eye of jealousy as they drank heartily from the oak water barrel next to the door.

"Don't you niggers get tired? I've been sittin' here fer quite a spell, an' I ain't seen you stop but once, an' that was only to wet yer whistle."

The tallest one spoke to Bill through his perfect straight white teeth, "You know, we have to work nonstop, or Mr. Harris, he'll beat us severely." The slave spoke better English than the majority of the white workers onboard.

The man had been given the name of Jonah since no one cared Thabo Mbekiuki was his real name. The biblical character that was swallowed by the whale was his name now and would be until someone else bought him and changed it.

Thabo had been working on the boat since it went into service, outlasting many others. His strong back and wiry muscles a allowed him to work continually with little rest while the others would work into an exhaustive state only to be beat for stopping. Thabo would just keep shoveling, not looking, as his compatriots were beaten to a bloody pulp. Thabo learned early in life to keep quiet and work steady. It did little good to complain as no one would listen to a slave anyway. His slender frame and bald head hid his age, which was well into his late twenties. The first mate would spy on them from around a bulkhead or from the top of a ladder, waiting to see who would slack off and who would work. It was always Thabo that never seemed to stop, or at least was never caught.

Thabo looked at the white boy before him, his short thin frame, his wispy blond hair, and his arrogant attitude. If they'd been in his home in Africa, he would take pleasure torturing this white man. Yes, he and his Zulu tribesmen could make this small one live for many days before allowing him to die. Maybe they would eat him or maybe bury him and let the huge ants consume him. Thabo could have killed him as easily as slitting the throat on a cow, but here sat the runt watching them die a slow death, making idle talk as they labored into the early evening.

But as for now, it was as if an imaginary shaman had thrown the bones of the future for him and his companions, causing them to be slaves to the boiler for the rest of their natural lives.

He had been captured from his village in Zambia by Arab slavers from the East. There was nowhere to run and nowhere to hide; his life now was work, and work he did, nonstop, trying to drown out the fact his life was over. He was dead for all practical purposes. No one was going to buy him; even then, what would it get him if he did get sold? He would be back under the sun, doing the slave labor on some plantation, picking tobacco, rice, or cotton. A new master meant new rules, and more beating as he learned. No, he would live his days out here, shoveling food for the fire gods. No way out, nowhere to run. If he escaped, they would come for him, maybe hang him, maybe not. There was the chance he could live out west with the red man he heard so much about from others.

Thabo thought, *this one is small but shows no fear. Hmm? His eyes do not look away when I look at his soul. Maybe I was wrong about his small one. Maybe he has a fighting spirit? I will never know.* He closed his eyes. *I will never know.* Thabo turned his back to Bill as he returned to the firebox before him, bringing his shovel to play once again. As he began to shovel coal into the open door, his mind returned to his African jungles, chasing the wildebeest, impalas, gazelles, lions, and the love of his wives. It seemed to Thabo that it was just a dream now, a time long gone.

Bill got up and left the workers, never to stay in one place too long as Harris was always on the prowl. He crept into the crews' quarters for a quick nap. Laziness overcame him quickly, and he fell asleep, unaware Harris had just stepped into the firebox looking for him.

"Where's that fucking runt?" he called to the back of the slaves.

"He was just here sir, you just missed him."

Thabo spoke without stopping. Harris was infuriated that he'd missed the slacker.

"Fucker!" he shouted as he grabbed the same bucket Bill had been sitting on and slammed it into the back of the nearest worker. The bucket hit Samuel's shoulder, knocking him down, but he was of little concern to Matthew as he crumpled onto the deck in pain. Now in a fit of rage, Harris continued his wrath on Isaac, the fourth man of the firebox workers, he quickly slipped behind Thabo as well to avoid the wild white man.

Swinging it again, the first mate landed a solid blow against Thabo's ribs. The black man grunted but refused to acknowledge the pain. Matthew hefted the bucket again, bringing it to land on the nearest man, Thabo's longtime friend Thomas. The bucket landed against Thomas's temple, causing him to crumple on the floor like a broken bag of sugar. The thin black man didn't move as Harris stared at him. As Thomas fell, Samuel crawled behind Thabo also as Harris went wild.

"Get up!" he screamed. The unconscious man lay quietly on the deck as blood seeped out of his ear.

The first mate was out of control now; he reared his leg back and landed a kick to Thomas's ribs. Thabo heard them break as the man went wild in rage. Harris pounced on the prone man's back; he grabbed the curly black matte of hair and slammed Thomas's head into the deck repeatedly until Thomas had no face. Thabo wanted to hit Harris with the shovel. He wanted it so bad he was willing to die to do it, but he didn't; he'd seen this before. He'd witnessed Harris out of control. No one would cross him as the man was crazy with anger.

Harris stood above the now-dead man, panting as if he'd just run a thousand yards.

"Throw this hunk of shit overboard." he spoke to Thabo, making sure the tall man knew he was still angry.

"Yes sir." Thabo answered quietly. The man was his friend, and now he was dead. Nothing to do but follow orders now; the river claimed another soul as Harris staggered away, rolling his shoulder against the bulkhead as he stumbled away.

Thabo watched him leave. It looked like he was wounded, but he knew better. Harris was drained of emotions as he was every time he killed.

An atmosphere of darkness crept over the firebox like a widower's veil at a funeral. Samuel and Thabo dragged their friend up the few stairs to the main deck and pushed him over the side.

They returned to their shovels. They looked to Isaac, the fourth man that had missed all of the anger; he looked to Thabo for a moment before he too returned to his task. Now with only three to do the work of four, they fell into the much-accustomed routine. No words were spoken. No eye contact was made. Thabo knew Harris would die, but he only hoped he would be the one to do it.

The runt. He will pay for my friend's death as will Harris, the tall thin man thought to himself as he listened to the night and the crackling of the fire. *Yes, the runt will pay.* Thabo would take great pleasure to make sure the small man became lost on a dark passageway at night.

The next day Harris had assigned a dining room server to take Thomas's position in the firebox. The man was Michael, not strong or tall but he had a good heart, which Thabo recognized immediately. His cinnamon skin was quick to cover in sweat as he began to bring in cords of wood.

"Work steady, not fast. We will help you." Thabo spoke in a hushed voice, his eyes darting to assure himself Harris was not near. The man looked at Thabo and the others. Nodding, he began his life of feeding the fiery dragon that made the ship live.

The young lad was oblivious to previous day's mayhem. He had no idea his laziness had cost a man his life. Thabo did though, and made it a point to stay away from Harris whenever he could.

***

Bill had reported late to the galley for his chores and did a poor job of it when he was there. After he'd washed the breakfast dishes and prepared the dining room for lunch, he meandered off to get away from the work.

It was early in the afternoon when he wandered to the fantail of the paddleboat to watch the west bank and listen to the fur trappers that booked passage to St. Louis.

Silas Becton, Murray Aston, and Two Thumbs McReady were the storytellers that the blond man had come to hold in high revere. He liked to listen to them tell tall tales of the beaver, Blackfoot Indians, grizzly bears, and the Indian women that kept them warm in the winter months. They would describe their adventures for Bill as they drank heartily from the badger-skin-covered porcelain whiskey jugs. Bill was always in amazement that McReady had two thumbs on his left hand. Two Thumbs would hold his hand up, wiggling the miniature appendage, as the Runt would stare slack-jawed.

"I got this here little one to tickle their assholes while I'm diddling 'em with my big un!" Then he would do a big laugh, almost rolling off the small French chairs that they had brought out from the dining room.

"You're so full of shit McReady. You told us you had that one sew'd on so as you stroke your bean better!" Silas would laugh and slap Murray on the back, and then they each would take a long pull on the jug.

"Well shit, you know no such goddamned thing you lily-liver'd polecat fuckers." Then Two Thumbs would pout as his partners laughed at his expense.

"What's it's like?" Bill asked. "Fightin' them Blackfoot? I bet they're meaner than a cat dipped in turpentine, ain't they?" His eyes shot from one to the other.

"Boy, just hope you ain't never got to face 'em. They's the devils own by God. Shit, I've seen 'em kill a man by stripping' his flesh off one or two strips a day." Murray answered quickly.

"Yeah, one of our partners got kilt that way. We had to sit back there in the brush, couldn't do nuthin' to help. Them red niggers was beatin' the brush somethin' fierce lookin' fer us, an' we could move nary an inch or two on 'count of gettin' caught our own selves." Murray continued.

"Well, if you hadn't kilt that goddamned kid, we wouldn't of lost Greaves, an' you know that's the gospel truth!" shouted McReady.

"Fuck you Two Thumbs!" With that Aston got to his feet and grabbed his buckskin crotch, thrusting his forward to show his displeasure to having the story brought up. He turned on his moccasin heel, leaving his partners.

"Goddamn Aston to hell." Silas said quietly, shaking his head, watching Murray walk away; he pulled the fur-covered jug to his chapped lips again as he watched Aston fade away into the early evening. Then he continued, "He was trying to get to one of the Blackfoot girls while she was taking a bath.

"Two Thumbs chimed in, "She wasn't more than ten 'er twelve.""

"Yeah, she was a cutie. Reminds me of my first daughter. Breaks Light, she's Crow, I cain't wait to see her an' her mom, Soft Eyes. Anyway that fucker Murray was trying to get her in the bush for a poke when she screamed an' brought the whole goddamned village down on us." Silas spoke quietly closing his eyes then he shook his head.

"Yeah damn, I was a scarit nigger. Well, we skedaddled out there 'cept for Mick Greaves. One of 'em got off an arrow inta his back. Knocked him down an' we couldn't do nuthin' but hide an' wait fer dark."

"Mick was a good man, kid. He loved chil'n. Hell, I've seen him pack his daughters for miles so they wouldn't have to walk in the snow."

"Hey, remember that time when Mick broke through that crick on the Musselshell right up his crotch? Shit! You oughta hear him a hollerin' aboot the ice freezin' his pod!" Silas laughed, taking another big pull on the jug.

"It was sumptin', runt. There was ol' Mick ass deep in freezing water, an' we couldn't do nuthin' but laugh! Hell, I wasn't gonna go out there an' break through."

"Shit, me neither." Two Thumbs smiled, shaking his head, his salt-and-pepper beard shaking slowly to each side.

"What happened?" Billy inquired further.

"Well. He got kilt!" Silas slapped Billy's back, almost knocking him off his chair.

"Hardy har-har!" They each laughed at the runt's gullibility. Bill was sassy enough to consider all the lies with no further weight put on the trappers' glorious stories. But still, the dress and mannerism made him dream of the adventurous life of the mountain man, living free and saying sir to no man. Billy wanted it so bad it seemed to burn his soul to stay on the *Alice Mae*. He would have to wait.

Bill didn't get along with the first mate; he considered him a hard case as he cut the young blond runt no slack whatsoever.

Matthew Harris was short in stature, and he was meaner than a drunken sailor and by far the hairiest person Bill had ever met with his curly black hair coming out from his cuffs, collar, and front of his shirt. The abundance of hair gave him the appearance of a small ape dressed in poor-quality clothes.

But he ran a taunt ship, barking orders to whoever was unfortunate enough to be in his path. Normally, this wasn't any concern for Bill, but Matthew had it in for young Bill as he remembered his deal with Fleming. So he was always after him for any violation he could muster up at the time. Anything from loitering on deck to pestering the guests, Harris had a habit of cornering the white boy. Then he'd beat the young man or chew his ass in front of the other workers. His actions caused Bill to have more than a few scars and bruises, but Harris's theory on humiliation didn't work on the runt. Instead of having Bill work more from fear of getting a whipping, the young white man did even less.

The supper was to be served soon, so Bill had acquired the knack of just fading away before he could be put to work. At times he was successful, and others he brought the wrath of the first mate as well as the head maître d' upon him. The supper on this particular paddleboat had been the talk of the river community since a French cook, Emil Rebedeau, had been hired to serve only the best that the Ultmans' wages could provide. The short thin cook would prepare all the delicacies that upper-class passengers desired. Steaks weighing in at eighteen ounces, an inch or more thick, pheasant that was cooked to fork-cutting tenderness, trout, with many varieties of game hens and wild hog. The cook would make fabulous meals aboard the steaming vessel all the while the eastern-living entourage would rave about the size and the quality of the food.

"Goddamnit! I've done everything that sand niggers has told me to do. I've swabbed the deck, served coffee, done dishes, made beds, or whatever Hamhead figured I oughta do. Shit, that ol'boy ain't gave me one thank you very much for all the work I do. Goddamned peckerwood." Bill bitched aloud to his fellow galley workers.

Bill had made a queer-some friendship with one of his fellow workers. Sheila from Baton Rouge Louisiana, black and six feet tall with an ample rump with big breasts that bounced and jiggled when she laughed. Her sharp nose and straight hair didn't give her appearance of a slave; in fact, she had never been a slave.

Whenever he could, the young runt would confide in her about what the poor treatment he was receiving from the Arab, hoping for some compassion from her.

Sheila was a strange woman too; she'd been a hired person that had made the Ultmans Transportation company some serious revenue. With her large frame and sassy attitude, she quickly won favor among the passengers. They would request her for the entertainment of the evening since her deep rich voice could carry a tune far better than the fat Italians that boasted heavily of their abilities.

She wasn't a whore, but she did bring one with her when she hired onboard, a beautiful fiery little redhead. The big black woman carried herself proudly and pompously as Mohammad, the maître d'. She was always sure to let everyone know who was in command as she floated over the teak decks.

Bill and Sheila got to be thicker than thieves, so when Mohammad gave him extra work at the midnight shift, she'd wait until the Arab was nodding off in his rack. Then she would come into the wash area to help the small blond man with his chores, wading right in, washing, scraping, and cleaning with the best of them. Bill never asked why she did it; he just accepted her help. When she had bed-making chores up in the first-class section, he'd fold a few sheets with her. So it worked out fine for an unlikely friendship.

CHAPTER 41

The late-summer drizzle had turned into a deluge by late afternoon, coming down in huge drops as it splattered on the hardwood decks. Bill stood at the door of the galley, watching it come down in sheets as he shirked his galley duties. The visibility had been reduced to less than a quarter mile now; he could barely make out the banks of Missouri as the squall showed no signs of stopping. Shaking his head, he returned to the deep sink and his work, the small blond man leaned his back against the sink. Hooking his elbows on the edge, he looked at his co-workers.

René and Rebecca. René didn't look at the runt as Bill looked at the red-haired lass across the small galley; she turned to meet his gaze, her amazingly blue eyes twinkling. Her simple white cotton dress uniform did her no justice as Billy noticed her perfect figure. His thoughts ran wild with imagination of her naked, enjoying sex with him.

René stopped working, looking at the runt staring at Rebecca.

"You best be careful of what you stare at runt. Her mistress will zee you. Oui. Then she will slap zee shit out of you!" He smiled, knowing he could shake the lad up. René was one of the many Frenchmen hired on as ship's company.

He was five feet tall, his Gallic features accented by a small mustache and lip beard; his frail appearance hid the fact that he was deadly with his feet. Billy had witnessed his savagery more than once.

In a grog house, René had nearly killed a man when they started with the name-calling. Soon it went to pushing and shoving, and then to follow were the punches. René would tell them to stop. He'd give them a fair warning. Then when they laughed and scoffed at him, he would snap and simply start kicking. When his opponents lay unconscious on the tavern floor, he'd ask if there were any more that wanted to call him names. It made Bill glad he was René's friend.

"Don't worry about her. Me an' her are tight." Billy smiled at his fellow washer.

"Oui, so I've heard." the Frenchman rolled his eyes, "over and over." René smiled, knowing he was about to hear another one of the runt's stories.

Billy turned to his sink as he began to weave a tale for his French counterpart.

"You know, René, one afternoon me an' Sheila was up workin' in the first-class section. Shit, I reckon we had close to fifteen rooms to do 'fore we had to be down here, you know, fer' the evenin' meal. So as I was workin' my ass off an' I kept lookin' at her big ol'ass cover'd up in the dress thinkin' 'bout a poke. So I figured, what the hell?"

"You did ask her, no?" René asked. Billy snipped back at his dark little friend, "If ya shut ye pork-eatin' yap, I'll tell ya." The blond runt paused, looking down at a scrap of food. He methodically pulled a hunk of steak loose and chucked it in his mouth, closing his eyes as he savored the taste. Then he went with on with his story.

"I sez to her." Bill stopped, staring at the bulkhead in front of him.

"Hey, Sheila, why don't ya slip off yer draws an' hike that dress of yers up so as I can make yer bed fer ya while ya fluff that there pillow?'" Bill continued his story as René rolled his eyes.

"Well, she looked at me with them coal-black eyes with a twinkle in them an' answered, 'White boy, don't say what ya can't back up.'"

The runt smiled a toothy smile at René.

"Shit, can you believe she said that? Goddamn I was surprised." Billy pulled loose another hunk of steak, admiring it slowly. Then he tossed it into his mouth. He stood back from the sink, putting his hands on his hips as he continued.

"So I says to her, I reckon I can slip right in while y'all is workin'. I won't even make ya miss a beat." Bill answered, placing his hands on her imaginary hips.

"Oh, is zat right?" René answered. Bill nodded. Rebecca looked over her shoulder at the storyteller.

"Yeppers."

Bill continued his tale, "So I says to her. I can if ya give me by yer leave.'" The runt smiled at René.

"You know what that ol'black girl did? She hiked that dress of hers up. Goddamn! She had nuthin' under it! Yeppers, she had no drawers on a'tall! I was takin' 'back a tad 'cause I was only hackin' on her when she was as serious as a Baptist preacher." He laughed, slapping his knee.

Rebecca, Sheila's whore, was on the other side of the small galley, scraping crusted pasta out of a large iron pan, as she only caught bits and pieces of Bill's yarn.

The lass liked him and wanted him, but he never approached her, whom she considered strange. *He must be scared of Sheila. That has to be it. She would definitely beat him to a pulp if he made a pass at me without her permission,* she thought as she went back to the chores, having the water occasionally splash up on her black apron. At times the water would splash up and miss the black apron getting her white uniform wet. She looked down seeing nipples clinging to the wet clothes visible for anyone to notice. *Oops, I hope that she doesn't see this, or she'll have me doing chores on her,* she thought as she returned to her work, but she continued listening for any thread of Bill's story.

Billy continued his story as René stopped working. He smiled as he listened to Bill's story. He liked the runt, and his tales were better than working even if they were all just that, tales.

"So she says to me, 'Well?' like she wanted it somethin' fierce."

"Can't hardly believe it was gonna happen. I mean getting' a poke with that ol'nigger.

"Okay, okay, let me get ol'John Thomas out, I says to her." Bill continued.

Rebecca had stopped working. She didn't turn, but she was listening hard for every bit of Bill's story.

"Goddamn she was a wantin' it bad by now." Bill smiled at René.

"Anyway, she wiggled her black shinin' rump up at me. Christ on the cross, I wasn't gonna miss this chance." The runt smiled at René as Bill began pantomiming having sex.

"You did it? You fouk her?" René answered as he licked his lips.

"Hell yes! I slipped inta her like a warm spoon inta puddin'." Rebecca heard that part, and she felt herself flushing.

"Well, there I was, slippin' an' slidin' like a frog in the mud while she was fluffing' that pillow up. You know, René, the thought of gettin' caught made it all the more excitin'. So I figured I better be quick 'cause this could get us both fired. Then as pretty as ya please she stepped away leavin' me quiverin' in the breeze." Bill stepped back up to the sink. He paused a moment, looking down at a food-encrusted plate.

"You know what she said? She said, 'You never said anything 'bout ridin' the pony to the end, sugar. You said you wanted to slip it in.' That's what she said." Bill spoke as he shook his head, remembering how close he'd been.

"Well, what do ya say if we go ahead an' finish this here right here an' now?" Bill continued to weave his tale. That ol'girl says to me, 'Now, lookie here, we got too much work to' do. You better get to it hear?' like she was the boss of me! Damn her eyes! That's what she told me right then an' there." He nodded to René as he continued washing, but all he could think of was stuffing his carrot in that black hole.

"Oh well, some other time." he spoke aloud as his mood changed instantly as it did on a regular occasion.

CHAPTER 42

Billy was on his way to the third-floor dining room, being very familiar with the routine of the ship, when something out of the ordinary caught his attention this particular evening.

He saw Mohammad heading to the fantail of the paddleboat.

It made the young blond runt wonder since he knew that Mohammad was due up in the main cabin for the captain's supper party. Being like a kitten with the ball of twine, Bill decided to investigate this strange behavior, so he quickly ducked behind a bulkhead to see where the Arab went.

"This is one nasty bastard." the small man spoke in a whisper as he rubbed his thin beard, watching the man that commanded others to do his bidding continue to slink about.

The Arab had a black curly beard that was always trimmed short. He was tall but not thin. What he lost in masculinity he made up with attitude. He was quick to chastise and slow to praise. He would threaten the crew with extra work or being fired and put to shore in a heartbeat if they didn't tow the line to his satisfaction.

It didn't bother young Bill to have a black man giving him orders though. Bill had nothing against the blacks onboard, and most of his whoring buds were blacker than a whore's heart. Mohammad had shifty black eyes as he was overcome with paranoia. The Arab made sure everyone knew he was in charge as he wielded his authority with an iron fist.

On the deck there were several stacks of mooring line coiled up. Bill looked at it, quickly calculating if he could fit in between them or not. Seconds raced by as his decision was made. He quietly slipped into one unnoticed, or so he thought. The runt spied through the small opening in the rope as he spied on his superior.

Squatting inside the coil, he waited to see what would happen next. Then Josh from navigation appeared. Josh was a tall college graduate with a quick smile and trim figure; there was no mistaking Josh for anybody else because he was taller than a lodge pole pine and whiter than a preacher's sheet with his sandy-colored hair cut crisp and close on the sides and back. Bill thought this was a tad off center, but it was none of his business. Yet. Then he couldn't believe what happened next. He blinked and rubbed his eyes a few times, then looked again to make sure. They had started to kiss. On the lips with open mouth, tonguing each other like a pair of lovers. Bill was too amazed to even believe this was happening.

As he stared in amazement, his mind raced, *no one's gonna believe this,* these two men were of the highest stature among the crew. Navigation meant he had to be able to read, write, and know the charts and maps. Good lord knows that only one of those traits was among the truly smartest folks onboard the vessel. The small white man watched the men that had the most control of this ship; perhaps these two men could make or break this paddleboat. Yes, the captain was in charge; but without Josh's expert knowledge of maps and the ability to read the surveying charts, the captain would be truly lost. Then there was Mohammad. His understanding of serving manners and table etiquette distinguished him from the rest of the serving staff. So the runt hid watching the show with total disbelief.

The two men began to grope each other as he stared in disbelief. Mohammad produced his long thick black penis to the tall young white man. Bill sat in shock seeing the man's penis. It was ever big as the late Ivory's had been. Josh went down on his knees, with his back to Bill. The runt knew Hamhead was getting sucked off right there on deck. In a short time Mohammad arched his back and grabbed Josh's head as his knees gave out, stumbling for a brief moment as he'd finished being pleasured. Josh backed off. Then he stood up and wiped his mouth off just like he had finished eating a portion of suet pudding.

Reaching inside his jacket pocket, Mohammad pulled out the biggest wad of cash Bill had ever seen. It was as big as a cinnamon rolls they made down in the galley. Grabbing Josh's hand, he put the whole roll of cash in it. They parted ways after mumbling something out of Bill's earshot. The runt was sweating now; he could feel the drops gliding down his back, sliding into the waistband of his wool uniform breeches, causing him to be more than a tad warm.

Bill didn't realize that Josh knew that someone was there watching. The tall white man had been aware of a person watching long before the show had begun. Josh had continued this exhibition to whoever was hiding, knowing that as soon as he received his wages for his performance, he would roust the violator and bring him before his dark lover for punishment. It made it all the better to Josh. Leaning over to Mohammad, he spoke quietly into his brown satin ear, "The one hiding? I will bring him to you in a short time."

"I think, like many times before, you enjoy being watched too much. Very well, do not tarry."

Then they parted ways. The runt was so shocked that he was unsure of what to do next. Waiting as the sun was completely gone into to the western tree line, Bill finally came out of his hiding position. His back and neck were stiff from being cramped up in the coil of rope; he really needed to stretch out after being scrunched up. *It smelled like a ton of rat shit inside that coil. I wouldn't be surprised if the deckhands didn't piss all over it when no one was around.* As he stood up, he arched his back, working the kinks out as he twisted in the cool evening air. He put one hand on the top rope coil as he smoothly glided over the top; landing cat like on the deck, he sauntered to the handrail as he leaned on looking west into the darkness that hid Missouri.

"What should I do? I wonder what Sheila will say." he mumbled, not hearing the movement behind him.

CHAPTER 43

The ship's life seemed to slow down for the runt, now armed with intriguing information; he wondered what to do with his ill-gained knowledge. Though men with men were about, not many held the high-ranking positions these two did. It put a whole different scheme of what to do.

Looking at the occasional lights that would be on a small dock or farmhouse, he wondered, *What're they doing? Was the ol' farmer slipping the wood to the big fat mammy in the back shed, or was the young daughter dreaming of meeting a sneak-away lover in the barn fer a bit of lovemaking?*

His mind was just drifting when he felt a touch on his rump. Billy jumped a foot off the deck as he spun to take a whack at the one that touched him. Squatted down, fists clenched, ready to dance, the small man had the heart of a fighting dog on a short leash. No oppressor too big to take on.

Josh stood looking down at the small river rat. Billy was only a few feet from him. *This small man, he's so, so childlike. I think he'd be fun to play around with. Hmm? Too bad,* Josh mind raced as he'd already formulated his move.

"You'll have to be careful with what you know. I would hate to see a cute boy as yourself disappear on a black night."

"What're you talkin' 'bout?"

"You were in that coil of rope, while I was doing." Josh paused while a smile crept to his thin lips.

"That." He hissed.

"Yer crazy as a brain-sick dog. I been in the galley peelin' taters with Sheila an' Rebecca." He lied like his life depended on it.

He saw the fist coming but he froze. *Duck! Duck!* His mind

screamed, but nothing happened. One to the gut and one to his face. He fell to the deck trying to get his breath when Josh kicked him in the face. He lost consciousness after that.

He awoke in a bed in the crews' quarters, shackled to the head rail, his head pounding like an anvil at the blacksmith's.

"What the hell's goin' on here?" he demanded. Speaking too soon, he could feel the bile rising in his throat as the words left his mouth. He immediately turned his head, waiting for the vomit. Dry heaves were all his body could muster up.

"Well, I see you are coming back to the world again." His Persian accent always pestered Bill as he couldn't understand some of his words.

"Yeah, I reckon." The runty white man ran his tongue over the edge of his lip until he found the open wound, *lip musta got split.* His tongue found caked blood in the corner of his mouth. *It sure as hell hurts. Oh yeah, back to the lover twins.*

He looked at Mohammad.

"You like to watch, yes?" the bearded man asked the small blond man.

"I still don't know what yer talkin' 'bout Hamhead." the White Man sassed the Arab, knowing it would no good to try to be nice at this point. Billy felt sure he was going to die, and he wasn't going to go quietly. Mohammad eyes flared, he hated the Western culture where nicknames prevailed.

Oh no, he's goin' to whack me again, Bill thought. He cringed and waited but felt no pain; instead he felt one of thirteen buttons on his britches being tugged on.

"Hey, leave that alone. Stop! Leave me be!" Billy barked, almost expecting his wishes to be honored. With that, Josh jumped up; putting his hands on the side of his face, he began to pantomime a startled and frightened look.

"Oh my, he said to stop. Oh, what will I do now kind sir?" Sarcasm was dripping from his voice.

"Stop playing you queer! Do as I have told you! Do it now!" Mohammad's voice rose.

With that, the look on Josh's face changed from a fun-loving prankster to a pissed-off man. He whacked the headwaiter in the gut just like he had done to the blond boy earlier. The man fell to the ground faster than a brain-shot cow, sprawling on the ground like a bag of sand. Bill's mind began to race of what the next move would be.

Josh looked at the downed man.

"I do what I do for money, and I will not be spoken to in such a manner especially from a scoundrel as this person." He reared his foot back and kicked the Arab in the face like he'd done to Billy. *Kick 'em again. Kick 'em again!* he thought as the Arab became the center of the abuse.

Josh knew he had gone too far with that last stunt. Looking at the chained runt and the black man on the floor, he began to formulate a plan. He would knock the runt unconscious, stab Mohammad several times, put the knife in the small one's hand, and then lead Harris to the theatrically setup scene.

"Josh, lookie here. What ya do fer spendin' money is yer business. I'll jus' keep it to myself. I don't particularly like Hamy there, but it's 'tween you an' him what ya do. So if ya don' mind, undo these here shackles. I'll be on my way to tend to this here split lip."

"Oh, is that right? I undo you and you walk off as pretty as you please and leave me with the angry one? Is that it?"

"Hey, what do ya want me da do? You sucked his dick."

Suddenly the door burst open as Sheila made her grand entrance. This woman had the brass balls of a drunken sailor. Coming from the waterfront, she could scrap with the best of them, sailor or skin trapper, soldier or constable it didn't matter to her. She feared neither man nor beast. But mess with her friends or property and disaster was soon to follow.

"Whatcha doin' with my boy here?" she demanded.

"Get out, you fat nigger bitch! This is no concern of yours!" The tall one stood with his fists balled, ready to dance with the large black woman.

That was the wrong thing to say to a six-foot-tall, two-hundred-pound black woman. She quickly swung a roundhouse punch, but Josh was equal on speed but not strength. His right arm came up to block the blow, but it did little good as Sheila's fist hit his arm, breaking it immediately. Josh screamed like a schoolgirl as he dropped to his left knee, cradling his arm as it lay at an unnatural angle. He looked up in time to see Sheila's left fist coming in at breakneck speed. The mighty fist connected with the side of Josh's pretty face. His jaw became instantly broken and dislocated as the handsome man was knocked into next week. As he spun around, he slumped upon the unconscious black man. There they lay in a big pile like so much dirty laundry.

"Sugar, what have you gotten yerself into?" the huge black woman questioned Bill as she stood there looking at the scene before her.

"It's a long story. Could ya help me out here?" the small blond man whined.

"First, tell me what was goin' on." demanded the huge-breasted woman.

The small blond man was going through all his options in a blink of an eye, his mind racing, *Do I tell her the truth or flat-out lie?* In the time it took to let a breath out, the decision was made. He would tell the truth.

"Well, I saw Hamhead here walk toward the back of the ship. So I decide to do some snoopin' an' see what he was up to." the runt blurted out.

"Well, when he got back there, Josh here showed up an' gave that ol'boy a knobber. By the way, that Ham's got a huge ol'bean too. Then he got a shitload of money." Bill nodded to Josh.

"How much?" she asked, her eyebrows rising with the mention of money.

"I mean beaucoup money. Like I ain't never seen that much money. Well, anyway, after they, he, was done, I come outta of my spyin' place. I was a lookin' out over at the shore when Josh whacked me. I came to jus' 'bout when ya came in."

The black woman appeared to be thinking very hard on this scenario.

Sheila looked at him. No twinkle this time. She leaned over to Josh; grabbing his broken arm, she rolled him off Mohammad. Then she searched in Mohammad's pockets until she found the key to the shackles. Making a face in disgust, she reached over to the shackles.

"You sure find a lot of trouble fer a little guy, don'cha?" she mumbled as she was undoing his shackles.

"Yeppers, I surely do."

"Jus' fer the record, I'm gonna make sure these here boys don't do anything rash." She reached down. Grabbing each one by his collar, she dragged them to the rack where Bill had been held captive. Pulling their arms around, she shackled them securely to the rack as she began to formulate a plan.

Mohammad started to show some signs of coming back to the real world. As he opened his eyes, he took in the scene before him.

Sheila looked at him and spoke quietly, "You be quiet there, Mohammad, and you'll live to see tomorrow. You understand?"

He looked at her with daggers in his eyes and slowly nodded.

She returned her attention to Billy. "Ya say he got a big ol' pecker?"

"Yep. He's got a black snake that would scare a horse. That's no bald face."

"Whatcha doin'?" he asked as she was undoing the flap on Mohammad's black wool breeches. The Arab was glaring at her and began to wiggle.

"Now you stop that. Let me have my fun, and you'll be out of here real quick like. Nod if you understand?" she asked him.

Watching Mohammad glare at her, he nodded slowly. Bill thought, *There's no way he'll live to another day. No fucking way.*

"Well, I wanna see fer myself."

She reached into the opening, fumbling around for a moment, and then her eyes twinkled. Out came her hand along with the human blacksnake. Mohammad's manhood was huge even by animal standards. Sheila fell back on her rump, staring at it. The huge penis was lying on the man's leg, almost touching the deck of the crews' quarters like it was a living being and on its own. Sheila composed herself before scooting back over to it.

"Lock the door." she commanded.

The lad walked over to the door on the cabin, locking it as he watched the big black woman stroke the man's pod, bringing life to the huge black monster that was before her. The small man rummaged through an unlocked footlocker until he produced two brightly colored bandanas that he could use to gag the men.

"I gotta gag you, Hamhead. You know why, don't you?" Bill asked as he held the handkerchief in front of Mohammad. The Arab nodded.

Sheila was squeezing the flaccid member like she was milking the teat of a young cow, pulling the skin down slowly as to reveal the shining head. With her eyes locked on it, a small smile crept across her face as she waited in anticipation for it to become fully erect. Her eyes glazed over with the desire to have her pink tongue wrap around it. Total concentration was on her face as the snake stood up, begging for attention.

Mohammad was hating this. *I will kill these infidels as soon as I can. For now, I'll do as she asks. I will take great pleasure killing her.*

"See that blackjack on the floor? Well, if either of these boys start to throw a fit, you smack them a good lick. Ya hear?" She wanted nothing to interfere with the task that was standing before her.

Mopingly the blond runt picked up the blackjack, watching her, thinking about how deep of trouble he was in.

"I reckon I could do that, but you would mind if I got some of that attention."

"Well, when ya get this big, I'll do the same fer ya." She chuckled.

Mohammad was at full erection with the big black head shining like a brass doorknob. She stood back up and stepped over the prone man. She carefully reached down between her legs, pulling her dress out of the way as she grabbed Mohammad's now-erect penis in her maul-sized hand and carefully guided it into her awaiting black briar patch. Slowly she sunk on the man as she leaned forward to balance herself. Billy was sitting in the presence of a master; she had done this many times before with much less of men. She leaned back, letting all ten inches bury it deep within her. Mohammad was concentrating to spill his seed as soon as possible. He wanted this humiliation to be over.

She turned to the young white boy.

"I ain't never had a root this long in me. Hell, it's almost too long. I mean it's almost hurting my pussy!" She smiled at Bill.

"Almost." Then she giggled. She raised and lowered herself again and again, picking up the speed as she was bouncing on the man.

"Oh! Oh! Darlin'!" She cried as she paused for a moment as she climaxed. Still the black man hadn't released his seed. She stood panting looking down at the rock-hard tool below her.

"Damn, what I gotta do to make that snake spit?" She smiled at Billy. Then looked at Mohammad.

"You holding back, are ya? Well, we'll see how long you can hold back." Mohammad was trying to release, but the thought of the woman was revolting. *I must release.* He closed his eyes, thinking of Josh and his mouth.

"I might as well keepa using it, huh, sugar?" She smiled at the runt. She was far from finished with the Arab. Once again she squatted over the man, her hand guiding him once more.

"I'm gonna shove it up my ass. What do you think of that, boy?"

Billy looked at Mohammad and saw his eyes closed, almost squinting in concentration.

"You gonna get shit all over his pecker." Bill answered, being very uncomfortable with what was happening. He thought of running, but with nowhere to go and nowhere to escape, he had to sit and wait.

She did as she said she was going to do. She placed the black monster in her saturated hole and then leaned forward. Slowly she guided the huge root to the wrong hole. Pain was on her face as she slowly lowered herself. Lower she went, her teeth clamped tight as she waited to be impaled. Then she stopped. Sweat was beading up on her forehead, dripping down on the Arab's face as she slowly tried to insert the snake. Lower, then she stopped, her teeth clamped shut, eyes squinted, and sweat running down her chin like a brook in the springtime as she continued an inch at a time. Then she sunk down onto the man. All the Arab's penis was buried into her.

"Oh boy, that does hurt." she spoke through her pursed lips. Up and down she went on the Arab. Each stroke she wanted to cry. It hurt so much. Finally she could take no more. She leaned forward until the man's penis broke into the air.

"I cain't do it. Goddamnit. It just hurts too much. I ain't never had a pecker that big in me, an' it'll be the last time too."

So the monster of a woman turned around to see the black pole waiting before her.

"I know what'll work, though." She pulled her dress up to the man's penis; she carefully wiped off the blood and excrement. When she was satisfied, she sat on the deck once more, stoking the man's bean slowly. She then lowered her mouth on it and began working slowly over the tip and shaft like she was eating a piece of hard candy. The small white man realized that the man had not moved since Sheila had started, but his manhood had begun to show signs of distress. In a short time the snake began spitting its life fluids out of the huge black sack hidden inside of the cataleptic man's breeches. Then she did what impossible to Billy, she forced the whole snake down her throat until her nose was touching his groin hair. She raised her head up and down slowly. Then she lifted her head up and more came gushing out, overflowing as it came out the side, dripping down her chin. She coughed a couple of times, then carefully wiping herself off on her dress as she stood her six-foot frame up from the messy task. She belched loudly, leaving his penis out for of all to see.

"Man's got him a prize piss'r there. I don't see why he's only usin' it on boys."

Billy saw Mohammad's face relax from his concentration.

Watching in all this in disbelief, the small man had a difficult time remembering this is the woman that he worked with and laughed with. They were good friends. She looked over to the small white runt sitting against the door. She smiled and held her palms up, "Oh well."

"Hell, maybe he'll give ya another poke outta of the goodness of his heart." the young white man sassed.

"Nah, he ain't. Neither is Josh over there. They's hard cases an' will surely kill us both when they get free. You lookie out the door there an' see if anyone a'comin'. You holler when the coast is clear."

Mohammad almost sat up with confusion on his face, mumbling.

"Cain't let you live. You'll kill us fer certain. You understand I'm sure." she spoke to him in a quiet and assuring voice. Hatred came back to Mohammad's face, *It was too good to be true. She'll die along with the runt.*

Billy looked out the door into the night; it was still raining like a cow pissing on a flat rock. It came as no surprise that no one was out in the torrential weather, and then a strong wind blew across his face as he peered into the darkness, *I wanna go west so bad. Goddamnit!* he almost spoke aloud.

Then he looked back only to see Sheila going through their pockets, putting whatever money he had in the front of her dress. *Damn! There sure ain't too much room up there.* She carefully pulled a huge brown breast out into the open air as Bill marveled at the size. She carefully lifted her breast up, putting the money in the fold of her skin, and then carefully put her massive mammary gland back into her white uniform dress. The small man was always amazed that her breasts were always about to fall out. *She seemed to have no problem with what had just happened. Hell, it was the middle of night who'd care anyway*, Bill thought. He looked up and down the passage way for anyone.

"The coast is clear." He loudly whispered.

The big black woman leaned down to unlock the Arab; her breathing was all Bill could hear as she went about the task before her. When Mohammad was free of his bonds, she relocked Josh. The huge woman took care to tie the Arab's hand securely behind his back. She reached down to the now-flaccid member on the Arab's pant leg, putting her fingertip on the end. Then she lifted her finger as the semen made a thin thread. She placed it in her mouth, savoring the last bit before the man would die.

"Damn shame." She shook her head. "Damn shame."

Then Sheila picked up Mohammad like he was a sack of potatoes and strolled through the door into the rain. She walked quickly to the handrail, then as slick as you please, she casually lowered Mohammad into the black water. There was no struggle or splashing, nothing, just the quiet river lapping against the hull of the ship. The man sank quickly, fading out of sight into the next world.

CHAPTER 44

As the water went over the unconscious man's face, it revived him. Mohammad kicked viciously against the strong current. He knew he wasn't to die a watery death. The man continued until he broke free of its black grasp. Into the night air, his face finally felt the warm air; a breath of the night air filled his lungs through the bandana as he turned to the see the twinkling light of the boat fading out of sight. Kicking, he began to tread water. He shook his head viciously as the bandana fell around his neck.

"You bitch! You'll die a slow death!" he called out after the *Alice Mae* as it vanished into the night. He'd almost wished he hadn't opened his mouth as pain shot up to his temple. His jaw wasn't broken or dislocated, but it hurt tremendously from the fist of the big black woman.

The Arab didn't give up. His new goal in life was to kill the two of them, and the runt and Sheila would die a horrid death for what they did to him. Rolling over on his back, he kicked to the west bank. Slowly he found himself creeping closer and closer to the black shoreline. What seemed like only a few moments was, in fact, all night. He looked to the east, seeing the false dawn creeping over the tree line. He was satisfied that Allah had seen fit to let him live, yes, live. To go on a quest to make those pay for what they did to him.

He felt the bonds stretching as he worried them, they slipped off as he was inching closer to the Missouri bank. What to do next was of little concern as he knew he was going to fulfill his promise.

He had no idea what was before him. He knew he was going to get his revenge, but he had no idea how long and how many miles he would have to cover to find them. The stinky mud of the

Mississippi touched his foot as he began to crawl up the shoreline. He stood up in the ankle-deep mud, looking up and down the shoreline, when he realized his penis was out of his breeches. He slipped it away as he buttoned his breeches, *that fat bitch will be killed a hundredfold for what she has done!* He thought as he looked into the blackness where he thought he go, turning his face to the river he looked into where the *Alice Mae* had vanished.

He hadn't always been a maître d'; he had survived as a slaver many a year, tearing people away from their homes like they were cattle on the way to slaughter. It mattered little to him as long as he did what the new owners requested. He had spent many a day living off the land with his nomadic kinsmen as they searched for villages to plunder. His association with the slaver had paid for his long journey from Africa to America.

He stood up looking into the black wall of trees before him. Taking a deep breath, he stepped in the inky veil of trees and disappeared from sight. His eyes became accustomed to the dim light in the trees; he was now able to see his new surroundings. Walking into the willows and the walnut trees, he soon found a game trail, a very well-used trail at that, *I will seek out the savages to do my bidding. Yes, they will be my tool of death for the black one and the runt. Ha! The runt, if it hadn't been for the fat bitch, he would have suffered greatly. Augh! It displeases me that hourglass of time had turned against me so quickly,* the Arab almost spoke, but his aching jaw kept him from talking. He knew his appearance would shock the local natives. That and with a few parlor tricks he had learned for the street performers in Cairo, he felt very sure of himself. He set off as bold as a peacock in the garden of a sheik as he began his trek to revenge.

Mohammad had no idea what was happening on the *Alice Mae*. He knew Josh would be killed as he was thought to be. Josh was an infidel; he didn't have Allah watching over him. So he will die. A touch of sadness came over him. He had grown fond of the tall white man. He used him as he would use any white man, but Josh had a way with his mouth, and Mohammad knew he would not find another like him for a long time. Perhaps he never would.

CHAPTER 45

"One down. One to go. Let's get to it." Sheila commanded the young blond runt.

As she entered the room, she shook the rain from her hair when she noticed Josh was awake. Pain was showing on his face from his broken arm and broken face, but fear was in his eyes. He began to mumble, grunting, trying to say something. The runt looked down at him. "I'll pull this gag down, but if ya start to hollerin', I'll whack ya a good one." As the bandana came off, the handsome man took in a deep breath, almost to the level of panting. The pain from his broken and dislocated jaws was so intensive each word was a struggle.

"I expect you are going to kill me." he choked out to Sheila.

"Yeppers." she replied matter-of-factly.

"I will pay you a very healthy sum of money to release me." The tall man was pleading for his life.

"Yeah? Is that so?" Sheila asked.

"You're a very intelligent and beautiful woman. We could get rid of the runt, and you and I could clean up on this ship. You know that, don't you?" he beseeched her.

"How much? How much money?" she asked.

"At least four thousand." he answered with authority.

With that news the small white man became nervous. She had just killed a man for less than that. Now here's a captive offering more wealth than either would see in a lifetime of scrubbing pots and making beds.

She looked over at the runt; a smile crept across her lips as she thought about killing the runt. She wouldn't do it, but she wanted to scare Billy. Then she looked back to the blond man.

"Where's the money?" she asked slyly with her eyes going into small slits.

"No, it does not work that way. You release me, and then I will give you some of the money. When I know I'll be safe, I'll give you the rest." he continued.

That was the wrong answer. With that, she quickly grabbed the blackjack from the blond man's hand; and in one fluid movement she whacked him across the temple, snapping his head to the side, saliva spraying across the floor as his mouth fell open.

"Hmm, how big is this un?' she asked Billy.

"Hell, I don't know. I ain't no goddamned pecker sucker! What? Are ya gonna inspect him too?"

"Yep. I wouldn't wanna waste a good load."

The scenario unfolded as before. Undoing his trousers as if she had been doing this for years. Quietly humming a little ditty to herself, she groped inside the man's garment. Finding what she was looking for, she paused, and she started to chuckle.

"He's smaller than you." She pulled the white penis out. Josh's penis barely lay on the side of his breeches and as soon as she let go it quickly returned to the hiding in Josh's garment.

"Too bad, another waste." she spoke aloud. She went through his pockets like she did the other, taking the money from him and anything else that looked of good enough to have a street value. Into the folds of her breasts it went.

Bill thought about bringing up the money but backed out of that when he thought about how this spider of a woman killed so easily. By his thinking, it was a good thing to be smaller than Mohammad's was but bigger than Josh's. Discretion took the better part of his decision making, so he declined to say any more on the subject.

"You lookie about fer anybody walkin' around . Now get. I'll put the gag back on this one here."

Once more he stepped out into the rainy night, looking to the right then to the left, listening for footsteps that would alert him to a confrontation with a crew member or a passenger. When no strange sounds came to him, he slipped back into the killing room.

"It's clear."

Off to the handrail, she went once more with the baggage over her shoulder, like so much dirty laundry, then a quiet splash. Another death came to the small paddleboat. All this happened because the small runty white man was too curious. His heart dropped on the ground like a lead weight when the truth had hit him. He reassured himself that he would get off as quickly as possible to start a new life away from the grasp of this woman.

"It's gettin' on to bein' late. Think ya could get that carrot of yer's to work quick like?"

"I ain't big like that there Hamhead was." the runt said as he nodded toward the handrail.

"Are you sayin' ya don' mind me not being big?" He asked.

"Nah, them big boys are only good fer one squirt. Then they's done a fer long time. You little guys, well, I can stick if anywhere I want without gettin' sore an' ornery."

CHAPTER 46

In the morning, the skies had cleared. There was an occasional cloud dotting the otherwise-deep blue sky. The boat was a shambles with no one to run the galley and dining room. Sheila and the small white man just did their respective jobs keeping their heads down while the search for a new maître d' was on. The owners got tired of the people running around like chickens with their heads cut off. When no one stepped up for the responsibility, Sheila finally conceded to take the job.

The small man was convinced that he would be removed from the tedious and boring chores to be placed in a position of authority. Bill felt remorse of his actions as he ate his breakfast of corn cakes and hardtack; he had no appetite as he remembered the quiet splash of the two men that were drowned last night. He figured the small boat would be a place he was from rather than where he wanted to be.

The day started differently though, to his surprise. Then to his dismay he was made to do all her work plus his own. No special treatment came his way, which truly surprised him. At the dishwashing deep sink, he spoke quietly out loud, "I figured I woulda been moved inta a position of authority since me an' Sheila went back a long way an' was fairly tight. I had dirt on her, but she had dirt on me. But no. That black bitch ain't cut me one inch o'slack. Damn!"

In the galley, the small man cleaned and scraped the remains of breakfast off the plates and   bowls, he decided that the next stop he would get the hell off this damned boat and find a new line of work. Meanwhile, the runt was destined to scrubbing like a new hire. Now that Sheila was the boss, Bill was stuck making beds, doing the dishes, and bussing the tables. Hell, nothing had changed except he was doing her work as well as his own. When Bill would make jokes and brush against Sheila, she would show no reaction to speak of.

Whenever Sheila was feeling frisky, she would wait until Bill had an armful of dishes. Then she would reach down quickly, grabbing the front of his breeches.

"Jus' makin' sure ya still got 'em." She would chuckle, "now get on back to work."

"I'll be right back." He spoke to Rebecca. While walking away, he could feel her eyes upon him. They looked as she wanted to tell him something but couldn't. *Women are so puzzling,* he thought. As he entered the passageway leading into the pantry of the boat, he heard footsteps behind him thinking it was Rebecca; he turned to see the black woman approaching him.

"Oh shit. What did I do this time?" he questioned her. His mind racing *I bet this's for me eyeballing Rebecca.*

She continued, "I want some of you. I figure yer 'bout to pop. You ain't got none in quite some time. Ain't that right?" She looked at him with soft doe eyes.

"Yeppers. That be the truth. The last time is when you an' me took care of that business." He nodded to the western side of the boat

"Yep. That's what I figured too. Unless you been sneakin' a poke with my girl." The soft eyes went to blazing fire and brimstone.

"No, no, I ain't done no such thing! I ain't never touched her 'er nuthin' I swear on my pappy's grave!" The small man was noticeably shaken over her accusation. They entered the small pantry where she turned to him and grabbed him under the arms, hoisting him up on top of a barrel of whiskey. She leaned over and softly kissed him on the mouth. Her lips parted his as her tongue dove inside of his mouth. Her breath tasted of coffee and smoke as her tongue roamed inside of the small man's mouth. Then she pulled back and gave a sigh.

"All right, I believe you."

"Let's see that pod of yer's." she said looking back at him with the soft eyes again.

Confused, Bill began to unbutton his breeches; he reached inside to produce his pink carrot.

"It's a tad small right now, but it'll be bigger in a few shakes. No bullshit." Bill told her apologetically.

"Now, don't you worry none 'bout that." she cooed.

Then he watched her face disappear while he felt the hot breath upon his pod. As he watched her head going up and down, he knew it wasn't going to take too long. The runt figured her talents were being wasted onboard this boat. He felt the tingling down deep in his groin as she proceeded on her mission to bring forth his seed. Soon he felt he was going to spew. She lifted her face up to his.

"Not yet. You understand me? Not yet. I'll tell you when you can pop. You got that?" Her eyes were blazing again. This strange woman commanded as God himself was the doing the deed. The small man nodded as he thought, *Gotta think about mud, dishes, going west away from here.* Anything that he could think that would take him away from her in his mind. Her head was a blur going up and down so fast.

"Okay, boy! Squirt yer squirt." she said from underneath the mound of flying satin hair. It didn't take Bill too long to do just that. As he felt his body tense and then relax, he was sure it was what she wanted. He felt the suction on his pod, thinking she was going to pull it right off. *Hell,* he thought, *I bet she could suck a turtle right outta its shell!*

Then her head came up; she opened her mouth, exposing her pink tongue, with his seed on it. Quick like a water moccasin striking a frog, she reached up with the hams she called her hands, grasping his cheeks. The runt fought furiously, trying to disengage her hand, but with no avail. She squeezed hard until his mouth opened. Then she placed her lips on his, forcing her tongue inside his mouth. The runt had his hands against her shoulders, pushing her away with all his might. No movement. Twisting his head to the side had no effect on the large black woman. Her thick fingers were too strong for the small white man. Bill instantly had the urge to vomit. She pulled her face away, watching his reaction.

"Now don't you go spittin' out my present to you, or I'll thump you a good one! Now you get back to work 'er I'll dock you a day's wages fer loafin'! You hear boy?"

With that she hoisted him back on the deck, watching him fasten his breeches as he scooted down the hallway to the galley.

When he entered the galley, Rebecca handed him his apron. Looking at his face, she could see something was wrong but was afraid to ask. As he tied the dirty apron back on, the thought was too much. He turned, running through the open door to the handrail; he began vomiting off the side like a boy who was recovering from his first drunk. While he was bent expelling the goo from his mouth, he had noticed Sheila approaching him.

"I thought I told you not to waste my present to you!" she bellowed.

"I ain't swallerin' that! You can whomp me if'n ya wanna, but I ain't gonna do that never again. So if'n yer gonna thrash me, well, get it over with, so I can get back to work!" he yelled back at her.

"My. My. You do have some sand after all." She chuckled. Then as if it was all a dream, she turned, floating away, leaving the runt and the redhead together. He turned to Rebecca, looking into her blue eyes. He wanted to tell her everything, but instead he turned back to his chores.

"The next opportunity I get, I'm jumpin' this goddamned boat an' gettin' the hell outta here." he mumbled to himself.

"What's that?" Rebecca asked.

"Oh, nothing." They both worked as the silence came to the galley.

"Hey, where's René?" he asked to her freckled back. No answer, just a shrug of her slim shoulders.

Bill worked until the pile of dishes had been reduced to but just a few.

"Hey, can you finish up here?" he asked the redhead.

"Sure. Where are you going?" she asked, her eyes pleading for conversation.

"I'm gonna go find Silas an' them trappers. Don't tell nobody, okay?" he asked softly.

"Sure. Just be careful." With that she turned back to the remaining dishes.

Bill had just gone out the starboard door when Harris walked in the port one.

"Where's the goddamned runt?" Matthew demanded.

"He said he had to take a leak. He'll be back quickly." she lied.

"Well, I'll just sit here and wait." He watched the young lass doing her work, the bare shoulders and the white skin with small freckles dotting her perfect complexion.

"Come here lassie." Matthew felt himself swelling.

"No sir. If you touch me, Sheila will know. Then she'll be a beatin' me. She doesn't want anybody touching me without her permission." she answered with her voice shaking.

"Fuck that nigger bitch!" he spat.

"What's that Harris?" Sheila had walked in as he finished his sentence; she had heard almost all the conversation, "So you wanna fuck me?" she asked smiling.

"Hell no. I ain't so desperate that I'd fuck a nigger!" With that he stood up and spit on the floor in front of her as he left the galley by the same door Bill had.

"He touch you?" she asked, with fire in her eyes.

"No, he didn't. He just asked." she spoke, her voice almost a whisper.

"Best keep it that way, you hear?" Then she turned and stepped out into the darkness.

Rebecca stood there trembling as the events sank in. She had been so close to being raped and beaten in a just a moment's notice.

CHAPTER 47

Bill had just missed all the action by a heartbeat once again. He wandered to the aft of the ship where the trappers stayed. They liked it back there, away from prying eyes and frilly guests. Here they could cuss, drink, vomit, and fight with no concern of the rest of the ship interfering. Many a life had been lost back here by the paddle wheel. Knife fights came often as the drinks increased. The trappers needed the fights. They had lived wild for too long, and captivity was taking its toll.

"Silas? That you?" Bill asked in the dim lantern light.

"Nah. It ain't." came a new voice.

"I'm lookin' fer Silas. You seen him?" Bill spoke at the shape slumped against the wall.

"Yeah, I seen 'em. I seen him sink inta the Big Muddy." the voice answered.

"You. You kilt 'em?" Bill asked in a hushed voice.

"Yeah, 'fraid he kilt me too. Nigger threw down on me during a game of euchre. He was too drunk an' couldn't fight fer shit. Come sit down, boy. I'm dying, an' I wanna talk to someone fer I go under." the voice called to him.

Billy walked to where the man was braced against the wall. He slouched next to the trapper; he could see a dark trail of blood leading away from the stranger's leg.

"Where he get ya?" Bill asked, hoping to see if he could help.

"Ol' coon stuck me in the food bag. I ain't long fer this world, so I'll tell you what I can 'cause Silas spoke highly of ya." The trapper coughed nosily and spit a glob of blood on the deck.

"Son, I be Isaiah Weatherspoon. I came to the mountains back in '23 with Ashley an' Henry. We had some shinin' times back then.

That's where I met Silas. He was my friend. Hard to believe that son?" He coughed again.

"It was just a bad turn of the cards, him an' me killing each other. He saved my hide more than once, was like a brother to me. But, well, well, he threw down, so I did the same.

"You see, son, he told me you wanted to be a mountain man. That the God's truth?" Isaiah asked.

"That's fer certain an' fer true." Billy smiled at the buckskin-clad figure dying next to him."Well then, there's few things I'll tell you that I feel is very 'portant. First, always reload after you touch one off. That'll save yer scalp more an' once. The next thing is sounds. The mountains will talk at ya. If ya listen, they be a telling you what coming an goin'." He coughed again. His head slumped off to the side.

"Isaiah?" Billy spoke softly as he touched the dying man's arm.

"Yeah, I'm still here. Not too much longer. Son, here take this." He unbuckled the belt with the elk antler-handled knife. Bill pulled out the eight-inch blade as it glimmered in the dim lantern light. The brown leather belt fell to the deck with quiet tinkle when the buckle touched the deck.

"I'd give ya my flinter, but I lost it to McReady already. Filthy nigger. Cheatin'est mother humper I ever played a game with. Son, don't trust nobody. They'll skin ya out quicker than a thievin' Bannock." Isaiah coughed again. More blood came up.

"You want me get ya a saw bones?" Bill suddenly felt nervous; he'd never been with a man that was dying.

"Hell, no. Dying's a one-man job son, an' I'm doin' fine right here. When I go unner, jus' pitch me off the side there an' let the turtles feed on me." He laughed aloud, coughing up phlegm and blood. Then his head slumped onto his chest as the life left him.

He looked at the man in the meager light, his gray beard, the long hair with small braided locks on each side dangling against the paling skin, India trade beads weaved in from his Crow wife.

His greasy buckskins had so many stories that would never be told. The White Man sat in the dim light looking at the knife, his only connection to the life of this man.

Looking out into the darkness when he realized someone was standing next to him. Bill had never heard the man, and now he was standing there.

He looked up, expecting to see another buckskinned trapper, but he recognized Sheila instead.

"Sugar, that man dead?" she asked quietly.

"Yeah, his name's Isaiah Weatherspoon. He's a skin trapper and mountain man. He went to the mountains with Ashley an' Henry back in '23. Him an' my friend got inta a knife fight. My friend, Silas, he's dead an' gone. I'm suppose to slip ol'Isaiah over the side." Bill spoke to her, looking at the ornate sheathed knife.

"Well, let's get on with it 'fore Harris comes snoopin' 'round. Have you gone through his pockets? He might have money on him." she spoke as she stepped over Bill to the dead man. She rolled him over to check what he had of value.

"Shit, he ain't got nuthin'. Not nuthin' a'tall." she said in a miffed voice.

"He tolt me lost everything gambling 'cept this here knife." Bill looked at her rump as she was going through Weatherspoon's pockets.

"Let me see that knife, might be able to get something for it from the damned chinks." She turned looking down at the elk-horn-handled knife.

"Nope. He gave it to me, you ain't takin' it. It's mine. You ain't takin' it." Billy White stood quickly, slipping the knife into his waistband.

"So." she stepped over the dead man, "you gonna fight me fer it?" She smiled in the darkness.

"If I have to. Yeppers. I will." Bill was so scared he felt like he was going to piss himself at any moment.

He never saw the fist coming at his head. Something happened to Bill that had never happened before. He felt her fist coming, his heart raced, and then he ducked. Sheila's huge fist went harmlessly over his head. It was like a blur for Bill. Sheila had never seen someone duck so quickly, but then she lost sight of the runt in the dim light. Bill was on the deck, and he could make out her form now.

"I don't wanna fight. Let's jus' ferget this, okay?" Now he scurried behind Isaiah's prone body. He heard feet this time; she wasn't so quiet as she searched for the young blond man. Now she was unable to locate him in the dim light, but the light behind her outlined her. Bill could see her just fine.

"All right, sugar, you can keep the knife. We'll talk later." With that, she vanished from the dim light, leaving Bill next to the trapper. He waited for a few moments to assure himself that she wasn't coming back before he stood.

Now he was alone with the dead man.

"Goddamn Weatherspoon! That was mighty close." Bill spoke to the corpse as he quit trembling.

"Here's one fer ya Isaiah, I felt her swingin' at me. Yeppers. Felt it an' ducked. I reckon yer mountain savvy went inta me when ya wen' unner. Well, I might as well get you over the side." Bill spoke as he picked up the man's legs. That's when the smell came to his nostrils.

Weatherspoon's bowels had released, and his stench was enough to make Billy work quickly. Pulling him to the side feet first, Bill pushed, pulled, and rolled him into the Big Muddy to meet up with Silas. Somewhere. He stood panting for the work. Looking west, he knew now he had to go. If not for himself, then for his friend. His hand caressed the handle as he turned to return to the activity of the boat and the evening.

CHAPTER 48

Several nights later the captain hosted a large party for the guests. People were all about the vessel like ants on a pile of sugar as the death boat crept slowly up the muddy waters. They were milling about, watching the black coast pass by, pointing occasionally at light or campfire that was visible from the handrails. With all the people, Bill figured it would be a good night to get lost. Nobody would even notice the small white man's absence. As he was formulating his escape plan, Sheila came over to where he was working, passing out punch and black coffee. She leaned over to the white man, her black shining hair falling on Bill's shoulder as she whispered,

"To night I'm gonna poke you so many times you won't be able to walk 'til Christmas."

Then she walked off as if she'd never spoken to the scruffy man.

"Ah, son of a bitch. Now what am I suppose to do? If I light out without gettin' a poke, it's no tellin' when I'll get another one. Shit! Shit! Shit!" he mumbled to no one particular. A guest dressed in a long topcoat with a beaver top hat walked by looking at him.

"Say, lad, were you speaking to me?" the guest inquired.

"Huh? No sir, I was jus' thinkin' aloud. Is that one of them beaver hats?" he asked, making small talk

"Yes, it is." The man removed it, admiring it from different positions.

"A damn fine hat, ain't it? Just think, boy, some nigger's freezin' his balls wading waist deep in an ice-cold pond getting them beaver so I can buy a hat. I par'ticularly like the way it sets on my noggin." The guest placed his hat back on his head.

"I'll have some of that punch, son." Bill ladled out a portion into his cup. He looked at the man's face. Many time lines had been drawn over his tanned hard-surfaced face. Some hid by the short-cropped beard; others were out for the world to see. Then Bill looked into the tall man's eyes. They were twinkling like stars in the sky.

"See son, year's ago go I trapped Kaintuck 'fore all this." He waved at the paddleboat's interior.

"Was all here." He reached inside his waistcoat to produce a small silver flask covered in inordinate scrollwork. Carefully he opened it, pouring the contents into the punch cup.

"Ah yes. Something to warm up the inside. Well, thank ye for the punch lad." Then he walked off, looking up and down the ship's walls as if there was story to be told by those paper-covered walls.

The drunken guests were becoming uninhibited. Some of the women were becoming very frisky with their escort or whoever was nearest to them, openly groping and enjoying long passionate kisses.

Bill was in awe at these parties he was required to serve. One of the most reserved female guests, Ms. Katherine Trip, got rip-roaring drunk, playing dare games. Soon she had her bodice undone and her white breasts were exposed as she openly groped a trapper's crotch. His finely decorated buckskins were undone, exposing his swollen member. The man lost no time with coy games; he buried his bearded face deep into her bosom, shaking his dark-red hair wildly as Katherine threw her head back in ecstasy all the time pleasuring the trapper.

The party labored on into the late night. The trapper with Katherine got up, slipping his penis back into his skins as he walked straight to Bill.

"Boy are you that kid Silas was talkin' 'bout?" the man inquired. His buckskin shirt was untied, hanging loosely from his broad shoulders. Bill noticed the scars on the man's chest as he reached past Bill to grab a bottle of bourbon from the table next to Bill.

"Yeah, who might you be?" Billy replied quizzically.

"Name's Dugan. James Dugan." He smiled as he stuck his hand out for Bill to shake it.

"I'm." Bill never got to finish he sentence.

"Come with me, you wild man. I have plans for you!" Katherine slurred.

"See ya, boy!" James hollered over his shoulder as he and Katherine disappeared through one of the doors into the night. The party was winding down, and Bill was thinking more of leaving.

Bill poured coffee, passed out punch, and mopped up spilled drinks, all the time thinking about when he'd make his break. He decided no poke was worth what Sheila was doing to him. The last guest was finally carried out so the cleaning could begin. What a mess the dining room had become, with tablecloths covered in spilled drinks, food smeared into them as the drunks wiped themselves as they continually ate.

Bill's task for the night was removing the tablecloths. He pulled and wadded them up and put them in large baskets so they could be taken to the laundry. When Sheila approached him from the port side staircase.

"Oh shit! What did I do now?" he had spoken aloud without realizing it.

"You done nuthin' wrong." she spoke in a soft voice to the small white man.

Rebecca watched from across the room as she mopped the deck, moved chairs, and began setting up the dining room for the next day. Little did the runt know she had watched him all evening from the time he spoke to the tall man with the hat until Katherine had dragged Dugan away. From a comfortable distance, she watched as Sheila had approached him. *There's something about this small man. He's scared of Sheila, but he'd only take so much from her before he bowed his back at her authority.* She reflected on Sheila's power as she drug chair after chair into position on the long wooden tables. *Sheila's lord and god over us workers. She can allow you to live or make you wish you were dead.* Looking down at the deck, she continued to watch as Sheila was approaching the small man.

She was curious to what her mistress was up to, but heaven forgive her if she even spoke out in question.

"Rebecca, you finish this mess. I need the boy." she spoke to Rebecca from across the room, but she was looking right into Bill's scruffy face.

"NOW!" Sheila spoke with a voice so sharp it would have cut the steel on a boilerplate.

Rebecca instantly moved quicker than she had all night. Bringing the wrath of Sheila upon her was not a good thing no matter what time of the day it was.

She watched as the big black woman ushered out the young lad. She wondered about the situation the little man had gotten himself into. *If he fought, he was done for. If he jumped ship, drowning was the only option. Poor man,* she thought as she slowed back to normal speed of cleaning.

She surveyed the dining hall as she laid the mop against the wall; she walked out of the large room into the night. Leaning against the handrail, she thought about the mess she was in. *Sheila rules my life. There's no two ways about it. Whether it's in the bed or at the galley, my life is to serve her. That's all there is to it. Maybe the White Man would kill her.* She smiled to herself. *That's a dream if there ever was one. Nobody's brave enough to go against Sheila. But the White Man did show some fire in his soul. He back talked her without getting whacked.*

René saw her watching where Bill had gone, "Do not worry. The runt? He can take care of himself. He will only let the fat bitch do so much to him before he fights back. You know he wants to leave very badly, don't you?" René asked.

"Yes, I can imagine, but he never said anything. He won't even talk to me." she confided to her co-worker.

"Oui, he's afraid of her. She will be hard on our White Man tonight. Very hard." René turned and went back into the dining hall, leaving her to her own thoughts.

CHAPTER 49

Bill walked away from the dining room not knowing where he was supposed to lead the mistress of pain.

"Where to, Sheila?" he questioned.

"Up to the captain's quarters." she whispered into his ear.

Oh shit, he thought as they walked up the ladder to the beautiful brass-inlaid door. Terror began to fill the small man's heart as the door appeared before him.

She has done spilled the beans, 'cept she told them it was me who did all the killing' an' she'll get away scot-free. Turning the glass knob, he opened the door and stepped in to the room. *Empty?* he thought. *Not a soul to be seen anywhere, no evidence of Captain Meyer's anywhere.*

"Where's everybody at?" he queried her as he looked about the large room. The big mirror on the wall took him by surprise. It had been so long since he'd looked into a mirror, seeing his blond hair lying on his shoulders, his wispy beard filling out on his narrow face. He hadn't seen his blue eyes in so long it took him by surprise the color of them. Like the sky on a summer day.

"It ain't no concern of yours. But if ya must know, the cap'n said I could use it as a." looking around the room as she smiled. Then turning back to Billy, she hissed like a cottonmouth snake, "Favor."

This woman had contact with everyone; no one was out of her reach. Sheila did as she pleased using sex and violence to obtain whatever her heart desired on the ship. Now Bill was looking at the captain's quarters, thinking that the world was going in circles. Nothing made sense to the small man as he turned back to his capturer. Looking into her eyes, he noticed that they had gone soft again. A sensual glaze had replaced the blazing fire.

"Take off them clothes an' put them outside the door. I'll get a chink to clean them up for ya." she commanded. The small man was undoing his tunic when some movement caught his attention out of the corner of his eye. She left the room; he could hear her at the laundry chute.

"Ming Yao, get up to the cap'n's quarters. There's clothes outside the door. Get 'em clean quick like!" Then she reentered the quarters as she closed the door behind her. His face went slack-jawed as he stared at her. He had just slipped off his shoes as he watched her looking at him.

"Take them outside an' leave 'em on the deck." Bill did as he was told. Buck naked he walked to the door, opened, and laid his uniform on the teak deck. He turned to close the door when he saw her. She was stripped down to the buff. Her mounds of brown skins didn't appear to be fat. She was just very large. Her huge breasts hung down to her waist with walnut-sized nipples sticking out from them. They were the biggest breasts that the young man had ever seen. His eyes drifted down to her honey pot, but nothing was visible through the coarse black briar patch.

"Why, boy, you's plum white." She chuckled as she watched the young man walk to her.

"Yeah, I reckon I don't get much sun workin' like I do."

The small man's breathing became quick as the black woman glided toward him, floating over the polished deck like a fog on the river in the early morning. So smoothly she moved that it seemed as though she was a black ghost waiting to take him to the netherworld. She wrapped her big black arm around the white runt as she picked him up like a rag doll. Over to the captain's bed, she carried him as if he wasn't even there.

"You know I can walk." he spoke boldly from under her arm as the odor from her caught his senses. Excitement was overcoming him now. He felt that he had to touch her but unwilling to override the survival instinct.

"I know, but I like to do it this way." she whispered to him.

She plopped him down on the large bed, looking him over as a cat does to a mouse.

"I think your cock is bigger than the last time I saw it." she said with a little surprise in her voice.

Sheila thought to herself as she drooled over the small white man before her, *My oh my, I's gonna enjoy this runt. God, I love that white boy's jism. I's hopin' he don't go a shootin' off too quick. I want him to do my butthole tonight. Yes sah, that's want I want. He better do it good, or I'll skin him my own self!* She was ready to begin when the runt spoke, not knowing what was going to happen.

Bill, seeing her looking at him with desire and lust in her eyes, figured he should say something.

"The pantry was kinda dark, ya know." he mumbled wondering what was going to happen next.

"Yeah, I reckon so." she answered as she wiped her mouth off with the back of her hand in anticipation.

With that, she sat down on the edge of the bed to begin their lovemaking. She reached down to his carrot and slowly pulled down the foreskin, revealing the pink head. She looked at him with a twinkle in her eye. Down went her black head until there was nothing to see but her shimmering black hair. Sheila became obsessed with making the young man come forth. *Oh yeah. I remember that from way back,* thought Bill as Sheila worked her magic on him.

"Ah, I'm gonna— Ah— I— ah" At that moment the young lad released the stream of life into the big woman's mouth. Gulping like she was swallowing a frothy beer on a hot July afternoon, Sheila continued noisily.

As the young lad pumped her mouth full of the sticky seeds of life, she was in a dream world where she was the queen over all. It mattered little to her who lived and who died as long as she could have whatever she wanted whenever she wanted. This small lad was only a diversion to her goal to run this ship. The captain liked her for a quick roll in the hay between ports. The damned chinks wanted her for protection against other clans on the docks. Harris. Harris was the only one she could not control. He would find himself out of a job soon enough. All she had to do was frame him so there would be no way out other than resigning or going to jail.

The way she figured, as soon as she lost interest in the small blond, he would join Mohammad and Josh. She smiled to herself as she wrapped her tongue around the quivering man's tool.

"Um. Um, you white boys is quick. But you's good. Better than them damned chinks."

"I was tryin' to tell ya I was gettin' close, but you was too fast fer me."

Bill had heard the last words from Sheila, but it didn't make any sense. *Was she doing the laundry help too? Yes. It had to be true. She had said, 'Damned chinks.'*

Shit! Bill's mind raced. *Is there anybody on this flat boat that she ain't sucked, fucked, 'er plucked?* He realized the depth he had committed himself to. There was no turning to anyone on the ship for help. Sheila had everyone right where she wanted them. Right there on the captain's bed, as his youth was being sucked from his young body, his decision was made. As soon as he could get free from this devil woman, he would jump ship.

"How many more squirts you got in there sugar?" she queried the runt bringing him back to the reality of sweaty, sticky sex.

"Hell, I can go all night." he claimed boastfully, hoping he could in order to save his own life.

"We'll see." she countered. Once again using the years of experience, she went down on the young blond lad, determined to bring to full attitude as quickly as possible. Her fat tongue twisted, tickled, and tortured the young man until she felt the small root quivering.

"You ain't gonna pop now, are ya?" She looked up for a heartbeat.

"Nah, but it's fairly close." Billy's young chest was covered in a fine sheen of sweat. Sheila put her hand around Bill's pod. His penis stuck out an inch. *Oh, this boy can do no wrong tonight,* her mind raced forward.

"Well, let see how the smart-assed mouth of yours works." Then as smooth as a white-tailed doe hopping through the brush, she was upon him.

"You stay flat on yer back boy!" she commanded. The young lad obeyed.

"Oh, I'm gonna like this." she murmured. She slowly squatted down on his face.

Bill was holding his breath, not wanting to venture into the black curly mess that was coming down to his face. It smelled like a bait boat, causing him to try to turn his head. It was too late. Her massive thighs captured the runt's blond head. Sheila could feel the breath of the young boy against her. She felt him try to turn his head, but she knew that it wouldn't be. He would do what the others failed to do. She would have her moment of ecstasy.

Almost gagging, Bill felt the wet stinky lips of the black woman touch his face. His eyes were open as he saw the huge hand come down to spread the rolls of skin apart. Great gobs of goo dripped down into his cheeks and chin. The urge to vomit was overwhelming to him. *I gotta do this 'er I'm a dead man. That's fer certain an' fer true,* he thought.

Bill reached up with his hands, putting them on her log-like thighs, gently pulling them apart more as he put what he was doing aside and concerned himself with living instead. His tongue went into the mixture of goo and sweat as he began pleasuring the mistress of pain. He touched the button that rules the world with his tongue. Violently he licked it as a cat would a saucer of milk.

"You best do a good job, sugar." she commanded. Not knowing if she was asking or threatening, he lapped, sucked, bit, and then licked some more. She was sitting upon him for what seemed an eternity when she quickly reached down. Gabbing a handful of his blond smooth hair with her meaty hand, she rammed his face deeper in to the black fur coat.

"Oh, yes'sah!" Sheila moaned as she fell off to the side of the small man. Her mind raced, *I ain't had it this good since that Arab. This is like a dream.* The big black woman was in bliss now, *That white boy has done so good.*

The small white man was relieved when the woman fell off him. Bill felt like he had stuck his face into a plateful of ham jelly. He brought his hand up to wipe off his face when Sheila reached out as quickly as a bat catching a mosquito to stop him.

"You done really good, white boy. Don't spoil it." With that, she swiveled around on her large black bum to face him again. Slowly she leaned over to his face to begin giving him a tongue bath. Sheila used her pink tongue to stroke up and down, back and forth until every last drop of her honey was gone from his thin beard and mustache.

Oh my god, I ain't believin' this! Bill thought. This was a very new experience. As she finished with her feline chore, she leaned forward, sticking her watermelon-sized breast into his face.

"Here boy, work on these." she commanded. Seeing the big brown pillows coming at him, Bill thought of the rock-hard nipples. He chuckled to himself. *They look like two thumbs sticking out of a big fluffy pillow.* As he touched them with his fingers, the big woman shuddered almost immediately. Bill was amazed the big nipples were as harder than an anvil. Leaning down she placed them in his mouth. The lad began to suckle as a small cafe would do, biting, then drawing the flesh deep in to his mouth. He raked his teeth across each one as he continued to pleasure the mistress of his domain. On through the night Bill performed, he was anxious to finish this chore.

"Well, it looks like yer still ready to go." she spoke matter-of-factly. She had been thinking of the small man's flesh tool. Reaching around, she rolled him over so he was on top of the huge mound of brown flesh. She was excited to the point of quick shallow breaths, with sweat dripping down the rolls of her body on the gray blanket of the captain's oversized bed. Bill was amazed at all the different faces that this woman would wear. Meaner than an alley cat one moment then as soft as a kitten the next.

"Boy, you best not squirt too soon. You hear me? Now get to work." the alley cat spoke. The runt obeyed his mistress quickly to avoid the wrath that would fall upon him for being tardy on this chore.

I figure I'll give this here nigger a run fer her money, Bill thought. He caught himself almost talking aloud. That would be the end of him if that had come out. Back to the task at hand. Concentrating, he began to stroke, with a little grinding off to the side, pulling it out; he rubbed his pod on the button of the universe until he felt her stiffen. Slipping it in slowly at first, he pumped savagely like a stud in the spring. His heart was racing as the black mistress reached around to his small rump with her huge hands to pull him hard against her.

Damn, this runt does a fine job. I'm gonna hate when he don't work no more! the thought breezed through her mind like a hummingbird on a hot summer afternoon.

She was sweating like a hog in the slaughter line. Bill resisted by arching his back and wanting her to work for this one. His thin, wiry muscles strained against the big black's grip as he fought the urge to release his seed. When the small man could hold back no longer, he released the stream of life deep into the black woman.

Her arms fell to her side as he slid from between her legs as he continued to ooze life onto her massive leg. To the small man's surprise, she sat straight up, sweat dripping down her nose, off her nipples, but she didn't stop. She continued to lean over as her breasts pressed against his thin white legs, pressing him onto his back so she could bring the small man's pod into her mouth. Not satisfied with the mounting, she wanted more. Pulling the small man to her, into the black hole of a mouth, went the blonde's quivering root. He could feel her teeth upon him as she drew the last drop of life from him. *I don't know how many more squirts I have left, but I cain't let this hell bitch know 'er she'll skin me right out,* he thought in a panic.

As the last drop was excreted from the youth, she lay back, sweating and panting from the pleasure the young river rat had provided her. *Shit, maybe she's was a dyin' an' I won't have to jump ship. Now that would be fine with me!* The young man chuckled to himself. However, she didn't. She sat back up, boldly looking him directly into his crisp blue eyes.

"Sugar, that's the best I had in a long, long time. But there's one more place I want to be poked." the kitten purred. Sweat was still rolling off her like a plow horse in the middle of a September afternoon. *I bet she wants me to poke her in the poop shoot. Ain't nuthin to it. I done it many a time 'fore,* reminiscing.

"I ain't never done that afore, Sheila. Will I get shit all over my piss'r ? Are you gonna fart on me?" Bill lied as he leaned back bracing his arms on the gray-blanketed bed.

"Hell, what are you worried about sugar? You'll do jus' fine. 'Sides I took me a big ol' shit earlier so you'll have nuthin' to worry 'bout. Now lookie here, boy." She opened the draw in the tobacco stand beside the captain's spacious bed.

"Take some of this cure-all an' rub it on yer pecker. Then take some an' smear it on my butthole. Now you do it right sugar." she purred.

Shiela rolled over and suck her butt in the air with her face laying on a pillow, the black hair covered rosebud was exposed. The young runt was in awe of how easily she moved. He could barely touch his toes on a good day, and here she was nimble like a two-year-old. He would have never guessed that she could have moved so fluidly especially being so big.

The lad got up to his knees as he began the chore that lay before him. The black briar patch lay open before him, seeing the life still seeping from her, dribbling out her black peach.

The sight made him nauseous, but he focused on living. That meant to keep this brown giant happy.

"Take yer piss'r an' poke me in my cootch first. Then when I tell you to, you shove it up my ass. You understand? Wait 'till I tell you." She made sure the runt understood her instructions.

"Damn, if this don't seem like work. Well, at least I ain't washin' dishes." Bill murmured.

"What's that you're mumbling 'bout boy?" she snapped, raising her head.

"I was saying I sure glad I ain't workin'." Bill answered quietly. *Whew! I gots to be watchin' what I be a sayin',* he thought.

Back into the black canyon of ooze he slipped. Smoothly he stroked. The previous lovemaking was slipping out as he continued. Bill ventured a look down only to witness the white stream of life puddling on the bedding.

"Okay, boy, slip 'er in real easy now." she commanded.

Out came the semen-covered tool of the White Man. He reached for the cure-all, proceeding to cover the head of his root with the clear suave. Not wishing to hear from the big black, he lathered up her dark hole. *Damn, I hope I do this right,* he spoke to himself. Bill kept remembering what happened to Josh and Mohammad. He put his pecker against the hidden entrance and began to push. Nothing happened! *Oh my god! It ain't workin'! I'm fish food fer sure!* his mind cried.

"Push a little more boy. Yes, that's it. Oh! Oh!" she whispered. *Mohammad was bigger and hurt. This little white boy is just right. I love this little boy. It's gonna be a shame when I tire of him. He so good, so ahh.* She couldn't finish the thought.

"Ooow. That's good." she claimed. *He's too good to kill! I'll have to figure somethin' else out fer him,* her mind wandered as

Billy proceeded on with his chore.

Bill had pushed against her opening with his pecker very slowly, with nothing happening. So, when she asked to push harder, he obliged. Then it happened all at once. It went in. Just a small pop, it was inside. As Billy moved slowly in, he noticed that Sheila was so quiet. *That wasn't difficult or anything,* he thought, but she wasn't moving or anything. She reached for her swollen clitoris and started to rub. She was matching her strokes with the small white man. Bill's sweat was dripping down onto the massive bum of Sheila as he continued to stroke the hair covered hole. As Bill stroked, he could feel her tensing. *Oh my god! This boy can do no wrong right now. Oh shit! Oh. Oh.* she dreamed to herself.

The blonde runt then slowed to give his mistress a moment of uncertainty. It didn't work as she picked up on the leisurely pace he exhibited. *Ha, that'll fix the ol'girl. Show her who's the boss fer a minute.* He chuckled to himself.

"Boy, don't you slow none!" her deep voice roared. *I guess I'm luckier than good,* Bill thought as she tensed back up.

"When I tell you, boy, you pull out that root of yers an' let me have it. You hear me?" she demanded between breaths.

"Yeah! I'll. Do. What. You. Say!" he panted. Then she did it. She tightened up, turning stiffer than a dried-out fence rail as her muscles tightened around his small manhood.

"Give it to me now." she said rapidly.

As Bill removed himself as she commanded, the enormous woman swiftly swiveled around, reaching for the small man's tool. Grabbing the erected flesh, she pulled on it until it was spewing upon her sweaty brown breasts and stomach.

"Goddamnit! Be careful! You'll pull the rascal off!" Bill cried aloud. It was going off like a snake with his head cut off. She took her big meat hooks of hands to begin smearing that spooge all over herself. Her eyes closed as she moaned a sigh. She stopped. Leaning back, she propped herself up on an elbow. Looking him straight in the eyes, she spoke deliberately, "I reckon I'll keep you around fer a while more. Ya did real well in all the right places."

With that Sheila sat straight up. Reaching out, she grasped the small man, giving him a bear hug.

"Goddamnit, yer smearin' that spooge all over me. Now I'm gonna need a bath fer sure." Bill cried out against the big woman.

"We'll see 'bout that. Only if'n I get to wash your sassy ass! Now go see if'n them goddamned chinks have yer clothes done yet. I hates them little shits, but they do a good job on the tablecloths an' towels. I figures that I'll have to put up with the good along with the bad."

Bill opened the door slowly to peek into the night. There was nothing there except the pitch black. The hot air of the riverboat seemed to suck the life right out of the lad as he peered out the small wooden door. He felt drained after the lovemaking with this pirate of a woman. The ship chugged on as they continued to the next dock on the river.

"Uh, Sheila, there ain't nuthin' there." Bill spoke over his shoulder. He wanted to leave, but the woman had made sure he would go nowhere until she deemed it so. He was in the captain's quarters naked as a jaybird, so he walked back over to the bed, sitting on the edge until the mistress of the evening gave him new orders. He had learned to be patient with her requests, not to ask too many questions. The white man was comfortable being naked, and it didn't bother Sheila as she lounged on the large bed with Bill, that is, she took up almost all of it.

As quick as a hummingbird and as smooth as a cat, she was up and off the bed heading for the door. Amazement was in the runt's face as the woman headed out of the room into the night buck naked. She was still dripping spooge down the side of her massive black legs. The white goo stood out like a sore thumb on her brown body as she went to create havoc upon the Chinese laundry men. Throwing the door open, she pranced into the black night.

Bill heard her bellow into the night as she had found the flap for the laundry shoot. Bill was once again happy to be in her graces.

"Ming Yao! Get yer stinkin' yellow ass up top to the cap'n's quarters with the runt's clothes! Right now!" After a brief moment of silence, she reappeared in the doorway of the stateroom. She reentered smoothly, leaving the door wide open, letting the fresh air into the hot, muggy stateroom. The light from the room reflected off her shining skin. *Shit, looks like somebody painted her with varnish!* He laughed to himself, not daring to show any emotions.

"I hate that bastard." The tone of her voice could have flayed a carp without the benefit of a knife. The runt looked at the trail the woman had made when she left as she had bounced about the deck. He figured, *She probably make me clean this place up. Bitch.*

Gracefully she floated over to sit down on one of the captain's velvet French chairs. She turned and plopped down in one swift movement. Slowly she draped one leg over the arm and commenced to masturbate. Bill couldn't help but stare at the black matted hair, seeing his seed dripping all over the beautiful red velvet. *That's gonna piss the cap'n off somethin' fierce. Serves the bastard right.*

"I don't why I'm doin' this my own self when I got you to do it fer me." Raising an eyebrow, she looked at the small white man before her.

"What 'bout Ming Yaw?" Bill answered back, trying to ignore the fact he was beginning to become aroused again.

"He can watch." She chuckled as she rubbed herself slowly, her eyes closing to small slits. Little time had passed before Ming Yao materialized at the door in with his hands behind his back. No knock or beg your pardon. He just stepped through the open door and bowed faintly. His presence didn't deter Sheila from her masturbation, and she wasn't about to stop for a laundry man. Bill was unsure of what to do, so he slowly pulled the blanket up over his nakedness. Gone was the erection that had been formulating in the young lad's groin.

"'Bout time ya got yer stinkin' yellow ass up here, ya son of a bitchin', cat fucking piece of shit. Where's the boy's clothes? I wanted them cleaned. Now where the hell is they?" She had stopped her masturbation, but instead she was rubbing her hand across her nipples, licking the boy's semen off as it was still beginning to dry.

"I have them right here, oh brown piece of dung!" Ming spoke out through a tight-lipped mouth.

With that, he whipped the clothes out in front of him; the laundry was in one hand, the other hand a forty five caliber French dueling pistol. For a brief moment, Bill's eyes were affixed to the contours of the pistol. The dragonhead hammer, the silver inlay on the front stock, as it sparkled in the dimly lit room. Bill had lost a moment of time staring at the gun, but he was brought back to reality of the situation before him.

"You have insulted my workers and I for the last time, oh black pig!" he yelled. Sheila was fast, but how fast Bill wasn't sure. She was on the Chinaman in a blink of an eye. The gunshot was barely audible as her mass muffled it. She engulfed the Chinaman in one swift movement. Bill was surprised that it actually sounded like breaking glass. Smoke filled the room as she landed on Ming. The bullet had punched out of her back sending a blossom of blood on to the captain's prize full length floor mirror as it shattered it into a hundred small shards.

Her momentum carried her forward, falling onto the small laundry man as they fell into the doorway. Her mass engulfed him as she landed on the wooden deck with a sickening thump. Bill sat there on the bed in shock. The gray blanket had slipped down, exposing his nakedness. He made no effort to retrieve it. Gone were the sparkling eyes. The laugh. The evil she could produce in a heartbeat. Dead forever.

Ming was under her but couldn't move. All that was visible was his arms and hands, which were thrashing on the dead woman violently as the life faded from him. Suffocation was overcoming the small man. He had come to do battle with the black monster. To kill her, to free himself and his countrymen from her tyranny.

Bill had seen enough by now; he scooped his clothes off the floor where they had fallen when the commotion had started. As he shook them out, a few small shards dropped to the floor, making a tinkling bell sounds. That's when Bill noticed no further movement from the flesh on the deck. Black or yellow. As Sheila's blood stopped flowing, the small laundryman's hands had fallen to the floor. The dueling pistol was nowhere to be seen.

"That woulda been nice to have. " he said aloud as he got dressed. He stepped over them into the black night. He turned to view the mess that had been over him. Once again he was in the hot seat.

"I cain't believe this." Bill mumbled to himself as he rested his arms on the polished handrail. He looked back to make sure that there was nothing that would tie him to this mess.

When he felt confident, he went in search of the captain or Harris. A strong breeze from the west blew in against his face. He stopped looking west. He strained his eyes into the darkness, and then a fragrance caught his senses. It smelled like freedom.

"I'm outta here! I'll get my ruck an' get the hell off this death boat. If I have to swim, then by god that's what I'll do! I gotta get shut of this disaster that had just happened." he spoke to the black night before him.

CHAPTER 50

Young Bill formulated a plan. If he got stopped by Harris, he'd say he was working with Rebecca in the galley when he had heard a commotion. He went to investigate, and that's when he found the bodies. As he thought about his plan, he decided he didn't want to get Rebecca involved, but if that's what it took, well, that's that. Hell, maybe she'd lie too. The lad was in a bad position as he pondered his next confrontation. He came to a flight of stairs, which he slid down effortlessly; he then strolled down the gangway leading past the main dining hall. Billy mumbled aloud as approached the doors to the main galley.

"I cain't see what good it could possibly do me to stay on this boat. Out west, Silas said it's a trapper's paradise. 'Course, Two Thumbs said that there's bears as big as wagons an' wild savages that eat people. On the other hand, there's land no white man has ever seen. Silas said that beaver an' other critters jus' waitin' to get in yer traps. Hmm, I wonder, how do ya trap? I reckon I'd have to learn from someone 'fore I left. I'm gettin' ahead of myself here. There's a bigger problem in the room I jus' left." he spoke into the darkness.

Now behind him was a dead woman and Chinaman. Both of these people meant something to the captain.

Bill continued to think, *The woman was a slut but ran his galley. I bet she was a sparkin' him too. She may have had some dirt on him 'er he liked to get some that dark meat whenever he wanted. I'm layin' odds it was she had somethin' on him. I don't know, but I'm willin' to bet a coupla weeks of wages that she was doin' him the same way she was doin' me.*

Now what 'bout ol' Ming? That feisty Chinaman. She mentioned that I was somethin' 'er the other 'bout the chinks. What the hell was it? Shit, I cain't member right now. Well, anyway, the Chinaman did a respectable job. No doubt, she had somethin' on him too. He did say he was fed up with her insultin' him an' his crew. Shit, it musta been pretty bad to have 'em shoot her. It was way too much thinking for young Bill. He had barely left the mess upstairs, and now here he was trying to figure it all out.

The whole crew onboard the *Alice Mae* knew what was going on. They had a good suspicion that Sheila and Bill were involved with the disappearance of Mohammad and Josh.

Bill walked past the main dining room, quietly trying to be unobserved. Just as he passed the doors, Harris came out, looking right then left. He saw young Bill going aft. He approached the rugged-looking young man quietly from behind, taking Bill by total surprise. He grasped his elbow, forcing the runt out of the passageway into a dark gangway.

"What the fuck did you do now, you worthless piece of floating scum?" he yelled at Bill then looked around to be sure no one had heard him.

Billy White's mind raced, trying to cover his ass.

"There's been a problem." Bill stammered.

"I was a workin' down below an' I hear'd a gunshot. I was gonna report it Matthew." Bill spoke his common name, knowing Harris hated to be addressed that way.

"What happened?" Harris asked through gritted teeth.

"I got no clue!" the runt whined. Harris spun around, slamming his fist on the bulkhead then turned to look out into the pitch-black night.

He spun back to face the small white man, "Goddamnit! I bet that chink had enough of that fat bitch! Were you in on it? I had a report from one of our guests that his firearm was missing!" he accused the runt.

"Jus' tellin' you that I heard a gunshot." Bill had turned his head to look west, wanting to jump right at that moment.

"If I find out that you have any knowledge and you're not divulging information I'll shoot you myself before they can hang you. I can't prove it but I know you and that nigger bitch had something to do with the missing of Mohammad and Joshua, but I just can't prove it!" The first mate face was red even in the dimly lit gangway of the ship.

"Get out of my sight. Better off, you're restricted to the galley until further notice. Now get out of my fucking sight, you piece of shit!" With that, Harris pushed Bill toward the galley. Stumbling, Bill nearly sprawled out on the gangway. As he regained his balance, he turned to say something but Harris was already gone.

"Bastard went to stick his head up the cap'n's ass." Bill cussed aloud.

***

As Harris entered the dining room, he reseated himself on the right side of the captain, arranging a smile to the obese woman across from him and the captain.

"Well?" Meyers asked without turning his head.

"The runt said he heard a gunshot. Dumb fuck. He wouldn't know a gunshot if someone shot him in the ass! I hate that motherfucker!" he whispered to the captain's ear.

"Really? I had no clue." Meyers answered back, his voice dripping in sarcasm.

"I thought you loved him like a son." He chuckled, "No matter now. Go up to my quarters. Sheila had the ragamuffin up there. Take care of whatever mess she's made. I'll be happy when she disembarks from this vessel. She's been a pain in the ass ever since she's come aboard."

"Yes sir." With that Harris excused himself left from the room.

The man did what he was told without argument. Meyers liked that. The other first mate had always tried to outthink him in some manner. This man was a follower. That's exactly what he liked about him. No questions, just did what he was told, keeping his opinions to himself.

CHAPTER 51

Bill walked into an empty galley, Rebecca was the only one working. Red head and freckles beaming about her. Her dress clung around her shoulders, tightening up at the waist revealing her perfect figure. She looked at Bill walking with the weight of the world on his shoulders. She thought, *This's a good man; he just seems to get into trouble easily. However, he is very cute.*

The runt looked upon this girl and wondered, *How does she always look so good working in a sty like this?* He noticed her red hair tied up in a bun, he imagined her white shoulders and the freckles; his mind was running wild as he forgot the situation he had just left.

"What happened up there?" she asked quickly.

Bill blurted out, "I ain't done nuthin' wrong. I'm jus' under 'vestigation, an' I'm down here 'cause goddamned Harris hates me. That bastard has it in fer me ever since I came 'board this shithole. I figure he's gonna slice my jugular on this one."

Then the galley door flew open, and an enraged Captain Meyers slammed the door open with such force it startled Bill to the point of actually jumping. His face was about as red as Rebecca's hair while his big purple nose was almost glowing from the excitement. Bill almost laughed. If he hadn't been in serious trouble, he would've gambled on the captain's nose popping. The captain still had his white napkin hanging from the front of his dinner jacket. It was unsightly with different food stains on it as it hung like a sheet on his enormous belly. *I guess that's not gonna get cleaned since his favorite chink is dead now. Maybe they'll give the work to Slim now.* Bill chuckled to himself at his private joke.

"Who in the Sam Hill do you think you are mister? Calling me out of my dinner party with accusations of gunshots! You call in a report like this! If you must know, a bird flew into my quarters and struck my mirror, and broke it. The next time you hear gunshots, investigate before you run around crying wolf! Good god, man, now I know what Mr.Harris was speaking about!"

Then Captain Meyers turned on his heel and vanished out the door so quick Bill wasn't even sure he had been there. The runt was stunned. *What 'bout the two bodies? What the hell is going on here?* Then the truth hit him.

"Sheila musta had had dirt on everybody, so it was hush-hush and over the side for her. It was too bad about the laundry chink." he spoke aloud.

"What? What's that you say?" Rebecca questioned him.

"Uh, nothing. I was thinkin' out loud." he quietly answered.

CHAPTER 52

What Bill didn't know was Harris was in Captain Meyer's stateroom, viewing Bill's mess. Harris gazed at the bodies and the disheveled room. His duty required him to protect Captain Meyers to whatever extent it took.

Harris hadn't been the only one onboard to protect the obese Captain Meyers. The earlier first mate, Dick Kuhler, got into a scuffle with a deckhand that was trying to gut Meyers on its maiden voyage. Meyers had promised the young Frenchman special treatment that never materialized. The voyeur took it upon himself to make sure it didn't happen to anyone else. Kuhler died of his wounds, and the Frenchman jumped into the Ohio to fight another day. Harris had been onboard and wanted the job. He wanted the position so badly he kept his deckhand wages to serve Meyers.

So now this situation had arisen, he had his chance to protect his captain from any disgrace that would ruin a captain's chance of getting a larger paddleboat. Harris was figuring that when Meyers left he'd take him along. At least he could hope, and he'd do everything to make sure it

First things first, he thought as he moved toward the dead woman. The big black woman had to be moved. He began the chore of dragging her toward the handrail. Grasping her thick arms, he strained to move her from the buried Chinese laundry man. Sweat began to bead on his forehead as well as it soaked his dinner waist coat. It finally sunk in that the huge woman would be easier to roll toward the handrail than dragged like he first planned. Slowly, one inch at a time, Matthew rolled the dead weight closer to the handrail. He rolled her over. Her arms and breasts would slap the deck as he continued. He felt the whole world would hear him following his orders. Though she was huge, he was amazed she didn't have as much fat on her as he had imagined. He leaned against the doorjamb catching his breath as he stared at the dead woman.

Her huge breasts were now nothing more than great brown pillows of flesh. The once-deep voice of authority lay before him now, her mount agape, with her pink tongue hanging out the side of her mouth. Sheila's dimpled rump lay on the deck now. Matthew noticed her legs; he'd never seen her naked, and now he was surprised at the thick muscular thighs.

"Damn, she's one huge nigger!" He sighed as he stared at her. Sheila had the last say though; her glassy eyes were staring at him. No sassing now, just the open eyes looking into Matthew Harris's soul. Matthew had the chills run up his back into his hair as he couldn't look away.

"Fuck you, bitch. You ain't gonna put no hoohdoos on me!" he spat at the dead woman. He returned back to the chore before him. Slowly he rolled, dragged, and pulled her out of the cabin as he looked at the handrail before him.

"How in the fuck am I supposed to get her fat ass over that handrail?" he spoke aloud as he panted, trying to catch his breath. *The top had to be at least four feet in the fucking air.* Harris stared at the brass handrail. His eyes drifted to the deck, then back up to the bottom rung. It looked to be at least a foot if not more. So the first mate walked over and peered down over the rail, estimating the distance to the outermost part of the paddleboat, *no way I can get this fat bitch over that fucking handrail and miss the bottom deck.* Now perplexed, he sat down on her head as he thought of a way to get her off the boat.

"You fuck!" He looked over his shoulder at the dead woman he was sitting on.

"FUCK!" he shouted out into the black night. He looked at the distance to the water, gauging the distance, I can drag your fat ass down three flights of stairs, then off to the fantail. Yes, that'll work. What do you think of that?" he spoke to the corpse. Then he realized he was talking to the dead.

"Aw fuck!" He looked over his shoulder at the dead woman he was sitting on.

"FUCK!" he shouted out into the black night. He looked at the distance to the water, gauging the distance once more, *what if I miss? I'll just go back to where she lands and push her off again. It's late. There'll be no guests out. This'll work. It has to!* So he turned and began the task.

Straining, he began to dead lift the massive 200 pound woman up to the top of the handrail. Harris's eyes were bulging. Blood veins were popping out of his face and neck as he lifted her upper torso to the top of the rail. Using her chin as a resting place, Harris took another deep breath as he lifted again. This time he was able to get her arms and the huge breasts over the rail. He was getting dizzy, so he paused as he balanced her on the handrail. With her arms and breasts over the top, he was panting heavily and assessing the situation for a brief moment. He decided the body was stable as he lightened his grip to recover his composure.

His heart jumped to his throat as she began to slip back to the deck. Quickly, he reestablished his hold on the dead woman as he stopped her journey back to the bloody deck. Using his back against the bulkhead, he strained as he pushed her back over the rail. Once again she was almost balanced. The first mate strained as he pushed her cold brown butt cheeks up higher toward the handrail. He felt he was making progress now. No one had seen this fiasco, and he was getting it all taken care of without any help. Matthew had his eyes squeezed shut as he pushed the black woman, and he paused, opening his eyes. There, not more than twelve inches from his face, was her black hair covered anus, still shiny with the blond runt's semen. Closing his eyes again, he continued to push the dead woman over the polished rail.

Slowly her stomach slipped over the rail as she began her

journey to hell. Relieved that his task was over, he looked over the rail to see how she fared.

"Oh fuck!" he cried out as he turned to the nearest ladder. Sheila had landed on the bottom deck's handrail, bending it and pulling all the fasteners out of one of the stanchions.

Her head, breasts, and arms were over the rail, and her legs had been broken from the fall. There she hung, perfectly balanced, awaiting her one-way trip to hell.

Harris couldn't believe his luck. It was shitty to say the least. He flew down the ladder to get her over the side as quickly as possible, running up to her, sweating profusely, his white coat now saturated in sweat and covered in her blood. He began to force her over the side. The woman had her right femur broken so severely that the bone had broken through the skin in a ragged tear. Then it was finally over. A noisy slap was heard as she hit the water.

Harris returned to the remaining corpse, his energy all but gone; he slowly trudged up the ladder to where the small Chinese laundry man lay.

"I don't think anyone heard the noise over the paddle wheel anyway." he spoke aloud.

Harris then reentered the captain's stateroom to retrieve the small Chinese man. Hefting him over his shoulder was as easy as picking up a bag of flour. He backed up a few steps, lifted the small man over his head, and ran to the rail. With all his remaining strength, Matthew Harris threw the last piece of evidence on the top deck of the *Alice Mae*. A quiet splash was all that was heard. All that was left was cleaning up the blood and glass from the scene of the crime. He looked at the deck, seeing the French pistol on the deck, now covered in blood. Bending over, he carefully picked it up, admiring the contours as Bill had done earlier, *there's no since giving this back,, I'll just keep it.* He smiled to himself. Matthew had never owned a gun, let alone one of such high value. He thought of how much he could sell it for when they docked.

It oughta be worth twenty bucks, if not more. He smiled again, thinking of how he would spend the money. He began stripping the bed, seeing the wet spots on the sheet had drained into the bed; he wiped the gun off with the soiled sheet. He smoothly slipped it into his waistband. He thought of a cheap whore and rot-gut whiskey. His eyes danced with delight.

The runt got some before she died. Too bad he didn't die with these others. After wiping the blood up, he threw the sheets overboard also. As he looked around the stateroom, all that was missing was the mirror and the sheets. Everything else looked normal.

"Now I'm gonna deal with the runt." he fumed.

CHAPTER 52

In the galley, Bill and Rebecca were standing across from each other, both looking at the floor, not saying anything. The silence was good as Bill had nothing to say and Rebecca had too much to ask. They heard footsteps coming closer to the galley. They looked at each other. Then the door opened slowly. As it came to a stop, a thin laundry man entered.

Bill called him Slim because he was skin and bones, but his given name was Sun Chung. The small man was standing before Bill and Rebecca in his traditional black frock and baggy pants. His tanned complexion was pasty white with his eyes having a hollow distant appearance. Sun Chung was so shaken he was quivering as he lifted his eyes to meet the white runt's gaze.

"Great shame is upon us." His voice was cracked and uneven as he stared at the two white people before him.

"What're you talkin' 'bout Slim?" Bill lied through sympathetic eyes.

He spun around to face the small white man.

"The great brown one is dead as is our head clansman. I stole the gun from a trapper down below for Ming Yaw to do the deed for all of us. Now he is dead, we cannot give honor to his death."

"What in the hell are ya talkin' 'bout Ming Yaw bein' dead?" The small man lied so often it came out sympathetic and sincere. He looked at the grief on this small man before him.

"Ming Yaw took the gun up when she requested your garments." His eyes went almost round with hatred.

There was no love lost between the Chinese and white workers. Neither had received any grace from Harris or Mohammad as work had been assigned.

"You're talkin' out yer ass shit fer brains. I had nuthin' to do with anythin'. I don't know nuthin'." Bill talked waving his hands around in front of him.

"The eyes of this vessel are upon you small one. You had better be careful of where and when you lay your head to rest. This crew has many bad memories of you and the great brown one. They shall not be put aside or forgotten."

Bill suddenly grabbed the small Chinese man in one fluid movement, slinging him toward the distant bulkhead. But before Bill could realize what had happened, he was facedown on the deck with his right arm folded to his back with excruciating pain in his wrist as it was only a breath away from being snapped like a twig on a December afternoon. The runt had no idea the Chinese man was schooled in the art of kung fu self-defense. As far as the whites knew, the Chinese were things to be used and discarded when no further use was found for them.

"Do not touch my person again. For if you do, it will be your last!" Sun Chung spoke in a whisper to Bill's ear. The pressure vanished as did the small man.

"What the hell had just' happened? One minute I was gonna kick the shit outta that little fart, an' the next minute I was lookin' up from the floor!"

"Well, what're you starin' at?" he snapped at the redhead that was looking at him with her mouth agape.

"It was so quick. I've never seen anything move so fast. One minute you had him going toward the wall and—and—and then there you were!" she said, pointing to the floor.

"You know, I was under Sheila's grasp also. I have no sorrow for her death. Ming Yaw was cruel to me also, with his sharp tongue and fire in his eyes. To hell with both of them I say!"

She laid her mop against the butcher block cutting table and took the runt's hand to lead him out into the black night. She looked around and then she walked to the bow of the paddleboat. As they sat down, he looked around. He swore it looked exactly like the same coil of rope that started the whole tale of debauchery.

The evening had cooled down as he noticed Rebecca shivering slightly. Looking around on the deck for something that would keep the redhead warm, he spotted a sweater on a chair from one of the guests. He quickly retrieved it, hanging it over her shoulders as he peered down the front of her dress, seeing her ample bosom only a few piece's of cloth away.

"Now, I don't know whose it is, but I'm sure they would mind a lick if'n you used it to stay a tad warmer. It's a far sight better than shiverin' to stay a tad warm."

She looked into the small man's eyes, seeing sympathy and adventure. The wild look was still there though, *It will take more than this death boat to quell this man's spirit,* she thought.

So Rebecca started her story. "You see, I was a whore working in the cribs on the Baton Rouge docks. That's when I met Sheila. Well, Sheila had been one of my regulars, and she was always really nice to me. Whenever she beat me, she always left extra money and said that she was sorry. She offered to take me away from the cribs, but I would have to service her free of charge and work in a kitchen. That's better than having trappers and drunks coming in for a poke. You know I have been poked, prodded, and groped by near everyone on this boat but you. Why is that? Is it because of my being white and you like the niggers? What have I done to cause you to look away from me? Did you know I had worked in the cribs, and that's what drove you from me?" she confessed to Bill.

"Hold on there. I've nuthin' against ya. Ol' Sheila kept her meat hooks on me all the time. If I started to flirtin' 'er anything, she'd cut my pod right off an' chucked it to the turtles, I swear. I like a poke jus' the same as the next guy, but I didn't want her comin' down on me fer doin' it. Hell, I figure you're the best-lookin' gal on this here boat. Ain't no bald face either. There's been a many a time when I looked ya over real good tryin' to figure what you'd be like with yer skirt all hiked up an' all. Say, is it red all over?" Billy asked quietly.

He was looking at her, and he just couldn't believe she had been a whore. Her skin was so perfect as were her manners. He thought of her as an educated person. He was still shocked she worked in the cribs on the wharves.

"Look, it's been a very trying time tonight. We can take care of this conversation some other time. If you don't mind?" Seeing his opportunity for sex vanishing into the black of the night he put his hand ever so gently on her arm.

"Don't go. I still wanna talk to ya."

He pleaded, "Rebecca, what do ya say about you takin' your bloomers off as I can see them red short hairs of yers?" He threw all the courting manners he might have ever had over the side of the ship like Sheila had thrown the two men earlier.

"Ha-ha." She laughed.

"How do you know that they're short?" she asked cutely. She too wanted to be bedded down by this runt, but she wanted it to seem like it was his idea.

"I don't. I was jus' hopin' to see if they'd be red. An' maybe ya would show me a trick 'er two that ya l'arn'd in the cribs."

She leaned over to him so her mouth was inches away from his ear. She whispered, "Well now, how bad do you want to? How badly do you want to fuck me, silly White Man?" She was so close Bill could smell the sweet fragrance of womanhood; gazing into her eyes on the dimly lit evening, he could barely think or even speak. Then she sat back to watch his reaction.

Bill was taken back by her forwardness as his jaw dropped for a moment. The girl before him didn't flinch one iota. Well, he wasn't quite sure of what to say, so he continued on with the same tack he had planned on.

"I'll tell ya what. I can poke three times in a row, an' you get yours every time. What da ya say to that?" the small white man bragged.

"I can get mine whenever I want. Every time. I don't need some runty white boy to do me any favors." Rebecca sassed Bill to tease him even more.

Shit, this girl's sassy! I've had jus' 'bout 'nuff of this, his mind raced.

"Don't ya like to poke? I mean most girls diddle themselves once in a while 'cept that ol'Sheila. She did all the time, an' she's dead." Billy continued, hoping for a break from the red-haired vixen.

"You don't have to remind me of her personal habits, thank you very much!" Rebecca retorted. The young girl stood up and slowly strolled over to the handrail, staring off into the western night.

I wonder what she's a thinkin'. I hopin' that she's thinkin' 'bout a poke. That's what I was a hopin', the blonde runt wondered as he looked at her.

She slowly began to walk away, humming, dragging her hand on the polished rail as she meandered aft. Bill was seeing his attempts at bedding the fiery lass fading away, so he jumped up after her. As he neared her, he figured a little honey never hurt.

"How old are ya?" he asked, trying to get personal.

"Twenty-two I think, my mother was never educated enough to keep track of such things. I came from the east, you know. Over by Nauvoo, Illinois, my father was a gunsmith over there. He had a good-size shop." There was a long pause.

"He even had an employee. Well, one afternoon there was an explosion in the workshop, and my father was killed. Michael, the employee, said my father was testing some gun powder or something, and it exploded. The shop was ruined, and my mother sold the property and moved to Boston. I didn't want to go, we had a very ugly argument, and I left. That's the last time I saw her. I started working in a pub serving food and drinks when a man approached me and said he knew how I could make more money than I'd ever seen." She paused, adjusting the borrowed sweater, she continued.

"I was getting pretty tired of waiting tables and getting yelled at by the owner. That owner always wanted sex. He said that if I gave him a poke, then I could live upstairs for free. He was fat and had terrible gas. It would make my eyes tear it was so bad." she continued.

"So I took Roy, that's the gambler's name, up on his proposition. He got me outside of town, and he beat me badly. I couldn't even see out of my left eye for over a week. He told me flat out that if I ever tried to leave, he'd blind me and leave me for wolf bait. I was scared because he already hurt me bad and the law doesn't do much for a whore as far as protection." Rebecca was quiet as Billy took all this information in, wondering about how much was the truth and what part was fictional.

She was staring out into the darkness. Bill didn't know what to do next. Was she expecting him to tell his story?

She spoke quietly, "I was working in St. Louis for a while and not doing too bad, and I had a little nest egg going. Well, Roy found it and took it, along with all my hopes of quitting the business and of becoming respectable. That's when I met Sheila." She paused looking west.

"She had been coming in often, and I did my best at servicing her. She liked me, so she spoke to Roy one afternoon, and that night I was on this boat. So there you go. I have told you my story. Now it's your turn." She turned her head, her eyes sparkling in the light from the small ship's lamp.

All the runt wanted was sex; it didn't matter to him if it was fact or fiction as long as it got the woman into bed. He could barely contain himself. His loins burned so badly for this young redhead, so he lied. It came easily for him as he used it frequently too, so he was very proficient at it.

Damn, all I want is a poke, an' now I have to do all this here jawin'. I'm so horny I think my pecker is gonna rip right through my breeches. I ain't tellin' her the truth. That's fer certain an' fer true. No tellin' if'n she'll use it against me later. His mind raced as he began to weave his tale of deception.

"I was born down in Louisiana I think. I ain't rightly sure to tell the truth. My mammy run'd off't an' left me when I was knee high to a toadstool. They told me she was a nigger, but I don't believe 'em 'cause my hair ain't a bushy an' black like them niggers workin' on them goddamned boilers. Ya know, I lived there for a long time doin' the work around the place. Shit, I done pull'd 'nuff weeds to hold me over fer a lifetime. That an' choppin' firewood. Yessiree, I was gonna make tracks the hell away from that place soon as I could saddle a horse by my own self. I started thinkin' real hard 'bout leavin' that rock farm. That's all that seem to grow there was rocks.

"Well, one night the night ol'lady that was my new mammy said I was a cutie an' that she'd teach me 'bout bein' a man an' how to please the ladies."

He paused. "She was wantin' to give me a bath, and I was hiding from her under the bed with all them spiders an' dust balls." He paused.

Then he looked into her blue eyes. "I saw her changin' clothes. Hell, I almost gave myself away wantin' to sneeze an' all. Well, anyhoo it wasn't a pretty sight. She was big an' fat an' had them dark spots on her. Kinda like a pinto pony. Damn if her tits didn't hang clear the hell down past her fat ol'food bag, but off to the side. Big ol'nipples." Bill held his hands up, showing Rebecca the size to be as big as a tea saucer.

"I ain't never seen such a thing. Ya know what else? Bein' down under that bed I was lookin' up I couldn't even see her pussy hair. That's right. She had a big ol'flap of fat hangin' plum over it. But when she sat down on a chair that night, she reached down an' pulled that flap right up." Bill winced at the thought of what it would have looked like.

"Rubbed her self real hard, right in her crack. Dug her fingers in an' all, scratchin' at it like she had poison oak. I ain't tellin' you no bald face here either. I could hear it sloshing like a milk bucket on the back of a wagon as that ol' gal went at herself." Bill paused for a moment to let Rebecca digest the tale. But she interrupted before he could go on.

"It doesn't matter how big or little a woman is. All women like to pleasure themselves. Some are gentle. Some are rammy and rough." she defended the imaginary mother of Bill.

"Hold on now. Let's get on with my story." the small man interrupted.

"So I said g'bye to that place as soon as she fell asleep. I got the hell out that very night. I wasn't too sure 'bout takin' the horse, but I did any ol' way. I figured no one would miss it."

Bill shook his head. "Damn, they wasn't too pleased with me fer doing that. The constable caught me under a bridge the next afternoon while I was snoozin'. He kicked the shit outta of me an' took the horse back. That rascal left me all tore the hell up under that bridge. I thought that he ripped my head off an' shit in the hole I hurt so much." Bill wove his saga as he watched Rebecca's reactions; he weighed his chances and where the story should go for the best chances for sex.

"Well, I met you an' Sheila near Hannibal, 'member? So how 'bout me an' you goin' in fer that poke now?" He was almost to the begging stage now.

"Is that all you think about? I swear. I thought there was more to you than that!" she exclaimed with false indignation.

"I still want a poke, an' I can really do it three times in a row." The young lad was running out of ideas, and he could see his chances of slipping into the bed of the young girl fading away.

One last chance he thought. *Pour some honey on it to sweeten the pie.*

"I think yer the prettiest gal I ever seen. Ya know that's fer certain an' fer true. I bet that me an' you would make a good couple.

With all yer learnin' an' me with my good looks, we'll we make a handsome pair. Don't ya think?" Bill was trying everything that he could think of now, certain the young galley girl was going to walk away from him.

"You really think that I'm that pretty? I mean, even with all this red hair?" Rebecca acted like an innocent schoolgirl. She was going to have her way with the small white boy, but she wanted to see him squirm first.

Now were talkin'. This pretty young girl had fooled Bill. So he laid it on as thick as molasses in January thinking he was pulling one over on the girl.

"Hell yes, you're a fine looker. That is a fact. I bet yer skin is as soft as a kittens tummy. I'd go as far to say that them blue eyes of yers would put the stars to shame with the way they sparkle an' shine. Your cheeks glow with the fire of a Indian summer at dusk."

"I'd say." Bill was on a roll now, but she held her hand to his lips.

"That's enough. Your certainly are a golden-tongued devil. Let's go see if you were telling the truth." Rebecca gave in, seeing the runt was trying so to woo her.

The young lad was ecstatic that he had finally got the red vixen to concede to the lovemaking he was proposing.

Yeehaw! I was startin' to wonder if I could keep bullshittin' long 'nuff, an' well, it worked

Bill thought that there must have really been a God.

They walked hand in hand back to her petite cabin. Her small room was in the middle of the paddleboat; it's strange the floating craft seemed so quiet as they walked to her door.

Rebecca produced a small key from around her neck to open her door to the meager room assigned to her. If it hadn't been for Sheila, she would have been put in the crew berthing where men and women alike were stuffed into the small cabin. She had heard of many personal effects being stolen or borrowed from the crew by the biggest and strongest.

Rebecca opened her door as she and Bill stepped in. The scent of this woman was over whelming as Bill tried to identify the fragrance. *It's musky. No, wait. I know this smell. It's sex. That's what it is. It smells of sex.* The blond man wondered if this was where she and Sheila did their lovemaking. *Two women at once. Now there is something I ain't thought of.* The redhead brought him back to reality as she turned up the wick in the lamp on the wall, illuminating the small cabin as he looked around. A oval mirror hung from the wall over a matching shelf. The runt looked closer, seeing the hairbrush, covered with red hair from Rebecca's thick mane. Bill wanted so badly to throw her down on the floor and ravish her with all his being.

The small man got her key, locking the door, when he saw the the dress hanging from a nail from the back of the oak door. He leaned forward seeing the small flowers on it. It matched Rebecca's personality. He looked left where he saw a small pair of black dress shoes unlaced sitting next to the door with the strings haphazardly hanging from the eyelets. *They must be her dinner serving shoes,* he mulled to himself.

"Nice place." the blonde runt said as he turned to face Rebecca.

Before Bill's lips had closed she was upon him. Her lips came against his fast and hard. Her hot tongue shot into his mouth so fast it just about gagged the small white man. Not to be outdone he rammed his tongue back at her with the same ferocity, not stopping until she forced him back with her arms.

"You do have a golden tongue!" she exclaimed.

"Damned right. I know where else it'll work!"

He unbuttoned the front of her uniform as it slipped off her slim shoulders, past her beautiful sculpted breasts. Down her freckled body it traveled, past her muscular arms, her narrow waist until it lay crumpled on the floor at her black shoes. He noticed her young body in the dim light of the lamp as she had a well-defined shape from hours of manual labor.

She stepped out of the dress, standing before him in her drawers, waiting for him to be the mystical lover. She almost couldn't bear the wait for him to finish off the chore he had started. There she stood in front of him in her underwear and lace-up shoes.

Bill slowly pushed her to the small cot behind her. He reached up with his hands, sticking his thumbs under the waistband of her bloomers. He began pulling them off as she lifted herself to ease the small man's chore. Then they were off and sliding down toward her shoes. As he got to her knees, he stopped. Looking up, he saw her red pubic hair, thick and inviting. *Not too fast,* he thought.

So he reached down to untie her working shoes. Fumbling with the laces, he finally got them untied. He pulled them off one at a time, tossing them next to the others behind the door. Reaching for her well worn socks, the small white man pulled each one off carefully as not to rip or tear them. Into the pile of clothes they went also. The mound was growing as Billy looked up to the next object in the way of his desires. Her thin undergarment was at her knees, teasing him now. *Damn! I want them rascals off so bad I can taste it!* Billy thought as he continued with his hands up until they touched the frail cotton bloomers.

Rebecca's breathing was coming quickly now as she didn't want to wait for this teasing the runt was doing on his mission to bed her. She felt his slender hand touch the skin, easing the bloomers off her legs. The hair so fine it was almost invisible to the runt.

"Oh, tear them off, you silly man, and get on with it!" she mumbled. Bill waited and pulled them off to join the rest of her clothes. Now sitting before him was the naked redheaded woman ready to see if he had what it took to please her.

The young lad placed his hand between her breasts and slowly pushed her back until her body stopped against the bulkhead. He then lifted her legs up, placing her feet on his shoulders. Ever so slowly he ran his tongue down the inside of her cool white skin. Billy hadn't noticed she'd sat up. He'd not seen the two hands coming around the back of his head either. Her hands grabbed a handful of smooth blonde hair as she pulled him to her.

"I'm tired of this! Get on with it!" she cried out as she rammed his face into her soft red hair.

Bill stuck his tongue deep into Rebecca's moist crotch and lapped like a thirsty dog on a hot July afternoon. He brought his mouth up to the pink button to start nibbling on it. She was thrashing about now. Her hands were rubbing all over his hair going from the front to the back. He brought his face away, but she rammed it back in.

Hold on now! If this is what she wants, then, well, hell, then I'll give it to her. Bill was in heaven to be doing this to the beautiful redheaded woman that had been out of his grasp for so long. He was licking, biting, sucking, and slobbering all over that red bush like a hound dog searching for the marrow in the bone. Rebecca felt the first orgasm come as she arched her back, experiencing her body quiver from the pleasure this blond runt had shown her. It had been too long since a man had been able to pleasure her in such a way. She looked down at the man to see her honey was dripping off his chin like a maple tree on a hot afternoon.

"You are good!" Rebecca exclaimed. Bill knew he was on a roll now. Lifting her legs off his shoulders, he stood up and began to undo his breeches. They fell to the floor in a whisper as he quickly used his heel to pull each shoe off. They joined the soiled pile on the wooden deck. He started on the tunic buttons as he had gained enthusiasm as he pulled the work tunic over his head; it joined the rest of the clothes on the vessel's deck. There he stood as naked as the day he was born.

She sat the rest of the way up and reached for his rigid penis. It was harder than a hunk of hickory as she stared at it lovingly.

"You might wanna be careful with that. It's gettin' pretty close to gonna off. If I'm gonna give ya three, well then, ya best not tease it." Bill reminded the excited woman before him.

"It'll go right off if I suck it?" she asked. *God, she had blue eyes. Even in this lamp-lit room* he thought.

"Yeppers." he bragged.

"Good." She smiled as she placed it in her awaiting mouth; down it went until his soft blond pubic hairs were against her lips.

"Whoa there, missy!" Bill gasped. That's when the gate opened. The whole herd got out. He reached down to the back of her head, holding it firmly with both hands as he released. She didn't let up on the task that was before her though; she kept sucking as the blond's testicles began to hurt. It was like she was kicking the pony until it was lying on the ground quivering. Rebecca didn't miss a beat. She finally brought her mouth up to the head of his penis that was in the open air so she could drip some of that white semen of life onto the head. Rebecca reached up to wipe her mouth as she noticed Bill's member becoming hard again. This was the moment of truth for the white boy.

Rebecca leaned back, exposing the red furrow to be planted.

"Slip it in." she spoke with spooge still between her lips. Rebecca couldn't believe it. *This small runty white boy's ready to go again, with no rest in between!*

Bill wasn't one to wait for annoying orders. With one hand on the wall, the other on his planting tool, he guided it into Rebecca's awaiting valley. He began to slowly grind from side to side, with a couple quick jabs thrown in for good measure.

He must think I like it slow and smooth. Damn him. Faster! Harder! But the words never left her mouth as Bill had increased the crescendo. He let it rip, like a mink in heat.

She lay still for a moment, feeling another orgasm coming upon her. *This is too much!* She suddenly wrapped her legs around the thin man as she squeezed so hard it actually hurt the lad.

Bill popped the cork on another one.

Doggone! I ain't too sure I can do one more of 'em! Those last ones just 'bout did me in,

Bill almost spoke aloud as he continued to fill her up. He was sweating like a hog in the butcher shop now, and Rebecca was heaving like a heifer in heat. But he wasn't going to tell the vixen under him that.

"Two in a row. Do you have the last one, or were you lying about that also?" she queried him.

"Well, if ya wait a minute, yer gonna find out." he retorted.

Bill pulled her head over to his pod and slipped it back in her awaiting mouth. She didn't even flinch about having her honey and his spooge all over it. She commenced to lap and suck like her next week's wages depended on it, bringing the runty white man back to an erection. Bill felt the tingling in his groin as he knew he'd be back in fighting form in less time it would take to skin out a potato.

"Well, I'm ready to go there." Bill was bragging.

"Do it then!" she said in a raspy voice.

Billy slipped it into the red gash of hers faster than a fox leaving the hen house. Rebecca was in bliss. She started rocking back and forth and wiggling around as Billy kept stabbing her with his blunt tool. The small man was sweating like a whore in church. This was no cakewalk for the young lad. Sweat dripping down on her breasts, she was rubbing it all over herself, fully engulfed in the lovemaking. The runt put one hand on the wall as his knees were shaky from the exertion he had been putting out.

"Now! Now! Harder! Harder!" Her voice was crackling and hoarse.

She was thrashing her head side to side; her hips were thrusting at Bill as the lovemaking became almost violent. Her hand reached up behind his neck as she pulled herself up until she had all her weight on him. Just about then Bill's scrawny legs gave out as they cascaded over into the cot, filling her up once again.

"I've gave ya everything I had. The well? Well, she's plum dry." Bill spoke in a ragged breath as he viewed his partner on her cot. She was panting as her chest was heaving. She rolled over until she was on her hands and knees. Rebecca then lifted herself up onto her knees. She then leaned back against the wall as she placed her hand on her pink button. Then she rubbed it viciously. She tossed her head back, whacking it on the wall severely, but that didn't stop her. She climaxed again. She pulled her hand away, sticking her fingers in her mouth, licking and sucking them until there was no trace of the lovemaking.

The young white boy couldn't believe his eyes. Here he was plum tuckered out, and here she was still masturbating like she was washing dirty socks on a washboard.

"Now, I'm done." she said as her voice trailed off and her eyes glazed over from the pleasure she had received from young Bill.

Rebecca could only think of the next time she and the runt could be together. It wouldn't be soon enough as far as she was concerned. Never had a man or woman provided her with that level of ecstasy. Three pokes, one after the next. She wouldn't have believed it if it hadn't happened to her.

"Well, I did get my three pokes in." Bill boasted as he surprised the lass with his cockiness. Billy knew she was as nimble as a minx, and from the exhibition he had just witnessed, he'd say she was definitely hornier than one.

Realization came back to Bill as he sat looking at the naked woman before him. She was covered in a fine layer of sweat. Watching this girl, he then realized he was supposed to be in the galley this whole time. Leaning over, he scooped his shirt up as he slid it over his still-sweaty shoulders. As he pulled his breeches on she asked him.

"You're not leaving are you?" she asked.

"Yep, I'm supposed to be in the galley if ya 'member 'bout what happened tanight." He pulled his shiny shoes over his bare feet.

"Did you do it? Did you kill all them people? Like Slim said?"

"Nah, I wasn't even near them people. That's what I tolt the first mate." Bill was lying like a politician now. *I always figured it's better to have lied an' lived then to die tellin' the truth.* So he left her room heading toward the galley.

CHAPTER 53

Sun Chung watched Harris enter the galley from the darkness of a hallway. Hate fumed from him as he felt sure the white runt was going to get away with murder. *It was because they were all white. They hadn't fought tooth and nail to get away from China to be a freeman. This white runt, he had no honor, nor did this man Harris. Tonight, it would be his last.* He clutched the stolen Green River skinning knife. *What a fitting end to this scum. Killing him with a passenger's knife would put the blame on someone else. He could sit back and watch the silly white people try to find the culprit. Such fools they are.*

"Tonight he will pay with his life." Sun Chung spoke aloud as he inched closer to the galley door; he put his small frail hand on the door as he slowly opened it as he looked in. Harris had his back to him, his hands on his hips.

"Ha! Now you die!" Sun Chung rushed into the galley, flinging the door wide open, surprising Harris. Caught off guard but not unaware of the danger coming his way, Harris spun around to confront his attacker only to receive a gash on his stomach for his efforts. The knife slit open Harris's tunic and stomach as easily as opening a game hen.

Sun Chung screamed, "Tonight you die!" He slashed again with the skinning knife. His first cut had struck Harris solidly as there was blood showing though his fresh white dinner coat already.

"Die! Die! Die!" Sun Chung cried as the knife plunged again for Harris's heart. Matthew was no slouch in a knife fight. He expertly caught the wrist holding the knife and spun under Slim's arm, carrying the knife-wielding hand back into Sun Chung's soft stomach.

Sun Chung's eyes went wide with the disbelief that he had failed. *How could it be that the white man could do this to me?* Death was on its way to Sun Chung as he slowly sunk to the floor. He could feel the coldness of the deck as he slumped. *This was not supposed to happen. I was to be victorious, not die on the floor as some street urchin.*

"Goddamned Chink." He spat as the Chinese man lay on the floor. Harris was holding his stomach as he spoke. His intestines were trying to come out, but his hand held them inside the no-longer-white dinner jacket, picking up the bloody knife and slipping it under his dinner sash.

"Gonna put you where I can come back an' carve you up real good after I get sewed up myself." Matthew grabbed Sun Chung's arm and began to drag him into the meat locker. He knew his wound was bad as he had become lightheaded.

Sun Chung could do nothing as he felt himself being dragged into the darkness of the locker. *This must be a dream. I cannot move my arms or legs, and it's getting darker.* Then he thought, *I must kill this white pig!* He couldn't feel the wetness in his garments as his bladder released itself. It was as if he was in a dream, watching from the outside.

The white man released Sun's arm as it fell to the floor. He looked into Sun Chung's eyes where a small sign of life registered.

He spoke as he coughed up globs of blood, "I'm gonna gut you shit fer brains! How do you like that, you yellow bastard?"

"I reckon I'll have to gut you first then get all sewed up." Matthew's vision blurred as he spoke to the corpse.

"It looks like you killed me, you yellow fucker!" The lightheaded first mate opened his jacket to observe the wound. A clump of his intestine unfolded into his hand.

"Yep. You killed me, you fuck!" Harris couldn't focus as he knew he was on the road to hell. He was going to make sure the Chinaman was going first, though. He pulled back the black frock to reveal Sun Chung's sternum. Kneeling down, he removed the Green River knife from the sash as he prepared to finish off the Chinaman.

"Hum. Most of my work's already done." As he raised up the skinning knife with both hands as his own intestines spilled out, he plunged the knife deep into the small man's chest. The small body convulsed as the last bit of life fled.

The mortally wounded man knew he wouldn't make it to sick bay to get sewn up, so he used his remaining strength to break through the sternum as he pulled the knife through the heart on its way to the groin. For a moment the hands of the Chinaman had moved, but now they lay lifeless on the bloody deck.

"Fucker's dead now!" Harris vision was blurred as fire shot through his body and life was seeped out.

He spoke in a ragged voice as he continued toward the groin of the dead man, "Gotta finish." He removed the knife to cut the dead man's trousers. Satisfied, the penis and testicles were in open view. Only then did he reinsert the knife back into the chest cavity to finish the morbid work he had started. The knife stopped on Sun's pelvis and fell onto the deck as he reached into the man's cavity and began pulling organs out.

"Almost done." Then Matthew slumped over his opponent.

"Gotta get out." he slurred as he rolled over onto his back. Slowly he continued to roll until he felt the cool deck against his face. Darkness was rushing toward him as his death was only a few moments away.

"I ain't dyin' in here with you! You prick!" He got to his knee, holding his intestines the best he could. He rose to his feet, weaving like a drunk.

"I've seen men live from worse." he slurred as he grabbed the handle of the door. It swung open as his grip failed. Matthew Harris stepped on his own intestines, causing him to lose his balance, pitching him into the corner of the flour bin across the room. *Hey, there's my pappy. Hey, Pappy, I'm here to stay. Is that Grandpa?* Matthew imagined his father and grandfather as he started his journey to the other side. *We've been waiting for you Matty.* His grandpa held his open arms to Harris. The first mate, Matthew Harris, life slipped away quietly.

CHAPTER 54

The runt pushed the galley door open, expecting to receive a tongue lashing for being out of his assigned space. The first mate surely loved to yell at the young man whenever he got the chance. Billy gave him plenty of chances too since he was always out of his workspaces gallivanting around the ship.

"Anybody here?" Bill called out. A chill ran up his spine as he looked around the small galley.

"This is spooky." the runt spoke aloud. He noticed a blood trail coming out of the meat locker so he gingerly stepped to see where it led. That's when he saw Matthew off in the corner.

"Jumpin' Jehoshaphat!" he cried out, startled by the man's situation.

Bill looked at where the once tyrant of the ship was sitting on the floor. He was whiter than the snow on a January morning, except for the puddle of blood he was sitting in.

"You don't look so powerful now, sitting in your own goddamned blood." he spoke venomously at the dead man. The front of his dinner jacket had a huge gash on it with dried blood on it. Bill saw the intestines hanging out, draping on the deck.

"Shit! That had to hurt a scoosh! Serves him right, the prick." Billy spoke aloud. Feeling somewhat more confident he stepped over to the dead man to kick Harris on the foot then jumped back, expecting Matthew to blink or show some sign of life; but nothing happened other than sitting there with his eyes open, staring nowhere.

The White Man's curiosity was getting the best of him now; he had to find out what killed the bully, so he went to the meat locker. Shaking hands reached to open the iron handle. Slowly he pulled the heavy door open. He looked down at his hand, seeing the blood wasn't dry yet; he opened the door more to let the dim galley light shine into the dark meat locker. That's when the smell hit him like a ten-pound sledge. The smell of death. It was that of intestines and excrement. Bill fell back stumbling as he tried to regain his composure. Still hanging onto the iron handle, he recovered his balance to finish this intriguing story.

The next sight shocked him. Sun Chung was lying on the floor but had been gutted like a two-year-old steer, and he had been slit from stem to stern with intestines and organs all over the deck in the once-clean meat locker. Once again curiosity came over him.

Now what the hell happened here? He shook his blond mane slightly,

"If this don't take the circle?" he was speaking aloud as he walked over to the sink.

Grabbing the iron handle, he pumped water to splash onto his face. He pulled a towel off the rung by the deep sink, drying his face and hands as he turned to view the scene. The runt tossed the towel over his shoulder into the sink full of dirty dishes, looking over the scene.

Harris an' ol 'Slim were having a heart-to-heart talk when it got ugly. He made out the scene in a pantomime.

I reckon Slim got in the first stick as Bill did an imaginary sword parry? *an' sliced Harris pretty bad. Matthew musta killed him.* Once again Billy was the swashbuckler. *Then gutted him fer his rude behavior an' then fell down over there an' died. I wonder what that was all 'bout. Oh, well, it weren't none of my business. I got me 'nuff problems of my own, an' I don't need to have more of this shit.*

Then he threw his hands up in disgust as he walked out into the night air. It was cool and refreshing after being cooped up in the small galley with the dead men.

Bill looked west, thinking aloud, "Hmm, let's see here; Hamhead, Josh, Sheila, Ming Yaw, ol'Slim, an' now that fucker Harris. I'm gettin' off this here death boat right now."

Bill walked quickly to the crews' quarters where he had been held hostage. He began looking over his shoulder often as he neared the small compartment. Slowly he opened the door.

There sat Thabo Mbekiuki, or Jonah as the owner' called him.

"Hey, why ain't you out there shovelin' nigger?"

"Why are you not in the galley?" Thabo answered boldly. He knew something was wrong when Harris never made his evening rounds. It meant only one thing. Harris was dead because in all the time he'd worked on the *Alice Mae*, Harris had never missed a chance to beat the workers. Never. Though he had no proof, there was a terrible spirit floating on this boat. *Very bad spirit,* he thought as he looked at the young blond man before him.

"Well, get the hell outta the way nigger, 'cause I'm jumpin' ship as soon as I can get my ruck together." He answered the tall Zulu. Billy kicked off his shiny shoes, pulled off his white tunic and uniform breeches. He pulled on his linen shirt, his shoes and his own breeches.

"Then I'll go with you." Thabo stated. There was no question of if. It was a brazen statement. He was going with Bill whether he wanted it or not.

"Hold on Jonah, you can't go with me. Shit, you're a goddamned nigger slave. Hell, they'll throw us all in the hoosegow if'n they chance upon us together." Bill whined as he packed quickly, grabbing a small brimmed wool hat and possible bag.

"My name is Thabo Mbekiuki, not this Jonah." Thabo stood tall, looking down at the now very small man before him.

"I don't give a rat ass what your goddamned name is nigger. You cain't go with me. Shit, you're a goddamned nigger slave. What the hell is I suppose to do with you?" Bill had stopped talking as he stood up to his full five feet six inches. He buckled Isaiah's knife to his waist as his eyes looked into the black man's sternum.

"Well, I think you can go, but if it gets shitty, you'll have to be on your own." Bill knew that this man could kill him as easily as breaking a chicken's neck, and now wasn't the time to argue. He slung the possible bag over his left shoulder and picked up his coat.

I wish I coulda got some of that money Sheila had snagged from Mohammad an' Josh. That woulda really helped out once I get off this here death boat. Well, that's jus' tough shit! Bill was get shut of the slow-moving vessel.

Looking at Thabo's eyes, he saw his eyes flick from side to side. He spun around to face his new intruder.

"Rebecca! Goddamn you! I could have stuck you fer sneakin' up on me like that! Now what the hell are you doin'?" He realized he had been screaming.

The redhead wasn't frightened one bit from the young lad's bravado as she stared at the Zulu warrior standing behind Bill.

"You're leaving." It wasn't a question. It was a statement just as Thabo had spoken. He looked into her blue eyes and couldn't lie again.

"Yeppers, I'm jumpin' ship 'rite soon."

"What are you doing with Jonah?"

"His name's Thabo or something like that. He's coming with me."

"I'm going with you too." With that she reached up to the front of her uniform dress, pulling hard. She ripped the cotton dress down the front revealing a linen work shirt. She shimmied it down to the floor. Bill saw she was in breeches similar to his.

"Well, hell's on fire and I got the shovel. Can ya swim?"

"You will soon see, won't you?"

"Damn, she's sassy!" Bill spoke over his shoulder to Thabo.

"Yes, but the fire hair is a good thing. I see her soul is strong. She will make you a good wife." Thabo smiled. Rebecca heard the comment as she smiled at Billy White.

"Are we going east or west?" she queried.

The threesome walked into the night. He was looking west.

"Yeppers, I reckon we'll be a goin' west. The land of savages an' wild critters. If yer up fer it?" he spoke, acting as tough as he could not allow her to see his fear.

"Hey, Thabo, can ya swim?" Bill asked as they all crept to the aft of the paddleboat.

"Yes small one, I can." Thabo answered as they neared the stern wheel. Bill noticed it no longer was thrashing the water. It was moving slowly now, and the boat was actually yawing to starboard as they made their way back.

"Something ain't right. We ain't gonna wait to find out either." he spoke quietly to his jump mates.

Thabo was thinking of his next move. *It will be no problem to kill the runt and the redhead will be mine!* The plan had formulated as soon as Rebecca had entered the crews' quarters. *Now all I have to do is make sure the runt drowns, which will not be a problem, then get the shore and run, after I have my long-awaited entertainment. Yes, it has been too long since I've had a woman.* Thabo had never had a white woman. *Yes, this is a good night.* Rebecca brought him back to reality.

"I can keep up with your scrawny ass! Now let's leave before someone comes to kill us too." she spoke as they neared the aft of the paddleboat.

Billy wondered if she knew what had happened in the galley. *She must have because that's where she spent most of her working time. I ain't gonna ask her. That's fer certain an' fer true,* he thought about the turn of events that were transpiring. Traveling with a woman? *Now I got a goddamned nigger. Christ! Things just got too complicated, but it'll be a plus to have her with me, someone to talk with and get a poke whenever I want.*

He went on daydreaming. *Maybe I can make Thabo to all the work. Hell, I'm white, an' I'll turn him over for cash money when the time's right. Yeppers, money on the hoof. That what them nigger's is. She can do all the cooking, and he'd supply all the meat for the fire.* Back to reality. *I wish I'd had time to steal a gun from one of the trapper's. It shouldn't be hard at this time of the night. I know where James is, and he wasn't with his gun. Katherine's got that man humpin' like a bull in the spring.* He chuckled to himself. *Hell, I'd like to be that way my own self.*

The trio crept back to the fantail, staying out of the light as they neared the paddle wheel. Bill looked around to make sure that no one was there to witness their escape.

Shit, maybe they would figure we'd been killed too an' thrown over the side. Bill thought as he leaned out over the side to make sure that they could get away clean and fast.

"Now lookie here you two. Soon as we get clear of the boat, we'll hang on to each other until we can get far from the boat. Then well make out fer the west bank." Bill had a plan, a thin plan but a plan nonetheless. He was hoping to instill confidence in his new partners as well as build his own courage up.

Rebecca wasn't too worried about leaving the boat or the hazardous water. She was hoping for the adventure and getting off this floating funeral precession.

I'll have to make the best of a bad situation, she thought as she grabbed Bill's face and kissed him passionately, forcing her tongue deep down the white boy's throat. She enjoyed kissing this runt of a man. When they got clear of this boat, she would leave him to seek new prospects. As much as she enjoyed his sexual prowess, he didn't have savvy to take care of them outside of this paddleboat. When she had finished, she looked at Thabo; he had a toothy smile showing in the dim light.

"Okay, let's go!" With that she slipped her leg over the side and was gone. Bill pulled his hat tight and did the same with Thabo following. The cold water took his breath away as he heard a quiet splash from the Zulu. His hand went up to his hat, pulling it tighter on his head as the cold water slammed him. His hand found the handle of the knife, reassuring it was where he'd left it.

"Damn, this is cold." He swung around to watch the paddleboat fade away and began to look for Rebecca. He felt a hand on his arm, and there she was.

"My, you can swim well for a runty white boy." She giggled.

"Seen Thabo yet?" she asked nervously. She had seen the look on Thabo's face, the same as others before him, and she knew it meant no good. She looked over to the west, and she could see no light to speak of when right in front of her the large black man surfaced.

"Ha-ha-ha! Did I scare you small one?" He smiled in the darkness.

"Nope, ain't no nigger scarin' me." she answered to the voice.

"That you Thabo ? Hell, you oughta smile so as I can see your black ass."

"Runt, there's no master now, so you better be careful of how you speak to me!" he scolded the small white man.

"Feisty nigger, ain't you?" Bill chattered as the slow process of hypothermia was beginning its attack on the small white man.

Hum. It'll be light in a few hours, and I'll be free again, she thought. Bill brought her back to reality as he spoke to her.

"Let be a gettin' 'fore we both go under." he spoke through chattering teeth.

They started swimming to the west That's when Bill noticed they were going downriver quickly.

"You okay?" he asked, concerned.

"Seen Thabo ?" he questioned her.

"Ha-ha! Small man, I am right behind you." That's when Bill felt the hand on top of his hat, forcing him under the black muddy water. The small man struggled as Thabo forced him to stay down. He felt the blackness was creeping into his mind as the cold water began to sap his strength.

Christ! I'm gonna die! No! I'm not gonna get kilt! Not now! Not after all the shit I've been through! All the thoughts raced through his mind as he struggled to get a breath of air, grabbing the wrist of Thabo, trying to release his grip.

Thabo was having no problem drowning the puny white man. He knew in few more moments the woman would be his. Then he felt a terrible burning in his stomach. Releasing the runt, he felt his stomach. Warm blood was seeping from a gash. That's when he realized the runt had stabbed him. Anger, not fear overcame him as he called into the darkness.

"You will die, runt! Not now! But you'll die from my hand!" With that final statement, Thabo floated away from the couple. Soon all that was left was the memory of the Zulu warrior.

The runt had pulled the knife from his belt as panic overcame him. He slashed wildly until his blade found the hard flesh of the African, tearing away at his opponent's stomach. Bill had no idea where or how bad he had sliced Thabo, but he knew he was alive and breathing now. He sheathed his blade and pulled his hat down over his ears.

"White Man, you there?" called Rebecca out of the darkness as they floated down the cold water.

"Over here." he answered his through chattering teeth.

"What happened?"

"That nigger was trying to drown me!" Bill fought the current as she touched his arm.

"Shit! How'd you get away?" she queried him.

"I stabbed the sumbitch. Then he let go an' floated downriver. Shit, I was a goner too. That was too damned close." Bill continued.

"Damn." was all she could muster up in the chilling water.

"That bastard will be looking for revenge. Shit! Now I wished I coulda kilt him outright."

Now that was over, he felt the adrenalin fade away from the moment of near death. He could feel current pulling him along swiftly. Rebecca was holding Bill's arm as she thought of her situation. This wasn't like swimming in a pond. This was liquid death waiting to whisk her life away if she let her guard down. Then an undercurrent pulled her down as she grabbed for Bill's coat to avoid being drawn down farther. Bill thrashed like a drowning dog when she came up spitting and coughing. She started to pull him down as well.

"Damn, woman! Ya scarit me!" he scolded her as he too struggled against the Big Muddy.

"Yeah, well, I didn't enjoy it too much either." she snapped back, spitting out the revolting, foul-tasting muddy water.

Bill started stroking toward the shore; well, he thought it was the shore. They were floating downriver, and he was going toward the west best as he could figure.

The runt felt a push from behind him and assumed it was Rebecca going under again, but as he turned to help, he saw it was a huge tree limb traveling as fast as them.

"Grab hold of this here limb, an' we'll get some rest." he spoke between breaths of air, spitting out the black muddy water that was so quickly trying to kill them.

I should have stayed on the boat, she thought as she wrapped her arm around on the stump.

Her teeth were chattering like a woodpecker on a dead tree. She was so cold her toes began to ache from the chilling water now. *Why had I listened to the runt? I could be alive and warm on the* Alice Mae. *I'd screwed the devil himself to save me from this. Unfortunately I can't go back now as the boat is gone forever.* All that was there was blackness and cold. They were trying to make it to dry ground.

Bill heard her teeth chattering, and he knew she had to get out of the water before the black waters took all their strength away. He looked into the night, and he could make out the tree line. It was getting closer. The night was ending, and his vision was improving. He could see shapes now. The river swung off to the left, and it looked narrower.

"Here's our chance! Ya gotta swim like the devil hisself was comin' fer ya. Do ya think ya can make it?" Bill asked the shivering lass.

"You keep your eyes on me, and you'll find out!" she responded with false enthusiasm.

"Let's go!" he shouted.

With that they shoved off from the security of the limb and went hell-bent for leather to the shore. Young Bill swam as he'd never swum before. Cramps came in his legs and arms, but he persevered through them until his foot struck solid ground. Not actually solid. It was soft. Mud. He was wading up the bank in mud. He was happy it was mud and not the cold river taking his life away. He looked down the river in the dim light of the early morning, and he saw Rebecca climbing out of the water onto the bank. Damn, she had found a rocky outcrop where she had escaped the bone-chilling water. Young Bill crawled and slipped until he was on the dry bank. Covered from head to toe with black mud.

"Whew, I stink somethin' fierce." he spoke the first words of freedom. Not very profound to start a new life off with admitting that the odor he was emitting was foul, but he was free, and that's what really mattered.

The sun was barely showing over the top of the forest on the east bank. It was a fine day being free.

"Well, we made it." He slipped off his coat and tossed it up the bank. Then he pulled his possible bag off and tossed in on top of the coat. Pulling off his hat, he began wringing it free of water. Satisfied, he slipped back on his blond matted hair, pulling it tight.

"You might want to consider where you put your belonging." She pointed in the early morning light.

"That's poison oak right there, and I'm not going in after it for you." she spoke with a sharpness in her voice that Bill had never heard before. She pointed to the dark-green leaves where his belongings were awaiting him.

"We'll see 'bout that." he snapped back at her. This wasn't going like he'd dreamed. He turned back to the water, scanning the water line, until he saw a long stick lying in the shallow water. He walked back down to the water's edge through the foul mud until he could retrieve the stick. Returning to where his ruck was, the young white runt then used it to lift his parcel free from the devil's own glossy green foliage.

"You think you're clever, don't you?" she answered to his ingenuity.

"Yep." he answered back without looking at her.

"We'll see how you do later." she spoke as she turned to head into the forest before them.

After a few steps, she turned to Bill and spoke, "Let's be off."

Getting Started

CHAPTER 55

Bill was stunned. Here was a sixty-four-inch lass barking at him like the late Matthew Harris did. Where was the red-haired vixen that had been with on the boat? Now in front of him was a redheaded bitch of a woman. She hadn't spoken to him this way on the boat

His confusion turned to anger. He dropped his gear and grabbed her water-soaked arm and spun her around to face him. Her long red hair now matted from the muddy water flung around to slap her across her freckled face as she stared into his blue eyes.

Billy whispered, "Who died an' made you God? Now lookie here goddamnit! Me an' you wasn't shit back on that death boat, but that all changed right here, right now! I'm runnin' this here show. It jus' me an' you. I'll take care of my end of the living! You take care of yers! I don't cotton to yer brow beatin' either. I may not be the biggest dick in the woods, but right now, I'm the only one! If ya wanna clear out, then git!"

Bill pointed into the forest as it started to rain.

"Best you remember that nigger I stuck in the water. You remember the one that tried to drown me, or have you already forgotten? He's out there. Now, if ya wanna stay on with me to give it a go out in the mountains trapping beaver an' livin' off the land, on our on hook, then by god, I'm happy to have ya along. Other than that, shut yer goddamn yap fer a while 'till I figure if we're alone." Bill finished his speech.

He looked into the deep brush, wiping the raindrops off the front of his small hat. He adjusted it, lifting the bill slightly so he could see a tad better. The daylight stopped at the edge of the vegetation. Darkness took over his vision. He tried to gain some knowledge of the landscape. It was just like when he had hunted for Ike. He knew there were people out there that could and would kill him if he gave them a chance. That's when Isaiah's words came to him; "Listen. Listen, and the forest will talk to you." Bill looked at her as she whispered.

"What do you mean?" she whispered back.

He held his hand to his mouth, telling her not to speak. There was too much happening too quickly. They walked a few steps into the black abyss before them; Bill then turned to her, holding his hand up to motion her to stop. The small man shivered as he scanned his surroundings. He put his hand to his lips as he stepped off the trail into a patch of stinging nettles. Squatting down she took his lead by doing the same. The small man turned to the red-haired lass to motion her to the ground. She complied as her eyes were darting side to side, not knowing what was worse, the danger itself or the uncertainty of what was going to happen. The small man disappeared in the nettles as he settled down on his stomach

Rebecca thought it a bad idea but followed like a sheep into the slaughterhouse. The nettles were like fire on her forearms as she crawled along, wondering why she had left the paddleboat, and now she was wondering if it was Thabo the runt had heard. If that was true,

"Oh God, please don't let that nigger find us." she wept aloud. The canopy shielded them from the rain as they crawled away from the river.

"Shush!" Bill whispered to her over his shoulder. When he turned to scold her, he felt the water run off his back and down his ribs.

Ain't this gonna be a good day, wet like a mop. He thought about the wet clothes and how uncomfortable they could be.

The couple kept crawling forward as Billy tried to mentally figure a plan out. Each time they moved the small pins of pain shot through their exposed arms. *But I'm sure I heard voices,* he assured himself. A few inches at a time they crawled hidden from view of the trail as they snaked their way toward a small group of willow trees. They would listen and then crawl. Listen and crawl. Then the small blond man rolled over to see where his soon-to-be partner was only to be shocked that she was behind him. *Hell, I bet if'n I farted she'd be the first to smell it.* He chuckled to himself, forgetting the predicament they were in. Brought back to the realization that they were in trouble he motioned for them to move more to the right. More stinging nettles to pierce the skin! The pain was as if fire ants were all over the exposed skins, biting viciously into the soft skin of the humans. Bill looked back to wave. Rebecca was out of sight. It was a wasted movement for she was already hidden. Slowly the runt pulled Weatherspoon's knife out.

That's when he realized he had forgotten his ruck from the ship. *Too late now,* he thought. He was getting ready to dance with their aggressors if necessary. Lying quiet. The rain found them through a section of foliage. Dripping wet, lying in the stinging nettles, made the wait seem like an eternity. Then the noise came clearly. Voices. *I knew it! 'Cept they ain't talkin' 'Merican. What in the hell are they saying?* Bill froze; he'd heard that language before, even those voices. Foxes! *It cain't be. No shit! What did Crossed Lance say? Black something. Think! Think! Black Tail that's it, not that it matters that I know who's gonna kill us.*

Rebecca too had heard the sound. She was so glad that she had listened to the runt. *Maybe this small man has what it takes to make it to civilization.* The fear aroused her. *What am I thinking? Here are wild men coming after us, and I want to have sex! Stop it girl,* she scolded herself. But it only made her even more anxious to get the runt for his three in a row. *Stop! Stop!* She squeezed her eyes tight, trying to relinquish the tingling in her groin and breast.

The voices were upon them. She dared not look as they were walking right by the two whites hiding in the fiery stinging nettles.

They's walkin' right to us, he thought. *How can they know?* He recognized two of the four men; they were the ones that had chased him back when he'd blown up Ike's boat. There was also one he didn't and one black man! *Holy shit! It was Mohammad! How in the tarnations did he live? I watched him die! Ah, christ, we're in a tight spot!*

He was holding his breath, watching those wild-looking men walk right by them as their concentration was not on the floor of the small glen that the whites were hiding in. Mohammad was close behind, watching the warriors intensely.

Mohammad had survived just fine. After coming ashore and finding the game trail, he followed it to the Foxes village. There he did a few parlor tricks convincing the natives he was a god from far away, searching for the death of white people everywhere.

The chief, He Who Walks Quietly, was confused at first. Why would this dark man come to him? If he was a spirit, then he would need no help killing the simple whites.

The senior warrior, Black Tail, spoke a few words of American he had learned from the prisoners they had tortured, so after listening to Mohammad, he spoke to He Who Walks Quietly,

"The god must get to the white man's settlement so he could continue his revenge for the ones that tried to kill him." Mohammad had no idea that Sheila had died and Bill had jumped ship. He had no idea he had walked right past his prey.

He Who Walks Quietly spoke to his tribesmen, "Take the dark spirit man to the white man settlements." He looked Mohammad's face as his mind raced, *This dark man had done many things that no man could do. He's made objects disappear, and then he would pull them from a child's ear. How could this be? No man could do these things, so he must be a spirit and treated with great respect. Who knows what he could do if he became angry?*

Black Tail and his companions traveled in a loosely formed line with Mohammad bringing up the rear. They all stopped as the leader barked and grunted to a younger man.

"Are you sure you saw someone on the bank?" Black Tail asked.

"Yes, I'm sure. But we passed them up before I could stop you." Blue Bird answered.

"We should be getting close to where they should be." Blue Bird spoke, unsure of his decision.

"Listen. Did you hear that?" Crushed Hand whispered to Small Otter.

"What's that? Did you hear voices?" Black Tail asked.

"Yes. It was coming from the river. It looked like two of the white people. Ha! Those whites are not too smart on the land. They fire the guns then run like squaws!" Blue Bird laughed.

"Yes. They do not fight well." Black Tail conceded, forgetting the embarrassment they had received from Billy not so long ago. If there were whites, that meant captives. The women would get prisoners to torture. They would get honor among the others for such a gift to the tribe. The dark man's journey would have to wait a little longer.

"I hope there is a girl. I have not had a white woman in a long time." Crushed Hand moped.

"You can't do anything with the woman you have at camp. What makes you think a white woman would be any different?" Blue Bird taunted his crippled friend.

"Stop your bickering. If there is a white woman, we will all have some fun before she goes under the knife." Black Tail instructed his friends.

Mohammad had listened to the bickering, not understanding the grunts, barks, and whispers of their tongue. He just wanted to get his revenge. *If it means I have to travel with a group of savages, then so be it. This small one in front of me has said nothing since we left the village. This one is shrewd. Walks quietly. Yes, this one is one to watch for later.*

It was like Small Otter had heard Mohammad thinking. As

he turned to look at the dark man, a small smile crept across the thin lips.

A chill went down Mohammad's spine as the small man returned his attention back to his trail. All along the trail, Small Otter was listening to his older friends tease one another. That was fine by him. *Better they tease each other than to tease me. Black Tail is getting sloppy on this thing with the dark god. All of them have been carrying on like meadow larks since they left the camp this morning.*

Bill couldn't believe these warriors were jabbering like jays as they walked by. But most of all, he was shocked at the sight of Mohammad. *No matter,* he thought, as long as we get away, *I don't give a good goddamn what they do.* He watched as the procession walked on. Then he realized what they were doing. *They're lookin' for our footprints! Oh shit! I didn't even think 'bout leavin' footprints. These people track fer a livin'.* He panicked. As the warriors turned out of sight on a bend in the trail, he motioned to Rebecca to get up to follow him. Sticking the knife in the sheath, he got to his hands and knees. Looking back to see where Rebecca was, he felt relief when she was still right behind him. The young girl was mimicking the small man as he arose to his feet.

"Let's git!" he whispered. Off they went at a full run. He thought for a moment that the girl would slow him down. It wasn't to be. She was right behind him as they ran down the trail. He ran out of steam quickly. He began to pant as the pace slowed. His mind was telling his legs to go faster but to no avail. His quivering legs had gone too hard too quickly and were now refusing to be punished any further.

Rebecca watched Bill run. *This would be funny if it weren't so pitiful,* she thought. Her legs and lungs were beginning to warm to a comfortable lope when Bill had begun to slow down.

It figures, she thought. *Now the red men will surely catch us.*

Bill heard them hollering. He then remembered his ruck from

the boat.

"Ah shit!" He panted, realizing his mistake, "I fergot my ruck by the river!" he spoke over his shoulder to Rebecca.

What a dumbshit. I can't believe this. Rebecca thought as she watched him ahead of her. Bill rounded the next corner where he could see two canoes pulled up on the bank. The only problem was the small painted man standing next to the water's edge. Luck was with the white people today. The guard was looking out over the muddy tributary, oblivious to the oncoming whites.

Seeing an opportunity to get away, the runt barreled into the unaware warrior at full speed. Well, as fast as he could go at this time, knocking the small man to the left into the muddy stream.

Arms and legs flaying, the warrior had no idea what had happened to him. As the warrior thrashed in the water, the white man ran over to the nearest boat, pushing it out into the water. It floated away slowly as he looked at Rebecca. She was watching to see what he was doing, and then she realized that he had saved them once more.

The couple pushed the front of the second boat into the current, away from the fallen man in the water as Rebecca matched his speed. The water got waist deep.

"Okay. Hop in!" he called in a panting voice. He hopped on one side, she on the other. Rebecca was like a yearling doe jumping over a fence. Bill, on the other hand, was like a bull in a china closet struggling to not flip the boat as it crept into the channel, pushing them farther from the bank. He looked for the first boat; it was at least a hundred yards farther down the river heading for New Orleans.

CHAPTER 56

Brave Dog had no idea what had just happened to him. One minute he was daydreaming about his girlfriend, Brings Water, and then the next he was waist deep in the water. His feet were securely entrenched in the deep gooey mud of the tributary. As he turned, he saw the small white man and a woman with red hair stealing their canoes.

"Hey! Bring back my boats!" He was screaming at the pair as they floated away. Then the small man in the boat waved at him like they were good hunting friends. To make matters worse, Black Tail, Mohammad, and the others arrived from the hot pursuit. Mohammad couldn't believe his eyes. There was the runt and Rebecca! He must have walked right past them.

"Auggghhhh!" he let out a deep roar that shocked the warriors to the point of stepping back, their jaws agape as they stared at this dark spirit. Seeing the spirit was angry, they too began yelling and taunting the whites to come back and fight as men. It did no good; soon the thieves were out of sight. After the shock of having their boats stolen had worn off, Black Tail looked at Brave Dog as he clambered up out of the stinky mud.

"What happened? I thought you were guarding the canoes?" he asked sternly.

"I was looking the other way. How am I supposed to know you were chasing a pair of white people? One moment I was standing here, and the next I'm in the water! Stuck in the mud! Do not accuse me of doing wrong. You're the leader of this hunt. How is it a small white man and a redheaded woman can get the best of the great Black Tail?" Brave Dog spewed.

He was tired of being thought the fool by his kinsmen. Just because Black Tail was his oldest cousin didn't make him the best. Many a time Brave Dog had outhunted and outran the older man. He knew soon he would be leading his friends on a scalp hunt of his own, and then Black Tail would be at the camp with the old men. Brave Dog was sure Black Tail was going to strike him from the demeanor of his stance. He was hoping he would, for he felt confident that he could best the older warrior.

"Be careful Brave Dog. He's not in the mood for us to tease him now. Let's go." Crushed Hand pulled his friend away.

They all turned to leave as Mohammad turned back to the water.

"If I found him once, then I'll find him again." he spoke quietly, and then he turned to follow the warriors back into the thick forest. *No Sheila? Hmm?* He turned once more looking at the river. But to his surprise, they didn't return to the trail. They were heading back to the Foxes' camp! *We must be going back to get more boats, so I can track down that worthless infidel,* Mohammad's mind raced as he had no idea what waited for him back at the camp.

CHAPTER 57

When they returned to the village, the chief, He Who Walks Quietly, was taking notice the dark god was still with Black Tail.

"How is it the dark god is still with you Black Tail?" Before he could answer, Brave Dog piped up, "He let our canoes get stolen by a white man and his woman with fire hair!" With the quick statement, Black Tail snapped his head at his cousin, quickly giving him a stern look. He couldn't strike him in front He Who Walks Quietly, so he bit his tongue. *Soon Brave Dog will know better than to speak out!* he thought of the punishment he would give his relative later.

"How is this? You lost your boats, and now you still have the dark god to deliver!" He Who Walks Quietly was showing fire in his eyes as he spoke with a firm steady voice.

Then the mood slowed as He Who Walks Quietly surveyed his position with his people. Showing anger was a sign of weakness; to be levelheaded all the time is what his people expected of him, not a young hothead like Black Tail or Brave Dog.

He looked at the party before him, his eye softening as he thought about his next move.

"Let us smoke and see what we shall do next." Then He Who Walks Quietly turned to his wooden lodge, he pulled the deer skin door to the side and vanished inside.

Mohammad looked at the lodge. *I've seen this kind of hovel before.* He quickly measured the lodge in his mind, *a low roof, about six foot tall. Interlocking round logs notched like the homes of the town people. An angled flat top roof with an animal skin covering the door way. They have left me with the bumbling leader, he is being punished for his failed mission. So pathetic these savages.*

Black Tail knew what smoking meant. It meant hours of doing nothing while He Who Walks Quietly listened to all sides of the story. He liked to smoke as much as the next man, but the small one and his woman were getting farther away as they wasted time here.

Black Tail motioned for Mohammad to stay outside as they entered the lodge of He Who Walks Quietly. His youngest wife, Red Fish, was serving a boiled venison stew as the guest sat around the small fire, waiting for their turn to speak.

"So, Black Tail, tell me, how is Morning Dove these days? I noticed she's not with child yet. Are you waiting until the time when the ponies grow lean?" He Who Walks Quietly lit his pipe, drawing it smoothly as he watched the younger man's eyes. He knew Black Tail didn't want to be here, let alone sit and smoke with an old man.

"I, we, have been trying every moment I'm in camp to conceive. She still has nothing to show for all our efforts. Owl says I'm too anxious and I should let things happen as the Great Father sees fit." It came out so quickly he didn't realize what he'd said until it was out.

"Yes, that's happened to me before." He Who Walks Quietly chuckled aloud, "I think it was Runs Like Water or was Sparrow Woman? Ha-ha! I don't remember. They are both too much for an old man like me. Perhaps you'd like to try with one of them? I do not mind. Never mind, I'll send Sparrow Woman to your lodge this evening to help out." The old man smiled as he lit his pipe again.

"Now that's settled, here, smoke nephew." He Who Walks Quietly was not his uncle; it was a way of showing respect. The pipe came around the fire to the older warrior; he took a deep pull on the sweet tobacco, blowing the smoke to the north, east, and west before passing it to Crushed Hand. It galled him that He Who Walks Quietly made such gifts for him. Now he could not speak out against the leader.

"Wait a moment." He Who Walks Quietly spoke.

"Red Fish, come here child." Red Fish was far from a child; she had celebrated her twentieth winter already and had given He Who Walks Quietly a fine son two seasons ago.

"Sit down here beside me, my wife." The raven-haired slender-figured woman sat next her husband chief, wondering what his request would be.

"Would you be kind enough to bear Black Tail a child? It seems Morning Dove cannot conceive." She was surprised at the request. She'd been listening discreetly, following the conversation, and she knew that Sparrow Woman was getting too old to conceive. She knew that Runs Like Water hated Black Tail from many seasons ago when he courted her and lost favor with Runs Like Water's father.

"Yes, my husband." she spoke as she looked at Black Tail.

"Shall we do it now? Will you mount me as a pony? Or would you like to go back to your lodge and have Morning Dove join us?" This was happening too fast for Black Tail. *One moment I was seeking revenge, and now Red Fish is opening her legs for me.*

The other guests watched his face; they knew he couldn't say no to either question. Black Tail was in a predicament. On one hand, if he turned Red Fish away, it would be an insult to He Who Walks Quietly. Then on the other hand, he would be thought a less man for turning down this attractive woman. Some might even say he had no seed at all. They would say he likes men, not fit to lead a scalping party.

Blue Bird sat quietly as did Small Otter. Each looked to Crushed Hand. Crushed Hand knew it would bad for him when it was all over; He Who Walks Quietly was all but openly chastising the older warrior.

"I will mount you here for all to witness that I have a strong seed!" He quickly stood, pulling back his breechclout as the guest moved away to give him room.

"Ah, I see you are anxious. Wouldn't you care for something to eat first?" He Who Walks Quietly smiled at the man as his penis was hanging out for all to see. As he became aroused, its dark brown head began to reveal itself under the long foreskin. Red Fish had made no move to accommodate the older man as she watched the man preparing himself for sex.

"Yes, I will eat, then mount your wife." Confusion was setting in to Black Tail as the turn of events left his head swimming. One moment he was ready to mount the wife of He Who Walks Quietly; then it was back to eating and smoking. A scratching on the lodge door was a signal someone wanted in.

"Small Otter, let the guests in." He Who Walks Quietly spoke quietly. The door opened slowly, and in walked Mohammad. He had been quietly waiting outside. The others entered behind him; Morning Dove, Sparrow Woman, and Runs Like Water. Black Tail felt no comfort seeing his wife. She would know soon enough what was going to happen, and this was going to be tough enough on the warrior. Morning Dove looked around as she sat on her plump legs, politely averting her eyes from the men in the circle.

"Dove." He Who Walks Quietly spoke to her, "good news, Red Fish has agreed to give you a fine child since you cannot conceive."

"Thank you, He Who Walks Quietly. I'm honored for you to share such a wonderful gift with my husband and myself. When are we to get such a present?"

Morning Dove had no love for Red Fish. Many times they had had harsh words between them. This must be Black Tail's punishment for failing on a simple quest, It was the only thing she could think of. She lowered her head but not her eyes. Hatred for Red Fish is all she could see at this moment.

"We shall witness Black Tail mount her after we've eaten this fine meal she's prepared for us. Black Tail, ask the dark god if he wishes to mount any of these women." As He Who Walks Quietly waved his hand toward the women, Black Tail nodded.

"You want woman?" Black Tail waved at the women sitting before them. Mohammad looked at the savages before him; they were distasteful lot; fat one, attractive one, and old one. But the one who got him excited was Small Otter; yes, that one was very nice.

"Tell your leader that the women are good, but I want the small man there." He pointed to Small Otter. No one knew that Small Otter understood American. He had painstakingly learned it from the captives that had died under his knife, but he kept it his secret. He knew what the dark god wanted. He would be put under the knife before he let a man have his way with him.

He Who Walks Quietly smiled at the request.

"I see. Then he shall have Small Otter." He turned to Small Otter.

"The dark one wants to ride you like a pony. You are to be honored at such a request."

"Thank you, He Who Walks Quietly. I'm honored he chose me over everyone else. I will do whatever is requested." He bowed his head, but Small Otter already knew where he would go and live. He would not be here in the morning when the camp awoke. He knew he'd be an outcast, but so be it. West he would go, to a new land away from his friends and family.

The night unraveled like a flower seeding itself in the spring wind. The meal came to an end as Black Tail knew what would be next.

"The meal was very good, Red Fish. Do wish to be mounted now?" He Who Walks Quietly asked.

"Yes, my husband." Red Fish stood and untied her white doeskin dress, letting it fall to the floor of the lodge, until all she had on was her beaded moccasins. Morning Dove stared at the younger woman's figure; slender with firm breasts that did not sag, her hair, thick and full. Red Fish stepped and backed away from the circle as she looked back at the robes scattered on the dirt floor.

"Do wish to mount me now Black Tail? I am waiting." She had no emotion in her voice. It was something that she must do. No pleasure was to be had from her, and she'd make sure of that. Black Tail looked over to Morning Dove. He saw her eyes, and it was as if a knife plunged into his heart. They both knew it was a sad day for them, but honor was honor, and this must happen. He walked over, pulling his breechclout aside, showing his rigid manhood. He was bigger than the average man, eight inches long and as fat as a summer squash. Mohammad missed a breath seeing the size of the man; he'd seen no other man as endowed as himself. Red Fish looked up seeing the size of Black Tail; her eyes bulged wide at the sight of Black Tail penis.

This man is too large for me, but I will not dishonor my husband by crying, she thought in anticipation of the man approaching her. Everyone's eyes were on the coupling.

Everyone but Small Otter. He was watching Mohammad, seeing his movements and his mannerisms. Looking for a weakness. Then he saw it; he stared at Black Tail's manhood. *Yes, that was his weakness, I'll use that later to either kill this man/god or find a way to dishonor him so he'll be cast out.* He realized he had thought that in American, not his native tongue. He'd have to be careful not to let it slip he spoke the language.

Black Tail put his hand on Red Fish's shoulder, gently forcing her to the robes. The men gathered close to watch, but the other women sat quietly off to the side. He Who Walks Quietly moved to the front for a better view. Red Fish lay on her back; she opened herself for the warrior before her.

This was new to her, being on her back with her knees up. He Who Walks Quietly had always mounted her like the ponies, which was from behind. There she lay waiting for Black Tail. With one hand on her knee, the other guiding the manhood toward her, she had become excited. She could feel her nipples tingling in anticipation of the great-sized penis approaching her. Black Tail was in no hurry.

I will make this one mounting no one will forget anytime soon! he thought to himself. He guided himself into the awaiting valley; the tip touched her lips as she shuddered.

Oh, hurry! she pleaded with herself.

Black Tail pushed slowly as the brown shining head entered her, pushing slowly until he was completely in. He knew she had to be hurting as Morning Dove had told him many times not to go all the way in as it hurt her too much, but this was going to be different. He eased himself out until he was completely in the air, then pushed again until he felt himself stop on her cervix.

Seeing her husband bury himself in Red Fish, Morning Dove thought, *She is a strong woman. I could not stand to have him all the way in. She must be in great pain.*

That was far from the truth. Red Fish loved this. Never before had a man, well, her husband anyway, do this for her. Then as she was relishing the moment, Black Tail pushed again but quicker.

"Ah!" came to her lips before she could stop herself. *That's what I want to hear!* Black Tail thought. Quickly, like a snake striking a field mouse, he backed out but not all the way. Then before she could ready herself, he rammed himself deep in to her. Her breasts went toward her head from the violent attack. Then as a bear would crush the head of an elk, he slammed into her time after time; because it was going so quickly, it was a blur to those watching.

In disbelief He Who Walks Quietly watched his wife being mounted like he had never seen before; looking into her eyes, he saw something he'd never seen before. *Pleasure, I see she's enjoying this too much. I will remember this.*

Sweating now from the rapidness of the coupling, Black Tail was dripping from his brow; Red Fish had a bead of sweat on her upper lip as the man increased even faster. The other men were in shock. They could do nothing like this, especially for this amount of time. As Black Tail rammed himself deep each stroke, her breasts flung toward her cherub face. In each stroke a small groan of pleasure came to her throat. She couldn't hold herself back any longer. Her legs came up as the strokes were being met, and she wrapped her legs around Black Tail as she achieved orgasm again and again.

Black Tail knew what he was doing too. As he felt her legs, he knew she was ready for his seed. One last stroke and then he plunged all the way in and stopped as he filled Red Fish up with his seed. Red Fish's legs fell heavily to the robes as she started to breathe again. The men all sat back and murmured to one another quietly.

"Never before have I seen such mounting." Blue Bird whispered to Crushed Hand. "Not ever." he replied."

"My wife, are you pleased?" He Who Walks Quietly asked quietly, seeing the glow on his youngest wife's face.

"My husband, only the flesh. My heart is for you only." she lied. She wanted Black Tail to mount her again, soon. The other women were jealous of the coupling, everyone except Morning Dove. She held her head high, knowing this was her husband, and yes, he mounted her the same way and brought great pleasure to her as well.

All were watching the two as they returned to their lives except Mohammad. He had watched long enough to be excited, but his thoughts were on Small Otter. He would show that young one how men were mounted.

"I am tired. We shall talk again tomorrow." He Who Walks Quietly spoke; the evening was over for the guests.

"Black Tail, ask the dark god if he requires a lodge for him and Small Otter."

"You sleep now?" Black Tail spoke, leaving the part out about Small Otter.

"Yes, I'll sleep now. When do I get to mount the young one there?" he said, pointing directly at Small Otter.

"Soon. I send." Black Tail answered.

"Small Otter, you will go with the dark god. Do not make him angry as we do not want his wrath upon us." He Who Walks Quietly spoke, smiling at Small Otter.

"He Who Walks Quietly, I will not dishonor you." Small Otter had no intention of letting this dark man violate him. So the night ended for the guests, but it was just starting for the men. Black Tail folded the flap open and led the procession out into the night air.

"You come." he spoke to Mohammad, pointing to a lodge.

"I send woman. Make fire. Bring robes." Black Tail pantomimed being cold. Mohammad smiled in anticipation. He could feel himself stiffening at the thought of the young man beside him.

"Morning Dove, go make the lodge ready for the dark god." he spoke with authority. It was all for show as she would have done it with a whisper as well. He watched her scurrying away, thinking about the child that would be in their lodge in the early spring.

"She say when you go." Black Tail spoke in his rudimentary English, pointing to his own lodge.

"How long will it be? I want the boy now." Mohammad answered impatiently. Black Tail knew Small Otter; he knew that it was not going to go well for the younger man, *I must try to make the dark god not want him,* he thought.

Small Otter decided it was time to reveal his secret, but before he could, Black Tail asked him English, "Does it still hurt when you water the bushes?"

"Yes." Small Otter answered in English.

Black Tail's head snapped at Small Otter. He had spoken English so fluently that if Black Tail didn't know him any better, he would have thought Small Otter was white.

"Um." Black Tail nodded, leaving the Arab out of the conversation on purpose. Mohammad caught a piece of the questioning; he thought he was being secretive hearing what he did. *I've known many a man that had died from such a disease.* He quickly entered into their conversation.

"Wait, I'm tired. I don't want the boy after all. Can we leave at first light?" Mohammad asked, avoiding the boy's eyes

"Yes. We leave sunup." Black Tail answered.

"Woman has lodge ready." He pointed to the empty lodge. Mohammad left quickly to avoid further questioning.

After the Arab was out of earshot, Small Otter spoke to his

older friend, "Thank you, Black Tail. I was not going to go through with it. It would cause shame and dishonor for me, but I will not be used as a woman."

"I know Small Otter. Nor would I." They watched the man leave into the darkness.

"When did you learn the white tongue?"

"I have known it for many seasons. I learned it from the men we tortured. I kept it as a secret, waiting for the right time to use it. This was the time, so I did." Small Otter spoke without looking at Black Tail; instead he watched the glow from Mohammad's lodge.

As Mohammad entered the lodge, he looked around at his surroundings. A few animal pelts on the dirt floor, a head of a coyote on one wall, and some feathers here and there.

"Savages. I've sold better people than these, but I do need them for now." The darkness enveloped the village as the fire burned out, leaving a serenity about the night.

What Mohammad didn't know was four slavers had accidentally stumbled upon him. From a distance they had watched Mohammad at the Foxes' camp. They had been traveling to St. Louis after a failed search for a slave that had run away from his master in St. Louis. They had been quietly making their way back to town when they saw Mohammad and the Foxes return to the village.

"We'll wait till the red niggers go to bed, and we'll snatch that fucker right out from under their noses." Billy Gaines laid out the plan. The three others nodded and settled in for the wait.

CHAPTER 58

"Any guards?" He asked his filthy black-toothed partner.

"Fuck no. These red fuckers ain't got no clue. Go tell Simon and Frankie we can get that nigger as soon as he's ready." Luke Finnegan whispered back. He never heard Billy Gaines leave. He was just gone.

In a brief moment they all return to spring their plan.

"Are you ready?" It was the whispering voice of Simon Breaker.

"Yeah. You got Frank?" He heard a murmur of acknowledgment from the darkness.

"We gotta be quick 'fore them red niggers wake up." Luke whispered back.

"I'll go in. Frank, you watch our back. Bill, you an' Luke watch out the sides. Ready? Let's go."

Then they were off. Frank Lisa stayed out of the light while Simon went in the door. Luke took up a position on the right side as Billy Gaines took the left. Simon's eyes were already accustomed to the darkness as he entered the dimly lit lodge.

"Have you found another man for me?" Mohammad said as he thought Black Tail had sent someone else. Then he realized it was a man dressed in store-bought clothes, not a buckskinned youth from the camp. Before he could react, the stranger was on him, wrestling him over to his stomach. Mohammad felt his hands pulled together as the man was trying to bind him. He was stronger than the raider though; he threw Simon off as he quickly got to his feet, crouched like a jackal, ready to fight to the death before he would be taken captive.

The raider lunged at him again as they crashed through the rotten wood wall of the old lodge. The village came alive quickly.

A shot was fired as Luke killed the first Fox warrior. Then another shot sounded as Billy Gaines killed another. With the surprise gone, Frank called out to Simon, "Come on, Simon, we gotta get quick!"

Realizing he would never get to take this man with them, Simon whipped out a pistol from his waist sash and shot Mohammad in the face at point-blank range. The back of Mohammad's head sprayed into the darkness as he died instantly. Simon stepped over the man as they hurriedly left the village.

"Augh!" Frank cried out as they retreated into the darkness's security. The raiders hadn't seen Small Otter; he had been checking his horse when the shots had been fired. The small man quickly ran to his nearby lodge to retrieve his bow and began sprinting to the old lodge. He got there in time to see the raiders shoot the black god in the face and then begin their retreat into the forest. As the last man was fading into the darkness, he knocked an arrow, aimed, and released in one fluid movement. The arrow flew straight and true as it struck Frank through the spine, punching out the front of his dirty wool jacket.

Frank looked down at the arrow sticking out of his chest. *Damn, this is where I die.* He was dead before he hit the ground. The rest of the raiders were gone into the night like ghosts. They had left behind four dead men though. Mohammad wasn't a god after all. Black Tail would never see his son being born, and Blue Bird would never see the next sunrise.

CHAPTER 59

The rain had stopped now, leaving a fresh smell in the air as Bill looked back at the small warrior he knocked into the water and waved good-bye.

The man was so stuck that he couldn't free his legs from the mud. As he struggled in the quagmire, the rest of the warriors came into view with Mohammad on their heels. They were all yelling, waving their arms, and screaming insults. The runt and the redhead continued down the tributary toward the Big Muddy. Bill was thrashing the water with the paddle trying to go faster, but all it did was make the small craft veer sharply. Bill was in his own world for a moment as his fear had become apparent to the vixen with him.

"White Man! Slow down!" Rebecca yelled at him.

"Match my strokes." she spoke calmly. As soon as Bill had slowed his strokes to match hers, the small boat straightened as they went into the main river. South, they went, but they kept the west bank close. Bill investigated the canoe to see a small parfleche lying in the rear of the canoe.

"Hey, lookie here." he called out as Rebecca kept the boat on course.

"What is it?" she called out over her shoulder.

"Hell, I don't rightly know." he answered as he slowly opened the folds only to see a goodly supply of jerked meat and some pemmican. He didn't know of pemmican, but he did know he was starved. There, in the canoe the couple enjoyed the first taste of the wilderness. *The venison got a different taste. It's some kinda strong compared to the tack I had on the ship, and this other stuff tastes flat-out awful.* He looked closely at it, seeing the small dried berries and grease that held it together. Rebecca, on the other hand, ate all she could without a murmur of displeasure.

"God, I needed that. Oh. Um. This is good." she voiced a final approval as the remaining jerky was eaten.

"Well, it weren't half bad. Them cake things might take a while to get useta, but I could. Get useta it I mean. There any left?" he asked as he looked at her back to see the hide food pouch fall to the floor of the canoe.

"Uh, nope. I finished off the last bit." she said as she licked her fingers clean.

They paddled for most of the day watching the sun begin its race to the western tree line. Rebecca was intrigued by Bill's statement of trapping for a living.

"So we're gonna go up the river to trap beaver?" she asked.

"Yeah, it was what Silas was telling me before he died anyway. Says if we go up the Missouri River 'till it stops, we can trap enough beaver to make a good living. Say sir to no man. Says the Blackfoot and the grizzly live there, but the Crows and the Flatheads are good to white folks." He looked at her back, waiting for a response, but nothing came back.

"I reckon we oughta pull in an' stretch a tad." Bill spoke as a command rather than a question.

Through the cattails, the small craft wove its way to the muddy shoreline. Rebecca remained quiet as she got out of the boat to help pull it ashore.

The day had been full for the two new travelers. All the killings on the paddleboat and bumping into the red warriors. Running for their lives, stealing a boat, and almost getting killed.

Then there was Mohammad.

"How long do you think we'll have before those Indians get a boat and come after us?"

Rebecca asked quietly as she waded in the water to the shore.

"Hell, they won't be after us." He paused.

"I can't believe Mohammad's alive. Christ, I thought he was dead." Bill spoke, shaking his head. She never looked back as Billy spoke of his disbelief. As he stood there in knee-deep muddy water her words made the young white man think.

"You know, you got a good point there." Bill stated while his mind was racing about the escape from Mohammad and the warriors. Would they get another boat and pursue them or cut their losses and return to where they came from?

"I think we should get back in this here boat an' paddle to the nearest town. I don't reckon it could be too far. I 'member seein' some places on the river 'fore we got to St. Louis. Then we could get some clothes. Might even look fer some work." Bill spoke quietly to the redhead, expecting to get more verbal abuse from the young lass.

"Do you think that those Indians will chase us into town?" she said, looking back over her shoulder.

"Nah. When we get to a town, we'll be fine." He spoke with authority. Bill wanted to make sure that Rebecca knew he was in charge, even though he wasn't too sure about his own orders.

Back out into the channel, the couple floated, paddling while they searched the shore for any signs of civilization. They meandered quietly along the river; Bill would look around behind them occasionally to see if they were being followed. The river's remoteness was all about them as they drifted farther away from the irate warriors, oblivious to the fact that the river dwarfed the small skin boat as the two continued south.

Rebecca swung around until she was facing the small man. Bill watched her as he kept looking at the shoreline, expecting to see a horde of angry warriors to come out at any minute to capture them. Rebecca broke the silence.

"I think I'll try to clean these stinking clothes. I know that they won't be good as new, but it will be better than they are now."

The red-haired lass undid the buttons on her shirt, pulling it off, revealing her dirty undershirt. Watching the runt, she pulled the soiled garment off as well. Sitting there naked from the waist up, she leaned over the side of the skin boat so she could scrub the linen shirt. Bill watched her sweaty, dirt-covered breasts sway to and fro, thinking about the red hard nipples just waiting for some attention.

"Damn, woman! Ya got yerself a fine set of tits there!" Bill spoke aloud as he pulled his cap off. Wringing it out, he laid it on the floor of the canoe. He ran his hand through his hair, combing it with his fingers, parting it in the middle, pulling the longer strands behind his ears.

"Well, thank you very much." With that she draped her shirt over the middle of the boat, turning her attention to her not-so-white undershirt. As she scrubbed, she paused, looking at the small white man. She had become attached to this runt, and it hadn't been that long, but he had shown some intelligence back when they stole the boat. She took the water-soaked undershirt and began to wipe herself off as she watched Billy stare. She washed her armpits, feeling the cool rag of a garment clean the sweat that had dried there. Her soft pit hair slowly became clean as she dipped the shirt, now washcloth, back into the muddy water as she rung it out a bit before continuing. She lifted each of her breasts up as she wiped the sweat from underneath of them, knowing Billy was watching the whole time. One by one she raised the red hard nipple to her mouth as she flicked it with her tongue. Knowing the runt was watching made it all the more fun, admiring her handiwork until she was satisfied with her cleanliness.

She spoke to Bill, "I'm not wearing this anymore." She let go of the undershirt, watching it float away in the swift current. One minute it was there, and then the muddy waters swallowed it.

Then she pulled the damp shirt on.

"Oh, this feels good." She only buttoned the bottom two buttons, leaving the top open for his inspection. Reaching down to the mud-caked shoes, she undid them one at a time. Knowing the small white man was watching her the whole time, she made sure her cleavage was visible. As the shoes came off, Bill saw the dried mud from the morning adventure caked in between her toes. He gazed upon this fair maiden as it came to him. That last night she was a fairly proper girl, working in a galley on a not-so-friendly paddleboat. Now look at her. The young girl was caked in mud from her knees down. She looked at Bill, and slowly she reached to unbutton the dirty breeches. She pulled them off so all she had on was the linen shirt and her tattered bloomers. Leaning over to scrub the soiled breeches on the side of the boat, she knew Bill was mesmerized by her actions.

The white man couldn't help himself from staring at her bloomers. The red briar patch was still in his mind. Bill almost imagined he could see the red hair was trying to break out. As Rebecca scrubbed, she would hold them up occasionally, admiring her handiwork. When she finished, she laid them in the center of the boat, looking at the runt.

"I suppose you would like to see me wash these too." she said as she rubbed her hand on her dirty bloomers.

"Hell, I'd give ya a tongue bath if'n ya wanted one!" the lad blurted out.

"My! Aren't you anxious for some of this?" she spoke as she slid her hand under her dirty bloomers, leaning her head back.

"Oh yes, I think it would be a very good idea if you got some of this." Her hand moved under the almost-transparent garment.

"Well, if'n ya wanna. Do ya know how to turn this here boat around ? See that away ya could steer while I could get me a snack." Bill asked.

"Sure, I can do that. Take your paddle out of the water, and I'll show you how." Rebecca ordered.

Bill did as he was told as she had the small skin boat flipped around until she was driving from her end of the boat.

"Where'd you learn that?" the small man asked, puzzled.

"I haven't always been a working girl. There was a time when I did other things. Now let's see if you can do as you bragged." she teased.

Bill crawled back to where she was sitting, slipping and sliding on the slick skins of the canoe. Unfortunately Bill was not as graceful as Rebecca. As he went back, he caused the small craft to rock from side to side, and the bow lifted drastically. Water splashed in over the sides, drenching his hat as the runt made his way back to the now stern of the small craft. She tried to lean back with her legs flopped over the side of the boat.

"Goddamnit! It's a rockin' too much!" Bill whined.

"Forget it. It's not going to work. You'll have to do it later." Rebecca pouted.

With that she stuck her oar in the water to flip the small craft around until Bill was once more in the aft of the small skin craft.

Rebecca then pulled her bloomers off, spreading her legs wide, giving air to the private section of her body. The young man stopped paddling and stared at the maiden's red hair twinkling in the afternoon sun. Then she leaned over the side of the boat with the bloomers and soaked them as she did the undershirt. The runt watched as she brought the water-soaked bloomers back into the canoe.

"I'll wash this." With that she took the wet underwear and wiped down her legs and knees, slowly moving to her crotch. Once again the rag went into the water. This time she spread her lips apart as she wiped away the discharge from the day.

"I think that's good enough for now." She inspected her work.

"I won't need these again." She let go of the thin underwear into the cool water. It sank out of sight the same as the undershirt. Then she leaned herself back on the boat. Slowly she reached over the side, scooping a handful of brown water she dribbled it down herself. With eyes half open, she rubbed herself slowly. She was watching Bill as she slipped her fingers inside herself. Slowly at first then faster. Then her eyes went wide as she looked at him. She knew the small man was staring at her enhancing her experience.

"Oh, that was a surprise. I sure came fast that time. My, that was fun. I think I'll have me another one. No, I'll suck you off and get me a snack for my trouble!" Rebecca flirted.

"Will I be able to drive this thing with you back here?" Bill inquired.

"I mean shit. I'd like to squirt my squirt like the next guy, but I don't wanna go swimmin' to get it."

"Oh. I guess you'll have to wait then." Then she winked at him as she picked up her breeches, slipping them on.

"I could stand some new breeches lover." she commented, staring at the worn-out clothes, "I think I'll wash these off too." Then she hung her feet over the side of the boat, one foot on each side, letting them soak in the muddy water. She then pulled them back into the boat, admiring her feet. All the mud was gone, leaving them to dry in the morning sun.

"I'll put these on in a minute." she said as she was a putting her shoes in front of her. Then she swung around to resume paddling.

They came to a fork in the river, taking the widest one; and in a short time they were on the very widest section of the river, floating south toward St. Louis. *Damn, this is a fast river,* the young lad thought.

"You keep yer eyes open fer sand bars, snags, an' such things, hate to get grounded out here." Bill spoke aloud, remembering his short time on Ike's flatboat and how the pilot expertly guided the craft south.

On through the day they paddled. Bill turned once in a while to see if they were being followed. A blast from a riverboat just about made him jump out of the boat. Out in the main channel, the craft was steaming toward St. Louis. Her twin smokestacks were churning out black smoke like a forest fire. *Ah, those were the days,* Bill thought, *the good ol'days. Hard work, getting a poke now and then. Oh yeah, the murders I had been a part of. Well, there's no one to tell on me. Shit, everyone that knew anything is turtle food. Except ol'Hamhead,* the young white man pondered as they stroked on into the day.

The couple kept paddling into the early afternoon; Bill was daydreaming when they came around a bend only to see a small town materialized on the bank. The town was a little more than a few buildings built in a recess from the river. A small pier outstretched into the river, its gray shriveled wood bobbing in the muddy water from years of neglect, rough waters, and frequent storms.

"Well, it's time to go back to civilization." Bill brought himself back to realization, speaking aloud; he put on his hat while he scanned the decrepit dock.

"I'm not looking forward to this one bit. But it is better than killed by some pissed-off savages." she mumbled as they came up to the pier, its mooring swaying in the brisk current.

"Hold on. Let me get these shoes on." Bill stopped paddling for a stroke while she slipped her white feet back into the shoes. Bill couldn't help not to watch her breasts fight to get out of the linen shirt.

The couple slowly pulled up to the small pier. As they floated to the wooden structure, Bill reached out to hold the boat so Rebecca could climb onto the flimsy dock. He could feel the water-soaked casing moving as Rebecca's weight settled on the oak planking. She was making sure he was watching as she wiggled her rump at him. After she was on the dock, she squatted down right in front of Bill, her knees out. Her breeches were barely containing her crotch as she was looking up at the town while she held the boat as Bill clambered onto the pier.

"Hmm. I wonder what we're getting into lover. There ain't but a few shacks, not much to speak about?" he spoke as he finished securing the boat. Bill used the horse-hair rope that was tied to the front of the boat to lash the small canoe alongside of the pulsating pier. The young man got to his feet as he stretched, looking for his new challenges in this little community.

The couple headed for what looked to be the largest shack. He turned to get a last look at the boat; at least we'd have it for later. He wouldn't be too surprised if someone didn't steal it as soon as were out of sight. Turning around to face the town, Bill noticed a small weasel of a man walking up to them.

Closing the gap on the new travelers, the weasel smiled through his rotted black teeth, his unshaven face, and hollowed yellow creamy eyes from too much booze. The man had been devoid of any nourishment for too long, causing his clothes to hang from the small frame, giving him a ghoulish appearance.

Rebecca recognized the type of vermin that was approaching them. She had to service many of his kind. Smelly small men that hated everything better than them, whatever they couldn't get they stole. She noticed his right arm was behind his back with his left hand stretched out.

"White Man, watch for a knife." Rebecca said as she covered her mouth, faking a cough.

"Well, I've seen that trick used by them Irish folks. See they grab ya with one hand. Then they stick ya with the knife holdin' in the other. Then they say, 'Lookie here, this man's sick an' hurt.' Meanwhile they take yer money bag, leavin' ya fer the dead. That about the whole story, lover?" Bill mumbled as the weasel came closer.

"Yes, that pretty much sums it up, runt." she spoke through a big smile.

The runt reached out for the living plague's hand and started pumping it like the handle on a dry well. Then, sure as if it had been a well-choreographed move, Bill saw his hand coming around with the flash of steel heading on its way to his heart. Bill was fast but not near as fast as Rebecca. She reached out and grabbed his arm faster than a preacher taking your money.

"Now what are you going to do with this?" she asked him as she tightened her grip. That six-inch bone-handled knife fell to the wooden deck as the weasel's eyes went wide.

"Hey, let me go you stinkin' slut, or I'll have yer tits cut off to make t'bacy pouches!" he screamed.

"Maybe you can do that after you get out of the river!" She looked at Bill. He nodded, and the pair manhandled the weasel to the edge of the shaky pier. Together they tossed the poor excuse of a human into the fast-moving current. He hit with a soft splash going under then surfaced quickly. The would-be thief was screaming something about not being able to swim as they watched him bob up and down, fading from sight. Bill picked up the knife and handed it to Rebecca. She slipped it under her belt.

"Ya know, I be this ain't the first time this has happened to that piece of trash."

"It won't be the last either." she responded as they headed to the shanties up the dirt path.

The couple approached the first shack as another man appeared. This one appeared to be dressed better than the first portion of the welcoming committee, his dirty white shirt under a vest and waist coat jacket. His stomach protruded like he'd swallowed a watermelon, and his five-day-old beard looked like the south end of a northbound mule. To top it all off, there was the derby sitting on his head that reminded Bill of a huge nipple on a fat woman's tit.

"I see you met Elijah. He says he can't swim, but he's in the water more than a huntin' dog. I'm McPherson, the town constable. If you can tell me what's goin' on, I'll think about not arrestin' you an' throwin' yer ass in the jail." he spoke as he ogled Rebecca, undressing her with his bloodshot eyes.

"Well, it's like this. That piece of shit went to carve my liver an' my wife here", Bill gestured to Rebecca, "stopped him. We chucked him in the water to keep from havin' to gut him outright."

the young white man spoke as he watched the constable's eyes for recognition. The constable looked over to see the bone-handled knife under Rebecca's belt.

"You have his knife. I'll take it back for him, you know, family heirloom an' all." the constable spoke smoothly as his hand went out, waiting to receive the knife.

"I'll just keep it safe fer him." Rebecca spoke tight-lipped, not making any offer to hand over the knife.

"Humph!" McPherson huffed. He went on, "Well, I guess that'll be fine." McPherson turned to lead them into the town as he spoke over his shoulder, "You know what's best for you an' yours I reckon." He stopped and turned to the river, shading his eyes below his bowler. He looked at the skin boat tied to the wharf, shaking his head. Then his gaze fell upon Rebecca and Bill.

"Where did you come by that there boat, son?" he asked.

"We stole it off a bunch of Injuns up the river a while back. Why?" Bill answered coolly.

"It belongs to Red Bow. Well, that's what I call 'em. I cain't pronounce his Injun name. Big fella too." He held up his hand, indicating the height he thought the warrior would be.

"What side of the river did ya get it from?" he questioned.

Bill wasn't too keen on being interrogated, so he stepped toward the constable.

"What's it to ya?" Bill said through a thin smile. Rebecca elbowed Bill.

"Sorry for my husband's rudeness. If the individual is an acquaintance of yours, then you may tell him that we have it and are keeping it safe for him." The words flowed like fresh maple syrup on a hot day.

"Oh? He ain't no frien' of ours. Wears a red bow in his hair sometimes makin' him look like a queer an' all. Big fella." he repeated himself.

"Anyway he's been raidin' both sides of the river fer weeks.

He surely causes some real grief among us. I was jus' wonder how you came by it. That's all. Ah, hell, I don't rightly give a rat's ass of how ya got it. It's 'nuff that ya got it I reckon. Come on, I'll buy ya a drink." he said, leading the way.

Rebecca and Bill followed the fat man into the town, all three buildings; Billy noticed that no one came out to see the visitors. *That's strange. People always come out to see visitors,* he thought as they neared the end of their walk.

It looked like a store, a bar, and a stable. They walked through the doors and down the two steps into the bar behind McPherson. Billy noticed the doors were almost ready to fall off the hinges, but onward they went through the into the filthy lamp-lit room where two of the foulest women he had ever seen were sitting on the stairs leading to the open loft above the bar.

The women had low-cut dresses on with ample cleavage showing. *The nearest one seemed to be half nigger from her cinnamon skin and green eyes. Her eyes looked as soft as a kitten's tummy with a beautiful smile,* Bill thought. She smiled her smile of seductiveness to Bill as she gawked at Rebecca. The other had red hair like Rebecca only matted together as the Jamaicans' do. *She looks rough. Too rough* she thought. The whore knew it too as she made eye contact with Rebecca then lifted her dress to show her the wares to the visitors.

Maybe she's showing off to the white man? Maybe to me. Good god, we made a mistake coming in here. We'll end up fighting to get clear of this rat's nest. I'll bet that crotch hasn't seen sunlight since it was shittin' green, she thought as she continued behind the constable. Except for the barkeep and the whores, the place was deserted. A plank across two whiskey barrels made up the bar, and a few empty tables filled the rest of the room. Bill looked around room noticing the whore that was flashing Rebecca.

"She needed to soak in the river fer a few days that one does." Bill mumbled to himself.

"Hmm? What's that?" McPherson asked as he turned looking at Bill as they approached the bar.

"I was saying I could soak in a hot tub fer a while. We been travelin' an' could use something along those lines." Bill recovered quickly, looking at one of the two windows. The wavy glass hadn't been wiped down in years; spider webs adorned all the corners, giving the place a look of a jail.

Even with sawdust on the dirt floor, there was a smell he couldn't place. The barkeep did have on an apron of some nature. It was as filthy as the whores on the stairs, and it appeared he hadn't shaved in several years from the length of his beard.

"Don't mind Sally an' Melissa. They jus' want your coins an' leave ya with some present. Hell, I'm still itchin' from that dern Sally." McPherson pointed to the disgusting redheaded one that had several fingers deep inside herself, making sure the new guests got a good view.

The constable ordered to the man from behind the bar, "Mike, two whiskey fer these travelers."

As Mike was pouring, the constable felt it was necessary to tell whoever wanted to listen what had happened down at the rickety pier.

Rebecca didn't take her eyes off the whores on the stairs. She put her back against the plank bar while she turned to watch the so-called liquor being poured into the shot glasses. She had seen enough men killed from backstabbing to know better than to trust these desperate women.

Bill held the glass up as he looked at the whiskey as did Rebecca. He could see small pieces of debris floating in the amber liquid. She looked around the small room as she summed up their situation.

She quickly chugged it down, making a face as the whiskey burned her throat.

"This has to be the best whiskey I've had all day." Bill took her lead, doing the same. The fire went down his throat like a hot knife into his stomach. The brown liquid burned so bad it made his eyes water as he finished swallowing.

"We'd like a place to stay the night and a hot bath. Are there any rooms that are available upstairs?" young Bill asked.

"Yeah, it'll be five dollars each!" spouted of Mike from behind the bar. Rebecca saw the whores' heads pop up with the mention of money.

"We'll pass fer that price. Thankie fer the drink, but we'll be on our way." Bill wrapped an arm around Rebecca, heading for the door.

"Hold on there. There's a fee for tyin' up at our dock." Before McPherson could finish his sentence, she interrupted, "That'll be five dollars."

"Each." smiled the fat McPherson.

This whole town was a carpetbagger's dream come true. Bill commented to himself, *We gotta get out while we can or we'll be dead before sunset.*

Spinning around, he grabbed McPherson, catching him off guard. Bill pushed him across the room until his back was against the wall. Bill had Weatherspoon's knife against his throat.

At the bar, the poor excuse of liquor fell over, causing Mike to stumble trying to grab it.

As he righted the bottle, he produced a small pistol from under his soiled apron. Like a cat, she was under the bar before the gun could be leveled on Bill, snatching the ornate gun from Mike's hand in a heartbeat.

Mike had no clue what had just happened. One moment he had his French pistol, and the next it was against his head. Spinning Mike around, she faced the whores as Bill held McPherson.

"I see what we have here is a little welcomin' committee? I bet that there ain't no Red Bow. These here whores will slice my throat as soon as my money pouch can be emptied. Then the nice constable splits the coins an' dumps us in the river. That's the way

I see it." Billy spoke to Rebecca around the constable's fat head.

"Let's get. You might wanna bring that pistol jus' in case these nice folks wanna invite us to stay longer." Bill continued. Then as quick as a ghost she was under the bar with the barkeep in tow, the gun on his temple.

The runt kept the knife on the fat man's neck as McPherson was dragged up the two stairs. Bill glanced at Melissa and Sally to make sure the whores wouldn't join in the fight. Then he pushed the fat constable into the room, causing him to stumble as he staggered to keep his footing. Almost cascading to the floor, he spun around with unimaginable dexterity as he glared at the young couple, realizing he was going to miss the opportunity for piracy.

"You'll not live through the night. I guarantee I'll have every pirate on the river looking for you before nightfall. You have my word on that!" McPherson yelled, pointing his plump finger at the two.

"You go right ahead. We'll wait fer them in St. Louis." Bill shot back. They backed out of the bar with Rebecca holding Mike as a hostage. As they went through the doors, she let go of Mike and pushed him back into the room with her foot, causing the man to lose his balance as he slammed into the filthy constable, almost toppling them over.

Bill and Rebecca turned and began the sprint to where they hoped the boat was still tied to the gray pier. Luck was with them as the boat was bobbing like a cork in the water as they'd left it.

"Be quick there, lover." she spoke anxiously as she slipped into the small skin boat; she was cutting the rope with the newly acquired knife as he stepped off the pier to join her in the skin craft. The town faded away after a few strokes until the sty was just a memory.

"Shit! That place sucked worse than a two-bit whore on nickel night." She paused, turning to look behind them.

"It's been a while since I've been in a predicament like that."

The redhead turned back to Bill as she pulled the paddle to the left, Bill to the right.

"I don't believe I've ever seen someone suck me off poorly now that you mention it, lover. Anyway, the sun's almost gone. Hey, that means we're goin' to be sleepin' under the stars tonight. Hmm? Then I can get you to suck my piss'r like you was a promisin'." Bill reminded the redhead.

"Well, as soon as we hole up, I'll do you up a good one. How's that sound?" she answered from the front of the boat.

"Real fine." he replied as they paddled on. The sun hovered over the trees in the west as they continued to float down the Big Muddy. Soon navigation would be impossible, and Bill had no intention of traveling at night on the river.

CHAPTER 61

The sun dipped into the trees now with a false dusk upon them. They rounded a turn in the river only to see a small light up on a hillside on the west bank.

"What do ya say if we pull in an' give that light a try?" Bill questioned the redheaded helmsman.

"Sure." she answered as the sty came to mind. *Hope it isn't like the last place we pulled into.*

They pulled into some cattails and stashed the boat out of sight as they looked for the light. The couple walked up the greasy bank until it opened into a small wild grass meadow.

"Hey, looks to be a trail." Bill pointed ahead of the dimming light, so the couple proceeded until they stumbled onto a dirt road.

"This looks promisin'. Keep that pistol handy and let's get 'fore it turns all the way dark." Bill motioned to the vanishing light. They walked in silence as a small white-picket-fenced yard came into view. They marveled at a piece of civilization in the wilderness.

"Hello, the house!" Bill yelled. Out came a man old enough to be his grandfather dressed in blue bib overalls and a dark striped shirt. Rebecca kept the pistol in her hand but behind her back as they waited for the greeting from the man.

"Hal'lo thar ya own self. Welcome to the Beck's. That's me." He turned toward the house as he began hollering.

"Get yer ass's out here goddamnit! Be friendly to these folks!" There was no movement in the dusk. The old-timer turned back to the house.

"Now goddamnit! Shit, kids these days. When I was a kid, I woulda got my backside tanned fer bein' rebellious. You'll have to 'scuse my girls. They's a bit shy." he apologized quietly. Slowly one girl then the next came out.

"This one's Mary Beth. That tall one is Ann." he spoke as his mind kinda drifted off. The girls were dressed in cotton dresses, low cut in the front and so short the bare butts could be seen. Rebecca slipped the gun in the small of her back.

Bill turned to look at Rebecca and she at him. Bill stuck his hand out to shake the daughters' hands. They took turns shaking Bill's hand with enthusiasm of a preacher at a spring social.

"Pleasure to meet ya." the tall one spoke in a husky voice. This girl was at least a head taller than Bill. Her coal-black hair fell across her brow, covering her left eye. Her stunning features were masculine; her full lips looked to be as desirable as Bill had ever had the pleasure of kissing. The other did a fake cough to get Bill's attention.

"Hi." the blonde-haired girl spoke silkily. The runt stared mouth agape at the large-breasted blonde girl; her impish smile set the tone for what she had in mind. Bill's eyes drifted down the front of her dress. All the buttons were missing, open at the top, exposing almost all her breasts for the young lad. That's when Bill noticed that the tall one's hand lingered as she shook with Rebecca's.

Bill remembered the Foxes that he and Rebecca had stolen the boat from. Shit, she could pass for one of the red niggers. He looked upon Mary Beth. Her hair was the same as Bill's, straight and blonde, but she was a tad pudgy and no taller than Billy himself. *I bet Ann got a black briar patch thicker than a wool sweater. Maybe I'll get a chance to take a peek tonight,* Bill thought as he disrobed the two with his eyes. He was brought back to reality when Mary Beth squeezed his hand.

"Ever since Momma pass'd Daddy ain't been right in the head. Sometimes he kinda floats off like that." Ann said when she noticed Bill was watching her father.

Bill looked at the shack they called home, the once white wash was almost gone, the front porch looked to be in fine shape. They walked into the house in single file, he noticed that there was very little in the house. Not at all like the place he had been raised in. Mary Beth excused herself; Ann stayed very close to Rebecca.

Damn, she's got a thing for Rebecca, he thought as Mary Beth came back while Mr. Beck just went out to the front porch to sit. He never spoke to anyone as he walked by. Plopping down with a sigh on a high back rocking chair by the door, he just sat staring out into the night.

"He do that's all the time?" the white runt asked.

"Yes he does. I have something I'd like to show you." Mary Beth asked with her head hanging low in an innocent manner.

"Sure. Hey I'm gonna go see what she's got back there." Bill said as he followed the blonde girl behind the blanket wall.

"Oh, take your time, Mary Beth. I'm havin' a wonderful time with Rebecca here." Ann's voice was smoother than silk.

They had barely got behind the curtain that separated the bedroom from the front room when Mary Beth turned, throwing her arms around the to-be trapper. Her dress hiked up revealing her plump butt; and then she began to kiss him, forcing her tongue deep into his mouth, catching him off guard.

"Whoa there, girl." Bill pushed her away, panting.

"My wife's right out there, ya know, an' I'm kinda of partial to her." Bill used false concern.

"Don't you worry 'bout your wife. Ann's has a thing for girls."

The white man turned, peeking out from the side of the curtain. Sure enough, she had Rebecca pinned against the wall in the small room, kissing her like there was no tomorrow.

"Hmm, if that don't beat all." Bill spoke aloud. Mary Beth pulled Bill's mouth back to hers. Her tongue continued to ravish Bill's. His hand slid down her back until he cupped her butt cheek. She wrapped one leg around him as they continued kissing. Bill pulled her away.

"What's down here?" His hand slid along her hip as it journeyed to her open crotch.

"It's my pussy. Stick your fingers in it." As Bill complied with her, he brought his mouth back to hers as he fingered her. She started squirming, and then she began thrusting forward as Bill met her strokes. Then she bit Bill's lip as she climaxed.

"Goddamnit. You bit me!" Bill exclaimed as she giggled.

"Come back to me after everyone goes to sleep." Mary Beth requested.

CHAPTER 62

The rest of the evening they sat on the front porch; Bill, Rebecca, Ann, Mary Beth, and Mr. Beck. The two travelers told of the adventures they had had thus far. Ann had cooked up a batch of biscuits and rabbit for everyone.

Bill chewed on a biscuit and thought, *It's strange that Mary Beth hadn't said a single word since we've been a sittin' here.* It became late, so everyone bid their good nights as Bill and Rebecca took to sleeping on the front porch. Bill had no intention of missing a good poke, so after the house had become quiet, he whispered to Rebecca, "Hey, you awake?"

"Yes." she whispered back.

"Is Ann coming to you tonight?" There was a long pause.

"Yes." There was no wishy-washy answer. Just a plain yes.

"I'm going for a poke with Mary Beth. I'll be back 'fore dawn." With that Billy leaned over to kiss her. As their lips met she wrapped her arms around Bill, pulling him close as she fished for his last meal with her tongue. As she let him go, she pulled him back, putting her lips to his ear whispering, "I want you now."

"I thought you was gonna be with Ann." Bill quizzed.

"I am. But Ann doesn't have a root to slip in me, and besides, I know you can go three times, so load me up. Oh, I just thought of something. Won't she be surprised when she goes for a snack and get a load of you? Oowwee! That's going to be a hoot!" She giggled into his ear.

Bill pulled his now-hard carrot out the front of his breeches as Rebecca pulled the pistol and knife out and laid them within easy reach. Then she pulled down her breeches, lifting her legs up to expose the garden Bill had become so superb at planting.

The young man stroked. Rebecca lay still as she climaxed quietly, waiting for the blond man to leave her a present.

"Here you go lover." Bill whispered as he filled her garden up with the seeds of life.

"Give her a good time." Rebecca said as she slithered into her breeches.

Bill said no more as he fastened his breeches; he began the journey inside as he listened for the snoring of the father. Satisfied there was no one about, Bill crept to the door. He pulled it open slowly, waiting for it to creak, but no sound was to be heard. *Sneaking is the key here 'cause Ann's cot is right next to Mary Beth's.* When he was close enough to see the outline of the black-haired one, he leaned down to her face waiting for Ann to wake. It wasn't long.

"What do you want?" she whispered.

"A kiss 'fore you go out to Rebecca." he asked, knowing he'd be denied. Bill was surprised when her arms came around his neck, pulling his mouth to hers. Her tongue shot in and out of Bill's like an egret snacking on minnows. Bill answered her kiss as he felt her hand going down into his breeches.

"I'll have these later." She squeezed his nut's sack hard. Bill's eyes went wide open when he realized she had been toying with him the whole time. Then she rolled off the cot and disappeared into the night.

Ann walked effortlessly out of the room to the front of the small house. Past her sleeping father, over the wooden floors that she had been born on, through the door she had run out of many a day to escape her father's molesting hands, past the dilapidated chair she sat on when she was a child, to find a not-so-asleep redhead.

"I see you're not sleeping. Care for some company?" Ann asked smoothly.

"What took you so long? I thought you weren't coming." Rebecca whispered in reply. Ann lay down next to Rebecca, reaching for embrace. When they found each other, their lips met as they began to kiss passionately. Rebecca felt Ann's thick hand slide down the front of her breeches, heading for Rebecca's moist garden.

"Don't waste any time with your hand, girl. Use your tongue!" Rebecca begged to her new lover. Ann was so excited about a woman other than her sister she complied exactly as she instructed. Rebecca felt her breeches being pulled down quickly, almost ripping them as Ann rushed to into Rebecca's honey pot. *I can't wait for her reaction when she gets a mouthful of the white man!* Rebecca was almost laughing aloud from the gag she was going to pull on this new lover.

Oh! This is going to be so good! I can't wait to bury my tongue up this redheaded whore's crotch! Ann's mind raced. Finally she got her breeches off and Rebecca's legs pulled apart. She couldn't see the valley of pleasure, but she knew where it would be. Not wasting time with any foreplay, she brought her face to the soft hair. When her nose touched the hair, she used her tongue to force open the lips. She drove her tongue deep inside as she wiggled from side to side.

What? This tastes like a man's cum! She lapped and sucked all that was inside of Rebecca. She felt a large glob of semen slide onto her tongue; she was going to spit it out but thought of a different trick. *Okay, if she wants to play a game, I'll give her a game!* Ann thought. She brought her face out of her crotch and pulled herself to Rebecca's face. She brought both hands up to her lover's face to hold her so she wouldn't be able to squirm away. As they touched lips she opened her mouth to receive Ann's tongue, not knowing Bill's seed was going be slipped in.

Oh, Bill! Rebecca thought as she tasted her lover's seed. This made her hot and more passionate than Ann could have ever done. Ann was surprised that it did the opposite on this girl. She expected it to be revolting to her, but it made her become as horny as a goat in breeding season. Rebecca wrapped her arms around Ann as she hugged her back, forcing her tongue deep into the black-headed one. Like a bucket of snakes, the two girls kissed and fondled each other. Ann wanted more of Rebecca's honey, so she forced herself from Rebecca to go back to the pond. Into Rebecca's honey pot she dove, ramming her tongue deep into the redhead as Ann worked her magic, nibbling on the button of life, gnawing on her sensitive labia, basically doing everything she could think of to bring ecstasy to this new girl as Rebecca came again and again.

"Enough! I hurt. Please stop!" Rebecca cried out.

"Here eat this then." Ann ordered as she wiggled up to Rebecca's face, forcing her black matted hair into Rebecca's face. The musky odor engulfed the redhead as Ann rocked forward and aft. Rebecca worked to bring a climax to Ann. Time after time Ann came into Rebecca's awaiting mouth. Rebecca felt the slippery cream of Ann fill her mouth as she sucked and chewed on Ann. Slowly it became lighter, showing the night was almost over.

"Come on, let's go down to the river and clean up before everyone wakes up." So the two strolled down to the bank hand in hand. Exhaustion was evident on Rebeccas' face as the dark circle began to form under her eyes. Ann was as fresh as the day before, showing she had been used to the late-night games.

When Ann got up to leave, that's when he felt Mary Beth's hand touching his backside. He turned as he began pulling off his thin linen shirt; Bill paused as he looked into the darkness. He saw her on the bed. The dim light revealed she was naked, only a wool blanket covering her legs. The runt unbuckled the belt and let his breeches drop to the floor. So intent with the thought of the up-and-coming events he'd forgotten Weatherspoon's knife as it clunked to the floor to join his breeches.

"I'm here." she said in an almost whisper. She kicked the covers off all the way waiting for Bill to crawl on. His hand touched her skin, as smooth as a mink. Not waiting any longer, she reached for him. Grabbing his pod, she began working him frantically.

"Whoa, there, that thing will go off if you're not too careful." Billy whispered. That didn't stop her one iota. While she was pumping Bill like a handle on a dry well, Bill brought his lips to hers as they began to kiss passionately. They kissed while the young lass pumped and strained Bill's manhood like the teat of a milk cow.

"Uh oh. The boat's pullin' up to the pier, an' it ain't slowin' down!" he whispered as he shot a full load into her hand. She then took the offending hand and rubbed herself with it. Then she pulled him on top of her. They were slipping and sliding around on that little cot like a cat on ice. In a short time it got a tad sticky, but that didn't stop her a bit. She was licking her fingers and French kissing Bill, making more noise than a dog with a ham bone. That's when Bill's hair stood up on the back of his neck.

"I heard some noise out in the front room." Bill whispered as a light went brighter in the other room.

"Jus' slip under the bed an' wait 'til my daddy goes back to bed." she answered. Bill grabbed his clothes and shoes as he rolled under the small cot.

The light got brighter when Mr. Beck entered the room with candle held high, her father walked up to her curtain and opened it.

"You okay? I thought I heard voices." She didn't flinch or cover herself, and she spoke in a soothing voice, "I woke myself up in a dream. Night, Daddy."

Then he went away, and the light went out. Billy rolled out and returned to Mary Beth to continued his lovemaking with the young blonde girl; he felt her slender hand grasp his once-again hard root. Mary Beth wanted to have more of the runt, so she proceeded to paw and jerk at his erect manhood with the vigor of a cat shaking a rat. Bill slid his hand down over her plump tummy going for the valley of life. Surprise came to him as he felt the wetness she was providing. *Damn! It feels like she jus' took a piss, but I know'd she ain't done that,* Bill thought. He slid his finger into the waiting void as she began to squirm. One wasn't enough, so two went in. Using his thumb on the button of life, he rubbed it with the same pace that she was using on his planting rod. One hand snaked behind his neck as the other continued to wreak havoc on the lad's root. Her back was arching as he worked the young maiden like a musician with a violin. Her enthusiasm was overwhelming as she pulled and yanked on the young man's flesh. Bill picked up on the spasms and inserted all his fingers now. It had no effect on the young girl as she rammed her tongue in and out of his bearded mouth. Pulling her mouth away, she brought her lips to ear.

"Use all your hand now!" She panted as she bit his ear. Not a nibble but a genuine bite to draw blood.

"Owww! You scamp! Here you go." he whispered in a harsh voice. Bill's hand was covered in honey by now, and it seemed there was no stopping this girl. So his thumb joined the rest of his hand, going deep into the young girl's cave. Mary Beth relinquished her grasp on his pod to aid him on his mission of ramming his hand into her. Obviously Bill wasn't going hard or fast enough for her, so her hand demonstrated to him the speed and roughness she wanted. It felt to Bill that he was all but punching her groin now, but she was lifting to meet every stroke now. Then she achieved an orgasm, viciously throwing her head back against the cot's hard surface, heaving and panting as Bill brought his hand out slowly. Mary Beth stopped his hand from retracting, pushing it in deeper as she whispered in his ear, "I have one more coming. Just go faster now!" So the runt obliged her by picking up the crescendo. Again her head went back as she rocked to and fro with a spastic climax.

"Pull it out slowly while you spread your finger." she spoke quietly.

"I want to feel all your fingers in my pussy. Make me feel them." she begged. Billy did as she requested. His hand spread as he pulled his slim fingers out, feeling the ribs of her birth canal. He removed his hand until the opening retracted to the original size of a young maiden in her late teens.

"I'll suck you now, now that I know you're not some Johnny come quickly." With that she unwove herself from the white man to put her face on his groin. Her garden was above Bill's face as she placed his pod in her mouth. Mary Beth was going through the motions of giving Bill oral sex now as she felt completely spent from the abusive hand sex she had just been bestowed upon, even though she requested it.

She didn't count on Billy wanting to continue. Bill brought his hands up to her rump. Reaching around, he spread the blonde girl open as he lifted his face to her now-seeping pond. Then she felt herself open as his tongue entered her. *Oh, this man's a bucket of surprises!* she thought as she plunged the garden tool deep in her throat. Down the tool went in her throat until her nose had his nut sack tickling it.

Bill could feel the young girl quivering as he worried his tongue all around the deep cavity before him. She continued with more enthusiasm now, aggressively forcing Bill's tool down her throat. When his sack was touching her nose, she would swallow over and over using her throat muscles to bring forth the seeds Bill had waiting for her. She felt her button being bitten and sucked as she brought her head up for a breath of air. As her mouth came off the shaft to get air, Bill unleashed a load of hot syrup into her mouth. Before she had a chance to swallow, it shot down her throat with such force she gagged. He bit and pulled her button the same time as she couldn't believe she had come again and so soon. The young girl arched her back, forcing her briar patch into Bill's face as she took a breath of untainted air. She flopped down on top of Bill, breathing in shallow breaths as Bill rolled out from under her.

"Lookie here. I gotta get. I'll see you after while." Bill spoke into the darkness as he patted her rump. Picking up his breeches, he slipped them on, adjusting the knife to the side. Then he squatted down to locate his hat, shirt, and shoes only to find a puddle under the cot where this girl had discharged so heavily it had seeped through the cot and dripped on the wooden floor. With his shirt in hand, he slipped it over his head, pulling the hat on. He carefully slipped his shoes on as he opened the curtain to sneak back to the porch.

Creeping out of the back room, he heard the father snoring from the far side of the room. Relief washed over him as he slipped out the front door. Carefully he closed the flimsy door to not wake the old man, not that he could or would do much to the runt, but it would be an unneeded confrontation. He found the porch empty, no Rebecca and Ann; they must be out having a bit of fun too as he lay down for a brief moment of sleep.

CHAPTER 63

In the morning it was like nothing had happened that night. No forlorn looks, no quick pinches. Nothing. Rebecca came floating around the side of the house; her face looked like she had been in a fistfight from the color of the dark rings around her eyes.

"I see you're up an' 'bout." Billy chuckled.

She looked at him then looked around before, leaning over to him.

"That girl has a wicked tongue. Goddamn. I musta came five 'er six times to her once. I mean she didn't stop. She told me you were in with the other one and she wanted fair time." Rebecca stooped down to retrieve the gun and knife. She carefully placed them in her belt as she looked out onto the river.

"You're okay with what happened?" Bill asked.

"We're supposed to be married, but we're not, right?" she spoke as she tilted her head quizzically. The morning started as it would on any small working farm. Mr. Beck went out back to do chores, and Ann walked out to the chicken coop. They could hear Mary Beth in the house rattling a few pans. The door opened as Mary Beth walked out, a fresh look on her face, almost glowing.

"I have some biscuits cooking. As soon as Ann returns with the eggs, we'll have them as well. That okay with you?"

"Sounds perfect to us. May I help you?" Rebecca asked.

"No, I'll take care of it. The biscuits are almost done, and as soon as Ann gets back with the eggs, we'll be ready." Then she turned to reenter the house. Bill and Rebecca sat on the porch watching the distant river.

"Hard to believe so much has happened in such a short time?" she asked quietly.

"So much." he answered.

"Good morning, runt. Hi, lover." Ann spoke as she approached the couple with a small basket with several eggs showing. She leaned down to give Rebecca a passionate kiss, ignoring Bill's eyes. She walked into the house with no more conversation to either of them.

"Tell ya what, if it's okay with you, it's okay with me." Bill commented as he stood up and stretched. Mary Beth called out from inside the small shack.

"Okay. Come on in. The food's ready." The couple got up, exchanging looks as they walked in.

"Is your pappy gonna eat?" Rebecca asked as she saw only four plates on the rickety table.

"Nope, said he wanted to chop some firewood, and then he walked out. He's like that. Sometimes he don't eat fer a day or two." Ann answered as she sat next to Rebecca, leaving a space for Bill and Mary Beth on the other side of the long maple table. They ate in silence as Bill savored the hot food. When all the food was gone, Bill stood up and stretched.

"I'm goin' out back fer a while, you know, help yer pappy out fer the hospitality." He turned to go out back of the house to see if he could help their pappy.

Bill found the farmer cutting firewood for the up-and-coming cold nights.

"Ya mind if I do that fer lettin' us stay overnight?" the white man asked.

"Why no I don't. I'll go out to the west field an' pull some weeds if you're willin' to do this." he said. Then he just walked off. The morning warmed up fine as Billy chopped steadily; log after log was split and stacked next to the house.

He pulled off his shirt and hat as he kept working on the woodpile but he had a strange feeling someone was watching him. He had felt that feeling several times now and he knew enough to pay attention to it. When he looked around, no one could be seen, but it felt like he was being watched. Then he looked to an open window at the back of the house and saw Mary Beth.

That's where I got that feelin', he assured himself. She leaned out of the window, licking her fingers ever so slowly. In and out they would go. Each stroke she would wrap her tongue around a digit to show her intentions to the young white lad.

Well, she has the right idea away, he thought as he looked around to see if anyone else was watching. With no one in the area, he turned to say something but she was gone. Sticking the axe in the stump, he walked to the back door of the gray house. Up the two steps into the same room he had been in the night before, there she was on the cot. She leaned back against the wall, propping one leg up on the edge of the cot, exposing her blonde briar patch. Bill felt himself getting hard already as he stood there, viewing the young lass before him.

"Daddy's out in the field workin'. Your wife an' Ann went down to the river to swim." commented Mary Beth.

"Well, what are we waitin' fer?" Bill asked.

"I was watchin' you through the window you know. You looked hot out there workin'. I wanted to make sure I would be really ready when you noticed me." the temptress spoke through her full lips.

"I believe you're gonna have to put a towel on the cot 'er yer gonna get it soaked." He pointed to her endless puddle.

"How about a snack?" he asked as he approached her. She just smiled asking if her flavor would be good enough. Mary Beth was wet for sure. She had been thinking about having the young white boy ever since he had left her bed in the early morning. Good lord, she could feel herself oozing as he came closer. Bill pulled his hat off and got down on his knees as he lowered his face into her awaiting honey pot. At this particular time, it really didn't matter to him. After a few minutes his ears were getting a bit sore from almost being ripped off every few moments. After the last climax

Bill stood and dropped his breeches. Hearing the heavy knife clank of the wooden floor, he reached down to hold his pod for her. The beast was fresh, all ready to go for a couple quick runs. She leaned over to fondle the head. She grasped it, shaking like a terrier does a rat.

"What do you think of that?" she inquired.

"I don't believe it'll run away 'anythin'.'" He smiled back at her.

"Oh good." she said. She put the head in her mouth as her tongue wrapped around it. She lifted her head off, letting the spit dribble down on it. Then she flicked the tip with her tongue. Then faster than a snake strike, she swallowed his whole root right down to the short hairs.

"That thing is goin' to go off in a second you know." the white runt warned.

"I know." She pulled her mouth off, looking up at him. Back on the root she went. Closer. Closer. Billy went off, and she didn't miss a beat. She backed up as she stared at Bill.

"I know how to make it work again." she said. She grabbed his ears again, forcing his face back to work in the honey mine. Two or three minutes in the open air were enough to get Bill's manhood back up to operating fitness. Rolling her over on the cot, he pulled her rump up so both her doors were accessible.

"You can put it in anywhere you want whenever you're ready."

"Seriously?" he asked

"Umhum. Anywhere."

It was slippery enough to make the choice easy, so he slid it in the honey pot first. He pumped in and out as she was wiggling and sweating, so Bill pulled it out, aiming it at the back door. He put the tip on the brown rosebud and began to push slowly. The door opened right up. Slowly at first, then he was giving it all he had. She was wiggling so much Bill figured they would fall to the floor. It didn't happen. He slowly pulled it out looking down at the gaping hole he had just left. *This ain't the first time I'm a thinkin'*, he assured himself. There was nothing on his root, so he slipped it back in the gaping hole. As he was pounding away, all he could hear was the slapping of his baggage against the cheeks of her ass.

"Don't come yet." she said. She pulled forward, leaving him in the fresh air. *Damn, I jus' 'bout went off when the air hit this here stick of mine,* Bill commented too himself. Going to her back, she grabbed her legs, pulling them up to her shoulders. She pulled her legs behind her arms, so her arms were free to press the button on the top of that soft pink valley.

"Now do one at a time." the contortionist spoke. Bill put the tip at the back door and applied some pressure, which wasn't very much, and it opened wide. After visiting for some time, he left, going to the front door. It was already open. She had pulled the soft red curtain back, leaving the door open for him to enter. She was using that button like she was kneading some bread dough.

"Eat it! Eat it!" she cried out. Bill needed no further encouragement as he went to the honey patch for a tasty snack. When she started quivering, her legs came down to wrap around his head. She was squeezing so hard Billy thought he was going to pass out.

"Fine job. Let me help you with that pecker of yours." Into her mouth it went all the way down until the baggage was bouncing off her chin.

"I'm ready to pop!" he said quickly between breaths. As he popped, she reached around, grabbing his bum. She kept sucking hard as the fire went out. She sat up and looked at him.

"You're a lot better than my daddy." she said.

"I'm younger." *That does explain how she is so good at what she does.* He stood up pulling his breeches up and fastening them while he looked at the blonde lass on the cot. She had reseated herself on the cot, spreading her legs, exposing her drenched genitalia as she pulled on the lips apart, making them lie flat to show her most delicate anatomy. The white man buckled his breeches and adjusted the big knife to the side.

"You know, don't get too many folks through here." she spoke as her fingers disappeared into the honey pot.

"Well, me an' Rebecca are gonna have to be movin' on today. We're on our way to St. Louis, so we gotta be a gettin'. Thankie ye fer the poke an' all." He grabbed his shirt and hat. He turned to the blond girl as he tucked in his linen shirt. He stopped and admired the landscape through the back door, the flowing grass of the field, and the rickety shed of an outhouse. He reached for his hat. He pulled it down as he pulled the hair behind his ears.

Her wet finger pointed at Billy.

"You'd better stay over again, or I'll tell you wife that you fucked me!" she called to him from her cot. Her eyes had gone to small slits, and her happy smile had disappeared.

"Go right ahead. We're still leavin'." the runt replied.

"I'll tell my Daddy you raped me!" she said quickly.

"I doubt your daddy can find his ass with both hands, let alone whip me fer forkin' your sassy ass." Bill chuckled. She was getting desperate. Bill surmised that she would be pulling a gun or knife soon to keep him from leaving.

"You'd better stay!" she screamed at him as he walked by her through the curtain into the front room of the small cabin. Looking at the sparsely furnished room, he figured it wouldn't be long before the pappy just walked away and never came back. When he pushed the flimsy door open, he saw Rebecca and Ann sitting hand in hand. They both looked up as he walked out.

"We heard it all. It's been real nice having you two around for a day or so." Ann said quietly. Reaching over, she put her hand behind Rebecca's head, pulling her close. She proceeded to tongue kiss Rebecca. When she pulled away, her cheeks were flushed.

"Thank you." Then she got up and walked into the house. Inside Mary Beth could be heard crying; Ann was telling her that there would be others.

"Let's get." Bill spoke softly to Rebecca. Rebecca thought, *I can't leave Ann behind. She means too much to me right now.*

Before she could change her mind, she blurted out, "I'd like to take Ann with us."

"What? We're going to be trappers up the Missouri an' all." Bill was definitely surprised by the turn of events.

"We still are. Just think if you have two women at your beckoning. Anytime too. Remember that we all can't be having our time of the month at the same time." she spoke seductively with her eyes half open.

"What 'bout their pappy? Who's goin'to take care of him?" Bill argued.

"Let's ask them." She stood up walking right past him into the house. Billy stood there on the porch, digesting all that had happened in a brief moment before following the brilliant redhead into the cabin. He pulled his hat off, running his fingers through his hair and then pulling it back on. He followed her in; as he entered, they all looked his way, waiting for the man of the group to ask the questions. Rebecca could see Bill wasn't too keen on what had transpired, so she took the lead on the matter.

"Girls, do you want to go with us and make a go of it, trapping beaver in the mountains? Say sir to no man and living on your own hook?" she spoke.

"I'll go." Ann said without thinking a lick. She turned and went behind the blanket curtain and returned with her thin blanket.

"I'm ready." she said.

"I don't know. What about my daddy? Can he come? Who will feed us? Will I have to fight Indians and skin animals? Will my daddy be safe?" As she spoke, he could tell she had no hankering to leave her place of security.

"See ya." The White Man turned to walk out. As he pushed the door open to walk out, he turned to see Ann kiss her sister for the last time. Then Rebecca followed her out. That was it. The last time he'd ever see that girl again. They all walked down to the skin boat without a word.

CHAPTER 64

"Where's the boat?" Ann asked.

"Right here." Bill answered as he pulled the boat out of its hiding place.

"You were telling the truth about stealing it from Indians! It's not very big, is it?" she commented.

"It's big 'nuff with a bit of room to spare." the runt responded as he began getting it ready for the newly formed trio. The runt pulled the paddles out of the reeds when he noticed Mary Beth walking toward them carrying a small bag over her arm.

"I'll go." she said matter-of-fact. No concerns of safety or food. *Just "I'll go."' Hmm, go figure,* Bill thought, holding the boat steady as the girls clambered in. After the last leg was over the edge of the small boat, he pushed it off as he slid into the front of the boat. Much more graceful than when they stole it from the Fox warriors.

Rebecca had taken the aft end to be able to guide the overloaded craft down the murky water of the Mississippi. *I don't even wanna know how this is gonna work. At least she wasn't bringin' her pappy,* he wondered.

"Did you tell Papa you weren't coming back?" Asked Ann.

"I told him me an' you was going away for a long time. He said okay. He said that he was going in to town to get some supplies then. That's it. That's all he said. He really surprised me. I don't know what to think. So here I am. Off become a trapper. I took what food we had left in the house. Daddy will have to do for himself now." As they paddled out into the channel, everyone was quiet. As the booshway of the newly formed brigade, the runt was thinking of how much money it would take to outfit them all.

All I know is I have three women to poke, well, two anyway. I don't know 'bout Ann. Her likin' girls an' all. Hell, maybe I can still get a poke in once in a while with Rebecca. Mary Beth is kinda moody. There's a good chance that I'll be plum wore out. He chuckled to himself.

"Hey, White Man." Ann said.

"Yeah." he answered, thinking, *This is where we get all the sleeping arrangements made.*

"Do you care for Rebecca? I mean I know you told us you were married. I know that isn't true. Will you, um, well, I was wondering, well, I like her a lot. I was thinking since Mary Beth came with us, you and her could be together and Rebecca and I could be together. If that's okay with you." she spoke in a firm voice, making sure there was no confusion on her request.

"To be truthful, me an' Rebecca are partners. We ain't got it all figured out yet, but that's the story. I know you have a thing fer her. I have a thing fer yer sister. We're all pretty open here, so this is what I'm puttin' out." Bill kept paddling, not looking back as he spoke. He'd have no idea of what their expressions would be with next part of the bargain he was about to put on them.

"I want a poke whenever I can get it. As it is, me an' Rebecca have been tagether fer quite a spell. What I was thinkin' is that if the situation presents itself to get a quick poke 'er a snack, then so be it. If it happens to be all four of us at one time, well, that's okay. If I'm a workin' an' you three want a rollin' the hay, so be it. Let's not get real attached so that we'll be a fightin' 'bout who screwed who, okay? How's that sound to you girls?" Bill kept paddling, looking at the shore, thinking about getting a poke whenever it worked out.

"Okay by me." Rebecca spoke out. *That's one,* Bill thought.

"I can do it with a man. Hell, you have to be better than my father." Ann spoke out. *That leaves one,* Bill waited.

"I can get it from whoever I want? You don't care if it's from my sister?" she asked.

"Sure, if she gives no never mind." he answered aloud.

"Here." She pulled out the meager food supply, passing the biscuits and jerked meat to her newly formed partners.

"Here Ann, I know you have a sweet tooth for this." She handed her sister a sugary biscuit.

"Thanks." *Well, this is going to be real different. Three girls with all different things on their mind.* He chuckled to himself.

"Okay, here's what's gonna have to happen. We get to some place where we can make some wages as it's gonna cost a lot fer each of us. I reckon I'll get a job on the docks. Maybe a eatin' places after hours. I'll try to make as much as I can. I figure we'll have to have a coupla hundred dollars apiece. Maybe more. It all goes inta the big pot. When we get 'nuff to outfit us all, then we'll get the hell out of here an' head fer them shinin' mountains. That's what I'm a thinkin'."

"We're going to have to whore, aren't we?" Mary Beth asked.

"Not this time. I have something much better than work." Ann said smugly. Bill craned his head around to see that she was holding a piece of paper.

"What's that?" Rebecca asked.

"The deed for my daddy's farm. Lock, stock, and barrel." she boasted.

"You can't do that!" Mary Beth screamed.

"That's Daddy's! It's all he has!" She was becoming frantic about now.

"Shut up Mary Beth! All he did was fuck us! Continually. We did the chores, and he fucked us. He fucked us in the mouth, the ass, and the pussy! Hell, anywhere he wanted to. All the fucking time! He owes us this. Either I took this or I was taking his life. I figure he got off easy! So shut up about it being his. Besides, I already got him to sign it." she bragged.

Bill turned back to the front of the boat. "Oh boy." Bill murmured under his breath.

"How did you get him to sign it?" Mary Beth was still screaming.

It must be quite a sight. Four people in a skin boat going down the Mississippi and two them yelling like they stirred up a hornet's nest, Bill thought, *oh yeppers.*

"I tricked him. I got him all worked up, and then before we went any further, I told him that I wanted the deed signed off to me since he was getting too old to run the farm. Hell, he was so horny by then he'd signed his own life away just to have a poke." She was laughing. *Well, I'm with a hellcat. That's fer certain an' fer true,* Bill thought.

It occurred to Bill that they were on their way as they were paddling down the west side of the river. *Damn, it hadn't even been a week since we'd skip the death boat. Now here we are going into the trappin' business.* Bill looked into the tree line, thinking about the savages and wild bears and such things.

The morning turned into afternoon as the girls and Bill paddled on. With all the food gone, he was becoming concerned as they traveled south. He occasionally pointed out of a paddleboat or turtles sitting on snags, anything to take their mind off being hungry. They rounded a bend when a small town came into view.

"Are you ready fer a stretch yet, girls?" Bill spoke without turning his head.

"I have to pee!" Ann said emotionless.

"Yeah, I have to water the bushes also. I figure this town should do fine. I cain't 'member if this place is Saverton or Petersburgh. Rebecca, which one do ya think it is?" he asked.

"It's Fort Mason." Mary Beth spoke up before Rebecca could answer, *she must know living in these here parts,* she thought.

"Let's pull in now so I can get the lay of this place for we go traipsing inta town with three women on my heels." Bill said, looking round the countryside.

The want to-be trapper paddled over to the shore, and he hopped out to wade up the slick bank. Bill, trying to be gallant, held the boat for Ann and Rebecca to jump out. They did just that, quickly wading in the soft mud up to the bank, but not Mary Beth. She made sure that she could step out of the skin boat without getting her feet wet. Ann and Rebecca were alike. Pants and shoes like a man. Mary Beth held on to her dress. *I reckon it'll be gone soon 'nuff.* Billy chuckled to his own joke.

CHAPTER 65

The small white man looked around on the bank for a suitable place to stash the canoe. His search was rewarded when he saw a dead oak tree that was lying half submerged. It would hide the small boat effortlessly. He began to drag the small boat into the broken limbs when Rebecca came to help. The two of them pulled and shoved until Bill felt the craft would be there for them upon their return, if they returned at all. Ann and Mary Beth stood by with their hands on their hips, watching the two strain to get the boat hidden. Not one ounce of help was offered by either sister.

"Well, that's done. I reckon we can head fer that town an' see what we can do fer supplies." The runt wrapped his arm around Rebecca's waist as he pulled her to him; burying his face into her neck, he nuzzled and kissed her. Rebecca lifted her head as he began to arouse her.

"Um." was all she could say. Ann looked on. Her face told the story, and she didn't appreciate the affection Bill was bestowing on the redhead one bit. The runt was satisfied that he'd pissed off Ann sufficiently and released his partner.

He spoke to Rebecca, not even acknowledging the others' presence.

"Let's head that way." Bill said, pointing across the small meadow; its long wild brown grass blowing softly in the early summer gave it the appearance of wind across the water. He paused.

"'Til we find a town 'er something. It 'pears to be someone's property, so we oughta find some crops 'er a road 'er something." Rebecca took Bill's hand, pulling him close until she could kiss him softly on the lips.

"You're the boss." Then she released her grip on him to begin her journey west with the rest of the party. Billy was bringing up the back as he watched three fine-looking women sashay through the meadow. He wasn't too far off as they stumbled into a freshly plowed field. Looking down the rows, he remembered the hard work it took for these farmers to get these rows this straight.

"Hey! You there! Get outta my field!" a voice called out. They all looked around until they found the voice. A rough-looking man sitting on a bay plow horse his feet dangling on the side showing tattered breeches and wore out ankle high shoes. His torn floppy hat and faded calico shirt told the story of near poverty. This was the farmer who owned the land or at least worked it. Bill was unsure of what would happen but stood his ground, waiting for the farmer to lay out the rules.

"I thought that we might skirt yer field to get to town sir." the runt spoke pulling his hat up a bit to see as the rider closed in on them. That's when the farmer noticed the girls and changed his mind about being a hard case.

"Tell ya what, son. If ya walk to the south along the field, ya'll hit a road. That'll take ya to town. Where ya'll from anyway?" the horseman asked as he kept his eyes on the girls, Mary Beth especially.

"Up by the Salt River." Ann spoke first as she stepped forward, touching the man's leg. *Whoa this is bold,* he thought. The horse rider was second-guessing what to do, thinking, and contemplating the next move.

"We thank you for the information, sir. Maybe we'll have a chance to say good-bye when we're finished in town. Thanks again." Ann turned, walking the direction he pointed.

The rider turned his big horse, walking the other direction. After he was out of earshot, the runt asked Ann, "I thought ya didn't like men?"

"I did that to ease the tension that was starting to grow. I could see he was unsure of what was going to happen with us three girls

and a scrawny white runt. Don't worry, we're all still here for you."
she said as if Bill was along as baggage.

"I see. I reckon you wanna run this here show!" Bill snapped.

"Don't go and worry your pretty little head, you're still running
the show." She led the unlikely foursome headed toward the town.

CHAPTER 66

Their walk was rewarded when a dirt road materialized out of nowhere. From the appearance of it, it hadn't been traveled too much as the grooves were only a few inches deep and there was deep-green grass growing in the center on the road.

"I'm going to pee. Come with me in case a wild animal attacks me." Ann said as she hung her head like a small child asking for a piece of candy.

"Only to pee. No sex, okay?" Rebecca answered, knowing exactly what was going to happen.

"I just want to pee. Mary Beth, come with us, won't you?" Ann asked.

"No. I'll stay here with the White Man and keep him company." With that she walked over to Bill, sliding her arm around his waist.

"Take your time girls." Bill was surprised as Mary Beth hadn't said three words since she voiced he intentions for her sister.

"Sit down here." She patted the grass next to her.

"I'll suck you off while Ann and Rebecca pee."

Bill wasn't too sure he wanted to have this girl suck him off right by the side of the road. It was deserted, and he seriously doubted anyone would happen along anyway.

"Okay, I reckon." Out came the soft member of Bill's anatomy. The open air aroused him almost immediately as his tool became engorged with blood. He anticipated what was going to happen next. Mary Beth got up and turned to face Bill. She held his root in her hands inches from her face. Then as quick as a hummingbird, she slid it in her mouth until Bill's breeches were touching her face. She didn't bob her head as others had done. No, this girl did it all with her throat muscles. Swallowing over and over brought Bill to a climax in a brief moment. The thing was there was no wiping her mouth or dribbling. She just backed up and stood. Bill looked down with his now-soft pod as clean as a whistle. Not a drop of seed to be seen anywhere.

"Thank you, Mary Beth. That was very nice." Bill said appreciably.

"Don't worry about it. I can't wait 'til you can slap that stick in my ass some more." With that she went back into her own world, her eyes glazed over as she stood there. *Now this girl is the damnedest thing I've ever seen!* Billy thought. He looked to where the other girls had gone, wondering their next move. The girls came out of the brush hand in hand a satisfied look on their faces. Bill knew Ann had gotten what she wanted and Rebecca couldn't resist a snack.

Now it was time to be off to the town to get previsions, Bill thought as they walked toward the town. After they'd walked for about a half an hour, Bill saw a couple of buildings on the horizon.

"I take it you've been here?" he asked.

Ann spoke firmly, "Yes. Many times. I know of this place well. You just hold back and let me do all the talking. You're still in charge, but I'm just helping out, okay?" she spoke to Bill as if he were a child. Bill could do nothing about it at this time, but he figured it would change as soon as they got provisions and headed west, but for now he'd have to take the abuse.

As they walked into the little town, Bill noticed this town was respectable looking, with women that weren't whores and such. He approached a dry-goods store on the right side of the town; the glass window had the name Basting's Dry Goods painted in big bold white letters. Blankenship's all over again, he thought.

"May ah help you ladies?" the storekeep asked as he was wiping his hands on his apron.

"Good morning, sir. You're Mr. Basting's?" Ann asked as she walked up the wooden steps that was shaded by the storefront awning.

"Yes, I am. May I help you, girls?" he asked.

"I'd like a set of men's breeches for my sister here. Please." Ann touched his arm as the sugarcoated words came out.

"Yes ma'm. Won't you come in?" he spoke as he led the way in.

"I'll wait out here." Bill said, knowing he'd be in the way. He didn't know how she did it, but she knew what she was doing around men.

Inside the cluttered store, he pulled some wool breeches from a stack. He called over his shoulder to the girls, "I think I have something over here." He continued, "She can try them on in the room in the back. I'd be happy to help if she needs any." he offered.

"Why, thank you so much. If it's not too much trouble?" she spoke with honey dripping off her words. In a short time she returned with the storekeeper in tow. His wool trousers hadn't been buttoned, showing his red long handles through the front opening.

"I don't believe there'll be a charge for these breeches. Isn't that right?" She looked at him, smiling.

He mumbled, "Huh. Un, no charge. That's right. No charge." There was a small stool by the wall near the door. He walked over to it then fell hard on it. A great rush of air came out of his lungs. The poor sod never moved again.

"Bye now." she said as they walked out. The owner didn't even look up. *Now I've seen it all, but this could be helpful,* Bill thought.

"Do you think you could do that for some horses?" Billy asked as he looked down the past the stores towards a sign, 'Blacksmith and Ferrier'.

"If it's a man? Yes. If it's a woman, it takes a little longer. Sometimes it doesn't work at all. It depends on their state of mind really." she said as they strolled toward the stable.

At the blacksmiths' forge, a huge burly man with a clean-shaven face walked out to greet them, dressed in a linen shirt with sleeves rolled up and a shiny leather apron. His wool breeches were stuffed into the top of his calf-high boots. The huge man stuck out a hand the size of a ham for Bill to shake. Young Billy wanted to impress this gargantuan, so he grasped hard and pumped the man's hand.

"Damn boy, what're you tryin' to do, break my hand?" the mountain of a man named Samuel Jenkins asked the runt. Bill immediately turned red from embarrassment. Quickly Bill changed the subject

"My friends an' I would like to look at some horses an' tack." the runty white man spoke clearly as he arched his back to appear larger.

"Your friends are very attractive. Are they all spoken for, sir?" His eyes looked up and down them. The smithy never flinched an inch when he spoke of the girls.

"I'll speak for myself." Ann said.

"Maybe you an' I could speak alone for a minute." she asked. He looked her up and down, weighing his options.

"Sure, I'd really like a word 'er two with the redhead there." he answered.

"How about you speak to all three of us at once? That way we can talk about business in a pleasant atmosphere." Ann smiled seductively at him.

"Whoowee! Hot damn! I reckon we can speak in the back for a few minutes." His face beamed.

It was as simple as that. They wandered off to discuss horses. Bill watched them all leave to the rear of the stables, thinking that this man had met his match with Ann. Looking about the stable, the small man took in all the smells and sights of the blacksmith's shop. There were broken wagon wheels, horse tack hanging from hand forged hooks, leaning against the wall long metal bars waiting for the master's touch.

The fire from the forge was radiating heat so extreme that even from the distance Bill was standing he felt uncomfortable. He stood near the anvil, feeling boredom creep in; he reached down to pick up the hammer the smithy had been using. Judging the weight, he picked it up; well, he tried to pick it up. Realizing he could hardly move, he slid it to the floor as he began his wait.

In an hour or so, out came the smithy with six horses with saddles and two with pack cradles.

"I don't know 'er care how they did it." Bill spoke quietly as he ran his hand down the withers of the brown horse before him. He knew it would surely make some interesting gossip to the town folk if they knew what had just transpired. Bill looked at the nonscript brown animal.

"This one is fine. No flashy horse fer me. Yep, this one will do." Bill spoke as he caressed the brown horse between the ears. The horse lowered its head so that Bill could continue.

"Now, if you ladies come back this way, be sure to return them fer some fresh ones, hear?" he spoke with a dazed look in his eyes.

With that he walked over to the forge, picking up a hammer off the ground. He picked a pair of long tongs and took out a red-hot shoe from the forge and began the steps to transform the the metal into a horse shoe. The runt was amazed at the strength this man possessed, but he could tell his mind was somewhere else, mainly the three girls that had left him. *I figure ya could take all his kitten-kaboodle an' he wouldn't even notice,* Bill thought.

"Well, it looks like we got this part done. What are you gonna do with yer pappy's deed?" Bill spoke as he threw a leg over his brown mare.

"You know, runt, if it wasn't for us women, you'd be out back of some livery stable shoveling shit. So don't worry about things you've no concern over." Ann spoke with a sharp tongue, making sure the runt knew who was in charge.

"Hold on there, I like my man, and I don't want you running him down." Rebecca spoke quickly. *Why does she hate the white man so?* Rebecca pondered as she studied the black-headed bitch of a woman.

"I'm just saying that he hasn't pulled his share of the work. That's all." Ann snapped.

"Look, he's like a hunting dog. In town he's just another dog. However, take him out to the woods, and things change quickly.

He's the one that'll save your ass when it comes time. I can attest to that. Why, once he stole a canoe right out from under a bunch of Indians." Rebecca bragged on Bill.

"Yes, I remember the story. Were they asleep or all cripples?" Ann laughed.

"Go ahead. Make fun of him, but I'm willing to bet my life on his skills." Rebecca defended Bill further. The runt could see that the girl was not going to let a sleeping dog lay.

"I'll tell ya what." the small white man spoke calmly.

"Do you girls want out?" Bill asked them, looking at Ann and Mary Beth as he pulled his hat off.

"Rebecca an' I have seen the territory an' made it out. Her an' me are a goin' back into it with you 'er not." He ran his finger through his hair. "I know you have a way with men. Hell, I admit it outright. But there's a fortune out in the shinin' mountains waitin' fer the pickin's. All we have to do is go an' get it." He slipped his hat back on.

"Yeah, there be Indians that'll want yer scalps an' animals that will wanta eat you. But take the risk and the rewards will be large. Ya know, if you girls get the rest of our stakes, I'll take us up the Missouri an' to them shinin' mountains. What do ya say?" He rested his hands on the horn of the newly acquired saddle. *Shit.* Bill shook his head from the speech he's just made.

He wondered if he hadn't made a mistake bringing Ann and Mary Beth along with them.

"Okay. You talk a mean show. Tomorrow we'll get the rest of our supplies. Then we'll go to the shining mountains as you call them." Ann spoke as she always did; in charge.

"I think I'll find us a place to bed down for the night. One that'll will ask no questions about three women and a runt." Ann spoke without even looking at Billy. *Damnit! I cain't do nothin' 'bout it in town! Once we get out of this place, I'll show them what I'm 'bout! Fer now I have to bite my tongue an' listen to her ridin' me like a whipped pony,* Bill moped to himself.

CHAPTER 67

Bill found a corral to put the horses in for the night at the back part of the abandoned store where they were staying. As he closed the gate, he looked to the west as a breeze came to his face. *Freedom, we're almost there. The night's still young, and the mountains are a day closer,* he thought.

Bill found the girls sitting in a small room, four walls and a place to lay their clothes for the night. She produced a small pouch she had got from the smithy. In went her hand, bringing out several bundles of bread and jerked meat. Passing it out to the other girls first, she held the last piece away from Bill to make sure he knew she was in charge. For the time being anyway.

They sat in silence, each engulfed in thoughts of the adventure that was awaiting them in the west. Bill took a pull from the canteen the girls had got from the smithies. The cool water soothed his parched throat.

"Damn, that's good. You girls want some?" Bill looked at Ann, then Rebecca, and finally he stopped on Mary Beth's blank stare. *Cain't figure her out,* he thought as he went back to see Ann staring at him with venom in her eyes. He knew she was mean, but he didn't really know how mean she could be.

After all the food was gone, Bill sat there in the room, watching the show of three women getting ready for the sack. Ann pulled off her breeches, letting her shirt cover herself as she looked over at Rebecca, hoping to get a look at the fiery redhead undressing. Rebecca kicked off her shoes and dropped the pistol and knife along with her breeches. All she had on was her shirt as she caught Bill gazing. The runt knew Ann had a thing for Rebecca. Meanwhile Mary Beth just flopped down on a blanket and was asleep before her hair settled. Rebecca walked over, sitting next to Bill on the blanket-covered plank floor.

"Would you like me an' Ann tonight?" she asked. Bill watched Ann's jaw spring open as he smiled, knowing she hated him for even considering it.

"I'm not too sure I want a man in my bed." she said quickly.

"This man can go three times in a row, and he has a golden tongue. I can guarantee that." Rebecca said.

"Why would I care for a man shoving that thing in me? I don't even want it once let alone for three times." Ann retorted.

Shit, she could put a dampener on an evening for sure, he thought.

"I guess you'll go without then." With that Rebecca put her arm around Bill and plastered a big old sloppy kiss on him; her hot tongue was searching for his as she used to do on the *Alice Mae*. Bill circled his arms around her as they rolled over onto the dirty blanket, hugging and groping as they had done when they were new lovers. Bill became so excited he thought he would explode right through his breeches. Rolling off, he got to his knees, opening his breeches to release the treasure inside. Rebecca's eyes went wide as she saw the fifth member of their entourage ready for business. She went up on one elbow, gently touching the lad's planting tool. She slowly slid it into her mouth. She was slurping and lapping like a kid suckling on a mammy's teat. Bill was getting real close.

"I'm on the way lover!" he spoke quickly.

"Hold on for a second. Lay on your back." she ordered.

"You want to join me?" She was looking at Ann.

"No, thank you." She was as cold as ice in January.

Rebecca began to stroke Bill's quivering pod.

"It's time!" Billy spoke in short quick breaths. With that, she grabbed the base of his gardening tool, squeezing hard. It didn't take long until the head started to turn red then blue and then purple.

"Hey, that's hurtin', ya know." the runt called out.

"Relax, I just want to see how far you can squirt." She giggled. Now that caught Ann's attention. Rebecca was watching like a dog waiting for a gopher to come out of his hole.

"You mean you play games with it?" Ann quizzed.

"Sure. Come on over and let's have some fun." Rebecca invited. Ann was reluctant but scooted over. Meanwhile Rebecca had a firm hand on his pecker.

"Okay. When I let go, it'll spurt up. Then you try to catch it in your mouth. If you miss, then you have to make it hard again so I can try, okay?" Rebecca said.

"He can do it over an' over?" Ann asked.

"Yep. The only man I've seen that can do it. Ready?" She asked.

"Yes. I guess. Does it taste horrid?" Ann quizzed.

"Hell, you've already tasted it. Remember our first night at your house? Besides, it's just a bit different than me or your sister." With that she released her grip, and a hot stream of white liquid shot up about three feet in the air. As it came to a stop in midair, Bill saw Ann's red tongue shoot out. She looked like she was trying to catch snowflakes with it. It hit her cheek and nose with the rest falling on the wooden floor.

"Your turn." Rebecca said.

"I know." Ann pouted.

"Does he take long? I mean will it be easy or will he fall asleep?" Ann asked.

"Just watch." Rebecca said.

Slowly Ann lowered her mouth on Bill's soft pod. As soon as her hot mouth covered it, she could feel the tingling start as Bill's tool came back to working form. Up and down she went, slathering the young man with saliva as he brought him closer to eruption. She lifted her head up.

"I would not believe it if I hadn't witnessed it firsthand." she spoke in amazement.

"Maybe we should wake up Mary Beth? She likes games also." Ann asked.

"Next time. Remember you have to squeeze really hard. Be sure to give me some warning so I can get ready." Rebecca requested.

"Okay, girls. It's time." Bill spoke in short broken breaths. *This is good. Gettin' blown under the disguise of a game. Maybe this won't be so bad after all.* About that time Ann let go, and Bill let another load go straight up. Not as far but a good two feet anyway. Rebecca knew what was going on as she swooped in like a bat getting a mosquito at night. Only one drop fell to the floor. She was licking her chops like a fat cat that just got a rat.

"I've had enough of this. Let's see if your tongue works like Rebecca says it does." Ann said.

She stood up sticking her thumbs in her dirty drawers. She slowly slipped them down, stepping out of them. Then she positioned herself over Bill, she stood before him in a worn-out linen shirt and nothing else. Try as he could, Bill couldn't see those soft red lips for all the black hair. He squinted in the dimly lit room. As she approached, all he could see was darkness, not like Rebecca's or Mary Beth's with their light-colored hair.

"You do that, and I'll do this." Rebecca said as she began to orally pleasure the young white man.

"Okay. Do your best." Ann said as she slowly stepped over him, squatting over his face. She lowered herself until the hair was touching his lips, forcing his hands up under her legs, touching the red valley of hers, pulling the briar patch apart. He barely got it skinned back when a honey dripped to his lips. *Hey, she tastes different than Rebecca. No matter,* thought Bill as he started working his magic. He pulled and teased the button hidden in the fur coat as he felt it become harder; it was as if a stream of honey was flowing down his chin running down the side of his face as he pleasured the black-haired beauty.

My, the white man is doing much better than I thought he'd do! Ann thought as she felt her body tighten up as an orgasm rippled through her groin. *She was a lot faster than Rebecca,* he thought. Rebecca was lowering herself on the small white man's planting tool. As Ann shuttered and fell away from Bill. He lifted his head to watch Rebecca. Like a choreographed dance she slid around, so her back was toward him, giving Bill a clear view of her hair covered anus. Then it struck him, a new idea. Timing her strokes, he stuck a thumb in his mouth, getting it slippery with saliva as Rebecca turned to look at the small white runt. She turned her head looking back at him.

"Good thinking." The whole time she had her hands on his knees, slowly rocking back and forth on him. When he had it lubricated well enough, he placed his thumb to where the rosebud would be and waited. His wait was short as the redhead came down on the erect thumb forcing it into her. She paused to enjoy the moment and then backed up, releasing Bill's thumb into open air. Forward she went until his pod was engulfed again; and then she quickly sat back down, forcing the thumb deep into her again.

"Do both thumbs when I tell you." she requested. By this time Ann had recovered, looking to pleasure Rebecca as she rode Bill. Watching her move to the front of the redhead he knew what she was up to. She was going for the appendage on the top of Rebecca's red garden.

Reaching down, she moved her fingers onto Rebecca's rock-hard clitoris; she began kneading it as if she were working bread dough. Rebecca's speed had increased as the thrill of having both thumbs cramped up on her became a realization.

"Okay. Do it now." she spoke in a raspy voice. Not wasting time, the runt locked his fingers together, pushing his thumbs into her as her red button was to be thrashed by Ann. She squeezed her legs as she spent herself falling off to the side, leaving Bill quivering in the open air, ready to go off in any moment. Ann, remembering the taste of Billy, didn't want to miss a drop of his vital fluids; so she leaned over, placing his root in her mouth. She worked feverishly to finish him off. As she wrapped her tongue around his pod, she pushed it deep down her throat as she began to swallow over and over as her sister had done. Bill could hold his seed no longer; he reached down to hold Ann's head as he brought forth a load of his finest down her gravelly throat. She kept swallowing like a raccoon would do a crawdad until she sat up, wiping her mouth off with the back of her hand.

She spoke, "Boy you do taste good."

"I've had 'nuff for tonight." Rebecca commented as she rubbed her butt.

"Damn I like it when it's happened, but afterward it makes me a bit tender."

This whole time Mary Beth had never stirred, but out of the clear blue, she awoke. As she sat up looking at the nearly naked people before her, she asked, "What are you doin'? Did I miss anything?"

"Nah. Go back to sleep." Ann instructed her. There was Bill with his breeches undone, both girls had their pants off, and she was wondering if she missed anything.

CHAPTER 68

In the morning after they all got dressed, the foursome headed for the dry-goods store for the remainder of their supplies. As Bill waited outside with the horses, all three girls strolled into the store. Bill watched the town become alive as the day opened up. The blacksmith had smoke coming from the chimney. Though the saloon was still closed. A few shopkeepers were opening their doors, preparing for the day's customers, sweeping the wooden walkway, and pulling out goods to entice customers. In what seemed like no time at all, she walked out with several burlap bags full of goods, with Rebecca on her heels with another stuffed bag. Mary Beth was the last one out, her two bags dangling from her arms. A plump woman in her early forties, her hair unfurled and with a glazed look in her eyes, followed them out.

"Ann, you and your friends will come back now, won't you? You did promise." she asked.

"Yes, Janie. It'll be in the early spring of next year. We'll come back to visit. Remember what I showed you, okay?" With that Ann threw a leg over her buckskin gelding looking at Bill.

"Ann, did you happen to get any long guns?" Bill quizzed her.

"That's taken care of. I truly hope you can pull your share when we get out of town." She turned her horse to the west and walked off. Ann turned and addressed the white man, "We'll get them later." *Damn, I'm in a tight spot, but there's nothin' I can do. Yet.* Bill figured.

They traveled onto Franklin, away from thefew small towns on the riverfront and the ever-present inspections by other travelers. The scenery was beautiful as they kept a steady pace heading northwest. The rolling hills were covered with thickets of maple, hickory, walnut, and oak trees. Beautiful green and brown grass fluffed by the easterly winds as they meandered on the dirt road. The clouds seemed to dance and weave stories as Billy watched them, almost oblivious to the surroundings, as his little group marched east to mystical Charlton.

They crossed the small tributaries of the Salt River. It seemed whenever their clothes were dry, they'd come upon a creek to cross. The wool breeches would chafe the tender skin of the girls, and young Bill was forever having to adjust his genitals as he was water soaked. Pulling out a rag, he was continually wiping his neck down to keep the small critters from deviling him as they traveled across the Missouri territory.

As they neared the Dry Pork River, the pesky mosquitoes were on the prowl for fresh food, causing Bill and the girls to become engrossed at keeping the flying devils away from their face and hands. Then as quickly as they were upon them, they were gone.

"Damn strange. Damn strange." he called out to whoever would listen. They rounded a corner. Seeing an orchard of wild apples, they decided to fill up with the fresh fruit while the opportunity presented itself.

Bill rode under the lower limbs so he could rapidly pluck the green and red fruit. Soon their little canvas bags were overflowing with the newest supplies. There were always the small sand flies that populated the water edges, but now they were replaced by the huge horseflies that bit the travelers continually.

They traveled through the day, seeing no one. Not horse, wagon, or walker. A dismal mood sat on Bill's shoulders as the next series of creeks came to them. The slow-moving Greasy Creek was next, known for its big catfish and turtles but only to the few pioneers that suffered out the lonely life in the territory.

The small brigade had no idea food was within arm's reach as they slogged through the deep muddy stream. The water in the middle was up to the top of their saddles, causing them to hang on for dear life as the horses struggled in the slow moving brown water. Coming out of it was as if they'd been in a rainstorm. Their clothes were drenched as every part of their belonging. Plodding on for twenty more minutes, Bill wanted to be away from the pesky mosquitoes.

Finally they holed up for the night in a small grove of alder trees a few miles west of the Greasy. The smooth bark and the beautiful deep-green summer colors were breathtaking as they set up their meager camp. Bill worked on getting the horses hobbled, pulling saddles and blankets off for the night to let them dry out. Rebecca and Ann produced a flint and steel. The girls worked on getting a small fire going to start the drying process that would seem to follow them continually.

When Bill walked up to the fire Rebecca had already stripped her wet cogs off. Her perfect skin and wet hair pulled back made Bill want her. *Always gorgeous,* he thought as he gazed at her.

Ann stripped cautiously, avoiding Bill's eyes as she too hung her wet clothes up. He noticed they had hung their clothes on the deadfall around the fire. Not one to be left out, Bill stripped his clothes off and hung them in a similar fashion over the crackling fire. He was glad it was producing plenty of heat and not much smoke. He pulled his knife out and wiped the blade off and stuck it in a piece of firewood near his clothes.

"You girls sure have got that fire making down." he spoke as he warmed his hands over the yellow jumping flames. Satisfied all was good, he pulled out an apple that they had gotten in the orchard. He munched slowly as his other hand began pulling on his bean, aroused by the naked women.

Soon forgotten were the pestering mosquitoes that had harassed them. Now they had a fire to drive the pests away. Bill's eyes wandered about the small camp. Rebecca sat naked, her arms behind her, elbows locked and her knees out, showing her garden to Bill and Ann. Not Ann, she had no intention of having Bill stare at her, so she kept her knees up with her arms wrapped around devoiding Billy of any eye candy. Mary Beth just slept near the fire, wet clothes and all; not a peep from her about the conditions. She just wanted to sleep and dream about a warm bed and hot food.

"Damn, I wish these breeches would dry sooner." Ann spoke solemnly, "I hate lying about so the white man can ogle my fine crotch." She smiled at Rebecca. She continued, "But you're welcome to taste the honey I have."

"If you won't share your bed with the white man, well, maybe I don't want in it either."

Rebecca stood up for Bill, slowly turning around so Bill could admire her fine breasts, firm butt, and her red-haired crotch. The small to-be trapper listened to Rebecca, wanting her very badly, knowing the apple was only a distraction.

"Fine, he can fuck me in the ass after you suck my pussy dry. How's that sound?" the hardened lesbian spouted to her redheaded lover.

"Maybe I want Bill to slip that hard bean he's been stroking in me instead. Maybe I don't want any pussy tonight. Maybe I want to suck him dry after he's slipped in every hole I have." She turned to Ann.

"Can you do that? Can you poke all open holes one after the other?"

"No! You know I can't, but I can give you a tongue lashing." Ann answered, desperately trying to get Rebecca's attention.

"I'll see how I feel after I finish with the runt." Then she walked over to Bill; she leaned down, pulling his hand away from his stiff member.

"Now, you don't have to do that. That's why I'm here." She squatted down in front of Billy, and then she leaned over, pulling on his erection. Slowly she leaned down between his legs, her mouth closing in on Bill's planting tool. As she began pleasing Bill, there was a strange sound coming from where they'd crossed the creek.

"If I didn't know better, I'd say that's a hog." Ann commented as she stood with her back to Bill. She had forgotten about her nakedness. Bill looked at her broad shoulders, her small boyish rump; her narrow waist. He saw her garden hanging down in the midst of the black matte of hair.

Damn fine-lookin' woman. Damn fine, he thought. The noise was getting closer as Rebecca stopped. She looked over Bill's knee to see where Ann was looking.

"You might wanna stop that." She looked down at her sister.

"Mary Beth! Get up. Mary Beth!" Ann nudged her sister. Mary Beth sat up looking around at the naked people; she looked up to Ann only to see her staring to the east. She sat there motionless for a moment, then got to her feet, and began running to the nearest tree.

"Huh?" Bill asked, turning his head to his naked friends.

"It's a wild pig. Best you get your ass up a tree!" she yelled at Bill as she scampered from limb to limb, climbing higher with each step.

"Hell, if it's a hog, all you gotta do is yell at it. Shit." Bill answered, annoyed.

"Not these." Ann scurried to the nearest tree, leaving her clothes. Threes steps later she was six feet up and climbing.

"You believing this? Shit, it's just a pig fer Christ sakes." Bill spoke without turning his head to Rebecca. But she wasn't there; she was on her way up the same tree as Mary Beth, climbing like a pack of wolves were on her trail.

"Eh? Rebecca? Rebecca?" He turned to see she wasn't there but up in the tree with Mary Beth. He looked through the brush, listening to the noise. *Shit, I was gettin' my piss'r sucked off right fine too. Now we've got a few dern'd pig disturbin' us,* "Girls, look it's just a coupla little ol'pigs." He pointed out to the pair of razorback hogs as they came into the light. They were tall with brown bristly hair and longer legs than a common farm pig, with wide flat noses' they had the beginning tusks showing on both sides of their muzzles. The pair dug and shuffled through the camp stomping and tossing the food and supplies all over the small crude camp.

"Shit! You were scarit of this?" He laughed. His hands on his hips, he shook his head slowly. But the noise continued after one of the small hog was walking closer to the fire and close

to Bill, grunting along as happy as a lark until it realized Bill was standing not five feet from it. Then it squealed loud enough to make Bill's ears hurt as it returned quickly into the nearest brush leaving the other one on its own.

The sounds were getting closer and louder. Much louder. Huh? It's most likely its brother 'somethin'. He thought, *Uh, that sounds big.* Bill started backing up toward the tree Ann was in. He was still over ten feet away from her sanctuary when a huge razorback hog busted out of the brush, running at Bill at full steam.

"Shiiiitttt!" Bill screamed as he covered the distance in two steps. In three steps he was on the first limb as the hog rammed the tree, knocking loose Bill's hold on the branch. He started slipping when the hog hit the tree again.

Violently it shook its head as it grunted deeper. Both of his legs were dangling three feet off the ground as he tried to hoist himself up; the hog saw his feet as it ran to them, jumping up as Bill's grip slipped. The hog's timing was perfect as it rammed Bill full-on, tossing him back toward the fire. Thankfully the two-hundred-pound monster had missed slicing Bill with its razor-sharp tusks. Bill landed on the clothes, breaking the small branches and limbs. Rolling over quickly, he got to his feet. He saw the hog turn to see where the threat had gone.

"Christ! Run! Run!" screamed Ann. Bill heard her voice and the sound of panic. *Now I know why Mary Beth skedaddled up a tree first thing,* he thought.

"Hey there, piggy! Come on! Come get me, you ol' piece of shit!" Bill yelled loudly to the pig. The hog shook its head, unfamiliar with the new noise coming from its next meal. It didn't stop it from charging Bill as fast as it could run. Bill waited as the hog closed the distance, five feet, four, then two. He saw the tusks, the coarse hair on its three-foot high back, and the wild look in its beaded yellow eyes. That's what he was counting on. In the next step he was out of the way, dropping his shirt over its head. He quickly sprinted back to Ann's tree. One, two, three, four limbs as Bill climbed. He stopped just under Ann.

The hog had gone mad with the loss of its prey. It shook Bill's shirt off as it spun wildly looking for the human. Then the razorback stopped. Slowly it began looking around the camp; grunting quietly the hog stopped and sat down and looked directly at Bill.

Grunting loudly the hog returned to its feet; then the monster of a hog ran at the tree at a good five miles per hour. Bill watched it close the distance as it rammed the smooth barked tree again. Ann was shocked at the force the creature could create. So huge and fast was this animal it could cause the small tree to shake violently.

"Not this time pig!" he called down to the hog. Flustered, it rammed it again and again. The smaller hogs came back into the camp as its mother grunted to it. When it failed to do as she commanded, she hooked the 100-pound pig and tossed it over by where the apples were. Stunned, the smaller hog sat quietly as its keen nose began sniffing the immediate area. The scent of the fruit got the hog's attention, and it began munching on the fruit. It chewed noisily as the apples were being enjoyed. The other smaller pig came out of the brush to join its sibling eating the apples and being out of its mother's way, but best of all they enjoyed the cool apples.

She heard the eating and stopped. She'd lost all concentration on Bill as she walked over to the bags of fruit. Down on her knees she went as she joined her daughter's eating. There sat Billy on the limb directly under Ann. She had both hands on the outreaching branches balancing her. She wanted nothing of what had happened to the White Man. Bill saw it as an opportunity, though. It the dim forest light, he could see her butt cheeks hanging off the branch with her legs on the other side as if she were sitting on a rope swing.

"Hmm? Looks like yer balanced just about perfect." Bill spoke to her backside.

"Damn! I figured that hog was going to kill you when she flipped you like that. There's been stories of them things killing people out here in the territory. They're mean critters. Satan's own, that's what I say." She had no idea what Bill was up to or about to get into. The runt leaned against the trunks as he started his hand toward her black briar patch. She flinched when she felt Bill's finger touch her skin.

"Don't! I'll slip and fall." She was almost crying now.

"Do it! Fuck her with your fingers!" called out her sister from the tree next to them.

"Please don't! I'm so scared." She was all but openly crying.

"Now if you hold still, nothing will happen." he answered her.

"Oh god, don't! I don't want that hog to kill me! Please don't." she pleaded. Bill was going to go through with it but decided that her fear was enough as a punishment for her rude behavior.

"All right. Christ, stop your sniveling. Shit. Hey?" he called to his lover in the next tree. His voice brought the hog's head around. It began testing the air for the human's scent. Satisfied it wasn't on the ground, it went back to eating their supplies.

"Think I could get a poke?" he called to her.

"If you want to outrun that hog, you can. You best be quick, or I'll have to find me a new man. Maybe I'll get one that go four times in a row!" she answered Bill, knowing full well he would walk through hell's own fire to have sex with her. Bill calculated the distance from his tree to hers and Mary Beth's.

Damn too far to jump, but I bet I can outrun that hog.

"Ann, if you won't give me a poke, then I'm gonna get one from Rebecca." he spoke to her butt as he couldn't see her face.

"Don't get down. Please don't. The hog. It'll—It'll—kill you sure as the apples their eating." she stammered through her crying.

"Don't you fret. I ain't gonna get killed. Not by a goddamned hog that's fer certain an' fer true."

"Rebecca, you best get that garden warmed up 'cause here I come!" he shouted. The hog turned its head again, but it didn't get to it feet. Not yet.

Bill slowly slid behind the trunk as he lowered himself to the soft-leafed ground. He slowly looked around the trunk to see where the hog was. She was still eating the apples. Bill judged the distance to be about twenty-five yards or so. He slowly brought his head back behind the tree.

One, two, three! Then he started his run. As he began his sprint, the hog was on its feet in less time it took to shake his pod off after a piss. She was quick too. Closing the distance three steps to his one. *Shit! She's fast!* was all he could think of as he sprinted to the other tree. He heard her coming fast. *Damn, it'll be close* was all he could think as he sprinted closer to the tree. In the last few steps, he could almost feel her breath on his heels. Then he launched himself for the highest limb he felt he could make. As he grabbed the limb, he swung his feet up as she went right under him, slashing her tusks from side to side. Bill brought his body back around until the bare skin of his stomach was on the smooth maple limb. Hoisting himself up, he threw his leg over as the hog skidded around, grunting and squealing at the loss of her prey.

The runt brought his legs up behind him as he hooked his feet on the branch; carefully he let go as he reached for the next higher branch. Lifting himself up, he began to climb to Rebecca.

"You ready to get poked?" He smiled into the darkness of the tree.

"Took you long enough. That ol' hog was just about to have you for supper!" She smiled at the man as he brought himself to her.

"But didn't." He leaned forward to receive a kiss from her.

"That was a fool thing to do. A fool thing to do!" Ann called across from his old tree.

"Maybe. But now I'll get my poke since you were being stingy an' all!" he answered as he pulled away from Rebecca's warm mouth.

"You want me to suck you off, or you want me to lean over this branch?" she asked, making sure the runt got his treasure.

"Just lean over, missy."

"You hard enough?"

"Like a axe handle." he responded. Bill slipped into her as the hog rooted around through their belongings, tearing the place up but good. Rebecca was as slippery as she was back in the room of hers on the *Alice Mae*.

"Oh, you runt!" Rebecca called out as Billy flayed away on her.

"Here. I. Come!" Then the runt released himself into her.

"Damned good, runt. Damned good. You missed out for sure." she called to her lesbian lover.

"You can have him! He's a damned fool! He'll get us all killed!" she chided an answer. Below the hogs had eaten all the food and were on their way out. The sow turned once more. Then she rammed the tree Ann was in once more before she disappeared.

"That ol'hog never even messed with the horses. Didn't give 'em a never mind, ain't' that strange?" he asked her as she reached into herself for her prize.

"Yeah. I mean yes, it is." she answered as she licked her lips and fingers clean. They stayed in the trees until the sun rose itself over the eastern trees to assure themselves the hogs had moved on. Bill could hear Rebecca shivering but not Mary Beth. She was enjoying being dressed. Bill climbed down the tree and waited to see if the monster pig was coming back. When nothing happened, he called up to the others, "The coast is clear."

They started by getting the dry clothes on; Ann was shivering as she pulled her breeches on.

"You're a fucking lunatic. If you'd gotten killed, we'd be out of luck for someone to harass.

"Oh, you're so kind."

"White Man, bring the horses in an' I'll give you a hand saddling them." Mary Beth called to Bill as he pulled his thin shirt on.

The camp was torn up. All the food was gone, and the burlap bags were ripped beyond repair as well. He found their pistol and his knife. Picked them up wiping the blade on his breeches leg and sheathed it, then the pistol under his belt. He looked for his hat. He found it torn into pieces. *It must smelled me. Pissed off something fierce,* he thought as he began the ritual of preparing to travel, which occupied the most of the afternoon.

"Let's get Bill." Rebecca called to him as she threw a leg over her gelding.

"Yeah, we can do no more here." he answered.

CHAPTER 69

The flies were harassing Bill continually as he rode in misery. They deviled him and the horses nonstop as they plodded north toward the next town, Franklin. The sun had begun to sink into the changing landscape. The groves of oak trees began to thin as they crossed the Peno Creek. Not as deep at the Salt River but deeper than the Cain Creek. They happened upon a small pond next to the road

The large oak trees dotted the landscape next to the road, fading out as the road crested the horizon. He considered riding all night to reach the next settlement but changed his mind before speaking. Feeling the roads would be hazardous for the small brigade to travel at night, not from four-legged animal but the two-legged ones that raided the roads close to towns. He figured it would best if they took a short nap off the side of the road until daylight and then continued on.

"Why are we stopping? We can be in town by tonight if we don't stop." Ann spoke aloud.

"Yeah, that's true. We'll be open game fer bandits too. They'll take more than our horses too I might add." Bill added.

"I'm glad we've not bumped into any so far." Ann spoke to her sister and Rebecca in a boastful tone, "All right then, we'll stay here."

"Oh? Is that right? Let's see." Billy looked up and down the road as it wove through the small narrow valley. There was a small pond of water on the south side and no cover for the horses as he surveyed the area.

"I'll be a movin' up there." He pointed north to the ridge across a small meadow with a dense thicket. Without further ado,

Bill looked to Rebecca. She nodded, and they rode away from the sisters, leaving them wondering if they'd make the correct decision. As they plodded away, the other horses began to cry out from being left behind.

"Hold up, I'll be a goin' back fer a minute." Bill sat there in silence, waiting for the two girls become uncomfortable with the loud animals, then turned back to them.

"No. I want to hear this." she said as she turned to go back as well, as Bill approached the black-haired bitch, he started his lecture, "Lookie here. This is how it works. I called the camp fer a reason. It ain't 'cause I wanna be the boss. Lookie roun' here. Ya got no cover. No place fer yer back. Yah got a pond full of skeeters. Ya got both sides of the road open. Up there." He pointed.

"Only one way in. We can keep track of what comes up an' down the road, okay?" Bill spoke to be authoritative but not commanding. He was hoping she took it that way.

"Oh, I didn't know why. I thought you were just trying to be an asshole." she said as she looked away. The whole time Mary Beth hadn't said a word. She just sat there with a blank look on her face. The sisters turned their noses to the meadow as they followed Bill and Rebecca to the secretive hiding spot.

They began the ritual that would become the way of life for the small brigade. Bill stashed the horses out of sight in the small thicket then, he walked outside of the thicket to see if his handiwork had paid off. Looking for any sign of the horses and not seeing any evidence, he felt content that they would be there in the morning. "Bill, I'm leaving the saddles and bridles on. We'll be leaving quick like soon 'nuff." Rebecca informed Bill. Ann and Mary Beth got a small fire going as they watched the night creep upon them.

He entered the small camp to find everything had been done, so all that was left was relaxing for the night. He sat back against a small crop of rocks to watch the sun sink into the west. He began to ponder his life at that moment.

"Are you okay? I could take your mind off your problems for a while if you like." Rebecca asked.

"Thanks. After a while, when the sun's gone. I really wanna see what comes down this here road." he spoke quietly.

"I know what can come." She put her hand on the front of his breeches.

"I love you. You know that, don't you?" Bill blurted out. She cocked her head looking at him and the dying sun's light.

"You mean it, don't you?" she asked, seeing Bill looking into the twilight.

"Yeppers." he said.

"I've been waiting to hear that for a long time." she said laying her head on his lap as she slipped into sleep.

Bill thought about the past events of the day. It had gone from he and Rebecca to three women. He was concerned knowing they had been traveling in Indian country with three lovely ladies.

The runt gazed over at Mary Beth as she slept on the dirty blanket she had picked up at the dry-goods store. Nothing stayed clean for the young trappers to-be. The ever-present dust and wind made sure of that. Mary Beth hadn't spoken but a few words, and now here she was on an adventure that could take all their lives in a blink of an eye. The youngest one in the party didn't seem right in the head. She hadn't participated in the games the other girls played out back with the smithy and even with the storekeeps.

Ann the hellcat, was fun as a ball of yarn, but she had a mean streak in her. It was as if she could read minds. Young Bill was looking at her when her eyes popped open in a split second, looking directly into his.

"You'll get yours." she said, lying her back against a rock staring at Bill. Into the front of her breeches went her hand to scratch. She had her eyes locked with Bill the whole time as she performed her necessities. Out came her hand. She paused looking at it. Then she smelled it. Nodding to him, she spoke in a hushed voice, "This is something you won't be getting much of!" Then into her mouth it went. *This woman is scarin' me an' I do believe she's a bit touched in the head,* Bill thought.

Satisfied she had made her point with the runt, she lay back down, closing her eyes. Billy let his mind drift for a moment as he pondered his running mates. He hadn't said a word the whole time. He just kept was watching her as she dozed off.

Sitting in their small hideout, Bill watched as the last sliver of sun dropped into the plains. A movement caught his eye down on the road. It looked to be a small cart going west. Pulling the two-wheeled cart were a pair of tired oxen. They plodded as they had been doing all day. Step after step they walked with no concerns other than a bag of grain or soft grass at the end of the day.

Bill's eyes sprang open as two men scampered out of the trees. He saw smoke then heard the gunshot. The wagon was hauled off the side into the trees that were lining that section of the road. The man leading the team had fallen to the ground as Bill watched as the family was being methodically massacred. Nothing he could do but sit there and watch. His stomach became queasy as he watched in the dusk of the evening. He looked over to see Ann watching the same thing. She turned her head toward him, giving him a smug smile.

"You're still an asshole." she said.

The runt closed his eyes for a moment but awoke quickly. Well, he thought it was quick. The sun was gone completely now as a chill came over the camp ground. Something had awaken Bill. He wasn't sure of what it was, but something wasn't right in their small camp. There was Rebecca on his lap. Over against the rock was Ann. He turned his head to see Mary Beth. No Mary Beth.

"Wake up." Bill kicked Ann's leg.

"Yer sister's gone." he confessed in concern.

"Oh." she said as she sat up and looked around in dark camp.

"I heard her get up to take a leak. Or at least that's what she said she was going to do. That was last night. I went back to sleep. She'll be all right. She's a big girl." She flopped back down on her back, snaking her hand down the front of her breeches to scratch herself again.

"I'll take a look to see if I can find her. Do you mind stayin' here while I look around ?" he asked.

"I'll be okay." said Rebecca as she sat up looking around.

"Oh my, I don't know if I can stand it with you being gone. Of course we'll be okay." Ann whispered that she turned her back, ending the conversation.

The runt thought about the pistol but decided to do this quietly. He walked out of the secluded camp, his eyes already accustomed to the darkness as he listened to the night. Quiet. Maybe it's the wind. Then he heard it; voices in the distance, very faint, but it was voices. He walked quickly to the sound as he thought of what to say and do. As he got closer he stopped. Shivers went down his spine as he stopped, thinking.

Not so fast here, Billy boy. Let's make sure of what's goin' on 'fore you go a traipsing in, he told himself. So the runt crept painfully slow toward the noise. When he had identified the noise, he got down on his hands and knees to get closer. It was men all right. They were laughing and carrying on as if they were having a shindig. Onto his stomach he went until he could peer out of the brush before him.

The young man watched as the small camp unfolded its story before him. From the look of it, these were the same ones who had plundered the wagon. Bill lay there listening to see if there were any more people outside the firelight. No noise or references were made to anyone else, so Billy crept even closer, careful not to make any noise that twould give him away. That's when he saw why there was so much commotion. There were three of them, but what's this?

There sat Thabo. He was shackled hand and foot, his bald head now covered with nappy hair, full of twigs and brush from many a bad night of travel and abuse. The three had a bottle of whiskey; they were passing it around as they watched one of their party hold a girl by the hair. It might have been a girl from the wagon, but Bill had no way of telling at this moment. The small girl looked to be ten or eleven at the most. The one holding her hair had his erect manhood protruding from his open breeches. He pushed her head towards it, a knife to her ribs with the other. Bill looked at Thabo, who sat staring into the fire with no emotion being shown.

"You best suck it good, darlin'. If you wanna live 'til mornin'!" The drunk sneered.

The young girl hadn't given up yet. She lowered her mouth over the man's tool. All Bill could see was her head going down, and then in the next moment the recipient cried out as the knife went into the girl's ribs. Her head came up with blood on her face as the man threw her to the ground to die with the knife still in her ribs. His breeches were soon covered in blood. Bill could do nothing but watch as the young girl died.

"Goddamnit! The bitch bit my cock!" he screamed as he began stumbling; he drew his foot back and kicked the girl so hard she was lifted off the ground. The unfortunate little brown-haired girl never moved when she hit the ground. She was dead before he kicked her.

"Damn, Luke, she jus' about bit your cock off!" the nearest one gaffed at him.

"Fuck you Billy Gaines!" Luke screamed as he stumbled to retrieve his knife from the dead girl. After wiping it off on her simple cotton dress, he slipped it in its scabbard.

"Serves you right. Ya shoulda left her be. She was only a little girl." Billy Gaines spoke as he gained his composure from laughing. The remaining bandit spoke, "You'll be more careful next time." Then he took a long pull from the bottle, liquid pouring out of the sides of his mouth saturating the front of his wool coat.

This must be the leader of these bastards, the white runt thought as he looked around. Then he saw another girl. It was Mary Beth.

"I think I'll kill this un too." Luke slurred as he had forgotten his bloodied penis.

"Luke, if you wanna kill her, you go right ahead. She sucks dick worse than a fuckin' goat." the one called Billy Gaines said.

"Don't go killin' her. We can get a good price fer her with them red fuckers up in the hills." Simon Breaker, the leader, spoke out as he drank deeply again. Then he held out the amber liquor to Luke, "You best get all liquored up so as your cock won't hurt zo bad."

Luke took the offered bottle, drinking in the same manner, swaying as he guzzled the booze.

"Hey! Leave some fer me!" Billy Gaines called out as he snatched the bottle from Luke. By this time Luke could barely stand. He stumbled over to a tree. He put his back against it and slid down to the dirt floor, his head lying off to one side. Out like a brain shot cow.

"Ol' Luke gonna have both heads hurting in the morning." Billy Gaines laughed as he pulled again on the almost-empty bottle.

The runt watched the mean one, mouth open, drooling as he slept. He saw the one called Billy Gaines staring at the fire, nodding off, the empty bottle next to him. Simon Breaker lay on a blanket next to the fire and was snoring in no time at all.

Billy inched back from the light to formulate a plan as he stared worriedly into the darkness.

If I untied Mary Beth, they'll most likely track us down then kill me and then the women. Then there's ol'Thabo. How in the tarnations did he end up with them varmints? No, never mind right now. Well, that leaves one option open to me. Start payin' fer my keep. If'n I was gonna be a mountain man, then I'd have to kill sooner 'er later. Might as well be sooner I reckon, Bill thought.

He crept back to the small pond where he pulled off his dirty linen shirt. Then he stuck his hand into the mud, pulling big globs of it out, smearing mud on his white chest and face. He pulled out the knife that Weatherspoon had given him, holding it out before him he stuck it in the the mud as well. Bill's hand was shaking like a leaf in a windstorm as he headed to kill.

I don't like the sound of that, but that's what I'm intendin' to do. Be a murder. A killer. The same. Maybe this was like killin' a wild dog. Yeah, that's it. Puttin' it out of its misery, he rationalized as he crept back to his hiding place with his knife in his hand, ready to deal a hand of death.

He could see Billy Gaines was still asleep right where he had nodded off; his head had fallen on to his upright knees. As slow as molasses in January, Bill moved until he was behind the tree where Luke was sitting. Slowly he reached around with his left hand. Grabbing Luke's mouth, he plunged the knife into the drunk's throat. Warm blood covered the runt's hand as the sleeping man died quietly. No thrashing. Bill let him slump over on his side. Then he smelled it. Death. He had to be quick now. Making eye contact with Mary Beth, he held his finger to his lips as he left the dim light of the fire.

Thabo had been watching without moving his head. *This looks to be the runt from the* Alice Mae, *but it couldn't be or could it?* His mind was reeling with the possibilities of being killed also. Circling the camp, the runt crept up behind the man that had nodded off. Holding the knife in his now-bloody right hand, he approached the sleeping man. The white runt grabbed him with the left hand, pushing the knife deep into his throat with his right hand as he had done earlier. The drunk was asleep like the first but reached up with both hands, trying to pry the runt's hand away. Billy Gaines's strength was too much for the runt, prying the white man's hand away. The second man died as he tried to speak; nothing but a gurgle came out of his mouth as his hands came up to his bloody throat. He was dead before Bill let him slump to the ground. As he backed into the darkness, death covered Bill's hand as he felt the sticky blood drying. His stomach was trying to revolt as he went about the sickening chore he had assigned to himself.

One left, he thought. Still Thabo hadn't made a sound as he had watched his two captors killed methodically.

Billy waited a bit and then left the security of the bushes, approaching Simon Breaker when he stirred. He rolled over and put his face to the fire. Billy paused in mid-step as the snoring resumed. The white runt kneeled down behind the remaining bandit. Taking the knife, he positioned it right below the last man's exposed neck. Then he swiftly pushed it in hard but the neck bones made it glance off, only partially severed his spinal column. He jumped back, leaving the knife imbedded as Simon Breaker began to scream, his arms moving but nothing else. He tried to move but nothing happened.

"Augh! I've been stabbed! My god! Luke, help me. I cain't move! Billy, help me. Help me." The leader was screaming in panic now but only his arms were moving. Then no movement. Bill looked at Thabo now, eyes piercing deep into the soul of the Zulu warrior. Young Bill rolled the leader on the fire, stomach down; Mary Beth was watching the whole time as the man began to burn alive. Satisfied the man wouldn't move any farther. He pulled his knife out of the wounded man and wiped it off on Gaines's grungy coat.

"Yer gonna be a smellin' yerself burnin' to death, ya prick. The fire will burn through yer clothes an' skin first. Maybe yer blood will put the fire out? But I ain't too sure. Maybe yer guts will put the fire out. But never mind that. You'll smell the whole thing. You're gonna die a miserable death. If you don't die from the fire, I'm laying odds a critter will come an' finished you off!" he chatted as he turned to Mary Beth.

She was securely tied to an adjacent tree, able to watch all the grisly things this lover of hers had done. While the young man cut her ropes, she stared at the burning man as he had ceased to scream. Bill looked at Thabo, then back to Mary Beth.

"This un do anything to ya?" he asked, pointing to Thabo.

"No. No, he don't even speak American. He just sits. I heard they were going to sell him later." she commented, looking at the slave.

"You don't speak American Thabo?" Bill questioned the black man.

"I thought you'd be dead by now, small one. Are you going to kill me as you've done these?"

"I ain't quite sure yet. Where the keys?"

Mary Beth spoke out before the Zulu could, "You ain't gonna kill again, are you?" Her voice quivered.

"Nah, I'm done killing." Before Billy could finish his sentence, she quickly spoke again.

"The keys are in his pocket." She pointed to the roasting one. Bill walked over to the man, flames were consuming his coat now, making it dicey to get the keys out of the pocket. He was still alive and burning slowly. The runt reached into a few pockets until he found the rusty key.

"Hold your hands up." he ordered Thabo. Bill unlocked the slave's hands; looking into the Zulu's eyes, he spoke, handing him the keys so he could undo his foot shackles.

"Here, hold on a second." Bill walked over to Luke and pulled the belt and knife off the dead man. Looking around near the man, he found Luke's pistol. He snatched it up along with the possible bag that had been next to Luke's small possessions.

"This'll be useful on your trip out west. Go get one of them horses. You're free to go. Good luck to you." Surprise was in the man's eyes.

"Thank you, small one. One day I will see you again." Thabo couldn't believe what had just happened. One moment he was destined to work the rest of his life, and now the runt he tried to kill was letting him go? *These whites are very different now. By honor I can't kill him, no matter what.* He did not wait around to see if the runt's mind would change. As quickly as he was there, he was gone, fading into the brush, gone from Bill and the girl. For now.

Bill turn to leave with Mary Beth, never looking back. The young girl was quiet as they walked to the outlaw's horses. Behind them the leader was screaming for Bill to come back to finish him off.

"Did they hurt ya bad?" Billy asked the blonde abused girl. She looked back to where the sound was coming from.

"Not as bad as that. You're a cold fucker, ain't you?" she responded as they approached the horses. The morning sun had broken over the eastern horizon, bathing the young couple with a soft glow and warmth. Bill looked around the massacre scene that the bandits had left.

"Yeppers. Mess with my girls an' death is sure to follow." The runt made sure she understood it was a promise, not just a cavalier statement.

"Let's get so we can pick up Rebecca an' Ann." Bill spoke to the young girl as he began the process of pulling the cinches tight on the bandits' mounts. The runt turned to where the man was burning as the smell of burning flesh wafted through the early morning serenity. He decided he would stay and begin burying the unfortunate folks.

"Ride back up to the others. I'm gonna bury the folks they killed." he spoke quietly to the blonde survivor.

The runt walked over to the wagon to begin the ritual. He stumbled a step back as he saw the family. There was a man, his wife, and one little girl. The daughter had her face caved in, and the father's head was barely on. He had been tortured and mutilated, just a quick glance and he knew what bestowed on the man. Bloody bib overalls were sliced opened and his groin. His belly and head been split open like a ripe melon. The image seared in his mind. *That man died horribly,* his mind raced. He turned away from the man and glimpsed at the mother for just a second and it was too long. The mother had sticks buried in her eyes, her dress ripped open, her bloomers torn bloody lay at her feet. Dried blood on her legs from matted her groin with both her breast's were cut open. Bill turned away and dry heaved.

"Burnin' that bastard wasn't good 'nuff. I wished I'd thought of somethin' else." he mumbled as he found a shovel in the back of the cart. He had to move the little girl, *at least she died quick, I don't see any thing else done to her.* Picking up the shovel he went to start the chore.

Bill began to dig the graves as he pondered the situation he was in, *I ain't the law in these parts, now who was going to believe a white runt with three girls? That nigger? Hell, he's long gone by now. Mary Beth could be my witness.* The shovel sliced into the black dirt with ease, *am I as bad as them now?* It was too confusing to Billy. He put it out of his mind as he dug. Shovel after shovel of the black dirt came out of the ground. He had his back to the girls as he heard them approach. He called out over his shoulder.

"I would like some help gettin' them buried, jus' be prepared for horridly mutilated people." he requested.

The black-haired bitch spoke to Bill in a civil tone, "I'll help. I've done this before." Then a long pause.

"Oh, thank you for bringin' my sister back. I was wrong about you, and I apologize." As she spoke these words, there was a different tone in her voice. Ann was actually being honest, showing she was a real person under that hard shell.

"Yer welcome." Billy answered as he kept digging.

"Damn, I hate this. I'd just like to be gone from here." Ann spoke quietly as she and Billy lowered the last body into the grave. She paused as she covered the mother with a quilt from their wagon. I've never seen anything like this. I hope I never have to again."

They finished the task about midmorning. Bill fashioned four crosses with supplies he found on the ground and near the wagon. They could see the belongings scattered all over the killing field, their oxen were dead and swelling with flies buzzing everywhere.

"Rebecca will you an' Mary Beth try to find out who they was so we can send word to their kin when we get to Franklin?" Bill asked his redheaded lover.

She and Mary Beth scoured the scene looking for any shred that would identify the family.

"There's nothing here." Bill looked over the area, rotten animals and personal effects strewn everywhere.

"I reckon I'll say somethin'." Bill softly spoke.

"They were good folks. Now they're dead. Let's get for the mountains 'fore we get killed too."

"Amen." Mary Beth whispered.

"I'm gonna go back to the bandits' camp and get whatever looks to be good, guns and such things." Billy spoke solemnly.

Billy walked away from the girls as he approached Simon. There was on the stench of burning flesh and no sound from the man.

"Fucker's done passed out." He said as he looked around the camp, seeing three pistols and two long guns. *These oughta work just fine. I wonder how much powder and shot they have?* Bill opened each bag to inspect them, *maybe twenty or thirty balls between them all, three horns, two more knives.* He brought each possible bag over his shoulder. *That should be it. Got guns and them horses. Yep.*

He returned to the girls, carrying the guns and supplies.

"I reckon we can be off to Franklin." he spoke to them as he pulled the horns and possible bags off and hung each one off a girl's saddle horn.

"Uh, you mind washing that mud off? We don't wanna be confused by dragging a nigger along with us." Ann laughed.

"Oh yeah. I plum fergot in all the confusion." Billy conceded. He walked back to the pond where he'd left his shirt. As he splashed the water on himself, he thought of the next step.

"Well, I'll figure it out when we get there I reckon. No one will have to know 'bout that goddamn nigger neither." Bill mumbled aloud.

"What's that?" Rebecca asked from above him. Bill hadn't said anything about Thabo to her yet.

"Thabo was one of 'em. I mean he was all shackled up back there. So I set him free." Rebecca stood there, her slender jaw hanging open.

"If you don't beat all?" She smiled at him.

"Good for you. Good for you."

"We'll ride inta town, report the murders, an' light out. Yeppers. That's what we'll do."

Bill was proud of himself for coming up with a plan that left Ann out. They all mounted and began the long ride to the nearest town, pulling the bandits' horses behind him. Bill rode in silence as he remembered the screams of the burning man, the small child that was killed so easily. He could do nothing for the girl as she had been murdered. As much as he wanted to stop the events from happening, he couldn't. *Damn them!* he thought as they rode on, but Bill continued to ponder what was going to happen in the next town.

CHAPTER 70

As the foursome entered the town of Franklin, Bill could feel the eyes of the town upon them. The crowds gathered as the blond runt and the three women pulling two pack horses and three saddled horses rode into town.

Samuel Blevins, the local saloon owner, spotted the girls and immediately saw dollar signs flashing in his eyes. The scarecrow approached Billy straightaway from across the dirt street. Bill was surprised the man could even walk with his gangly appearance. He was a tall thin man dressed in a poor fitting black suit, with a hollowed-out face from years of drink. The gaunt man held up his hand to stop the runt on the fine-looking mare, not to mention two extra horses and gear to boot. *Must be a pack of runaways, easy picking for me, except they're all armed.*

"Hello, I'm a lookin' fer the constable of this town. Could ya point me in the direction of his office?" the runt asked.

"You want to sell those women?" he asked and looked back at the girls with his hand caressing the mare.

"No, I don't wanna sell my friends. Leave my horse be." Billy said as he pulled his horse from the ghoulish character.

"Where's the constable?" Bill asked bluntly.

"You don't have to get snotty, you runt. He's over in that buildin'." He pointed to a small office building down at the opposite end of the small town, "over there."

"Thankie. Let's go, girls." Bill turned his small brigade toward the door of the constable's office, leaving the saloon owner in the center of the street.

"I'll be here if you happen to change your mind." he repeated.

"I won't." he called over his shoulder, leading the horses and the girls down the street; people were gawking as they plodded down the center of the dirt street. As Billy reined up at the wooden rail in front of the constable's office, the girls fell in beside him at the hitching rail. Sliding off the mare, the runt stretched his five foot six frame as he twisted around, feeling the kinks fade away from the day of riding. He pulled the horses up and tied them next to his mare.

"Goddamn, my rump's sore from sitting." Ann spoke to no one particular. Rebecca pulled her left leg over the saddle horn while she watched the antics of her companions. She felt fine. The ride had been easy as they never seemed to go more than a trot the whole time. It was evident Ann and Mary Beth were unaccustomed to sitting for this length of time. They made faces of discomfort as they touched the ground.

The runt slipped under the handrail as he looked up and down the wooden walkway. Satisfied no one would accost them, he opened the door to the office and entered the dimly lit room. There was a man behind a small cluttered desk, his white shirt button up to the top with a small ribbon tie dangling from under the last of many chins. His sweat was apparent as Bill closed the distance to the law keeper desk. The stale smell in the air brought back memories of the Hannibal store as his eyes adjusted to the room's light.

"I reckon yer the constable?" the runt asked quietly.

"That would be true, sir. What is it I can do for you on this fine day?" Frank Low asked. The constable was in a fine mood. His wife had just fed him a wonderful meal, and it was time for him to take his afternoon nap. He was slightly put off that this runt had shown up at an inopportune time. He decided to humor the boy then send him on his way.

"Well, we have a problem. See, we're on our way west. Last night we were campin' an' we saw a robbery. One of my friends was kidnapped." He looked around the jail, shuffling his feet a bit, and then got the courage to finish his story, "Well, the bandits are dead as are the party that was attacked. I have the horses an' gear, but everythin' that was on the wagon was plum torn up. They killed the man, woman, an' two small girls. They killed the oxen an' destroyed everythin' else." Billy was rambling, hoping to get all the facts out in one sentence.

Frank looked over his small round glasses at the runt before him.

"Let me get this straight. You and your friends were camping. Is that right?" He looked at the shabbily dressed man before him.

"Then you witnessed a robbery? Then the same people that kidnapped your friend. After that, I'm a little confused on what happened." Frank asked.

The runt became more confident since the constable spoke to Bill in a civil voice, not like the others on the *Alice Mae* or Stillwater back in Dallas City.

"I went down to get my frien'. There was as fight. I have my frien' back. The others are all dead." Bill slowly let the words dribble out of his mouth, watching the fat man's face for a response. Now it was Bill's turn to sweat.

"You killed all them bandits did you?" he asked as he rocking back in his chair, looking at this small white boy before him while he began weighing out the story.

"Yeppers. I did." Bill spoke as he looked into Frank's eyes.

"The people in the wagon, you buried them? Christian like?" he humored the boy more, and then it hit him; *a man, and two girls? Could it be his brother Markus?*

"Yeppers. A man, woman, an' two small girls." With that the constable's eyebrows went up and his ears went back.

"Two girls, 'bout yeah high." Low held his hand up from the floor.

"Well, I guess that's 'bout it, if you were to lay 'em out proper like, yep." The man before Billy went pale as a fresh winter snow as he pulled his glasses off and put his hands to his face, covering his round features. A loud rush of air escaped Frank Low's lungs as reality stomped on him.

"That was my brother and his family. His name is, was Markus Low. I'm Frank Low. How do I know you didn't kill them and these other folks you're speaking about?" he asked.

"Lookie here. If I did what you said, an' I didn't, why would I come a paradin' in here to tell ya all 'bout it?" Bill responded.

"Sorry, son. It's just a shock that's all. You say you have all the bandits' gear?" Frank asked. "Where are the bandits?"

"I left them where they died, around a small fire pit across from the pond."

"I'll have a look at it. Maybe I can identify some of it." the constable replied. All thoughts of a nap had vanished.

"Well, we got three pistols and two rifles." Bill watched him rock back in his chair.

"Possibles too?" Frank asked.

"Yeppers, they's on the horses out yonder." Bill nodded over his shoulder as he watched the man slowly get up from his chair.

Frank sized up Bill and then walked to the door. As he opened it, he once again looked at Bill White. Stepping out into the bright day, he was taken back when he saw the girls. Rebecca's red hair gently blew in the afternoon breeze, causing her to look as stunning as always. Then there was Ann. Her sharp features and jet-black hair was shining and luxurious as any proper lady. Mary Beth was standing beside her, giving the complete contrast to her sister, like salt and pepper. He turned looking at Billy.

"Son, are you a gambler? Are these your whores?" he asked, looking at the gorgeous dirt-covered girls.

"No. These are my friends. Can you identify anything here?" Bill asked, perturbed.

Frank waddled over to the horses slowly; he walked around them, touching each one cautiously. He reached the last in the line, recognizing it as his own. He stroked the horse slowly. As his hand went to the flank, it immediately kicked.

"Son, this is my horse. It was stolen a few nights back. If the other one has a mark on the inside of the front leg." He paused. "Well, it's stolen too." He walked over to the two animals, bending down on one knee pointing to the leg. Breathing hard, he spoke wheezing.

"This un's Olof Andersen's. That's his mark. He owns the dry-goods store across the street. Let's see those pistols and those rifles." Frank spoke as he looked at the plain leather shooting pouches.

"Hold on." Bill stepped away to his horse and retrieved the long guns. Frank's mind seemed to ramble as Bill returned.

"These are trash. Hell, I've seen better possible bags on them Injuns on the plains." Feeling the awkward silence, Frank made some chitchat, "Gonna be a hot one this month." No one replied to his casual remark.

It was the first time Bill had looked closely at them; squirrel guns, one with a broken lock and the other not far from being trash. He handed them to Frank one at a time.

"These guns are pretty used up, boy. I'd be surprised if they even fired. Ike Barlow, our gunsmith, could fix them up, but it'll cost more than buying new ones. You got them pistols?'

Frank handed the guns back to Bill. *Shit, this ain't going too good. Both free guns are done for.* He got the pistol from each girl and began showing them to Frank.

"These have seen some use as well, but I do believe they fling a ball down range. You got molds or anything?" Frank asked as he looked up to meet Ann's mesmerizing eyes. He stared at her, not moving.

"Nope. All we have is in them shooting bags. Might be something in 'em." He saw what Ann was doing.

"Ann." he spoke to her, but she didn't acknowledge Bill's words.

"Ann!" he spoke curtly to her this time. She broke off her stare with Frank.

"What?" she answered in a huff.

"Look in them bags for bullet molds." Bill ordered the black-haired girl.

"Oh, all right." She changed to the soothing pussy cat that she could be in a whim. Rebecca had been watching the whole event. *That Ann has a way with men. I don't know how she does it, but she surely does.* Ann rummaged in her and Mary Beth's bags, coming up empty.

"Just them balls and a few flints." Ann purred as she went back to controlling Frank.

"Rebecca?" Bill asked.

"I already looked. Same as Ann's." Rebecca watched Frank snap out of his trance.

"There you go Constable. About the horses?" Bill asked.

"I'll go speak to Olof right now." With great effort, Low shuffled to the dry-goods store.

"Thanks Constable." Bill spoke as the fat man walked off. In a few minutes a tall thick man came out of the store, his white apron on. Mutton-chop sideburns adorned his square smooth face, his black hair parted in the center and plastered to his head. The tall man shaded his eyes as he spoke to the constable. Then he turned to go back into the store. Not a word was spoken to Bill or the girls.

When Frank returned, he spoke to Bill as he looked at the girls.

"He says this is his all right. Take 'em over to his store, and he'll make it right with you. Said he'd make a deal for the guns as well. I told him this saddle wasn't mine, so you'll have that to barter with." Then the constable held out his hand to Bill to shake it in thanks. Bill grasped it firmly. Shaking it he spoke, "If that's it, we'll be on our way." He said.

"I'll get my horse later. You can leave it here. Alright. I'll pick it up later." Then he turned to his office and stopped and turned to face Bill again, "Can you tell me where my kin is buried? The missus would most likely to go say something over them, you know, pay our respects." he said.

"Sure. It's outside of town 'bout an hour 'er so. On the opposite side of a pond." Billy was pointing to the south.

"The wagon should still be there. The oxen an' the bandits should be stinkin' to high heaven by now. I'm sorry this has happened to ya. If ya don't need anythin' else, we'll be on our way." Bill said as he was nervous being in a town.

"Tell you what, son. See that house way down there by the end of town?" He pointed to the cottage with a small white picket fence around it.

"That's where I live. Before you leave, stop by. My wife will give you some of the best hot food that you ever tasted. I don't think your friends have had a hot meal for some time by the looks of them." he said.

"What 'bout you an' yer wife goin' to see 'bout the dead?" Bill asked.

"If you've already buried them, then we can go tomorrow." he answered.

"Well then, thankie ye kindly. I reckon we'll see you in a bit."

CHAPTER 71

Billy led his party to the store across the street to meet the mystery man. As he closed the distance the man came out of the store, he looked up and down the street and introduced himself, "I'm Olof Andersen. I zee you aft mine horses." he spoke with a strong Norwegian accent.

"Is this here your horse?" Ann asked politely.

"Yaw. Dat isht mine. Se der mark? Yaw, der shame as does." He was pointing to the stolen horses that was tied up next to theirs.

The White Man looked at the marks where Olof was pointing, agreeing that they were the same.

"Here ya go then." Billy handed him the reins.

"How 'bout we trade for some supplies? These rifles, pistols, the saddle an' tack for some good blankets and," Rebecca asked as the man began to walk away.

"A good long gun, maybe a Hawken?" Bill interrupted.

"Yaw, ve can do zat. Go unt my store." With that he walked away with the two horses back to the back of the store. Over his back, he called out again, "Go unt in, ya? I vill be back unt moment." The shop owner vanished from sight with the recovered horses.

The little brigade entered the small store as Bill noticed the same odor as the constable's office, musty and stale. The foursome walked through the store looking at the wares on the shelves when from behind the curtain door in the back of the store Olof walked in.

"I 'ave looked at der tack of dose horses, unt I sink I can give you unt vair price. Vhat kind ooph zuppllies do yew vequire?" he asked in his accent.

"We're goin' trappin'. So anythin' along thata way would helpful." Billy answered, figuring he might be sounding ignorant, but he was unaware of his needs, just what the skin trapper on the riverboat had told him.

"Vell, let's see. Two saddles, same amvount of reins, some blankets. I vill give von vifty dollars credit in my store, or I vill gift you vifty cash mouney. Vat vill it be, youngt man?"

Bill's mind raced, *Damn, his accent is strange. But credit is credit.* Then Rebecca remembered the pistols and rifles.

"What about these guns?" Rebecca asked as she laid them on the counter.

The store owner picked up each pistol working the action of the hammer and the pull of the trigger, and then he walked over to a section of the store and held the guns up to the light coming through one of the side windows, inspecting the bores. Then he returned to handle the long guns, frowning as the constable had done earlier.

"Vel, dees gunts are no gunt. I vill give each, pistol only. Ya? The rifles? No gunt. Kaput. Ow aovt der vone dere?" He was pointing to Rebecca. She had the French pistol that she and Bill had gotten back on the Mississippi slipped in the front of her breeches.

"Not for sale or trade, but we'll need a mold and flints for it, if we can work out some deal." Rebecca answered smartly.

"Girls, what do ya want?" Billy asked. At first they went right to pretty clothes and hats.

Then slowly one by one they went to supplies. Ann was the first to speak.

Well, here we go, Bill thought, *she's going to whip out that deed to take care of this. Then again, it's Ann. She'll mostly "talk" the storekeep out of everything. Again.*

"Four rifles and pistols an' possibles to go with 'em." Bill blurted out.

"Ah, you vant lead in der bar from France or America?" he asked.

"I don't know the difference." Billy stammered.

"I zee. I tell you vhat. I give galena. Ist der best, or zo I ear.

Vhy don you valk 'round unt get vhat you thinks unt put dem here ven you're done, I vill tally it up unt ve vill go from dair? Zound good to you?" he spoke with some frustration.

Galena? Shit, wasn't that just down the river from Hannibal? Hell, he was the one holdin' all the cards. I don't see why he has to be so testy, Bill thought as he watched the pile grow.

"Sure thing."

Billy stacked four half-stocked octagonal-barreled flintlocks on the counter, one E&W Bond and three Hawkens complete with double-set triggers, and patch box built into the right of the tiger striped curly maple stock. All in the popular fifty four calibers. On top he laid four fifty four-caliber Kentucky flintlock pistols. He was satisfied with his choices. He continued walking around until he found the molds as he saw Rebecca put down several four-point blankets. Ann brought over a coffee pot and sugar. Mary Beth had a bunch of needles with several spools of colored threads. Bill went to gathering up more supplies. As he browsed through the small dry-goods store, he paused for a moment.

"Well, lookie here."

"What's that, runt?" was the reply from Ann.

"This here hat." Bill slipped the notched crowned wide-brimmed hat onto his head.

"I found a hat to replace the one that hog got." he said as he admired himself in the silver-rimmed mirror on the distant wall. Removing it he admired the hat, the brim had wire sewn in so the wearer could style it.

"You ain't really gonna get that, are ya?" was all that Ann could muster up at the time.

"Why, yes, I believe I will. What do ya think?" he quizzed his better half, "Look good?"

"Yeah, looks good on ya." she answered as she went back to shopping, laying a mold for the French pistol on the pile.

"Well, y'all get one or two. We got no idea of the winter out here. I figure to keep my noggin warm."

"Well, fer once you gotta yerself a good idea. Shit, hey, how's this one?" Ann held up the brown wide-brimmed hat.

"Damn, if I didn't know better, I swear you was a man." Rebecca laughed as she too pulled a brown hat from the stack; the wide brim would keep the rain from going down their backs as well as to protect them from the sun and winds.

"Mary Beth? You gonna get one of these?" Ann asked her sister.

"Nope. I'll get a bonnet, something nice. Not an ol'shit ugly hat." she spoke over her shoulder as she fitted a nice blue-and-white hat on herself.

"Shit, that won't hold up in the mountains, girl. You best get a good hat." Bill tossed another wide-brimmed hat to her.

"No! I want this one. And I'm keeping it!" She huffed as she turned her back to the others as she pouted. Not to be put off, Bill added the extra hat to the pile. The young lad thought, *She may not want it now, but she'll be lookin' fer it later. That's fer certain an' fer true.*

Bill continued with his shopping; farrier pliers, a hoof file, a handful of hoof spikes, butcher knives, possible bags for all of them, camp axes, and ten number four Newhouse beaver traps. The pile was huge by now as Mary Beth added more to it. Looking at the supplies, Bill knew it was more than fifty dollars. Olof came to the room as he saw the pile of goods. He spoke slowly to be sure the travelers could understand him.

"Vell, you 'ave much more zan vifty dollars here. But I tell you vhat. If dees girls vould like to verk for me for one year, I vill give you everyting do 'ave here. Dat isht vat I vill do." The tall man smiled a smile of deceit to the young people.

"Oh, is that right? I'll tell you what, Olof. It's Olof, right? I'll spend an hour with you for all this stuff. I guarantee that you'll be wantin' to give me your store when I'm finished with you. So what do you say to that?" Ann spoke out in confidence.

"Ha. Acht, I can do you unt zes oudors whit no problems." He waved to Mary Beth and Rebecca.

"If you can't?" Rebecca broke in.

"You get every zing." He snapped back, "But I Vill. You vell get nausing unt I get to keep all oof der credit. Yaw, ist dat good?" The weasel smiled.

"Okay, Olof." said Ann as she held out her hand. Olof grabbed it, shaking it firmly.

"It's a deal." he said as his Norwegian accent vanished. He pulled Ann close, quickly kissing her before she realized what had happened. He all but threw her to the floor when he released her.

"You stupid sluts, I'll be whoring you out before the sunup tomorrow! Ha-ha-ha!" he barked.

"What 'bout yer accent an' all?" Billy asked innocently.

"You dumb fuck! I only use that for drifters and trail trash like you losers!" Olof barked.

"In the back, girls! And drop your drawers quick like. I'll fuck each of you a couple of times before the sun goes down. This is gonna be better than I thought."

He herded the girl to the back room through the curtain that went to the back of the store. He stopped turning to Bill.

"You don't go anywhere. I've got work lined up for you as well!" Olof spat as he vanished behind the girls.

The runt stared at the curtain as he thought of Ann. *She's our ace in the hole. If she could do that mind trick on the asshole storekeeper, then we'll have a chance to make out.*

The runt strolled inside the store as a rack of smoking pipes caught his attention. Reaching out, he picked a small clay one off the rack, admiring it for its simplistic look. Having never smoked he had decided it was time he tried. Looking around the store, he found a small container of smoking tobacco. Carefully opening the canister, he retrieved a twist of the sweet-smelling tobacco. Slowly and meticulously he began filling the pipe bowl as he looked for some fire. The runt figured he'd get some extra while the getting was good, no telling how things in the back room would pan out. Before he put the canister lid on, he reached into the jar to take a handful of the soft-smoking tobacco. Looking over his shoulder to see if anyone was watching, he put a few plugs in his breeches' pocket. Bill looked about the store until he located a small lantern; carefully he lifted the glass off. Looking around, he noticed a burned stick that was on the counter.

This'll work jus' fine. He lit the small stick.

Billy lowered the fire to the tobacco as he drew in deep as he'd seen others do. The smoke went into his lungs, causing no pain whatsoever. Then out of nowhere he began to cough. He kept coughing until his eyes were in tears, almost vomiting from the convulsions.

Goddamn! This isn't like what I thought it was gonna be. He took another draw. This time he didn't take it so deep. Surprised at the taste, Bill took another puff. A small cough echoed as he practiced the smoking technique.

Satisfied with his newfound skill, he strolled to the front of the store. Slowly he opened the door. Looking both directions, he waited. Satisfied he wasn't going to be arrested for the theft of the tobacco, he walked outside. Standing under the broad awning on the plank porch, he noticed two chairs in front of the store.

Plopping down, he rocked back against the wall as he watched the town's activities. He pushed his new hat back as he pondered the next move he and his small brigade would make, considering the girls could pull off this feat of black magic.

If Ann can pull this off, hell, we'll be set up fer the mountains. I wonder how long we'll have to go. I've no real idea of where we're supposed to even go. Silas said it was at the top of the Missouri River. Hell, I wonder if we could tag along with a reg'lar brigade. They'd want to poke the whole time. He drew on the small pipe again. *Now there's a thought. The girls could charge 'em a coupla beaver fer a poke, maybe a muskrat for havin' them purty lips wrapped around their pecker's. I'd have to be on the lookout fer the crooked type in this type of trade. If we did well, I could see makin' 'nuff to cover the trouble. Hell, what was I werkin' fer in the first place? Hmm, if we make a lot of money, what do we do next? Do we keep getting' ready fer trappin? Hmm. I hadn't thought this out far 'nuff. Well, I reckon I'll load this here pipe again.* As the pipe's fire went out.

His attention was struck as he heard some movement inside the store.

Out came Olof. Bill was surprised; it hadn't even been very long at all. The runt looked him up and down. *Looks like he's been down five miles of bad road.*

"Shit you look like a derned porcupine." Bill commented when he saw that Olof's hair was no longer plastered down but instead it was sticking straight up. Olof stared into the afternoon sun with no quick-witted remark.

"I reckon you like it rough?" Bill continued to ask him.

"Huh? Oh, I thought they were normal girls." Then he walked over to the other chair, falling into it. The impact made Billy wince as he thought the small sitting chair was going to shatter from the force.

Without turning his head, Olof asked, "Where did you get those girls?"

"Oh, they're jus' frien's of mine. We still got us a deal?" Billy asked as he got up to light the pipe again.

"Huh? Yes, we still got a deal. Where did you get those girls?" he stammered.

Bill smiled as he returned into the store. Closing the door behind him, he looked over to see Rebecca sitting on the counter with a huge grin on her face. To the right Ann was looking through some cast-iron skillets and Mary Beth was a holding up a dress she was admiring.

"How'd it go?" Bill asked Rebecca as she spread her legs to let him wiggle between them.

"He went once with me, and then Ann got him. Then it was all over. Mary Beth got to sleep the whole time. She isn't right, you know? But do we still have a deal with ol'man Andersen?" she asked as she pulled his new hat off lying it on the counter next to her. Smiling at him, she wrapped her arms around him, pulling him closer to her. Her fragrance was of sex, and it was driving Billy silly. He wanted her right now as he felt his breeches filling up.

"Do you want to go out back?" She had read his mind. Then she opened her shirt, pulling out her ivory-white breasts. She offered them to him. Taking the red nipple in his mouth, he gave it a quick suck as he raked his teeth gently over it. He brought his head back. Bill felt her stiffen up as her legs began to encircle him.

"I sure do! But we have to get this business taken care of first." As he was talking to her, Andersen came in.

"Where did you get these girls?" he asked as the runt plopped the other breast in his mouth, suckling like a newborn calf. Billy turned to him, leaning his head back between the white pillows shaking his blond dirty hair between them. Rebecca whacked on his top of his head, pushing him away. She didn't bother putting her ample bosom away as she watched the events unfold before her. She leaned back against the countertop, locking her elbows. They lay perfectly on her narrow ribs.

Ann had watched the whole thing as her cheeks flushed red like fresh strawberries.

"That's not important right now. We need to get settled here so we can be on our way." Ann spoke out before Bill could speak.

"Take whatever you need. I'll be out back." The store owner wandered through the curtain to the back of the store.

"We'll need a bill of sales." Bill called to the curtain.

The voice answered, "Just write one up and I'll sign it."

"How we doin' here anyway? Do we got everything we need?"

Rebecca asked her cohorts. Ann walked to Rebecca and planted a solid kiss on her.

"That's all I need."

"What do you think? Should I do him a little extra?" She giggled.

"Sure, but just enough." Rebecca answered.

Then she was gone in the back room. When she returned, she was leading the once-slick salesman with his wool breeches unbuttoned open with his shrunken manhood hanging out, traces of semen still showing on his breeches as well as dripping from the tip.

"Olof wants to say something." Ann said.

"I do? Oh yeah. Thanks for coming into my store, and you're welcome anytime." He was staring off into the distance. He went behind the counter to sit. He just stared a blank look, never bothering to fasten his wool breeches up.

The trappers to-be spent the rest of the afternoon getting the pack animals set up with all the possibles that they could use. Bill's eyes wondered around the store as his hand went to the possible bag he put his personal things in it. Flint and steel, a ball puller, a pan pick for the ignition hole, a small screwdriver, and small spring pliers.

"Better do this for the girls too. Shit!" Bill exclaimed as we went to each bag, adding the provisions.

It was late afternoon before they started to Frank's house.

"How long before he comes to his senses?" he asked her as they slowly walked down to the constables house. She just smiled at him.

"I don't even wanna know." As Billy looked into her eyes, they were as black as the hair hanging around her face, no white, just all black. That's when he saw it. Evil. She winked at Bill and the white returned to her eyes. The young runt had a bad feeling in his stomach, ever since the first meeting on the front of their porch of her home on the river. *This here girl's jus' pure evil waitin' to pounce on the first thing that gives her a reason,* he thought as he tried not to stare at the town folks as they went down the dirt street.

"Hold up a minute." Ann slipped off her horse and ran back to the store.

"What the hell?" asked Rebecca as she turned in her saddle to see where her lover had went. She returned carrying an armful of thick multi-colored wool scarves.

"Here, these will be good for something later." She passed them out to the small brigade.

"Thankie." Bill held it to his nose, smelling the musky odor of the store.

Bill and Rebecca pulled the two packhorses, he looked at Mary Beth. A vacant stare was all he could see in the young girl's eyes, the once-antsy blonde girl was now a shell of her former self, and Bill had no clue of how to repair her broken spirit.

CHAPTER 72

The small brigade neared the constable's house as Frank and his wife came out. She was a plump short woman with a big smile across her round cherub face, her cooking apron pulled tight around her, her graying hair pulled into a bun on top of her, *this is what a mother should look like,* thought Rebecca, seeing the spark in her eye and the bounce in her step.

"Hi kids! I'm Eva. Climb on down and come on in so I can feed you! Oh, it's so good to see so many young faces! I have corn on the cob, potatoes, pork stew, and hot biscuits. But for dessert I've made a few blackberry pies! Please come on. Come on." She latched right onto Mary Beth, wrapping her arm around her and hugging her like a long-lost daughter. Frank held the door open as the small procession walked by.

He nodded and smiled to Bill. "I see you made out all right with Olof."

"Yeppers. He did right by us." Bill said as he entered the small home. The meal was more than the to-be trappers had eaten in days; soon all of them had their buckles undone as they leaned back in their chairs.

Young Bill excused himself as he strolled out to the front of the small home for a newfound diversion; smoking. Rebecca watched him leave the table as Ann was scooping another piece of the excellent pie. Staring at the opposite wall, Mary Beth hadn't even taken a bite. Her full plate sat in front of her as it cooled in the early evening.

"You better eat girl, or Daddy's gonna tan your hide!" Ann snapped.

"I'm not hungry, an Daddy cain't hurt me never again." Mary

Beth retorted to Ann's sharp tongue.

"I do as I please." With that she got up, walking to the back of the home near the fire, staring into the bright flames as the room became uneasily quiet.

Eva approached Ann, "Your sister, she's your sister, isn't she? She should stay with me. You know that, don't you?"

"Ask the White Man. He's the boss!" With that she cut the conversation to a stop. Eva figured her for a hard case, and she wasn't let down by her abrupt manners.

Out front, Bill lit his pipe from the lantern as Eva came out of the house, letting the heavy wooden door shut slowly behind her. She walked up to him. No misinterpretations were given. Standing next to the runt, she turned to look into his face. The small lantern light made his blue eyes sparkle. "That girl isn't right, is she?" she asked straightaway.

"She was kidnapped an' ain't been the same since." Bill replied.

"She should stay with me. I need a daughter, and she needs a mother." she said quietly.

"I'll speak for her as I know she'll most likely not give you an answer. Yeppers, she should stay on with you as I know it's going to get rough for us as winter closes in." the runt answered her as he drew again on his clay pipe. He was staring out into the night as He heard the wooden door quietly closed. Bill finished his small pipe, staring out at the stars. *Shit, I got more on my mind than them twinklin's up there. I got two women in there behind me wantin' to go up the inta shinin' mountains an' all. I ain't never been poked so many times in all my born days. That Ann, well, I figure when she wants to get a poke, well, she'll can be a real she-panther. I believe she'd jus' as soon carve my liver as get a poke. But she does like it up the ass, an' rough too. That's fer certain an' fer true.*

Bill tapped his pipe clean as he turned to the open door.

"I'm callin' it a night. See ya'll later." he called to whoever was listening. No movement or acknowledgment was heard as the door shut.

CHAPTER 73

Walking over to his horse, he pulled his cinch loose as he untied his bedroll and headed to the meadow behind the house. It was peaceful out in the open for the young man. Crickets could be heard, and the fireflies were out. There was serenity in the air as Bill called an end to a long day.

Billy lit a candle inside a glass lantern and set it in front of him and opened his newly acquired supplies. He fished out a ball for the pistol Rebecca had gotten from the riverside bar. He poured out some powder in his hand then funneled it down the barrel. He looked around; confident he was alone, he placed a ball in the barrel and carefully used the ramrod to push it home. He stopped for a moment and stared at the stars. Picking up a small powder flask he proceeded to pour a fine powder into the pan and snapped the frizzen shut. *That ought to do it in case Olof comes snooping around.* He blew out the candle and laid back and relaxed. The runt had just dozed off when he heard a movement close to him; pulling the pistol from the covers, he waited for the noise to identify itself.

"White Man, where are you?" the whispering voice called out.

It was Ann. "Over here. Somethin' wrong?" Billy asked, concerned.

"Hell yes. I need some of that white meat of yours shoved up my ass!" she whispered, giggling like a school girl. *Did I hear what I thought I heard? Did she say that?* Bill thought.

"Well, pull them breeches down an I'll slip some into ya then." Not wanting to miss a chance for sex, no matter whom it was from.

"Listen then, I want you to use that golden tongue of yours first. Then you can stick it in, okay?" Ann was using the innocent voice that comes and goes faster than a quart of moonshine at a barn dance.

Ann wrapped her arms around the runt as she placed her lips on his. Parting them, she forced her tongue deep into the blond man's mouth. She was flickering that hot tongue of hers in and out as her breathing was getting faster and faster. Bill slipped his hand down the front of her breeches to rub that red button. Slowly first. Then he rolled it between his fingers. She pulled back from his embrace as she laid on her back, folding her arms behind her head.

"Do my tits." she begged. As he lifted up her shirt, Bill's wet fingers caressed her hard nipples. Her honey was on his fingers, making them slippery as he manipulated, rolled, and tugged on them.

He then lowered his mouth on them to suckle and rough them up with his teeth. Her hands came around to hold his head down on them. Bill forced himself up as pulled them together so he could do both at once. She was squirming like she had rolled into an anthill. Her breathing was coming in small pants now.

"Use your tongue on my pussy." she said between breaths, "I want that rock-hard tongue of yours shoved up my hot dripping pussy." *This girl likes to talk,* Bill thought as he obeyed.

When he pulled her breeches down to her ankles, lifting her legs up to put them on his shoulders, it occurred to him she was dripping like a milk bucket with a hole in it. *Hell, it felt like she was takin' a piss, like her sister. But it was only that sweet honey of hers,* Bill's mind raced as he sucked and licked like a hound dog sucking the marrow out of a bone. He lifted her legs higher so he could stick his tongue up her ass. She had so much honey dripping that it was already dribbling down her butt cheeks. The runt rolled her over on her side, pulling his root out; he began to probe for an opening. She pulled one leg out of her breeches, giving him a better target. Bill was very anxious, ready to go off at any moment. Feeling her hand pull her ass cheek open so he could perform easier, the young man began pushing very gently on the black-haired one's anus, not wanting to injure her.

"You don't have to be gentle, I've been poked there many a

time. Ram that cock in hard! I want your rock-hard cock shoved up my hot juicy ass! I want your balls banging off of my ass cheeks! Do you hear me?" This was different than what he was accustomed to, so he responded to her commands quickly.

Bill could feel his scrotum flapping against her rump as he performed. She had let go of her leg and was using her hand on herself now. He couldn't see, but occasionally he would feel her finger touch his pod, so that's what he figured she was doing. She was thrusting her rump to meet his every stroke when a pair of hands covered his eyes.

"Guess who?" the voice said. It was Rebecca.

"Don't stop on my account." Rebecca continued. Bill strained his eye to see the redheaded form in the moonlight. He saw her white rump as she moved to Ann's head, and then he saw her form lower on Ann's head.

"Hey, eat this bitch!" Rebecca ordered in a hushed voice as Ann's head vanished under Rebecca. The fiery redhead didn't miss a good licking when she had a chance. Ann's hand was thrashing herself like scrubbing clothes on a rock. As Ann climaxed, her legs closed around Bill and her butt tightened up. Bill exploded inside the evil woman below him, filling her up with his seed. He kept stroking until he was as soft as a fat woman's ass.

"Oh. Oh. Oh." Then Rebecca fell over.

Bill was wiping himself off with his shirt as he noticed the sun was on its way to a new day. The girls saw it too as they were pulling themselves apart from the late night's activities. Then, as quick as a snake, they were up heading toward the house; little did they know Eva had been listening most of the night through her bedroom window, which just happened to face the meadow.

CHAPTER 74

Those youngsters will be better off without Mary Beth. I expect they'll be getting ready to leave, she thought as she pulled Frank's arm from around her.

Quickly she got up pulling her robe around her. *Hmm? What's this?* Her hand lifted her gown so she could touch herself.

Well, I'll be 'et for a tatter. I haven't been wet like this since Frank courted me years ago! Well, she thought as she looked at the sleeping man on their bed, *Nah, I'll let the ol'goat get some rest.* She headed for the wooden door. Just before she opened it, she stopped. Turning, she looked again at the sleeping man.

No, I'm going to wake him up with a surprise. Walking back to the bed, she dropped the robe and her nightgown to the old wooden floor as she slipped in beside him. Gone were the firm breasts and the tight little rump he had married nearly fourty-five years ago. But her heart was filled of love for this man, and she was going to have him right now. Her hand slid down to find the opening on his long handles as she watched his face, still asleep.

Good, she thought. Her finger found his manhood as she caressed it, feeling it begin to swell. She kept a smooth movement as not to stir the old man next to her. As it grew, she guided it out the front of the underwear until it was completely erect.

Slowly she stroked it as it hardened more. Eva lifted the covers as she repositioned herself to have her face inches from his penis. Carefully lowered her mouth over it as it crept down her plump throat. Her lips closed on him as she raised her head up and down, slowly bringing the constable closer to firing a load off. She began pulling the covers down, she slowly brought a leg over the sleeping man, careful not to awaken him. Yet.

Leaning forward until her large breasts swayed to and fro as she guided her man's root into her, sitting down slowly until he was completely buried. She knew him to be a sound sleeper; so she continued, up and down, up and down. Then she felt the tingling that hadn't been there for many a season.

"Frank, it's time to get up." she whispered in his ear. Slowly he stirred, and then his eyes blinked open as he figured out what was happening.

"Eva? What in tar feathers are you, " He didn't get to finish as Eva lowered her mouth onto his, forcing her tongue into his mouth. Frank was old, but he hadn't forgotten how to make love. His arms came around her as he matched her strokes, her pillows of breasts smashing down on him as she climaxed. Frank felt himself spurting away inside of his wife, filling her up with his love.

"Damn, Eva. That was nice. We should do that more often."

"Yes, we should." As she got up, she placed her hand to catch the dripping semen. She bent over, picking up her nightgown. She wiped herself off and the smell of sex filled her little room. Too long they had gone without that smell. Frank saw her plump backside as she bent over; he noticed the hair-covered peach he used to enjoy as they were young lovers. *Yes, we'll do this more often.*

CHAPTER 75

Billy watched the two girls leave as he pulled his belt and knife over his shirt. Satisfied he slipped the French pistol in across the left side. He was sure they were off to the mountains today as he rolled his bedroll up and hung it over the rail. He looked at the horses standing in the small corral. There were many things to do before they could leave, he began the soon-to-be routine of preparing the horses every day. Today, though, there would be no brushing the horses as they were still saddled from last night. He grabbed the nearest bridle and walked to the nearest horse. The horse stood still as he put the bridle on and he began thinking about the oncoming journey. *Damn, there is a shitload of stuff to be done 'fore ya even throw a leg over these nags.* Bill turned as he heard footsteps. It was Mary Beth.

"I'm going to stay here." Mary Beth said, emotionless. Then she turned walking off toward the house, not another word to be said. Ann and Rebecca came out of the house with a bundle of food and a smile on their faces. Bill, seeing the smiles, knew there had been some mischief. They shook hands with Frank and Eva as the constable ensured the trio that Mary Beth would be well taken care of. With promises made, they rode west, never looking back.

"Frank said that if we head due west, we'd bump inta the Missouri in a week 'er so. Then follow it north. The way he was talkin' we'd find a brigade 'fore we even get out of Missouri." the runt blurted out as they rode west.

Bill thought about the trip ahead of them. St. Louis was ruled out now as they found they could head due west to find a brigade of substantial size. Billy still remembered the Indians and the fierce wild animals they had heard of.

"Well, I've already been bloodied, an' I reckon I'll do it again if my girls get in a pinch." he spoke to the open prairie before them.

"What's that?" Rebecca asked.

"Nuthin'. Jus' thinkin' out loud."

"That's a joke, you thinking! Just keep that piss'r of your's handy, and we'll be fine!" laughed Ann. Rebecca soon joined in the joking too.

The days and nights began to blend into one after another as the end of summer raced to meet them. After a few nights it felt like they'd been doing this forever. The chores of packing and watching for highway men and Indians were a pain in the ass to the young blond man. The girls pulled their weight and did their share of night watch's. Bill would wake up to do his shift, and there would be no one to be seen. But as soon as he got his rifle, a body would show up like a ghost.

In the three weeks following the departure from the Low's, they encountered many more creeks and streams. The town named Florida lay before them now. They entered the town just as they had been doing for days, no one gave the small brigade a second look. On the contrary the folks they did meet would wave and greet them with enthusiasm of a long-lost relative. Bill and his girls kept their noses pointed west. Soon they crossed the Salt River from the east side of the town of Florida. Once they were across, they were in the west side of Charlton. Everyone was saying that's where the real frontier starts.

The Great Plains

CHAPTER 76

The trio rode into Charlton in the midday heat; sweat had soaked through his hat and was dripping down his back into his already-soaked breeches as he surveyed the tent town before him.

The last two weeks the temperature had been hovering in the low one hundreds, causing a great deal of chaffing on tender skin as the young brigade tramped across the open plains, heading to the elusive shining mountains.

"I'm strippin' this goddamned shirt the hell off!" the runty white man blurted as the sweat dripped into his eye from under his wide-brimmed hat.

"You best be leaving that rag on your back. You're so dern white that you'll scare every critter off for miles." Then Rebecca laughed and winked at Ann from under the brim of her hat.

Bill felt the sting from the two sassy women. He decided to leave his shirt on as he walked the mare up to the first dry-goods store on the edge of town.

Ann took charge, as always, speaking to the clerk that was sweeping the wooden walkway in front of his tented store.

"Say, mister!" The clerk stopped, looking up at Ann; his old eyes twinkled with beauty of the young girl before him.

"What do you want, you sassy girl?" he spoke harsh, but his eyes reflected a different thought.

She tilted her hat up, "My friends an' I want to go up the Missouri fur trapping." she spoke blatantly loud.

"Is that a fact? I suppose you want me to tell you how to get there, ain't it?" he retorted, holding his broom close to his chest.

Before he could snap more responses to Ann, several skin trappers who had been sitting on barrels in front of the store overheard the conversation. They approached the small brigade with mischief in their eyes. Apathetically they looked at Billy and the girls, their eyes dancing with lustful thoughts.

"Well flatlander, Ashley be a goin' up tomorrow. You might be able to werk fer him. 'Cept them women ain't gonna be able to go. You'll have every nigger in the brigade fightin' fer a piece of tail." the nearest greasy bearded trapper spoke to Bill; but as his eyes were dancing with the girls, his hand rested on Rebecca's gelding as he drooled over the red-haired girl.

"Where's this here Ashley? I'll be askin' him personal like." Billy spoke, reining his horse between the trappers and his girls.

"He's on the outside of town." He was pointing north with a bit of disgust for the white runt ruining the fun for him and his partners.

"But it won't do you no good." he called to Bill and the girls as they left.

"Thank ye." Bill spoke as he backed his mare away from the newly formed crowd.

The trio rode out of the town to hoots and hollers of the crowd about coming back to show off the girls' skills. Indecision was bouncing around in the young man's head as they traveled in the direction the trappers had given them.

"You know, we could make a lot of money right there. Them ol' boys need a poke bad. Hell, who knows what we coulda got from them?" Rebecca spoke as she looked back over her shoulder at the disappearing tents.

"Listen, girl." Ann answered, "I ain't gonna start whoring." Ann spoke with the usual authority, "Not until we absolutely have to."

"It might be fun. Maybe one of them old codgers got them a fat ol' dick." Rebecca sassed her lover.

"Now that wouldn't be half bad then. Big old squash-sized prick. Yeah, I can feel it up my ass already. Um, good." She laughed as they left the town.

Billy just shook his head as he led them northwest. The sun peaked in the sky as the morning became afternoon. The sweat had soaked through Rebecca's thin linen shirt, outlining her nipples as Billy looked admiringly over to her. She winked at him as Ann watched, her white face reddening. The horses had become as sweat soaked as the young trappers, but they plodded on methodically to the commands of the young riders. Bill wasn't sure what was going to happen when and if they reached Ashley, whether they would get welcomed or run out on a rail. He was guessing the first.

"There be the camp." Bill pointed to the small columns of smoke spiraling to the heavens as the trio entered the makeshift town of canvas tents. The skin trappers and camp workers stopped working to view the sights of Rebecca and Ann as they crept closer to Ashley. Bill looked at the grizzled trappers and the fat camp workers. Suddenly, he felt as out of place as a preacher in a whorehouse.

Bill's mare became nervous with strange noises and smells that had caught her attention. Her ears laid back flat on her slender head. She began to prance. The runt patted her neck, comforting her as he approached the man wearing the clean white high-collared shirt with a waist coat as black as the soot from a chimney.

"This has to be Ashley." he spoke to Rebecca without turning his head.

"You Ashley?" Bill asked as politely as he closed the distance.

"Whom may I ask is inquiring?" he spoke with even looking up.

"I'm askin'." Bill replied, pushing the brim up on his hat.

Ashley had been leaning over a deer-skin table covered in maps; he stood tall as he looked the trio over as he lay a pair of dividers down.

"I don't want women with my trapping brigade. If that's what you're inquiring about. If you want to be in my employ, then I'll pay you a fair wage to do camp work to the mouth of the Missouri and back. If not, you may leave my camp." As he spoke, a crowd gathered around.

"Leave that redhead fer me an' I'll make sure she has a warm place to sleep. Ha-ha." A deeply tanned buckskinner laughed, his red voyeur cap bouncing playfully back and forth as he mimicked having sex with her.

"Well, thank ya kindly jus' the same, but I reckon we'll be on our way." Bill said as he backed his horse into the girls. They all turned to walk out of the camp.

"Come on back when ya can stay a little longer." the buckskin-clad trapper shouted, and then the camp went up in a roar as they walked out of the camp.

"Don't give them the pleasure of riling us up." Ann spoke without turning her head.

"I hope you have a plan, Mr. Hunting Dog." she chided Bill.

"We'll jus' skirt them sumbitches. Ain't no worries. We'll jus' skirt 'em." he spoke confidently. *But damn! We're in a mess now,* he worried.

CHAPTER 77

The trio made camp within view of Ashley's large brigade, just to be sure they wouldn't leave without them. Then on a hot August 18, Ashley packed up and began his journey to the headwaters of the Missouri, taking twenty-five skin trappers, fifty packhorses and mules loaded heavy for the trappers, and countless camp workers.

Traveling twenty-five miles the first day, they had gotten within a few miles of a village of Pawnee Indians. The runt knew where the village was, but no white trappers came up to advise them of the situation with the Indians. Billy, Rebecca, and Ann made their camp and cooked their meager meals over a brush fire.

Bill sat by his small fire watching the other white people as the weather continued to change. It dropped from eighty-eight degrees to thirty-two degrees in a moment's notice as a layer of thick clouds engulfed the prairie. He lay another piece of wispy scrub bush on the fire, causing the flames to warm up the immediate area as it sparked and popped from the sap.

"I don't like all those red niggers being so close. Do you think they'll bother us?" Rebecca asked with a worried look on her face.

"Hell, I don't figure that there be any problems, but we'll just keep our eyes wide open and keep them guns close." the runt answered with confidence. His gaze fell over the distant village as his lips finished the sentence. The village was huge, and there was no way the natives didn't know the young trio was bivouacked on the distant hillside.

Bill and the girls made a meager camp that evening. There was no fire, and the once-new blankets were pulled tight against the evening winds.

"I hope it gets better than this. I'm freezing my twat off." was Ann's only comment the whole evening as she painfully fell asleep.

Rebecca remained quiet and thought *Bill said it was gonna be hard. This is hard, and we haven't even got to the mountains yet. God, what have I gotten into? The* Mae *was warm. Sheila would be cussing now. She hates being cold. Ha ha. I remember that, Sheila. She was,* Rebecca dozed as the wind blew in from the northwest. Bill curled up like a cur dog, his blanket pulled over his hat and scarf as he wondered, *This is gonna be rough. I hope Rebecca and Ann can make it. I don't wanna turn back. Maybe this is just a quick snap. Yeah, a quick snap. It'll be nice tomorrow. These blankets aren't as warm as I thought they'd be. Nope.* He squeezed his eyes shut and drifted to sleep as the winds raced across the prairie. Their horses turned their rumps to the winds, heads hung low as they weathered winter's early visit.

He got up in the morning and stepped outside his small camp to water the bushes. He marveled at the vastness the plains offered as he spread his stream in the direction of a clump of dry grass. Concentrating on his game, he failed to notice the handsome Pawnee warrior that materialized before him.

The sight took Billy by surprise as he had no weapons with him at the time. Still he marveled at the man's garb. His bald scalp was colored red and black, the black made him look like a coon, with a greased roach of hair standing up in the center going from his brow to the nape of his neck; it was decorated with feathers that gave the appearance of a breast of a peacock. His brightly decorated buckskins were beneath an elaborate breastplate made of bird bones and India trade beads. Around the neck of the five-foot-ten-inch man hung a necklace of badger or bear claws and more India glass beads. The long fringe on the arms of his war shirt waved in the air like prairie daisies in the spring as the man raised his hands in a gesture of peace. Bill slipped his pod away and buttoned his breeches as he watched the man.

"Gotta remember to take a gun with me next time I gotta pull on this here root of mine." Billy spoke aloud as he held his hands away, showing he had nothing to fight with. The native was making signs with his hands, quickly pantomiming to try to get the young trapper to understand his wishes. As the runt watched, he slowly began to grasp the hand signals, so he used his fingers and arms to convey his message back to the native before him. The warrior picked up two sticks, then pointed to his chest, signing that his name was Two Sticks, and he wanted to trade. Before the White Man could answer, the Pawnee turned and walked away, leaving Bill in a quandary. *What in tarnations is goin' on?* the runt thought.

Two Sticks reappeared with three fine ponies trailing behind him. The runt's heart skipped a beat when he saw the mounds of buffalo robes and deep-yellow buckskins piled on the backs of the horses. The cold wind blew across the high plains, bringing Bill back to the reality of being almost frozen, so Billy did the only thing he could think of; he led the Pawnee back to the tiny fire Rebecca had started.

Two Sticks surveyed the small camp; seeing the women with their blankets wrapped around them with their hats held down with the wool scarves, he held out the reins for two completely loaded ponies while pointing to Ann.

"You ain't trading me to some filthy red nigger White Man, so you can just forget it!" the black-haired bitch snapped, her eyes shooting daggers as her hand rested on her pistol butt. Billy held his hand up, indicating no trade. Not to be put off, the dark trader increased his wager to three ponies. Billy was surprised by this bold movement but still held his hands up to show no trade. Finally Two Sticks got the point. So the Indian sat down to the fire, holding his hands out to warm them. Once again he started hand signals. The runt watched patiently as Two Sticks began the trading sequence. Billy watched, nodding his head as he watched the signs. Billy signed back slowly as he watched Two Sticks's eyes for approval.

"Three ponies?" the Indian signed. Billy watched closely.

"Still want her?" he spoke aloud as he signed the best he could.

Two Sticks nodded slowly, his eyes dancing on Ann's blanketed shape.

"Don't you do it White Man. I swear by all that's alive I'll kill you dead an' shit on your grave!" Ann chimed in when she saw Two Sticks eyeballing her again.

"Likes girls." Bill continued showing his fingers; he mimicked two V's intersecting. The Pawnee nodded an approval.

"You told that Injun I was a lesbian, didn't you? Fucker!" she cussed.

"Shut up Ann. This guy could kill us an' take all of it for himself. So just shut up!" Bill spoke over his shoulder at the black-haired one. The trading started.

"What's that White Man?" Rebecca asked.

"Nuthin'. Jus' thinkin' out loud."

"That's a joke, you thinking! Just keep that piss'r of your's handy, and we'll be fine!" laughed Ann. Rebecca soon joined in the joking on Ann, he shook his head.

"What did he say?" Ann snapped. Bill called over his shoulder to the whining woman.

"Too bad we're gonna get scalped by the derned Blackfoot.'" Bill continued to rile Ann.

"He says it a waste of a good woman.'" All that Two Sticks had really motioned was his rump was sore from sitting, but Bill wanted to stir Ann up some.

He started trading. The Pawnee was pointing to the small iron pot that lay next to the fire. Billy nodded.

"Cook tools?"

"Warm clothes."

Out came the beautiful buckskins and the robes for the trio to admire and lust over.

Two Sticks asked, pantomiming drinking.

"Coffee?" Bill asked.

Two Sticks nodded.

"Moccasins?" Bill replied, pointing to his tattered shoes. The Indian nodded, producing ankle-high moccasins. There were six pair laid before the young white man. Bills picked up a set and held them to his foot.

Bill nodded and called the girls, "Come fit up these here moccasins girls." Each woman tried on the shoes until they settled on two pairs each, leaving the last one for Bill. He picked up the last set and measured them again.

"Too big." He sighed. *Hey, I wonder if they'd fit over the others.* He slipped the smaller into the last pair. They fit perfectly. Bill nodded as Two Sticks smiled, knowing he was getting a deal from the young white travelers.

He called to the girls, "Make sure yer moc'sons fit inside each other like a snow boot."

Each girl called out, "They do!"

"Five pounds for three pairs." Billy held up five fingers on one hand and three on the other as he did his best poker face. He could see the trader was thinking hard and then he shook his head.

"Five pounds coffee and five pounds of sugar. All shoes." He pointed to the stack of sugar and coffee and then pointed to the shoes. Two Sticks nodded.

"Rebecca, fetch five pounds of coffee an' five pounds of sugar fer this gentleman, would ya please?" Bill spoke over his shoulder.

"You don't have to do squat for that peckerwood Rebecca." Ann snipped.

Rebecca sassed back, "Shut up Ann, I wanna get warm, so if I have to get stuff for the White Man, then by god I'm doing it. You know, you could help a little." Ann just pulled the blanket tighter as she sneered.

On went the trading. Billy would ask, Two Sticks would respond with a marginal item. It was up to Billy to up the ante to his level.

If Bill made no qualms about the price, Two Sticks would smile and nod. If the price wasn't to the Indian's level and Bill wouldn't come down, Two Sticks would sit cold faced and wait. Billy would take the item away as he would caress a knife or pan as he watched the Indian think. Finally, when he was almost sure Two Sticks was going to get up, the Indian would nod and the trade would continue.

The young lad had done well trading with Two Sticks. He had gotten them warm clothes, footwear to ward off the cold of the up-and-coming winter, along with tomahawks for each of them with several extra hand-carved handles and nice buckskin covers for the four rifles.

Finally Two Sticks stood again, holding out his hand. Bill grasped it, shaking it firmly; Two Sticks placed a hand on Bill's shoulder and nodded. He then turned, picking up the bounty he had traded for, and began loading the ponies. The items he traded for were not as bulky as the buckskins and buffalo robes, but they would be worth two or three times that to other whites later. Satisfied with his packing, he waved good-bye, vanishing from sight. The morning was gone and the afternoon was waning as Bill's trio had gotten all they had desired. Gone was all the tobacco, all the coffee and sugar, the cloth, India beads, vermilion, and the only mirror this side of the Mississippi as far as Ann was concerned. They had one cooking pot and two camp axes left.

The small trio quickly shed the ragged clothes they had been living in. The soft linen had become threadbare from hours of use, and Billy's was in horrid shape from his encounter with the hog. They all had a smooth yellow breechclout that took them a few tries it get right. Each pulled on the leggings, that had six inch fringe on the outside from hip to ankle and thigh-length buckskin shirts with fringe on the outside of each arm. The front were plain smooth buckskin with a fringe buckskin bib that they could remove. On went the thick-soled double-layered moccasins as Bill felt his feet immediately get warmer as he pulled the thick strings tight on the ankle-high shoes. Then the over moccasins shoes. Last were the thick buffalo coats that had cost them so much. The shirts hug down level with the bottom of the coats, assuring their rumps would be warm as they rode.

"Rebecca, let me see you in your new skins." Bill was admiring the shirt. It hung low enough to be a dress; the shoulders of the doeskin were died green with long fringe on the arms. Bill admired the shirt as the wind caused them to flutter like bird feathers; the small shells and beads tied in the fringe tinkled as the winter began its onslaught on the prairie.

"Goddamnit! I'm freezin' my ass off here!" she said through her chattering teeth.

"You can wait until spring to get the rest of yer show!"

"You can just forget me prancing around for you. There isn't any goddamned way I'm going to walk around and freeze my twat off just so you can ogle me!" Ann spoke sharply as she pulled her wide belt around the big buffalo robe. She slipped her tomahawk in the back and her pistol in the front. She put the powder horn over her left shoulder and the possible bag over the right, completing her mountain-man ensemble.

"Ya know, I'm glad we met Two Sticks. I bet that red nigger trades all our stuff an' doubles his money doin' it." Billy spoke as he and Rebecca mimicked Ann's dressing style.

The small brigade settled in the routine of traveling. Now that they were dressed as the plains Indians, their chances of survival had improved immensely.

CHAPTER 78

They traveled northwest following the thin ribbon of a trail that was left by the larger brigade. The wind blew into their faces as it commenced to snow, coming down in what seemed like a huge blanket covering the ground quickly.

Billy had his new buffalo robe coat pulled tight but could still feel the wind buffeting him. His breath froze on his wispy mustache, looking like he has a white caterpillar on his now-wind-burned face. He was glad Ann had thought of the wool scarves as he had his around his hat as the girls had done.

The girls kept to themselves, bundled up in their robes as the horses followed Bill's brown mare into the white frozen wasteland, each lost in the mindless tramp across the frozen prairie. Step by step they traveled just within sight of the larger brigade.

Bill watched his horses' ears as they traveled. They would twitch this way and that as sound would come across the snow. The humans couldn't hear the sounds, but the horses stayed on guard as their lives depended on it. The lack of food, combined with the biting cold and howling wind, assured them they were in for a long winter. The early winter claimed the last day of October.

The white man and his wives traveled on through the bleakness, only occasionally catching a glimpse of Ashley's large brigade. They had been following Ashley's group, and when they got to the site of the abandoned Pawnee village, deserted of all life now, they entered what used to be the center of it.

The trio had left Charlton with no idea of how or where they would get food for the horses or themselves for that matter, and Billy was hoping for the Ashley group to help them out as they traveled, but the large brigade stayed away from the runt and his girls. The landscape was bare of game as the horses grew leaner by the day; their ribs were now showing as they plodded on through the deepening snow.

I reckon most of them critters left fer warmer weather. The way I figure it, them red niggers followed 'em 'cause there ain't shit here, Bill thought as they entered the remains of the camp.

As they entered a small glade of cottonwoods that had acted as a snow break for the village, Bill surveyed what was left of the defunct camp. All there was left were blacken holes in the ground from the camp fires. He didn't even dismount as they followed the trail of Ashley's horses. There about an eighth mile out in front of them, Bill spotted the large brigade.

Rebecca stared at the men in the distance as she spoke, "What in tarnations is them white niggers doin'?"

"I don't know, but I hope they have a fire. My ass is so cold I think it'll take a pry bar just to open it up to take a shit." the muffled voice of Ann spoke from inside her buffalo coat.

Bill looked across the meadow to where Ashley's men were feeding their horses bark from the trees.

Billy spoke as he watched the faraway men feeding the saddle horses.

"Lookie there. They's feeding their horses bark off'na these here trees. Well, I'll be cooked over the devil's own fire. If'n it works fer him, it'd work fer our horses too."

Billy White had no idea that cottonwood bark was the easiest food he could get for the horses, though it did nothing for his and his wives' stomachs. He dismounted, feeling pain as his feet touched the frozen ground.

"Come on down girls an' give me a hand feeding these here cayuse's." Bill spoke without turning his head.

"You can kiss my frozen ass if you think I'm climbing down off this bucket of bones, you sawed-off son of a bang tailed whore of a runt. You make a fire, then, I'll climb down. Then I'll lend a hand feeding the horses." Ann mumbled inside her warm coat.

"Bitch." Bill spoke quietly, and then he heard movement as Rebecca had come over to help with the chores as well.

"Thanks lover." Bill smiled through his white chapped lips.

"You'll owe me a good tongue lashing this spring, hear?" she spoke loudly enough for Ann to hear. The horses ate as quickly as Bill and Rebecca could peel the eatable bark. Bill's mare stepped over to a tree and used her yellow teeth to pry more as the white couple pulled long slivers off. Ann never dismounted; her black hair covered her face in the wind as Bill fed the horses. When the trees were skinned down, Bill and Rebecca mounted to continue after the large brigade.

Following Ashley's brigade, they were wondering if they were going to survive. The horses were doing better now that they had a source of food, but the young people on the other hand, were not doing as well as the weather was battering them. Bill turned in his saddle to look at Ann; her black hair blew in the wind, reminding Bill of crow's feathers the way it fluttered in the brisk wind. She looked up from inside her robe coat. Her eyes met Bill's, and she smiled through her cracked and dry lips. He leaned over to look past Ann to see Rebecca and the packhorses; she had her scarf pulled tight around her hat, keeping her ears warm as well. Seeing Bill had turned to check on them, she lifted a hand to wave to him, assuring him she was okay. He waved back as he thought of his lover often now as the bleakness of the prairie invaded his mind. All he could see was that red hair and those blue eyes. She was a looker even in this cold weather.

It snowed continually now. The large drifts made the tired horses stumble, often catching a weary traveler by surprise. Bill or Ann would catch themselves as the horse would leap or bound through a drift, causing the riders to cling to the saddle horn to keep from being tossed off. The two packhorses were straining to keep up as the trio plunged deeper into the frozen white tundra of the open prairie.

Rebecca's gelding was the best in the bunch. She had traded places with Bill as her geldings sure-footedness was obvious. It chose its steps well even when exhausted. It never stumbled or tried to unseat the redheaded rider. At times Bill lost sight of the other skin trappers, letting him wonder if they all had gone under.

Finally they stopped on the Loupe fork of the Platte River not more than a rock throw of the Great Pawnee village. The terrain had changed. Gone were the huge snowdrifts, replaced by barren landscape with jagged rocks and devoid of any life.

The cold weather had killed several of Ashley's horses, and many more of the haggard beasts were on death's doorstep as Billy and his partners skirted the village.

"We'll hole up here on this here bluff. I wanna see where they is." the black-haired bitch spoke with authority. Billy looked at Rebecca who shrugged her shoulders as if to say, "I don't know."

As Billy looked out at the other trappers, it occurred to the young lad the strangeness of these men. They had been traveling behind the large brigade, and not once had they made an attempt for conversation or provisions.

"You know, them white niggers is a passel of strange folks. Hell, they ain't come around asking fer a poke 'er whiskey, not that I gots any. It's like we ain't even here." Billy spoke through the frigid air, "You think it might be because it's colder than a preacher's wife on her wedding night. I mean that might be the reason they ain't came up." he stammered on.

"They won't come up because of Ashley's a hard ass. He keeps them on a tight rein. The poor bastard's probably have to get permission to take a piss. Ain't none of 'em gonna jack off without that prick allowing it either." Ann interrupted before the small white man could ramble on.

The night closed in on them as the temperature plummeted once again. The stars came out in a beautiful show that night. With a cloudless sky, Bill stared in amazement of the beauty the open plains offered them. True, it was colder than a well-digger's ass in January, but the breathtaking views always settled him down.

Across the landscape, clumps of trees could be seen. They would sprout like weeds in a garden; miles with nothing, and then a few acres of trees would dot the horizon. He and Rebecca once again got a fire going using the deadfall that littered the floor of the small timber they had found. With the fire crackling and popping, the night crept in and reminded the trio that they had no food and one more night of biting-cold pains would pierce them.

In the early-morning darkness, he woke up Rebecca. With a slight nudge of his moccasin-covered foot, he whispered, "I'm gonna go bag us some meat."

"I want some of this meat." She reached out with a mitten-covered hand to Bill's buckskinned crotch.

"Later."

He got up, grabbing his possible bag and his rifle; as he vanished, it began to snow again. In the time it took Billy to be fifty feet from the camp, a white blanket covered the landscape.

CHAPTER 79

The runt headed into a stand of oak and poplar trees, hoping for some luck. It had been dismal so far, and he and the girls really needed some fatty meat to survive. Slowly he entered the small forest of trees as he froze next to a tall thin oak tree. Its black bark and barren limbs reminded Bill of the dismal life the prairie offered. He stood motionless for an eternity, or so it seemed. Listening, he waited for an animal to reveal itself. His patience was rewarded as the canopy above him became alive with activity. The squirrels began to bark and scamper between trees, paying no mind to the human in their presence. Sounds filled the woods, and sounds meant food. He was ready to shoot squirrels if it came down to getting something to eat, but he stood like a pillar of salt, waiting for a large game creature to show itself.

His perseverance paid off as a large gray white-tailed doe walked out in front of him, not more than fifty yards up wind of him, grazing on the last of the grass under the fresh snow, oblivious to the threat standing a few yards from her. The runt slowly slipped his mitten off, feeling the cold against the rifle. He slowly raised the gun sighting down the iron buckhorn sights to bear on the beautiful creature before him. When he pulled the set trigger, it made an earth-shattering click. Her head lifted quickly as she scanned for the sound, her ears flipping to and fro, trying to identify the sound. She heard the report of the big bore rifle but couldn't identify the danger.

The round ball ripped through her heart as she was looking the wrong way, flinging her five feet across the brush. The beautiful animal tried to stand one last time, but it was a feat in futility. Bill waited as he reloaded his Hawkens. He made no movement other than the simple loading and priming. Quietness came about the forest again. Still he made no movement toward the animal. Bill spoke to himself as he listened to the forest, *No hurry to field dress this here deer and head back. Just wait, boy. If there's a doe, maybe the buck's around here as well.* Slowly the forest came to life as it did earlier. Squirrels barked and scampered from tree to tree as Billy slowly leaned against the tree and waited. Then the wind reversed itself. *I reckon that's it. Might as well go get this over with,* he thought as he leaned away from the tree. His small movement was enough to startle a twelve-point buck up from its resting bed. As it came to its feet, it froze, looking Bill straight in the eye. The runt didn't flinch as he sent another round ball into the chest of the two-hundred-pound deer. The impact lifted the deer off its feet, throwing it into a back flip from the impact. It never felt the landing. *I can pop a few squirrels too? Naw, that's 'nuff fer now I reckon.* Isaiah Weatherspoon's dying words chimed in his ear, "Always reload after you touch one off." Advice he used every time he pulled the gun out of the buckskin cover. So true to the word of mentor words he reloaded. He approached the two animals looking for signs of life.

He found the buck deader than a doornail as he moved over to the doe. As he approached it, he heard the wheezing of the dying animal. He pulled the big knife and kneeled down to finish her off. Looking into her eyes, he watched them glaze into dullness as she died.

"Well, get on with it" he spoke aloud as he laid the rifle against a fallen tree and stripped off the buffalo coat and his buckskin shirt. The young man began with the grizzly chores of gutting the animals. The buck was first; he cut off the scent gland's tossing them over by his gun, then he turned his attention to the belly and was careful not to rip any of the intestines, he slit the big animal carefully. Then he reversed his knife and ripped it through the sternum. He poured the guts to the floor of the forest. Switching to a small butcher knife, he removed the penis and scrotum, tossing them aside. He pulled the liver and what was left of the heart out and put them aside.

The runt stood, catching his breath as the blood froze quickly. Pulling out his tomahawk, he broke the pelvis of the big buck. He moved to the big doe and repeated his process on her as well.

I reckon I should be getting back. He turned to see the animals on the ground. "I'll be back." he spoke quietly as he washed his hands with the snow. He began getting dressed and gathering up his rifle and possibles, Bill stepped to the edge of the small forest looking and waiting to see if the shots had aroused any attention. Satisfied he began his walk back to the small camp for a pair of horses.

The runt approached the small camp whereupon he heard the click of a hammer being set.

"Hold on there girls. It' jus' me. Now hold your fire. I'm back to get a couple horses so I can bring you back some venison." Bill said as he waited for the girls to respond.

"That you, you sawed of runt?" Ann's sharp voice came across the crisp morning air.

"Who else would it be with my voice, you dern idgit?" This was the first time Bill had spoken back to the black-haired vixen.

"I got to shoot a coupla of big ol'deer and spent most of the morning field dressin' 'em fer us. I need a horse 'er two. Now let me in the camp." *I've had 'bout 'nuff of her sharp tongue. I'll take no more of it. Unless she wants to lash at my root with her tongue!* He chuckled to himself as he entered the camp to find a fire going and a small game hen on a spit.

"Damn, that looks tasty. Save me a piece while I go back an' get those deer."

He paused, "No. I'll take a taste right now." Rebecca pulled a leg off and handed it to him.

"Thanks." He stood there relishing the taste until all the meat was gone.

"Goddamn that's good." Bill spoke as he grabbed the halters of two packhorses.

"Glad they ain't saddled. Hate to get gore all over 'em that way. I'll be back soon." Then he left, heading back to his rewards.

***

"Do you really think that shit for brains really killed something?" Ann mouthed off to Rebecca as Bill was soon out of earshot.

"He said he did, and he did take two horses. Anyway, why are you always down on him? You haven't cut him one iota of slack girl." Rebecca asked her partner.

"I don't like him pawing on you. I kind of want you all to myself, and it grinds me the wrong way knowing he's touching you. That's all. It's, well, I'm jealous, okay? There I said it." Ann's shoulders fell as if a burden had been lifted from her.

"Don't fret it lover. There's plenty for everyone, okay?" Then Rebecca leaned over, kissing Ann gently on her cracked lips. Ann responded back, opening her mouth feeling Rebecca's hot tongue enter her mouth; she met it with her own.

"That'll have to be enough for now. We have plenty of work to do when the White Man returns." With that Rebecca pulled out the bone-handled knife and a wet stone she and Bill had gotten back on the Mississippi. Ann watched Rebecca begin to put an edge on the unique knife.

"Where'd you get that knife?" Ann asked, passing the time.

"Bill an' I got it back on the Big Muddy. A little weasel of a man tried to stab the White Man. Me an' him persuaded the varmint into the water or the White Man was gonna carve his liver." Rebecca smiled as she held the knife up, admiring it.

"No shit, the White Man was gonna fight to protect you. Shit, I figured he'd a run like a sissy." Ann smirked.

Rebecca held her tongue and continued sharpening the knife.

What seemed like an eternity was less than a few hours until Bill returned.

"Hello, the camp! Don't go a shootin' me Ann!" Bill called out once again.

"You're fine. Come on in!" came back the familiar voice of Ann. Bill was almost expecting to be gut shot from the young woman. He knew she disliked him and didn't wish to provoke her needlessly.

Good thing Rebecca had worked in the galley because she knew her way around those animals. It took the red-haired lass but a few moments to have a large chuck of red meat sizzling on the fire. The fat from the doe was dripping in the fire, popping, crackling, and sending a tantalizing aroma in the air. Bill cut a large chunk off, handing it to Ann; he knew if he kept her in a subdued demeanor, he could relax the rest of the afternoon.

"Oh my god, this is so good! I'm so hungry." Ann mumbled through a mouthful of the venison. She had juice dripping down her chin into her buffalo robe coat, but she refused to slow down eating. So Bill tossed her more and then cut off a chunk for Rebecca. She took the piece in her mouth, pulling on it with her hand. She sliced between her lips and hand.

"Yeppers. This is the best deer meat I've had all day. Thank you very much White Man." She then stuck the knife in the prone animal as she wiped her mouth on the sleeve of her buffalo robe coat. The red-haired lass sat back against a saddle as she let out a loud belch.

"Damn, that felt good. If it wasn't so cold, I could stand to have some of that root of yours filling me up there, you blond-headed runt!" She smiled at the young man as he placed a small chunk in his mouth. He blew her a kiss as Ann watched in disgust. The trio ate continually until the choice pieces were gone.

"We'll save the other one." Bill announced.

"Yeah White Man, we'll dry it over the fire slow like. And by the way, thank you for the deer." Ann spoke, looking into the blue eyes of the runt. She really didn't hate him as much a she was jealous of him being the apple of Rebecca's eye.

Rebecca finished the second deer as fast as the first one, rolling up the meat inside of the green hide.

"I'm gonna drag these carcasses away from here an' give the coyote's and wolves something to fight over." He laughed aloud at his humor; it was lost on the girls. *Damn them wolves. They'll kill each other to get this. Should be a sight,* he thought. When he returned from the chore, the sun was falling into the western tree line. Looking around the camp, he saw the stack of firewood. Bill dragged a large chunk into the fire, dropping it into the red-hot embers. He watched the sparks fly into the darkness. As he stood there mesmerized by the show, his mind had gone blank as the cold began to wrap its fingers around Bill.

"White Man, you coming in here with us?" Rebecca asked from under the thick black buffalo hide.

"Yeah, let me drag a few more pieces into the fire." He walked back over to the stack Rebecca and Ann had made. Rummaging through the pile, he found another large chunk. The blond runt let out a deep sigh as he dragged the broken limb into the fire. Once more the fire put Bill at ease as he looked into the black sky watching the sparks disappear. Satisfied he began snapping large pieces into more manageable pieces for later as the big limbs would be burned down. When he was content he had enough to keep the fire going all night, he looked at the girls. They were snuggled together, just a big hump in the black robe.

"Too damned cold to do anything anyway." He pulled off his robe coat and laid it over the girls. He crawled in next to Rebecca.

"Night." she spoke softly.

"Go fuck yourself White Man." Ann spoke from the other side of Rebecca. Bill wasn't surprised anymore by this woman. He just let it lie and drifted off to sleep.

CHAPTER 80

As the moon peaked in the night's sky. Red Blanket and his close friend Cut Finger of the Grand Pawnee snuck into the young trapper's picket line to steal the horses from the whites. It would bring great honor to their family if they brought a string of horses in, especially if they were from the stupid white people. While they were quiet and stealthy, some the horses were not familiar with the scent of the Indians. Snickering and foot stomping became more and more evident as they worked to cut the hemp rope.

Bill got out the robes quickly but not quick enough to stop the theft of one horse. He quickly grabbed his Hawkens and ran to investigate the ruckus. As the runt closed the distance to the picket line, he was able to see one of the horses being ridden away with a second dragging its lead rope. The second horse, Rebecca's gelding, hesitated being led by the unfamiliar human, stopped, and backed up, turning in circles as the human tried in vain to lead him away. *Smart horse I reckon that's one less horse, but ain't gonna send a red nigger to hell this close to his own camp. That would most likely be some bad shit fer us.* Quickly the young trapper gathered his and his partners' mounts to return them to his picket line before the cold bit further into his hide.

"What was that all about?" asked Ann as she stood there in her robe coat. Bill was surprised she didn't bitch him out for letting one of the horses being stolen.

"Them thievin' red niggers done stole a pack horse. Sumbitches!" Bill answered as he walked into the small camp.

"Well, only one got stolt. Next time don't go traipsing out in the dark after them fuckers. I don't want to see you killed." Ann sat down staring into the small fire; she turned her face up to meet

Bill's eyes. Even by the night's fire, he could see the concern in her eyes.

"I'm going out tonight and try to steal our horse back. We really cain't 'ford to lose a single horse, ya know." Bill spoke slowly as he stared into the fire. Rebecca had gotten up in all the commotion and had figured out what was going on. Listening to Bill and Ann, she gathered what was on the young man's mind.

Rebecca jumped into the conversation, "Lookie here, if you go out and try to steal that ol' nag back, you'll lose the horse an' all yer hair an' I'm fixing for you keep both of 'em. We might be inviting more trouble than we need. Let it go. We don't have so much we can't spread the load out. Ann and I need you here. We might be able to get it back if we go to the village and explain to the chief that we need it desperately. I'm sure that he's an understanding man." she explained as her breath hung in the freezing air.

"Well shit, what we got to lose. Might as well." With the decision made, Bill lay back against a saddle, pulling a robe around him to ward off the remainder of the night's cold.

CHAPTER 81

Early the next day they rode right down the middle of the camp of the Grand Pawnee. The Indians were astonished by Rebecca's red hair as they stopped moving and just stared. The trio rode into the crowd as it parted. The quiet was overwhelming as the young trapper led them through the Pawnees. Bill had no idea that they'd never seen such red hair as they entered the center of the encampment. Bill saw why everyone was quiet. There sat Ashley sitting with the chief of the Grand Pawnees. Bill looked into Ann's black eyes and asked her, "Do ya think ya could do yer magic on a red nigger?"

"If he likes women? Yes, I can." she spoke quietly. Bill was the only one to dismount; he handed his reins to Rebecca then walked over to where the two leaders sat.

"Hello Mr. Ashley. I didn't 'spect to see ya here. I would like to speak to this great man here, if ya don't mind." Billy spoke politely.

The chief looked up at Bill and then over to the girls and once again to Bill, "I speak your tongue small one."

"Me an' my frien's here, well, we was out yonder." Bill pointed to the south, "Well, one of our horses came up missin' durin' the night. I was wonderin' if ya could tell me how I might go 'bout findin' it. See we ain't as set up as well as Mr. Ashley here, an' we need it somethin' fierce. Now I ain't sayin' yer folks found it, but I was jus' wonderin' if you might be able to point me in the direction that I might try to get it back." Bill stammered. The young lad's knees were shaking under the strain of diplomacy.

"It is good that you came to me first. Stealing ponies is the measure of a man in our land. I have many young warriors that like to play tricks on the white people." he spoke slowly and made no mistake that the whites were the intruders here. Satisfied he had made an impression on the small white man, he quickly spoke to a small man of his tribe. When the brief exchange was over, the small warrior vanished into the crowd. Bill wasn't too sure what was going to happen next, so he held his ground, trying to appear strong. Ashley broke the uncomfortable silence,

"We too have lost some of our provisions son. This is Bright Horse. He's the leader of the Grand Pawnee. He's a fine man, and I call him my friend." Ashley did a small bow toward Bright Horse.

"Yes. We are friends, Ashley." He pushed his chest out to appear bigger than he already was.

The runt interrupted, "Did you say Grand Pawnee?" Bright Horse paused looking at the small man before him; here was a man no bigger than a young warrior of fifteen winters. Bright Horse continued to evaluate Bill. *The heavy coat hides his size, and the hat hides his hair but not his eyes.* There Bright Horse could see determination as well as courage. *This white man does not look away or hang his shoulders. No, this is a strong one.* So in the briefest moment, the Grand Pawnee had summed up Bill. The old warrior answered, "Yes."

"Do ya have a feller here named Two Sticks? He an' me did some tradin' an' would like to wish him a warm winter." Billy spoke with genuine friendship in his voice, letting a big smile come across his face.

"You know Two Sticks?" Bright Horse asked, eyebrows going up.

Bill smiled a toothy grin. "Yeppers. I do."

Once again he spoke something Billy couldn't understand, and another Pawnee vanished. In what seemed like forever, the crowd parted and Red Blanket and Cut Finger entered the scene with the stolen horse. Bill was shocked to see how young these warriors were. The two walked over, handing the reins to the small man. Billy nodded, showing his approval. He figured he should give something to the chief, a gift for returning his horse. He had to figure out what he would trade since he had already traded all the tobacco to Two Sticks already.

"Thank you very much. You're a man of great honor. I would please me to call ya my frien' also." Bill stumbled with the words, looking at the two young men at the same time, seeing the awe in their eyes.

Before Bright Horse could speak, Two Sticks appeared.

"White Man! It makes my heart soar to see you again. Do you have more to trade with me?" Billy's jaw dropped open when he realized Two Sticks spoke fine English. So Billy held out his hand to shake the hand of his new friend. The Pawnee shook it vigorously with a large smile on his face also.

"Nah, you skinned me out pretty good the last time we met." the runt told him.

"Hold on fer a moment." he told him. Then he walked back to where Ann and Rebecca were waiting on their mounts.

"What do you think we should do? We gotta give him a present fer gettin' our horse back. Do we have anything a'tall?" Billy asked.

"You still have that pistol from the river bar." Rebecca reminded the small white man.

"That's the last thing we have from our life," he waved his hand at the supplies on the remaining pack animal, "back 'fore all this."

"I didn't think of it that way. Do you want to keep it? I mean, we don't have to give it up. Maybe we can find something else." Rebecca spoke as she watched Bill open the flap and rummage through the supplies until he produced the pistol, powder flask, shot pouch, and bullet molds.

"Nope. This is all me and you have left from the river." She nodded, realizing Bill had made the decision and was going to go through with it. Bill turned and began walking back to the chief with the pistol lying flat, hammer up showing the intricate engraving on the lock. He presented it to Bright Horse.

"Bright Horse, this is for helpin' us find our lost horse. There's a mold and a few balls, and a powder flask too. Thank you." As Bill handed it to him, Bright Horse's jaw dropped open. Ashley was watching the whole time. He slowly stood up and grabbed Bill's elbow, leading him out of earshot of the chief who was turning the pistol around, admiring it.

"Son, you may have just got us all in some very serious trouble. He did you a favor with that animal of yours, and you've insulted him by giving him a gift. Now I may not be able to trap and survey these mountains because of you." He let go and turned back and smiled.

Meanwhile the chief had been holding counsel with some of his peers. Then one of the older men left, and the tone got very somber. *Goddamn it seems everybody is a coming an' a goin' around here,* Bill thought to himself.

In a short time a beautiful woman walked up to the chief. She was dressed in a thick buffalo robe that was decorated with horse hair, beads, quills, and shells, very similar to the ones he had traded with Two Sticks. Her black hair hung around her smooth bronze skin of her sculpted neck, and her black onyx eyes sparkled with mischief.

"Here is my daughter. She is to be your wife. You must be a good man for you have two wives already. They look strong. You will have many fine sons." he spoke with a big smile. Then Bright Horse spoke to the gathering. Then the camp erupted in clapping, hooting, and hollering.

Oh no! He's givin' me his daughter fer a wife. Goddamnit! Bill was scared now with the thought of having another woman, but he knew Rebecca and Ann would give her a warm place in their small brigade.

"Thank you Bright Horse. What am I to call yer daughter?" Billy asked, trying to sound brave.

"Her name is White Moon, but you may call her whatever

you wish. You may take your new wife into the marriage lodge." he spoke, pointing to a tipi lodge at the far end of the village, and then he turned to Ashley.

"Ashley, we give things you need." Then he got up walking away, taking the majority of the council with him into a lodge behind him, and it was over. Ashley nodded as he got up and signaled his men as they moved out of the Indian encampment back to where his trappers had made a small city once again.

CHAPTER 82

The rest of the village faded away, except for White Moon and Bill's girls. White Moon had a buckskin bag adorned with beads and piping, telling stories of life in her village. She walked over to the returned horse and proceeded to put her possessions across the back of the animal. Then she turned, looking at Rebecca and Ann; she stuck her hand out and spoke clear English, "I will be happy to be with you. Let us all go to the marriage lodge."

She was looking at Rebecca when she quizzed her, "Are you his first wife?"

"Yes. My name is Rebecca. This is White Man's next wife. She is called Ann. How is it you speak American so well?" she asked.

"A man like you came last season, and we learned from him. His name was Jedediah Smith." she spoke looking deep into the redhead's eyes, "A Christian man. We are Christians now. Are you Christian also?" She was looking at them smiling. *Oh shit! We had never talked 'bout religion an' such things. Goddamnit, we're in a tight spot. If we say the wrong thing, hell, she might go tell her pappy an' get us killed.* Bill could see Rebecca looking at him for an answer.

The runt shrugged as if to say, "I don't know."

"It is something that we don't do. Praying and that kind of thing. Is that going to be a problem?" Ann asked.

White Moon walked over to where Billy was standing. She leaned over. Speaking in his ear, she said, "I am glad. I grow weary of it. I liked it the old ways. We could do as we pleased with whoever we wished." She stopped for a moment as she took in the camp's life, smoke coming from the tops of the tall buffalo lodges and few dogs running about playing in the chilling air.

Then she continued, "That is if his wife did not mind. We should go to the lodge now." With that she turned and led the horse toward the outside of the village to the prescribed lodge. Bill and his girls followed as they had no idea of customs that should or would be used in this newest addition to the trapping brigade.

The young trapper noticed a lodge pole in front of the marriage lodge as they closed the distance. He looked over at the other lodges. Seeing the horses tied to them, he figured out what they were for. He tied the geldings up to the outside and the mares to the inside. As Rebecca and Ann entered the lodge, White Moon turned to Bill.

"I will tell you when you may enter." Then she opened the decorated flap. On it was a sun, moon, and stars. Bill acknowledged the order as he went about hobbling the horses for the night. As he tied the knots, he thought about the coming events. The mountains were right before him now. It wouldn't take but a few weeks and they would be in prime trapping streams or so he'd heard. The young runt had no clue where they were going, but he knew that they were close. A cold breeze blew in from the west and made the young man shiver under his heavy buffalo robe. He stared at the saddles. Thinking of it would be worth the trouble taking them off or leaving them on for the night. If he left them on all night, it would be one less thing to do in the morning, but if it snowed at night, it would make the gear wet, might even ruin it.

"Fine! I'll take 'em off!" He mumbled aloud. As he reached for the cinch strap on the gelding, he heard a voice from the lodge.

It was Rebecca, "You can come in now."

"Lordy, what am I in fer?" he asked her as he walked into the lodge. It took a couple seconds for his eyes to get accustomed to the dim light. They had a small fire going with sage smoking on it. The smell caught the small man by surprise as he looked around.

"What's that on the fire?" he asked. White Moon answered with a smile, "It is sage. Do you not like the smell?"

"Nah. It smells right fine. I reckon we'll have to figure what we're gonna do now. The way I, " The young Pawnee stopped him in midsentence as she leaped off the robes like smoke coming off the fire, covering the distance quicker than a coyote snagging a field mouse from under the snow.

He heard a whoopee from the other girls as White Moon's hand was groping under his breechclout, trying to release his hidden gardening tool. Bill reached around behind her head, grabbing a handful of her black satin hair; he pulled until her lips came away from his. The runt caught some air as he released her to continue with the passionate kissing. The young couple fell to the floor of the lodge, intertwined like a pair of courting snakes. White Moon brought Bill's arms above his head as she continued with her insatiable appetite for the white man. Bill felt hands pulling his pod out into the open. *Good god, when was the last time I got that thing out without havin' it freeze?* he thought as White Moon's tongue dove deep inside his mouth. Then Billy felt the warm of a mouth upon his tool while White Moon kept his lips busy. The aspiring mountain man was getting close to eruption now. Just when he thought he was going to unleash himself upon the perpetrator, she backed up.

"We are going to have fun now!" With that she undid the thin buckskin string holding her dress on as it fell to the animal skins on the floor. There she stood before Bill, bronze skin contrasted by the white brain tanned leggings. Her short hairs were as dark and thick as Ann's that she could have passed for her sister.

"I'll have some of that." Ann spoke. She pulled off the war shirt, and soon she was in the same dress as White Moon.

"Well, I don't want to be left out!" So off came Rebecca's long shirt. The contrast was striking; black, red hair, bronze and white skin as the three girls began their investigations of one another.

"I am to be ridden first since I'm the new wife." White Moon spoke boldly. She didn't know about the young white man's ability to go three times.

"Well, isn't that like the new girl." Rebecca laughed. White Moon stood over the small man as she lowered herself onto the waiting runt as she leaned forward guiding the white tool into herself. Satisfied, she leaned back, burying the tool deep inside her. Ann had seen an opportunity for some action, so she walked over and stood over the runt. Then she lowered herself until her black hair covered his face, letting those swollen lips part as the honey began to flow. He did not know where Rebecca had snuck off to. Bill's curiosity was soon abated as he felt her hand guide his into her garden. Bill followed her lead as he stuck his fingers deep inside the slippery valley. As he found her red button with his thumb, he forced his remaining finger up into her awaiting brown rosebud. The runt really had to concentrate, one riding his pod, one girl sitting on his face, and his hand working wickedness on the third girl as White Moon ground on. The young lad felt himself beginning to tingle. He arched his back as he released into her.

White Moon lifted herself as she felt the White Man filling her innermost sanctuary. Standing slowly, she pushed her pelvis forward to let the white semen of life drip upon the runt's stomach. Then Ann arched her back and rolled off as she too climaxed. The runt lifted his head to watch White Moon turn around and commence to lick up the white life on his skin. Then, as if it had been choreographed, Rebecca moved in behind the brown wife, burying her face in White Moon's rump. Feeling the attention to herself, she rolled over, pulling her legs on top of Rebecca's shoulders as the white girl ate noisily. Not to be left out, Ann got up and crawled behind Rebecca. She rolled over on her back as she began to shimmy under Rebecca to pleasure the young redhead. Seeing Ann was open for more attention, Bill quickly slipped over to her. She opened her legs to let the runt gain entry.

Bill was ready for action as he slipped his white pod into the black briar patch of Ann. Bill closed his eyes as he performed on Ann. He couldn't believe he was still on God's green earth. Three women at once, all ready to partake in lovemaking at his request. Even Ann was receptive tonight. White Moon let out a scream, grabbing Rebecca's head as the young Pawnee climaxed. She howled as she threw her head back against the skins she was lying on. Then Rebecca sat up as Ann was still in her honey pot. Ann had both ends covered now. Rebecca reached orgasm, releasing Ann, her eyes closed. That left Bill and Ann in the coupling. As Billy lifted Ann's legs, the black-haired bitch raised her head, her face still wet from Rebecca's entertainment.

"Ready?" Billy asked in between breaths.

"You bet, you ass-fucking runt!" She gasped. Reaching down, Bill slid out his tool from the dripping one to the rosebud of Ann. Pushing slowly at first, he wanted Ann to beg for it. Bill's wait wasn't long. Up to her elbows she came, sneering at the man between her legs.

"Ram it in hard! Fuck my ass hard!" she called to the runt. The runt did just that, not slow and methodical but vicious as a terrier with a rat. Billy was slamming into the black-haired vixen with so much force her eyes opened as big as milk saucers. Staying up on one elbow, she reached down with the other hand to knead her swollen red button. Her hand was a blur as Bill thrashed away in the deep recesses of her anatomy.

"Faster!" she begged. The white runt already had his scrotum slapping against the white cheeks of this hell bitch. She cried, tossing her head back and forth, "Now! Now!" Bill released himself into the poor excuse of a lesbian. As he retracted himself, his member wasn't through as it spewed on to her coal-black curly hair. The vanquished young lass reached down and began to smear his seed over her valley and her belly. Then her other elbow gave out, falling. He began to pant, taking in huge breaths of the musty smoke-filled air.

"Son of a bitch, you do that so well!" she murmured with her eyes half closed. White Moon was watching the whole time as was Rebecca.

"You will have to do that to me sometime. I have never had it that way. Ann, does it hurt you?" White Moon asked.

"Hell yes. But god, does it feel good." She chuckled.

"I do not understand. It hurts but feels good?"

"Well, it's like, hmm, let's see. It's like when you do something very difficult that when it's over it was a good pain. Does that make sense?" Ann asked as the spooge was dripping on to the robes. Rebecca had scooted over to the mess that was still oozing from Ann; she slipped her fingers into Ann to extract more semen. As her fingers came out with the prize, she slowly sucked them clean. Bill watched all this while he wiped himself off on his war shirt.

"If you girls don't take the cake, this is the damndest thing I've ever saw. But I believe I can get used to it." He smiled at the naked girls around him.

White Moon continued, "It must be like when I scrape a hide. It is very difficult, but when I am done and have a fine robe, the happiness is great within me." White Moon spoke as she opened her own love lips with her fingers to probe inside, smearing herself with her own honey.

"Well, that sounds like it a bit. You'll find out when the White Man does you." She smiled, lying back. Rebecca, with a big glob of spooge hanging from her lip, leaned forward and kissed Ann on her open mouth. Ann wrapped her arms around her as they hugged. Billy pulled on his breechclout and shirt as he planned the next chore before him.

"I'm gonna have to get our stuff ready to leave tomorrow girls. Take yer time an' enjoy yer selves." he spoke to no one particular.

The young lad slipped his robe coat on to enter the late-afternoon's cold. He pulled the flap on the lodge open as he stepped out into the cold. The cold wind slapped his face as he walked to the horses; slowly he walked around each animal, checking for anything out of place. He would pull a cinch strap here or check a halter, look at the hobbles to assure that his possessions would still be there in the morning. His mare nuzzled his bare hand as he stroked her between the ears. Leaving the muzzle, he walked along her flanks. *I can't leave this tack out. I know it will be fine, but we'll need it for too long to mistreat it now. "* His mare turned to look at him as he spoke to her.

Off came each saddle and blanket as he stacked them like cord wood outside the marriage lodge. Satisfied the runt undid a robe from the back of the top saddle and spread it out hair down over the saddles. Confident it would be fairly dry come morning, he returned his interest back to the mare. Approaching her, she bowed her head for the man to scratch again.

"You like that, don'cha? It's gonna get worse 'fore it gets better girl. I hope you an' your brood hold up to this harshness we're 'bout to get into." When the small man assured himself all was well, he turned to reenter the marriage lodge.

As his eyes adjusted to the glow of the lodge, he couldn't make out who was who. There were the three women engaged in mutual lovemaking. Billy's eyes strained to discern what was going on, and then he put it together.

Ann looked up from the crotch of Rebecca with honey dripping off her chin. Rebecca had her face buried in White Moon, and White Moon was using her fingers on Ann. Bill peeled his robe coat off to join in the foray when Ann spoke, "You just sit there and watch. Pull on that root of yours if you want. But this is just for us girls." Then she stuck her face back down into the honey pot. By this time, White Moon was three fingers deep in Ann and was using her thumb in her butt. Rebecca arched her back as she climaxed causing her legs to go limp. White Moon brought both hands up to Ann's backside in order to use three fingers in both holes. Then Ann's legs closed as she lifted her head up showing her eyes, which had gone wide open. White Moon giggled. *That does it for them,* he figured. They were flopping around on the robes with honey dripping off Rebecca and Ann. White Moon's brown skin was shining in the dim light of the fire from the sweat of the lovemaking.

"Your wives are much better than I would have ever thought. Most of the whites I meet do not have the playfulness that is here. I am happy to be one of your wives." With that she rolled over on a robe and closed her eyes. Bill thought about his situation as he tossed some more wood on the small fire. As warm as it was inside, it didn't take long for the cold to creep in under the edge of the leather lodge. He lay next to Rebecca, resting his hand on her bare flesh as he stared into the fire.

"You want something lover?" she asked quietly.

"Nah. I was jus' thinkin' 'bout tomorrow. I think we'll head out with Ashley then peel off later. It looks like this weather is common up here. I'm gonna try to talk Two Sticks inta goin' with us. I mean if'n you girls don't mind?" Bill spoke in a low voice.

"One more piss'r to play with." She giggled. The young man chuckled aloud as he closed his eyes thinking about the coming day.

CHAPTER 83

Bill's mind wandered as he listened to the night's sounds. A horse grunted, a quick bark of a guard dog. *This place is good, the dogs, the people, the whole village. Yeppers, pretty damned nice.* Sleep invaded his mind as he began to see the trip to the mountains in a dream. *Gonna have a fine time, yeppers, a fine time.* He began to snore lightly.

Rebecca didn't sleep. Her mind raced with the uncertainty of the journey before them. Under one arm was the Pawnee, her black-haired lover at her foot, and her blond man next to her. She had wanted sleep, but the sex had sharpened her awareness. *I see White Moon an' me doing this, but I can't see Ann going all the way. I love her dearly, but,* she paused as Ann stirred. *Can she do it? Can she stay with me even when it gets shitty? I don't know.* The hog experience flashed before her when the black-haired woman had cried in fear. Then in an instant she flashed back to the time Bill had killed the deer. *She was ready to put the White Man's lights out when he got them two deer too.* She shook her head. *It doesn't make sense. She was none too anxious to have him go after the horse. Shit. That's what started this whole thing.* She looked at White Moon in the glow of the fire. *She's beautiful. No, stunning is better. Yeah, stunning would be it.* She brought her hand up to White Moon's face and carefully pulled a loose hair back. The Pawnee opened her eyes and looked at Rebecca.

"Do you wish more?" she whispered to the redhead.

"No, you're just so beautiful. I just want to look at you." Rebecca whispered a reply. White Moon slid her hand under the robe to Rebecca's groin and paused, looking for a sign from the redhead to continue.

"That's all right." The white woman pulled the Pawnee closer. "We should sleep."

"If you wish." But White Moon left her hand on the edge of Rebecca's red triangle. Neither woman knew Ann had been awake and listening to the whole scenario. *She better not take up with this Injun. I'll have her tits if she does. It's bad enough having the White Man groping all over her.* Ann reached out and slid her hand under the robe to Rebecca's feet and gently rubbed the woman's feet, caressing each slowly and methodically hoping to get a rise from her lover, but no response from Rebecca made Ann feel comfortable that the white woman was still hers. Rebecca was startled but didn't move, *Shit. Ann musta heard me and White Moon. She want's to play more. I've had enough playing around for one night.* Rebecca had no idea what was going through the mind of the lover at her feet. Ann left her hand on Rebecca's ankle, assuring the redhead was hers. Rebecca slid her hand under the robe and under Bill's breechclout and left it there as she fell asleep. Bill slept through the quiet exchange of emotions, not knowing the intimate decisions that had been made in a flash of a spark. The night crept on, ebbing its way toward morning. The horses stirred, and chill entered the lodge as the morning started a new day.

CHAPTER 84

Bill awoke with the hand of Rebecca under his breechclout; he looked at her seeing her mouth open and lightly snoring. *Damn, she had her hand there all night. I better see to the horses.* He pulled the robe off and adjusted it on her. *There, that oughta do her fine.* The young blond man got up and pulled his belt and Weatherspoon's knife on as him looked at his wives. *Damn, these here are some shining times. Well, here we go.*

Bill opened the flap and stepped out into the daylight. The young runt noticed Two Sticks by one of the village fires, so he approached him.

"Hey, Two Sticks. Why don'cha come with us fer a season 'er so? I got them three girls that plum tucker me out. 'Sides I could use yer help on goin' north an' all."

"No thank you small one. I have a life here, and besides, north are the Crow and Blackfoot. They do not like the Pawnee, so I will keep my hair and stay down here on the plains with the buffalo. We will meet again. I know you have some things that I can trade for. Ha-ha!" He offered his hand for the white runt to shake. As the two shook, they smiled at each other, knowing it may be the last time either would be seen alive.

Bill wandered over to the council lodges to listen to the old men as they spoke of past conquests and victories. They noticed the white man squatting near the door. In clear English, an older councilman spoke to Bill, "Come in young one. How does a man with three wives find time to visit with us?" An old warrior laughed, showing his toothless smile.

"I'm surprised he's not resting after White Moon was finished with him!" They all chuckled an inside joke on the young man.

"Why don't you stay here with us this winter White Man? It's not as cold down here, and your scalp will stay on your head!" A young council member laughed.

"Yes, it would be a good thing if the fire-haired one would come to my lodge!" the younger man spoke, laughing and kidding the runt.

"What's yer name?" Billy asked.

"I am called Running Dog. Why do you ask?" Running Dog answered, still smiling.

"Well, I'm wanting to know so I could send my other wife to you. The black-haired one, she's called Ann. She'll make you want to beg to leave. The fire-haired one is too much for a young man like you!" With that the crowd roared in laughter at the joke that had turned around on the warrior. Seeing he was getting made the joke of, his demeanor changed instantly.

The smile now gone, replaced by a sinister frown. "Are you saying that I am not man enough for the red-haired one?"

"Hmm? Can you go three times in a row? If you cain't, well then, you'd be no good to that woman 'cause she'll not let you leave until you do!" Then the crowd was quiet, trying to figure out if it was more of a joke or a truth.

"No one can go three time." Running Dog answered.

"I can. That's how I can keep all them wives!" Bill laughed, slapping his knee loudly. The crowd sat stone cold for a moment. Then relieved they had a joke played on them, they all busted out laughing. Running Dog looked around feeling that he was not the brunt of attention. He laughed with the rest of the council members. Bill was relieved the atmosphere had lightened.

"I'm gonna get folks. It's been a pleasure, an' maybe I'll see you in the spring." Bill smiled as he stood to leave.

"Come back and tell us more jokes young one." the oldest-looking one spoke as Bill lifted the flap to leave. Bill felt the stinging cold as he scanned the village looking in the direction of Ashley's camp. He walked to the edge of the Grand Pawne camp. Seeing the smoke from the white men's he felt the cold wind against his face as it started to snow.

"I'm glad I got these here buffalo robes 'cause it's too goddamned cold." he mumbled as he walked to the trapper's camp. As he neared, he could see Ashley giving an ass chewing to a fat camp worker. Joseph Champeau scowled at Bill as he approached. *Hmm, what's he piss'd at me fer?* Bill wondered as he closed the distance to the booshway.

"Be leaving soon?" Bill asked.

"As soon as I finish this coffee we'll be heading out. You want to travel with us I suppose? Just keep your women away from my brigade. If you do that, we'll have no issues to attend to." Ashley spoke as he started kicking snow over the dismal fire.

"You'd best get your women together or get left behind." Ashley continued.

"I'll catch up with ya then." Bill turned, walking back to the lodge.

The young blond man was approaching the marriage lodge when he saw White Moon was packing the possessions on the horse she had claimed. Bill saw Ann pulling the cinch straps tight on his mare as he closed the distance.

"What's left to do inside?" Bill asked.

"If you were here, you know that it's empty. Where the hell you been anyway?" Ann asked, looking over the top of Bill's mare.

"Knock that shit off right now Ann. You coulda sat on yer ass in the lodge, ya know. Nobody forced you to get up off yer lazy twat to do this. So shut the hell up!" Bill snapped back at the rough lesbian. Ann was taken back that the runt had spoken harshly to her. She was going to snip back but saw the White Man was not going to take any abuse from her; she finished the task before her in silence.

"Oh, there you are White Man." Rebecca called to him.

"Did you get a chance to find out where Ashley is going?" she asked as she tied her sleeping robe on the packhorse.

"Nah, he never said. He jus' said to catch up with them when we're done here." Bill answered as he scratched the muzzle of the mare.

"We might as well get on with it." he said as he threw a leg over the saddle. Arranging his coat to ward off the cold, he turned the mare to where Ashley had been. He didn't need to coax the girls along. If they didn't go, they'd stay with the Pawnee and become wives to some arrogant warrior, doing all the chores with no rest to speak of. He rode for a moment in quietness as Rebecca reined up next to him.

"I'm happy to be on the move again. I was getting sore in that lodge, doing nothing but getting poked by you all night an' day." She laughed through the falling snow.

From behind him, Ann spoke loudly, "Hey! Fuck you!" Bill didn't even turn around as he responded, "Nah, you'd like it too much!" He looked over, winking at Rebecca seeing her smile.

CHAPTER 85

Traveling for most of the day, they saw that Ashley had bumped into another large band of natives. The small brigade tracked them up the fork of the Platte river as it continued to snow. As they crested a small knoll, Bill saw the village. A huge settlement by anyone's standards, they had tipi lodges standing haphazardly with smoke curling out of the tops of the skin structures. Dogs and children ran about, playing in the snow as the day waned on; to the east a column of riders moved toward the village. Bill picked out Ashley. The man broke off from the main body as he rode down into the village. The column had stopped as the white booshway held council with the chief of the village.

Billy White and his girls rode solemnly into the column of white trappers; neither Bill nor his small brigade averted their eyes from the stares of the trappers. They had been on the same tramp as the large cumbersome brigade and had held their own through thick and thin.

"Ashley gone on down to parley with them red niggers?" Bill asked one of the black camp men.

"Yes'ah. He done gone down to have a talk with 'em. Yes'ah that's where he go." the black man answered as his teeth chattered. The camp worker still hadn't become accustomed to the cold, coming from the jungles of Africa less than a year ago, so this whole adventure was far beyond the black man's comprehension.

"Hmm. Well, thank ye fer the information." Bill backed his horse away from the cold man, *it's gonna be a hard row fer that man. It's cold mosta the time,* he thought as he worked his way over to his girls.

"Ashley's down havin' a parley with them red niggers. That the fer certain an' fer true. Let's not get too comfortable here. I wanna take off from this here brigade, if you don't mind." he asked them, looking into their eyes for acceptance.

"Sounds good to me." Rebecca answered quickly, looking at the column of ragged trapper's ahead of them..

"I don't mind White Man, as long as we find a warm place to hole up and get fat." Ann answered.

"I am your wife. I go where you go." White Moon answered, sitting straight in her saddle. It appeared to be a pleasant day for her, not letting the cold or discomfort show on her beautiful bronze skin.

"Okay, it's settled. As soon as Ashley comes back, we'll cut loose." Bill spoke, showing his leadership skills the best he could.

Seeing Ashley return later in the day, Bill walked into the camp. Looking directly at the leader of the brigade, he spoke quickly before he changed his mind.

"It's been a hard row followin' you an' yer men. Me an' my wives are strikin' out on our own."

Bill stuck out his hand. The booshway grasped it and shook it firmly.

"You have been tenacious as a tick hanging on like you've done. Are you sure you don't wish to accompany us farther on my adventure? I think you should travel with us. You and your wives would welcome by our fire. I will not, however, condone the sale of services if you decide to travel with us." he spoke with his hands on his hips, showing Bill he was in charge.

"Well, you won't have to worry 'bout it. I don't want no booshway tellin' this nigger what he's a doin' an' where he goin'. I don't wanna be beholden to no man. I'm a free trapper by god!"

Bill spoke loudly, and then feeling a bit pompous, he changed his demeanor rapidly.

"I figured we could go to the head of this river an' head into the Yellowstone country in the spring. Thanky fer letting us tag along." He dipped his brimmed hat as he led his mare to where the girls were waiting.

"Let's get 'fore I change my mind." he spoke quietly to Rebecca. She knew his heart better than the rest of the girls.

"Wait there, sir! I meant no disrespect. It would be to our best interest if we travel together. I'll not put any regulations on the women." Billy knew that had to hurt.

"Okay. But lookie here. Me an' my wives will pull our share but you don't have no say over us. If that sounds like a deal, then we'll travel with ya." Bill sure hoped this works out. He quickly calculated his situation. *Them hellcats I'm sleeping with would have a man's nuts if they did something out of line.*

"Deal." He stuck his hand out. *Now I don't know if I can trust this here booshway, but it's all I have fer a while anyway,* Bill thought as he pumped the offered hand vigorously.

CHAPTER 86

Ashley's men had been suffering from the weather all the way from the Grand Pawnee's winter camp, losing horses along the way. Ashley went ahead, trading for more horses and food. The man had a golden tongue; he could sell rocks to a farmer. The young lad was standing next to the fire when he heard him say that they had two hundred miles to go and he wanted to be well provisioned. Bill listened to a young warrior, Broken Feather, as he described the next section as having no wood for fires or horses and very little in the way of game.

In the encampment Bill and White Moon joined Ashley at the Loupe's Grand Pawnee chief Gray Hawk's lodge for negotiations. They all sat around a fire inside of the lodge. Bill and White Moon were sitting closest to the door, not near the fire like Ashley. Since he was the booshway he had the respect of the leader. Bill listened to Ashley speak to Gray Hawk about how the great father out east would see favor with the way they had been treated.

"I hear the words, but he is speaking too fast. What is he saying?" the white man asked curiously.

"He was saying that because of his help, his people will see favor with Ashley's great white father in the east." she whispered.

"That's the biggest pile of horseshit I've ever heard. After Ashley's gone, them sumbitches back east are gonna send a shit load of trappers an' other such people out here an' trap an' kill everything that walks, crawls,'er flies. They won't give a good goddamn 'bout a bunch of red niggers either. They'll say this an' that an' take their land faster than fire to dry kindlin'. I saw it back east with them red niggers on the other side of the river." After the meeting, Bill got a cup of coffee and decided it was time to split up.

"Why don't we jus' stay here fer a while? I'm mean shit. We're freezin' our asses off as it is. Might as well git up there", he pointed west, "and get froze jus' as well as we go up there. Well, you know it won't be all that comfortable." Bill blurted out laughing.

Ashley looked up from his coffee.

"I do not require your counsel sir. We shall remain here until I determine that the animals are strong enough to travel. Thank you very much!" he snipped back at the white man.

Bill had been hacking on the booshway, but the elder had taken it to heart. He was actually happy to stay where they were because of the game and food for the horses. He thought about Rebecca and the Ashley men.

Bill pondered as he stared into the fire. *Hmm, no problem there. She'll screw 'em outta whatever wages they've already got. Not to mention get some stuff to trade with Two Sticks when they see 'em next time. Ann won't have no problem and we're most likely gonna have all the grub we could stand.*

The days turned into weeks as they waited for a time to leave. After a month of sitting around, the day finally came to leave. Most of the cottonwood trees had been stripped, and the hunt for game was taking the hunters farther and farther away from the camp.

Bill and his girls rode near the front of the large brigade, an area reserved for leaders and visiting dignitaries from outlying tribes. In the rear, the wranglers had their hands full keeping track of the twenty-five new horses Ashley had acquired.

"The first chance I see, we're gonna skin out from Ashley an' be on our own. I don't like the way he rubs me." he confided in Ann as they rode out into the bleak prairie.

Now that Ann is something else, Bill thought as he smiled at her. She looked at the young lad riding next to her with the old twinkle in her eyes.

"I love it when you fuck me in the ass." Then she licked her cracked lips and winked at him. Bill felt himself swelling in his buckskins. *That'll have to wait.* Then he chuckled to his own joke.

"You're a bitch, ain't ya?" Bill grinned at her.

"You know it White Man!" She smiled.

Bill was too confused to worry about a strange girl.

The weather was glorious as they traveled into the foothills, leaving the flat prairie behind them. Big game became so common that the hunters began to wait until the evening meal to kill anything. They had been out for two weeks since leaving the Loupe with the route being favorable to the large brigade. They had been fortunate that none of Ashley's men had approached the girls for sexual favors. Bill had already figured out that it was business and not let it get between him and his wives.

Bill had listened to the other trappers speak of the relationship between the trappers and the Pawnees. Then there was no alliance with the Arapaho, Kiowa and the Blackfoot nation's. This was strange for the young trapper. Why they felt compelled to tell Ashley all about the treaty they were about to make left Bill in confusion. The confusion didn't last long as a scout from Ashley's brigade appeared from over a hummock riding hell-bent for leather. He said he'd seen a shitload of red niggers all painted up and looking for a fight. Bill was shocked in the time it took from the report to having the camp perimeter set up with fighting stations.

"I'll say one thing 'bout yer boss. He can set up fer a fight right quick!" Bill told Jerome, one of Ashley's hunters.

"Yeppers. That nigger knows how to fight. I'll say that fer 'em." Jerome replied as he checked his pan to assure himself of dry powder. No fight materialized. The war party skirted the white trappers to pursue some other foe.

"I figured we'd be a dancing. I reckon it's best to save lead an' powder." Jerome spoke to Bill without turning his head.

"Anything to take their attention away from us is fine by me." Bill answered back as the afternoon's sun raced into the not-so-distant mountains.

At night Bill would pull the buffalo robes over him and his small brigade so they could snuggle up for warmth in the bitter cold of the plains. There were times when the girls would play pranks with the young white man, especially White Moon. She was the trickster. She'd leave her hand out in the cold, then she would stick it under Bill's breechclout to watch him jump. Bill would cuss, and she would giggle.

One cold morning it started snowing. At times the flurries came so hard that the young trapper couldn't see the mitten in front of his face. The wind would howl as it raced across the foothills as it battered the brigades. Rebecca felt the wind against her robe as she dipped her hat into the wind and thanked God that Bill had traded away the provisions for the warm buffalo coat. She sat in her thought as the wind pressed against her with such force she felt she was going to topple off the sure-footed gelding she had been with since Missouri. Sitting on the horse, she thought about her life what seemed like years ago on the riverboat. Her life of whoring on the river and meeting the young to-be trapper had gone differently than she had first thought it would. She realized, *I don't even know his name*. Strange, it really didn't mean too much to her at this moment. She giggled to herself thinking about the little town where they met the whores and stole the gun. She realized it was a lifetime ago as she was brought back to present day as the wind buffeted her violently; her gelding, sure-footed as ever, never missed a step as they plodded along.

Ashley had a couple of horses that wouldn't move any farther, so he just left them for the scavengers. Bill watched as he approached the horses. Camp men were securing the provisions from them as his small trapping brigade passed the nearly dead animal.

Humph. A bear 'er wolf would get 'em 'fore the next mornin'. That's fer certain an' fer true. Bill's mind drifted as the bleak landscape past beneath the mare.

They were following buffalo tracks all day because they trampled everything that got in their way. Without the hairy animals, they would have been stuck for sure. Every once in a while, one of the hunters from Ashley's would strike out at dawn to pursue the huge shaggy creatures. As the brigade would catch up with them, they would have it butchered and cooking over a fire. The meat was tender and juicy laced with globs of fat as the young trapper sliced off chunk after chunk.

Billy and his entourage were camping right in the midst of Ashley now. The men made no moves or advancements toward the girls. It was as if they took them as one of their own now. They would talk of past whoring or hunts, old friends, wives, and children. Rebecca and Ann would sit quietly listening to the men, occasionally speaking an opinion when called upon. Not young Bill. As he sat with Rebecca in his lap, all he thought about lately was sex. Three girls at once was consuming his every thought. He'd run his hand through the red hair of Rebecca as she would lean her head into his hand as he did, smiling through her chapped bleeding lips at the white runt above her.

White Moon had no worries with this weather; she just sat there straight as a dinner chair, looking out at the white landscape with her robe pulled up tight, and her coal-black hair would flow in the breeze like a wild colt's mane. Watching the meager fire burn, she would look at Bill and Rebecca and smile a toothy grin thinking of all the mischief she was going to get into once it warmed up.

In the morning they would climb up on their steeds for a long day of traveling. The foothill had turned flat, and it seemed the mountains moved farther west every day. Time would crawl by as they advanced to the distant mountains. Ann began keeping to herself more and more as the miles crept slowly by. Bill would ride next to her and wink at the black-haired one, but she just stared off into the white of the rolling hills. Once in a while, she would recognize Bill's mischievous smile and her eyes would twinkle like the old days before the cold.

CHAPTER 87

That night at the fire, Ashley walked up to the runt and girls; looking at the foursome, he made his speech.

"I am taking a small group of men in my employ and am moving into the mountain range to find a suitable pass. If you and your party wish to stay here or to travel with us makes no difference to me. But mark my words. If you accompany me, you'll be under my jurisdiction. What I say goes without report or discussion."

"Well, how long 'fore ya need my answer?" the runt asked.

"We leave at first light." Ashley responded. Then he turned on his heel, walking away with no further conversation.

Billy looked at his girls sitting by the fire. Rebecca spoke quietly, "If we go on with Ashley, will we find a place to hole up fer rest of the winter?" She looked to Bill and her traveling mates.

"I ain't got a clue. I'm hopin' to get in these here mountains an' findin' a place where we can make a life fer ourselves. How's that sound to you girls?" he asked.

"I jus' want to get warm and full of food for a while. I don't care about trapping or hunting. I'm so tired of sitting on that fucking horse. I know I can't stop, but I wouldn't mind a place to get strong again." Ann spoke a muffled voice from inside her buffalo robe, her face hidden by her hat, her eyes barely showing.

"I have heard of this place from the elders. They say if we travel up the Platte river, we will find many beaver and buffalo." White Moon spoke as she stared into the fire."

"Okay, we'll break off here then, make our way from hereon out." Bill snuggled up to all them as the fire died down and the cold invaded the camp.

Ann leaned over to Billy, whispering, "I'm really tired, but if you want some, well, I'll oblige you."

"You rest girl." he whispered back as he kissed her bare forehead.

CHAPTER 88

In the morning Bill told Ashley that they were going to break off on their own and the best of luck with his adventure. He stuck his hand out.

"Best of luck sir." William Ashley shook Bill's hand.

"Thankie ye kindly, Mr. Ashley. Good luck to you as well." Bill turned and returned to his brigade.

"That's done. When yer ready, we'll get." he spoke as he tossed the well-used saddle over the back of his familiar horse. After months of repetition, he had gotten a system down that worked efficiently. He would do his first then move on to White Moon's, then Rebecca's, and last he'd do Ann's mare. The horse was high strung for being an older horse; it continually pranced nervously as it turned into him. It made Bill chuckle that the horse matched its rider, being unpredictable and temperamental. If he did hers first, it would pull on the lead rope, making a pain to do the rest. After a few moments of the horse's shenanigans, Bill spoke coarsely to her, "I oughta trade the you fer a Indian pony. I think I will the next chance I get. Them Indian ponies are smarter than you bag of bones!" He finished with the horse as he spoke to Rebecca, "I cain't cuss it too much, it did make it all the way across the prairie an' to the mountains. That ol' blacksmith that Ann an' you girls worked on sure gave us some good stock. Maybe I won't trade after all." he continued as he placed bridles and hackamores on the familiar horses.

"You know, they have done us a fair service. I bet if they get a belly full of food, they'll change their disposition a shitload. What the hell am I talkin' 'bout? These are horse's fer Christ's sakes. They ain't people 'er anything. I think that my mind done turned to a puddle of shit here." He shook his head as Rebecca smiled at him.

They rode slowly in a single file toward the headwaters miles away upriver; he and the girls had good luck finding firewood and cottonwood for the horses. After a day or two they pulled into a small grove of poplar and ash trees as the brutal cold finally let up. Then, the clouds parted and the sky turned blue as they wandered out of the plains into the foothills of the Rocky Mountains.

The Rocky Mountains

CHAPTER 89

The foursome went to the south of the largest peak, and true to the mountains, the weather changed in an instant. Soon it was freezing cold, but just for the fun of it, it rained instead of snowing. Then it snowed. Then when they were all wet to the bone, the temperature dropped severely, freezing the buffalo robes to the buckskins on the young trappers. Moving slowly into the mountains, they happened upon a small valley.

"White Man, let us turn in here. It appears to be a pleasant valley. See the wind has slowed." White Moon spoke, her breath hovering before her face. There was no arguing; Ann was exhausted and ready to fall at the slightest misstep of her horse. Rebecca surveyed the area as well, nodding with approval.

"At least the snow has stopped." Ann chimed in.

As they traveled up the valley, Bill noticed something. Trees became more abundant, and the wildlife seemed to come out of nowhere. They looked around for a while until they found a small recess in the hillside where the wind was calm.

"Figure we can make some kinda lean-to 'er somethin'?" Bill asked his traveling companions through chattering teeth. No answer came to him.

"Look at the trails! They're worn down smooth. There must be buffalo and elk here." Rebecca spoke as she scanned the faraway hillsides.

"There is good firewood too. I will get a fire going for tonight." White Moon spoke as she slid effortlessly off her gelding. The temperature dropped quickly as the bronze beauty produced a horseshoe-shaped steel ring and chunk of flint.

"Damn it is hell cold." She spoke as she flicked a few sparks on the dried moss he had in her small fire bag.

"Well, I see you got to work on yer cussing. It should be 'It's damned cold,'" Rebecca chattered. A few strikes on the flint and she had the dried moss smoldering. She blew carefully on it until a yellow flame licked up.

"There. A fire. Now we can get warm or at least warmer." White Moon waved her hand across the little fire, bringing the flames higher.

"Here's some kindling lover." Bill laid a few small twigs next to her.

"I like that. Lover. That is the same as wife?" she asked as she blew onto the smoke, producing a yellow flame.

"Sorry, I'm just tired of being wet. It was fine till it rained so fucking much. Damned I'm soaked to the bone."

"Hurry up Moon!" Ann chattered.

"I'm going as fast as the wood will burn Ann." White Moon responded as she fed the twigs to the yellow flames.

As the fire leaped up, the heat radiated, and the green brigade huddled together, trying to ward off the blast of cold air that had started up again in the valley.

"I don't know horse shit from hog jaws 'bout buildin' a shelter." Bill confessed from under his wet robe coat.

"I have been around the building of many a wooden lodge. I can help. But I can tell you, I think we have waited too long to build. All the ground is too hard, and the cold will make building very hard. We should look for a cave instead. There must be some caves in this valley. Maybe we can find one with a bear, and then we will have food also." she spoke like it was nothing, finding a bear, killing it to have the warm cave.

Bill's mind jumped back to hunting for Ike an the crew, *it ain't gonna be easy as that black bear I kilt in Missouri.*

There was no conversation for what seemed like an eternity, and then Bill spoke out, "Well, you girls go on yonder side of the valley an' I'll go on this here side. If I find one, I'll come an' get ya. You do the same." Bill spoke of the best plan he could come up with, not having any bear-hunting experience.

He laid his Hawken in the crook of his arm as they struck out in single file to a point where they could split. The girls where ahead of Bill by twenty yards. It seemed like the thick brush engulfed them as the river had swallowed Rebecca's underwear a lifetime ago.

Hmm? What do I look fer, seeing Rebecca running at him, *What the hell's got inta her?* Then as she ran by, he looked down where they had come from and saw the biggest bear he'd ever seen. *Christ! It must be bigger than a barn.* Bill's mind jumped into fighting mode. He pulled his rifle up smoothly and sighting in the chest of the enormous creature approaching him at a full gallop.

"I hope that ball does somethin' to this critter." Bill spoke aloud as he squeezed the set trigger. Ann and White Moon ran by, but he waited until the gruesome monster was just a few paces away. Then he pulled the main trigger. The rifle roared as it rammed against his shoulder. White smoke hid the bear as Bill brought the gun down looking into the cloud that hit the devil creature that was before him. Then out of the smoke the huge animal crashed into the small man, knocking him onto his back, flinging his rifle out of his hands as the huge bear slashed at him with paws the size of a dinner plate. The bear was covering the small man, jumping on him with its front legs, lashing at him with paws and its long teeth with the speed of a terrier. He felt the sharp claws and teeth ripping away at the buffalo robe. Into his shoulder sank the teeth, going into the collarbone. The bear raked its teeth over the bone, its claws digging into the robe as they pierced his soft back flesh. It roared and threw Bill in the air like a cub.

Bill felt himself being lifted and thrown. Then he saw the ground below; he realized he was in the air flying down the small embankment, *damn, there's the ground. I reckon this'll hurt a tad,* the runt thought as he was sailing down the hill. He hit the ground fifteen yards down the embankment from where he'd shot the grizzly. The noise it was making was worse than when a riverboat rubbed its keel in agony as it ran over a submerged snag. The injured white man got to his knees, looking back up the hill he had just been thrown down. The distance looked immeasurable as he watched the fight materialized on the trail above him.

The big bear was standing, pawing the air, growling, swiping the air, its froth-covered muzzle snapping. Then another gun went off. The seven-hundred-pound animal continued batting the air for the invisible flies that continued to pester it. Another gun went off. It turned to see where the irritation had come from, growling horribly as it walked on, shaking its huge head as it approached toward the nearest human, *If it gets into the girls, it'll be real bad fer 'em,* the injured runt thought. Looking down at his available weapons, he quickly formulated a plan.

He used his good arm to pull his tomahawk out from the small of his back as he got to his feet. Weaving from the loss of blood and pain, he began to make his way back to the battle. Swallowing down the bile that was threatening to come to his lips, the young man called his reserve courage and ran at the big silver-tipped cinnamon creature from the netherworld. Luck wasn't on his side as he waded into the boar grizzly bear. He was almost to it when his moccasin slipped, sliding him unto his back into the bear headfirst. It might have been comical except the runt was going to die in a heartbeat.

The bear stopped growling and looked down between its legs at the small trapper lying on the ground looking up at it with the blue eyes. Bill was unsure of what to do next, so he did the only thing he could think of; he used both hands to swing his tomahawk with all his might at the bear's genitals. The sharp steel buried itself into the groin of the eight-foot-tall creature with a sickening thunk. He quickly crawled away from the bear.

The girls had watched in disbelief as the small man lay there on death's doorstep. Not giving up, he had changed a bloody death into a few more moments of life.

"Quick! Shoot it before it kills the runt!" Rebecca called out. All three girls fired one at a time, each ball hitting the thick hide, causing puffs of hair to fly as the large balls ripped into the bear's beautiful thick fur.

The grizzly dropped to the ground, ignoring the blond human that had caused it unknown pain. Rolling over on its back, the creature began to howl, thrashing in a frizzy, trying to dislodge the pain in its groin. Without hands it couldn't grasp the tomahawk to wrench it out.

Bill crawled over to where his gun had dropped and with blood-covered hands began to load it. Barely able to pour powder, the runt kept his eyes on the thrashing bear. Another shot went off as Rebecca fired a round ball into the groaning bear. Once again a tuff of hair flew into the cold air as life began slipping from the almost prehistoric animal.

"I—Almost—Got—It." he mumbled as another shot rang through the trees. He finally got it loaded when Ann's gun sounded in the chill of the day. The shot made a puff of hair on the bear's back go up. Feeling life was slipping away, the bear made one last attempt to quell the cause of its pain. Standing once again, it shook its head, flinging saliva across the blood-covered snow as it staggered at the runt. *That looks painful having that 'hawk buried in his balls,* Bill thought as it rapidly approached him. On its last quest, to kill the small man before its life seeped outs the holes all over its immense body. Bill aimed at its heart, squeezing the set trigger. The bear was almost running now, growling and snarling like it was the devil himself as it closed the distance to the white runt.

At just ten feet away Bill's gun roared. This time he wasted no time moving out of the thrashing creature's reach. It was a good thing he had moved too, for the bear ran through the smoke, expecting to find the runt like the first time. Another gun sounded. It was Rebecca's. Her bullet went directly into its right eye. All this time White Moon had been trying to get a shot in without hitting Bill. When she finally fired, the kick just about knocked her down. As she began to reload, Ann's gun sounded. Bill saw the bear's head jerk back. It paused for a moment then fell over. It clawed at it eye thrashing as its life ebbed away from the king of the forest. Slowly it stopped moving, no breath freezing in the air as Bill loaded another ball.

"Load up girls! No tellin' what this critter's gonna do!" he yelled to the girls. Bill aimed at its remaining glassy eye, and then he fired again. The bear didn't move as the ball smashed out the back of its head, spraying gore across the snow. It was finally over.

"Hold on there. Don't waste any more balls on this ol'boy. I believe he's a goner." Bill spoke in a ragged breath.

"This had to be the biggest bear in the world. I'm sure of it." Bill spoke as he felt the adrenaline leave and the dizziness overcome him.

"Girls! I hurt!" the runt spoke as he dropped next to the bloody snow at the bear's side; he passed out from the loss of blood, going into shock, as the sun fell from the sky.

CHAPTER 90

He awoke with a searing pain in his shoulder. Billy White screamed, "Goddamnit! What the hell's goin' on?" His eyes were wild with fever; it didn't last long as he passed out again. In Bill's fever-ridden dreams he saw stars, small flat-bottom boats floating listlessly on the clear river, green trees of the Illinois side of the river with their red, gold, and green leaves. All the little children with brightly colored summer dresses with bonnets carrying flowers; they were going to a tall steeple church near the shore. The sun was out, and it was a beautiful day. Then the bear came from the water.

"Run! Run!" he screamed, "The bear's coming to get you!" He wasn't fast enough. The bear had the face of Matthew Harris as it was screaming that it was going to eat all the children. Bill couldn't move to help as Sheila was holding him down. When Bill awoke, the sky was clear and his body hurt worse than anything he had ever experienced.

"Goddamnit I hurt." Bill wept.

"You must lie still. It takes many days for the medicine to heal you. We have closed the big wound, but there are many angry wounds that will not go away." It was White Moon speaking to him as he looked over to see Rebecca and Ann. They watched White Moon use the poultices on the runt. *What a pretty face,* he thought as he closed his eyes, thinking about what was going on.

Then he opened them again, seeing darkness. He saw the images outlined by the small fire. Smelling the meat cooking, he felt hunger pangs in his empty stomach.

"Girls, help me up." Bill called out in a weak breath, "I want some of that meat."

Ann brought him some bear meat dripping with grease, black

and burned on one side and red on the other. Bill didn't care. He was ready to eat anything that didn't move. Stuffing the big chunk in, he chewed vigorously; as soon as he swallowed it, he felt it rising back up his throat. Coughing he spewed out the greasy meat onto the snow-covered ground around the fire pit.

"The meat is rich in fat. Eat smaller pieces and chew it slowly. You will not get sick that way." White Moon spoke as she watched the runt's antics.

"Damn, it's greasy." Bill commented as he looked down at the chunk he'd spit out. A white glaze had already formed as the cold changed the warm meat into a chunk of frozen flesh. Rebecca stared at the meat, mesmerized by the changing of its structure. She didn't know if it was the fat that made it white or the fact that it was freezing so quickly.

Throughout the next days they sat around eating bear watching the snow drift around the small camp. Bill got stronger and more mobile, not back to fighting condition but able to move without help. He continually rotated his shoulder and arm, working out kinks and the stiffness.

"Feeling better, my strength is returning purty quick. 'Fore you know I'll be chasing your scrawny ass around Ann.

"Hey, did you ever go look fer the cave, you know, the one the bear was in?" Bill asked. He remembered the reason they had separated in the first place.

"We were afraid." Ann spoke, staring into the fire. *Is this is same Ann? I didn't think anything would scare her,* Bill almost blurted out.

"I wasn't sure of what to do. If we found the cave, we couldn't move you there, so there was no hurry in finding it. It'll be there after you are well enough to travel." she continued.

"Hmm, I reckon ya have a point." Bill looked into her black eyes, seeing no life, no sparkle, just depression.

"Ann, how are ya feelin'?" Bill asked, concerned for his friend.

"Well, let's see. I'm in the middle of nowhere freezing my tits off, just about got killed by a bear the size of a small town, I'm on my 'time' and have blood freezing in my buckskins. Now how do you think I'm feeling?" she shouted.

"You don't have to bite my head off. I was jus' askin' that's all." Bill said meekly.

"Stop your groveling. Shit! Just like a man. The first sign of a fight and you roll over like an opossum. Rebecca, ain't that like men?" she asked, looking for some backup.

"Not this man. He's done everything in his power to keep us alive and fed. I for one don't particularly like you hacking on him when he was just trying to be nice to you." she answered back but not looking up from the fire.

"Well, you can all kiss my ass! I'm out of here the first chance I get. I don't give a good goddamn if I have to live with the fucking Pawnee as long as I'm not freezing and starving at every crook in the mountains." she spouted.

Hearing this, White Moon spoke up, "I miss my people. I will take you out of here when the weather breaks, that is if you do not mind?" She looked at Billy. " It is a long journey, and we should have no problems finding the fork of the Platte where my people are wintering."

"What're you gonna tell your pappy? He'll be after my hair fer lettin' ya go, won't he?" Bill, asked concerned.

She spoke as she stirred the broth in their remaining pot, "No, many times a man and wife do not get along. Then one or the other leaves, and things go as normal, and nothing is done to either one." Bill looked at the Indian maiden he had taken for his wife. She was still as gorgeous as the day he had received her from Bright Horse.

The moon was racing the sun as the afternoon ended abruptly. The to-be trappers began to pull out their sleeping robes in anticipation of another freezing night. Rebecca and Bill cuddled up as did Ann and White Moon

It got a little warmer during the night as it had quit snowing, and by late morning it had turned into a beautiful day. The valley was still as nothing moved, covered in a white blanket. Bill could see buffalo and elk on the far hillside. It was like a painting on the wall on the ship. It was so pretty. Bill watched Ann from across the camp as she threw her saddle blanket on the back of her horse. Then she walked over to where Bill and Rebecca sat. She looked down at them.

"I'm taking my horse and one pack animal. You got a problem with that?" she spoke with ice in her voice. Then she walked over to her twitchy mount as she began to saddle it. True to form, the horse pranced about as she worked in earnest to saddle the cantankerous horse. Shying away several times, she finally got it saddled. Then the hackamore bridle. This particular horse didn't let the black-haired one get by with anything as it continued to fight even the simplest operation. Finally she had the saddle and bridle on. She looked over at Bill with evil spilling from her face.

"Hold on a minute, I want some stuff off the pack cradle." Bill spoke as he started to the pack horse. He pulled the traps off, Mary Beth's Hawken, her possible bag and the extra pistol.

"I'm keeping the cooking pot too." Bill's mind was racing about what was in the pack. *I cain't recall what's in it so I reckon we'll get by without what's in it. Our pack horse has the flints, powder and tools.*

"I ain't gonna miss that nag one bit." Bill spoke out of the side of his mouth to Rebecca. "I'll miss the horse though." Then she grabbed the halter line, speaking to White Moon.

"Well, just like I said last night. A coward to the end. Fuck you and your redheaded whore!" Then she mounted and looked at White Moon.

"Get on your horse and take me away from this snivelin' worm!" Then she pulled the lead rope of the packhorse and led it away with no more to say. White Moon stood there with tears in her eyes.

"Hold on now! Let me get you a cup'a coffee an' maybe a cinnamon roll before you run off." Bill looked back at Rebecca as she covered her mouth to avoid being seen laughing as Bill continued to make a joke of Ann's harsh demeanor.

"Jus' be careful with my wife there. She likes to have coffee with me in the morning." Rebecca had her mouth covered, and Bill could see her shoulders bouncing as she tried not to laugh aloud.

"What, no kiss?" Bill hollered to her back. White Moon stood there watching the black-haired monster walking away. She looked at Bill and Rebecca.

"I will get Two Sticks, and we will come and find you in the spring." Then she kissed Bill on the mouth, her tongue diving deep as she choked down her welling tears.

"I will miss you Rebecca. I will think of all the tricks you will teach me this spring. Ann will not be like this when we return to my village. She will find a woman. Yes, that's what she needs. There are some who will take her in. Good-bye." Then she turned to Rebecca, kissing her in the same manner as Bill. Then as quick as an eagle catching a rabbit, she turned to her horse, throwing a leg over it in one fluid movement, she lifted her hand good-bye and rode away.

Bill sat watching everything go to hell in a handbasket. Then it was quiet, just he and Rebecca with the whole Rocky Mountains in front of them. Bill looked over at her.

"Well, yer stuck with me now girl. Are ya up fer it?" he asked. She watched the figures get smaller and smaller, and then they were gone. She turned and walked over to where he was sitting, sticking her cold hand inside of his robe.

"The question is, are you up for it?" Rebecca asked jokingly.

"I reckon I can take care of that request." Bill smiled, feeling pretty good from the medicine White Moon had used.

She brought her robe over as she crawled under it with Bill. The late morning was shaping up fine. The sun was warm as he could feel the heat on the buffalo robes they were beneath. He felt her cold hand creep down under his breechclout as he did the same to her. She was as wet as the snow in April as Bill slipped his fingers into her. Feeling himself getting close to eruption, he whispered in her ear, "I'm ready to go off girl."

"I'll let you have this one, but I get mine the first chance it warms up. Deal?"

"Deal." Bill White mimicked.

She pulled his penis out of the breechclout; slipping her leg over him, she reached down to guide his pod into her as she sat down slowly.

"Think you could go for a while or are ya gonna toot your whistle?" she asked.

"Damnit, girl! It's feelin' like the kettle is goin' to whistle any minute." he spoke in a shallow voice. She started rocking, moving up and down, staring into her lover's eyes.

"Oh, I can tell you're on the way." Then as quick as a shooting star, she was off and had his pod in her mouth. There'd be no mess today.

"I cain't believe how fast you are girl." Bill wagged his head.

She wiped her mouth on the back of her hand. "Thank you kind sir, for the compliment."

CHAPTER 91

With the lovemaking done for a while, it was time for the couple to find a place to winter up. Bill rotated his arm feeling the stifness fade away, *Moon did me right with the medicine she knew 'bout.* They began packing the remaining horses; Bill looked across the valley where they had started the search for the bear. *How many days have I been out?*

"Hey, lover, how many days was I out anyway?" he questioned her as she adjusted the packhorse's cradle.

"Three days." she answered as she tied the bearskin on the packhorse; it was so big it was hanging down the flanks on both sides of the animal.

"Well, I got my work cut out for me this winter, eh White Man?" Tying the lead rope on the horn, she looked around the small camp once more then threw a leg over her gelding.

"Eh?" he questioned her.

"Tanning this bear hide for us. What do you think? Sleeping robe? A couple sets of leggings an' a vest for each of us?" she called as she pulled her buffalo coat tighter.

"Leggings would be good. There's a lot to be done. I'll help ya." he called over his shoulder.

They commenced to look for the elusive cave. As they moved through the valley, she saw plenty of life. Animals were everywhere. Squirrels, rabbits, and deer. Everything that they could possibly want was here for the taking.

"Hey, look over there on the hillside." she called out, pointing to a distant hillside. There on the hillside was a cave about the size of an outhouse.

"Check yer powder lover. If there's 'nother bear, I don't wanna be surprised." The journey took them most of the day to get to the other side of the valley, and by the time they stopped below the cave, it was late afternoon.

"It sure didn't look that far." Bill spoke to Rebecca's back as she had been leading. After finding suitable cover for the horses, Bill turned to survey the trail they just made. Comfortable their location was concealed, they quietly walked to the entrance of the cave. He peered into the black hole as his vision became accustomed to the darkness. Inside, he could see no movement as he waited for Rebecca to join him.

"It looks empty." she whispered. Bill motioned for her to follow him back down to where the horses were.

"Let's get a torch made so we can see if there's any varmints inside." Producing a flint and steel, he soon had a small fire going. He continued, "Yeppers, no surprises fer us?" Bill laughed as he lit a dried branch to use as a torch.

"You get ready to shoot if 'nother bear comes out." he whispered. As the fire illuminated the sides of the caves, he could see that the cave was empty of all life. As they walked in deeper, the light had shown they had not been the first to use this cave. Looking down at the very old fire ring, he began to feel confident that they would be safe. Rebecca took his elbow and lifted his arm higher to see farther inside the cave.

"It's deep 'nuff that we could pull our horses in and no one would know we were even here." she commented, letting Bill's arm go.

"Let's get 'em. Son of a bitch, what a relief it'll be havin' a place rest without freezin' our asses off." she called out as she was leaving the cave to get the animals.

In the evening, they had a warm fire going, producing good heat with little smoke; Bill lay back against the rocky wall as he began to ponder their next move.

"You know we can hole up here fer quite some time. We've got game down in the valley an' bet we can find some good trappin' come spring. What do ya think?" the runt asked his lovely cave mate.

"It sounds like a plan. It'll give me a chance to work on that bear skin 'fore the thaw." she spoke as she walked to the back of the cave where she had left the horses.

"How is it you learned to do hides?" he asked.

"Moon showed me. I did a small piece of bear while you was all pass'd out. I jus' figured to do the same but bigger." she spoke over her shoulder.

"Come on, let's get these horses unsaddled and hobbled. You know we're gonna have to find a place to feed 'em regular like as well. You see anything that was suitable fer 'em?" she asked over her shoulder as she neared Bill's mare.

"Come on, let's take care of these horses."

"There must be some cottonwoods, and I bet we can walk 'em down to find something to eat." He folded his arms, making no movement to help her as his head began to slink onto his robe coat.

"Get yer ass over here an' help me, or you'll get no blowjob and you can ferget about a poke too." She stopped and turned to see Bill had all but fallen asleep.

"Shit." Rebecca looked onto the cave floor until she found a sizable rock. The redhead hefted it in her hand, tossing it in the air for weight a few times. Then she arched back and threw the rock at the sleeping man. It struck Bill solidly in the shoulder, ricocheting up and knocking off the wide-brimmed hat.

"Jesus Christ!" Bill screamed as he was on his feet pulling his knife and tomahawk in one fluid movement, looking at the entrance of the cave.

"What the hell?" He moved on the balls of his feet, ready for a fight, when he realized the shoulder that had been hit was on the cave side.

Bill turned to Rebecca. "Did you chuck that at me?"

"Yeppers. Now get yer ass over here an' help, you sawed-off shit bag." She turned to leave Bill in a confused stupor.

"Goddamnit. You coulda just asked. Didn't have to chuck a rock at me fer Christ's sake." he mumbled as he went back to help.

"You wouldn'to got up. You're getting lazy." She didn't turn to him as he neared her.

"Humph. Well, you coulda asked. I ain't lazy neither. Just not too anxious to do any work right now, that's all." He passed her to get the bear skin off the packhorse.

The couple began the routine of day-to-day living in the mountains, feeding the horses being the most important part of their day. They had to make sure the cave's location wasn't compromised with each trip to get them fed. On days when the rain or snow was too bad, they would go out and bring in as much food as they could carry. The horses suffered, but by no means were they starving. Each trip out Bill or Rebecca would keep a lookout for any sign of invaders into their sanctuary as the other gathered feed.

Once a week one of them would take a horse and venture out to get them meat. A fat elk or a tasty mule deer would keep them fed throughout the cold times of the mountain winter while providing skins for future clothes.

Bill was amazed by Rebecca at the tedious work she would do in the dimly lit cave throughout the winter months. He'd never get a chance to call her lazy as every free moment she was working the hides. True to his words, he helped her on the working of the skins. Rebecca staked out the hides on the dirt cave floor near the entrance where she worked diligently, scraping them clean of any fat or flesh as she planned for more buckskins.

The redhead had the big bear staked out near the others, taking turns with Bill to scrape the huge skin. He wasn't as quick or as skilled as her as she would have an elk done by the time he would have scraped a small section of the bear. By January she had produced a set of half legging and a warm vest for each of them as well as four tanned elk skins and six big mule deer.

Then the weather started to break. Warmth came more often as the season changed.

"You reckon we'll be outta here soon?" he asked her one warm morning.

"I don't think we have to wait too long. This morning it was actually pretty nice. I bet we'll see spring soon, and when we get ready, we'll have a good time in this valley."

The runt thought about what she said, looking forward to a new season.

CHAPTER 92

The days got longer as Bill thought more and more of leaving.

"Let's get out of here an' inta the rest of these here mountains. I wanna see more before the season changes much more." Billy spoke to her one warm afternoon.

"Okay by me. I'm ready for a change. The cave has been okay, but I'd like to move on, see something new." she said looking out at the now-speckled-green valley.

"I reckon we can leave in the mornin' if ya wanna." he spoke, looking out into the scenic valley. He walked back into the depth of the cave. He started packing the hides she and he had worked on all winter. He left the animals and walked to the front of the cave as he looked out at the valley again. Now that the decision had been made, he was ready to leave.

"Let's leave now. Let's jus' get the hell outta here." Bill spoke quickly.

"You mean ride out in the afternoon and camp somewhere else?" she queried.

"Yeppers. What do ya say?" he answered.

"Fine by me." Then she turned, grabbing her blanket and saddle. She threw it on the horse in one fluid movement. When she was satisfied with her saddling, she turned to load the packhorse. The meager reserves made it a quick chore as well. Gone was the huge grizzly bear hide, replaced now by the bulky elk and deer hides. Bill was amazed. This woman was so quick. One moment he had been talking about it. Not more than a breath later she was all but on her horse. When the hackamore was secured on the gelding's muzzle, she slipped on its back. The packhorse was pulled up to her as she smiled at Bill

"Let's go." She smiled at Billy White.

"Okay, okay." Bill said as he put his blanket on the brown mare that had been with him since Missouri. Lifting the saddle over the back, he let it settle on her. Pulling the cinch tight, he relaxed, turning away from her as he always did. Waiting for her to exhale. Damned horse always held her breath as he saddled her. Making him wait, she would play this game every time. Bill rotated his arm, feeling the old bear wound while the animal turned to look at him as if to say it would be okay to continue with the routine. His shoulder hadn't hurt since that damned Ann left.

"I wonder how Ann an' White Moon did on the way back." There was a long awkward pause.

"Oh well, nuthin' I could do 'bout it now." He looked over to Rebecca. She looked away at the mention of Ann's name. Bill had noticed that the cave rats had been busy on the leather. There were small pieces chewed up on his saddle.

"Damned rats, that's gonna happen anywhere we stay." he continued making idle conversation to get Ann's memory gone again.

"Yeppers." As he pulled the cinch tight, he looked at the smoke-covered walls. They'd have to come back next winter to stay here. It worked out fine for them. Riding out of the cave, Bill pointed them north, up the valley. He watched the mule deer and buffalo wander in and out of the green trees, making him glad he had jumped that riverboat last year. Glad that this red-haired vixen had joined him.

The night approached quickly. He found a grove of pine trees deciding to camp in. Bill tied the horses up very close to the campsite as it had been some time since they had been outside the confines of the cave.

"I'll get us a rabbit or hen." Rebecca spoke over her shoulder as she wandered away from the camp. Bill wasn't concerned, but he knew eventually they'd bump into some Indians. He plopped down on a fallen oak limb as he watched the sky turn red in the early evening. It seemed like only a moment since she had left, and she was back already with a plump cottontail in her hand.

"It was too easy. I walked right up to it an clubbed it with a stick, damnedest thing I've ever saw." She quickly skinned it outside of the camp as Bill watched admiringly. They watched the sun set in the western skies as another beautiful spring day came to an end.

"God, this place is a far cry from the last winter ain't it?" Bill asked as he sat next to Rebecca, eyeballing the young redhead for a trip to the robes. Then he saw something that got his interest. Down in the end of the valley, Bill saw some other riders. They didn't know that the young couple was in the grove of pines as the natives rode by. Bill couldn't tell if they were Crow or Blackfoot, Pawnee, or Sioux; but he did know they were on a mission as they prepared to harvest an elk that was grazing in the end of the meadow. Bill watched in awe as they circled the huge gray creature driving it to the warriors that were waiting in a populace of trees for the ambush. Arrows flew with pinpoint accuracy as the once-magnificent animal was soon on the ground, completing the circle of life.

"Well, what do ya think of that?" Bill asked her.

"They do seem organized, don't they? I think we'll either avoid them or make friends. I vote for avoidance." she said as she got a small fire going. Then she rammed a green stick through the animal as she hung it over the crackling fire. Normally the smell would draw every prying nose in the countryside, but not tonight as the others were predisposed with their own supper.

"You know, I bet they get so full that they'll fall right asleep. Then we could play a trick on 'em an' steal their ponies." Bill said as he stroked his thin wispy beard.

"Are you crazy? Why in the hell would you wanna steal those ponies from them? They've done nothing to us. Hell, they'll hunt us down and kill us for doing something like that. Remember the Pawnee gave our horse back, so we should leave them be."

"If it presents itself, I wanna steal 'em." Billy spoke as he watched the smoke spiral up through faraway canopy.

"You're gonna get killed. That's what you're get, an I'm going to be a slave or worse. Them red niggers is gonna fork me nine ways to Sunday. I just know it." she whined shaking her head from side to side.

"Don't worry. It'll be fun. After we get 'em an' make sure that they're followin' us, we'll tie 'em up where they can get 'em back. That'll throw 'em fer a loop. He-he." The runt slapped his buckskinned knee. He pulled off a leg of the rabbit, tossing it to her.

"You want to do all that just to give them back?" she said as she chewed slowly on the tender meat.

"Sure. Jus' fer some fun. Hell, maybe they be too embarrassed to follow us after that." The small white runt giggled as he pulled a leg for himself. Chewing slowly, he smiled at her.

"You're getting stranger and stranger all the time. But if that's what you want to do, let's do it." she said as she looked up to the sky, shaking her flowing red mane.

"Here." He tossed her a front leg, shoulder and all. As she ate it quietly, she studied the runt she had thrown it with. *He's sassy. That's for sure,* she thought. The remainder of the rabbit was consumed as they waited for the evening to finish so they could begin their games with the Indians down the valley.

Bill looked down at the hoof prints on the worn trail. Then he walked back to his mare. It was a dead giveaway; the Indian ponies were shoeless.

"Rebecca, let's take a break. I wanna pull these shoes off the horses." Bill spoke as he pulled out his ferrying supplies.

"Why in the world? Oh, I see. So our track won't be so easy to follow. Ain't that right?" she asked.

"Yeppers." The runt was quick pulling the shoes off, stashing them in the pack animal's cradle. He was attempting to do the brown mare when it reached around, biting the fringe of Bill's shirt.

The runt reached around, whacking her nose as he continued his work. In a moment he felt its hot breath again. He waited to see if the horse had learned anything.

"She's going for it again." Rebecca spoke softly. She just nibbled on the fringe of his shirt a bit, then lost interest. She turned back to the front. When Bill had the three horses done, they mounted up to continue on with their mischievous plans. Rebecca smelled the smoke before they even saw the camp of the natives.

They waited until it got dark and the snores were as loud as thunder from the camp. Bill walked in on one side of the line with Rebecca from the other side. Cutting the horse-hair rope, they led the ponies away from the slumbering camp slicker than a carpetbagger's tongue. The Indian ponies didn't even make a sound. When Bill and Rebecca got to their horses, they mounted and quietly rode off into the darkness away from the sleeping warriors.

"To bad we cain't see them red niggers in the mornin'. They'd whack each other an' blame someone fer they're not thinkin' of guardin' the horses." Bill laughed aloud.

The young couple rode into a meadow in the early morning, finding a small bluff to watch from, wishing to see the embarrassed natives come looking for their ponies. Bill tied them to a small stand of cottonwoods while Rebecca climbed a rock outcropping to watch for the pursuing Indians. Bill figured when they found the trail, they'd find where they had been; but by that time, he hoped to be long gone.

As Bill climbed the rock face, he saw Rebecca on her hands and knees, her butt beaming in the morning sun.

"Say there miss, do you mind if I have a poke while we're waitin' fer them red niggers?"

"Well no, I don't good sir." With that she turned, exposing her most private area for the young man. The young to-be trapper slipped up behind her, his right hand resting on her backside while he used the other to guide himself into her. It was like putting on a familiar glove, snug but not tight. As usual, the young girl was dripping wet as the young man began to perform his mating ritual.

Rebecca always wanted the young man. She often thought of him as she rode through the forest. She thought of the their lovemaking from the riverboat, the small room where she and Ann played games, the times when White Moon was learning their ways, all the cold nights in the cave. Then she came back to reality. The young man was thrashing away behind her now as she reached down to her button of life to enhance her pleasure as Billy continued.

The runt didn't know how she could always be ready, but he was sure glad she was. He looked down at his root going in and out, seeing her red haired rosebud. It was as if it was begging for his attention. The young blond man pulled out his tool. Dripping her honey on the back door, he pushed gently. It was a tad tight, but she opened right up. In he went, like a kingsnake after a gopher. She was wiggling her rump back and forth and side to side as Billy pummeled her.

"Oh. Oh." He felt her stiffen up. Seeing she was climaxing, Bill went ahead and filled her awaiting cavity up with his life-giving seed. The young lad pulled out, leaning back on his legs, letting the cool morning air-dry him off. Then Rebecca turned to look at him.

"Here's a kiss for your effort White Man!" Then she farted a big old juicy fart, blowing spooge all over the half-naked trapper. She thought that was some kind of funny as she began to laugh. She continued laughing as she rolled over on her back, kicking her legs in the air as she continued.

"You enjoy that, ya little scamp!" Then he whacked her leg with an open hand, not hard enough to hurt but it did make a sharp crack.

"Oh, you're a mean one!" She kept laughing as Bill wiped himself off on his war shirt; she relaxed, spreading herself, exposing her briar patch for the morning sun to dry her. They sat on the bluff overlooking the meadow for what seemed like hours. They waited looking north from where they'd come, seeing no movement to speak of. The waves of grass looked like water on a calm lake as the sun shone on the young couple.

"They ain't comin'." Bill spoke to her without turning his head.

"I really hope that they've given up on getting their horses back." Rebecca spoke as she looked anxiously at the faraway opening of the meadow.

"How 'bout a blowjob?" Bill figured. *What the hell, all she can say is no.*

"You just got a poke. Aren't you a little bit tired?" she answered.

"Hmm, let me think fer a minute. Nope." He grinned at her.

"All right. But just a blowjob. My rump is still sore from where you poked me."

Producing an already-erect member from under his breechclout, he watched her expression as she saw him ready to go. The cool air felt good as he waited for his partner. The young man dreamed about getting sex whenever he wanted it, and now it was happening. Rebecca leaned over plopping his pod in her mouth, she began to lap on it like a piece of hard candy. She had a hold of the bottom of the shaft, squeezing it until the head would turn red then purple. Then she sucked on it. She sucked his nut sack a while and then back to his pod. Then like she had renewed her interest in her duties, she increased her crescendo. Her redhead began bobbing like a cork being pulled by a bluegill. All Bill could see was a red blur of the lass performing her well-practiced role of pleasure giver to the young lad.

"Here it comes darlin'." he spoke in short breaths. Then she pulled her mouth off and squeezed the bottom hard. Bill was watching all this, just like when she and Ann were playing. She put her mouth over the tip and released her hand, letting the load shoot down her throat.

"I like that. I like the way you squirt. It's fun to play." she said as she wiped her mouth on the back of her hand, then wiped it on her leggings. Then she burped a loud rolling belch.

"Oh my, excuse me for being rude. My, where have my manners gone? Did you want some of this?" She held out her hand to him.

"Nah, maybe later." Bill avoided her hand as she finished wiping it off. Bill watched all this in amazement.

"Rebecca, if you don't take the cake. Yer funny an' I do enjoy yer company."

"Well, thank ye white boy. I think we ought to clear out pretty soon an' find a place to bed down for the night. What do you think?"

"Yeah, we'll have to be on our way. It looks like them red niggers ain't a comin' after their ponies after all."

Some movement caught his attention down on the tree line. It was the Indians tracking their horses. They were Arapaho, but they didn't know that.

Rebecca touched his arm pointing to the other side of the meadow. Turning his head, he saw another group coming from the east, on foot also. They were Crow.

"Good god, we're in some deep shit here lover." he spoke quietly to her as he continued to watch the interaction as it unfolded. They stopped a few feet from each other; soon arms were animated as the two groups had a serious disagreement. Each pulled out war clubs, and then the fight started. They were throwing tomahawks, spears, and shooting arrows at each other.

Bill was watching this whole thing and couldn't believe that they were witnessing a battle firsthand. The Arapaho that was following them got completely wiped out. The Crow had one warrior left. Bill saw him staggering away as he was trying to walk, but he stumbled and slumped over, lying motionless. All was quiet.

Bill looked over at Rebecca. She was staring at the massacre and then at him, then back down.

"I'm a thinkin' we ought to haul ass down an' get as much plunder as we can. They most likely got food an' gear that we could use."

"Do you think it'll be safe?"

"Hell yes, they's all been wiped out! We could use some of their gear. They got knives an' bows an' clothes."

"How 'bout if we stay up here? I'll give you another blowjob. You can poke me in the ass if you want. As many times as you want! We can stay up here for a while, okay? I'll let you do anything you want."

"No, it's time we started livin' like them red bastards. Let's go."

"I'm not sure about this, but if you say it's time, then so be it."

"Okay. This is how it's gotta work. No one lives down there. If ya can't do it, then jus' grab whatever ya can, okay?"

"Wouldn't it be better if we got one of them alive? We could nurse him back to health, and then we could learn some things from him. He would be happy or thankful, and maybe he would teach us things. Maybe they're from White Moon's village." she pleaded.

"Maybe when he got well, he'd slit my throat an' take ya back to his people as a prize an' they'd all be a pokin' ya, Then ram a pole ass an' burn ya up an eat ya."

Her face turned whiter than a preacher sheet with that tit-bit of information.

They left the bluff, walking down toward the massacre. Bill was thinking about the action that had just happened. *This's a violent place. That's fer certain an' fer true.* He turned around to see how Rebecca was doing, noticing she was shaking.

"You gonna be okay?" he asked.

"Yes." she whispered.

They slowly entered the scene; bodies were hanged in the deadfall along the trail as if a whirlwind had come through. Walking quietly they approached the carnage in awe. Rebecca walked up to the bunch that was after them, staring blankly at the faces painted in pain, jaws open in silent screams, eyes staring into the dirt or the heavens above. Then she rushed to the bushes vomiting violently like she had swallowed a bucketful of buffalo spunk.

"You all right?" Billy asked as he gazed over the massacre.

"Yes, I've never witnessed suck gore. I wasn't ready for it. But I'll be okay in a minute." After she had recovered, they began to look through the possessions of the nomadic warriors. Out of the corner of his eye, Bill saw some movement by Rebecca. Then he saw the hand move. Before he could help, she grabbed up a war club and began to smash the man's head in. Brains and bones were flying all over the scene as well as covering her shirt with gray matter. Bill stood there watching. Not a damn thing he could do either way. Seeing she had everything under control on her side, he turned Back to the matters before him.

"Do ya need any help?" he asked over his shoulder.

"No. I'll take care of this."

"You gonna be okay?" he asked, concerned.

"No." She sighed in a heavy breath. Reaching down, Bill pulled a bit of plunder out from under a body. and then stood straight. He looked at the bodies covering the meadow floor. Shaking his head in the loss of life, he commenced to step over others to continue his pillaging. The arrows were sticking out of the warriors at haphazard angles as he saw the glistening blood drying in the late-afternoon sun. Once they were slippery from all the blood, flies and other insects began to dominate the exposed gore. Rebecca reached down to move an arm to gather more weapons when an arm came off in her hand. It seemed it was only being held on by some skin. She laid it next to the fallen fighter as she put another knife into her bag. Separating herself from what she was doing, she continued to concentrate on the task ahead of her.

"Damn, this is a mess." she spoke to Bill's back.

"I finished my side, an' I figured I'd give ya a hand." Bill spoke as he turned to her.

"Thanks. This stuff is pretty heavy. It looks like they were gonna follow us to hell an' back to get their horses. There's all kinds of food in these bag and a coupla gourds of water too. I have

five really nice skinnin' knives an' at least two bundles of arrows."
As she was going through the list of stuff, Bill noticed that she
still had the remains of the man all over her shirt and on her face.

"Let's get some water an' wash yer shirt off." he said.

"We're not done here yet." she replied.

"I know. But I want to wash that blood off ya 'fore the flies
start to devilin' ya." She pulled her shirt off and gave it to him.
The runt opened a gourd and began pouring water over the blood
on the shirt. Satisfied he had it wet enough, he pulled a handful of
the wild grass and began to scrub. When he'd finished, he went to
hand it back to her, but she had wandered off back to the battlefield.
She was picking up trinkets, feathers, or jewelry.

"You wanna put this back on?" he called to her, holding the
leather war shirt out to her.

"I like it this way. Thanks for washing it, but I think I'm going
go like this for a while, if you don't mind?" she answered back
from the killing field. He took the shirt over to the pile of goodies.
Dropping it, he called back to her.

"Shit, darlin'! You can go bare-assed naked if ya wanna. But
let's get this taken care of an' be on our way." he called to her.

The red-haired lass returned to where the runt was going through
the piles of prizes. He looked up as she returned.

That's when Bill noticed her nipples were sticking out like a
sore thumb. She sat down across from him; he flicked one of them
with his finger.

"What are ya thinkin'?" Billy quizzed her.

"Well, what do ya think? I'm thinkin' about you." She leaned
over to him, kissing very gently.

"There, that's much better. Now let's get finished here." she
commented as she lifted an armful of plunder to carry back to the
packhorse. Bill stood there, his jaw gaping open. Never had he been
around such a woman. She walked away, and the contrast hit Bill
like a sledgehammer; a white woman with red hair in the wilderness.

When she returned, she sat down looking through more of the Indian's ruck. Bill walked over to where she sat looking over the plunder. There was food, weapons, leggings, extra moccasins, and a bag of roots used for medicines. She was squatting down on her haunches with her red crotch hairs gleaming in the late-afternoon sun. The lips of her valley were spread a little bit, showing a slit of her briar patch. Her tits were resting on her knees as she was going through the bags of gear.

"I think I'll wear these leggin's, an' these moccasins an' nothing else. At least while it's warm. I found this leather shirt that's too big, but I think I can make it smaller. There's a bone needle an' a repair thread in this small bag." She held up a decorated buckskin bag.

"Do you think a breechclout, or should I go for a long war shirt as a dress?"

"I like to see ya naked, but we are gonna be in the bush. I think the war shirt as a dress will keep ya from getting all tore up in the bramble that we might ride through. Tell ya what. We have enough, that if ya wanna ya could cut the sleeves off, an' then cut it off jus' below yer tits. That way we'd have spare buckskins fer repairs, an' I can still grab a handful 'er suck on 'em if'n I get a hankerin'. With no breechclout I can get a poke real quick when the opportunity arises." Bill winked.

"Well, you think you've gotten it all figured out, don't you?"

"Yeppers." With that he leaned over to kiss her mouth, sticking a couple of fingers deep inside her.

"Hey! Don't start what you can't finish!" She pushed him back on his rump. *Damn, she's sassy.* Bill chuckled to himself.

Billy brought one of the Indian horses over and began tying the plunder onto it. The booty slipped off easily. *Damn.* He tried again. *Damn!*

"I'm gonna have to make another pack cradle." Bill spoke to her back.

"Can you do that?"

"I reckon I can use ours as a sample, we have plenty of spare leather and the forrest will provide the rest."

Bill rummage around the meadow to find a few pieces of wood that's close to the shape of the cradles. Rebecca task was to make cinch straps and breast straps. She brought over a saddled an Indian pony looking at it and compared to theirs. *Pretty damned close. If I take some of the bags from the stuff we found, tie 'em together we'd have...*

"White Man stop looking. We have everything we need right here."

Billy returned carrying some curved wood. He looked at what she had laid out and dropped his wood outside her work area.

"What can I do to help?"

"See if you can find any more bags like this one?" She held up a large bag.

"Alrighty." Bill set off to find what he could.

Rebecca began to tie the components together, making long thick straps with the plunder they had amassed into a close replica of their own.

Billy returned with several bags for her to choose from.

"Thanks White Man. She took a large one and made a few cuts here and there, tied some pieces there and deemed it finished.

"Let's put it on, make sure everything will work together." Billy pulled the saddle off and prepared to put the new one on. Together they put the new hybrid saddle-pack cradle on the pony and cinched it tight. It looked better and was easier to use than the one they had gotten from Missouri.

"Lets pack up an' mosey outta here." He said as they began to pack the new cradle as well as to their own pack animal. The sun crept into the western sky, Bill had become oblivious to the smell of the waste and blood as he swung a leg over his mare, taking once last look at the battlefield before they began their wandering north.

"Life's short." he spoke aloud.

"Huh? Yeah, it is." she replied.

They each had three new knives, two in the belt and one under the leggings; extra 'hawk each; a bow and quiver full of arrows; a war shirt; an extra pair of moccasins and leggings; all the food and two gourds of water; and the small bag of medicine. Not to mention the three rifles, and three pistols. Billy looked back at Rebecca to see how she was doing; there he saw she had the bow and quiver over one tit, the powder horn and possible over the other one with her pistol hanging off her waist belt.

"What about them horses?" she asked.

"Let's turn 'em loose. We got no need fer 'em." he answered as he leaned over to untie the horse-hair lead rope. The horses didn't run off; they just ate the long grass as the couple rode away.

CHAPTER 93

They rode into the forest, listening to the mountains around them.

"We're doin' jus' fine there lover." Bill mused as he watched the trees weaving in the late afternoon. They had food, water, extra clothes, weapons, and medicines for healing themselves, although he wasn't too sure how or what to use them on. But after that run-in with the bear, he felt Rebecca had a handle on their uses.

Rebecca was thinking about Bill as they rode into the trees. *He's proven himself over and over to me. His lovemaking is unbelievable; his tracking and mountain skills are advancing quickly, and he could read the signs on the ground as well as anybody as far as I know anyway. Now here I am looking for a place to bed down with this runt. It sure has changed,* she thought.

As they rode on through into the early evening, they found the clump of pines that was perfect. It had a low canopy of limbs to ward off rain if it happened and dense foliage surrounding the perimeter. The young couple tied their mounts up as they unsaddled them, laying their possessions on the needle-covered floor.

"Let's go out an' see what we have around us. Hell, we might even find some good trapping ponds." the runt spoke out as he looked around the newly formed camp.

"Sounds good White Man. Take your bow an' leave your rifle. We don't need unnecessary noise. Not yet anyway." Rebecca said as she hooked the quiver over her breast. The young couple looked around one last time then left their camp in search of nearby adventure. As they walked through a nearby meadow, they came upon a game trail.

"We're not going on this are we?" Rebecca asked.

"Well, I thought we might. Why?" Billy asked as he looked at the well-used trail.

"We haven't been here before, so we don't know anything about who travels these trails. I was thinking that we should hide to see who or what uses these trails." she said, pointing to a little clump of trees.

This woman is learning fast, Bill smiled. *Damn. I surely do love her,* he thought as he headed to the surveillance spot.

"Ya know, after seeing those other red bastards in that meadow down there, I'm a thinkin' that their friends will miss 'em an' comin' a lookin' fer them." Billy pondered aloud.

Bill got down on one knee to inspect the ground, just to see if he could figure out who or what had been there before. Rebecca was watching him analyze the marks on the trail. Then she too squatted down on one knee to look at them. Bill's eyes wandered to her red crotch hairs sticking out like a sore thumb.

Seeing Bill's eyes stray from the ground, she spoke out, "Ahem, ain't we supposed to be looking at these tracks?"

"Oh yeah, the trail. I reckon someone has been through here 'fore us. I don't know how long ago, but there is some hoof prints. Let's get while we have some light."

So they zigzagged off to the trees to watch the trails. As they entered into the foliage, the darkness swallowed them faster than a hog eating last night's meal. Bill turned to observe the path they had just taken to ensure they would have no one following. The soft grass of the meadow had sprung back up like no one had traveled on it. Satisfied he and Rebecca sat and began the wait.

The sun dropped into the western tree line as the couple waited. Nothing had come on the trail as the darkness came over the small valley.

"Let's get back to camp." Bill whispered to his mate.

"Sure." Rebecca pointed to a small opening on the opposite side of the trees.

"That trail's purty damned close to our camp. Didn't realize it when we're snooping for campsite." Bill answered as they walked in silence back to their camp. The forest was coming to life as the light faded. Squirrels barked, elk bugled, an occasionally an owl hooted as they entered their meager camp. Rebecca looked around to assure nothing had been tampered with. Then she stretched. Her arms went up and out to the side, causing her firm breasts to heave up and down as she made her swan-like movements.

"I was figurin' to lay down fer a nap, but you go ahead an' sleep fer a while an' I'll watch the trail fer a spell."

"Okay." That was it. She just plopped down on the pine-needle-covered ground and was asleep in nothing flat. Bill looked down at the sleeping woman; she was curled up like a little baby except her white butt was open for viewing. Bill admired his partner's rump as he rummaged in the bags for some of the newfound food. He found some of the Indian pemmican the natives used to supplement the diet of meat.

Tastes awful, but damnit, I'm hungry, he agonized as he swallowed each bite. He'd already forgotten the pemmican they ate back on the Mississippi when they had stolen the canoe.

The sun was almost gone as he saw some movement on the trail. Sure as shit, there were eight or ten men who came walking down the trail. They were socializing and jabbering like a bunch of bluejays. It didn't seem to matter one iota who heard them. They walked right the hell by and didn't flinch a lick at where Bill and Rebecca had left the trail. The last one stopped for a second and looked right at where they were. Then he took a couple steps, and then he stepped off the trail and stood there. Ahead of him, the others stopped. Then the leaders came back. Then they all walked toward them and stopped. Then they circled the area a couple of times and lay down. Right there in front of the green trappers.

Well, I reckon they don't know we're here, he thought as he put his hand on Rebecca's shoulder. Rebecca woke up and leaned over to him, whispering in his ear, "I'm scared."

"We'll be okay." he reassured her.

The light was completely gone as they huddled together in the clump of trees. Bill lay back against a tree, staring out into the darkness. Vision was gone but not the sounds of the forest. The nightlife was playing a symphony as he stared at where the natives were sleeping.

I'm sure glad our horses are quiet an' all, he thought as he dozed off. The quiet awoke him. Bill touched Rebecca's arm. He couldn't see if her eyes were open, but he felt her hand touch his.

"Somethin's happening!" he whispered in her ear. Then he heard a mountain lion.

"That's a big 'un, like the ones I saw the trappers loading on the boat. I reckon one of those would surely devil ya if it caught ya. The sound was comin' from across the meadow." he whispered. Then he heard an awful scream as death came to the Indians in the meadow next to them. The sound gave Bill goose bumps, knowing it could have been him or Rebecca that was getting mauled. God, it sounded terrible. The runt pulled his knife as he took Rebecca's hand and put it on hers.

"Put yer back to the tree till we can figure out what's goin' on." he whispered.

There was a shitload of noise and commotion going on out in the meadow. That cougar had gotten a late-night snack out of the local natives. Then it was quiet. A painfully long quiet came over the forest as the sun slowly came up to bathe the meadow with a new day's light. Bill reached behind him to wake Rebecca.

"You awake there darlin'?" Bill whispered.

"I am now. Anything else happen last night?" she replied back in a hushed voice.

"Nah, it's pretty still out there."

She went to stand up, but he touched her arm and motioned her to stay seated. Leaning over, he pulled a few branches aside to see if he could see what was happening out in the meadow. The natives were still there. Over at the other side of the meadow, Bill watched a couple them whacking down a few saplings. Those others were tying some tree limbs together. Then they put one of the smaller men on those limbs and started to drag him away. They went the way they came from; soon there was nothing in the meadow. The others had continued the way they had come from. As Bill watched the scene before him, he felt sure that the cougar had got one of them last night. They were gone in no time at all, but he wanted to wait until the birds and the forest critters came back to life.

"Damn, that was closer than I like." he spoke quietly.

"I have to pee!" she whispered. With that she scampered over to a bush and turned around to face him as she squatted down, making her water. Bill looked over to her, admiring his woman when she winked at him. He felt the pang of a full bladder also, standing up slowly, stretching the muscles in his back. He walked over to the brush to relieve himself. As he urinated, he spoke over his shoulder to the red-haired one.

"Let's get packed up an' get a move on."

"Don't you want a poke first?"

"Nah, not right yet. I got a bad feelin' 'bout last night. I don't know where they're a goin', but when they find the mess, they'll definitely start lookin' around. It'll take 'em a while to round up them horses as well. I know we hid our trail, but they'll figure it out, an' we'll have to be gone by the time they get back here."

"That means I can't even give you a quick one?" she asked.

"That's right. Things are different now. We could go under from a piss-poor decision. Hell, we got them red niggers all over the place. It appears to me we're right in the middle of the hornet's nest, okay darlin'?"

"Well, if ya get a poke, then you'll die a happy man. If we get caught, well, we can deal with that when it happens."

"You have a different way of thinkin' Rebecca. But it's still no. Get yer horse saddled an' let's put some time 'tween us an' our neighbors yonder." He pointed to where the warriors had gone.

Hell, he wanted a poke something fierce, but the men behind them would kill them for sure. They made a living killing, so it wouldn't be any problem to kill a couple of green trappers. Following the trail of the wounded man, they plodded on quietly as the day closed. On through the day they rode, nice and enjoyable with no thought of the warriors that were sure to be lurking about.

In the late afternoon they stopped and looked for a place to camp. Bill found a secluded section of small pine trees that would hide them from prying eyes. Making a cold camp they lay down on their saddle blankets listening to the nightlife begin to call to the hidden creatures.

"Well, tomorrow we'll look fer some grub an' start lookin' fer a place to trap. What do ya say to that?" No answer. Then he leaned over to see her face. *Yep, asleep. If that don't beat all.*

She's plum tuckered out. He chuckled.

CHAPTER 94

In the morning she was up and as fresh as a daisy. Standing and stretching, she headed for the edge of their camp. Squatting down, she made her water.

"Hey White Man! You wanna a poke? I need somethin' to plug this hole of mine up! Seems it's flowin' like a river in the spring." She giggled.

"Sure, bring yer flea-bitten, crab-infested crotch over here, an' I'll take care of it." he retorted. Not worrying about the Indians in the area, he felt pretty safe in their little hideaway.

She walked over and plopped on her butt in front of him. Lying on her back, she pulled her legs up, exposing Bill's playground.

"Breakfast is served." she huskily whispered.

The young blond runt lay on his gut so he could shimmy over to where she waited; burying his face in her honey pot, he started to snack away. Rebecca wasn't lying about her being wet.

Christ, Bill thought. *She's flowing like maple sap on a hot summer day.* He lapped, sucked, and nibbled on the red button of hers until he felt her tense up. Then, as quick as a jay snagging a horsefly, her legs came together and just about broke the young man's neck.

"God, you do that so well!" she said between breaths, "You know, if you don't mind, I'd like to be poked."

"Yes mam!" Billy slid out his root and planted it firmly in her garden. After some work, the seed was planted.

"There ya go, mam. Garden's all done." He stood up, his manhood still dripping from the gardening chore. He watched the red-haired lass sit up and reach for her toy.

"Don't wanna waste any of this now, do we?" She smiled up at him.

After they had tethered the horses well, the couple assembled their gear and struck out on the trails in the area for a scouting trip to see what was available to them. They had scouted untill the sun reached the highest point in the sky, Bill heard a familiar noise.

"Listen." he spoke to her.

"Voices?" she answered.

"Let's get!" Bill spoke quietly. So they turned and started back down the trail like the devil himself was pulling on their breechclouts. Well, his anyway, as Rebecca had nothing on except the damned leggings and a buckskin half shirt. Bill was trying to formulate a plan as they beat feet for some kind of safety; his possible bag was flopping to and fro as the young white man ran for his life. He looked back to see how his woman was doing. It was a wasted effort on his part. She was loping along like a young doe. She had the bow and quiver tied down tighter than a nun's tits as they ran on the narrow game trail.

Bill didn't know how much time they had before the warriors on the rescue trail would cut their's. As he was running by a briar patch he stopped.

"Hey let's take this way, they'll will never know we were here and if they do will be gone before they can catch us."

"All right let's hurry up before they catch us now."

They stepped into the briar patch and vanished. He's stopped in a small growth of birtch trees and turned to her. In a whisper he said, "They won't know if we get off the trail not, it's fairly covered with tracks already. They won't even know we're here!"

"Do you really think they'll run right past us?"

"Yeppers!" he exclaimed.

"If they ever figure out where we went, we'll be inta the next valley by then. I'll tell ya what. I'm so sure that this'll work that I'll give you that poke. We'll go up higher so we can see, an' as soon as them bastards is gone, I'll pull ol'John Thomas out an' thrash you soundly. Now what do ya say to that, missy?"

"You better be right! I don't like being teased. I only got one poke this morning, and I'm getting used to being poked reg'larly, you know." She giggled.

"Damn, yer sassy." he spoke through a huge grin.

Bill figured it would take those warriors quite a while to even figure out if they had even been there, let alone stepping carefully through the briar patch. That's if they stayed where they were. He figured if they did come after them, they'd beat feet along the ridge line before they even saw them. The young man changed his point of view; he was actually enjoying himself now that he wasn't being directly threatened. It wasn't like being hunted. Not like before. This time he figured the bastards would have to work to get his white ass.

"Hey, ya know, they don't even know we're white. They most likely figured some of them other niggers lived to tell the tale an' they was ready to even that score with 'em!" he spoke in a hushed voice. Lying on their stomachs, they watched the trail. The view was almost perfect.

"Lookie. There they are. Shit! They are really makin' some time." he whispered. There were five Arapaho following the trail of Bill and Rebecca, and they were running hard. He could hear them before he saw them. They were speaking as they ran, not that any of it was understandable to the young couple. They didn't look that much different than regular folks, just a tad skinnier. Darker, of course.

As sure as the nose on his face, the red bastards ran right by their briars. They didn't even flinch a lick at where they'd stepped off. They waited until they were gone before either of the whites made a move, and then it was Rebecca. She slipped her hand in between Bill's legs, her slim hand gliding past his scrotum on its mission to find the planting toy she so enjoyed. Bill felt her hand. He turned to her seeing a huge grin on her beautiful face.

"Time to pay up White Man." she whispered. Billy rolled over on his side, looking at her. He chose his words carefully.

"Look, tell ya what. Ya can give me a knobber, an' then we'll move on up the hill an' find some cover. Then I'll give ya everythin'. How's that sound? I want to get out of this par'ticular area now that them red niggers had gone by."

"No! I want a poke." she protested, folding her arms over her chest and sticking her bottom lip out in a fake pout.

"That trail ain't too far, an' ya know, how would ya feel if'n I was a pokin' ya an' then niggers showed up to join in an' all? That kind of ruin the mood, wouldn't it?" He was stalling a bit.

"Hmm You do have a point. Okay, then let's get while the gettin's good." With that she leaned over to kiss his mouth, her tongue went sliding down his throat like a frog getting a fly.

"That'll hold me over until you can pay me properly." Then she whacked his ass with an opened hand, making a sharp crack.

They moved away from their hiding spot and headed up to the ridge line above them. He stopped in his tracks. The young white man was standing directly in the middle of another trail. He looked off to the left and to the right when the conclusion made his heart sink. It appeared to be the same trail that had been below them. Bill felt a tingling on the back of his neck.

"Rebecca, I think we're about to get to learn how to shoot these bows." Billy said nervously.

"What're you talking about?" the sassy red-haired vixen asked.

"Them sumbitches that we saw down there? Well, they'll be here in a few shakes. Get a handful of arrows ready. Get yer knife ready too. As soon as ya see 'em come around that bend, well, start to screamin' an' runnin' right at 'em!"

"Are you crazy? We've ain't even practiced let alone trying to shoot at a moving target!"

"There's nowhere to hide, an' I think that they'll be here faster than a bluejay robbin' eggs. Remember, scream an' fight like yer life depends on it 'cause it does!" Looking over at her as she was shucking the top, exposing her breasts to the world, she commented,

"That'll give them red niggers something to take their minds off us for a second." She chuckled.

Smart girl. Damn, I love her! he thought.

There she stood butt naked except for her leggings. White breasts gleamed in the broken rays of sun as her red hair waved in the early morning breeze.

"That'll get them niggers attention, not to mention the two of us screamin' an yellin' at the top of our lungs." He smiled at her. He didn't noticed she had dropped the bow and arrows behind her and pulled a knife and tomahawk instead.

The wait wasn't long as the white trappers saw them before they were observed.

"Ready?"

"Yeppers lover." she answered.

"Here we go!" he shouted over his shoulder.

They took off at them like a bull that had its nuts tied tight. Yelling and screaming at the top of their lungs, the young couple started the battle. The surprise worked. The Arapaho hadn't ever thought of seeing such a spectacle in the forest, let alone attacking them.

Cut by the Eye didn't know what to think. One moment he was on a rescue for his friends, and next there were two wild people attacking him. He wasn't sure if they were spirits or real people. The one had fire hair, and it screamed like a woman giving childbirth. That was enough to frighten him.

He turned to run, but Heavy Hawk was in his way, and it caused Cut by the Eye to stubble and fall into him. As Heavy Hawk stumbled and turned to run, he felt his head being pulled back. Heavy Hawk felt the air knocked out of him as his back hit the ground. He opened his eyes only to see a knife plunging toward him. He froze, unable to move. He died as the knife ended his life.

Bill barreled into the first warrior. As the Indian stumbled falling backward, the runt stepped on his back and kept going. The next one wasn't as fast as the last three. Bill reached out, grabbing his long black hair; he pulled hard, causing the warrior to fly off his feet, hitting the ground with a sickening thump. Bill slid around, his knife already out; he stabbed the prone man in the right eye. The knife stopped as the hilt hit the eyebrow bone. Leaving it in, Bill quickly got to his feet to continue the chase. The first two were gone like a mourning dove in a lightning storm.

That last one. Well, that man had some sand in him. Flat Lance skidded and turned to face his attacker. That was a bad choice. The white terror didn't. Billy bowled into the senior warrior. Both were knocked down to the fern-covered ground. They both immediately jumped to their feet as the warrior pulled an eight-inch butcher knife. Both men were panting like a couple of lung-shot bucks now. Bill could see the warrior's salt-and-pepper hair shining from the bear grease the warrior used to adorn himself. The sweat was running down his painted face dripping on the dusty trail. Bill looked down at the knife and saw the smile come across his opponent's face. He reached down to grab Isaiah's, only to find it missing.

"Oh oh!" Bill spoke aloud. Bill stood there panting as the Arapaho slowly moved to wade into Bill's liver. The white runt had a backup knife stashed under his legging though. He quickly reached down to retrieve his weapon. Flat Lance's smile faded as the white runt leveled his knife at his aboriginal opponent.

"No matter! I will eat your heart today and prove that you are nothing but a puny white man!" he screamed in his native tongue.

Bill couldn't make heads or tails out of the fighter's screaming; he knew it was a threat of some kind. Then the warrior ran straight at Bill, slashing quickly at the runt. As Flat Lance went by, Bill sidestepped the rushing man, kicking him in the butt as he went by. Thrown off balance by the kick in the butt, Flat Lance spilled into the dirt of the trail, his hands going down to keep his face from smacking the ground. He rolled over; jumping to his feet, he cussed the small white man.

Billy figured he was still cussing from the tone of his voice. The bad part was he didn't know Rebecca was behind him. All of a sudden, his gut shot forward as he tried to reach his back with his hands. Of course, they didn't work that way. He fell on the ground belly down, trying to scream, but all that came out was blood and foam. Bill quickly ran over to the fallen warrior to push Rebecca's knife in farther. Then he pulled the man's head back, exposing the now-dead-man's throat, and sliced the man's exposed soft skin. Blood oozed out mixing with the sweat on the dirt. The smell of the warrior's bowels releasing was more than Rebecca could stand. She backed away, turning as she vomited on the side of the trail. Bill released the greased hair. The head fell crooked off to the side.

"The other'n?" he asked, "Ya kill the first 'un to fall?" He knew she had before he asked.

"He's back there, same as this one you did." she said with no feeling as she wiped her mouth on the back of her hand.

Reaching down, the runt pulled Rebecca's knife out, wiping it clean on the dead man's back. He stood looking around for the knife that had fallen at the beginning of the skirmish.

"Sure as shit, it fell out when I rammed that bastard." Bill commented as he retrieved the big bone-handled knife from the trail.

Bill rolled the dead man over and looked at how his knife was in there. *Oh? A sheath.* It was decorated with all kinds of beads, paint, and fringe.

"Very purty." he spoke as he pulled the sheath and belt off; he pulled it around himself, admiring it. Pleased with himself, he slipped the dead man's knife in its home.

"Let's go back to the others an' get what we can off 'em." Billy spoke as the his breath released in a rush of air. *What a day!* he thought.

They got back to the one with the knife in his eye. He had squirmed around but was as dead as a drowned cat by now. Bill rolled him over, pulling the dead man's sheath off. He offered it to Rebecca. It was decorated also, but the colors were arranged differently than the one Bill had gotten.

"Here ya go sweetie."

"Oh, how nice. A gift."

The tone of her voice said more than the words. The small white warrior pulled his knife out of the man's eye, putting it in the sheath in the small of his back. He stuck the third knife in the sheath under his leggings.

"Did ya have any problems?"

"Does it look like it?"

"What got yer hackles up?" he asked.

"Well, in case you have to know, I was scared shitless. I have no idea how to kill. Okay, I clubbed an almost-dead man to death, but that's nothing like what we just did. I don't like it. I just want to get our stuff and leave.

"Look, if we didn't kill these niggers, they would have sliced out my gizzard an' killed you real slow!" Bill told her.

"You don't know that!" she screamed.

"Oh! Well, feast yer pretty blues on what was on that nigger's belt!" She took her eyes off Bill, looking down at where he was pointing. There on the ground where his belt had been was a clump of blond hair.

"Does that make a difference to ya now?" he asked softly.

"Oh my god, I didn't know. I just thought— I thought that— well, they wasn't gonna be mean. I thought they would be like the ones I saw at White Moon's camp. I—I" Then she walked over to a sapling. Leaning against it, she began to sob.

Billy walked over to her and put his arm around her as he spoke firmly, "We can't stand around here darlin' We got to get away from here. They know were whites an' that they're gonna be back with more of their red frien's. Let's do like ya said. I wanna get."

Bill stuck her knife in her waistband, tying the new sheath onto her. She turned wrapping her arms around him. Crying, she stepped back with tears dripping down her cheeks. They were landing on her tits, making their way down her stomach right down to her red briar patch. By this time Bill was all bent over watching the tears enter the red hair going right into that red valley of hers. She put her hand on his shoulder, pushing him back on to his rump.

"You still owe me a poke asshole." she said between sobs.

Bill realized that she was going to be okay. He was scared also but didn't want her to know, not yet anyway. Rebecca recovered the bow and arrows and her half shirt. She slipped it effortlessly on then strapping them across her chest, the string making a neat *x* across her breasts.

They headed up the trail that the others had run away on, looking warily as they traveled on into the afternoon.

"This trail looked fairly well traveled on. The groove from everyone walking on it is as deep as my ankles." Billy commented.

Rebecca had stop sobbing as they walked.

"You know White Man, life's fucking' cheap out here!" she blurted out to his back. Billy White stopped in his tracks. Turning, he looked at her. She usually didn't speak like that. She usually spoke pretty refined. Now all of a sudden she was talking like a gutter tramp.

"What the hell's got inta ya?" he asked.

"We just killed three fucking people! On the boat, well now, there was six goddamned fucking people killed that we know of. That's what the fuck I'm talking about, you fucking white asshole!" Her face was as red as her hair as she spat these venomous words. At first he was taken back by her insults. Then he thought about what she was saying. He pondered it for a moment before he spoke. Bill thought of the words he was going to use, so he spoke carefully.

"Is all this commotion 'cause ya didn't get yer poke like I was a promisin' ya?" Bill asked. She stumbled back a step. Her mouth dropped open.

"What? You think I'm all riled up because your scrawny white ass didn't fuck me? What the fuck do you think? No, who the fuck do you think you are? You're a filthy white river rat who can't take care of himself. You had to jump the boat because you're afraid of the authority! No, I don't give a rat's fucking ass if you fuck me again or not! What do you think of that, you putrid hunk of shit?" she bellowed. *Hmm, she can chew ass better than that ol'Matthew Harris,* thought Bill.

By this time she was screaming so hard that her blue eyes almost popped out of her skull. He thought about whacking her upside the head but figured it would make things worse.

"Are ya done?" Billy asked quietly. She just stared at him slack-jawed, no fists flying. Her eyes held a blank stare.

"Yeah, I guess I'm pretty much done. Sorry, I could only stand so much, and I had to yell and scream. You're the only one available, so you got the full load. I didn't mean any of it, okay?" Then she stuck out her hand for a handshake. The young white runt reached out, grasping it firmly as he would any man he had met.

"We should get off this trail 'cause it looks to be used a lot. What do ya say if we head north? I was thinkin' maybe we could hook up with one of them trappin' brigades that I heard from Ashleys group." Bill questioned her, waiting to see her reaction.

"Okay, sounds good to me. Do you think that they'll make me wear clothes?"

"Yeppers. I don't know why. Best goddamn tits I've ever seen. I don't wanna see 'em covered up. No siree. Not ever. If I have anything to say 'bout it. But they're your tits an' if ya wanna leave dem out, well then, by god, by all means leave them sumbitches out fer the whole world to admire." Bill spouted.

CHAPTER 95

After retrieving the horses and gear, the couple rode just under the ridge line, with their noses pointed north. Bill stopped to look out over the valley below; the sun was sinking in the west as the orange light came cascading through the trees. It was almost dark as they traveled slowly on into the new reaches of the valley.

"Ya see any place special that ya wanna stop fer the night?" the blond runt asked over his shoulder. She looked around for a while, spotting a clump of maple trees.

"Those look good to me." she spoke quietly. As they entered the little clump, Bill noticed that all the grass was lying down like someone else was there before them. Then he spotted some deer pellets, figuring if it was good enough for them, then it would good enough for a couple of white folk. Pulling off their saddles and flopping them on the brown and decaying leaves from last winter, he looked at the backs of the horses.

"Shit, I imagine them horses felt as light as a feather gettin' them saddles off. They's purty heavy with all of our ruck an' possibles in dem. I figure we'll have to even more when we start trapping." he spoke as he looked over to her. He dug in the pack cradle getting out a curry brush where he proceeded to brush all four horses down. Then he picked up each foot to examine the hoofs in the waning light.

"Cain't see a dern thing." he mumbled.

"Might as well hobble these critters." he called over his shoulder to her. No answer. Finished as he could be, he went to where she was and dropped down. Billy hit the ground hard as he relaxed. He watched her rummage around in her bag for some grub. As she dug her hand, she stopped then pulled out some jerky to offer her partner. As the white runt leaned over to get it, she grabbed his hand, pulling him over on top of her instead.

"This is what I want to eat." She giggled. She rolled him over onto his back, she pulled the half top off, tossing it over by the saddles. She reached down for her prize under his breechclout. It didn't take a whole lot to get his carrot out. She had her left hand on his bare chest with her right she was skinning that carrot down to expose it to the world. Then she leaned over, she slowly moved toward his groin and her play toy. She was using her tongue as a teaser. She brought her left hand up to meet the right, squeezing hard, she placed her lips over the tip, letting saliva dribble onto it, then released the root from her grasp as she went down. All he could see was red hair flying this way and that as the fiery maiden worked her magic. Bill could feel himself getting close to popping.

"I'm gettin' close there darlin'."

She brought her head up, looking Bill in the eye.

"I know you can toot more than once." With that she put her right hand back on and started pumping it like a handle on a well. Then in a few seconds Bill's pride and joy went to squirting like a geyser. It was going everywhere but where he figured it should go.

"Uh oh. Did someone go off?" She giggled as she was wiping it off the side of her face, rubbing it into her red hair. She then plopped his pod back in her mouth to ready him again for her enjoyment. It wasn't too long before he started feeling that familiar tingle of getting back to fighting form.

"This time I want to use it fer myself." she spoke to him in the dim light of the early evening. With that she swung a buckskinned leg over him. Leaning down, she closed the distance from her garden to her toy, so close Billy White could hear her breathing.

"I'm going to have me some fun now." she whispered in his ear. With that she snaked a hand down grabbing his pod. Holding firmly, she slowly slipped it inside of her, rocking back on him until her thighs were touching her calves. Slowly she leaned forward until his carrot almost fell out. Quickly she sat back down fast. Then back up real slow. Just before Bill slipped out, she plopped back down so hard her knees came up off the ground. She kept doing that until he could stand it no longer.

"Woman, the boat's pullin' up to the dock an' the payin' passengers are fixin' to get off."

"Oh! Is that right?" With that she lifted herself off and turned around, sticking her red briar patch right in his mug. That thing was dripping like a water barrel with a hole in it.

"Damn, girl!" Bill spoke as he buried his face into her sloppy wet garden. She rammed that red muffin down hard, smearing it all over his face. Meanwhile down below she was sucking, lapping, and licking like a hound dog with a ham bone. He felt his piss'r getting closer to popping. He wanted to scream, and then she leaned forward so all that was touching him was the red dripping valley of hers.

Then she spoke, "Bite! Bite! Do it now! He did as he was told; he could feel her tightened up for a second then fell over to the side, panting like she had just outrun a hundred red niggers. *Well, that don't do me no good,* Bill thought. She was lying there; her tits were heaving up and down. Her eyes were closed, so he rolled over. Getting to his knees, he quickly brought himself to popping. She opened her eyes looking over at him just as the runt blew the whole load right in her face. *That'll teach her to leave me hangin'!* he thought.

"Um, a snack. Thanks white boy!" Then she leaned over. Using her hand, she grabbed his pod. Holding on with both hands, she stuck it in her mouth. She sucked until the last drop was gone. Then she rubbed all that slimy stuff from her face to her once-ivory-colored breasts. He was stunned. Again. *Damn, this woman surprises me all the time.* She lay there for a while as the small man got up, arranging his pod back under his breechclout. Then he walked to the other side of their little camp, peering out into the darkness. He could barely make out the trees and shrubs of the forest. *Tomorrow we'll have to kill a large animal for food, an elk or mule deer. Something as the booty food is all but gone,* he thought as he placed his hand on his growling stomach.

He walked back over to her, looking down; she had her eyes closed, appeared to be sleeping. All the spooge was gone, and her arms covered up her ample breasts, but he could still make them out in the fading light.

"Shit, if that don't beat all." *She's plumb tuckered out* as he leaned against an old maple tree. The young man was desperately trying to figure out his current place. He knew they were northwest of the Platte, but he didn't know how far. He didn't know if every band of savages they had met were out to kill whites, just the ones that they had tangled up with. He laughed aloud; he really didn't know too much at all to tell the truth.

He put his back to the smooth bark of a near by tree, *Hell, I know I got a good partner as any man could ask fer. She can screw like a mink, sassy as a store clerk, an' she can kill like a fightin' dog. I reckon the last one is fairly important since we're hell an' gone from any white folk to speak of. The more I think 'bout it, the more I'm startin' to like the red man's way of doin' things.* He continued to ponder, *Eat when ya want, raid some, screw whenever I could get her to, an' run wild through the woods. Sure has changed from washin' dishes takin' orders from a booshway that I would rather spit on than obey. Now Sheila, she was a handful an' I truly miss her at times 'cause she had a sense of humor.* He slipped down on the tree, resting his head against the trunk. He dozed off thinking about Rebecca and the soft red lips.

In the morning he awoke still against the tree. The young lad stretched his legs out as his rump tingled. *Dang if my butt didn't fall asleep.* My, he looked at Rebecca sleeping soundly. She was still on her side, and her butt was beaming out. The scratches and dirt didn't hide the fact that she was white. He moved in behind her and gently touched her butt with his hand. He pulled his breechclout aside as he thought of mounting her again. She stirred a bit rolling over to her back. She opened her eyes. She rubbed them, hoisting herself up on her elbows, looking at what was before her.

"Well, what's on your mind white boy?" she asked.

"I figured I give ya a poke the first thing." he answered.

"Let me pee first, or I'm likely to piss all over you while you're poking me."

"By all means." She leaned forward for him to pull her to her feet. She did a big stretch as she yawned. As the young girl stretched, her breasts lifted, showing almost no fat left on her. The miles of riding and running had leaned the woman out. Around her slim waist was the belt of leather that held up her leggings, her feet still covered by the moccasin they had got from the plunder. *By god, she's gorgeous,* he thought as she walked over to the edge of the trees. Turning to face him, she squatted down on her heels.

"Hey, White Man!" she called out. She leaned back, balancing herself with one hand. With the other one, she reached down to spread those soft red lips of hers. Then she pissed. A yellow stream sprayed out two or three feet toward the runt.

"Well, what do ya think of that? I bet you figured just you men could do that?" she asked.

"Well, you do take the cake Rebecca. If you're 'bout finished, I reckon I want to slip this carrot of mine into the beautiful hole of yours." Bill spoke, pushing on with his mission.

"Okay okay, here I come Romeo."

"Who?" Billy asked.

"It's an old love story I read once." she answered. She sidestepped her piss, coming over to where the blond runt was waiting. Then she lay down on the soft grass and leaves, pulling her legs up to reveal the red wet canyon of hers. She then grabbed each ankle. Rocking back a bit, she opened the garden for young Bill.

"There you go son. Do yer best!" Sliding up to her, the runt aimed his pod right up to her hole; slowly pushing, he wanted to savor every moment with her. But she had other plans.

"Come on, do me real hard!" she ordered. With that note Bill started stroking a little faster and then faster. Soon he was thrashing as fast as he possibly could. Each stroke he buried his tool deep. Each time he saw her tits fly toward her head from the force. By now he was sweating like a whore in church, getting ready to release his seed into her. Rebecca had her eyes closed, enjoying every moment with her blond runty lover, and then they flew open.

"Bury it deep. Give me the full load lover!" She was sweating like a dog passing a peach pit by now.

"After you come, don't stop. I want to be full of you." she requested. That was all he could stand, one final thrust and he filled her garden full. Not wanting to stop, he kept stroking until he was softer than a rotten squash. Backing out, Bill plopped onto his rump; his carrot was still quivering with spooge dripping off the end. She rubbed her hand down in the valley, getting a few fingers into herself; she pulled them out and placed them in her mouth to appreciate every drop.

"Umm. You taste good in the morning as you do in the night boy." Then she stood up bending over a bit to watch the spooge dribble down into her leggings. It left a wet trail where it ran down. Then she looked over to him.

"I always like when it runs down my legs. It reminds me of you as it dries."

"We oughta get packed so we can get the hell outta here." Bill spoke as he looked around the small cold camp.

"We're gonna have to kill some grub today. My belly thinks my throat's been cut. Do ya think ya could that bow to work?" the runt asked.

"Why don't we shoot something? I mean I can figure that bow out, but a gun would be quicker." the redheaded minx asked.

"I'm guessin' we don't need any attention to tell them red

niggers where we is." he answered. With that she walked over to the bag with the ruck in it, pulling the bow out with four arrows. She walked over a few paces, putting an arrow on the right side of the bow. Then, putting her fingers on the string, she began pulling it back. Then she released the string, and an arrow flew off to the right.

"Hmm. Let me try the arrow on the other side of the bow." This time she put the arrow on the left side, she placed the arrow knock between her first and second finger as she pulled the arrow back. Then she let it go. Damn! The arrow flew into the tree across the camp.

"Well, I'll be! You do that right fine girl! Can ya show me the way to do it?" Billy asked.

"Sure. If you promise to give me a poke later."

"Damn, girl! You drive yerself a hard bargain, but I'll take ya up on that."

She then instructed the small white man the method she had used. His didn't go as straight like hers. The string hit his arm. He could see right away he needed more practice and something to protect his arm. Walking over to his possible bag, he pulled out a chunk of soft buckskin. Carefully he wrapped his arm where the string had hurt him. After inspecting his work, he picked up the bow to try again. This time he missed the tree but not as much. He kept flinging arrows until he finally hit close to center.

"Well, I reckon we can use these here things just fine. Let's get all these arrows picked up and skedaddle outta here." He was pulling the arrows out of the tree. The shafts came out but not the head.

"Well, shit!" he complained as he pulled his knife out. He began prying out the black obsidian arrow tips out. He find got two out but the third fractured.

He looked up and out where they were as the sun began its race around the world.

"Well, there something we'll have to take care of later. I reckon we can't be a shootin' these things inta trees an' such things, broke one of 'em." he spoke aloud; actually it was to himself than to Rebecca as she was already saddling her gelding. Bill inspected the arrows to see that the heads had been tied to the shaft using sinew. Bill looked back at Rebecca; she was fussing with some stuff in the one of the pack bag. She was bent over. He could see her rump clearly. He kneeled down, looking at that valley of her just hanging like a coat sleeve. *Good lord, it does look inviting.*

"Hmm, that would have to be later." he mumbled. She slipped the bow over her shoulder. The string went right between her tits. Next came the powder horn. It went over the opposite shoulder with the strings crossing into the center of those perfectly shaped breasts. The sun was up fairly well by now, so he figured that they could ride just below the ridge line to not give a silhouette.

"Ya know we're getting short on water. If we could find a brook 'er a stream, we could fill up the gourds maybe wash up some. Hell, maybe wait fer an' ani'mule to come down fer a drink. Then we'd have some to keep my guts from rumblin' so much." No response from the woman sitting next to him. They rode for most of the morning without seeing anything except a couple squirrels, a bunch of jays and starlings.

Just before dusk, a whiff of smoke flittered in the air. Bill stopped turning to look back at Rebecca; she nodded as they started toward the smoke. Soon the smell of meat cooking accompanied the smoke as they neared a row of trees. They stopped and stashed their horses. They did a slow crawl to see what was going on inside the small fort of trees.

CHAPTER 96

Inside the camp were white people. Not store clerks but skin trappers. He looked over to her then back down to the people before them. She leaned over to his ear whispering, "Let's wait for a while. They may be a bunch of bandits or highway men."

"Uh, lover, we're miles an' miles away from any known white folks. That's fer certain an' fer true. They ain't bandits. Who'd they be a robbing?" the runt questioned his lovely partner.

So the young couple waited, watching the men below for quite some time. The men ate when it was almost dark. Then they lay around like sluggards. Still the couple made no move to introduce themselves. The evening fire was stoked and hunger was getting the best of the young couple.

"Brazen sumbitches! Gettin' a fire that big." Bill whispered to his red headed lover. Then a pair of men entered the camp carrying pelts over their shoulders. They flung the rolled objects to the ground, Bill noticed the men were wet from the waist down. *Water's a good sign. That's taken care of,* he thought as he watched.

"I'm a thinkin' that these are the genuine article. That's what we wanna do." he whispered without turning his head.

"Well, do ya wanna go down an' get some grub jus' slip off real quiet like?" she asked, and then she continued, "I'm hungry. Let's call to the camp. If they'll allow us in, then we can socialize with 'em fer a while. But am I your wife? Sister? Lover? What?" she queried the young blond runt.

"I reckon yer my wife. I like the way that sounds too."

"Should I use your name, you know, Mrs. White Man?" She giggled.

"Oh, all right. My Christian name is William White. So I reckon you'll be Mrs. White. What's yer last name? You've never tolt me." Billy smiled in the darkness to his redheaded lover.

"It's Magnuson. Rebecca Alma Magnuson. I've been with you this whole time, and this is the first time you've asked me. I believe I could be a little put off by that, but you're too cute to be mad at very long. So I've been callin' you by your name all the time, an' you never said anything. Ha-ha. That's a good joke on everyone."

"Well, you never tolt me yers either. Anyway, let's get then, Mrs. White."

"Ok Mr. White." So the young couple slid back down to where they had stashed their gear.

"I'll hide the horses, an' we'll go on down. How's that sound?" he spoke as he picketed the animals in a thick patch of trees. When he was finished, he looked at the lovely lass he was traveling with, making out her shape in the darkness.

"Hmm, you ain't hardly got a stitch on there girl." Bill admired her brazenness but wondered if it was too much.

"I'm a free trapper by god. I'll wear what I want." With that the young girl spun around, heading for the not-so-distant camp. He ran a few steps and stopped her, "Here, he handed her a tomahawk and her pistol. She slipped them in their perspective homes.

She wants to be naked. Well, so be it, Bill thought. He stuck his tomahawk in the small of his back under his wide belt, and the pistol in the front under his belt. Satisfied her hand found his as they closed the distance to the camp.

"Hello the camp!" Bill called out. They all grabbed their guns, standing up, looking their direction.

Bill called out again, "Hello, the camp! Do ya mind if'n we come in to visit fer a spell?"

"I heard ya the first time. Ya ain't got to be a blarin' all over the consarned valley! Stop flappin' yer jaws an' come on in."

So the young couple walked right into the camp full of skin trappers to say a how-do-you-do. Rebecca held back a step, she didn't want to show everything at once.

"Well, what the hell have we got here?" The voice came from a tall black bearded man with a big smile. He was standing with both hands crossed over the top of his Derringer rifle.

"I reckon we got some greenhorns here boys." He laughed.

"Oh, sorry, I fergot my manners. Name's Daniel Rose. I'm the booshway here. Glad to meetcha." His eyes dancing over Rebecca faint figure, he continued,

"That over there is Mel Bridges an' his brother Dirty Billy. That guy cookin' up the stew is Alison Staily. The Norwegian bastard over there, well that's Shannon Lief. Now that we got that over with, why don't ya sit yer ass's down an' get some grub? Then ya can tell us all 'bout yerself." One by one they sat back down. *This is going better than I figured,* Bill thought.

Bill squatted next to the fire as he watched their jaws drop as Rebecca walked into the campfire light. She kept that knife handy and her pistol with-in easy reach as she squatted down, accepting the metal plate the Daniel handed her. Then Alison just about missed the metal plate staring at Rebecca's crotch and tits.

"Son, yer woman here, is she a whore? No offense now but she jus' ain't got too much on the way of clothes. Well, we ain't seen a woman in a coupla months, let alone a neck'd white one." Daniel spoke slowly, trying to be polite.

"Nah, she ain't no whore. She's my wife, I rec," Rebecca broke in just then.

"I understand your confusion in this matter of traditional coverings. I choose to avoid wearing those garments that other women have been instructed to adorn themselves in to appease their strict Christian ethics. It's a personal choice, and if it's offensive to you or if it's going to become a problem with you and your associates, then my husband and I will bid you adieu." Bill was dumbfounded as his wife spouted off. She was speaking like a politician, not a prostitute.

"I don't see it bein' that simple. There's only two of ya, an' there's five of us. Ya got be braver than a bull in the spring 'er dumber than a box of dirt to bring a neck'd woman in here with the bunch of us'n." He waved his hand, then resting it on the big knife as he spoke.

Before Bill could say anything, she threw the plate down and was on her feet quicker than a gambler taking his wages. That caught them by surprise; the only one that wasn't startled was Daniel. He never moved one inch as the young redhead challenged his authority.

"I see. If I'd come down in to your camp wearing a dress of cotton and hard-soled shoes with a pretty bonnet, then you would have extended me all the pleasantries of uncomfortable conversation. But all the time you would have been wondering if I swallow or if I take it in the ass. If I refused, then you'd rape me and kill my husband. That's about it, isn't it?" she spoke thin lipped to her oppressors.

"Damn! You gotta a sharp tongue! Well, you know, that's 'bout the whole shitery right there." Daniel was doing all the talking, but the others were still standing, not knowing what to make of this recent event.

Dirty Billy, a foul-looking short man like Bill White, was making some animal noise, sticking his tongue out. He was trying to get the last drop of honey out of a mason jar. Good god, he was an ugly varmint, with crooked and black teeth. His black eyes were darting from side to side as he spoke. His greasy black hair was hanging over his face, mixing in with his scraggy beard. Bill thought, *He's just about the filthiest human I'd ever seen, bar none.*

"I say we gut the runt! Then do as we please with the bitch." Dirty Billy spoke out.

"Now hang face fer a second." Daniel spoke quietly while he kept his rifle handy.

"These folks could have gone right by us an' not said a by-yer-leave 'er anything, but no, they came in to be social. I reckon we can show that we're not all crazy ol'coons. Tell ya what, son. If Dirty Billy can gut ya, well then, it's our choice to do what we please, but if the young un get the worse end of the deal, we drop it. Ya can take his place in the trappin' line with all his traps and gear. But if he wins, we're gonna have some fun with your woman there. That's sounds like a fair deal? 'Course, I'll get to introduce myself to yer woman first. Ha-ha!" He laughed as he rocked his head back, his black beard shining with grease.

Bill looked at Rebecca; she had the wild look in her eyes, like when they had met the warriors on the trail.

Then she spoke out, "I thought you men were going to be different than the river scum I had met earlier. But alas, I'm incorrect. Your man there, Dirty Billy is it? I will fight him for my place in your trap line. I'm not to be doled out as a piece of meat at the supper line. I am married to this man, but I fight my own battles. I'm to be no one's prize." she spoke clearly, her voice cutting through the evening's air like a lightning storm in the summer.

"Hold on now!" Daniel cradled his rife in the crook of his arm and walked toward them, holding his hand out.

"Son, are ya gonna let this here split tail speak fer ya? Hell, what kind of man are ye to let a squaw fight fer ya? I suppose ya squat to piss too!"

Bill was cool enough not to get goaded into a fight. He figured Daniel wanted to make sure the woman would be intact for the trapper's to use later.

"Well, Dan'l, I've seen this here woman kill. I ain't too sure 'bout yer runt here. But I know my woman, an' she's a killer. That's fer certain an' fer true." He was hoping that they would simmer down some because he was hungry, and all this bantering back and forth wasn't helping any.

The White Man kneeled down on one knee, commencing to eating his food, after chewing for a moment, he stopped looking up at the nearly naked redhead.

He spoke to Alison first, "Alison, you make good grub. Thank ya kindly. Rebecca, go 'head an' kill this runt. Best be quick 'bout it if ya don't want yer food to get cold." Bill couldn't see all the guns, but rest assured they were easily accessible.

The runt was hoping by acting nonchalant they would forgo the fight. Well, that might make them accept them into their little band of trappers.

Daniel held his hand up to stop the ugly runt from carving up the beautiful woman. The older trapper could have killed Billy White in a heartbeat and raped the woman, but this seemed to add something to an already-boring night.

"You're sayin' that this here sassy assed-naked woman is gonna carve Dirty Billy's liver? You're gonna sit an' eat while she does it? Son, am I readin' yer tracks right?" Daniel was almost laughing. The white man looked into the fire for a minute before he answered, "Yeppers, that the tracks I'm a leavin'.'"

Dirty Billy's eyes were darting from Rebecca to Daniel then to the White Man, looking for guidance in his quest to kill something.

"Dan'l, what'll I do?" His voice was quavering.

"Well, Dirty Bill, are ya up to beaver? I ain't never seen ye draw blood, but ye say ye have. She's a pretty thing. I reckon one-on-one is fair. We are sorta fair here. Damnit, there's nuthin' better then to havin' a white woman around to take yer mind off them red devils. But I reckon we can get by if we have to kill these two. Damn, I think I'll have a smoke an' think on this fer a bit."

Dirty Billy just didn't know what to do. Meanwhile Rebecca was standing on the balls of her feet, ready to dance with that white runt. She'd drawn the bone-handled knife from the riverfront weasel. She held her knife by the handle with the blade pointing down, ready for blood. Those others just sat there, not saying a word. Just sitting there.

"Mel, if ye brother gets his hair raised by this here squaw, ya gonna kill her fer doin' it?" Daniel asked.

"He's up to beaver. He fights his own fights. I'll not take up the fight if he loses to a woman, but I've seen Billy fight. Seen him raise hair 'fore. It's too bad 'bout yer woman. She is a real looker." Mel spoke with no remorse as he too picked up his plate to eat. There stood Rebecca, tits shining with sweat in the light of the bright fire, nipples erect, sticking out like two horns on a bull. Bill thought of his lover as he looked at her ready to go into battle, *I bet she's wet too, jus' drippin'. I know fer a fact that when she gets all riled up she gets thata way.* He smiled to himself. Dirty Billy hunched over, starting toward Rebecca.

"Hey Dan'l! What kinda traps does my wife get?" Billy White asked.

Dirty Billy snarled looking at the White Man, "She'll be a doomed beaver in a few shakes, an' this child's gonna skull fuck her right in front of ya. Then I'll cut yer heart out too!" he spat.

Rebecca thought of the Frenchman she'd seen knife fighting. She remembered how smoothly they danced with the knife. No slashes, no grunts. Just smooth, efficient killing, like a dance, smooth steps, wait for the right moment, then finish the dance. *That's what I'll do, dance with him, then finish it when the opportunity presents itself,* she thought.

This's un a bad un, the White Man thought. She really had her hands full with this disgusting rascal. Dirty Billy's attention went back to her. He faked a jab with his right hand. She ducked smoothly. He whacked the back of her head with his open left hand. The slap put a dampener on the evening, that's for sure. She spun on her heel from the impact catching her balance. As she began to turn back to Dirty Bill, she saw his blade coming toward her heart. She sidestepped the lunge but still got a slice on her right breast.

It didn't start to bleed right away, but it looked as it would at any minute. As Dirty Bill lunged again, she spun around, kicking him in the butt as he went by. That sent him sprawling in the dirt. The camp went up in a roar of laughter. Bill thought, *By getting your opponent upset, they don't think straight and make a mistake. Then they die.*

True to form, Dirty Billy jumped to his feet, turning to rush right back at her. His knife was slashing from right to left. Too bad for him. As his right arm went wide to the left, she simply stepped into his side, grabbed his greasy black hair, and pulled his head back, slicing his throat like she was cutting the throat of a chicken for supper. Those of them that were watching all jumped back when Dirty Bill's blood went spurting out across the camp.

White Man finished his plate of grub as he looked at the mess she had created; he got up to fetch a plate full of stew as she wiped the blade off on her leggings, slowly slipping it away.

Then she walked over to the fire to sit down cross-legged on a coyote pelt.

Those other trappers walked over to Dirty Billy. Alison bent over to inspect the dead man.

"That's some damp powder fer sure."

Then his brother bent down, putting his hand on young Dirty Billy's shoulder as his life slipped away. He bowed his head in a silent prayer for his brother. He then got up walking out of the firelight in to the darkness without a word said.

"Ol' Mel is takin' it hard." The words slipped out of Shannon's mouth as they watched Mel Bridges fade out of the light.

"Well, he ought to. It was his kin an' all. Damn, an' kilt by a pilgrim white woman. A naked one at that. I do admit that if I was gonna go under, a naked woman would most likely be the best way." Daniel claimed.

Bill got to his feet and walked over to sit beside Rebecca. She put her head on his shoulder as she whispered, "I was scared shitless." She whispered.

"Where did ya learn those moves?" Bill asked.

"I just thought them out, kind of like learning dance steps. I think there's gonna be bad blood between them and us now. I think we should leave pretty quickly." she spoke in a hushed voice, her eyes watching Daniel.

"Yeppers." Bill conceded. About that time Daniel walked over to where they were sitting, causing them to rise to their feet, hands closing in on knife handles. The couple was ready to dance.

"I'm surprised it came out this way. He had a real mean streak, that pup did. But he was on his own hook. Well now he's gone under 'cause he was a hot head. I'll stick to my word."

He let out a sigh, "Yer wife here gets all his trappin' gear an' his scalp. She put his lights out fair an' square."

"No. I don't want that reminder of the savagery that I was involved with."

"It's most likely a good thing since his brother is still with us an' all. But it's the way things are done out here missy. The stories are gonna be told of how this happened. If some sassy naked redhead kills a seasoned trapper an' don't take his topknot, well, that leaves ya open fer a lot more fights. But if ya have his topknot hangin' from yer belt 'er off yer saddle, well, that says to anyone walkin' by ya got 'har of the bar', an' ya'll take no shit from man nor beast. Now that's jus' what this ol'coon here has seen in these here shinin' mountains." Daniel said.

"I'll take my chances. I don't believe I want a white man's topknot at this time, and I'm not a squaw. I'm a free trapper by god!" she said, looking up to meet his eyes.

"We'll see about that later." With that, he held out a big ham of a hand. Rebecca reached out to shake it. Then Daniel walked over to where Dirty Bill was lying in a puddle of his own blood. Bill could see Rebecca shaking as the events continued. Daniel turned to his men, speaking bluntly, "Let's get this here ol'coon buried." Looking into his mate's eyes, he saw a vacant stare rather than the sparkle he was accustomed to seeing. That look of battle was gone.

"Rebecca, let's take care of the cut on yer tit." he reminded her of the wound.

"It's starting to hurt now that you mention it." she whispered.

Bill went over to his possible bag to retrieve the medicine bag he had got from the Crow war party as the others continued in the darkness burying one of their own. As he opened it, he realized he had no idea of how to use any of the ingredients. There was a deerskin pouch that had bead work and colored porcupine quill in an arrow head design. In it was something that looked like a cure-all, so he smeared some in the center of the buckskin pouch. As he was preparing it, he wrinkled his nose at the smell.

Rebecca had to sit back down closer to the fire so Bill could see to fix her up. She watched him approach with something in this hand. As he closed the distance, the odor came to her nose.

"Christ!" She pulled her hand back from Bill's hand.

"What the hell are you trying to put on me? God, that stuff smells horrid. Take it away right now!" she bellowed. Hearing the commotion, Daniel walked over to see what was going on with the greenhorns.

"What's the problem here?" he asked as he stood over the two.

"You see, I'm still the head nigger here, an' I'm also the sawbones among us. You wanna fix that cut on yer tit. Is that it?" he asked.

"Yes." she answered.

"Well, the stuff yer husband was gonna be puttin' on ya would fix ya jus' fine." he said, pointing at the clump of poultice.

"'Cept if ya chew that there 'baccy it'll help a bunch. That concoction is called a poultice, an' them Injuns larn'd me how to use it. Is that where you got that medicine bag? Injuns?" he asked.

"Yeppers." Bill conceded.

"If ya sew it up, it'll heal up real good in jus' a few days, most likely won't scar as bad to boot." he told them.

"Why are you helping us? I've just killed one of your men." she asked, eyes pleading for answers.

"I tolt ya it was fair an' square. That young bull was itchin' fer a fight. You jus' happened to be the one that came along. I ain't gonna hold it again ya. Now do you want yer husband to sew you up 'er me to do the deed?" he asked.

"I suppose you can, if you say you're the doctor in this group." she said.

"You hang face right there." With that Daniel got up. He walked over to his kit and pulled out a bag similar to Bill's. Bill watched Daniel pull out some thin thread and needle as he hummed a little ditty.

"Most likely this'll hurt a lot, so jus' don't jerk around 'it'll make it worse than it already is." he said. For a mean-looking man, he had a tender side as he reached for Rebecca's white breast.

"Here we go." Then he stuck the needle into the soft flesh. Her eyes went wide, but she didn't move. Again and again he poked that needle through her soft skin. Then he tied off the end and pulled a small sharp-boned knife from the front of his buckskin shirt to cut off the extra thread.

"There ya go. It should heal up fine, an' ya can save yer poultice fer a real cut or a bullet hole. By the way, missy, ya have very nice tits." Then he got up and walked back over to where they were digging Billy's grave.

"Come on, let's get comfy fer the night." Bill whispered to her. Rebecca lay down, so her ass was facing out from the fire. Then as the young Bill sat down behind her with one hand on her rump, the other created mischief. She rolled her head back, speaking to the runt, "You know I like that, but this bunch isn't stupid. We may end up fightin' again before the evenin' is finished."

"We'll wait an' see." He leaned down, kissing her shoulder. When they had finished planting the foul-smelling runt, they all walked over to the fire, shovels clanking behind them as they plopped down. No one spoke. Mel had returned to the camp. He sat down staring into the fire, and then he reached over and threw another chunk of wood on the fire.

"I didn't want to fight your brother Mel. I had to defend myself." blurted out Rebecca.

"I ain't holdin' a grudge if that's what yer thinkin'. I'm sad 'cause he was my kin. He was my only kin. That's all. He always wanted to fight. Anybody, anytime he was ready to fight. It's jus' yer a better knife fighter than he was, I reckon."

"That was no fun a'tall." said Alison.

"So! Sit yer asses up! Tell us a yarn to lift our spirits from doin' such a melancholy chore. I know ya ain't a sleepin', so get yer ass's up!" Daniel bellowed.

"So what do ya wanna hear?" Bill asked.

"Tell us 'bout the land yer from. Tell us the adventures ya 'ave endured!" Daniel spoke loudly to them as they sat up. Bill had been deviling Rebecca's crotch the whole time, and she was sloshing like a bucketful of milk in the back of a wagon.

"I'll tell you a story!" With that she spun around, rolling over so her legs spread wide open. Leaning back she began to tell the tale of the misfortunes on the paddleboat, of how the bear mauled him, and the fight with the Arapaho. The whole time she was putting her knees together, and then she would spread them apart until her knees would touch the ground. She kept doing this as the tale was being woven. Then she told the part of their lovemaking. She was telling how Bill was good for three in a row.

"That so boy?" Daniel asked.

"Yeppers. It is a fact." Bill answered matter-of-fact. With one hand, she took to rubbing herself as she told the tale of sex and adventure. She would throw her head back, saying how good Billy White was. Then she would look at the hardened skin trappers. She would speak slowly about how he this or she that. All the time her fingers were busier than a five-year-old in a candy store. Finally, Alison could stand it no longer. He reached into his buckskins, pulling his pecker out. He started stroking it as if he was sharpening a knife. The others looked at him.

"It ain't like ya never seen a man stroke his bean? Her storytellin' is too good." he claimed. Rebecca was sweating by now. It was running down between her breasts as it continued down to her navel. As it filled, the sweat would spill off the sides, dripping into the pelt she was sitting on. The others pulled their pods out and started pulling on them too since the ice had been broken.

Here's these seasoned trappers, the wild of the wild. They's sitting around pulling on their beans to a story that was being told by a naked redheaded woman that just killed their friend! Helluva story at that, Bill thought.

Rebecca was doing her self-hard by now, telling of Bill's poking and this and that. How she was continually giving blowjobs.

"White Man, come do me now! I can't wait till later." she pleaded. He looked at the others. They were getting as worked up as her. So he slipped his pod out and scooted over to her.

"Lay back an' grab yer ankles darlin', so these gents can get a good view." Bill spoke calmly. She did just that as she pulled one leg up as Bill moved into her. She was dripping all right.

"Here. I. Come!" she cried after but just a few strokes. She wrapped her leg around him, almost pushing him over backward. *Damn, that hurts!* Bill thought, not wanting to say anything aloud. Then she backed off, watching him the whole time. She rolled onto her hands and knees coming over to him. She pushed him onto his back as she put his carrot in her mouth. Bill was so close she could have just touched him to make him go off. Bill released his seed into her mouth. He looked over to the others as Rebecca sat up, wiping her mouth off. Alison blew his load, rolling over, letting it drip in the dirt. Mel? Well, Mel was just Mel. His hand must have slipped or something because his spooge landed up all over his buckskins.

"Here ya go girl!" Daniel shot a load across the fire, landing on her breasts. *Hell, it's at least four feet across the fire,* she thought.

"Damn fine shooting kind sir!" She giggled. She opened her mouth, dribbling the spooge down her chin onto her breasts. Then she rubbed her hand on her mixture from Bill and Daniel. She then licked the stuff off her hands until they were dry.

"Shannon? What happened to you?" she asked.

"It jus' went soft. I don't know what happened." He sighed.

"Too bad. Looks like you need to work on that." She giggled.

"I reckons we'll get along fine, that's if yer worth yer salt fer trappin'." Daniel said he stood up so he could straighten his buckskins.

"We can hear some more of yer stories some other time. See ya in the mornin' folks." The men grabbed the robes and proceeded to lie down around the fire. Soon snoring was all they could hear from their new partners.

"Is the rest of the evenin' ours?" Bill asked.

"Yes lover, let's take this robe out of the firelight, an' I'll do you proper like." Off in the darkness the couple slipped until the early hours of the morning when the brigade awoke for the day's trapping chores.

CHAPTER 97

Bill slept in a fitful rest. New faces and places made him a light sleeper. He heard a person approach, so he tensed up with a hand on his knife, ready for any sign of confrontation. Then he heard Shannon call out at a safe distance.

"Missy, it's time ya got up. Time to go to work runt." Shannon continued.

"Hell, I can't even see." Bill whined.

"Ya don't need to see. Jus' get yer possibles an' come with me." There was a pause.

"Missy, ya hang face here. Daniel will be over in a few minutes to take ya out fer yer schoolin'." the voice said. Bill sat up and then rolled over to stand. Stretching his sore back, he remembered his breechclout was still off. He had a piss erection he could hang a flat tail off. *Good thing Rebecca didn't see it, or I wouldn't get out of here fer a good half an hour.* He chuckled to himself at his so-called misfortune.

"Wait a minute" she said

"What's it?"

"I want a kiss before you go." she requested.

So he bent back down, kissing her on her open mouth. Rebecca's breath had a strange taste. Then he realized it was his own taste. *I don't want to ever taste that again, that Sheila did that once to me, an' it ain't gonna happen again.* She continued to kiss him passionately. She rammed her tongue as far down his throat as possible. He pulled away, looking at her in the blackness of the morning, wishing he'd have time for a poke.

"Hurry back and I'll give you a surprise." She giggled. The young man couldn't figure what a surprise could possibly be as he walked to the edge of the camp to relieve himself.

"Do I got time to take a piss, Shannon?"

"Yeah, but don't doddle." The response from the darkness.

"Hey, Rebecca! Heres a kiss fer ya!" Bill ripped a loud rumbling fart.

"Thank you, asshole." she chimed back from the darkness. Off they went into the early morning on his first day of trapping, Bill following Shannon like a small puppy. The young runt already had his rifle, powder horn, possible bag, and then he remembered his tomahawk.

"Hang face Shannon." Bill whispered using his newly acquired slang.

"Now what?" the teacher asked.

"I fergot my 'hawk. I'll be right back." Bill turned and ran back to camp. There next his bedroll was his 'hawk.

"What are you doing back? Come back for your surprise already?" Rebecca asked jokingly.

"No, I fergot my 'hawk. See ya shortly." Then he sprinted away into the darkness. As he ran, he stuck the 'hawk in the small of his back next to his extra knife. Bill walked on behind Shannon, wondering if there was anything else he'd forgotten.

"All right, let's get." Shannon spoke in a frustrated voice as they walked down a dark trail away from the campsite for the better part of an hour. Bill decided to break the silence as the false dawn was upon them.

"I reckon I'll be doin' this by myself the next time?" he asked quietly.

"Got yerself a real looker, that wife of your'n." Shannon replied, obliviously not thinking about the teaching of the young man the ways of beaver trapping.

"Yeah. I love her dearly. I said I reckon I'll be doing this by myself next time?" Bill pressed the question.

"Yes goddamnit. You'll be own yer own. I don't par'ticularly like showin' greenhorns how to trap, but ya have showed that ya have some sand. At least yer wife does." the older man answered grumpily. Bill stopped in his tracks.

"Hey, Shannon! You wanna dance right here? Right now? I ain't no greenhorn! Jus' 'cause I ain't been trappin' like you don't mean I don't know which way the stick floats! Now if you don't want us around , then we'll be takin' our leave. Goddamnit!" Bill spoke in a hushed voice, but he made sure Shannon understood the tone.

"Hey runt, keep yer voice down. Do ya wanna scare every varmint off in the woods?" he scolded his young protégé'.

"Now lookie here. I don't wanna fight ya. I didn't mean anything against ya. I jus' feel bad 'cause you get to poke all the time, an' well, my pod went soft on me in front of everybody." he moped.

"Well, I feel bad fer ya. But don't go puttin' bad words on me 'cause of it, all right?" Billy whispered.

"Yeah. All right." Shannon mopingly replied. Neither one wishing to speak, they walked on in silence. The dawn light came cascading over the eastern tree line, chasing the chill from the early morning. The crisp morning air felt good as they continued. Bill could see fairly well by now and chose his steps well. He was able to make out things on the stream bank, mainly deadfall to step over and briars to miss. Once they walked away from the camp to the beaver ponds that seemed too hidden away.

"This sure is better than that riverboat." he spoke aloud.

"We're gonna be at the trappin' spot real soon. Okay, this is how it works. Ya cain't leave yer scent anywhere a'tall, no spittin' in the water 'er touchin' trees. Nuthin' to give them critters a reason not to come to bait. Now this bait is some beaver oil that comes from a little spot near their ass. It's all brown an' orange an' stinks to high heaven but them beavers love it." he spoke in a low voice.

He stopped dead in the trail, motioning to Bill to get down. The older trapper turned to Bill, holding his fingers to his lips, indicating no noise. Then he pointed up the trail.

"We're gettin' robbed. I guess we'll get to see if ya have that sand you were a spoutin' 'bout. There's three 'er four of them red niggers up there takin' what ours out of them traps. Now, I'm a goin' in from this away. You circle in back of 'em. When ya hear me a hollerin', well, they'd be a headin' fer ya. Kill all them bastards. You got it kid? All of 'em don't let any of 'em by, hear? If ya do, they'll be back to devil us." he whispered.

Bill obeyed the older man as he walked into the stream of icy water. Quietly he climbed the bank as he watched the thieves a short distance away. He was hoping to be around them before Shannon started his attack. Hell, they were so busy taking the beaver out of the trap that they never even looked up. He crossed the stream again, slipping onto the trail. Bill prepared himself for battle. Carefully laying his rifle down so he could get it quickly, he pulled out his tomahawk and knife. Bill was figuring the men to come running and not even be aware of the small blond man hiding in the brush next to the trail.

Them red niggers ain't got no clue what's 'bout to happen to 'em! He was almost laughing at his plan when he heard Shannon let out a scream like that sent shivers up his back. Bill heard the commotion as he crouched in the brush next to the trail. Then he waited. His plan was simple; when the Indians came by, he could trip the first one. The way he saw it, the rest would fall on top of them. He'd have the advantage of still being on his feet so he'd be able to kill them before they realized what had happened. That's the plan anyway.

Sure enough two of the buckskinned warriors came running right down the trail toward him, hell-bent for leather. Bill's plan sprang into action. He tripped the first one. Down he went. The next one wasn't ready for that and stumbled, falling right on top of him. Before he could move, Bill was on his back, swinging the 'hawk with all his strength at the fallen warrior.

His 'hawk found its mark in the back of the Arapaho's head as it buried itself up to the handle. The bottom one was trying to crawl out from out under the mess that was on top of him.

Funny, it reminded me of a cat with a broken back, trying to squirm with nuthin' happenin', he thought. As he watched the man below him start to make progress, Bill rammed Isaiah's big knife in just below the ear, pushing it in until the hilt was covered by blood and hair. He went to pull it out, but it too was stuck.

"I'll have to get that later. Any more of them niggers a comin'?" he whispered aloud. The man with the knife in his ear wiggled a bit but died quietly. Not a sound except for the crack of that head being split open. The next thing he knew he felt a burning in the right side of his ass. Jumping off the now-dead pile of men, Bill turned to see a third man pulling back another arrow.

"Shit!" Billy screamed as he pulled his other knife as he stood to run at the warrior before the arrow could find its mark. It was a bad move on Bill's part, as the pain caused him to stumble. The next arrow went harmlessly over his head.

Slips in the Night thought of his next move, *I will toy with this puny white man. I will put one through his leg. Then perhaps I will cut his arms off before I send him under. We shall see how he fares after this.* Then Slips in the Night released the arrow into Bill's left leg.

"Goddamnit that hurts!" Bill looked down, seeing the arrow coming out the back of his right calf. But he screamed as he continued his course to ram the warrior before him.

The arrow in his right butt cheek broke off as they crashed to the ground, grappling with the Arapaho warrior. Each vied for control. Bill hobbled to his feet. Standing there panting, he looked at his adversary. That's when he realized he had dropped his knife. The runt couldn't bend down to retrieve the knife under his legging as the pain was too much for him. Then Slips in the Night smiled at the runt. Speaking in his native tongue, he motioned to his hair and then small white to-be trapper.

Then to Bill's surprise, the Arapaho spoke 'Merican, "I will cut your heart out white man. Then I'll lift your hair for my lodge pole."

"Well, you can kiss my ass, you red nigger. I'll have yer topknot hangin' from my saddle this afternoon before I have me a poke, you black-hearted son of a bitch!" Bill answered his opponent's threat with his own verbal abuse.

Billy White went down on one knee, reaching back until he felt the arrow protruding out of his calf through his buckskin leggings. He pulled; blackness and nausea overwhelmed him as he pulled on the blood-covered arrow out a few inches.

Then Slips in the Night, seeing his chance to kill the white runt, ran at him like a crazed horse. In a few quick lunges, he was almost upon the white trapper. He didn't realize the runt had pulled out the arrow enough to break it off, giving Bill a formidable weapon. Bill looked up in time to see the Arapaho coming at him. He couldn't run, so he waited for the impact.

Slips in the Night ran into Bill like a bull into a rotten fence, bowling them both over onto the moist floor of the forest. As the warrior rolled over on top of Bill, the Arapaho wedged Bill's arms under his knees, preventing the small white man from striking back. Bill could see the hard features of this killer above him, the black eyes and hideous smile. But the eyes, the eyes were wild, like a rabid dog on its final hour of life. The runt knew that the warrior was fixing to put his lights out as he was pinned down, but when the red man lifted his arms to run Billy White through, the runt broke his right arm free just in time to stop that knife from going into his throat. Instead it went through his right arm. Bill saw the blade come out through his sleeve on his war shirt as the man on top of him continued to push.

"Goddamn, I ain't doin too good on this one." Bill spoke to his adversary through ragged breaths as he used his free hand to prevent the knife from going into his throat. Seeing the problem, the warrior was taken back by the event. He went to pull the knife out, but it had become fastened securely. The hilt was caught in Bill's war shirt's sleeve. He had both hands trying to pull the knife out. It became apparent that it was securely stuck, so the warrior released it and quickly went to choking the now-weary white man. As he was choking the small white man, the Arapaho had no way of knowing Bill had broken off the arrow. As the last moments of consciousness were leaving the small white man, he used all the strength he could muster, swinging his left arm up, and rammed the broken arrow point into Slips in the Night's eye! The wounded warrior let out a howl, falling backward, grabbing the shaft that was sticking out of his eye, screaming like a cat that had his tail under a rocking chair. The poor soul was rolling on the ground, thrashing like a coyote with a broken back.

Bill's vision returned as he looked over to see the man stop moving. Concerned that more of the damned Arapaho would be coming his way, he slowly stood. Pain swept through his body as the remains of supper came up. Leaning over, balancing himself with a limb he vomited until dry heaves took over. Then dizziness washed over him as he quickly began to sweat.

Finally he regained his composure as he assessed his situation. *Shit, I'm in a tight spot here. I gots an arrow in the ass, one through my leg, and goddamn knife buried in my arm. But I ain't dead.*

"It's gonna take more than that to kill this white nigger!" he screamed into the forest.

"Shit, I hope there ain't no more a comin' at me 'cause I couldn't do nuthin' 'bout it if they did." he slurred, feeling the loss of blood taking its toll.

The runt started hobbling back to get his rifle and nearly passed out from the pain of retrieving it from his hiding place. Using it as a crutch, it was off to find Shannon.

Bill found him all right. He and the other Arapaho were both dead. The man had Shannon's knife in him, and Shannon's head was caved in. *What a mess. Rebecca was right. Life's cheap out here.* That's when he remembered his knife that he had lost.

"I ain't goin' to go lookin' fer it. Hell, I can barely stand up let alone goin' to get some damned knife." the runt spoke through the drool as his life ebbed away. He plopped down on his right knee next to the dead warrior and pulled Shannon's knife out of the lifeless form. He tried to slip it in his sheath, but it was too big. He tried several times as his focus kept leaving him. Finally he just stuck it under his belt. Standing up, he leaned against his Hawken for the long hobble back to camp, one step and then next. That was as far as Bill White made it. Two steps. He spiraled to the moist trail of the forest as the loss of blood and shock took over.

CHAPTER 98

The young lad woke up to a blue sky; he lay there for a moment remembering what had happened, last to him. The fight. Then he was walking, well, really hobbling back to camp. Slowly he turned his head to see Rebecca looking at with the bright-blue eyes and smile on her face.

"You'll be fine in a while, then I'll thrash you soundly." she spoke through her beautiful smile.

"Where'm I?" he asked, confused, through his dry parched lips.

"Back in camp. Daniel went out and found you and Shannon just before dark. He brought your rifle back and the other stuff you left lying around. He also brought these back for you." Then she held up three blood-encrusted scalps.

Bill looked at them feeling his stomach convulsing. He rolled over to hurl. His stomach was empty, so all he could muster up was the burning bile.

"What the hell are them fer?" he asked, wiping the saliva off his mouth. The familiar voice of the booshway came to him.

"Son, out here when ya put someone's lights out, ya take their topknot as a trophy. You have to show them other niggers ya got some sand, so as they don't mess with ya. Jus' like I told yer wife the other day." Daniel answered back softly to the convalescing man.

"Can I get a drink of water?" Bill requested.

"Better than that, here, have a nip of this John Barleycorn. We keep it around fer medicinal purposes. You surely made a fine mess back on the crick, what the hell happened?"

Billy sat up taking a pull of the skin-covered bottle, leaning over on one elbow, his throat burning. His eyes watered, and he felt the elixir begin to work he began with his tale.

"Well, we was a walkin' to the traps when Shannon saw them red niggers stealin' the beaver right out of 'em. So I went down stream apiece when Shannon hollered. Then I was to stop them from gettin' away. Well, the way I see it, that one that got kilt by Shannon kilt him. Them next two came at me, so I kilt them. I caved in one's head with my 'hawk, an' then I stuffed my sticker in the other's ear. Then that third one, well, the red nigger didn't agree with that, so we had a few words 'bout it. Then I send that sumbitch to hell! Rebecca, damn it hurts bad." Bill complained.

"Son, you do have some sand in ya. You may not be able to trap fer shit, but ya can fight." the older trapper praised him.

Each day Bill would make an improvement of how much he could move his arm or bend his leg. The pain slowly easinged up, and Daniel had the runt working on the traps; Mel was showing him how how to service the spring leg trap, to clean the locks on the rifles that they all carried, as well.

"I might as well be in a goddamned gun an' trap establishment in Missoura." the runt whined. He knew it was busy work the things that needed to be repaired and maintained.

The spring traps were touchy, so if he didn't take care with them, he could easily lose his finger from the jaw's powerful grip.

Daniel spoke to the runt after a week of busy work, "Figure yer 'bout ready to start earnin' yer keep, yer dern'd midget." Daniel continued, "You just go along with yer wife an' watch her. Nuthin' else. She's a scrapper an' stronger than a bull so don't go feelin' like ya have to help her. You just walk along an' watch a master trapper." He laughed.

In the next breath, he spoke solemnly to the small white man, "That's what your wife is, ya know. She's a master at what she does. She takes care to do exactly what I taught her, an' then she added some to it. Shit, she brings in more of them flat tails than any of these coons." He waved his arm at the rest of his small brigade.

The day slowed to a crawl and soon the evening fire was crackling from the fat dripping in it from the several squirrels that were hanging from the green spits.

"Hey, Daniel, where the hell are we? I mean I know'd we's in the mountains an' all but jus' where is here?" he asked, staring in the fire.

"Boy, you's in the Rocky Mountains! Off to the west is the great divide. Down south is Taos. I ain't never been there, but I've been told its down in the greaser land. Down there they got Apache, Comanche, not to mention the Mes'can Army. No. This child stays right here in the Rocky Mountains. Up north's the Wind River, the Powder, an' the cussed Blackfoot. It's them bastards that'll truly devil you. You gotta be extra careful up there. You know that, don'cha boy?" he spoke, staring into the fire.

Billy nodded in the light of the fire, *ok here we go,* he thought.

CHAPTER 99

In the dark of the morning the day started by Daniel getting up to relieve himself. Then Mel made his move to do his business; slowly the small brigade was coming to life. Alison crawled over to the embers of the fire and stoked them up by blowing into a brass tube pointed at the bottom of the fire. Soon the fire jumped, lighting up the area. Alison laid a few pieces of tender on the small flames, causing them to snap and crackle as the flame intensified.

Rebecca's hand crept down onto the small man's root, feeling the morning's erection.

"Oh my. What do we have here?" She giggled.

"Your play toy, darlin'." he spoke quietly.

With that she slipped her head under the robes, commencing to give the recuperating man pleasure right there in the dim light of the campfire. About that time Daniel walked back into camp.

Seeing what was going on, he spoke to the frolicking couple.

"Hey there, missy, ya can do that after ya run yer traps. Now get yer possibles ready." The bobbing blanket stopped moving. Slowly her head came out.

She brought her lips to Bill's, kissing him, "You still get that surprise I spoke about, you know, I aim to keep my promise too." Then she to went to the outside of the camp, she squatted down. Bill could hear the spray of her making her water in the quiet of the predawn.

"Hey White Man, here's a kiss for you." From her direction a loud rumbling fart came across the camp.

"Shit! That woman can put a man to shame with her farts." chuckled Alison.

"Here's one for ya." Then a loud pop came from Mel's corner of the camp.

"Fer Christ's sake will you yahoos get ready?" Daniel scolded.

"Son, get yerself ready." Daniel spoke quietly, directing his orders at the white man.

Bill slowly stood, testing his leg. It was fine; he was just apprehensive about going out after the last time. Slowly his erection softened so he could relieve himself. Bill stood staring out into the darkness. *Wonder what people was a watchin' the camp from a distance.* As far as anyone could tell, the bunch he and Shannon killed were't out for stealin'. The small white man pondered for a moment, *I like this life, running through the woods free as a lark. Calling no man sir. Enough of this daydreaming. Get on with life. Yep, get on with life.* That's when he heard some steps behind him. Turning his head around, he recognized the shape of Rebecca carrying his possibles.

"Here ya are William." she spoke loud enough for the rest of the camp to hear. Then she snaked her hand around his waist with his belt, buckling it from behind him. Bill felt the hawk go into the small of his back, then the tug of the knife accompanying it.

"Here. Turn 'round so I can put the sheath on your leg." The runt stepped back, turning around to face her. She leaned down, pulling up his legging. As she tied the knife in place, she looked around Bill to see if she could spot Daniel. Seeing his back was to her, she quickly pulled out Bill's root, placing the soft member into her mouth. She worked her magic. The young man was so aroused by this he reached down to hold her head firmly. He popped, and she didn't stop sucking.

"There you go, are gonna ya need some help walkin'?" she spoke aloud once more; they turned their heads to see the couple as they finished their coffee. Billy White, green trapper, bear killer and Indian fighter, hobbled into the light.

Daniel spoke gruffly, "Well, I hear ya got what ya wanted there Rebecca. I reckon there ain't no stoppin' a woman that has that on her mind. Since ya wanted suck rather than get some hot coffee we'll be on our way. Let's get."

Then he looked at Bill with a scorn. *Hell, I knew what he's thinkin'. It ain't my fault she wants to please me an' not him,* he thought as the brigade shuffled out into the blackness of the early morning.

Bill thought of the last time he did this. He ended up plucked full of arrows. After they had walked for less than hour, they came to the area when the fight had been, yet the brigade continued without a step being missed.

"All right, you take yer man an' go run yer traps. Me an' these two yahoos are goin' go to do ours. Stay quiet. See ya back in camp an' keep yer dick tied down while yer workin', will ya?" Then they were gone, leaving the man and woman to their own demise.

Once again he could almost see in the false dawn. He walked up next to Rebecca and slid his hand against her flat stomach; slowly it reached her briar patch.

"God, I want you so bad. I want that tongue of yours deep inside of me." Then she touched his hand, gently pushing it away.

"Daniel knows how long it takes to run these six traps here and the five on the other side of the pond, and if we're late, well, he'll come looking for us. Then he'll know what we're doing, and then he'll be giving us extra work for being slackers."

She continued, "I learned a new way to walk. See, white folks walk heel first and roll to the ball. Injuns step lightly on their ball of their feet, and it doesn't leave as deep of a track." She showed the runt as they walked away from the intersection. Bill watched her walk; it reminded him of the way Sheila could glide across the floor. It looked like she hadn't even touched the ground. Bill tried, but his stiff muscles in his calf cried out. As he gave up on the floating, the couple continued as the sun shown over the eastern tree line. By now, the sun was blanketing the large pond. Walking along, they could hear the forest; birds, squirrels, and other varmints were out in force, making a commotion as they closed the distance to the first trap.

"Okay, here's our first one. Smell that? That's beaver. They stink to high heaven. Now look over here on the bank." She was pointing at a sapling stuck into the bank.

"That's where I put the bait. Now see that stake out away from the bank?" she questioned.

"Yeah."

"See that stick floatin' out there? That tells us we got a flat tail, that stick is attached to the trap. See we cut a little ledge under the sapling so the beaver will crawl on the ledge, trying to smell the scent. When a beaver gets caught in the trap, that rascal will swim for deep water and safety. They won't make it because the chain won't let 'em. They can't get air and drown. So we wade in the water, pull the beaver up, undo the trap, bring it to the bank, reset the trap, put it back under the sapling, and put new bait on the sapling. The whole time you have to be careful not to have the trap go off while you're putting it down. Pretty easy. The real hard part is coming in and out of the water. It gets real cold. I'll do this one, then I'll show you how to skin it and cut off the tail." she explained.

Billy White watched as she made her way in to the water, first her leggings, then the bottom of her war shirt. As she went to the float stick, she reached her arm below the water level. Then she froze and slowly pulled the chain up. There in the trap was a sleek fat beaver. She undid the trap and pulled a cord from her waistband and began tying it to the critter's leg. When she finished she wrapped it around the pole so as not to lose it in the cold water.

The whole time he was watching his woman in action, it made him so proud. *Damn, look at her, my partner and lover, ass deep in water. She knows her way around a trap. I can say that for her. Damn, she's a looker!*

She sprung the leg trap open and flipped the set pan under the latch. She laid the chain over her shoulder and carefully began walking back to the bank. She put the float stick under it and slowly lowered the trap into the water onto the ledge. She rose up and reached up to the small vial that was hanging around her neck. Undoing the top, she dribbled the foul smell on the sapling. She made an awful face at the smell as she held her wet hand up to her nose, shaking her head. She fed the chain smoothly into the water as she backed up. When she got to the stake, she undid the animal, and waded back to the bank. She stood there dripping and started to shiver.

"Damn, this's cold!" She shivered to the dry man before her.

"Here let me warm ya up a tad." he volunteered.

"No. We can get warm later. We have work to do first." With that she picked up the animal walking about twenty paces away from the water. She looked back to ensure that the runt was following. Sure enough, like a puppy hunting a nipple at feeding time.

"This is far 'nuff lover. See, if we skin it too close to the shore, the others won't come to bait. This way a coyote 'er a wolf, 'er a bear will find what we've left and eat the evidence when we leave. First things first." She leaned over and kissed him on the mouth, her hot tongue darting in and out of his dry mouth.

"There. That's better. Now we can work. See ya have cut here an' here." She showed Billy the place around the back legs.

"Then around the tail like so." Her knife was flashing in the sunlight.

"Then down the gut and round the front legs and around the muzzle. Then as we pull the skin off, we make sure nothing gets torn and, " She stopped talking and was pulling the skin right off the critter.

"There. One skinned beaver. Now, we need some beaver bait. Ya start back here around their asshole, then ya feel around 'till ya find their scent glands. Here we are," she used her knife elegantly to trim the meat away from the two pear shaped bags, "make sure ya don't cut into 'em." She pulled and cut until the scent glands

were out. "Then we cut 'em off, an' put 'em off to the side here."
She laid them on the grass.

"Now we need some oil to be able to mix it up." She felt around
until she found a small sack near where the scent glands were.
"Here we are." Once again in the flash of her knife she had the oil
sack next to the scent glands. We don't need these from every one
of 'em. Just a few now an' then."

"I'll show you how to make beaver bait later. Now, we roll it
up fur side in an' stick it in our rucksack. Oh, I almost forgot the
tail." She pulled her 'hawk out. Swinging it expertly, she severed
the tail.

"They others say the fat will help keep us warm later when we
start up the Yellowstone to better trapping grounds."

The young trappers continued on through the eleven traps,
doing the same each time as the first. The sun was slowly creeping
up to the high part of the day, when they started the return trip
back to the camp; Bill felt the warmth of those golden rays as they
marched on, those afternoon arrows piercing his cold bones as they
trod through the forest.

"We did good William. Eleven traps an' every one chocked-full.
Well, I hope one of the other got some supper and hot coffee for
us." Bill looked at her, admiring the way her nipples were poking
into the soft-skinned war shirt. He could hardly wait to get under
the skins to sample her goods. Between the load of wet skins and
the injuries, he couldn't walk as fast or as easy as Rebecca. She
was floating along like a mist in the morning. Bill thought, *What
a mink. She could poke all night long, get up in the morning, and
then do this work like it was nothing at all.* He noticed that the
skins she wore were almost dry already.

*That's the nice thing 'bout buckskin. It keeps ya fairly warm,
an' it dries real fast compared to wool,* the small man pondered
as he watched his partner sashaying ahead of him. That's when he
noticed that the forest had become quiet.

CHAPTER 100

Rebecca noticed it also. She stopped in the trail, motioning them off to the bushes on the side of the trail. There, concealed they waited for the forest to reveal the story to them. Their wait wasn't wasted. A huge war party of Arapaho came by.

"Oh! There's fifteen 'er twenty of them bastards!" he whispered close to her ear. Her hand came up to his mouth, shushing the young man as the war party marched through. Then Bill saw it, or them. Scalps! Three scalps, dripping with gore, were tied to one of the biggest one's belts. The warrior was bigger than Daniel by a foot or so and appeared to be the leader of the scalp hunters. Bill watched the rest of the warriors go by with all their supplies.

Well, I didn't see the guns 'er possibles, but I could have missed them, he thought as he watched in awe as the Arapaho killers went by.

Bill went to stand, but Rebecca motioned him back to the cover.

"Wait a little more, lover." she whispered to him. A good thing they had waited as the two stayed back to assure that they weren't going to be backtracked. Amazed at the level of preparedness these warriors were showing, Bill could hardly contain himself. When these men were out of sight, Bill almost stood, but the forest told him there was more in store for he and Rebecca.

"Let's wait till dark 'fore we go back to see what's left." Bill whispered again to his redheaded vixen.

"No shit. That had to be the biggest goddamned war party I've ever seen." She looked into his blue eyes, not seeing fear but anger.

"What have we gotten inta this time lover?" she continued, looking back at the trail.

Before she could say anything more, he broke in, "I don't want to wait that long. Let's get while the gettin' is good." She reached slowly over to his arm, gently restraining the blond man.

"Not yet. Listen to the forest. It's still quiet." she whispered. Two more painted killers came running by with their guns and bows. Bill couldn't stand it any longer, so he pulled his 'hawk and knife as he jumped into the trail behind the Arapaho warriors.

"Hey, you red niggers!" he yelled. Rebecca wasn't ready for his attack, but she filled her hands also. She stood next to her lover.

Running Bird and Crossed Arms had stayed behind to bring the last of the white trappers' gear. The scalp hunt had gone well. Two Wolves had killed the white trappers easily, and none of his companions had been injured. The whites never knew what hit them as it was over before it even started.

But now there was a new situation. The only redhead they had ever seen were the Hudson Bay skin trappers; and now before them was a redheaded woman, with a knife and tomahawk challenging them to combat.

They looked at each other and smiled. They started toward Bill and Rebecca, grinning like a cat that had a mouse cornered. The one on the right spoke to his friend as he sized up the prey.

"Wait until Two Wolves see what we have brought back."

"Yes, let's take the woman back alive. She will give us great pleasure as we take our turns mounting her." he spoke as he pantomimed mounting her as they moved closer.

"I'd say they wanna fork you there lover. When I say throw that sticker hard as ya can at the right one an I'll take the left one, make sure ya hit on center." he spoke slowly and clearly. The young runt didn't realize the Arapaho could speak American.

"This silly hair face is going to throw these weapons! This will be easier than I thought."

Running Bird spoke in Arapaho to his compadre. Crossed Arms laughed with his friend at their good fortune as they threw the whites' ruck in the bushes and filled their hands with weapons. They were about fifteen paces away and getting closer. Ten paces.

Then the warriors burst forward like racehorses covering the few remaining feet to the soon-to-be white captives.

"NOW!" Bill screamed as he threw with all his strength at the approaching Arapaho. Running Bird ducked to his left, but Bill's throw was wild to the right, not thrown like a warrior but with an odd side-arm throw. It found its mark as his 'hawk spun one revolution as it struck the oncoming warrior in the side of his face, killing him instantly.

Crossed Arms bowled over Bill on his way to get the redhead. Her 'hawk had bounced harmlessly off his arm as he leaped at her. In one swift movement, he was on her. He hadn't noticed her knife in the other hand. When he knocked her over, it was then he became aware that there was eight inches of steel buried deep in his heart. He wasn't dead yet. He leaned back to cuff her, but his life ended before he could follow through. As he cascaded over to the side of Rebecca, she helped guide him on to the ground and off her. Both of the the warriors were dead now.

Bill stood there in a trance looking at the two dead men. It all happened too fast. Coming back to reality, he walked over to Rebecca, offering her a hand to her feet.

"Damn, that was close lover." he spoke and let a breath out.

"Would have been nice to know that you were going to do that. We could have gone under you know." she said.

"Look." Bill defended his actions.

"If they got away with our gear, we couldn't even defend ourselves when the time came. Against red 'er white! Now we ain't got no time to argue 'bout this right now." Bill spoke firmly.

"Let's get our ruck an' get the hell outta here." he spoke to her as he hurriedly walked over to the dead man. Placing a moccasin on the skull, he pulled, removing the grisly killing tool. He looked over to see Rebecca was doing the same. Bill's partner leaned down to cut a circle on the Arapaho's head. Then she put her knee on the back of his head and began pulling. *Pop!* was heard as the scalp came loose. She swung the grisly trophy around, throwing blood and gore all over the scene. Then she stuffed it in her belt. She went over to get the rucksack with her bow, guns, and possible bag as if she had just gone to the dry-goods store. Bill looked down at his opponent; he started the chore of scalping. His trophy didn't come off very cleanly as half of the man's skull was caved in. What he did get, he stuck it in his belt as he walked to recover the remaining gear in the bushes.

As Bill walked away from the scene she called out to him, "Wait a minute. Mel told me 'bout this. He says it put the fear of God in them when they see this. He says that they won't be able to have sex in the afterlife an' won't be able to see the sprit horse when it comes from them."

Then she pulled the breechclout out of the way, grabbing the dead man's penis and scrotum. She took her knife out and cut them cleanly off, just like she was skinning a beaver. With that chore finished, she took a finger and stuck them in the eyeballs. She pulled them out, tearing all veins with them; admiring her work for a moment, she then tossed them in the bushes like a dead cat. She stuck her knife in the man's mouth, prying it open so she could stuff the dead man's privates in it. She stood looking at her work.

"There. Not pretty but it might save our lives or at least buy us some time. Now you do the same." she spoke. No response from the runt. She looked over to see young Billy, he was white as the snow in January.

"William! Get a grip! Now do it!" she barked. Bill felt queasy and was ready to hurl as he watched the mutilation of another human. *Hell, it hadn't been that long ago that I'd been on the other side of the fence telling her to get ahold of herself. My, how things change.*

"I'm all right." he mumbled as he also began the task. As he did this, he thought about how it was on the boat and remembered the safety. He knew he was as good as dead on that boat as on this trail in the Missouri River country. He finished the chore wiping off his knife on the dead man's leggings.

"Let's get back to our camp." he spoke solemnly.

They hurried to the camp and saw why the last two were here. All three bodies were naked, mutilated worse than the two they left back on the trail. Naked, blinded, slumped over a log, stomach up, lay Daniel. His penis and nut sack were stuffed in his mouth. They had had built a fire on his stomach. They had baked him first and then cut his throat. He heard Rebecca hurling in the bushes as he looked at the barbaric scene. Alison was hanging from a tree limb, blackened feet and legs with a smoldering fire under him. Blinded and cut in the same manner, not a piece of skin on him. Mel got off the easiest. Looked like he tried to outrun a tomahawk. It found its mark in the back of his head. Thankfully he never knew what they did to him.

"See if ya spot anything that we could use?" Billy asked. She wandered around the small camp, looking at this and that. Then she came back to where he stood.

"There's a dead horse over by the stream. A bunch of meat was carved off it. We might as well do the same. At least we'll get some food for a while."

"Damnit!" Bill stomped.

"I hope we can get back two of 'em anyway!" he spat referring to their horses.

"Relax. We're going to have to go back for the traps, you know. We might find some tracks. Then all we'll have to do is follow them to our horses. I know where some of the other traps are also. We should use the ridge line back to the pond. Their friends are going to backtrack to find those back there." She nodded the way they had come from.

"The way I see it, I figure we should be away from here. What do you think Bill?" She asked.

"Bill?" He asked.

"Yeah, I like the way it sounds. Maybe I'll call you Wild Bill 'cause you're a wild man with that pecker of yours." she said, smiling.

"I ain't too wild right now. I'm scarit shitless! Let's get." he spoke to Rebecca as he looked around the camp; he was getting the feeling something was going to happen.

"Let's go out past that horse and head out from there." Together they walked to the quickly ripening horse. As they stepped past the dead animals, they heard voices.

"Down!" they spoke at the same time as they spun, dropping down behind the bloating carcass. They waited to see what was in store for them next. The flies were already covering the open wounds as nature worked its magic of the mounds of horse flesh. The wait wasn't long as they saw seven Arapaho warriors run into the now-empty camp.

Rebecca wasn't surprised that they were tracking them. They were speaking quickly to one another, pointing at the ground and to where Bill and she had been standing. A fat one motioned to where they were hiding. A tall one shook his head, motioning toward the pond behind him.

The other five were taking turn, throwing the 'hawks at Alison. When the 'hawks hit the body of the trapper, they could hear the sickening thunk as they tore into the mutilated man. Then the fat one walked toward them. Bill reached for a couple of arrows, getting ready to dance as he watched the fat man walking their way. Scooting down, he made eye contact with Rebecca. Motioning to the guns, she nodded. He brought up the well-used gun, checking the pan for powder. He looked at Rebecca as she did the same. She looked over, nodding. They laid the guns against the dead horse as they knocked the arrows, preparing for the fight.

The others were arguing with their backs to Bill as they cut on the now-dead white trapper. Bill touched Rebecca's arm, getting her attention. He then mouthed out the words, "One, two, three."

She nodded and waited for the count. Bill started the countdown as she waited breathlessly for the action to start. Finally three came close enough, and they rose up, letting arrows fly.

His buried itself in the heart of the warrior nearest to Alison, he quickly knocked another arrow. He saw Rebecca's arrow plunge deep into the spine of the farthest warrior. Loading another, he released the messenger of death; it found the one bent over Daniel's body. Rebecca let loose another arrow. One more fell. That left three. No noise from anyone white or red, as the minutes ticked by. The Arapaho's quickly ducked behind the log where Daniel was staked out. When an eternity had passed, the warrior on the left decided to die. Bill made eye contact, motioning to the guns. The warrior had failed to realize Bill and Rebecca had brought their gun's into the deadly game.

They swung them onto the side of the horse and waited. It wasn't too long before the one on the left got up the nerve to run at them. Tomahawk in one hand, knife in the other, screaming like his nuts were caught in a briar patch. Rebecca's gun went off. That Indian flew back about five paces, deader than last night's supper. That must have spooked the last two as it got quiet again.

The couple waited for the two to make their next move. His wait wasn't long as a head popped up to assess the situation. His mistake was he took too long; a third eye appeared on his forehead as a fifty-four-caliber galena ball took the top of his head off. That left one. Rebecca already had an arrow, ready to go.

She stood up walking toward the remaining warrior, giving him a chance to fight her. She screamed, "Hey! You goddamn piece of red-fucking wolf bait! Get your fucking ass up and fight me! You miserable excuse of a human being!" She stepped again, arrow at full pull. Waiting.

Soft Belly had been along on the hunt because his uncle Two Wolves assured him it would be an easy kill. A few whites that would run like girls at the first sign of battle.

It wasn't like his uncle had said at all. Crossed Arms was dead as was Running Bird. Now he looked around seeing six of his best friends from childhood were deader than the buffalo at last night's supper. He remembered that the whites had thrown their hands up asking for mercy, so he figured that would be his next action taken. He stood up with his hands empty, reaching for the sky. The fear was showing as his eyes were darting from Bill to Rebecca.

Soft Belly began chanting his death song as he already figured his mistake out. The arrow went deep in his eye, coming out the back of his head. He fell onto the ground, wiggling like he had ants in his pants. Rebecca calmly walked to the prone man, releasing another arrow into his crotch. Soft Belly never felt it as his body took on the appearance of a porcupine. Bill put his hand on her arm.

"Lover, I reckon this 'un's dead."

"Possum fucker! I hate them all!" she spat.

"Let's get our arrows an' get 'fore they come a lookin' fer these too. I 'magine those shots were heard in the next valley. Shit, we've killed a passel of red niggers in the last hour. Damn! Shit comes in barrels sometimes. Let's get these scalps an' be gone." He whistled.

"Now you're talking." Out came her knife, and she was scalping faster than the hummingbird in the swarm of gnats. She had five of the scalps off before he could finish his second one.

"Here. You killed three, you get three. Better get quicker if you want more." She handed Bill the gory scalps.

The woman was changing into a native more and more. He took the bloody scalps and swung them around to get most of the gore off, and then he tied them to his possible bag.

Bill began pulling arrows out of the body when he noticed one was still breathing. He pulled out his knife, plunging it into the quivering heart. The warrior had been quiet even though he'd been scalped and shot. When an arrow yanked from his body, he didn't move.

Bill thought of the day and let it be. *Hell, I still had some white left in me, unlike Rebecca, who was becoming more and more native all the time.* She was busy getting her arrows and mutilating the dead men. Billy looked around for the warriors 'hawks and knives. Too bad he couldn't find any of the other guns.

"Let's get." Bill spoke as he looked around the now-bloody camp.

"Okay."

As they walked back up to the dead horse, they grabbed the guns. Bill took his knife out, carving a hunk of the quickly fouling meat, slipping it in his almost-full possible bag.

They were about twenty paces outside of the camp when she turned.

"Hang face there White Man." Running back to the scene, she began kicking one of the dead men. No movement, just a thump of her moccasin connecting.

"What's that 'bout?" he asked. She called over her shoulder, "I'm just pissed 'cause they killed our friend's, that's all."

"Let's load these right now." Bill motioned to the guns.

"Why? Are there more coming?" She spun around holding the gun waist level at the forest.

"That wouldn't do you no good." Bill spoke, nodding at the gun.

"Why not?" she asked.

"Sugar, it ain't loaded."

"Huh? Oh yeah. Now I know why I keep you around. I thought you were good for more than a good poke." She laughed. *Shit, here's death an' gore everywhere. She's laughing like she's on a picnic. Hell, I wouldn't be surprised if she didn't want a poke right now.* Bill amused himself with a quick fantasy of getting sex at the moment. He remembered about having hot embers in the bottom of the barrel. Bill brought the gun barrel to his lips and blew hard. Nothing at first. He continued, his face turning red. Then a small poof. A small volcano spit out the burned residue from the touchhole. Bill let up for a breath and then went back at it until there was air rushing out, unobstructed. The whole time Rebecca was watching, her jaw hanging open.

"What the hell's that about?" she asked, Bill took a minute to explain the procedure as she listened patiently. After the impromptu lecture, she tried to do the exercise on her rifle. Nothing. She tried again and again, but nothing came out the touchhole.

"Hold on. I'll help ya soon as I get this loaded." Bill continued with his loading, powder and patch with a ball, and then ramming it down until it seated itself on the powder. Laying the gun in the crook of his arm, he lifted the frizzen, pouring fine-grain powder in the pan. He snapped it shut. Carefully he slowly let the hammer down. Satisfied with the procedure, he handed the gun to Rebecca.

"There. That 'un's loaded." he spoke with a rush of air.

"Let me see yer gun there sweetie." As he took her gun, she reached for his, cocked it, then leveled at the way they had come from.

"Just in case, lover." she said. Billy White rummaged in his possible bag, his hand smeared with the coagulating horse blood. He found the small toolbox he had been using for the repairs. Carefully opening the box, he found the small pin to unclog the touchhole. He looked around for a moment, then placed his lips on the gun, and blew. *Poof!* Air rushed out the touch hole as it had done on his. Bill went on with the loading procedure as he had done before. After he primed the gun, he commented, "That's that."

Rebecca looked over her shoulder and nodded. Then she returned her gaze to the back trail.

"You can use that one 'er this one. It don't matter to me." he spoke quietly.

"This 'un's fine." she spoke without turning her head.

She continued, "How much powder did we save from them killing bastards?

"Well, we have the three horns, maybe four pounds. Looks to be three pounds of balls an' a handful of flints. We got 'bout twenty arrows between us, two guns, six knives, an' four 'hawks. I reckon we can make war on some of 'em niggers if that's what yer askin'.""

"I want to go to Yellowstone. The trapping Daniel was speaking about, I want to go up there and make a life out of trapping. Well, I would like that. What do you think?"

She's rambling, but I know she wanted to get the hell outta of this little valley an' away from these niggers that been hauntin' us. Bill's mind wandered a brief moment.

He spoke as he looked at the dead horse, "Sounds good to me. Are ya gonna get some of this horse meat too?"

"Yeah, watch the back trail." she ordered as she produced her knife and commenced to slice that horse up. She's quick with a knife; she had a slab of meat off, slipping it in her bag in before Bill had even turned to guard the back trail.

"You know, Wild Bill, I was thinking. Maybe we ought to ambush some more of them niggers. See we could set a few traps for them. When the stepped on them, we could stick them with some arrows. They won't see 'em coming, and we can pick them off one or two at a time. Hit and run. Hit and run. 'Till we kill all them that's tracking us. Then they figure were bad medicine and leave us the hell alone. Then we can get back to trapping and some serious sex!" She was smiling.

The way she was going on, she could be a general in the army.

He acknowledged. "I reckon we could get on each ridge an' set the traps in certain places."

"Okay, then how 'bout this? We leave real sloppy tracks. Ones that are so easy to follow that they'll let down their guard and come a running after us." she asked.

"That might not work either. They will see this mess an' be cautious 'bout followin' us." Bill squinted his eyes.

"Hell, we've killed a shitload of them red niggers, an' they'll be lookin' fer ways to even it up. The way I see it we skedaddle up there." he pointed out a ridge line to the north, "We can watch to see what's gonna happen. I don't wanna be lookin' over my shoulder the rest of my life out here. If the chance comes where we can put some lights out, well, then we'll do it on our terms. That's what I'm thinkin'." Bill spoke.

"Good 'nuff for me." She walked over to Bill White wrapping her arms around him. She gave him a passionate kiss right next to the stinking dead horse. Rebecca could isolate her emotions whenever she wanted, whether it was in the robes or next to a bloated horse.

So up the ridge line they went. Walking up the north trail, he began looking for ambushing sites. When the runt found some dead trees that had fallen seasons ago, he decided to make a stand behind them.

"Ya hang face here 'an keep a sharp eye out. I'm goin' up the trail more to see if'n there's a trail fer our retreat when we need it." He turned to leave when she slapped his ass. Not hard but a small crack was heard.

"Hey!" He turned back in a false challenge.

"Hurry back." She winked. Bill scouted out the small trail that went up and away from the scene below them but in the direction of the ponds. Satisfied, he turned to his lover.

"I was ponderin' somethin' lover. If these folks are half smart, they'll be seein' where our traps are, then set up an ambush of their own. They know we'll come back fer our traps. Then we'll be in a pickle fer sure." he spoke as he lay against the log, looking back down the hill.

"They don't know we're here. All they know is that a shitload of their friends haven't come back from a simple raid. As far as our traps go, we'll just have to make sure that we're not seen." she spoke as she turned to view the back trail. They sat there most of the afternoon watching the sun go into the treetops in the west when their wait paid off. Eight men of different sizes came into view. This time they were leery walking up the trail.

"Shit! Here they come. I say we pop the two small guys as soon as we can. They're the trackers. Then that'll buy some time.

See it'll be dark quick like an' they won't be able to track at night. Then when mornin' comes, we pop a coupla more. We stay jus' outta sight an' keep doin' it 'til we can get a shot at that big son of a bitch." Bill instructed.

"Okay Bill, let's do it." she said.

Two Wolves walked into the trappers camp looking at the dead white men, then at his dead friends. He walked toward the horse where they had been hiding, surveying the killing field as he continued to the edge of the defunct camp. The others were looking at the ground where the whites had been hiding, when several men started speaking, motioning the to the trail that they had come from. Without any warning he whacked Sings Well across the face, sending him spiraling to the ground. The others shut up fast, averting their eyes to avoid his further wrath. There was not a sound from the rest of them. He pointed to the horse, speaking loudly. Those others cut some more meat off the rotting horse.

Two Wolves eyes searched over the hills to the north, when he saw the trail leading up the hill. He called over his shoulder to two smaller warriors. The warriors came up, looking at the ground, jabbering like jays as the pointed to where the whites had gone. The big one nodded. The chase was on.

CHAPTER 101

Sitting behind their little log fort, they waited as the avengers came up the ridge. It was a race to see if they got within shooting range before the sun went down. The sun's rays were just starting to touch the top of the trees on the eastern side off the valley. When the two trackers were about fifty yards away.

"Ready lover?" he whispered.

"Yeppers." she answered.

"I'll take the one on the right, an' you get the other 'un."

"Ready, set. Now!" Both guns went off together in one loud clap. In a cloud of gun powder smoke, they scurried up to the next fort.

Two Toes and his younger brother Owl had no idea what had just happened. One moment they were following the whites. Then Owl felt himself being thrown back down the hill with a burning in his chest he had never felt before. He looked to his right where he saw his brother, Two Toes, but he had no face, just a bloody hole below his hairline. That was the last thing he saw before he met the Great Spirit.

Young Bill had his legs going as fast as he could, ahead of him Rebecca was loping along like she was on a picnic, her possibles and bow lashed down tight. His bow and possibles were flopping around as he tried to keep up with the small redheaded woman. *What a mess I'd be if'n I fell down,* came to Bill's mind as he ran behind Rebecca.

"Hold up a few shakes. Let's reload these smoke sticks while we get set up again. Watch the back trail." the runt commanded as he took her gun and quickly reload it. Handing it to her, she pulled the hammer back flipped the frizzen up to check the pan, sinking to one knee in a silky smooth motion. *God, I love this woman,* Bill thought as he watched her from the corner of his eye.

Darkness was covering the forest as the sun touched the western tree line. Bill finished just as a deafening roar rang through the forest. He looked up to see one more Arapaho keel over backward without using his feet.

Sings Well felt he was going to kill the stupid whites as he watched them crouch behind a small group of deadfall. He had no clue death was rushing toward him as his feet never completed its mission to carry him up the trail. He was dead before he hit the ground.

Bill handed her the primed rifle and then began the ritual again. As the smoke cleared, Bill watched two warriors as they began to flank the white runt and his redheaded partner.

Bill looked down the trail to see the large warrior walking toward him like he was a god.

"Damn lover, he got balls the size of a boiler!" Bill exclaimed.

Two Wolves had a special medicine. Old Bull, the shaman, had given him the medicine to make him invincible to the white man's bullets. He had already proven this when he had killed the others. The only part he didn't know is when Daniel had shot at him the gun had misfired and only the powder in the pan went off. No bullet had left the barrel. All that Two Wolves knew was the white man had shot him and no lead ball came to hurt him. So his special medicine had worked.

Now he was walking toward the weak trappers above him.

"They will die as the others. I will eat their hearts as I show them I am the strongest." he spoke aloud to the forest as he walked up the trail.

Bill could see that the two were coming on fast to flank them as he and Rebecca waited. She saw the biggest one still walking up the trail. Sure enough, he was walking right toward them. Movement caught Bill's eye as he looked to his right, seeing the two were making good time to get behind them, but they stopped.

They were waiting.

"Them two ain't moving. Lover, you reckon this big 'un must be the booshway over this scalping party?" Bill asked as he kept track of the warriors.

The flanking two had no desire to have Two Wolves's anger upon them. Rebecca looked in the shallow light as Two Wolves approached them. Off to her side Bill sparked a command at her.

"Rebecca starts puttin' balls inta the big bastard. I'll keep a loadin', you keep shootin'." he spoke quickly.

"He must think he got the hoodoo 'er somethin'." Rebecca said as she leveled her gun on the massive man marching up the trail taking each step deliberately. Her gun sounded as the bullet hit him in the chest. He stopped for a second, then picked up his pace, walking faster.

"Here! Shoot!" Bill was on the edge of panic now. Another ball hit him. He had his primed and ready when she reached for it. The following ball went right in his crotch. He went down on that one. Then he stood up, taking one more step as he closed the distance to the white couple. Now he was close enough to see the hatred on his face as he continued toward them. But he didn't go but one more step before he fell over. His hands never came out to stop his fall. The large man landed face first on the trail with a loud thump and didn't move again.

Bill handed her the loaded gun as he loaded his. The forest went silent. Bill watched the other two as they closed the circle on the runt and his partner. Bill leveled his weapon and waited, squeezing the set trigger until the click was heard. Then he waited a heartbeat and tickled the front trigger. As Wounded Bear lifted his head for a peek, a round ball made a third eye in his forehead as he began his journey to the other side.

Wounded Bear's third eye ended his life. As he felt his life end, his mind wandered. His mind's eye witnessed the blackness coming over him. Then there was nothing.

Rebecca leveled her gun and waited for the other warrior to get a little closer. Then she fired. Talks Allot's foot slipped on a dead branch at that same instant. The ball went harmlessly over his head.

At the bottom of the hill, behind the two dead trackers, Fat Belly had watched them all die; then he turned tail and ran like he had seen a ghost. That left the clumsy one on their flank and one more coming up the trail. Billy handed Rebecca a freshly loaded gun while he watched their flank. Then in the dimming light, he saw the flanking warrior throw his bow down and run for his life. Bill pulled his Hawken up, and in one fluid movement, he pulled the set trigger. It clicked. He raised it a tad over the man's head as he squeezed the main trigger. His gun roared as the fifty-four-caliber round ball entered the running warriors lower back, exiting his stomach, taking his small intestines and his liver on its way out.

Sharpen's Knife blacked out from the pain. He never heard Talks Allot die, never knew that Fat Belly had run for help. All he knew was he was dying and could not move but an inch with pain, making him lose consciousness.

She waited for Talks Allot to reveal himself again. He rose slowly with an arrow in and ready to go. He didn't even get the string taut before Rebecca's ball went into his mouth, shattering teeth as it exited the back of his head, tossing him back down the embankment. She traded her empty for a loaded one. The sun was gone by now, and darkness had covered the forest.

"Let's hang face right here. At least fer a while an' listen. We'll be able to hear what's goin' on." he whispered.

"I say we collect our scalps and move on to our traps. The way I see it, it would be big medicine for us to get those scalps before daylight. That way when they came for their dead, it would really shake 'em up. I still want to get out of this valley an' to the Yellowstone country." she spoke convincingly.

"All right. Here's how we do it. We take the knives an' go quick like. Nuthin' fancy, jus' scalps an' get the hell out, right?" he asked.

"Yeppers Bill." The young couple bared themselves to a minimum as they slithered and crawled down to where the big one should be. He was gone. Feeling the ground, Bill found where the ground was warm and sticky. A blood trail. Everything was looking like people now, and he was getting nervous. Then his hand touched him or his foot anyway. The large man was lying on his stomach trying to crawl away, but he was still breathing. Barely. Slipping his knife out, Bill was preparing to put Two Wolves's lights out when he stopped.

"What are you waiting for?" she whispered.

"He ain't dead." he responded quietly.

"I wanna scalp him alive an' leave him alive to tell of how his enemies are strong." He continued.

"Serves the prick right then!" she answered.

"You hold him down, and I'll do the deed." she said.

"Ya ready?"

"Go!" Bill leapt on his back, holding his tree stumps of arms down. Rebecca scurried around in front and grabbed his hair. As quick as a shooting star, she had that wounded man's scalp in her hand. He was so weak from blood loss the Arapaho couldn't fight back.

Rebecca went to gather the trackers' scalps, when their topknots were collected, she passed by the huge man and stopped. She started cutting on the man, slicing him from the waistline to the bottom of his skull.

"Fucker." she said as she began to crawl back to their guns and possibles.

"Hold on." she spoke quietly. He turned, but couldn't make out where she went.

Rebecca went back to the big warrior, squatted over him, she began to urinate on the scalped mans head. Satisfied she returned to Billy.

"Where'd ya go?" he asked.

"I went to piss on the big 'un scalped head." She answered.

"Ha-ha, piss on 'em Billy!" She laughed as they were leaving the scene.

"That son of a bitch has a bad time ahead of 'em." he said to her as they went up the hill away from the death below them. As they retrieved the guns and possibles, they headed toward the pond and their traps.

"We'll haves to pass on the rest of 'em. They's too far in the brush to get. We might as well get the hell outta of here. Too bad them rascals stole our horses. If we happen to find 'em, that would make it a lot easier to travel." he commented.

"Yeppers." was all she said.

CHAPTER 102

On the trail out, Bill found a dead tree that had fallen over to hide under.

"Let's hole up here fer a while." he spoke more of a question than a command. So he slipped under it and offered a hand to Rebecca. She slid in next to him as the nightlife chimed in around them.

"Bill, hope you don't mind, but I'd like to sleep for a while. I'm plum tuckered out from all that's happened today." she said softly.

"No problem. I'll jus' rest here too. There's plenty of deadfall 'round here to make noise if someone comes a callin'." With that he lay back, listening to the night.

Rebecca was shaking Bill awake.

"Damn, I musta dozed off." he defended himself.

"Bill, there's something out there. I heard it moving around, snapping sticks and making a hell of a ruckus." she whispered. Looking out into the darkness, he could see nothing.

Then he smelled it. *Bear. Goddamn, them things stink to high heaven. Rotten flesh. That's the smell.*

He touched Rebecca and said, chuckling, "It's a bear, I think that ol'boy has one of them niggers we killed yesterday an' is lookin' to have himself a snack."

"We should leave as quickly as we can." He felt her starting to get up.

"Hang face a sec, if'n he stays around here, well, that ol'boy will work for us."

"Are you crazy? That damned thing is going to eat us too!" she was a little more than concerned. He could tell by the sound of her voice

About that time he heard it growl. The moonlit night offered just enough light to make out the image of the monster across the small killing field having a snack.

"All right, let's get." he whispered, remembering the last bear that had nearly killed him. Leaving the dead tree, they headed for the ponds where their traps were in. The couple walked as the false dawn crept up to the eastern tree line, shedding an eerie light on the forest. As they walked on, the forest came alive with critters barking and chirping away.

"Ya know, we had us a bad scrape, but we're on the move again." he called out over his shoulder. They walked up the valley where their traps were and waited in a thicket opposite to the trail. The noise in the valley never stopped. They sat there for the better part of the morning with nothing happening out of the ordinary. He signaled to Rebecca that they should continue onto the ponds. As they got up to go, some movement caught his attention, so he motioned her back down.

"On the trail. I cain't believe our luck. Them red niggers is a riding our cayuse's." Bill spotted his familiar brown mare as well as Rebecca's gelding. Rebecca nodded. Then she whispered back, "Look at all the traps. Ours plus some. Bandits! That's what they is, bandits."

"Holy shit, some of 'em is white!" Bill exclaimed.

He counted four thieves as he motioned for Rebecca to get ready. He then signaled he would take the lead and she was to get the last one. That would take care of the white men. Then they could use arrows on the red ones. As they closed on the ambush, Bill counted to three. Then they both fired. The front man rolled off the horse backward as the last one did. The two red men came off the horses in a blur. They were looking at the smoke figuring how to get to the bushwhackers. Bill had stayed in one spot too long as he heard an arrow whiz by his head. Down on all fours, he crawled over to the right as Rebecca went left. Bill heard a scream, which meant that Rebecca had another one down.

One more to go Bill counted. The remaining one dropped everything as he was running like the devil himself was on his heels. Before Bill could even get up, she was on the back of her gelding, chasing the lone bandit down. Another scream echoed in the forest. Then it went quiet.

Bill took a moment to reload as he looked over the mess they had just made. The horses were uneasy with the smell of death in the air, so he grabbed the halters, walking them away from the gore on the trail to be tethered to a large hickory tree. He tied the horses up securely as he scratched his mare between her eyes. She remembered as she lowered her head for him to continue.

The runt finished tying up the horses, he turned and walked back over to see the bandits. They were white all right. Their aroma filled the air as he neared them; dirty, smelly, toothless, bearded old-timers. Bill pulled his skinning knife and methodically scalped the three men lying on the ground. As he was slinging the gore off, she came riding back to him, a fresh scalp hanging from her belt.

"That nigger wasn't faster than my horse." she said matter-of-fact.

"Looks like all the traps are here plus some extra ones. We have more than we'll need." he said to her without looking her way. He rummaged through the pack horse until he found their pistols. He pulled each one out, tried the action to assure that they had not been compromised.

"I see you already got the scalps. Which ones are mine?" she asked. *She's sensitive about her scalps,* he thought.

"Here, this is yours." He handed her the loaded gun, "and these are yours. That's two. Countin' the one you chased down, it makes three."

"Damn, you're good at this line of work." Bill said matter-of-fact.

She slid the pistol under her belt, "I do what I have to. I don't really enjoy this. No, that's not true. I like the battle. I get excited, and it makes me wet and hungry for you!" She was looking at the dead men before her.

"No. It's jus' what we have to do. Am I going crazy? To want to kill?" She continued looking at the bodies on the ground.

"No. It's jus' what we do, to keep even around here. If ya steal from us, well, you'll most likely die fer doin' it. It's simple as that. Let's get." They turned walking away from the mess. He untied her horse, handing her the reins for hers and their pack horse

"Well, that gives us one extra horse, two more long guns, our three pistols and possibles, four more 'hawks, four more knives, two more bows, and at least forty arrows, a shitload of traps an' plunder. Not to mention all our pelts plus our friends."

Putting the morning events behind them, they started looking for a place to trap. Not to be let down, they stumbled on a sizable pond.

"Damn, what's that smell" Bill asked.

"Somethin rotten, its gotta be the horse meat." she surmised.

"It's the horse, I'm chucking it." she dugs hers out and winched at the smell.

"You got that right." he kept his nose away from the foul rancid meat as he threw his piece as far as he could.

"We aught keep moving away from that smell, whoowe that's putrid?"

"We're gonna have to clean out the possible bags tonight, they's gonna be ripe." Bill commented, waiting for reply from Rebecca but none returned.

CHAPTER 103

Bill pointed them northwest. They began the ride through the canyons and valleys of spectacular beauty. The snow-covered peaks, contrasted by the green meadows as the wind began to blow the fields to look like waves in the afternoon breeze, accented by the blue sky. The song birds orchestra saranaded them as the they rode north.

On they traveled listening to the mountains and watching for signs of man. Later the next day they came upon a sizable pond.

"I reckon we could trap here fer a while. Then follow it up to the head waters." he spoke with authority.

"I believe we'd be better off to keep moving. Look over there." She was pointing to the fallen trees.

"There's no life here. Maybe a coupla beaver." she said, looking out over the pond.

"How are ya so sure there missy?" he asked belligerently.

"You don't have to get snotty. Just look out in the pond itself. There's no life. There's no building, no smell, no tail slapping when we rode up. Nothing but quiet. I believe this place has already seen man's hand. I'm not saying we have to, but I believe we should move on." she said, gazing out over the pond.

Bill thought about what she said. It really made him take notice of the things she spoke of. True to her words, there was no life to be seen. Bill had no idea why he was so sharp with her.

"Sorry I was bein' an asshole, lover. I jus' thought I was the brains. Well, you've proved that we're a team. I reckon we'll move if ya think so." he answered mopingly.

"Oh, fer Christ's sake. It isn't like I just tanned your hide for forkin' someone else. So stop your moping and let's get!" With that she clucked her horse, leaving the melancholy runt to himself for a moment.

I'll have to work on not bein' so sensitive. It seems that when I ain't right, then I get all defensive, he spoke sharply to himself.

CHAPTER 104

The couple rode through the passes, keeping their noses pointed northwest. After about a week, they stumbled upon a medium-sized stream that wasn't moving real fast, but it was moving.

"If we go upstream, we'll find a pond." she said.

"How'd you know?"

"Look at the water. See, it's not movin' real fast. There's stuff floating in it. Look right there." She was pointing at some small wood chips floating.

"See, that's what beaver does. They cut with their teeth, and small pieces float past their dam and down the stream. If you keep looking, you can see where the animals live before they see you. Daniel taught me before he was kilt."

Well, true to her words, they pulled into a small valley where the pond was twice as big as the one they trapped with Daniel and the others. They sat for a while just watching. She was right. The beaver was here, dragging trees and broken limbs all over the place. The fish were jumping here and there. It was right pretty place.

"Hell, I kinda hate to trap here. It's so peaceful. But that's what we're here fer. Let's set up camp away from here?" he asked her.

"Sure. Sounds good to me. Let's find a place that we can watch the valley." she said as they looked up and down the valley.

"Look. Over there, by that clump of trees. See, there's a hill. The hill will be to our back and the trees will hide our smoke. We'll be able to see both ends of the valley. What do ya say there sweetie?" Bill asked her for approval.

"We could graze the horses at night and bring 'em at daybreak. It'll be fine. Good job Bill." She reached over and patted his arm.

"Well, here we are at our own trappin' spot." he spoke aloud.

Into the trees they went looking for just the right camping spot. When it was all said and done, they had found a suitable place to stash their goods. After tying up the horses, they went about the chores of getting firewood for the night. As they worked, they would occasionally hear an elk bugle in the distance.

"Damn, they do make some kinda ruckus." she spoke as she hefted a large piece of wood. Then there would be quiet as the couple labored. A reply or challenge would come from across the valley.

"If someone could imitate them critters, you could trick in to comin' closer." He paused, "Then it would be elk steaks fer sure." Bill spoke aloud as he dumped an armful of wood into their new camp. As he stretched his back, he turned to see Rebecca dragging deadfall into the camp. The tree limb fell to the ground. She followed it down with a plop.

"Damn! That was a heavy piece of wood!" She had hiked up her war shirt, pulling her legs up as she rested her elbows on her knees, exposing her red briar patch along with the sweat-stained leggings.

"Say there, sweetie, you look good 'nuff to eat." he teased her. With that she scooted away from the deadfall, lying back on the soft grass. She lifted her head up to speak.

"Well, what are you waiting for? An engraved invitation?"

"On my way lover!" He dropped to his stomach as he leaned into her red waiting valley.

"Woman, I don't know how you do it but you always smell so good!" With that he stuck his tongue deep in that crevice as he lapped and licked like a thirsty cat. As he worked on her, he felt her hands on his head. Firmly she held his head as he performed for her. Then her legs came together hard enough to hurt the young blond runt as the woman climaxed. She then lifted herself up on her elbows.

"Wild Bill, think you could get that piss'r of yers out? I think I'd like to enjoy some of it." she asked.

"I reckon I can do that." the wiry runt answered as he got up on his knees. He reached inside his breechclout for her toy. He wrestled ol' John Thomas out into the open air. It seemed the tool of Bill had a mind of its own for as soon as the cool mountain air touched it the tool sprang to life.

"My my, aren't you quick? You going to go fer the full three or just a quick one?" she asked.

"I reckon a quick one." He leaned into her slippery briar patch, slowly at first, then ramming it in hard. He was anxious as he pumped violently right from the get-go, and when he couldn't stand it any longer, he pulled back until he was almost out. Then he slammed it for all he was worth. Not moving, the runt felt himself fill up the redheaded partner of his. As he pulled out, the river of life followed him out.

"My, you had a bucketful today, didn't you? I know you got more, but we really should get this camp ready to start working tomorrow." she said. She looked down at the puddle still growing under her.

"Shit, how much did you put in me?" she quizzed.

"'Nuff I reckon." He laughed as he put his pod away as he walked toward the horses. He looked back at her as he began hobbling the animals. She was still dripping as he finished the last one.

"Well, I can't be waiting all night for this to stop!" So she got up straightening her shirt. Off she went to bring in more wood.

He got the bag with the traps along with the mallets to drive the poles into the pond floor. When he had everything he could think of, he sat down on a log for a moment.

"How much food do we have left?" he called out to her as she returned with another armful of wood.

"None." she answered, "I'll go get a coupla rabbits before dark. Hand me my bow will you?" she said. He reached over behind a log next to her saddle, retrieving her quiver and bow, as he handed her the weapons, she spoke matter-of-factly to him.

"I'll be back after dark, keep the fire hot." With that, she walked off into the meadow. Billy White wasn't worried as she vanished from sight. He knew she could take care of herself. But in the back of his mind, he kept thinking, *We've seen the Pawnee an' Arapaho. Not too sure bout the ones that rubbed each other out when we stolt them horses. Shit, that one 'Rapaho ran away.* He was hoping, no, praying, to some great being above that no harm would come to his woman. She's a good hunter and excellent in the woods. Dismissing the thoughts from his mind, he went ahead and proceeded getting the fire going. He began peeling some green sticks to hang the rabbits on.

Satisfied with his progress, he began to pull limbs off the deadfall, stacking them for the upcoming night. Listening to the oncoming night, Bill began making a lean-to to keep their gear out of the elements. He stepped back, looking at it. Most likely it wouldn't keep all the rain out but it would stop a great deal.

While he was on a roll, he went to the deadfall and started cutting poles to hold the traps in place once they were set. What seemed like forever was only a half hour until he had twelve poles cut and ready for use. As Bill sat on the large buckskin pallet by the fire pit, he thought about what else to do, *the possible bags, damn.* He brought them out and dumped them on the pallet he was sitting on. *Shit not as bad as I thought,* he reached for a small piece of cloth they used for wadding for the guns. Wiping everything cleaned he reassembled each one an laid them off to the side.

He got the guns out to do his cleaning ritual. One by one he cleaned and reloaded each gun. Once they were all cleaned and primed, he turned his attention to the skinning knives. One by one he sharpened the wooden-handled knives from the Arapahos and the dead white trappers as the sun was dipping under the western tree line. Bill sat listening to the night when a noise came to him. Slowly he picked up a rifle and slid his pistol under his belt, with a few steps he faded into the darkness outside of the small camp to wait for the intruder.

Rebecca stepped into the light, carrying two large rabbits. She looked around slowly.

"Bill? Billy White where are you?" She looked about nervously.

"I'm here." He stepped into the light.

"Christ, Bill, you had me scared." she answered.

"You know, we still got them goddamned 'Rapaho out there." he answered defensively. She nodded approvingly at him.

"Shit. These here varmints are huge. I hope the beaver is as big in this valley." Bill commented as he did the skinning. They sat in the evening eating the rabbit while watching the stars. It was a perfect night with all the nightlife around them raising a ruckus like they do in the spring. Rebecca figured it was because they were horny, just like her.

"I'm callin' it a night, lover." Billy said, looking into the fire.

"You don't want a poke?" she asked.

"Nah. I was thinkin' 'bout jus' gettin' some sleep 'fore we go out into the valley in the morning." he spoke as he lay back.

"I didn't figure I'd ever hear that from you. I think my crotch won't know what to do with itself." She smiled at herself as she hiked her shirt up, speaking to the red garden Bill loved to play in.

"Ya hear that? Ya get a night off. What'cha gonna do with yerself?" She laughed as she pulled it back down.

"Okay, I think I could use some sleep too." she answered. She lay back against a pack. Her snoring began almost immediately. The couple each thought about how far they had come. Bill thought if he'd do it all over again. *Would I? Yeppers, but I think I'd left that damned Ann sooner though.* The young trapper drifted to sleep as the sun raced around the world to wake the couple in the morning. But before it cast its blazing light on the two, she was waking Bill up.

"Bill, time to go to work." she said quietly.

"I jus' got to sleep. Hell, it ain't even light out yet woman. How we gonna set traps if we cain't even see? Shit!" he whined, "All right, I'm gettin' up. Shit. It's blacker that a nigger's heel." he continued to bitch harmlessly. He used the brass tube as he had seen

Alison do, blowing on the embers and made the fire come to life.

"Now we can see and won't be stumbling around like a couple flatlanders in the dark." He whispered as they prepared to harvest the flat tails.

"You sound like a calf looking for a teat. Is that your problem? You need a poke to get you going in the morning. Every morning you get yer poke, then yer the best friend to have round. No poke, you're a little kid."

Laughing at him, she continued, "I believe you're spoiled White Man." She sat down. Then she picked up the front of her war shirt, relieving the dark valley where he played regularly.

"Get on with it, Bill. I want to be on the pond by first light." she said. Not needing a second invitation, he pulled his breechclout over to the side. He reached down to pull out his soon-to-be hardening pod. Just the thought got him stiffer than a hoe handle. He kneeled down, slipping between her legs. It felt so good to be in her as she wrapped her legs around him.

"Billy White, give it to me hard and fast." she whispered. He did just as she requested. Soon he was heaving like a bull in the spring.

"Here. It. Comes!" he said between breaths. That's when she squeezed with her legs as he unloaded all he had stored up into her. Her legs dropped off as he backed off, wiping his pecker on his breechclout.

She stuck her fingers inside herself, pulling out the goo, wiping it on a clump of grass.

"My, you were full. This will probably draw every critter in the woods." she said looking at the globs of white life on the grass.

"But I still love it." she said as she licked her fingers.

"Now we can go trapping." She hopped up, grabbing her possible bag with her pistol, bow and quiver.

"You takin' yer pistol an' bow?" he asked.

"It's quiet but I want some back up if'n I need it. I want to get some grub for supper without having every swinging dick in the valley comin' 'round investigatin'."

"Sounds good to me. Hang face fer a shake." he called to her. She turned to Bill, waiting. He grabbed up a thick strand of buckskin and made a hoop around the barrel and one around the stock and passed it to her. She held the gun waiting. He quickly made one for his.

"Sling it over yer shoulder along with the powder horn an possible bag.

"I'd hate to lose these again." he said as he got his in the same position as hers. Then came his bow along with all the traps. He almost fell over, picking them up.

"We'll have to make a couple trips to get these poles." she commented.

"Hmm? I don't think so lover. Hold up. That's a great idea. Let's just strap everything on the horses, 'cept the bows an' arrows. Let the horses do the work an' lead 'em around with you. What do ya think?"

"Sounds good I reckon." she answered back as she dropped everything to retrieve a pair of horses for carrying the ruck to the pond.

He turned to look over the camp as they left. He was very pleased that they had located this hidden spot. He felt that it wouldn't be found unless someone was looking very hard or stumbled into it. They walked in the predawn light. He saw all kinds of life. Squirrels were up, giving them hell as were the jaybirds. He shook his head at the commotion they caused.

They got to the pond in a short time. Rebecca thought it seemed farther yesterday. The more they walked around, the more she was getting familiar with their little valley. As she looked out over the water watching the pond come to life, the beaver were thick here. They didn't know that Bill and Rebecca were here yet. The rascals were sliding down the bank swimming on their backs acting like a bunch of kids. She felt bad knowing that they were going to kill most of them here. The young couple surveyed the surrounding area as they plotted out their working areas. As soon as Rebecca walked into the opening, the slap of tails could be heard all over the pond as the beavers went to water. They worked their way around the pond as the sun began its journey to the west side of the mountains. Bill went one way and Rebecca the other. She had six as did he. Afterward they met back at the trailhead about midafternoon to walk back to camp. As they walked, she began gathering more firewood as well as saplings to make the stretching hoops that they were going to need for the beaver hides. They were both stacking wood and branches on the pack animals as they got closer to the camp.

When the runt and his partner entered the camp, two raccoons scampered off at a full run.

"I wonder what them scamps were up to." Bill said aloud as he surveyed the camp.

"Bill, it seems that I'm not the only one who enjoys you." laughed Rebecca, pointing to the ground where they had had sex.

"Hell, it was skinned down to bare dirt." She laughed.

"I'll have to use that lovely mouth of yours more often there lover!" He chuckled.

"Sounds good to me. You ready right now, Bill?" she said coyly.

"Christ, woman! We have to do some work around here gettin' these stretchin' hoops ready for tanight. I thought you'd get a couple more rabbits 'er something fer supper?" Bill spoke through a smile.

Was that me talkin'? Sayin' no to a blowjob? I didn't even feel like one right now anyway, he answered himself. *Twelve traps twice a day, twenty-four beaver at five pounds piece.* He was sure glad they had the horses to tote the plews.

"I'm getting these wet leggings off. If we're gonna be going in twice a day, I'll be a using them leggin's we snatched back in the meadows last spring."

"Good point. I'll get some dry ones as well. You know, if we do as good as I think we will, we'll have to go to one of those rony'viou Dan'l was talking 'bout." she said, pulling the quill-covered Crow leggings out of her rucksack.

"When did he say anything like that?" Bill watched her white skin in the afternoon light.

"Hell, I never heard anything like that. Sounds to me like you were pretty friendly there woman." Bill spouted as he pulled on a similar set.

"Why Bill, are you jealous?" She giggled.

"I was wonderin' why he was tellin' you all these things. Shit, he never said nuthin' to me the whole time 'bout no rony'viou?" he asked, not looking up.

"Hmm? Let me think for a minute." she said, tilting her head as she worked on the hoop for the beaver.

"I recall someone who was shot the hell up. Hum. I remember someone who was unconscious for quite some time. Now who do you think that was? I didn't sit on my hands the whole time you were healing. Where do you think I learned to trap? How about skinning and hunting? I sure didn't learn it being a whore on a riverboat. I didn't learn it from you either. Sure I got friendly. He was a nice man. I know he wanted a poke. He knew you and I were together, so he never tried anything. He knew I'd gut him from asshole to eyeball with a green river knife if he tried to!" she said boastfully.

"He knew I killed that scamp, what was his name anyway? I already forgot his name. You know, I've lost track of how many men I've killed. Shit, listen to me. I'm rambling on now."

She lowered her eyes back to her work, letting her speech soak in.

"Well, at least one of us knows horseshit from hog jowls." He chuckled. She got up to hang a rabbit on the spit over the fire as she gathered up the saplings to make more stretching rings for the skins they were hoping to get. *She has fast hands,* Bill thought. As he had one done, she was already beginning her third.

They worked by the glow of the fire, the meat sizzling and snapping as fat dripped into the fire. His mouth was watering with the thought of getting some grub into his gut as a strange noise came in from across the pond.

"Ya ever heard that 'fore?" he questioned her.

"Sounded like a screech owl but bigger, you know, deeper, like a big fat man." she said.

Then it happened again but closer. The sound sent shivers up the runt's spine, making his hairs stand up on the back of his neck. He looked at her and she at him. Both of them put their work down and slowly picked up their rifles, each checking the pan to assure dry powder was ready. *There it is again, real close this time.* His mind raced, *It sounds like it's right outside the camp now.*

The deadfall outside of the camp was breaking and snapping like a wagon was rolling over it. Closer it came. Then the sound came through the trees, right in front of them. That screech, like fingernails on a chalkboard. Loud enough to hurt his ears. Rebecca got up, scampering over to his side of the campfire. They both leveled their muzzleloaders and waited. The young couple pulled the hammers back in the exact same instant, so close it sounded like one click. The noise stopped. It just went quiet. Silence was deafening. Then they heard it, the breathing. It was just outside of the firelight. Like a bull that had just pulled out a stump. Loud and deep. The brush started moving, breaking branches and limbs as it came closer to the white trappers. Then Bill had to look way up into the night to see its yellow eyes. Something wasn't right as it came into the light. The couple just stared at it. It was huge. Eight or ten feet tall covered in brown hair like a grizzly bear, walking on its hind legs. Its face was almost like a man, with its huge eyes with a pointy nose, looked almost like one of the Africans that was on the paddleboat but bigger. Really bigger. Bill was so scared he couldn't move, but Rebecca kept her wits about herself as she lowered her gun.

Slowly she reached over to Bill's, pushing his barrel down.

"Well howdy, why don't ya sit yer ass down an' have some grub?" she spoke in a firm voice.

"What are you doin'?" he spoke quietly without turning his head.

"You're not going to hurt it with that. Just follow my lead." she said. The thing was standing there breathing out its nose in great rushes like a horse in the cold. It was just looking at them. It tilted the shaggy head back and let out another screech, and then it slowly squatted down before them, staring intently. Rebecca was looking at the creature before them. It was covered in coarse hair. The yellow eyes didn't dart about like a scared animal but looked at each of them slowly as it appeared to be thinking of what to do next. Rebecca's eyes lowered to its loins. She could see the huge hair-covered penis as it sat there on its haunches. *What am I thinking?* she scolded herself. *Oh my god!*

Bill was figuring that this was it for them. Slowly, ever so slowly, it reached out to the rabbit. Then with a lightning-quick movement, it snatched the meat off the skewer as it kept its eyes on the couple. It slowly stood and shook itself like a dog that had just come out of the water. The whole time it kept its eyes on them. Then it vanished into the night. That left Bill and Rebecca speechless.

"Did we jus' see somethin'?" he asked.

"I believe we did. I don't know what it was we saw either. Christ almighty, what was it?" she asked.

"I ain't leavin' my trappin' grounds 'cause of a hoodoo!" he spit out.

"Oh, is that right? I believe that thing could of had us both for a snack. There was nothing we could do to stop it either." As she finished speaking, the screech happened again, except this time it's way across the other side of the pond.

"How the hell does it travel that fast? It hadn't been but a coulpa minutes, an' it was already on the other side of the pond?" he asked her, looking into the darkness.

"Ya reckon we should tell anybody 'bout this?" he asked meekly.

"Why not? Are you afraid of what people will say?" she challenged him for his weakness as she continued.

"What people? We haven't seen anybody else since Dan'l an my friends were kilt."

"Hey, they were my friends too! I like them all, okay?" he snapped.

"Whoa! Hold on. I didn't mean anything bad by it." Just then the hoodoo let out another screech, except this time it was from afar. Bill spoke quickly to change the subject, "Good god, that thing can travel. Maybe it was a bear we seen. Yeah, that's it! It was a bear." He looked into the darkness.

"I bet White Moon or Two Sticks would know. But they're not here, so we're not going to worry about it." she said to Bill as much as to herself.

"Damnit. The rabbit musta fell in the fire when I wasn't lookin'. I'm plum hungry too! We'll have to cook up the other'n fer to'night, an' get somethin' fer the mornin' after we run the traps?"

"Sure, Bill. Do you want a poke or anything?" she asked as she stirred the embers of the fire. She spoke without looking at the runty white man.

"You know, I'd feel a better if'n I know'd we'd be all alone when I was slippin' the wood to ya. I wouldn't wanna be bother'd by a overgrown hunk a rug or something."

"I don't think we'll have that problem. Why don't you show me how you can go three times there White Man?" She smiled.

It jus' like her, Bill thought. He went on with his pondering, *When we have something that is scary or life threatening, she gets all worked up. Shit, I'd like a poke, that's fer certain an' fer sure, but damnit, that hoodoo is plum scary.* He pondered to himself

"As much as I wanna, girl, I ain't gonna. Not right now. I don't think my piss'r would work anyhoo." he defended his actions as he looked out in to the night.

"I kept thinkin' of how fast the critter was. Christ! It would bein' the next valley before you could even draw a bead on it. Was it a boar 'er a sow? Hell, I didn't even think 'bout askin' it. It? Naw, it was a thing. How do ask a thing if it's got a dick 'er a slit? You don't. Ya keep yer mouth shut an' hope it don't make you a meal? It took that meat sure as shit, though!" he spoke to Rebecca as he felt a hand snake around from behind him, working its way down to his breechclout.

"What do ya think yer doin' there?" he said.

"It was a boar. I saw its huge root. It was as big as my forearm." she answered.

"You looked?" he asked.

"Sure, I wanted to know so I looked." she answered.

"I wanna see if it's really not gonna work." She giggled. She pulled him around, forcing him to look right into those deep blue eyes of hers.

"Shit, here we go." he conceded aloud.

"I think I can get it to work Wild Bill, you sit your ass down and let me work my magic." So he plopped right down next to the fire and watched his redheaded lover work her magic. She then untied the breechclout drawstring, letting it fall off to the side.

"There. Now I have some room to work." She sighed like it was a major chore she had just accomplished. She slowly wrapped her hand around the soft white root while she stared at it. Then as quick as a snake striking at its prey, she engulfed the white member. The young lass usually took her time but not tonight. Bill was watching as he contemplated, *She must be drippin' wet down there ta night*. Rebecca continued like a terrier thrashing a rat. A blur was all Bill could see of her head. He thought of a trick to play on her. *Let's see if I can keep it soft while she's a playin'*. So he thought about shoveling horseshit and trapping in cold water. It was working.

"Bill! You stop that right now." she scolded.

"Huh? What do ya mean?" he snickered.

"I know what you're doing, and you stop it right now!" she said. With that she swallowed it all, plum down to the short hairs. Up she came until the tip was in the air. He was up on his elbows, watching all this before him. He couldn't keep it soft with her working this hard at it. So ol' John Thomas sprang to life, and in an instant it was harder than an oak plank.

"That's better! Now I can properly work on ya. Remember way back I was gonna give a surprise? But you went off an' got shot the hell up?" she asked.

"Hell, woman, that's a lifetime ago. But yes, I do 'member that. Is it time?" he asked.

"Yeppers. It is. Now you just watch because I have some fun planned for you tonight." he said as she slipped the skinned-down penis back in her mouth. Slowly she came up until the head was out in the air. Then she took the tip of her tongue, forcing it down the tip of his root. Then her whole mouth went over it until all he could see was the top of her head bobbing up and down. She rubbed his nut sack as she did her magic, causing the young runt to get closer to popping. She rolled them around like a bag of marbles. It was not hurting him, but he knew she was doing it. Up came her mouth, and then onto the sack she went. It didn't feel like much to him, her doing that, but then she lifted his right leg, the whole time not stopping on the sack of his. *Pop* was the sound she made as a nut popped out of her mouth. Then she took her tongue down to his butthole! Then he felt it. Her finger went right into his anus! *Wow! What the hell? I ain't no sissy man!* he almost called out. Then she came back up to his piss'r swallowing on it. The whole time she had a finger or two up his ass. *It didn't hurt,* he thought. Then she touched his prostrate for the stimulation, and he blew a load almost instantly! The runt didn't even feel like he was close, but she knew exactly what she was doing.

"What do you think of that?" she asked with spooge dripping out of her mouth.

"Damn! Woman!" was all he could say.

"I know. You had no idea, huh?" Then back to work she went, slopping and slurping. Now he felt her finger for sure, and it didn't feel painful. But he was back to fighting form quickly.

"Hold that thought!" she said. Then she jumped up, pulling her war shirt off. Now she was naked from leggings up.

"I have more fun planned out for us tonight lover." She walked to over him, squatting down until her dripping valley was over his white stick. She reached back with one hand, balancing herself. With the other, she guided the planting stick into her red garden. When she felt comfortable, she lowered herself down the rest of the way, rocking back and forth. She began to grind on the runt. He felt the tingle coming quicker tonight than usual.

"I'm ready to plant sweetie." he called to her.

"Fill me up there lover." She sighed. He did just that. He kept filling until it was oozing down between his legs. She reached down her hand, covering the hole as she leaned forward. Standing up, she pulled her hand up, showing him the white life dripping from her hand. Then she wiped her butthole with it.

"Now I want it up the ass! With your cream for the starter." Sinking to her hands and knees and began to revive him for the third time. It took a tad longer than usual as he felt her lips surround the third member of their little group. He looked up as she was on him. Her red dripping valley was smeared with the white seeds of life. Mesmerized he watched it dribble on his white chest in the dim firelight as she licked and swallowed away on him. *Oh, this's too good,* he thought as she made his life's member grow. It made him want to do her in the ass somethin' fierce. He was almost panicking now.

"Get up! I'm so close I cain't stand it! Hurry!" he spoke between breaths.

"Only if you use that tongue on me first!" She panted. *Shit! I ain't got time to do that.*

"Sorry there lover. I ain't got time to do that." he blurted out. Then she was up, turning around, she dropped to her hands and knees. She grabbed his planting tool, forcing him into her brown rosebud! He hadn't even done a few strokes when he released into her. She waited a moment as he kept filling her with the white seeds of life. She leaned forward panting. Then she was up and turned around. She leaned down, kissing him full mouthed, hot tongue driving deep down his throat. He didn't care. He just wanted her so bad that nothing else mattered. He tasted himself as they continued kissing. Her scent was strong, but the taste was more than he could stand. He pushed her mouth away. She stood up over him, she said, "That's your surprise lover." She wiped her mouth off with the back of her hand. He did the same looking down and seeing his own mess on the back of his hand.

"Is it as bad as you thought it would be?" she asked.

"I wouldn't go outta of my way for it, if that's what you mean." He sat up the rest of the way and looked into the black night, wondering if the creature had come back to watch them. He could go a lifetime without seeing that thing again.

CHAPTER 105

In the early-morning darkness they headed off for the traps. He wondered if they'd see the tracks of the creature that was there last night. All the traps were chock-full of beaver. The young couple had done so well they had to stop several times along the trail back to camp to rearrange the loads on the horses.

Back at the camp, they changed into yesterday's leggings and moccasins. Then they started stretching the skins. Stretch and scrape. Scrape and stretch. The runt's fingers grew tired as he worked. At least his moccasins were dry. He looked at the wet leggings hanging from the firewood.

They were always dragging in the dirt from being wet all the time. Rebecca's war shirt was gone by midmorning; and she sat there in her leggings, moccasins, and nothing else. Bill had a hard time not staring at her tanned breasts as they would sway from side to side as she worked the raw skins. Her red nipples stuck out in the afternoon sun. She would look up at him with that innocent face of hers. What a beautiful smile she had. Her straight teeth, full lips, and her blushed complexion. Damn, he wanted a poke already. Then she'd lick her lips and winked at the runt. She was so talented. Christ! She had two done to his one as far as scraping and stretching went. He spoke to her, "I wanna go out an' look fer them tracks that thing left last night."

"Why, I reckon we could as we run our traps again." she said as she walked over in front of him. Then she turned and bent over in front of him, looking back between her legs. All he could see was her butt and the red bush hanging down.

"I think you should forget that we ever think we saw something." With that she reached back, grabbing her butt cheeks, pulling them apart. Ever so wide. Inviting.

"Do you really want to think about some hoodoo? I think you want something else." She was wiggling back and forth as she spoke. Then she got down on her hands and knees, leaning down so her forehead rested on the ground. Then she reached back, spreading herself again.

"Come on Bill, show me how you can do it." She was taunting him.

"Damn! Not now." Bill was teasing her. At least he thought he was.

"Please, Bill!" she whined.

"Oh, all right." He pulled out the smallest member of their brigade and put him to work. Bill was stroking with his eyes closed, enjoying himself to the utmost.

"White Man spends too much time mounting the redhead!" he heard the familiar voice. He spun around, shooting spooge all over her backside.

There stood Two Sticks and White Moon.

"Well, I be 'et fer a tater! Two Sticks an' White Moon." He was too shocked. So surprised.

"I never heard you walk up. Damn, it's good at see you!" He walked over dripping pecker and all, sticking his hand out to shake his friends when he remembered his piss'r was hanging out.

He quickly slipped it away, wiping his hands on his leggings. He offered his hand. Rebecca rolled over onto her back and propped herself up on her elbows with a frown on her face.

"Two Sticks, you should have of let him finish." Then she hopped up, giving him a big hug.

"The White Man can do it some other time. He will get more chances. It will not be trouble for him to do it later. Your breasts should be covered. Your white skin will turn angry in the sun." said Two Sticks.

"Bill likes me this way. I'll be careful in the sun." she answered as she backed away. White Moon had been watching him put his stick away. When he looked up at her, she smiled.

"It would be good to do it like before I took Ann away." White Moon smiled.

"Whatever happened to Ann anyway?" Bill asked, looking at both of them.

Two Sticks spoke with no emotion. "She is living with the trappers at Fort Atkchinson on the Platte. She came to our village with White Moon as a visitor, but she has a bad spirit. Not a man or woman could stay with her. Bright Horse told the trappers to take her away."

"I know'd she was a bad apple when she left us, she was fun in the robes though. I didn't figure that she'd have a problem if she got warm clothes an' some grub in her gullet."

"We will speak no more of her. Let us sit and smoke for a while." Two Sticks said as he produced a large decorated pipe bag.

"Rebecca got us a coupla plump rabbits last night, so we can have the other'n now." Bill told the trader.

"Your woman hunts for you?" he asked with his eyebrows going up.

"Ah hell, Two Sticks, things have really changed since you left us back on the Platte.

We've bumped into bad sorts of yer kind an' had to rub a passel of 'em out." Bill spoke, looking at his eyes as he spoke.

"They were Pawnee?" he asked.

"Nah. Rapho's. I know'd that they was gonna devil us somethin' fierce though. Hey, show him that bunch of scalps!" Bill asked. She got up walking over to her pack and produced two handfuls of dry shriveled scalps. She tossed them on the ground in front of Two Sticks.

He looked at them then at her and back to Bill. She was still naked, standing there. Her hand went to her red garden as she absentmindedly scratched herself.

"Your woman has killed these men?" he asked as he looked at the scalps.

"Yeppers. She most likely killed three fer my one. Hell, we was on a ridge a while back. I loaded, she shot. I believe it was eight 'er nine that time. On the trail back to camp, she killed two more. Then before that, I cain't 'member how many it was that time. Two 'er three anyhoo." Bill rambled on.

"Hey, don't forget them two trappers and their little friends." she chimed in.

"You killed whites also? Do you remember what they looked like, how they were dressed?" he asked slowly, looking at them then to the scalps on the ground in front of him.

"Whites were dressed in skins like me an' Rebecca. But the others, no, not really. These here are the scalps of them red niggers. I left the doodads in 'em." Bill pointed to the grizzly remains of a man to him.

"These are Arapaho, they have the allies up north, the Blackfeet. Have you heard of them? For they are fierce. Do you have anything else?" he asked.

"Hold on. The white men had some traps mixed in with ours." Bill answered.

"They was jus' a tad different than ours, but I didn't put too much stock in it though." The runt kept speaking as he watched his friends' eyes.

"Those white men were with the Hudson Bay Company. They have been down here hunting and trading before. Tell me, were they old and toothless? Smelling bad?" he asked.

"Yeppers. It's them all right. You know'd them?" Billy asked.

"Yes. Jean Bouchard was the one with no teeth. The other was his friend Luis Sanchez. They have children in many villages, but they claim no wife." he spoke with no emotion in his voice.

"How many moons ago did you do these things?" he asked.

"I don't rightly know. Why?"

"You have stirred a nest of hornets. You will not be safe again. Not in this valley. We travel to the Willow Valley to go to the White

Man's Rendezvous to trade. You should come with us. We have been before. Other skin trappers are there. Do you have many skins to trade?" he asked Bill.

"We'll have a coupla bundles." Bill pointed to the pile they had stacked under their lean-to. He got up walking over to them. He went through them, inspecting each of them slowly.

"Did your woma." but before he could finish his words, she cut him off.

"Goddamnit, Two Sticks! My name is Rebecca!" Her voice had some ice in it.

"Rebecca, you do fine work. I have seen such work only by the old ones in my village."

"Oh, sorry and thank you." She made a little face of being embarrassed.

"Lookie here, Two Sticks. What do you say if we trap here a couple more weeks then head off to this here rony'viou yer talkin' 'bout?" he spoke to him as he watched him and White Moon take his answer. He leaned over to her. They were whispering.

"We should leave now. Can you get your traps out soon?" he asked. *Well, now this is strange,* Bill was thinking.

"Yeah, I reckon. But why are ya'll fired up 'bout leavin' so goddamn soon?" Bill pressed. Two Sticks got up and walked out side of the camp.

"White Man, Rebecca, come here." he requested. So they got up following the Pawnee. He felt Rebecca's hand touching his.

"So what are you gonna show us?" Bill asked again.

"Look to the north." he said, pointing to the distant mountain range.

"Yeah." Bill answered.

"That is the land of the Blackfeet and the Crow. They are all fierce warriors. But the Arapaho? They have been stealing from the whites since they came to the mountains.

"But when they come again, there will not be one or two. But more than the birds in the sky. They will seek you and Rebecca. You say one or more ran away? They are the ones that will lead them back here to you. We have little time to leave this place. It will not take them long to be back. So we must hurry." he spoke, looking north.

"You have been lucky to fight and defeat those Arapaho." He pointed back to the camp. They walked back to the fire. Bill grabbed a couple of lead ropes off the pile of their belongings to retrieve a pair of horses. When he got back to the smoldering fire, she had the packsaddles ready to go on.

"I ain't gonna carry them traps an' the goddamned plews. Here, have a horse." He handed her the lead rope as she got a pack cradle on one of the extra horses. He went back for her gelding and his mare. When he reentered the camp, she had the camp packed up.

"Damn. That's fast."

"How long will it take you to do traps?" Two Sticks asked.

"Couple of hours. Why?" Bill asked. Rebecca thought it was strange of Two Sticks to be so concerned.

"We'll hurry. How's that?" she answered.

"It's your scalps." he answered to their backs as they left the camp. As they walked the animals to the pond, Bill spoke quietly to her, "I thought we had it good too."

"I was thinking the same thing. See ya back at camp." she said and peeled off to do her set of traps.

This time he was looking over his shoulder all the time.

"Forget the hoodoo. Shit, if them Arapaho was as bad as Two Sticks was talkin' 'bout, we're in some kinda deep shit." Bill mumbled aloud.

The runt had every trap full. He tried to go quickly, but the animals were waterlogged and very heavy. After skinning and rolling them up, he headed back to camp. Traps were banging off his horse as he entered the now-empty camp. They were all saddled up waiting for him as he returned.

"Bring that pack horse up will ya Moon?" Bill asked.

"Sure thing White Man." She brought up the Indian pony turned pack horse. Bill worked diligently loading plews and the traps.

"That pony, it has a notched ear. How did you come by it?" Two Sticks asked.

"We stole it from a bunch'a 'Rapahos a while back. Stole the whole string we did!" Rebecca laughed.

"Well that adds on much to your story with them. Did they come after them?" Two Sticks asked.

"Well now that you mention it, they did. They went head to head with a different bunch of niggers. It was a horrible battle. None survived. We got these moc's an leggin's from 'dem too." Bill chimed in.

"The horse." he pointed to the Indian pony, "is a buffalo runner. It has been trained to run next to a buffalo without shying away. A very valuable horse worth more than all of your horses."

"What happened to the other horses?" Two Sticks pressed the interrogation.

"We turned 'em loose. Just needed one to replace the one Ann took." Bill defended his action.

"Why did you steal them?" the Pawnee asked.

"Fer the fun of it. Jus' fer the fun of it." Bill answered as he approached his horse, "Haven't ya done somethin' fer jus' fer fun?" he said annoyed as he threw a leg over his brown mare.

"Damn." Bill spoke as air rushed out of his lungs as he settled on his mount.

"Okay. Now where do we go? I mean to this here rony'viou." Bill queried his new partners.

About that time Rebecca gave him a sharp look for being shitty. *Damn, I was feelin' right spunky too,* he thought.

"We go west through the South Pass. Then it will not be far to the Green River. It is in the land of the Shoshone. They are friends to the Pawnee. But not the Crow, they dislike us. I have traded with some Shoshone for many seasons. I know some of the warriors also. We'll have no trouble." With that little speech they set off to their first Rendezvous.

The Rendezvous

CHAPTER 106

With the peaceful little valley behind them, the foursome headed west going from the mountains in Colorado to the flatlands of southeastern corner of Wyoming. Lucky for them that Two Sticks was along to show them the way as they had the packhorses heavily loaded down with fresh plews. Rebecca kicked her horse up next to his as she listened to Bill quiz her bronze friend.

"Hey, Two Sticks, how is it you know so much 'bout this here country anyway?" Bill asked.

"I have traded with many tribes all over the mountains. The Crow will steal from you while shaking your hand. The Nez Perce have fine spotted horses. The Flathead have always been a friend to me. They are good people. The Black Robes have taught them French, and many of them believe in your god. The Bannocks are generally poor and steal everything they can find. The Blackfeet have many smaller tribes inside one large one. They have the Piegan, Gros Ventres, and the Bloods. Some of the Arapahos stay with them in the winter." he spoke without turning his head.

"Our friend told us we was in the Rocky Mountains. Well, he got kilt so I never got to hear more." Bill persisted.

"I will show you places as we travel." Then Two Sticks said no more. Too many new names and places for the runt to memorize. He just listened instead, turning around occasionally to see where they'd come from. After a period of time, he gazed out over the high prairie, thinking back to the last trapping grounds they had been chased out of.

"We hadn't been there long enough to clean the place out, so now we got a spot to go to if no one else finds it. Shit, it'll be prime beaver." he spoke aloud. No one said anything to the young man's mumblings; the Pawnee didn't want to offend Rebecca by asking about the small man, *the White Man must be touched as he speaks to the wind. These whites are always strange,* Two Sticks thought as they traveled on through the day.

They crossed river after river. Their buckskins were barely dry when they would plod through the next river or stream. White Moon looked at Bill and smiled.

I'd like to get the runt to poke me. A far cry better than Two Sticks. But she said nothing as she let her mind wander as the monotony played out.

"Two Sticks, I see ya ain't got yer wife with ya. What happened to her?" Bill asked as he and Rebecca listened.

"She has gone under." he said with no emotion in his voice.

"Oh, sorry my friend." Bill answered mournfully.

"It is rude to talk of the dead. But you are new to our ways, so I will tell you. She was gathering wood for our fire when she stepped into a hole. It broke her foot. The bone came through the skin and became angry. A wound that would not heal." He paused, looking away from Bill and Rebecca.

"She died from it. She had a mean spirit, so I did not mourn her." He finished speaking and turned to Bill.

"You are still White Moon's husband. You are now a rich man with two wives." He chuckled, turning back to the surrounding landscape.

Bill looked at Rebecca as he saw her smile.

"It's prime beaver?" asked White Moon, joining in the conversation in her newfound American slang.

"Now you got two of us to do your work for you. 'Sides we'll have more fun in the robes too." Then she giggled. *We're gonna have some fun now,* Bill thought.

"What do you say 'bout all this Two Sticks?" Bill asked, thinking he would want some too.

"They are your wives. Do as you please. I have shared my robes with White Moon many times. You will be happy to know that she has shown me many things that she has learned from you." he said as he smiled at Billy.

Billy White looked over at Rebecca as she too was smiling and she had that twinkle in her eye. Then she rode up next to White Moon.

"White Moon, I have some more tricks to show you. Tonight we'll get these men and really show them what fun is." she said as she turned and winked at Bill. Slowly Two Sticks turned his head to Bill.

"These new tricks will have to wait. We must ride all night. It will be bad to be caught out here in the open. There are Sioux and Cheyenne out here. They do not like when white men come on their land. We will be safer the closer we get to the South Pass. Then we can have time for games."

He rode in silence for a long spell, then turned to Billy, and asked, "What does she mean new tricks?'" He had a curious look on his face.

"Well, she has more than one way to skin a cat, my fren'." the runt answered.

"A cat? What is a cat?" He asked.

"It's like a small Lynx or bobcat. Folks back east have them around the house to catch mice and rafter rats. But when we say skin a cat they're referring to a catfish. There's many ways to skin them rascals. So Rebecca has tricks she lern't while she was a sportin' girl."

Two Sticks thought about what Billy had said, "Blue Nose does it with the ponies. No one cares because he is ugly. They don't want him coming around anyone's daughter. So when he does it with his ponies, it keeps him away from the young girls. He is a good warrior and counted coup many times, so he is left alone. This is something that is not good. Does your kind have these kind of men?" he asked. It surprised Bill of his emotionless tone.

"Yeah, we got some fell'r's like that. The men'r run out on a rail when someone finds out. It's a bad thing to the white people. Men with men ain't tolerated." As soon as those words left his mouth, the thought of Mohammad getting pleasures from that tall white man popped into his mind. *Zach 'er Jack. Was the hell was his name? Josh! That's it Josh. Now that was some kinda of queer. He kicked the shit outta me. Good riddance, that's what I say,* Bill thought. Rebecca noticed his mood had changed with the mention of the ghosts.

"Are you okay?" asked Rebecca.

"Yeppers. I was thinkin' 'bout Hamhead an' Josh. That's seems like a lifetime ago."

"Who are these men you speak of?" asked White Moon.

"They were two polecats back from the riverboat where me an' Rebecca came from. They liked men. One of 'em had a pecker 'bout this long." He held up his hands, showing the length.

Two Stick got reeled in to the story telling, "They were bad men?' What did they do? Did they steal your horses? Perhaps they raided a village and took some prisoners that were relatives of yours?"

"Nah, nothin' like that. They went under 'cause they kidnapped me. They was fixin' to put my lights out me when my frien' Sheila came in. She sent them both to hell." That's when Billy felt the eyes of Rebecca.

The runt sat there for a minute thinking then looked over at Rebecca. The horses plodded along as the scenery came and went. The mountains were still in the distance, now they rode on the high prairie with the long-flowing yellow grasses.

"You know, Two Sticks, this's the first time I thought 'bout them bein' bad. They weren't the bad ones. I was. They was doin' what they wanted. I was sneakin' a peek. Bein' a busybody. What they did was between the two of 'em. I made it my business. I got 'em kilt. If'na I woulda minded my own business, they'd still be kickin'. I'd still be bussin' dishes an' Rebecca here would still be workin' in the galley. Shit." Bill went on.

"Have you learned anything from this?" Two Sticks asked.

"Yeah. I reckon I should mind my own goddamned business." Billy White sullenly responded. Rebecca clucked her horses to ride up front. She didn't speak to Billy the rest of the day. The foursome rode in silence into the dusk as the night cascaded upon them like a waterfall in the spring.

"I'm glad these horses can see 'cause I sure cain't." Bill spoke to nobody in particular, hoping for an answer. Nothing.

"Hey, Two Sticks, I'm jus' 'bout ready to fall off this here goddamned horse. Do ya reckon we could stop so at least I can take a piss?" He was hoping Rebecca and White Moon needed to also.

"We cannot stop yet. You will have to hold it or go while you ride." he said. Bill saw Rebecca's turn to look at him. He couldn't see her eyes, but he was hoping she had to go as bad as him.

"I reckon I can wait." he said as he watched the last ray of sunlight sink into the western mountains. Hours passed as the unlikely brigade rode farther into the Wyoming plains. Bill had been watching Rebecca through the bleak light. He came up next to Rebecca, catching her just as she began to fall off the horse.

"Huh? What's happened?" she spoke groggily.

"Relax, lover. You were fallin' off. I jus' held you up." Bill answered in the darkness to where she sat.

"I appreciate that." She yawned and stretched.

"No problem?" He made small talk.

"You still have to pee?" she asked.

"Yeppers."

Off in the distance, an elk bugled. Then another one answered. *Closer to us than to him.* He figured they'd get some grub, but it wasn't meant to be.

"Goddamnit! I had 'bout nuff of this horse-ridin' bullshit. I ain't sure where this South Pass place is, but we better stop soon 'er I was gonna have to piss myself." Billy spoke to the wind.

On into the late evening they rode. The stars were hidden by the deep black clouds, giving the plains an eerie inky atmosphere. Billy saw some movement from Rebecca, but before he could close the distance to help, she fell off. She hit the ground with a loud thud. *Funny though, she didn't even move after she had hit the ground*, he thought as he rode to her. As he approached her, Two Sticks came back looking down at Rebecca.

"Put her on with you so we can keep moving." Then he turned his horse and walked off. White Moon hadn't even stopped. She just kept plodding along. Bill did as he was instructed; he got down and tried to lift her up to the saddle. The small man failed miserably in this attempt as his brown horse shied away at the different rider as she awoke.

"What the hell happened?" About that time she realized that she was on the ground.

"I fell off, didn't I?" she asked quietly.

"Yeppers." he answered her in the darkness.

"Where are the others?"

"They kept movin'. Here let me help you up." Bill lifted her so she could sit backwards on his saddle. Then he grabbed her reins as he mounted behind the fiery redhead lifting her legs over his. He clucked his horse to move along, and soon White Moon's white buckskin dress shone out in the darkness.

Funny it stands out like that. White buckskins. Now ain't that somethin'? he thought. Rebecca had fallen back to sleep as she slouched over in his arms.

"Two Sticks, we really need to stop. These horses are gonna fall over soon, ya know." Bill spoke in frustration.

"White Man." He paused in the darkness.

"Our lives will be worth little if the Sioux find you out here. White Moon and I are in good favors with them at times, but you, well, they do not like the hair faces. If they find us together, it will be a slow death for all of us. It is better to be uncomfortable for a few nights than to go under forever." he spoke to Billy in the darkness.

That shut him up. On through the night they traveled. The horses didn't fall over, and they didn't go under.

Sometime in the early morning Rebecca awoke.

"Billy."

"Yeah."

"Thanks for helping out back there. So that's what really happened on the *Alice Mae*. Well, that's quite a tale. Any more dark secrets you want to tell me?" she asked.

"Well, now that you mention it, I have one."

"Don't tell me you like other men?" She laughed.

"Nah, nothin' like that. Remember all the stuff 'bout not havin' a real ma an' that stuff 'bout the big fat woman that wanted to poke me?"

"Yes." she answered quietly.

"Well, the truth is my mother and father were farmers. I didn't wanna farm, so I tolt 'em so. My father was a strong Bible man like you wouldn't believe. So one day our mule kicked me somethin' fierce, and I yelled Jesus Christ!' and my father said that was the last straw and tolt me to get. He gave me credit over in Dallas City to get a start. Well, my mother didn't like that as I was her son but not my father's." He paused.

"You say you were your mother's son but not your father's? You mean someone else poked your mother? Before your father?" she asked.

"Yeah, my grandfather. Damnedest thing. She and David, that be my grandfather, had a fling 'fore she hitched up with Matthew. She married Matthew, and I was born, and he thought I was his.

Anyway, when he kicked me out, then him an' her had a fight. He slapped her, she whacked him with a frying pan, so he kicked us both out." He stopped speaking as he thought about Ells.

"There's more, ain't there? You got a story to tell, ain't you? An' you wanna make sure I wanna hear. Damned runt." She leaned back and kissed his neck.

"Well, might as well keep telling it. Ain't got nuthin' else happen'." she spoke as she saw the white dress of White Moon slow to listen too.

"Is this the White Mans history?" she asked.

"Yeppers. It is." he answered back.

"Well, go on." she answered back from the side of them.

"Well, my grandfather passed away, and I was supposed to help bury him, but like I said, I got kicked out. Now my mother got kicked out as well. So we took off for Dallas City. Well me and her got to a field of wheat and she kissed me on my cheek and walked away.

When neither woman made a comment, he continued, "Anyway, that day we split up. I went'to old man Stiffer's to get me a poke with Katie, see I'd been pokin' the shit outta his daughter. God, she could suck a walnut through a keyhole. Anyway, he tolt me Matthew got kicked by Joe the mule. Kilt him dead. Well that ol'cuss Stiffer try to kill me. Chased me with dogs he did. Well now, I climbed a big ol'oak tree to hide in. Them Miami's found him, I think they was Miami's. Any way they kilt 'em and his fine pointer dogs." He paused, recollecting the story.

"The town of Dallas City was bad news fer me. Damned near got kilt again. Anyway I wandered next to the river 'till Beulah and Mary Jane found me and took me back to their fort. I couldn't believe it, Ells was the booshway there."

He coughed a few times clearing his throat, "Anyway them red nigger's attacked that night and me and her an' one nigger lived through it. We headed back to Dallas City to get our horses that got taken by the assholes in Dallas City. Anyway Ells and Ivory, that was her nigger's name, got kilt, and I skinned out." He paused.

"Go on." Rebecca asked almost immediately.

"Hold on. Hold on. I'll keep goin'." He reached up with his free hand and grabbed a fistful of red hair and pulled her back to kiss her on her lips, his tongue going into her mouth. She responded back. "Now where was I?" he asked.

"You and Ells and Ivory were goin' back for the horses." White Moon blurted out.

"Okay, we got back to town, and we found the store owner and the barkeep having them a bit of fun. Well now, Ells asked them nice where our horses an' deed to the property was, and sure 'nuff they was assholes about it. So Ells she broke the barkeep's arm and leg an' almost cut his piss'r off. She went off to the Justice of the Peace while me and Ivory went fer the horses. Well, Ells got killed, as did Ivory. I barely made it out. But I went back after dark to get my revenge."

He paused a bit then continued, "Yeppers I did. I made some snares up so that when someone opened the door it would rip his pecker an' nut sack off. At the same time, another rope would pull on her big ol' floppy tits an' run the hemp rope right through her fat twat. Figured it make up fer killing my mother." Billy stopped and let it all settle.

"That's how it all happened." He listened to the wind and waited for the story to steel in with the girls.

"There has to be more. So go on." Rebecca requested.

"Well now that you mention it, there is. See, I hooked up with some riverboat men. We got into a few fights with some Injuns an' one of the men got an arrie in the back. Put a damper on the boat too. See the way they worked it was pretty slick. They pull in to a little quiet area on the river an' I'd hop off. Then they'd go down river a few miles an' tie up an' wait fer me to find them with fresh meat. This par'ticular time I didn't get there quick 'nuff an' the Injuns found them first. Kilt them all, chopped them all to pieces too. I made an ambush with gun powder after that, blew 'em up purty good too, so after that, they left me alone.

I made it to Hannibal and got into trouble with the town bully. But." He waited for a moment, no one spoke and Billy knew they were hooked for the story, "I met a town cook, Maria. See she had been poked by some young buck, slam bam thanky mam an' didn't know about real sex like we have. Well, she was a looker too, but she kept herself all bundled up so no one really knew she was quite attractive. There I was, new face in town an' hornier than a two pecker'd billy goat. I got to show off all the stuff I had learn't. Damn girls, she got four 'er five outta me. She never knew 'bout her own little button, had no clue 'bout it. She got real good at finding an' using it by the end of the night. She wanted to get pregnant, said she wanted something that would always remind her of me. Anyway the town folks were in a tight spot. Me to leave on the *Alice Mae* or the bully of the town would throw the good folks out on their ear. Well, the rest is history." He waited and listened to the wind, but no sound answered.

"How about a poke?" Bill asked his lover and friend.

"I thought you had to pee. Do you think it'll be safe? I mean what if the horse spooks or we bump in to a bear or something?" she asked.

"Hell, we been sittin' fer a long time here. Let's go find out." Bill squeezed his thighs to his horse, causing it to change its pace. The three came even with Two Sticks. Bill asked, "Do ya reckon it'll be quiet fer much longer?"

"You should stop talking and listen to the night. It will speak to you if you listen." That was it. Question-and-answer time was over.

"So much fer a poke. You wanna get back on yer horse?"

"Yes. If I sit here much longer, I'm going to want you in me." With that, he pulled up to her horse until it was even with his. Then as graceful as a tree squirrel, she was off his and on hers. Bill laughed aloud.

"What?" she asked.

"If'n I tried that, I'd be flat on the ground like a sack of taters with everyone a laughin' at me."

CHAPTER 107

On into the predawn they rode. Then the sun came up. It was hotter than a two bit whore on a nickel night. Bill thought of pulling his buckskin shirt off, but he remembered the story of his white skin scaring off all the game. White Moon rummaged in her saddle pack and produced some pemmican to pass around.

"Well I'll be 'et fer a tater, looks like the same thing we ate a lifetime ago down when we stole that skin boat, lover? It still looks like a puddle of dog shit. Damn, it tastes purty good." Billy commented. The good thing was it filled up the hole in their gut.

Sometime in the late morning Two Sticks pulled up his horse, sliding off in one fluid movement. Being an excellent horseman, he never paused as he hit the ground. His eyes were searching, searching for something that wasn't right. As Billy watched, he figured it was a good chance to take a leak. As quickly as he dared he was off, pod in hand, showering the prairie dust with his urine. He watched as White Moon squatted down to make her water as did Rebecca.

Two Sticks was looking down at the ground, touching it softly. He turned slowly, looking all around them. The Pawnee stopped moving. Using his hand to shade his eyes, he looked to the east. Standing up, he rubbed them and looked again it appeared, he was straining to see the far distance. In quick clip of Pawnee, he spoke to White Moon as he threw a leg over his horse and rode off to the east.

"What's all that 'bout?" He asked her as she watched Two Sticks turn into a small speck. The runt looked to where the trader was going. That's when he saw the small specks.

"Holy shit, them Sioux?" Bill asked.

"He didn't know fer sure. We're to travel this way. Fast. Let's git." White Moon answered as she swiftly threw her leg on her mount, grabbing the packhorse's and moving off at a trot. He looked at Rebecca and she at him.

"Let's get!" he said as they both mounted. Catching White Moon was no easy chore either. She had her horse doing a full gallop as did he and Rebecca. Bill ventured a quick look back only to see Two Sticks coming after them hell-bent for leather. His black hair was flowing straight like a ruler as his horse ran like the wind. Bill figured that the Pawnee must have the fastest horse on the whole prairie the way he was catching up to them. The small white man stole a look back to see the specks were closing the gap.

"Aww, shit! So much fer not gettin' caught. Think you can shoot while we ride?" he yelled.

"I'll give it a try!" she screamed above the thundering hooves.

By this time Two Sticks had caught up with them as the others were closing quickly.

"Shit! Them boys have some fast horses. Is they Sioux?" Bill yelled.

"Yes!" yelled Two Stick as they galloped away for their lives.

"What do they want?" Billy looked over his shoulder and back to the Pawnee.

"Your scalps!" he shouted a reply.

"Rebecca! When I say, grab yer possibles an' pull up! We cain't outrun 'em. Let's fight! What do ya say?" he screamed. Two Sticks heard all this, his jaw dropping open.

"There are too many. We will go under if we stop!" Two Sticks yelled out.

"Rebecca!" Bill waited until they passed a buffalo wallow.

"Now!" Bill yelled. The Sioux never expected a redheaded woman with a white runt to stop and fight them. But that's what they did. Pulling around into the small buffalo wallow, they skidded to a sloppy halt. Bill grabbed an extra gun as did Rebecca along with their pistols and possible bags.

"Not too soon, lover!" They were coming at them in a full gallop. Bill didn't know about counting coup. All he knew was he was in danger and about to fight for his life.

"It'll be a cold day in hell 'fore them red niggers take this child's scalp!" As he was spouting, she fired. The blast from her flinter peppered the left side of his face, making him go deaf for a moment.

***

The Sioux warrior Red Calf had been blessed the morning of the hunt by Great Horn, the shaman. He was told he would get many of the shaggy beasts for the camp. Now he was dead; a fifty-four-caliber round ball removed the top of his head. He never even felt the pain or the fall to the ground.

Bill squeezed the set trigger, then let out a half of breath, and squeezed the front one. The roar of the gun almost surprised him as another Sioux went spinning backward off his pony with a crimson blossom on his chest from the large caliber ball that had just flew through him. Long Bow had no idea the whites could shoot that far. One moment he was going to lift hair, counting praises for him and his friends, and then he felt himself falling to the ground. Darkness crept into his mind as he waited for the grandfathers to come to him. Stands Tall and his three friends were becoming unsure of this buffalo hunted that turned in a scalp raid. So far Long Bow and Red Calf were both dead. Great Horn had said nothing about white men when he blessed the hunt. Now they looked to Wolf Killer for leadership.

Wolf Killer had no idea what to do other than kill the white men to add to his already great list of accomplishments.

"What are we to do, Wolf Killer? Do we leave to fight another day or rub these pesky white men out?" Badger asked. Badger was the youngest of the hunters. He was barely fourteen winters; this was only his second hunt with his uncle Red Calf. He only heard stories from his uncles of the white people on the prairies. They never said they would not fight. They said they ran like girls and messed themselves when they died. Now he looked over to see Red Calf, the top of his head gone. Long Bow's gaping chest wound was large enough he could see it from his horse. The uncle that had taught him to see visions now lay dead.

"I counted six when we started. That leaves four." Bill was calculating.

Wolf Killer made the decision, "No. We will not run. I'll show you my strength is great. Great Horn has told me I will not die today." With that the Sioux warrior kicked his pony viciously, sprinting to the wallow where the white people were making their stand. Rebecca fired her remaining gun, dropping Wolf Killer as he was beginning his race to death. He hadn't make it ten feet before he cartwheeled off the back of his spotted horse. He too died almost instantly. Billy's second gun misfired. The remaining three wheeled their horses around, running out of rifle range. Poor bastards didn't know about Rebecca. Their ponies raced off to the east at full speed, trying to outrun the lead hornets that were about to sting them. They pulled up and turned to see where the white people were or if they had remounted and began to run away.

Some movement caught the runt's eye. There was Two Sticks with his bow standing next to the runt, his chest heaving as he was catching his wind. He turned to see White Moon holding all their horses.

"Howdy Two Sticks." The blond runt smiled.

"Rebecca, think you could drop that horse closest to us?" the blond fighter asked. In her response, she hefted up her rifle to let a shot go. It was a sight.

Stands Tall was in charge now. He thought they were out of range of the white men now; he had no idea that a gun could shoot that far. The impact didn't killed the pony as it threw the rider to the ground. It was thrashing from side to side and finally died. Stands Tall stood there looking at his now-dead war pony, trying to think of what to do next.

"Here. Do another one." Bill gave her his now-reprimed rifle. She shot again. Badger's pony fell to the ground. No thrashing, a clean head shot. The young lad had just barely got off in time to avoid having his leg crushed by the falling horse.

"These white people are not men! They kill our ponies as they are afraid to fight!" Badger's pony may have been dead but not the young warriors spirit.

"Take the fight to those women White Bird! Show them they are no match for a Sioux warrior!" Badger was almost screaming as his oldest cousin. White Bird turned his horse and began to race toward the white men as fast as his horse could muster up.

"That makes three men an' one horse." Bill spoke to Two Sticks. Bill had been reloading the guns when Rebecca called to him.

"Mount up lover! Let's finish this!" she screamed as she yanked off her buckskin top while the runt was grabbing their mounts from White Moon. Two Sticks had never been around a woman like this. She was bare to the waist, her tanned breast beaming in the late-morning sun as she quickly threw a leg over her horse and was off to bring the battle to the Sioux.

Two Sticks was looking at the white trappers and then at the dead men out there trying desperately to get a grasp on what was transpiring before him. Then they were gone. A runt with a naked white woman taking the fight to the remaining Sioux warriors. He stood perplexed, thinking, *Never has such a thing ever happened, especially against the powerful Sioux. The white men always ran when a fight happened. They never attacked. It just didn't happen.* But here it was happening right before him. He went to speak, but there was no one to speak to. Rebecca's gelding was faster than Bill's mare, so she was on them before the white runt. White Bird had some sand as he was racing full tilt directly at the redheaded vixen. Two Sticks couldn't imagine what the warrior must of thought, he chuckled in the midst of the irony. Imagine what he was thinking seeing a redheaded bare-chested white woman closing to do battle in the heat of the day. He could only watch from a distance as the two crashed. The impact sent the two horsemen sprawling over the prairie.

White Bird saw the topless white woman riding at him, and he knew his medicine was strong today. *There was no way a white woman can best me!* he thought as the two horses crashed with such an impact they both flew off onto the brown waving grass. Rebecca felt the impact against her face as her gelding's head reared up, smacking her solid as she tumbled to the ground.

She got to her feet in time to move from the slicing knife of the Sioux warrior. White Bird had jumped to his feet and ran at the woman with his knife out as he slashed wildly at her. He got quick slice on Rebecca's breast as he turned to face her again. Then she was on him like a bobcat on a bear. He swung wildly. She didn't, and Rebecca's knife gutted him like a yearling calf. He looked down seeing his intestines spilling out onto his hands as he sunk to his knees; he looked up in time to see the red-haired woman's knife coming fast toward him. *Her hair is as red as vermilion. Her eyes are wild and as blue as the sky*, he thought as his life of sixteen winters flashed by.

Bill rode right past them as he went at the other two that were running toward Rebecca. The rifle roared as Bill gut shot Badger from the hip and pulled his pistol for the remaining. Badger never got an arrow loose as he prepared to aid White Bird. He was hoping Stands Tall would be next to him. But now his stomach was falling out into his hands as he looked down when he fell to his knees. Nausea came over him as he began to be aware he was not going to return home. He was going to die out here on the plains with his cousins and uncle, he never got a chance to sing his death song.

He fell to the dry grass as he saw the small white man ride by;

he noticed how weak he looked, his yellow hair flowing in the wind, the yellow hair on his face, and the blue eyes.

Bill fired the pistol at the running man. The ball struck the dirt in front of the Sioux. The warrior never flinched as the dirt peppered his bare legs. Bill continued on, swinging his rifle wildly at Stands Tall. Billy missed as the red man ducked and rolled, returning to his feet, never missing a beat.

Turning the horse, the blond wild man went directly at the running Sioux warrior. Bill's horse shied away from the human for a heartbeat, but Billy White reined it into the upright man, causing the horse to knock him over. Bill's horse caught on to kill after the initial impact. It jumped, bucked, and kicked the life out of the now-prone man.

Stands Tall was hoping to spook the horse and kill the rider when he fell off, but to his surprise the horse didn't flinch as he'd hoped. The last thing he felt was the unshod hoof crushing his head.

Two Sticks stood watching in disbelief in the wallow. Never before had he seen a horse kill. It was as if this horse had an evil spirit that was allowed free for the first time. Too many things had happened today that he was not ready to accept. The white runt fighting viciously, a horse that was evil like a rabid wolf, a redheaded white woman that liked to fight. He shook his head as he looked back at Bill's other wife. She stood there as quiet as a rock. No movement as her lover and husband wreaked havoc on the unsuspected Sioux warriors.

Bill timed the jumps and twists of his brown horse as he prepared to jump off; as she went to turn inward, he slid off to the outside, landing on his feet and did a quick double step. The raging horse continued to trample the now-dead Sioux warrior as Bill made his way to the gut-shot man.

It didn't stop his horse from continuing kicking and stomping the remains of a man. As he approached the almost-dead man, Bill noticed the man was trying to crawl away.

"Hell, you ain't goin' nowhere." Bill spoke to the wounded man, and then he rolled him over to look at his face. The boy's eyes glazed over as his spirit faded away.

"Hell, you're my age. Dumbshit." He shook his head.

"You shoulda stayed home today." Bill spoke in a low voice.

Badger felt he could crawl to safety, but he did not move when the yellow-haired man rolled him over. *He's so young,* Badger thought as he waited for his grandfather to come for him.

He's deader than last night's supper, Bill thought as he stood up looking over to see how Rebecca was doing with the other warrior. That's when he heard Rebecca scream holding up a scalp. *Damn! She's a mean one when she's riled up,* he thought as he went to scalping the now-dead gut-shot Sioux. Grizzly trophy in his hand, he approached his horse, which was now standing over the mangled body, pawing at it. Gore dripping from the scalp into the prairie dust, he approached the horse, speaking calmly to it.

"Well, did ya kill 'em good girl?" The horse looked at him, eyes wild. Bill thought for a minute. She was going to continue her rage on him, but she blew through her nose, showering the dead man with mucus. It nodded to Bill as he reached for her halter.

"Did I see you nod?" he asked, not sure of what he saw.

"Nah. You're a good girl, ain't ya?" he spoke softly as he caressed her ears. The horse bowed her head to let the man scratch more efficiently. He moved back to the saddle to tie the trophy on a narrow leather wang hanging from the side.

"Well, I best get what left of this here red nigger." he spoke soothingly to her. There wasn't too much to cut as the scalp was almost torn off. The lad hung his rifle on the saddle horn next to the bloody scalps. Hearing a horse, he turned to see Rebecca ride up leading the remaining pony. Bill walked up, reaching out to stroke its neck as it tried to back away from the strange new smells. He looked at its notched ears and wild eyes as it seemed to test the wind for a chance to break away.

"I reckon one more horse won't be a problem?" Billy smiled as he continued to try to caress the horse.

"Yeehaw! We showed them red niggers? White Man." Her right eye was turning black and blue from the horse crash.

"Hey, ya got a big ol'slice on yer tit lover!" Bill noticed as he mounted his own horse. The Sioux pony pulled free of her hand, running off to the east.

"Damnit! It looked like a good pony too! Ya know, looks like yer tit is always getting some attention!" Bill smiled at her.

"Let's get back so as I can scalp the others!" she yelled.

"Yee-hee. Hi-hi-hi. Yip-yip-yipee!" She was screaming, dancing her horse around in a tight circle. Her blood was running down to her waist, but she didn't seem to mind the black eye or the gash.

"Hurry up, Bill! I want to make sure Two Sticks don't take my scalps!" With that she turned her horse, galloping in the direction of the wallow.

"Hell, I hardly got in two words." Bill muttered. He looked over the battle scene. Then he looked down at his two scalps on the horn of the saddle.

"It was going perfect until the red sumbitches show'd up. Hell, I was close to a getting a poke too." he spoke to his brown horse.

"If I know'd Rebecca like I do, she be drippin' like a broken well pump." he continued to speak to her as he adjusted himself in the saddle. He rode up to the scene as he saw Two Sticks hand Rebecca the bloody trophies.

"Thank you for saving us. I was not sure if we could outrun them. But when you and the White Man stopped, I knew there was going to be no running. It is a good day to die, but you two fight as fierce as anyone on the plains!" As he spoke, Bill could see he was definitely glad they were the ones doing the fighting. His eyes were darting back and forth from the dead warriors then to the white people. Bill's buckskin shirt was soaked through in sweat as late morning had turned into early afternoon. The sun was racing once again for the distant mountains. Early evening wasn't too far away now, the South Pass was at least a week away.

"Let me sew up yer tit there, lover. Hell, lookie here! The two scars are so close that it looks like a bear marked ya. But we know different, don't we lover?" As Bill spoke, he pulled out his medicine bundle. Laying it down on the bare ground, he opened it up. Bill noticed Two Sticks had real interest in it as Bill began preparing his sewing kit.

"What?"

"This medicine bundle. Where did you get it?" he asked.

"We saw a fight between two tribes. Well, when it was all over, we walked in takin' what we wanted. Why?"

"This is Great Owl's medicine bundle. He was a great medicine man of the Crows. You say he was killed?" he asked.

"That be the tracks I'm leavin'." Bill answered.

"The others. Do remember how they were dressed? Like us?" He was pointing to himself and White Moon.

"Nah. These here moccasins are what they was a wearin', almost as good as the ones we got from you. Used 'em for a long time too. I suppose you knew where they came from too." Bill said as he threaded the needle.

"They are Arapaho. You have a way of seeing many tribes in a short time. Now you know what? Pawnee, Sioux, Crow, and Arapaho. The more you learn, the longer your scalp will stay yours." he said as he put his bow over his shoulder. Rebecca sat down as he got ready to start.

"Wait. I'll sew for you." White Moon took the needle from him.

"You jus' wanna hold on to her tit." The small man gave his good seat up.

"Yes. I like holding Rebecca's tit, but I can sew well. I can show you many things about making shirts and leggings. If you'd like to learn." Then she winked at the White Man.

Hell, he wasn't taken back one bit by her forwardness. *She's mighty good in the robes, and I still liked to see her naked butt.* Before Rebecca could worry about the pain, she was done with Rebecca, wrapping the extra sinew around a small stick.

"There. It'll heal quick now." Then she leaned down, circling Rebecca's red nipple with her tongue.

"Oh my! Two Sticks, let's stay here fer a while. These here women want something we can give! What do you say?" He was looking at Rebecca's nipples getting hard. Bill's pod was beginning to grow like green grass in the spring.

"I believe if you look out in the prairie, you will get your answer." he said, pointing out to the east. Bill shaded his eyes looking past the dead men; farther out he saw the movements of other riders.

"I see 'em. Sioux?" he asked.

"I do not want to wait to find out." was the reply Bill heard as Two Sticks was already mounted, heading toward the distant mountains.

"Girls, saddle up quick like. We gotta get the hell outta here." He grabbed Rebecca's horse for her so she could hop on.

"Let's git!" She mounted without another word as did White Moon. Bill threw a leg over his mare looking back at the eastern horizons.

"Two Sticks, how long do you reckon we got until were deep in the mountains?" Bill quizzed.

"Not soon enough from what I see." They took off for the west at a ground-covering lope. Rebecca had put her war shirt back on, the long fringe on the arms flowing in the breeze.

"Could you see them, or do you feel them coming?" she asked Bill as they rode.

"Saw 'em. It will take 'em a while. It might wear their ponies down tryin' to catch us. Them rascals will most likely have caught that pony that got away by now. That'll help 'em out jus' fine too." he spoke to her as they rode west.

"Hey, I couldn't do anything about it. The one I had was too strong to hold, okay?" she spouted.

"I wasn't talkin' ya down lover. I was jus' makin' some cipherin'. Now lookie here. We'll have to load as we ride. I plum fergot to load while you was gettin' sewed up." The runt spoke as he pulled the possible bag around in front. Bill began the chore of loading as the horse loped along. It was difficult. He'd handed one gun after another to Rebecca as she hung it from her saddle horn waiting for Bill to finish the first. As they rode, Bill loaded. He spilled a lot of powder and dropped a couple of balls but got all four long guns loaded. With the last one loaded and primed, she handed Bill back his second weapon. He hung it as Rebecca had done. Then he reached for his pistol. Balancing the butt on his leg, he loaded it, spilling powder as well as dropping two balls in the process.

"Finally. Shit. Rebecca. Hand me your pistol." he asked as he shoved his into his wide belt. She reined her horse closer to her lover to make the hand off. Bill loaded hers in the same manner but didn't drop a ball this time.

"Here." he called to her in the late afternoon.

He looked over at White Moon as she rode along, pulling the packhorses. Bill pondered, *Damn, she reminded him of that consarned Ann. Ann could be nice when she wanted to, but most of the time she was as mean as a wounded badger. I'm glad to be shut of her.*

CHAPTER 108

On through the afternoon and into the evening they rode. Finally Two Sticks reined up to walk the horses. The animals were covered in lather as they had been used hard. Billy had kept looking back to see if he could spot the Sioux that had been following them. Nothing was visible. But that doesn't mean the warriors weren't after them. As long as they were leaving tracks they'd be followed.

"You reckon they lost interest or went back for more help?" Bill asked Two Sticks as the sun turned into an orange orb in the western sky.

"I would say they went back in shame. They lost six of their fellow warriors in a simple hunt. These things are very bad medicine for anyone, let alone the brave Lakota Sioux."

"Humph." was all the bored runt could muster up, but he still looked over his shoulder for any sign of pursuers.

***

The days began to bleed from one to next as Suiox/Cheyenne threat diminished. Now they could travel carefree and relaxed. The antelope and huge jackrabbits filled their bellies as they plodded through the high landscape. The small goat like creatures were not familiar with humans and horses. Bill could walk up within rifle range easily as they would flip their ears, trying to figure out a horse and rider.

"Them antelope as sure a curious critter, ain't they?" Rebecca asked Bill one evening as they had one of the goatlike creatures cooking over a buffalo dung fire.

"I cain't say I really like it. Maybe it would taste better cooked over some wood instead of these buffalo shit pies." Bill answered.

"I like it. Tastes goddamned good. Fucking excellent." White Moon chirped in. She'd been enjoying the use of the American slang for months now and was becoming proficient at her choice of words.

"Christ, Moon, you can cuss right fine." Rebecca smiled at her brown-skinned lover.

"Thank ye kindly Rebecca." White Moon smiled at the compliment. That night they set up a cold camp, far from where the fire had been. Each had the lead rope around their waist and tied to a saddled horse.

***

In the morning they hit the saddle again, heading west. Once again rolling hills awed them as they traveled through the waist-high grass; a light wind blowing the grass made it look like waves made the traveler feel as if they were riding through an ocean of grass. Not to be left out of the show, the bright sun baked them as they closed the distance to the South Pass with the high winds and temperatures dropping every night. It kept them forever adding and shedding clothes. They rode to the south end of the now Laramie Mountains. Then they turned north. With the Laramie Mountains on the east side and the Medicine Bow Mountains on the west, they closed the distance to the South Pass. The daylight began to fade as the scenery changed from prairie to scrub brush. Then it went to rocks and trees to just wonderful tall trees as they proceeded toward the Willow Valley in Utah.

"We will stop soon. It will be good to have a safe camp for us." Two Sticks paused waiting. He knew it get Billy's curiosity.

"Now why is that?" Billy asked curiously.

"We are in the land of the Snakes or Ute's. They hate the Sioux, and the Sioux knows this. Their heart will burn with revenge, but they will not come with a scalping party. Blanket Chief is a friend of the Snakes, so they will not harm you as you are white like him." he said as he pulled up into a grove of pines and oaks.

"Who's this Blanket chief?" Bill White asked as Rebecca was craning her neck to hear the answer as well.

"The white man called Bridger." he answered as he dismounted.

"Hey! I've heard of him. That's the fell'r them skin trappers was always jabberin' 'bout. They called him ol'Gabe an' was always yarnin' 'bout him. They was always sayin' he was the shit in the mountains." Bill rambled on as he began making a picket line for the horses.

"These thing you say are true." That was that. He turned his back to Bill as he began unpacking his mount. *Hum. Maybe now I can get some grub an' a poke. Hell, maybe two pokes.* As he reached up to help Rebecca down, his hand slid under her shirt. It didn't go as the young trapper thought it would. When her weight came down, it pulled the white lad's arm out from under her, where it was about to create mischief.

"You'll have to wait for a while until the camp set up." She leaned over, kissing him. She was gone before he could grab a handful of her.

"White Man's in a hurry to get his honey dobber wet, isn't he?" White Moon spoke matter-of-factly.

"I'll do ya both! So don't go waitin' too long, ya hear!" Bill smiled in the darkness at the two women. Rebecca had a small fire going in nothing flat as the light soon filled their small camp, bringing some warmth to his tired bones.

"Hell, listen to me whine. I ain't twenty-two yet I'm a soundin' like an ol'timer." Bill spoke aloud to the small fire.

"You are like a stud in the spring White Man. You cannot think of anything except mounting the young fillies." Two Sticks's voice came from the darkness.

"Don't tell me you don't get horny. Shit! That's all I think 'bout when I ain't bein' run down by a bunch of them murderous red bastards out there in the prairie. No offense Two Sticks." Bill quickly added.

"None taken." Two Sticks answered from the darkness. Bill continued, "I was sittin' on the goddamn horse fer so long I figured my piss'r done went back to St. Louis fer lack of attention." Billy laughed aloud.

"You privates cannot leave you unless someone cuts them off. Then you should be dead. No man wants his manhood cut off." the voice said as he came into the light.

"Hell, I wasn't serious Two Sticks. I was jus' sayin' I want'n a poke somethin' fierce 'bout now." Bill reminded himself that sometimes the language barrier was there. He thought, *Two Sticks is way too serious. Shit, he wasn't that way before. Or was he?* Bill pondered. *All we did was trade, making small talk back on the Lower Platte.*

"Goddamnit, Bill! I'm tired of you belly aching about wanting a poke. White Moon, would you mind getting the camp going while I poke this miserable peckerwood?" Rebecca said.

"Only if he fucks me afterward!" She laughed.

"Hot damn! That's what I wanted to hear!" Bill called out.

"You are going to mount both women? How is it you can do this? The Snake are sure to come to investigate the smoke. It is better to wait until the rendezvous. It is only three or four moons away." As he spoke, Bill was pulling his root out, stroking it slowly, bringing it to life. It didn't take too long until it was stiff as a hickory stick and waiting to slip into some wet valley. Rebecca had lain back with her war shirt hiked up. As sure as the snow in the pass, her red valley was dripping wet. Her slippery wet hairs were reflecting the light of the fire as he walked over to her, reminding him of wet grass in a meadow.

"What are you waiting for? Come an' get with it!" she said in a sweet voice.

"Fuck her hard Billy White. Do it's upright." piped in White Moon as he slipped into Rebecca.

"Yeppers." The hot juice slipped around the stick he was planting, adding a sensation that Bill hadn't felt in quite a long time. He went slow at first as Rebecca rose up to meet him on each stroke. As her breathing sped up, he pressed faster. The white lad plunged deeper into the red garden of hers. Sloshing noises of sex made him go faster with each stroke.

"Hear. I. Come!" Bill called out in short breaths.

"Not yet! Hold on." she said.

"Okay. Get ready. Now!" she yelled, thrashing her head violently from side to side. He buried the root deep, planting the seeds of life into his redheaded partner.

"Umm. That ye kindly young man." she said with an old woman's voice as she stuck her fingers inside to pull out her treat. Into her mouth it went. *That Rebecca don't waste none of that stuff. That's fer certain an' fer true!* Bill thought as he watched.

"You ain't forgotten me, have you?" White Moon asked. Her voice was so smooth when she spoke to Billy it always made him smile. He turned to her voice, seeing she was in the same position as Rebecca was, except she was on the other side of the camp.

"Nah, 'ain't fergot ya." He hobbled over to her on his knees.

"I'll help your soft piss'r." As she grabbed his pod, she started stroking it back to life. He looked down at her black hair. It looked thicker than a blackberry briar patch in the summer.

"Damn! Did'ja grow more hair since I saw'd you?"

"Hell no, come on, fuck me like you did that goddamned Ann. Come on, slip 'er in my asshole, you little white prick. Do my ass like you did Ann." With that she turned around as she put her forehead on a coyote skin. Then she spread her ass cheeks for the white trapper.

"Ann taught you real good 'Merican Moon."

"Never mind that. Give it to me, you fuckin' runt!" she pleaded in her best American slang. He reached down, spreading a little wider as he slipped in her garden first. Stroking slowly as to get her riled up, Bill plunged on. Looking down, he dribbled a stream of spit on her brown opening as he continued. Black hair hid the dark slippery entrance as Bill pulled out; he put the tip on her opening and pushed slowly. Rebecca looked at Two Sticks; he was mesmerized by the show before him. His mouth was hanging open in awe. Then pop. He slipped into her, starting his journey to heaven. As Bill stroked, she crawled over to White Moon and reached down under her to rub the button of life. Billy continued as he felt her tighten up.

"Oh, oh" was all she said as she lunged forward, causing Bill to spray her bronze backside with a stream of seed.

"Ann taught me how to be ass fucked. It hurts so good. Do it again. Don't wait until later. Do it again." she begged as her hand rubbed the spooge on her backside.

"I have never seen such a thing. You have gone from one to the other without waiting. How is it you can do this? You have strong medicine. I shall call you Two Times. It is a name that honors you." he spoke watching the show.

"Come back here, Bill. I want some more of you!" said Rebecca. So back he went to her. Rebecca spun around, slithering up to him. She stuck her red head between his legs, pulling his nut sack into her mouth while stroking his pod. It wasn't too long until the white runt was hard again, but she kept after his nut sack just the same. Movement caught Bill's attention as he noticed White Moon go for a snack at Rebecca's red garden. Her black hair covered the crotch of his redheaded lover, but Rebecca kept after his pod with quick jerks.

"Oh, here I come Moon." Then she pulled hard on his root as she arched her back. White Moon came up looking like a glazed ham on Easter Sunday.

"You taste goddamned good, not like the other bitches in my

village. Now I have Bill to finish." With that she straddled Rebecca, her briar patch dripping on Rebecca's stomach. Then she leaned down to put the runt's pod in her mouth, which put her tits right in Rebecca's grasp. As White Moon was slurping and slopping, Bill White looked over at Two Sticks. The native was sitting there slack-jawed at the fact that Bill could do it three in a row. Rebecca came out from under him looking at Bill and then at him.

"Two Sticks, why don't ya come poke one of these fine women." He stopped mid-sentence as Moon gave Bill her full attention, "Oh my! White Moon, you got a way with yer tongue." Bill shuddered as his bronze wife wrapped her tongue around the hoe handle of Bills.

"You do not care if I mount one of your wives?" he asked.

"Better than that, Two Sticks. I'll poke you until you can't walk. Now how's that sound?" Rebecca called out as Bill's nut sack slipped to the side of her face. It was too much for Bill, "On the way Moon" as he unloaded down Moon's slim throat. Not missing a beat she swallowed effortless.

"Thanks Bill, that was perfect." his Pawnee beauty spoke.

"I will need to walk in case the Snakes arrive unannounced." he spoke with no emotions.

"Goddamnit, Two Sticks! I'm not saying you won't be able to walk. It's just a way of describing the pleasure that I can show you. I ain't saying you won't be able to walk." Each of them wiped off and began getting dressed and arranging the the camp. Her sentence stopped without finishing. White Moon heard the horses nickering and spoke quietly to Bill, "Bill, someone is coming." With that, she slowly pulled her dress up to allow quick movements .

CHAPTER 109

The White Man had noticed the horses' uneasiness also as the strange smell came on the breeze. *That's white men,* he sniffed again, *yep filthy ones fer sure. Most likely trappers fixin to bushwhack us.* He made eye contact with Rebecca motioning her to slip away. She picked up a pair of pistols and vanished like a ghost out side the firelight. He made eye contact with White Moon as she smoothly filled her hands with a gun. Two Sticks had been oblivious to the horses or Rebecca fading from sight. Bill cradled his gun across his arm and mentally prepared himself.

Sam Baker and Russell Kincaid were trying to creep up on the camp and hadn't counted on the horses being a nuisance. They had smelled the smoke and decided to make and easy score. How hard could it be, a few white people that were most likely on their way to the rendezvous. *That means pelts, lots of pelts*, Sam Baker thought.

"Not sure about how many they be, so Joe, you and Loui circle aroun' back of 'em and we'll keep 'em busy. When I holler out ya'll be ready. Got it?" they leader whispered.

"Got it." They nodded in the dark. They never saw the redhead vanish and they never realized the little brigade had prepared for the worse. The bushwhackers figured they'd surprise them, take everything and kill everyone. When they were sure they had the camp surrounded, they made their announcement.

"Hello, the camp!" a voice sounded from the darkness. Bill pulled the hammer to full cock.

"Speak yer peace!" Bill bellowed out in his most threatening voice. He quickly thought, *Hell, most likely sounded like a Sparrow Hawk or something.* Nevertheless, he was serious. The men began entering the camp. Bill looked over to see that Two Sticks's bow had filled his hand.

"Sam Baker an' Russell Kincaid. We'd like to come in a parley a tad." the voice said. The runt looked over to Two Sticks. He nodded.

"All right come on in." Billy White returned the call as he pulled the set trigger; it went unnoticed as the visitors filed in, the first white men they'd seen since their friends had been butchered. They weren't much different than Bill, maybe so a couple of inches taller and a few years older. Both of them had dark hair with shiny beards from lack of cleaning and from the grease of many a meal. Their dark-stained buckskins had fancy quill work with beads near the fringe, showing that they lived with or been around some bands of Indians, though Bill couldn't tell which ones.

"I'm the White Man, and this is Two Sticks." Bill pointed to his Indian friend.

"This's White Moon my wife." Bill spoke, not lowering his gun. Something wasn't right. Bill could feel the hairs standing up on the nape of his neck, just like when he was getting ready to get into a fight.

"Lookie here, we don't want no trouble. We's on our way to the rendezvous. We saw yer fire. Well, we was jus' lookin' fer some traveling company. Now if'n you folks don't want us, well then, we'll skedaddle right gone." The taller of the two spoke. He smiled. His rotten teeth glimmered in the firelight.

"Here, let's have a smoke to relax a bit." he spoke too smooth. Something wasn't quite right, but Bill couldn't put his finger on it. *Now I remember. Dan'l had said not to trust nobody too far. Well, 'till you knew 'em anyway,* came back the instructions from his long-gone friend.

"You wanna call yer frien's in from outside the camp. I 'magine they'd want a smoke too." Bill spoke to Sam, not moving an inch.

"How is it you know that's more of us?" he asked.

"It jus' goes to figure. That's what I'd do. Leave some outside case it goes to hell in a handbasket right off the get-go." Bill spoke to Russell this time. The partner turned his head, calling out,

"Come on in boys!" From outside the camp, two more buckskin-clad men came in, their fur hats hiding most of their faces. *Looks like a coyote an' a gray fox. Right nice ones too,* Bill thought as he watched them walk in.

"You folks had a good season of trappin'." Sam mentioned, pointing at the bundles of fur.

"Fair. How 'bout you?" Bill replied, not taking his eyes off Sam. Something just wasn't right. He couldn't put his finger on it, but it didn't set too well. Bill was glad Rebecca was outside the camp waiting.

"We did fine up on the Powder 'til the goddamn Crow stole our horses an' plews!" said one of the new faces.

"I heard them Crow will do that kinda thing." Bill said, still holding his gun on those supposed bushwhackers. Then it all came together. They were fixing to skin them out for everything they had. That's the only thing Bill could come up with.

Shit maybe not, maybe they's jus' had hard luck. If the Crow did all that they say, then it's a rotten shame. Two Sticks said they's steal the shirt off your back if'n a body wasn't careful. Bill was confused as he stared at these men, trying to make the right decision, but he could see the Crow stealing traps, and the Arapaho were doing that exact same thing when he and Shannon surprised them. *It could happen,* he thought. *But I just don't feel right with these fellers. Damp powder fer sure losing everything.*

"Ya know, Sam, this child's gots a problem." Bill spoke to him as the other walked up next to Sam. Rebecca had been watching and listening to the whole conversation and didn't like the way it was turning out one bit. She cocked each pistol quietly. She kept her eyes on them as she rested on the trigger guard on her forearm waiting for the situation to change from bad to worse as the last one stood in line with Russell.

That's poor judgment call on their part. She calculated the shot as she watched the men forming a crude firing line. Bill spoke as she readied herself for the battle, "I'm figurin' on which one of you niggers is gonna go under first." Then Rebecca stepped out, pistol pointed at Sam.

"You cain't get us all." Russell spoke out pretentiously. Bill wasn't relieved by this statement. He was hoping for them to call it all off, say it was a mistake on their part and have a peaceable smoke in friendship.

"No. But I reckon you'll be the first. After that, you won't care now will ya?"Bill saw him bring his gun up a smidgen, so the barrel was slowly aiming toward him. Bill didn't hesitate. He pulled the trigger, blowing Russell off his feet, and in a heartbeat later Rebecca's pistol went off almost the same time. Sam joined his friend on the ground like a mule had kicked him.

"Hold on! Don't shoot! Don't shoot!" Louis Osborne called out, his voice crackling. He and Joe Roushe dropped their rifles, raising their hands. The roar of the guns had left Bill a tad bit deaf. *All I could see was them two rascals raise their hands through the smoke.* One was moaning on the ground.

"Bill, grab their guns." She kept her loaded pistol on the remaining men.

"White Moon, do ya think ya can finish that'un off?"

"Yeppers Billy." Then she vanished. Then the noise stopped.

"Mister, you're a coldhearted fucker. All we wanted was to smoke to get frien'ly." Louis was making his speech as Bill brought the extra gun into play. He checked the pan for powder; seeing it was good in the dim light of the fire, he listened. Rebecca had picked up her rifle and checked it also.

"I'm figurin' to send these pricks to hell with their frien's." Rebecca recovered her weapons as Bill covered the men who had botched the bushwhacking.

The whole time Two Sticks didn't know what to make of all this with white men killing one another. He thought the White Man and his wife had lost their minds, but these men had come here to murder them all just as the Sioux or the Arapaho had been trying to do.

"Are you going to kill these white men?" Two Sticks asked.

"If I don't, they'll be prisoners the whole way to the rony'viou. They'll make up some cock-an'-bull story, shoutin' it out to whoever will listen. They ain't no better than the ones I kilt in Missouri. They're sumbitches that rob honest folks, then lie to whoever 'bout how they bought everything fer a fair price. Yep. I reckon I'm gonna put their lights out." Bill was fixing to spout some more, but Rebecca's gun went off, splattering Joe's heart into the darkness. That left Louis standing alone and visibly shaken. He was looking to Two Sticks for any sign of help, and then he pissed himself as Bill pulled the trigger. Four shots. Four dead men.

"Damnit! Death does follows us like the plague, eh, lover?"

"You didn't have to kill them all. You have become as evil as the Blackfoot or the Arapaho." said Two Sticks as he turned walking out of the firelight.

"Yeppers I have. But I'm alive to spin the yarn. These here fell'r's came here to kill an' rob us, an I for one ain't ready to die."

"Grab their possibles. You get your two scalps and I get my two. Well, if White Moon wants one, I'll give her one of mine. She did finish the one I shot after all." Rebecca said matter-of-factly.

"I'll get my own Rebecca. I gots to keep my image of being Billy White's wife. Wouldn't be no good to him if I didn't pull my share. Ain't that right?" Moon said and returned with a dripping scalp. She tied it to her belt as the blood and gore dripped on her white dress. She began picking up the bandits possibles.

"Rebecca, when are we gonna meet more good folks like Dan'l, Mel, an' Alison? I mean Two Sticks is a right fine man, but there has'to be some good white niggers. Don't there?" he said somberly as he started dragging the dead men out into the night. As he was walking back, Two Sticks fell beside him.

"White Man, I think you were wrong to kill these men. But I also know now that they would be doing evil to us later. There was no good way out. Tomorrow I will leave you. You kill too easy. I am a trader, and I do not want to be around you when others find out their friends are dead. I will leave in the morning." With that he vanished in to the night. Bill walked into the light as Rebecca was inspecting the locks on the rifles they had just got.

"Bill, you know we now have eight rifles? Shit! We must have more guns than most folks will ever see." Rebecca said proudly.

"White Moon, are you gonna stay with us or go off with Two Sticks?" Bill asked her.

"Hell no! I'm your cocksucking wife goddamnit. I'll never leave you." she spoke as she went about the task of pulling Louis Osborne's carcass out of the camp. When the last of the corpse were gone, he looked at his wives, thinking about how things were going for them.

"White Moon, we're gonna teach you to shoot tomorrow. We've got 'nuff lead to spare. Rebecca, let's go get them fur hats off them dead niggers. They appear to be of good quality. I 'spect we'll needin' them come the first snow." With that he turned walking out into the darkness to retrieve the hats from the corpses. As he bent down, he heard Rebecca walking up.

"Them rascals were going to kill us, weren't they?" she said as she stood there watching him with the light of the campfire illuminating the chore.

"Yeppers." he answered as he turned to walk back to camp.

"They weren't lying about no horses or gear. They were poor, I reckon that explains why they turned to desperate acts."

CHAPTER 110

The trio got snuggly for the night, one woman on each side of him but still no Two Sticks. Bill figured he had no stomach for fighting. The runt could see his point though. The Pawnee wanted to trade with everyone, and if he was involved in a skirmish, well, no telling who would be the last man standing. But he was hoping to sell to the victors. Then he realized how vulnerable they really were.

"Do you reckon we oughta have someone stay up to keep a look out?" he asked his partners as he felt a hand going for his breechclout.

"I'll stay up and keep the first watch. When I cain't keep my wits up, I'll wake one of you." Rebecca volunteered.

"But how 'bout getting a taste first?" She asked.

"Sure thing lover." She was under the robe in an instant pulling Bill's stick out and placed in her mouth, true to form she made Bill pop quickly. Then she was up as fast as a summer storm, letting a cold rush of air go under the heavy buffalo robes as she went to stand watch.

"How about my turn there Bill?" White Moon asked. The blond man smiled as White Moon opened her arms to Bill, "Ah, my work is never done." He rolled over into the Pawnee'sweet garden. Just like always, she was ready to go.

He was awakened by the smell of meat sizzling on a fire. The songbirds were up, making their presence known by filling the air with joyful songs.

"Christ! Don't they ever get tired of singin' an' whistlin'?" the runt began bitching. He looked up to see both of his wives were preparing the morning meal for him, but on the left sat Two Sticks.

"What the hell? I figured you'd skinned out last night?" the white runt slurred, yawning as he stood to go to relieve himself.

"I am going to stay with you and the women. It is better to travel in a group than by myself." he called out to Billy White as the runt pulled out his erect manhood.

"Damn, if Rebecca sees I got this hard-on, she'll never let me get any grub." he spoke quietly as he closed his eyes and thought about the oncoming day. Then he felt her hand.

"Aw, goddamnit!" he mumbled, more amused than upset.

"Jus' wanted to take a leak an' eat." he whined.

"You didn't figure to get away with that, did you?" she asked as she slid around in front of him on her knees.

"Rebecca, I gots to piss real bad." he continued.

"You can piss after I had myself a snack. White Moon! Do you want any of this?" she bellowed out from around Bill.

"Yes. Don't let Billy White spill a drop on the ground. I'll be there in two shakes." she said as she finished her cooking chores quickly. The runt figured Two Sticks wouldn't be happy with this turn of events. *The hell with him! I like to have my root sucked on whenever I can.* He watched Rebecca's mouth engulf his swollen member. Slowly her head began to bob for a few strokes. Then all he could see was a red blur as she went about her morning chore. Closing his eyes, Bill relished the feeling of oral sex as he heard White Moon walking up. She too squatted down on her knees before the young blond trapper, waiting for her turn to pull on the young man's pod. Rebecca pulled her mouth away, giving White Moon a turn. They were taking turns when he looked up to see Two Sticks approaching. Bill figured he was going to start bellyaching about being in Snake country or something, like he always does.

"I have thought about the way you do things White Man. Perhaps it is better to have sex today, for tomorrow we know not lies in our path. If your offer still stands about having sex with your wives, then I am ready." They both stopped, turning their heads, looking at him then at each other.

"You want'a a go ahead and finish the White Man, I'll do Two Sticks." Rebecca said. Bill was pleased that White Moon had learned from Rebecca as she now had a way with her mouth. It wasn't anytime until he felt the tingling of a load getting close to coming out.

"You ready there, girl?" She nodded without missing a stroke. He popped in a heartbeat after that. She stood wiping her mouth off on the back of her hand.

"You got a good taste. Now you can take yer piss." She turned walking back to the sizzling meat.

Damn. It don't get no better than this! he thought as he looked over to see Two Sticks grasping Rebecca's ears. *Damn, if he ain't careful, he'll pull them rascals off,* Bill thought as he watched his wife. He turned toward them as he relieved himself. He wasn't even done pissing when ol' Two Sticks unloaded on her. Rebecca's head jerked back as she coughed up a load onto the ground.

"Good lord! When was the last time you got some?" She kept coughing up the white seeds of life.

"Many moons." he said as he was putting his penis away.

"Well, you should pop your load more often than that. Shit! You damn near drown me with that!" She stood up, wiping her mouth.

"Damn! That White Moon's in for a surprise today." She laughed as she whacked her knee. The whole time Bill was watching, he finally laughed aloud.

"I do believe this will work out jus' fine." he spoke to the trio before him.

"What's the joke?" asked White Moon with her back to Rebecca.

"You'll find out when it's your turn to pull on Two Sticks's pod." Rebecca answered.

"Oh, you mean because he squirts more than a young bull?" she answered without turning away from the cooking chores.

"You knew? Why didn't you tell me?" she asked with her hands on her hips.

"You didn't ask, bitch." She chuckled.

"Well, you got me there." Rebecca chuckled, "you black-haired slut!" Then she walked over to White Moon. Leaning down, she planted a big sloppy kiss on Moon. She sat down next to her as Bill walked to the fire to take a piece of meat from the green sapling over the fire.

"Damned fine cooking girl."

"Your wife is strange. One moment she says strong words. Then she shows affection. I do not understand." Two Sticks said as he took a small chunk of antelope, shook his head looking at the two.

"Your wives cook good."

"Jus' be glad your on our side. She can be mean as a wounded grizzly when she wants to be." Bill stood looking at the girls.

"Last chunk here girls." The remaining piece sizzling over the fire.

"Yes, I have seen her angry. There is all that's left of the ones who have crossed her." He was pointing to the scalps on top of her saddle.

"How much longer 'fore we get to this here rony'viou?" Bill asked. As he waited for the answer, he went on, "How 'bout givin' me some of yer 'baccy? I ain't had me a smoke in a long time."

Two Sticks got up to go to the bags where his goods were stored.

"Go head Bill, I'm good." Rebecca called out."

"I'll take that piece White Man when I start tearing down the camp." White Moon chimed in.

"Maybe three moons." He handed Bill the plug of the tobacco, and as he went to put the plug in his pocket, Two Sticks's hand went out.

"What? You want the plug back?" Bill quizzed the Pawnee.

"Yes, I will sell it at the rendezvous to the other trappers." he said solemnly.

"Well, I know there's gonna be whiskey an' such things there, but what else?" Bill asked the pair of Pawnee's sitting with him.

"There will be games of chance. I'll show you a few so you will not lose everything. Then there will be fights over whiskey. There will be many tribes there also. The Shoshone, Snake, Crow, Sioux, Nez Pierce, and maybe some Arapaho."

"Hey, I thought they was the ones we jus' killed on the way here?"

"They were Sioux. Everyone puts aside their differences for the rendezvous, they all want to trade with the white people. For the whiskey, tobacco, cloth, vermilion, buttons, and tools." he answered.

"Let's get away from here. Them niggers is smellin' powerful bad." Bill had barely closed his mouth when the girls started breaking camp.

"I'm glad you finally said something, I don't think I could stand the smell too much longer. Maybe we should have buried them? At least they wouldn't be stinking to high heaven." Rebecca complained.

"I'm glad we're getting the hell outta here." White Moon said as she flung a leg up on her saddled horse. She bit the last portion of the meat and tossed the remainder in the smoldering fire pit. Bill watched his well-oiled machine perform. The camp was cleaned up in a heartbeat. Not a speck of their existence was left. A few hoof prints and some moccasin tracks. As Bill threw a leg over his mare, he looked around.

"Yeppers, death does follow us like a bad storm. Off to the rony'viou girls." he called out as he clucked his mare to leave.

CHAPTER 111

They rode throughout the day, not seeing hide nor hair of a single human. Plenty of deer and elk were everywhere; they even saw some grizzly bears off on the hillside. The small brigade rode through the day and into the night, chasing the sun into the western mountain when Bill marveled at the view.

"God, it's so pretty. Not like back east with the red an' yella leaves an' such but jus' the size of everything kinda takes yer breath away." he spoke aloud not to anyone in particular. They pulled under some ponderosa pine trees and began the ritual of setting the camp up again.

"My rump is sore from sitting, Bill. I think you're gonna have to rub it for me tonight." She giggled.

"He's gonna have to do mine as well, but I want my pussy rubbed instead. That's where I'm sore." she said with head lowered, her eyes looking up at Bill shyly.

"Hey, Two Sticks, these here women folks is all tired from ridin'. They's needin' some attention. You may have to help." Billy White called to his Pawnee friend.

"I too am tired. When you have finished the girls, I will already be asleep." he spoke as he pulled the pack off his ponies.

"What's yer pleasure tonight there, ladies ? Elk? Deer? Rabbit? Turkey?" Bill looked at them as he spoke, catching a glimpse of flesh from Rebecca, making him want her for supper with White Moon for dessert.

"It's too damned dark for you Bill. You won't be able to see once you're out there. I'll go after I get this fire going, okay?" Then she winked at the blond man standing there with his bow and quiver in his hand.

"Damn, that girl is sassy." Bill spoke as she faded out of sight in to the near darkness.

"You do not worry about her?" asked Two Sticks as he slumped against a packsaddle.

"Nah. I worry 'bout the rascals she bumps inta." Bill answered as he reached out to the Indian with his palm up. Two Sticks looked at the runt waiting for the young man to speak. Bill finally broke the silence.

"How 'bout givin' us a plug there, Two Sticks?"

"I will have to start charging you for tobacco soon. You are smoking up my cache of trade goods." He laughed, tossing a plug into the young man's hand.

"Thank ye kindly." Billy said and sat down with his back against a tree to watch White Moon do busy work around the camp.

"White Moon, what do ya say 'bout takin' yer dress off? Then runnin' around here buck naked?" he joked with her. Two Sticks's head just about snapped off. It went to look at Bill so quick. Never before had he been around such people.

"Sure thing Billy White." She walked over to the place where her pack was. She stood on some furs that were lain out and dropped her dress. All she had on was her thigh-high legging and her moccasins.

Bill was in awe over the sight of this Indian maiden before him. Her inky black hair hung past her shoulders, cascading over her perfectly shaped breasts and onto her well-formed ribs. His eyes continued to follow the beautiful hair as it flowed to her narrow waist, curved hips, and her deep black groin hair. It was so thick it hid all the secrets Bill wanted to see.

"You know, Moon, I think I'm gonna give you a haircut. What do you say to that?" Bill asked her.

"I don't reckon it couldn't hurt, now that you mention it, this goddamned hair is thicker than a buffalo hump." With that her hand went down to the black mound, pulling it apart to reveal the dark moist valley Bill had become accustomed to playing in.

"Two Sticks, you got anything to cut hair with?" Bill pondered, rubbing his wispy beard.

"I have traded for something that might work for you. I traded two foxes for them. I will get them for you." Then he was up and gone faster than a weasel stealing an egg. He returned with a set of small hand-forged black scissors, handing them to Bill as he looked at White Moon standing in front of the runty white man.

"I know'd what you're a thinkin' 'cause I'm already there White Moon." Bill nodded to White Moon.

"Plop yer brown ass down here in front of me an' lay back. I'm fixin' to do some barber werk on ya." She did as Bill directed, pulling herself up on her elbows to watch. Bill reached down, running his fingers through that thick black matte of hair, thinking what was hiding down there.

"Bill! What the hell are you doing?" Rebecca's voice came across the camp. There she was holding two huge rabbits.

"Hey, yer jus' in time. I was fixin' to trim some of this hair back so as I could see the finery this here maiden has hidden. You wanna help?"

"Not right yet, ya know, I've heard some of them French sporting girls do that. You go right ahead. I'll get these rabbits cookin' then come over to have some fun." she spoke as she began skinning the rabbits. The redhead was fast with a knife, and in a short time she had the rabbits hanging over the fire. Then she stripped also to join in the haircutting session.

"If I like what I see, then you can do mine next." she said. So Bill cut and trimmed. Then he cut some more. Pulling the lips out to trim closer, he worked diligently on the bronze maiden's pubic hair. Slowly the bush was trimmed down so the deep-brown skin of the valley could be seen. A pile of hair grew off to the side as Bill worked. When all that was left was a little clump on top, he stopped to admire his handiwork.

Then he said, "Roll over an' stick your butt up." She did as Bill asked. He continued his barbering on her brown eye 'till it was hairless as the front.

"Damn, I like that!" he exclaimed as White Moon's hand came down to touch her now-hairless region.

"This's fucking good, it'll be easy to touch myself also." she commented as her fingers went in.

"Yes, I like this."

"Do mine next. Except I want mine trimmed really short. No, wait. I don't want any hair down there to get in the way when you're going for a snack!" she said. Bill looked into her face, seeing becoming flush with excitement. White Moon got up as Rebecca lay down next to the mound of black hair on the ground.

"This feels strange. I like it." She rubbed her hand down the slit, brushing off the stray hairs. Then she went over to Rebecca to begin lowering herself until Rebecca's face was gone except her chin.

"Don't you go jerkin' lover 'er I might cut you by accident." Bill called out as he began cutting the bright red hair from his partner's crotch.

"Dof muf busf" was all Bill could make out as White Moon rocked over the white girl's face. Soon all that was left on Rebecca was a few stray hairs. Her hand went down as her fingers went into herself. Quickly she rubbed the button of life as White Moon rocked and swayed from front to back. Then Rebecca's hands went up to White Moon's breasts, grabbing the big brown nipples, twisting them hard as she orgasmed. White Moon let out a squeal, flopping off the side the redhead. Rebecca sat up, admiring Bill's handiwork. It had been the first time she could actually see into herself.

"Do my ass too." She asked.

"Well roll over an' stick it up." Bill cut hers as he had done White Moons." When he was finished he tapped butt cheek, "all done there missy."

"I like this, Bill. I want to watch you do me." she said as the color came to her cheeks again. Her face was shining from White Moon in the light from the fire. The young white trapper hadn't even got his manhood out when Two Sticks interrupted.

"You want your hair trimmed too?" Bill asked Two Sticks, "I don't know, I think not yet."

"I would like to be the first one." he said in a deep voice.

"Hang face there a minute." She got up, picking up the coyote pelt she walked away from the camp and shook it vigorously. "There. Now we can have some fun." She laid the pelt down and sat on it.

"Well, I haven't had two men in a long time. I guess now is as good as any. Here's how we do it. Bill, you lay down here on these furs." She arranged the pelts in a loose rectangle shape.

"Let me have you suck my twat for a few minutes to get me ready. Then you slide your piss'r up my puss. See, then Two Sticks comes in from behind and sticks my ass. Then we all come together and make one hell of a mess!" She smiled as she prepared herself.

"Is there something I can do?" asked White Moon.

"Sure, you can plop yer brown slickery spot right here." Bill pointed to his mouth.

"No, not yet. Let him get me hot first. Then he can do you, okay?" She kissed her on the mouth, running her fingers into White Moon's bare wet valley.

"I'll wait." she said quietly, faking a pout. Slowly Rebecca lowered her now-bare bottom onto Bill's mouth. The white lad began to nibble on her pink button as she rolled herself on his face.

"Hold on." he mumbled from under her. His hand came up, pulling a stray hair out of his mouth.

"Okay, come on back down." She then moved down so Bill could finish his task.

She slid down Bill's chest until she was right where he could stick his root into her garden, leaving her exposed brown rosebud so Two Sticks could get in. She then slid her legs up, so she was on her hands and knees. Bill began to move in and out as Two Sticks pulled on his root to full stiffness.

"Okay, Two Sticks slip it in." With one hand balancing, she reached for his pod. She aimed it to her rosebud; she waited when she felt the large knob's pressure against her, then as smooth as a beaver's belly he entered. The excitement was more than she had bargained for as she climaxed almost immediately. Rebecca thought it was too good to be true, two men at once. Her rump was being stretched by Two Sticks as Bill matched the Pawnee's rhythm. The two men increased their speed as Rebecca became more excited.

"I'm on my way." Spoke Two Sticks.

"Can you wait fer a spark? Bill, quick, pop inside me." she spoke inches from his face.

"Okay." Bill concentrated on releasing. He felt the tingling quickly.

"Okay. Here ya go." he came on command.

"Okay, Two Sticks, soon as Bill drops out, you come inside as well. Bill was barely out when Two Sticks entered her.

"Yes. I. Oh." He filled her with a great load of semen. He slowly pulled out as Rebecca reached down with her hand to hold both loads inside. Rebecca sat up, her hand holding the men's semen in.

"White Moon, you lay on your back right here." She nodded to the robes. The dark girl obeyed with a smile across her beautiful face. Bill leaned over on one elbow to watch. White Moon got all laid out as Rebecca stepped over her as she removed her hand. The spooge began to dripping into her open mouth. Now, Bill understood why she wanted it all in her. She was going to share. As it slowed to a drip, she lowered herself until all that could be seen was the top of White Moon's head at the edge of Rebecca's stomach. As she became empty, she stood up, allowing White Moon to do the same. Then they leaned forward until their lips met. White Moon's mouth opened to give back what Bill and Two Sticks had deposited. They finally pulled apart from the passionate kiss and turned to smile at the men.

"That's why we keep you men around, for a snack an'," Rebecca smiled, "this." She spread her arms open, revealing her finely shaped breasts.

"This is for my husband and his frien's to enjoy."

"Well, I be 'et fer a tatter. Thankie kindly, girls." Bill smiled from the compliment.

"You have fine wives Bill White. I have never been with a woman and a man before. You and your wives have taken the cloud from my eyes. I have been too busy with trading to see the other side of life. I vow to change all this from this day on!"

"Shit! I cain't believe it. One romp with 'Moon an' Rebecca an' this here Pawnees is ready to change his whole life. That shines!" he spoke to White Moon as he sat down next to her.

"Oh ma god! I forgot about the rabbit!" said Rebecca as she scampered over to the now- blackened carcasses. With her bare rump facing them, she bent straight over. She turned her head off to the side.

"These are gonna be tough but eatable." she said as she tore off a leg, tossing it to Billy White. Bill bit through the blackened skin into the tender rabbit.

"Here you go, Sticks." She tossed him a portion of the blackened rabbit.

"Much thanks." he said as he took the food and began eating as he leaned back.

"Tomorrow, when the sun rises, we should start seeing others on the way to the rendezvous. You will find others that will be good men to trade with. Not all white men are like those earlier. I rest now." With that he rolled over to go to sleep.

"Are you gonna stay up, girls?" Bill asked as he began to spread his robe out.

"I'm kind of keyed up from the fun. I think I'll stay up for a while. What do you feel like doin' Moon?" she asked the other naked woman.

"I'm not tired at all. White Man, do mind if I smoke from your pipe?" she asked straight out.

"Hell no. You'll have to get that plug from Two Stick though. See you girls in the mornin'." As the runt rolled over, the girls began their mischief.

CHAPTER 112

Bill lay there thinking about the days that had gone by. The trapping in the cold cold ponds. The endless hours of sitting, stretching plews, and the never-ending scraping that went with it. How he sat on the horses, plodding ever westward for days on end. He was glad to be out of the plains into the mountains where the trees offered color and game, not to mention a windbreak. Then there was the killing; he'd done his share. Behind him, near the fire, he heard the giggling of his wives.

Those scamps, he thought as he wondered what were they into now. He rolled over to see what the commotion was all about. Well, the girls were still naked. White Moon would take a draw of the pipe, then put her lips to Rebecca's snatch, and blow smoke up her. Then Rebecca would roll back with her legs in the air in order to make puffs of smoke come out. Then they'd giggle, trading places. They took no notice of the runt as he watched them.

"Blow smoke up my ass." Rebecca laughed.

"Don't fart on me, you redhead slut of a bitch." White Moon laughed. So on went the game.

White Moon would draw a deep breath of smoke, put her lips to Rebecca's ass, and blow. She would have enough time to clear away from Rebecca as the redhead would fart a huge cloud of smoke. Then they laughed and started it over again.

"Hey, Bill, how long have you been watchin'?" she asked with one arm around White Moon while the other was rooting around inside of herself.

"I watched 'til you was doin' the fartin' thing. Did ya figure all that stuff out by yerself 'er did you have help?" he asked through a smile.

"By myself. We're havin' fun without you Mr. White! I bet you've never seen us blow smoke out of our twats, have you?" she asked with her head tilted in a quizzical manner.

"Not 'til tonight." he answered as he lay back.

"Well, we're gonna play a game, Bill. It's called pass the smoke. And you're playing?" Recbecca asked.

"Here's how it works. You take a big old draw. Then you blow it up my pussy. Then White Moon will suck it out, blow it your mouth. Then you blow it up her pussy, and I suck it out. Then I blow it in your mouth. We keep passin' it around until it's all gone. Then we change the person who smokes first, and we play it again! I can't wait until you have your lips on me!" She giggled.

"Christ, woman! We got a long day ahead of us tomorrow!" Bill whined a fake whine as he rolled over, waiting to see if they were going to call it a night.

"Pist." She touched his arm. "Bill, roll over." It was Rebecca whispering in his ear. As he rolled over, he opened his eyes to see White Moon's hairless crotch coming down on him.

"Suck, Bill! Suck!" Rebecca shook him as she chanted. He felt the musky smoke enter his lungs. Then as soon as he had it in his lungs, she was up only to have Rebecca's hairless twat coming down on him. Her scent always was so good. He blew the smoke into her as her hand came down to plug the opening. As soon as she was full, she was over to White Moon to continue the game.

"What is all the noise?" asked Two Sticks from his side of the fire.

"These two minks ain't tired, so they decided to keep us up with some games, ya know? It's kinda fun. Ya oughta come over an' give it a try."

"I guess one more day on the trail will not be a problem." He rolled over to get up. Soon they couldn't tell who had smoked and who didn't. The place had so much smoke coming and going. The girls had smoke coming out their twats and asses at the same time.

They were blowing up one at the same time, getting some up theirs as the night came to a close.

"Well, we've been up all night. Might as well saddle 'em up an' head fer that there rony'viou." Bill said as he expelled smoke from his lungs.

"Mifgth asht welth." came Rebecca's voice from White Moon's crotch.

"Goddamnit! We are in for a slow day. But it was worth every moment."White Moon finally spoke as she pulled on her dress as she became proper again. But not Rebecca! No, the fiery redhead did whatever she wanted. No man or woman was going to say different to her.

She proceeded to dig in her traveling bag until she located the half shirt from what seemed a lifetime ago. Then she slipped it over her shoulders, arranging it properly. The one by one she tied her legging on to show off the most of her fresh haircut.

"Well, I reckon we'll have a handful of fightin' if'n we meet some white men." Bill mentioned as he saddled his mare.

"I say bring it on, goddamnit! I'm a free trapper by god, and I dress any way I see fit!" she rebuked anyone else who said different.

"Your wife has much fire. Mark my words. We will shed blood today." Two Sticks threw his leg over his mare.

"Yeah, I figure that out too. I'm jus' hopin' it don't take one of us along fer the ride." Bill called out as he grabbed the lead rope of the packhorses.

They entered the Willow Valley in the early evening as it struck Bill odd that they had not seen a single soul on the way there. As they started down the last hillside, Two Sticks pulled up next to Bill, pointing out a small glade of grass.

"We should camp there tonight. Then you will be able to see the lights from the camps below." he spoke as he pointed to the floor of the valley.

"I'll get us some supper." White Moon called and vanished into the tall trees.

"You will be very impressed as the noise is great from the trappers as they become drunk with whiskey." Two Sticks spoke as he watched the Pawnee woman vanish.

"Well, I'd like to be one 'em being drunk. That's fer certain an fer true." Rebecca chimed in. She had the small camp set up in a few minutes as Bill and Two Sticks pulled the pack down to check supplies. Bill looked up to see White Moon ride in, a large turkey tied to her horse.

"Here we are." White Moon tossed a large turkey down in front of Bill.

"Get busy Billy White, save the feathers." Rebecca said as she smiled to Bill. She knew he would be slow and she would end up doing the bird anyway, but she enjoyed watching Bill try his best to help. As sure as the evening sun dropping, she ended finishing the bird as she and White Moon began the cooking.

Now they had supper cooking, they listened to the noise from the valley below. They watched the sights below as the lights twinkled and glared in the darkness. A few huge fires were going, and all kinds of hooting and hollering could be heard from the encampments. Bill sat there watching the commotion. He heard someone approaching from his own fire. Looking over, he made out Rebecca's form as she plopped down next to him. She had put on her long war shirt in favor of the half shirt. Bill smiled at her in the dimness of the evening as he resumed watching the rendezvous.

"Here, Bill." She handed him a leg of the bird. He took it and pulled off a bite. Savoring the taste, he began to think aloud, "Well, lover, we've made it from that goddamned riverboat to our first rony'viou. Whatcha got to say 'bout that?" he asked her, looking down at tomorrow's adventure.

"It seems like we've gone along way. Remember, the first night on the boat? How about the river rats an' them mangy whores on the river? Don't forget that hog we bumped into over on the Greasy, or was it the Sugar? Then there was that big bear on the North Platte. Shit, we almost lost you on that one." she continued.

Bill took another bite and chewed quietly. After swallowing, he answered her back, "Not to mention when you waded into a passel of Arapaho niggers. That one really scared me." She wrapped her arm around Bill as she stared into the distant light.

"Oh, well, let's not ferget the time you went to dancin' with Mel's brother. I had a knot the size of a quarter rope in my gut when you was tradin' blades with that nigger." Bill looked into the darkness at his redheaded lover as he threw the bone into the brush.

"There's been too many close ones." Bill lay back, looking up at the evening stars twinkling overhead. He felt her head rest on his chest, her arm lying across his legs.

"Bill." she said.

"Yeah."

"I love you." Then she wrapped her arms around him. She squeezed his chest hard.

"But if you go to screwin' any of those squaws down there without invitin' me along, well, I'll use your nuts for target practice." Then she was quiet.

"Hmm. Well, I know where I stand here. That wasn't too subtle 'er anything." He chuckled to Rebecca as he looked at the stars. He was thinking about how many of them were up there when it turned black. *Huh? What the Sam Hill is goin' on?* he quizzed himself. Then he smelled the fragrance of White Moon as her bare snatch touch his face. Then he felt a hand on his piss'r.

Them girls! Cain't get no shuteye in this camp! He chuckled to himself.

CHAPTER 113

In the morning they saddled up to begin their journey downhill to see how bad the traders were going to skin out Bill and his small brigade. Rebecca had put her long dress on. Bill was so glad because he knew there would have been plenty of blood spilling if she hadn't. When they neared the encampments, Two Sticks called to his white friends.

"White Man, Rebecca, shoot your guns in the air." Two Sticks said

"Why would I go an' do that?" Bill asked as he looked over at his friend.

"That way it shows that you are coming in unarmed. It is a sign of peace among the traders." he answered. Bill looked at Rebecca and pulled the trigger, feeling the kick of the large caliber against his thigh. Not more than a millisecond, her's went off.

In they rode past the tents of Crow, the Nez Perce, and the Snakes. Then the Flathead, the Bannocks, the Pawnee, and finally the Arapahos. Then it was the free trappers' lean-tos they saw next. They were yelling and waving at them to come over for whiskey, yelling for the girls to come over for a poke.

Rebecca looked at the men before her. They reminded her of the men they had to kill a short time ago. They were dressed in dark-stained greasy buskins, some without shirts, showing the tribal tattoos on their white bodies. There were many who had hair longer than hers, some braided, some unkempt and scraggy. Others had eastern haircuts, showing plenty of white skin that hadn't seen the light of sun for many days. But no women. She scanned the area as they plodded through the free trappers. Occasionally she'd see an Indian woman come out from a lean-to. The maiden would straighten her doeskin dress as she headed back to her camp with her hands full of beads or other trinkets from the whites.

Hmm? I reckon that's how they do it. A poke for beads or trade trinkets, she thought as she looked over to Bill, thinking on how good he was to her. She watched another Indian come out from a small tent. She stared at the bronze woman as they walked slowly by, thinking how much she looked like White Moon, but this woman had a dazed look as she staggered for a bit, trying to right herself. Then a man followed her from the small tent, his penis still out, taunting her to come back again.

"You come back to Bud Warner again now ya hear girl? I'll give you more of this for that." He shook his soft member at her while holding the kettle up. The Indian girl turned to look at the man and nodded. She took but a few steps before falling facefirst in the dust. Her hands never even came out to stop her fall.

"Bill." Rebecca called out as she slid off the right side of her horse, tossing the reins to her husband. The runt grabbed her reins as he watched her going to the side of the fallen girl. The trapper stood there staring at Rebecca, not believing what he was seeing. A white woman!

"Christ almighty! Micah, you gotta see this!" he called out to his friend in the tent. Micah St. Clair crawled out looking at the sight. His shrinking pod was returning back into his buckskins as well.

"Well, the Lord works in mysterious ways." He smiled.

Billy looked to White Moon.

"Think you can parley with the drunk girl, at least see where she's going or at least where she's from?"

"I'll give it a lick Billy White." answered White Moon. He looked at Two Sticks.

"What do ya think, Two Sticks? 'Rapaho? Snake?"

"All I see is trouble for you. I'm leaving to trade. I will find you later." The Pawnee dismounted and walked into the gathering crowd, leading his horses, quickly becoming engulfed by the crowd in a few steps.

"Just like the other niggers." she spoke to White Moon.

"No one should be treated this way." They rolled the girl over to inspect the damage. Her flat face had dust on it but no blood; she was breathing normal, just passed out from too much of the cheap trader's whiskey. White Moon spoke to the girl but got no response.

"Anybody know where she's from?" Rebecca asked the crowd. No one came forward.

"Goddamnit! Nobody knows nuthin'?" A few minutes went by before someone spoke out.

"I know her." the trapper that had been with her spoke up finally.

"She's from them Snakes. Her name's Small Doe. I'll take care of her. We just got carried away. Lookie here. She just drank too much, that's all. We done gave her a passel of foo-fer-ah already. Didn't rape her. That's the gawd's truth too. She spread her legs fair an' square."

By now the crowd had left, leaving just Bill, his wives, and the trappers before them.

"We'll take her back after she sobers up some." He looked at Bill and then to Rebecca.

"Who the hell are you anyway to give a good goddamn about some squaw?" Rebecca stood up walking over to the man. She looked in him the eye, fists balled up, ready to dance in a heartbeat.

"I'm the one that's gonna carve your liver if you don't do as you've said. That's who!" she spoke tight-lipped, almost quivering from the rage she had boiling up inside of her.

"Do we know you? I ain't never seen no white woman in these parts, much less a mercy queen." The man didn't back down as his hand was slowly inching its way to his bone-handled knife. Before his hand could finish its journey, she had her six-inch bone-handled knife out and under the man's penis, lifting slightly to let him know that a wrong move and he'd be a eunuch. The world stopped as he froze.

"I reckon we'll be sure to take good care of her. Why don't you put that away an' have a snort with us instead?" The man was actually trembling now. He had no idea how the knife had gotten to his pecker. All he knew is he was in a tight spot.

"No, we'll move on. We have trading to do as well. But when I come back, I better find that no wrongdoing has found its way to this young girl. Do you read my tracks?" Before he could answer, the knife was in its sheath as she was backing toward her gelding. White Moon was moving as smooth as silk, never a wasted movement as she took her reins from the ground where they dropped.

"Remember what I said." Rebecca took her reins from Billy White as she stepped into her right stirrup, swinging her leg over the well-used saddle.

The trio moved away from the two trappers as the eyes of the adjacent tents followed them.

"I couldn't sit here an' watch that behavior Bill. Jus' rubbed me wrong." she spoke without turning her head.

"Yeah, I noticed. Wonder if we'll be catching shit from that the whole rony'viou?" he answered back, surveying the area as they walked on toward what seemed the center of the encampment. Men were passed out everywhere it seemed. Next to lean-tos, in the dirt by trees, passed out everywhere they looked or so it seemed.

Bill stopped a bare-chested man wearing nothing but a breechclout and moccasins, adorned with tattoos and earrings, his long braided hair hanging down to the center of his slender back.

"Where be the booshway of this rony'viou?" But before the man could answer the question, a tall man in a crisp white shirt and beautiful cream-colored buckskinned pants answered, "I can answer that lad. Down to the end, turn right. There's a big tent at the end. That's the trader tent. Good luck, son!" He had a deep commanding voice.

"What's beaver goin' fer?" Rebecca asked him.

"They're going for $5 a pound or somewhere about $3 a plew." he answered.

"Are you a trader?" Bill asked.

"Matter of fact I am. I'm Bill Sublette. I just bought out Ashley. You must be free trappers." He stucky out his hand to shake.

"That I am, Mr. Sublette. This is Rebecca Alma White. That's my Pawnee wife, White Moon of the Great Pawnee, out of the Platte River. I'm the White Man. Pleasure to make yer acquaintance." Bill said as he reached down to shake the booshway's hand.

"Your first year trappin' son? Did you say the White Man? Also know as Billy White of Missouri fame?" he asked as his smile went wide, showing straight white teeth.

"The same white man that was with Ashley last summer and early winter. You the young lad that took off on yer own? The same one that got mauled by ol'Ephraim? Then killed the same bear that got you? That white man?" he asked, pumping Bill's hand vigorously.

"How's that you know me?" Billy asked.

"Ann Beck. You remember Ann? Her and I became friends. She has told me of your adventures with the bear, the razorback hog and scoundrels that captured her sister. Now look here. I'll give you top dollar for your beaver. You'll not pay for a drink for the time you're here either. You read my sign son?"

"Well then, I reckon I'll see you at yer tent." Bill turned his horse in the direction that he had been given.

"Son." he called out. Bill turned in his saddle looking back at the tall man.

"You tell my clerk that you spoke to me and that he's to give you top dollar. Okay Bill. You tell him that. You stop by later and we'll share a cup." He turned and walked off.

"Now why in tarnation did he go an' say all that? Hell, he don't know me from jack an' here he is sayin' all this shit 'bout top dollar." he asked Rebecca.

"I do believe he has heard all 'bout you from Ann. I reckon she tolt some stories 'bout you. That's all I can come up with."

So off they went, wandering down the rows of tents and lean-tos looking at the sights, watching the trappers having a hoot. Then they turned right like Sublette had said. They pulled up, and Bill handed his reins to White Moon as he surveyed the area.

The man standing there in his cotton shirt with the high collar and plastered-down hair looked Bill up and down as he rode up.

"You a free trapper?"

"Yeppers." Bill answered

"You're the White Man, ain't you?" said the clerk.

"I'm to give you top dollar. According to Mr. Sublette, you're a real hero. Now what do you have, sir?"

"I got these here plews." He reached up to untie the bundles of beaver hides.

"These are prime, sir. Who did the scraping? A squaw? By the look, these were done by an experienced hide person."

"Well, thank you young man!" Rebecca stepped up in all her glory.

"I scraped an' did the work myself!" She bent over, showing ample cleavage. The clerk just about came in his breeches.

"Now lookie here. You give the White Man a good price so I can hump the hell out of him, hear?" Then she winked at him. The poor fellow didn't know what to do after that. But he took each bundle apart, inspecting each and every pelt.

"I make out you have two hundred pounds of hides here. There was two of less than perfect shape. So I'll give you $3 a pelt for 198 hides. That's $590. Then there's the two, which I'll give you $2 for, so that's $4. So I'll give you a total of $594 of credit to be used in this store." he spoke as he kept his eyes away from Rebecca.

"Give him an even $600." came a voice from behind Bill; he turned to see Bill Sublette walking up.

"Give him an even $600 in store credit."

"Thank ye kindly sir." Billy said.

"No, thank you Billy. These are prime beavers for sure. Only the best trappers bring in this quality of fur. You want a job booshwaying for me? I'll pay top wages! You know, I could use a man of your skills." he said loud enough for all to hear.

"You know, Bill, I'll tell ya secret." The trappers within earshot came closer with the chance of getting some secret news.

"My wife is the one who did almost all the trappin' an' scrapin'. You might wanna offer her the job 'stead of me. The girl got some sand. That's fer certain an fer true!" The trappers that were near all took a step back as the story was being told. Then they looked at Rebecca in her long war shirt.

"Guff. That's what I say! They's stole them pelts an' brought 'em in fer cash money! That's what I say! Ain't no woman can trap better than a man!" a grizzled long-haired man with battle scar's spoke out.

"Lookie here. I don't know you from a stump, but I ain't tellin' no bald face here. My wife is the master trapper in our outfit! I think you might wanna put that tongue of your'n back in its sheath mister! She's likely to have you fer supper if'n you rile her up 'fore she gets her afternoon poke." They all laughed, slapping one another on the back, walking away, except the man that made the accusations. He was looking at the trio's gear when he spotted the rifles Bill had taken from the dead men.

"Hey, lookie here! I tolt ya they were a bunch a pirates. Here's Russell's gun! An' lookie there. That's Sam's Derringer. What else you got that ain't your'n mister?" he spouted.

Bill was ready for this, so he looked at Rebecca then Bill Sublette. By then even Sublette was curious.

"Son, how's it you have those men's rifles? Tell us what happened." he spoke loud enough for everybody to hear. But before Bill could start the story, Two Sticks appeared from the crowd.

"I will tell you all. I am Two Sticks of the Grand Pawnee of the Platte River. You all know me from before, and you know I speak the truth. I have traded with you many times, and we have been friends for many seasons. Even before the traders come to the mountains. Now hear my story, for it is the truth. Three moons ago we were at camp when two men came into our camp. They said they had lost everything to the Crow and only wanted to travel with us. Two of their friends stayed in the darkness while two did the talking. When talk of a fight came, the two you spoke of made the fight first. The white man defended himself. Afterward it was clear that they were going to rob us and declare all the beaver as their own. This is how it all happened." he spoke to all the men standing in a loosely formed circle. They nodded, mumbling. About then a tall thin man appeared.

"I know Two Sticks. If'n he says that's what happened, well, there ya go. I say go get yer cup an' I'll buy y'all around at the traders' tent." The young man was talking, and the trappers all left except the accuser.

"Jim, you know'd these Injuns are all liars. This here sumbitch is in cahoots with that. You kin see fer your ownself!" The man wouldn't let it go.

"I said this man don't lie." The young Jim Bridger stopped in his tracks and turned to Bill's accuser.

"It's the truth mister. I don't know you, but that's how the tracks were laid an' that's how they stay!" Bill spoke forcefully but loudly.

"Bridger, we all knows yer the biggest liar in the mountains. So yer expectin' us to believe you an' a red devil? Waugh! I'll carve this runt's liver fer killin' me friends!" The crowd had gathered again.

"Goddamnit! Here we go again." Bill looked at Rebecca as he rested his hand on the hilt of the knife he'd been given by Isaiah Weatherspoon.

"Ben, these people defended themselves. It ain't no call to go throwing down on them!" Sublette called to the revenge-seeking trapper.

"If they killed Ben Harris's friend, then they got a fight with me!" the man spoke, pulling a big knife.

"Oh shit! It seems trouble just follows us, Bill?" Rebecca shook her head.

"You want me to kill 'em Bill?" asked Rebecca.

"Nah. I reckon I'll jus' go ahead an' kill 'em my own self. Goddamnit! All I wanted to do is trade an' move on. Mr. Sublette, is there gonna be bad blood 'er we still welcome here?" As Billy spoke, he was watching his opponent weaving, switching the knife from one hand to the other.

"I say to all that are here; this man is defending himself. You have a problem with him, then you'll have a problem with me!" Bill Sublette's voice boomed out.

"The same goes for Jim Bridger!" Then another trader stepped forward.

"That goes for Davey Jackson as well!"

"If thou has slapped my friend, then thou will surely find the wrath of God upon you!"

"Jed, you got no call to defend this here sumbitch!" Ben Harris called out.

"If my friends stand with him, then I stand with him!" spoke out Jedediah Smith. Then there was a commotion with the crowd parting. Out came none other than William Ashley himself.

"What's the ruckus about here?" Ashley called out.

"Well, finally someone on my side." answered Ben Harris.

"These here niggers killed Sam 'an Russell an I'm fixin' to even the score." Harris was flicking his knife continually.

"Ben, I suggest you put your knife and differences away. This man will kill you." Ashley spoke slowly.

"Ben, may I introduce you to Mr. Billy White of Missouri fame." At that moment the trapper went white.

"You mean this here runt is the White Man? Billy White?" His voice quivereing

"Shit, how is it all these folks know me? I ain't nuthin' 'cept a man wantin' to trap an' live free an' all. Now this nigger wants to carve my liver?" Bill asked Rebecca out of the corner of his mouth.

"Well, my apologies, Bill. I reckon I made me a mistake. I didn't mean nothin'. I was only funnin' ya." He put his knife away, offering up his hand in friendship. As these events transpired, the crowd went wild, hooting and hollering.

"Let's get them drinks you niggers!" hollered out Bridger. Off everyone went except for the runt and his wives.

"We'll be along directly, Mr. Sublette. I jus' wanna get our supplies. Then we'll be over." Bill spoke, shaking his hand. When it was quiet, he finally let his breath out.

"Damn. I don't know what Ann tolt Sublette, but it must be a yarn of all yarns. Christ, just mention my name to these people an' I get all kinda of special treatment. I cain't figure it out." he spoke to Rebecca as she looked around at the trade goods.

"What's powder going fer?" Rebecca asked.

"Two dollars a pound."

"What kind?" Bill asked.

"English."

"How much we got left White Moon?" he called over to her.

"Let me look." After a brief moment, she came back.

"We got about five pounds left."

"Okay, give me fifty pounds."

"What kind a lead?"

"Galena." Bill quickly remembered Maria in Hannibal.

"Give me twenty pounds." he paused, "What kind of flints?"

"American an' French." Bill picked a flint admiring the dark sharp object.

"I'll take a bucketful."

"We don't sell them thata way, mister. I sell them by the dozen.

"Oh. All right, give me five dozen of 'em then."

"I'll take fifty pounds of coffee, ten pounds of sugar, twenty twists of tobacco." He was still going when Rebecca pushed him aside.

"I'll take twelve three-point blankets, four pairs of scissors, twenty yards of blue cloth, twenty yards of scarlet, some of those beads. Do you want some of this stuff?" Rebecca asked.

"I that need some beads an' blankets. Some vermilion would be nice. A big goddamn cooking pot would be nice also. Yes, that's all I'd like." she said as she looked around.

"Well, tally that up an' see what my damage is storekeep." Bill sternly looked at the clerk behind the plank counter.

"Let's see here." he mumbled as Billy watched him do the ciphering.

"The total is eight hun'ert an' seven American. Now, sir, you only have six hundred in credit. You'll have to take two hundred and seven off your list." he said.

"Hmm. Too damn we didn't have tAnn with us right 'bout now." Bill whispered to Rebecca.

"How about if my friend an' I treat you to something special?" Rebecca asked seductively.

"No, thank you, mam. I'm a married man, and I don't do things that would disrespect my wife. Thank you for the offer, but no thank you. You'll have to take some things off." he said that as he crossed his arms sticking his lip out.

"All right, cut the coffee in half as well as the sugar. How's that?" she asked.

"Well, sir, you're still a hundred seventy-nine over." he said, looking at the trio.

"Hmm? Okay, take back all that fancy cloth." said Rebecca.

"How's that look now?" Bill asked.

"Sir, you have twenty-one in credit." he spoke, looking at his tally sheet.

"You give me a paper showin' that so I can go have me a drink 'er two." The clerk wrote something on a piece of paper with Sublette's crest on it.

"There. That will buy you whiskey. Good day, sir. Next!" Bill and his wives loaded all the goods on their horses and went looking for a camping spot.

"We did good, Bill. You know we only got to really trap for a short time. We coulda really brought some fur in if them damned 'Rapaho hadn't been so fired up to get ours scalps."

They walked in quiet for a spell as Bill noticed a spot that looked too good for them to relax i

"Lookie here. I reckon this place will work. It's got some cover so not everybody will be a watchin' while I'm slippin' the wood to you minks." He turned and winked at them both.

"Now what makes you think I don't want anybody watching us?" the redhead asked.

"Maybe I'd like to show off my new haircut to some of the other niggers. Maybe we can get a couple of young bucks that can go more than just three times." Then she winked at White Moon.

"Oh, I get it now." Bill caught on, so he leaned back in his saddle as he listened to them go on.

"Yes, the white man must be getting old. He can only ride the pony three times. We may have to find a new man to please us." said White Moon as she was unloading the new stuff they had bought.

"Well, I'll be. I believe you gals is tryin' to get my goat, ain't ya? Well, I believe yer both getting a tad too sassy. I gonna have to poke the shit right outta both you minks. Now what do ya say to that?" Bill looked at them with a fake annoyance.

"Oh, kind sir! Do you really think that you can poke the shit outta of both of us fair maidens?" Then Rebecca put her hand to her forehead like she was fainting. White Moon didn't know what to think of all this play-acting. But she did the same thing watching Rebecca out of the corner of her eye.

"Oh, kind sir, please poke the shit out of me." White Moon said. It was a tad funny because she only had a fair idea of what the game they were playing was.

"Oh, all right if that'll shut up from yer consarned whinin'." The threat was as empty as a beaver trap on the bank.

"Let's get back down to the festivities girls. I'll poke ya proper to night." Bill spoke as he grabbed his rifle and possibles.

"Ya know, this would be a fine time to teach White Moon to shoot proper like, don'cha think Rebecca?" He laid the rifle over his shoulder.

"Good idea there Bill. But let's go to the trader for that drink first?" she asked.

"Should I stay back here with the new supplies?" asked White Moon.

"Nah. I reckon they'll be okay out here. Ya know maybe we should move in closer to the funnin'. Wouldn't have to walk that far if'n we tied one on?" he asked them.

"All right. Let's move then." With that, the two girls turned around and packed the whole kit and caboodle in a heartbeat.

"Lead the way, Bill." Rebecca said as she was pulling the horses behind her.

CHAPTER 114

They walked closer to the activities as Bill looked around the campsites until he saw one that looked friendly. They waved at Bill and his entourage.

"Howdy there friends. You niggers new to the rony'viou?" asked a round little fart. *How the hell he gets up an' down the trail I've no clue,* Bill thought.

"By george we are. I'm the White Man. This here is Rebecca. That lovely woman walkin' up, well, that's White Moon, my Pawnee wife." Bill smiled, realizing he'd made the right choice.

"Is the redhead yer wife too?" he asked, rubbing his hand through his shiny close-cropped beard.

"Yeppers they's both my wives." the runt answered. Something looked familiar about the man, but he couldn't pick it out.

"Well, hell! Sit yer ass's down an' have a cup with Joseph Champeau!" *That name. Where've I heard that name?* Bill asked himself, going back in his memory, trying to associate it with the face, but from where?

Joseph called to his partner, "Barnett, get yer stinkin' ass out here an' be sociable! He got inta his cups this mornin' an' was filthy drunk a'fore lunch!" He slapped his knee while letting out a big-bellied laugh. That took the edge off, making Bill more at ease. A dark-bearded thin face came inching out from behind the animal skin door. As slow as a turtle in March, a long tall man crawled out. He stood up stretching.

"Well, howdy. I'm Talbot Barnett." He stuck out his scrawny hand, letting Bill shake it firmly. *Well, ain't this a pair. A tall skinny man with a short fat man. If this doesn't take the cake,* Bill thought to himself.

"I'm." Bill was trying to speak, but this new face cut him off before he got the words out.

"Yer the White man, ain'tcha? Him, Billy White." Barnett said as he shook the blond runt's hand.

"I thought you'd be bigger, to tell ya the truth. It has to be the truth 'cause there's that redhead that travels with ya. Is all the shit true they'd be a sayin' 'bout you? You know 'bout killin' a bear that was bigger than a barn? What 'bout all them, them 'Rapahos an' Sioux? I heard you killed fifty of the niggers at one time?" he asked.

"Who's been tellin' ya all these here yarns?" Rebecca addressed the tall thin man.

"Billy Sublette was tellin' us over to the traders' tent a while ago. He said a witch told him." Then he looked Bill and back to Rebecca.

"Hey, is it true? You was a whore. I mean it ain't none of my business an' all, but I figure if you're gonna camp with us an' all I was jus' wonderin' if'n we be able to trade for some pokes?" Barnett said as he poured a cup of coffee from a blackened beat-up pot. Then, looking up at her with a quizzical look on his face, he stopped mid-sentence as Rebecca interrupted.

"Yeppers. I was once a whore. I fucked more men than you'll ever know. I've had a man every way possible. I done things that is only whispered behind closed doors. If that what's you wanted to know. I've had 'em black, yellow, an' red. Half breeds too! I've had 'em up the ass, in the mouth, three at once. In the water, in a tree, over a horse. Naked, dressed, an' in the breeches. Preachers, carpetbaggers, an' constables. Tall, short, round, and thin. I've fucked men an' women of every size an' shape." she said with her hands on her hips. Bill was shocked at first, but then he figured it out. If there was going to be stories about them, well by god, she'll give them some. She'd make even better stories than they'd ever hear.

"But I'll let you on a secret. I can outshoot and outride any nigger in these here shining mountains. I've got the prettiest horse, meanest dog, an' the best husband this side of the Mississippi!" she said as she threw her red head back, laughing deeply.

"You boys got any whiskey you'd like to share with me an' the White Man here?" They just looked at her. Finally, Champeau rummaged around until he produced a small tin bucket with some of the foul-smelling whiskey in it.

"Here you go." said Champeau. Bill noticed the air had changed. He couldn't quite pick up on it, but something had changed, and that face. It was really bothering Bill now.

"Don't worry, boys. I like you just fine. If you'd pissed me off, well, we'd have some words then." She lifted the tin to her mouth and drank heartily. Whiskey ran over the edges of her mouth and down her buckskin dress, leaving a wet trail. It went right down between her breasts as the soft deerskin began to soak the amber liquid up. *I'll bet a nickel to a plug dollar she a drippin' wet as the dew in June!* Billy White thought as he watched his wife drink her fill.

"Good god!" she shrieked. She let the bucket come back to rest on the ground. Then she let out a loud barking burp.

"Whoowee! That's got some punch to it. Do you boys mind if we set up camp with you or you rather we move on?" she asked as she shook herself from the feeling of the whiskey. It was a sight to behold too. Those tits of hers were begging to be set free the way they were a sashaying inside that long buckskin war shirt. *Shit, she's getting lit. I wonder how she'll be after she gets a good drunk going,* Bill quizzed himself. The only other time he'd seen her drinking was in Missouri, and that was some really horrid concoction.

"Holy shit! You're quite a woman! I ain't never seen a woman drink 'er talk like that! We'd, me an' Barnett, would be honored if'n you would stay at our camp site. Shit! Billy White, right here in our camp! Sumbitch, that's some beaver, eh, Talbot?

"Hell yeah! Some beaver! Shit! Do ya mind if'n we accompany you folks when you go a visitin'?" asked Barnett.

"By god yer a friend. That's fer certain an' fer true." answered Rebecca. Bill was glad they were treating them as friends, not as strangers.

"Gimme some of that hooch, will ya, Talbot? I gots me a powerful dry comin' on." Bill lifted the bucket to his lips and drank.

"Son of a bitch! That's awful-tastin' concoction!" Bill coughed. But he could feel the poor-quality booze taking effect immediately.

"Well, do you want a snort of this who kicked jack?" Bill asked White Moon.

"Hell yeah, I wanna get shitfaced with the rest of ya." she answered back.

"Do you mind if'n my other wife has some hooch?" Bill asked.

"Hell no! Do ya think we could trade something fer a poke with her?" Barnett asked.

"I don't think so. That wouldn't be a good idea. See, she's my wife. I don't trade her for pokes. Let's pass that pail around ." Bill asked, holding out his hand for the pail.

"So you want our licker, but you won't share yer women. Is that the signs you're leavin'?" Champeau asked, holding back the pail.

"I take it you boys are a thinkin' that share an' share alike is the way it happens. Them the tracks yer leavin'?" Bill became sober quickly.

"That's right. You can get more Injun gals. I jus' came from another camp over thata way, where they was pokin' a gal jus' fer beads an' cloth. So I figure that you'd be a doin' the same. I didn't mean harm by askin', did I?" Champeau asked.

"Ya know, I believe we'll pass on yer licker frien'." Bill looked at the girls.

"Girls, let's get our belongings an' move along." he spoke. As he stood, a slight dizziness came over him from the traders' whiskey.

"You still owe us fer the licker you drank, you saw'd-off scumsuckin' rat fucker of a runt. So I'll take a poke with yer squaw fer payment." Joseph said as he rose to his feet. One of his hands was resting on the hilt of a big butcher knife, the other making a reach for White Moon.

"Uh, let it go Joe. This ain't a good idea." Barnett said as he put his hand on his friend's shoulder.

"Aww, what are you worried 'bout? This here runt an' his two-bit whore? I betcha all them stories is jus' yarns anyhoo. He don't look so tough. I believe I'll gut him from asshole to eyeball. Then we kin do as we please with that whore an' Injun." Champeau was speaking as if they had already won the battle. Out came the knife, and it was time to dance for the runt.

"Whatcha say, squaw man? Ya gonna draw yer blade 'er ya gonna run off an' hide?" he sneered.

"Bill, do you want me to kill him for you? I'll give you his sassy tongue if you want. An it'll be for less than the two bits that fat fucker can scrape up." Rebecca said as she stepped forward, her hand caressing her bone-handled knife.

"Nah, that wouldn't be up to beaver to do that, lover. Barnett, you're the witness to say I didn't cause this here fight." the blond runt spoke, not taking his eyes off the fat man.

"I'm a seein' it. I ain't stayin' here. Most likely you'll kill him. Then you'll kill me fer jus' bein' his partner." Talbot said in a shaking voice.

"Nah, I ain't gonna kill you. Shit, I don't wanna kill Mr. Roly-Poly here neither. But he done pulled his sticker out wantin' to wade inta my liver. I reckon he wasn't satisfied with our conversation, eh Rebecca?" Bill joked with her.

About that time Mr. Roly-Poly lunged at Bill, missing him by a large margin.

"Lookie here, Champeau, let's put these pig stickers away an' go to the traders' tent fer a cup of his finest. Hell, I'll buy. What do ya say?" Billy asked the fat man, sidestepped another swinging attack; he'd not even pulled a knife as Bill tried to reason with him.

"Augh!" went the fat man as he swung again and stumbled, falling flat on his ass.

"What's going on here?" a familiar voice invaded the small camp.

"Well, how do Mr. Sublette. I was tryin' to convince this here feller that we oughta go to yer tent fer a cup of yer finest, but he's sworn on runnin' me through!" Bill spoke, looking at Joseph trying to regain his footing. Champeau rose to his feet. He was breathing so hard it sounded like he was going to pop.

"What's this all about? Talbot?" Sublette began interrogating Champeau's partner.

"Well, Mr. Sublette, Joe wants a poke fer givin' them." he was pointing to the trio, "a drink. The runt there said he don't give his wives out fer drinks. Joe here says he's gonna kill the runt an' have the women any ol'way. You walked up as Joe was getting the best of 'em too." Talbot defended his partner.

"The. Nig. Ger. Has. Two. Wives. He. Oughta. Be a. Sharin'. 'em with. With. All. Of. Us." he said as he sunk to one knee, wheezing like a lunger.

"Billy, do you want to share your wives?" Sublette asked Bill.

"No sir. I do not!" Bill answered with his arms crossed over his chest.

"Lookie here, Bill, we was a walkin' by an' these fellers was a wavin' an' smilin' like we was long-lost kin. Well after a cup he wants to screw my wives. He's wantin' a poke somethin' fierce I reckon. Shit, there's plenty of Injun gals out there wantin' foo-far-ah! Hell, I'm here fer some fun jus' like the rest of you niggers." Bill waved at the growing group of skin traders.

"Why, hell I was even willin' to buy drinks fer the shits." He pointed to the kneeling fat man and his slender partner.

"But hell no! He wants 'em all fer his ownself. Damn! Damp powder fer sure Bill." The white runt watched Champeau trying to regain his composure.

"When you catch your breath, come to my tent. I told you when you came you could have some fun without killing each other." Sublette spoke as he steered the runt and his wives away from the crowd toward his tent.

Leaving the fat man, Sublette spoke to Billy and his wives, "Billy, would you and your wives be so kind as to join me for a drink at my tent?" Sublette asked.

"It would be a pleasure sir." the runt answered.

"I'll grab the horses." Rebecca volunteered. "I'll bring the pack critters." Moon commented as they fell in step with Bill Sublette.

"Well, at least we didn't unpack all our stuff." Rebecca said as she kept an eye on Champeau.

"Ya know, Bill. How in the blue blazes does that man get up an' down mountains to trap? Christ! He was outta breath jus' tryin' to slit my gizzard." the runt spoke to the trader as they walked through the other tents and camps. As they strolled back to Bill Sublette's trading tent, people continually called him to come over to their fires for drinks and story telling.

"Well, he's not a trapper. He's a camp man. He does the chores around the camp while others are out in the streams trapping. He scraps hides, gets firewood, sets up camp, and breaks it down. As well as packs the horses and mules for the trip. He's been a thorn in my side since he's been in my employ. Mr. Ashley spoke to me about him when I bought him out. Apparently he's been somewhat of a problem since they left Fort Atkinson. But he don't work for me."

"He broke open some of the whiskey on the way here. Ashley fired him and gave him his wages when we got here. He's a rough one. He'll try to get to you on your blind side. Fights when your back is turned. I wouldn't be too surprised if he didn't bushwhack you and your women later." His voice had no emotion to speak of.

"Now I remember! I saw him way back on the Platte gettin' his ass chewed by Ashley. That's where I saw him. It's been pestering me ever since I laid eyes on him today. Thankie kindly fer the advice an' the warning, Bill." he changed the subject.

"Are most of these men workin' fer ya then?" Bill asked as they walked closer to Sublette's tent.

"Only the ones close to here. The rest are free trappers. You'll find no better man in the mountains then a free trapper. They're honest and loyal to each other. If I had a dozen of them, I'd be able to clean out a valley in half the time my trappers do." he spoke to Billy and Rebecca as they walked up to his tent. Bill noticed that the men in the area scurried and ran about like mice after fallen grain with the arrival of their employer. It made the runt wonder if Bill was a fair booshway or a downright asshole. They approached Sublette's tent. Billy wasn't too surprised that it was clean and organized in comparison to the other camps in the area.

"Ah, here we are. Home away from home." Sublette waved his arm at the tent. A black man was in the opening of the tent when they walked up.

"Louis, bring some whiskey for my guests an' I." he spoke gently to the tall thick black man. What shocked the runt was this man's name. It wasn't Louis. It was Thabo! He hadn't seen him since, shit, since last summer, or was it longer? But here he was pouring drinks as a man named Louis. Instantly the man disappeared only to return carrying a large silver flask.

"Here you go, Mr. Sublette." He was pouring the amber liquid looking into Bill's eyes, looking to see what the runt would say.

"Are these the folks you've been speaking about?" He nodded toward the trio.

"Indeed they are. The one and the same, Billy White, Rebecca, and White Moon. Where's Two Sticks?" he asked.

"He's out there skinnin' these here white folks out of their provisions no doubt. That man is a sharp trader. That's fer certain an' fer true." Bill said as he accepted the glass tumbler half full of liquor. He sipped it slowly, expecting the same punch as the first drink of the day had been.

"Whoowee! Damn! That's some strong hooch!" Billy White cried as he had tears running down his cheeks. He was just about ready to cough when he looked over to Rebecca. She saw the reaction he had. She looked down at it then smiled with her eyes twinkled. *Oh lordy! We're all getting a poke tonight,* Bill thought as the glass came to her lips, and then she threw her head back with the whole load. Nothing. She smiled as she looked to White Moon; the Pawnee just drank it like warm water. No coughing, spitting, or hacking. No visible signs of distress.

"Hmm? Go figure." mumbled the white runt.

"Ah. Now's that's some fine liquor, Mr. Sublette." she said as she pulled her hand across her lips. Out came her glass for another round. Bill Sublette didn't know what to expect from the runt's redheaded woman.

"Ah-huh! This is very easy to swallow, like you, White Man. So I'll have more." said White Moon.

"You drank that like it was mother's milk. Didn't bother ya a tad? Hell, you got a glass down already!" he said to her, looking down at his half-full tumbler.

"Damn! This is gonna a be a short night!" Billy White slurred.

"You know, Mr. Sublette, this is mighty fine refreshments that you're serving here. I haven't had good whiskey since I was a working girl." Rebecca said.

"Ann said you did some sparking on the river. Was that the Missouri or Mississippi?" he asked as he took a sip from his glass.

"Mississippi. That's where I met William here. I couldn't get along without him now." she said as she threw the next round of hooch down her throat.

"My my, I see you drink quickly." He motioned for the servant to pour more in her glass. Bill watched him looking at Rebecca as he poured another glass full. He was almost staring at her.

"Miss, I don't believe I've ever seen hair so red before." he said as he stepped back out of the way

"I don't know if I should be flattered or just what. Where did you get your man here?" Rebecca asked Sublette, not recognizing Thabo.

"He's not mine. He joined up with us outside of St. Louis. He's working for his keep on this trip, says he's going to be a free trapper. He's free to go after the rendezvous." Sublette said as he turned his head, holding out his cup.

"That's right. I'm to be a free trapper, say sir to no one. I'm going to be a skin trapper like Davey Jackson and Jedediah Smith. That's what I'm going to do." he said, showing a mouthful of straight white teeth.

"Well, I reckon that shines. I ain't never been a slave owner. A bunch of 'em was on the riverboat though.

"Hey, 'member Hamhead? That nigger was from Prussia. Remember we saw him when we stole that skin boat." Bill finished off his first glass, holding it out for Thabo to refill. Thabo quickly poured another. Then Bill drank his quickly so as not to fall behind too much in the drinking bravado. But Rebecca was up by two cups already, and hers was out again.

"You know, Bilth, I mean Bill, this is some very good with'skey. But, I lieveb. I mean, I mean, I believe it'll sneak up careful if you be. Aw hell! This 'ish good stuff." the white runt slurred.

"White Man, don't you go getting too drunk on me. I got plans for you tonight." Rebecca said resting her hand on Bill's leg.

"That is right. I wish to ride the pony many times also." White Moon said. *Damn she's smiling too* was all Bill could think as he passed out, slumping off the small stool he had been perched on.

"Well, looks like William will be relaxing for a time. Girls, would you." that's the last thing Billy White heard. What seemed like hours were only a few minutes until Bill sat up.

"Christ. Did I miss anything?" he mumbled, cotton mouthed.

"Nope. Have a drink William." Rebecca answered, handing him a half filled glasss of the fine whiskey.

"Damn, I'm going a tad slower." Bill sipped it this time.

"You gonna be able to slip us some of your wood there White Man?" White Moon asked.

"Yeppers. Let's get 'fore this stuff really kicks my ass!"

"Mr. Sublette, thank you for the hospitality. Could we interest you in some evening frolicking?" Rebecca queried.

"No, I'll have to pass this time but come find me later." he smiled to Rebecca.

Bill and his wives bid Mr. Sublette a good night and made their way to a quiet section of the rendezvous.

"This oughta do just fine?" Bill asked as he stared into the dark section of trees.

"Billy, let's just put down a robe and go from there. I don't wanna set camp up." Rebecca asked, swaying slightly.

"I'll do it, R'roundbecca." White Moon slurred as the fine whiskey was getting to her as well.

"You's get a fire going, see if I can find some firewood for tonight." Bill spoke as he wandered out into the darkness. After stumbling over several dead limbs, he found plenty of wood to burn. Bringing an armload, he plopped it down and turned to go back for more when White Moon beckoned him.

"That's 'nuff, Bill. Come slip me some ov yer root." He looked over to see her naked. She had her fingers plunging in and out as Rebecca was suckling on her brown breasts.

"Sure thing Moon." Bill unbuckled his thick belt, letting the knife and pistol drop and as he undid the the leather wang holding his legging on as well. Two more steps and his shirt came off. He stumbled and fell. Rolling over, he pulled each leg out of his leggings along with his moccasins. Bill got up on his hands and knees and began crawling over to Moon's smooth crotch.

"Here, let me do that." He pulled her slippery fingers away. In went his tongue, burying it deep as he sucked her honey out. She just kept oozing as his blond beard became saturated.

"Do it now! Stick it in now! Please, Bill, do it now! Please!" White Moon was begging now. Bill raised himself to his knees with his smallest member was as stiff as a hunk of firewood. One hand on her knee, the other holding his root. He guided into her. She didn't wait for him to initiate the movement as she thrust forward in a blur of movement. Rebecca could hear her pelvis whack hard against Bill.

"I want it next. But you gotta hurry!" Rebecca begged as she too was using her fingers on herself. Bill began to meet White Moon's action with his own, slamming hard against her as violently as he could, pumping away in a blur of movement he popped a load into White Moon. The Pawnee wrapped her legs around Bill, arching her back off the robe.

"Give me more! Give me more! Don't stop! More! I must have more!" she asked whimpering.

"Let me squirt some inta Rebecca. She's been waiting." he answered as he turned to the redhead.

"Hurry, Bill! Hurry!" She rolled over to her hands and knees. Bill was so anxious that he was hard in just a few moments.

"Do my pussy hard. Make it hurt! Do it so hard you hurt me! Do it! Do it!" she was sobbing now. Not one to be asked twice, he did as she asked. Bill came over to her with his erect pod. He aimed himself at his partner.

"Here you go." Then Billy began his rutting. Plunging deep with the first stroke, he heard her let out a shallow whimper. Then, pulling almost out, he rammed his pod into her with such force her arms buckled, ramming her face into the buffalo robe. Not to be quelled, she turned her head.

"Harder, Bill! Harder! Make me remember this night." So Bill thrashed her so hard he had to wrap one arm around her waist to keep her from falling on her stomach as he slammed into her.

"Now! Now please fill me! Fill me!" Bill released himself into his first wife with every ounce he could muster up. Sweating heavily, he fell back on his calves, panting like he'd just outrun a pack of Arapaho.

"Now come! Do me again!" White Moon slurred as she pulled him over, slipping his still-dripping piss'r in her mouth.

"Here! Let me help!" She gurgled and sucked. It took Bill a little longer than usual to get back into fighting form but a credit to his reputation; he was rock hard soon.

"Pound my ass! Don't even wait! Do it. Do it now!" She was almost crying as she went to her hands and knees like Rebecca had done.

"Here you go, Moon!" Bill bent down her butthole, dribbling spit on it. Then her musky smell got to him. He stuck his tongue into her butt. Doing small circles, he couldn't wait any longer. He put one hand on her butt cheek and guided himself into her. As he was slowly entering her, she rammed back with such force Bill almost lost his balance. The next time she did that, he met her with the same force, knocking her to her belly. He raised her back up with an arm under her as he continued to pummel her.

"Harder! Harder, Bill!" she demanded.

"Here! You! Go!" He shot a load into her. She kept wriggling her rump as he withdrew. As quick as a snake, she rolled over, pulling his pod into her mouth; luckily it had no shit on it. She wanted it in her mouth. Bill could feel her hot mouth bringing him back to hardness already.

"Do my ass now!" pleaded Rebecca. Not one to leave out a request, he crawled over to her as she lifted her legs toward her chest, pulling each ankle up until her rosebud was available to the runt. *This'll be four!* Bill thought. He knew what she wanted and she wanted it as hard and as violent as the last time. Concentrating as hard as he could, he managed to get erect. Two quick strokes in the seed-dripping hole was enough to get him slippery. He aimed, and then without warning he rammed into her.

"Oh god, Bill!" was all she could say as she writhed in passion. Billy White pulled completely out and rammed into her soft skin as hard as he could. Faster and faster he went. He could hear his nut sack slapping on her ass as he got closer and closer. Sweat was dripping down onto her stomach as he continued to mate with her.

"Oh! Oh! Now, Bill! Now!" she cried out. It was soon enough as Bill started squirting and kept going until his pod shriveled up and he fell back on his knees. White Moon pushed Billy out of the way as she quickly stuck her mouth to Rebecca's freshly filled hole. She sucked hard, sticking her tongue deep inside the redhead, getting all she could. Rebecca's hands came down to pull White Moon up to her mouth.

"Give me some of it!" she cried, tear running down her cheeks. White Moon opened her mouth to share with her lover. Bill sat there panting, exhausted.

"Do me again. Do it quickly!" White Moon begged.

"Yer gonna have to wait a tad. It'll take some kind doing to get it going again. I just might be played out, girl."

"I can make it work." She slid back over to him, pulling the blond lad into her mouth; she lapped and sucked until Bill started to feel the tingling. *This'll be five!* As he hardened, she kept the same bravado as earlier.

"Do me again in the rump. But harder this time!" She rolled over, pulling her legs up like Rebecca had done earlier. *Here we go.* Bill placed himself on her brown hole and pushed in; when she felt him in, she pinched her muscles tight.

"Now ram it hard, Bill. I want to hurt from you tonight!" Not needing any more encouragement, he did as she requested. What looked like a dog breeding for the first time was what Bill did. A blur was all Rebecca could see as she touched her butt, feeling the tenderness from the lovemaking. She felt more tingle as she slipped one finger in, then two. She watched Bill thrash away on Moon. Soon she was craving more from Bill. Gone was the tender hurt skin replaced with desire to be hurt again. Bill was watching her as he did White Moon.

"Here I come!" He squirted a small amount this time.

"Hurry, Bill, I want it again!" she pleaded.

"I don't think I got any left. That one was just a dribble I'm 'fraid."

"We'll see!" The redhead pulled him into her mouth, trying to get him hard for one last time. But it wasn't going to happen. His pod stayed soft as a puppies belly, no matter what she tried.

"That's it fer now I reckon. I'll poke you in a while, but for now, it's used up." He looked over to see White Moon was already asleep. He could make out a small amount of seed dribbling out of her as he sat back, elbows locked, watching Rebecca lick and suck the remainder of his seed from her fingers.

"Thanks Bill, never before have I had such a wonderful time." Then she too lay back as naked as the day she was born. Bill sat there drying off in the cool night air. *Whooooweee. What a night!*

He was going to get dressed but decided to wait until after he had the fire going. With a shower of sparks from the flint onto the dry moss, the small flames licked into the black night. He carefully added a few small twigs until it grew. In a few minutes he had a fire going that would be good enough for warmth as well as a good base for cooking in the morning. Now he could relax. He looked over to his naked wives and decided to cover them up with his new blankets. Satisfied with his chores, he sat in front of the fire. Still naked, he looked across the fire to see two white orbs reflect in the firelight.

"You wanna warm up or sit in the cold?" he asked the mystery person in the dark.

"I'll warm up." answered Thabo as he approached the fire. Bill made no attempt to getting dressed. He sat in front of the fire cross-legged as Thabo approached the fire, his eyes shot over to the girls and then to Bill's nakedness.

"How long you been sittin' out there?" Bill asked his old shipmate.

"Long enough to see you have your hands full. I counted four times. Four times in a row. I've only heard rumors you could do that. Now I've seen it firsthand, it's no longer a mystery."

"It was five, Louis, five times in a row, so, are you an errand boy for Sublette, or you here on a social visit?" the runt asked the huge black man before him.

"Social. Both. I need to know something. Why? Why did you cut me loose back in Missouri? Why didn't you tell Mr. Sublette my real name?" The ebony-skinned man asked as he stared across the fire at the small naked man.

"My my, you sure got a lot of question for a nigger, don't you? Okay let's see if my tracks are gonna be easy for you to follow. I figured you was a prick for trying to kill me back on the Big Muddy, but after me an' Rebecca saw ya drift away, I felt sorry for yer black ass."

"Sorry? Why would you feel sorry? You barely knew me, and you still don't!" Thabo sassed Bill.

"If ya want me to answer yer questions, then shut the hell up." Bill fired back at the Zulu. After the man was quiet.

Bill continued, "Lookie here, ya was a slave. I figure ya ain't always been a slave. I figured ya was somethin' else 'fore ya got snatched away. Am I right? Maybe you was a chief or some big man in yer own land? My tracks plain?"

"Yes. I was the war chief of my village in Africa. I come from the warriors called Zulu. We had conquered many tribes and enjoyed living like gods."

"See, that's what I figured. See, I figured you needed a break. You'd been chained down too much fer any man to tolerate. So I figured I'd let ya be free, not bound to no man." Billy smiled at the man from across the fire.

"I'm gonna get some duds on 'fore these girls wake up.

They'd have me forkin' them if they see me naked." He laughed a small laugh.

Now Thabo realized why his journey through life kept leading him to this small white man.

"White Man, I know why our paths always meet." Thabo spoke as he looked into the fire.

"I am to be with you not as a servant but a guardian of your life. You have done so many things for me without thought of yourself. So that is how it will be." Thabo realized he wasn't going be a slave, but he was bound to this runt.

"Huh?" Bill asked as he tied his leggings on. He reached down to pick up his breechclout.

"Yer gonna to stay with us? Hell, how am I gonna feed ya? Ya must eat a shitload of grub." Billy's mind was racing now; *How'd this huge black man pull his share of the work? Would he want to fork his wives? Did he have his own horse or camp gear?*

"Well, this adds a new touch to our little brigade." he kept talking as he pulled the 'clout up, adjusting his privates. Picking his moccasins up, he slid each one on then quickly tying them.

"I can carry my share of the work. Do not worry small one. These things will work out. I will go to Mr. Sublette now. He has been good to me, and I know he'll release me from his employ." Then he got up, did a small bow, and vanished into the predawn light.

Bill's head was spinning. *What would the girls say, having a nigger in their midst? Would they fork him like they'd been forking me? Do I want him to slip in some of that dark meat? I'm gonna sleep on this.* He pulled his wide belt on and adjusted it touching everything in the right place. Bill pulled a blanket over himself and quickly fell asleep.

CHAPTER 115

In the morning the girls woke red eyed. Neither of them were perky as they'd drank too much, with throbbing heads and tender backsides. They huddled together under the new blankets.

"That little varmint. Goddamned, that man can fuck, cain't he Rebecca?" White Moon said as she inched her hand down between her legs and touched herself gently.

"Yeah, I ain't gonna shit straight for a week." she answered.

"Let's get a bucket of water an' douse him. What do ya say?" Rebecca asked her lover.

"I'm gonna pull something on, or he'll be humping us but good." White Moon said as she got up in the early dawn light. She quickly picked up her doeskin dress, slipping it over her slim shoulders, adjusting it properly. She looked over to see Rebecca pulling on her leggings and a similar dress as well. They both pulled on the belts and knives with Rebecca slipping her pistol under her belt just in case another trapper wanted an uninvited poke.

Down to the stream the pair went with an empty bucket; leaning over the cold stream, they pulled a bucketful of Utah's coldest. Now armed with the bucket of cold stream water, they prepared to drench the soon-to-be-sober runt. Carefully White Moon slipped next to Bill and ever so slowly pulled out Isaiah's knife.

"Where's his pistol?" she mouthed out the words. Rebecca pointed to the rifle and pistol; both were within Bill's easy reach. White Moon slowly inched them away from the sleeping man. As she backed away, she nodded to Rebecca. She leaned back and hurled the water on the relaxed little man.

"Christ!" Bill exclaimed as he leapt to his feet, his hand going for his knife, but all that was a there was air. He finally focused on his attackers; White Moon and Rebecca were standing there with big grins on their faces. *Shit, I just barely got to sleep! Goddamnit!* he thought quickly.

"Good morning, Billy." The white man turned to see Sublette walking up.

"Good morning there Bill." Billy White greeted the trader through chattering teeth.

"I thought I'd stop by an' see how you fared last night as you all were pretty well into the cups. Here, young William, drink some of this." He held out a tin cup.

"Why thanks Bill." The runt took the tin cup and sipped it slowly.

"It's some of the hair of the dog that bit you!" Sublette went on.

"Christ! I ain't even sober from last night." Bill coughed a few times.

"Whoowee!" He coughed until he had tears running down his face.

"Here, have another taste, son." Sublette filled the cup again as Bill swallowed another mouthful.

"Hmm? That wasn't as bad as the other'n." he called out to the crowd that had formed around the small white man.

"Hell, that ain't half bad." he started to feel the whiskey warming him already; he already forgot the wet buckskin shirt he had just slipped on a few moments ago.

"Maybe I can get some use out of you now Bill!" Rebecca said as she had a deep-bellied laugh out of Bill's recuperation.

"The white man lives! Goddamn, I figured you'd gone under! It's good you're still alive. Now I can go under you!" White Moon smiled.

"Well, I leave you folks to your own demise. Good day." Bill Sublette waved as he turned and faded into the crowd.

"Okay, which one of you wants it first?" he asked his wives as he started feeling himself getting hard already.

"Damn! I never thought of drinkin' again so soon. Did taste good after the first cup though." he spoke to Rebecca as White Moon piped up. "You can do me first, but no back end today. You did us up good last night." she said, staring at Bill with the soft doe eyes.

"Well, you know, you're goddamned wicked when you've been in the cups. Four times in a row!" White Moon exclaimed.

"No, Moon, it was five! Five times! Shit, I only dreamed you could do that an' lookie here. Plugged me twice an' you three. Damned fine, Bill, damned fine." chimed in Rebecca as they all headed back to the robes and horses.

"I reckon we could set up a proper camp today, girls. Damn I feel like I could go off if ya jus' touch ol'John Thomas." he said as he locked an arm around each woman's waist.

"We're gonna have some fun now. That's fer certain an' fer true." Bill's spirit was soaring now that he was on his way for a romp in the robes with his wives.

"Hey, you there! Are ya Billy White?" the voice called out.

"Goddamnit! Now what?" he answered as he turned the girls around so they could see the caller.

"Yeppers. What can I do fer ya there, frien'?" Bill answered.

"Well, I got me a cup of John Barleycorn that says I can throw you down." he said as he stood there looking at Bill. He looked like every other trapper Bill had met. Greasy buckskin leggings, long greasy hair pulled back into a tail. No shirt. Purple scars adorned his torso from past adventures.

"Why wouldja wanna do that, frien'? Hell, me an' the girls would happy to buy you a cup. We ain't gotta fight fer it." he answered.

"I was jus' lookin' fer some sport. I figured you'd be a hoot wrestlin'. So what do ya say there Billy? Ya ain't scarit of a little wrestlin', are ya?" he said with a big grin.

"To be honest with ya, I was fixin' to get me a poke here with my wives. Maybe we can get to fight later. How would that be, frien'? Hell, what's yer name anyhoo?" Bill asked.

"Oh shit. Sorry 'bout that Billy. I'm Johnny Cottoné." The

caller stuck out his hand to be shaken. As Bill shook it, the caller continued, "So will ya fight me fer a cup 'er not?"

By this time several onlookers had gathered. They all started whistling, hooting for Bill and Johnny to take up a wrestling match.

"Go fer it, Billy. I betcha you can throw ol'Cottoné down in nothin' flat." a bare-chested white man hollered. Before Bill knew, they were circled by free trappers and camp workers alike.

"Now yer ain't get all riled up an wanna skin me out if'n I win, are ya? That goddamned Champeau was wantin' to carve my liver fer not sharin' my wives." he asked as he released the women's waists.

"Hell no. That prick's a backbitin' son of a bitch. You best watch yer back trail with that nigger. He'll bushwhack ya fer sure." Johnny said as the crowd murmured their agreement.

"Is there any rules 'er is jus' the first one to be knocked down? I mean is it fistfightin' 'er jus' fun-time wrestlin'?" he asked as he pulled off his war shirt to reveal the scars from the bear and the Arapaho fights. Murmurs went around as people saw that this really was the man that survived the grizzly bear attack. Johnny saw them as well.

"Them the scars the nigger bear left on ya?" he asked, pointing to Bill's shoulder.

"Yeppers, basterd's in hell now. Is this wrestlin' where the first one down loses? No fists 'er kickin' with yer feet like them pork-eatin' French basterds." Bill answered.

"Yes sah, first one down loses. No fist 'er feet. How's that sound?" he asked with a big grin. Bill was glad to meet this man; *maybe we's finally met some good folks.*

"Okay. Let's dance!" he said as he started circling Bill. Cottoné jumped forward, throwing his right hand behind the runt's head. With the other, he grabbed Bill's left arm. The white runt mimicked the move as he danced in a small circle, each man looking for the opportunity to throw his opponent down. Bill thought for a moment then quickly released his grasp, stepping inside to bear hug Cottoné. It caught Johnny by surprise as he tried to wiggle his arm inside to break Bill's grasp. Bill felt this and began to spin. Around and around they went four, five times. Then Bill released his competitor and quickly backed away. The trapper couldn't get his balance so he plopped right down on his ass. Then he grabbed the grass to keep from spinning around even more. The crowd went wild with laughter as Johnny finally regained his footing.

"Well, I'll be. That's the first time that's ever happened. Ain't no man ever beat Johnny Cottoné in a wrestlin' match! Here, have a cup. You won fair an' square." he offered it up as they shook hands.

"Thank ye kindly, Johnny." he answered as he handed the awful-tasting concoction back to his new friend.

"Hey there! I'm next so don't go a get all licker'd up." A new opponent stepped forward.

"Hold on now." The runt held his hand up.

"I ain't gonna have to fight all you niggers is I?" Bill asked, laughing.

"Nah. I'll be that last one 'cause I'm gonna toss you in to next week, son." This trapper looked to be quite a bit older than Johnny. Bill and his new opponent sized each other up. He was as big as Sheila but not black. His red and gray hair hung loosely down his shoulders with a great lock touching the middle of his back. The man before Billy smiled, showing his missing teeth.

"Who might you be, frien'?" the runt asked as they circled each other.

"Clay Meyers at yer service." Squatting down in a crouch position, he answered with never-ending smile.

"Meyers? Hey, wasn't that the captain's name on that ol' paddleboat we was on?" the runt asked over his shoulder, never taking his eyes off his opponent as he watched this grizzled older warrior circle him.

"Yeppers. It surely was. You watch your ass, Bill. I want it next! You hear me!" she snapped. The crowd went up in wild laughter. It had grown from a couple of trappers to a sea of men and Indians.

"Meyers. You got any kin piloting a riverboat on the Mississippi?" Billy asked. He stood up surprised. He was taken aback that someone from the settlements would know of his family. As Clay went upright in shock, Bill leaped upon him, plastering a huge kiss on his lips. It took Clay by such a surprise he stumbled back a step, lost his footing, slipped, and plopped right down on the ground. Once again the crowd went up in a roar.

"I'll be 'et fer a tatter! That ain't never happen 'fore." Then he commenced to start laughing and hugging his stomach. He was laughing like there was no tomorrow. *Another good trapper,* Bill thought to himself as he watched the man before him enjoying a belly laugh.

"That riverboat captain is my brother. Ezekiel. How was the ol'salt anyway?" he asked as he stuck out his hand to Bill to be pulled up. The runt took the raised hand, pulling him to his feet.

"Here ya go. I keep my bets." Clay offered Bill the pail of amber liquid. The runt swallowed a mouthful, anticipating the burn.

"Augh!" he choked out as he handed it back.

"It's a long story. I'll have to tell ya sometime. All right, who's next? Let's have some fun boys! Come on, who's next?" Billy White asked, smiling and thinking that these were good ol'boys. The crowd parted, and Champeau knocked people aside as he walked up.

"You're fuckin' dead White. I'm gonna break you in two for getting me thrown outta here!" he spat at Bill. Before Bill could say anything, Clay and John stepped between them.

"If you got a problem with Billy, then you've a got a problem with me." Clay spoke, pointing to himself.

"That goes fer me too!" John chimed in.

"Get outta of the fuckin' way, you corn-crackin' flatlanders, 'er I'll break you in two." His voice was deep and menacing. Then out came his pig sticker. Clay or John had no knife. So they parted, letting the fat man come through. No Sublette this time to save Bill's ass.

"Bill!" The runt sidestep Joe's first lunge. *This time he ain't drunk. He moves quick for a fat man. Almost too quick! Christ! He moves fast! An' I already drank too much hooch!* Bill thought as he crouched down to see what this killer's next move was going to be.

"Joe, I'm gonna have to kill you, ain't I?" Bill asked the man circling him.

"I'm gonna gut you! Then I'm gonna give those sluts to the Blackfoot jus' to watch 'em bein' skinned!" he answered in a raspy voice, a mean scowl coming across his face.

"No. I don't believe you'll be a doin' that, you little fat shit. Hell, you'll have to put your guts in to yer boots jus' to walk outta this here camp!" Bill spoke, hoping to upset the man into making a mistake.

"I'm gonna slit your throat an' skull fuck you!" With that he leaped at Bill. He faked to his right, switching the knife to his left hand. It was a blur for Billy White as the whiskey started really kicking in. He swirled around following the movements of Joe. *Damn, my arm's burning.* He looked down to see a deep slice on it. Blood was freely flowing from the gash. *Aw shit! I didn't even see it comin'. This basterd's too good fer me. I can already see that he's got a shitload of tricks an' he was wantin' to try on me. Hmm?* Bill thought through the fog that was taking over his mental alertness. He rushed again, so Bill dropped to the ground as he went by trying to trip him. The fat bastard jumped like a cat as his knife cut the top of the runt's head.

"Damnit, that hurts!" Bill cried out. Blood was running down the side of his head into his ear. Then Joe cleared his throat, spitting at Bill, the lunger landed on Bill's chest. He never looked down and he kept his eyes riveted on the menacing man before him.

"That all you got, runt? I gonna slice every piece up so you're nothin' but a bloody stump of shit!" he roared at the smaller man.

Bill judged the distance, thought about the throw, and hurled the knife at his fat opponent. It went by Joe, falling to the ground skittering and out of sight.

"Well, ain't you a dumbshit? I thought you was dumber than dirt. I reckon you really are." He swung again, but Billy was able to lean back enough to miss getting sliced.

"You can only go so long 'fore I cut you again runt!" He started laughing at Bill's misfortune. He lunged again, so Bill rolled out of the way to the other side of the circle of trappers forming a crude fighting ring. As he turned, Bill picked up his war shirt from the ground. As Champeau came at him again, Bill caught the knife in the leather war shirt. Finally he was able to do something right. The knife came out of Joe's hand as it was flung to the ground with one swift movement. Billy White was getting dizzy from the loss of blood, and he knew he had to do something quickly or he would go under for sure.

"Well well, you know one thing." He reached behind his back, producing another knife. Bill fished around in the shirt until he found the knife. This time Bill feigned a slash. Champeau didn't move as quick this time.

"Oh, you think you're gonna gut me with my own knife, do ya?" He swung wildly. His aim was off. That's when Bill remembered when Rebecca fought the foul runt a lifetime ago. So he watched him move. *All I gotta do is make him go left, step inside, an' do the deed,* Bill almost spoke aloud. *It's like he's reading my mind,* Bill thought as he planned his final steps of the knife fight. Bill faked to the right. Joe saw it coming and swung to the left to counter Billy's move; but before he could right himself, the runt stepped in, pulled his head back exposing the fat neck. Then Bill pulled the knife across the slippery white meat, slicing the throat as Joe's weight swung working against him. *Oops!* Bill's timing had been off as Joseph Champeau rammed his blade into the runt's thigh just missing the main artery as his life was ending.

"Yow! Christ! Now that hurts." he looked down at Champeau as he was squirming, trying to breathe through the new mouth in the middle of his fat neck. He lowered his head, and it quit bleeding! He even made it to his feet but fell flat on his face soon after that. A big puff of dirt went into the air as the fat body settled down on to the ground.

"That rascal ain't gonna devil me no more!" Bill took his knife, hobbling over to where the fat man lay, kneeled down on one knee with the knife still buried deep in his thigh. He lifted the knife high, and with all his remaining strength, he buried it into the back of Joseph Champeau. The runt kept pushing as it went into the spinal column and through the ribs into the back of the dead man's heart.

"Sumbitch ain't got no hair to even scalp!" Bill laughed a small chuckle. The crowd was quiet as Rebecca and White Moon came to his side quickly. Bill was confused by the quietness of the crowd. *This fat prick was trying to kill me. Now that it's over, they're just stared at me and that fat bastard.*

"It's true. This is really Billy White." It was the last thing Bill heard as his wives took him away, and he passed out from the loss of blood.

* * *

He awoke in Sublette's tent with his wives looking after him.

"Hell, I'm a thinkin' ain't this a familiar story. My head hurts lover." Bill complained.

"Bill, you oughta be dead from all the blood you lost. I can't believe you tried to throw your only knife. You coulda been killed, you little asshole!" she burst out.

"Not even a how-do-you-do? Nothing? Just an' ass chewing right from the get-go?" he spoke through dry chapped lips.

"What the hell were you thinking? All you had to do was wear him down. Couldn't you see that? Christ, Bill! We almost lost you.

You. You white runt." She started bawling as she wrapped her arms around the small invalid man in front of her.

"Is the White Man alive?" he heard the voice of White Moon.

"Hell yeah, ain't no fat fart camp man gonna make this child go under!" he quipped as Rebecca moved over so White Moon could sit next to them. Her eyes welled full of tears.

"Now lookie here, girls. I ain't dead. Jus' cut up some. 'Fore long, I'll be well 'nuff to fork you both! How long have I been here anyhoo?" he asked.

"Bill you were almost dead from the infections in your leg." she wept.

"Bill, they cut your leg off!" she cried.

"What are you talkin' 'bout? I can feel my toes jus' fine girl. Lift me up so as I can see." They did. It was.

Bill sat up quickly sweating.

"My leg! My leg!" he screamed.

"Bill, it's okay. You're dreaming!" It was Rebecca holding him down.

"Don't let 'em cut off my leg! Don't let 'em cut it goddamnit!" the runt called out.

"Bill, your leg is okay! You got a fever. You're gonna be okay. Here, have some this."

She held up a cup to drink. He took a sip of the warm, foul-tasting concoction.

"What the hell's that?" he questioned.

"It is medicine. It'll help the healing from the inside as well as the outside." White Moon answered.

"Is my leg okay lover? I gotta know." He sat up looking down to see his scrawny feet sticking out from beneath the thick white, red, and green trade blanket.

"Bill, it was only a dream. You rest now." she said as she placed a cool rag on his head.

"I don't wanna sleep. They're gonna cut my leg off if'n I sleep. Cain't sleep. They'll cut it off." Bill drifted off unconscious again.

He awoke in darkness; a lantern by the cot illuminated the figure of White Moon.

"Hey there, lover. How you doin'? I could sure use them lips of yer's around my pod 'bout now." Her eyes opened like big milk saucers as she leaped on him, smothering the runt in kisses.

"Rebecca! Come quickly. He lives. He lives!" she cried out. Bill saw Rebecca come in, her eyes black and hollow from the lack of sleep and too much crying.

"Hey, if'n yer not too busy, I'll let you thrash me soundly girl. You ain't been poked in a while, have you? Lest you been gettin' it from Louis." Bill joked, causing his dry lip to crack.

"He ain't half bad, but he can't go three times." She smiled teasing Billy.

By now it had been seven days since Bill had been cut in the knife fight. The infection from Champeau's knife had almost taken the life of the little blond trapper. Bill Sublette had brought every medicine man and semi-practicing saw bone to help with Billy White's recovery. But it was White Moon's medicines that helped the runt from Missouri cheat death again.

They stayed with Sublette as Billy did his convalescence. Day after day he felt better; soon he could put weight on his leg and began testing its strength.

"Ya know, girls, I can walk pretty good. Is Bill around?" He queried them about Bill Sublette.

"Not right now but I reckon he's not far away, why?" Answered Rebecca.

"I was wantin' him to inner'duce me to some of them there Crow from the Absoroka's so we can have a place to winter up."

"I'll go find him." Louis piped in on the conversation. Then Billy watched the Zulu fade into the sea of Indians, trappers and mountain men. Bill sat on one of the many wooden folding chairs that encircled the fire pit.

"Girls, thanky fer patching me up." He addressed his wives.

"Ya ain't gotta do that William, yer our husband. We'll do what ever it takes to keep yer scrawny ass safe so as ya can slip that hunk of hickory in us reg'lar like." Rebecca said.

"Ha ha, fair 'nuff." He looked around them to see Sublette returning with Louis.

"What can I do for you Billy?" Billy White stood up and addressed the booshway.

"I was a hoping ya could inner'duce us to some Crow's, so we'll have a place to winter up." Bill asked the trader.

"I can do that, come with me. I'll introduce you to Iron Hand from The Many Lodges tribe of the Crow nation and you can parley with him." The trader said.

"Can my wives come too?" The runt asked.

"That would be grand." Sublette answered.

They walked down the row of the free trappers. They all stopped to see Sublette and his entourage walk by, set on a path to the Crows, *I don't know what's goin' on with these folks a starrin' at us*, past the Arapaho's and their venomous stares, the Pawnee's looked at White Moon but made no visible greetings. Past the lowly Bannocks that barely acknowledged the foursome, the Flatheads, the Nez Perce with their fine spotted horses and finally stopping at the Crows. All the people were dressed in their best regalia, the women had white doe skin dresses with long fringe coming from their arms. They used fur, beads, feathers and dyed porcupine quills to accent their magnificent dresses.

A tall man came out of a teepee lodge and noticed Sublette walking towards him, "Sublette its good to see you." Iron Hand spoke in perfect English.

Rebecca watched Bill Sublette reach out to greet the chief but Iron Hand looked past his friend to see Billy and the girls. *He didn't stop to greet me, he walked right past me to the trio.* Bill Sublette thought.

He was six foot tall and towered over the short trapper. Bill had to look up to make eye contact with the exquisitely dressed man. On his head was a eagle feathered headdress with white feathers with contrasting black tips, the bottom of where the feathers met the headband were wrapped with some brilliant red cloth. The forehead section had, red, blue, yellow, and green glass beads wove into an arrowhead design. The headdress was so long that flowed over his shoulders. A necklace of grizzly bear claws hung from his chest. His white brain tanned buckskins shirt was dyed a deep blue on his shoulders that faded into moss green near the bottom, it had two woven designs with glass beads, horse hair, colored porcupine quills and small puff of animal fur wove into a striking pattern. The bead work came from under the headdress to just above his waist line. The fringe had been decorated similar to the soft leather buckskin shirt, with horse hair, colored quills and beads. On his left hand was a Spanish conquistador steel glove that was highly polished to a mirror finish. Bill took in the spectacular man. *This mus' be Iron Hand. Damn this fell'r knows how impress folks, that's fer certain an' fer true.* Sublette caught up with Iron Hand and introduced the White Man.

"Billy, may I introduce Iron Hand of the Many Lodges band of the Crow nation." Sublette stepped back allowing the chief to stand alone.

"Howdy Iron Hand, I'm Billy White."

"You are the Arapaho killer." Not a question but a statement.

"Yep, that be me."

"Sublette has spoken to me about you, you wish to winter with us in the Absoroka mountains."

"That's fer certain an fer true Iron Hand."

"How many enemy of my nation have you rubbed out?"

"I lost count after ten."

"My wife, has killed that many, maybe a coupla more if ya wanna count the Sioux warriors." He turn and pointed to the red head. Iron Hand looked over to the white woman. *Her hair is like fire, she is a warrior.*

"Sioux warriors?" He asked.

"Yeppers. I believe it was six of them."

"Once we saw some Crow fight the Arapaho in a small valley a while back, it was a bloody battle, all were killed. We needed clothes an such thing so we removed what we needed. We have a medicine bag from Great Owl. It's saved us many times from wounds them 'Raps have given us."

"Do you have it?"

"Yeppers."

"I wish to return it to his wife, Spotted Owl.

"Hang face fer a lick an' I'll go get it."

"Not now, you may bring it later or when you winter up with us."

"Thank you fer allowing us to stay with you. You say yer in the Absoroka range? We'll see you then. Thank you Iron Hand."

Then they shook hands the Indian way, half way up their arms grasping firmly. Iron Hand walked away and Billy was able to see the back of the headdress that went down his back, nearly to his waist. *Well that was short and sweet.* Billy thought. Sublette stayed a few minutes longer talking with Iron Hand. Then he caught up with Billy and his wives.

"That went well don't you think?" Sublette commented.

"Not sure where the Absoroka mountains is but I figure them Crows will find us or the Blackfeet. It'll be a fight if its them Blackfeet. You know, Two Sticks told us that there be three diff'ernt tribes all rolled up in one." Billy said to Sublette.

"That's true. The bug boys' is what the free trappers call them. The Piegans, Gros Ventre and the Bloods. Better hope it isn't one of them, they're a mean bunch. You could bump into more Arapaho's."

"That'll be damp powder fer sure if we bump into them rascals." Billy commented.

"That's true." Sublette said as neared the Arapaho's camp.

"Hang face girls." He called. Sublette turned to see what was going on.

"Whatcha up to White Man?" White Moon turned and walked back to Billy.

"These's 'Raphos right?" he quizzed her.

"Yeppers, that be fer certain an' fer true." She said as she watched Billy thinking, *Now whats he doin'? Hope he don't get us killed.*

Billy walked into the Arapaho's camp and watched it became a bustle of activity.

"What do you want?" A very menacing tall man dressed with the Arapaho headress of eagle feathers and red cloth similar to Iron Hand's with intricate beadwork. His headband was simple red crosses and a white background. His war shirt was not dyed, it had trade beads and horse hair on all the fringe.

"You the chief?" The runt tried to make himself looked bigger.

"I am Gray Wolf. You are Billy White, the Arapaho killer. You have rubbed out many of our warriors. Two Wolves is my son, when I heard that you dishonored him and let him live my blood boiled for revenge. But you had fled our land. Running away like the coward you are. You are fortunate we are here, not on our land where I would kill you and your women."

"Well now, yer son lives? I bettcha he hasta keep his noggin' covered up." Bill chuckled, "won't be bedding women I wager!" Billy laughed in Gray Wolf's face.

The chief took a step towards the White Man, Billy was not intimidated by this man, he didn't flinch or blink. Gray Wolf was shaking with anger. *He is an arrogant little man,* he thought when he tried to bully the blond trapper.

"I see we got the politeness out of the way. I wanna hunt an' trap without lookin' over my shoulder all day an' night, 'cause fer you fell'r's trying to rub me out. I reckon we're not to have peace between us." The runt asked.

"No." Gray Wolf gritted his teeth and crossed his arms on his chest to keep from attacking the smaller trapper.

"Yer sure?" Billy smiled at the Arapaho.

"Yes, you are going north as many trapper's do. You will try to stay with Iron Hand, the Crow, for the winter or north to the Sparrow Hawk band of the Crows. We will make sure you never make it! If need be, we will rub out the Crow to get to you.

You whitemen are all the same, kill our beaver and buffalo, spit on our land. You are like a sickness spreading across the mountains. You will be hunted day and night, you will never know saftey. We have allies, the Blackfeet Nation, they want to rub you out. Yes. You Billy White. The White Man. You and your fire haired woman will be tortured and not allowed to die. The Pawnee will be my slave, many of my people have a hatred for the lowly people of the plains."

"So its jus' a matter of time 'till you find us." Bill said not backing down, "that the tracks your leaving? How 'bout me and you dancing right here right now?" Bill taunting the chief.

"No, we have an agreement with the traders not to kill while we are at the rendezvous. I will honor it. I will kill you later." He arrogantly sneared.

Billy looked at each warrior standing with Gray Wolf, trying to memorize their faces, *I cain't really tell 'em apart. Look at their faces. Their eyes. There. Now I see the difference.* "So be it. Yer women are gonna be without a son 'er husband." Billy backed away into the crowd that had gathered. No one spoke as they vanished into the mass of people.

The atmosphere was tense when they returned to the traders tent. No one spoke, it was like a funeral with no wake.

"Thanks for introducing us to Iron Hand, Mr. Sublette." The runt broke the silence.

"No problem Billy."

Addressing Louis, Sublette asked, "Louis, bring some of my finest whiskey for us to be sipping."

"Sure thing Mr. Sublette." He bowed, turned and went into the big tent of the trader. He returned with the liquor and four glasses.

"So, what was that about? With them Arapaho's?" Rebecca asked

"Jus' what I asked. If we could let bygones be bygones." Bill sighed, "he made it clear, they all wanted to rub out the White Man."

"Wait, back up. You said they all?" Sublette asked.

"Yeppers. If'n they come after us, their women will be in mourning fer sure." The White Man stated. Not gloating. But the straight truth.

"Are you and your wives that good to be able to take a complete tribe of Arapaho's?" Bill Sublette asked astonished.

"That be the tracks I'm leaving. See we fight on our terms not their's. If we know our surroundings better than them, well, I gots a few tricks of my own." the White Man stated.

"Well shit." Moon entered the conversation, "that Gray Wolf is a big fucker idn't he."

"Damn right." Rebecca smiled

"Remember that big 'un we killed the ones that killed Daniel, Shannon and the others. Somethin' like four 'er five balls to bring him down." Bill reminisced.

"One to the balls worked didn't it." Rebecca recalled.

"Ha ha, fucker thought he was invincible." Bill chuckled.

"Did you hear Two Wolves was Gray Wolf's son. I bet he shit when he found out he was scalped and shot to hell." Bill chuckled.

"Fucker's got no balls or pod now." Rebecca laughed.

Sublette hadn't forgot about Louis standing there, he didn't want to disrespect Billy by breaking into his story. "No, we'll be drinking from tin cups, Louis." Sublette requested.

Louis smiled to all in the small group, "Yes'sah." He answered in his house slave voice.

When he returned the ex-slave passed out the stained and battered cups, then presented the ornate bottle to Sublette.

"Now, Mrs. White. How about a drink? White Man I know you're ready."

"Are you up for it White Moon." Rebecca turned and asked her close friend and lover.

"Fucking right I am."

"My my, you have a very exquisite and colorful way of speaking."

"I learned it from my man." She nodded to the White Man.

"Holy horse shit Bill! Brinin' out the good stuff fer us?" The White Man exclaimed.

"As White Moon would say, fuckin' right!" Bill Sublette quoted. They each received a tin cup and then it was filled to the top.

"Hold on Mr. Sublette, Louis get yerself a cup an' join us, I mean if yer host don't mind?" Rebecca called out.

"Sure, sit on down, you might as well have a drink as a free man." Sublette spoke to Louis.

Well, thank you very much." Louis answered. He quickly returned with his cup and wooden chair. He poured it like the others.

"Mr. Sublette, when was the last time you had sex." Rebecca asked point blank.

That took Sublette by surprise as he pondered the question. *Now when was it? I know it was in St. Louis with my wife, but I can't recall after that.*

"It was months ago in St. Louis." He said he looked into Rebecca's blue eye's.

"Well what if me and Moon were to take you into the tent right there an' show you the time of your life?"

"Whooo!" He exhaled, "That does sound exciting, I imagine you can show me things that most men would only dream or lie about. What do you think about all this Billy White? You have no problems with the wives having sex with me without you being there?"

"Who said I wasn't gonna be there? I want a poke somethin' fierce, hell we might even get Louis in there." The White Man smiled looking at the black man.

"No. No Louis. He may be a freeman, I don't want him in there with me engaging in sex. I just can't do that Billy."

"That's okay Mr. Sublette, it would be strange for me as well." Louis said.

"If I were to accept this offer, it would only be with Rebecca. I could only handle one, that would be quick I might add. No offense White Moon."

"None taken Mr. Sublette." White Moon answered as she walked over to the White Man and sat down.

"I'll do fine right here with my three shooter." She put her arm around Billy and squeezed.

"Three shooter?" Sublette asked.

"Yeppers, my little white man here can pop three times in a row with no rest between. Shit, me an' Rebecca got five outta him last night." She rested her head on his shoulder.

"That true Billy White?" Sublette asked.

"Yep, that's the gospel truth right there." Answered her movement by resting his on hers.

White Moon was on a roll now, "Hell, I might fuck ol'Louis right there outta the goodness of my heart. Hmm, now that you mention it. Louis, show me what ya got hidden in them fancy breeches?" She asked.

"Right now, in front of everyone?"

"Ya ain't shy are ya?" She asked. Rebecca turned to see as her interest was piqued as well.

"I feel awkward doing this." Louis said.

"You wanna a poke?" Moon asked.

"Yes very much so."

"Well, skin 'er out fer me." She asked.

"Yes mam." He stood and undid the buttons an pulled his black penis out, it started to swell almost immediately. He pulled the long foreskin down to show the black shiny head.

"Shit! Damn and hellfire! I ain't never seen anything that big. Ever." Rebecca said.

Meanwhile Bill Sublette was having mixed feeling about having sex. *I want Rebecca so much it hurts, but my wife. Well she's not here and no one to tell her, but I'll know. I've always been honest with her. I want to but I know I shouldn't.*

"Rebecca, I'm going to have to take a pass for your frivolities, I'm a married man and I just can't do this. If I were going to do this you'd be the first and only choice." He spoke solidly, not pioused about how the evening was shaping up.

"No worries Bill." she spoke looking him in the eyes seeing his indecision as she'd seen so many times before in married men.

"You can put that thing away Louis, I ain't gonna be using you tonight, 'sides yer scaring the mares." Moon laughed slapping her knee. The big black man stuffed his erection back into his breeches. *I'm relieved not having to perform in front of these people.*

"Shit fire Bill, pour me another cup of yer fine hooch." Billy White asked.

"Hell ya, I'll take some more too." Rebecca's held out her empty cup as well.

They drank well into the night, philosophizing and telling stories of past adventures and lovers. When Bill Sublette told Louis to get another bottle Billy White said, "That's it fer me Bill. I gotta be able to walk back to our camp, 'sides these scamps will wanta have some attention too."

"That be true Bill, if he's too drunk me and Moon will doin' most of our sitting on one butt cheek as every hole will be sore."

"Well lets get to it!" Billy announced. They said their good byes and bid Bill Sublette a good night. The girls were ready for a romp in the robes.

They arrived at the camp and inspected their goods to assure nothing had been tampered with.

"What say we do this, we each get to pull on William once. Then we play the who's who game?" Rebecca giggled.

"What's that?" Moon asked.

"We blind fold the white man here an' he has to tell who's who without touching either of us, if he gets it right then he gets a poke with that 'un."

"That ain't too hard. Shit. I can tell by your sweet aroma." He pointed to White Moon.

"Hmm, set back." Rebecca said.

"How about this. You each get a poke then snuggle up and enjoy each other's company fer a bit." Billy suggested.

"Well, I guess." Rebecca grudgingly agreed.

Bill stripped down to his legging and moccasins and brought Rebecca into his right arm and White Moon to his left.

Satisfied with the arrangements. He leaned over and kissed each of their heads.

"Bill, this's nice. But I'm not nice. Get your pecker out and put it to use, we can do this after you poke us proper." Rebecca commanded.

"She's right White Man. Come on. Thrash us somethin' fierce!" White Moon joined in. He sat up and got on his knees and began to shuffle girls an' pelts in order to poke each one.

"Moon, yer here, ass in the air. Rebecca you do the same right next to her." He pointed to a place next to Moon.

"There. I can go from one to the other'n without missing a beat."

"Rebecca?" he paused, "Are you ready?"

"Yes I." Bill didn't wait for her to finish her sentence as he rammed her straight away. In he went deep and rough. She was taken by surprise and her instinct was to pull away, but Bill had his arm around her waist preventing that movement.

"I'm coming! I'm…" she squealed. She no longer had said the words and Billy was out and did the same to Moon.

"Ugh! Oh fuck yeah! Harder you sawed off prick!" She cussed as she felt her orgasm coming quickly. Then bam! She came. As soon as she quivered he was out and into Rebecca. He whaled on her with the veracity of a terrier with a rat. This time he unloaded into her. Still squirting he came out and into Moon. Once again he pumped savagely. He saw her back arch knowing she was orgasming as he popped inside her.

He quickly pulled out while he was still squirting, a long thread of semen followed his pod as it came out. Not slowing down he aimed at Rebecca's anus. No teasing or careful insertion. He leaned back preparing to plunge into her. Rebecca read Bill's mind and she put her forehead on the soft pelt as her hands came back grabbing each butt cheek she pulled them apart giving Bill an excellent target.

"Read my mind." He said.

"Do it" she spoke in a short quick breath.

No more coaching was needed as he ripped into her.

"Owww! Harder! Harder!" Bill was going at top speed and he popped his third one into her. She fell flat on her chest heaving for a breath of air as she had been holding her breath.

Once again he repeated the same steps. This time it took more concentration but Bill rallied to give Moon the last one.

"Fuck it hard White Man! Rip it! Make me remember this day!" She pleaded. Not one to step away from a request he pushed harder and faster inching closer to his fourth explosion.

She felt her groin tingling as her next orgasm was coming hard.

"Do it! Squirt now!" She demanded.

"Here. You. Go!" As he gave her his last semen. He fell off to the side as White Moon rolled next to her redheaded lover.

"Goddamn he does that so well." She spoke in a ragged breath.

"You got that right Lover. No one can do what that little shit does. No one." Rebecca answered.

"There, are you scamps satisfied?" He asked as he ran his hand down Moon's back then gently across her butt cheek.

"I can't even begin to describe how I feel Billy. Can't do it." Moon confessed.

"In all my years as a sporting girl I've have a lot of men, most are quick shooter, once in a while one go fer a quick minute but none can do what you do Mr. William White. Rebecca rolled Bill over and gently began to caress his pod. Slowly it began to swell.

"You got more for us?" Rebecca asked.

"Unfucking believable." White Moon's interest was piqued by Rebecca's getting Bill to go for one more.

"Think you can get one more runt?" Rebecca asked.

"You keep going like that and you'll have a snack to share with Moon." She worked feverishly trying to get one more but Bill's garden tool simply went soft.

"That's it." He said as he laid back and laced his fingers behind his head and exhaled. The women went to each side of the runt as they drifted off to sleep.

In the morning each shuffled about slowly as the night of frolicking began to take its toll on them. Each had a job to do as they readied themselves for the day that already started.

"Let's pack up an' get to Yellerstone. I heard from some of them folks it has big pools of stinky water that gushes up inta the sky. They say that water is hot an' crystal clear. I bet that we'll find a shitload of beaver up there. So what do ya say? Ya wanna move on 'er stay here fer some more fun?" he asked them as he watched the rendezvous going on in full swing. Trappers were doing horse races, playing shell games, drinking, throwing tomahawks, and, the most important thing, bedding down every squaw they could lay their hands on.

"I'd like to see Yellowstone. It's a place I've heard much about." White Moon answered, "besides if I stay here any longer I won't be able to sit on a goddamned horse." Both girls got a chuckle out of that.

"Hell, Moon, I figured you'd been there. I was a hopin' that you be able to lead us up thata way." he answered as he waved to a group of free trappers as they staggered by, heading for the nearby stream.

"Two Sticks would know. Is he still here 'er did he vamoose, too?" Bill turned to his redheaded partner.

"He's long gone. After he skinned out what he could from the free trappers, he skedaddled back to the Platte. Says it gets too cold up this way. We should find a valley to live in while we trap on the way up." she said as they watched some of the Crows doing horse tricks.

"Glad we'll be able to winter up with them Crows. Iron Hand seemed like a purty good fell'r. Jus' gotta watch our horses, Two Sticks said they like to steal horses."

"That band lives very far north. They're next to the Blackfoot. They raid each other continually for slaves. It could be bad going with them." White Moon spoke emotionless, "but to be able to winter up, its worth the risk."

"Well, that's settled. Let's pack up an' get!" Bill said as he walked about the camp organizing things in his mind.

"Shit, I figured it would take a long time to pack but with all three of us it won't take no time at all." He said.

"It's my good fortune to have a medicine woman that loves a good snack!" He hugged the bronze Pawnee.

"You'd like to give me a snack right now?" she asked, surprised.

"Yeppers, I would." He thought of the pleasure before him.

"Too bad, you get packed instead!" Rebecca sounded off as she slapped his ass with her hand, making a loud crack in the now-quiet camp.

"Damn, girl!" He walked off, rubbing his rump in a fake pain.

As he walked toward the horses, he noticed how fat they had gotten from the lack of exercise and the abundance of thick green grass from the meadow. He put his hand on his mare, she turned to nuzzle him.

"Rebecca, bring that curry brush over please will ya? Ya know the one we use fer the these cuyuse's? These horses ain't been brushed since we got here. Been too busy slipping the wood to you minks."

She produced the brush from their kit. As she walked to Billy, she looked at him holding the mare's foreleg. *What a man, not much of a knife fighter, but I can't wait until he used his root on me or his golden tongue for that matter.* She could feel her nipples rubbing her dress as she closed the gap between her and Bill.

"Here ya go, Bill." He stuck his hand out without turning his head. She lifted her dress, slipping the handle into herself, letting it dangle like an obscene penis.

"Here ya go Bill!" she said in a firm voice. Now he looked over to see where the brush was.

"Good lord woman!" He dropped the leg as he reached for her. Laying her down slowly so as not to have the brush fall out, he made sure her dress wouldn't drop back down.

"What's going on here?" White Moon questioned in false accusation.

"I'm going to handle her." Bill smiled, not taking his eyes off her.

"Well, I'll see if she's hungry for some wet Pawnee!" White Moon lowered herself onto Rebecca's face. Her dress covered all that was happening. Bill worked the handle in and out as White Moon received her pleasures. It was too much for the white girl. Her hand went to the button of life and began to rub it with veracity. It seemed like an instant of rubbing when she went stiffer than a stretched beaver dollar. Bill pulled out the slippery handle as White Moon continued to be serviced. Seeing Rebecca's garden open, she leaned over to continue to pleasure her partner. Bill watched over his shoulder as he worked on the horses. When the last one was done, each woman lay on her back hand in hand, breathing slowly, eyes closed as the warm day continued.

"You're not leaving without me small one." Thabo spoke as Bill was saddling the brown mare.

"What? I know'd you's freeman, but coming with us?" Bill asked as the girls set up looking at each other. They quickly got to their feet and approached Bill and the big black man.

"Rebecca, meet Thabo." Bill said as Thabo smiled.

"Louis don't ya mean?" She quizzed him

"I was Jonah on the riverboat." He tried to jar her memory.

"I thought you looked familiar. You the same nigger that tried to kill my Bill last summer?" she accused the Zulu.

"Yes. That was a long time ago. He has saved me several times since then. I owe him my life. I will be his guardian until my debt is paid off." he spoke solemnly, making sure the redhead understood the seriousness of his words.

"You gonna be with us from now on?" she asked.

"Yes." he answered back emotionless.

"He's welcome fer me, biggest pecker I've ever seen." White Moon smiled at the huge black man.

"What's with you niggers an' your big dicks?" Rebecca asked.

"Do all niggers have horse-sized cocks or what?" she asked, her hands on her hips, looking into his black eyes.

"Not all men can go three or four times in a row. Some of us just go once. But it's an unforgettable once." He laughed.

"I believe you'll do just fine. You got a gun or any gear?" she continued.

"No. All Mr. Sublette gave me was a horse and saddle. I have nothing else. But I can learn, and I can work." he spoke, his eyes searching for some approval.

"You'll do just fine, Louis, or what do you want to be called?" White Moon asked.

"My name is Thabo Mbekiuki, but I like Louis. So I will be Louis." He smiled shown his perfect white teeth.

"I'll fetch him one of our extra guns an' I'll be sure to get him all set up, with a good knife an 'hawk as well." Rebecca assured Bill.

"White Moon, you an' me are gonna finish these horses."

"Sure thing Bill." She went about the business of getting the horses ready for traveling.

The morning was gone, and the afternoon sun was already racing toward the western tree line.

"Let's get. I'm glad we got all that extra supplies from the tradin'. Billy Sublette was sure kind to us, eh, lover?" They rode away toward the ridge they had come in on. There above the rendezvous they stopped one last time. Rebecca started shedding clothes faster than a dog shedding his winter coat. All she had on was her leggings by the time Bill had finished his small pipe of tobacco.

"Well, what do you think, Louis? Think you could get useta traveling with naked women?" he asked without taking his eyes off White Moon, who had shed her hot clothes.

"Yes. I can get used to this very easily." He smiled as he admired White Moon's perfect figure. The rendezvous was far from over, but the trappers would soon be back to the mountains and the cold streams in hunt of the elusive flat tails that had brought them together.

"To the Yellerstone, girls." With that they walked out, heading north.

The adventure continues with Bill, Rebecca, White Moon and Thabo in

All That Glitters

CHAPTER 1

Billy White, Rebecca, White Moon, and Louis left the lush ponderosa pine trees that lined the Cache Valley in northern Utah. Louis was leading the packhorses carrying all the belongings Bill and Rebecca had acquired by trapping for the fall of 1825 and the spring of the following year. It took two horses to haul all the trapping supplies to ply their trade as fur trappers. Billy White pointed their noses north to Idaho, Wyoming, and Montana.

They had made it to their first rendezvous. The unlikely threesome had gone through hell and high water together. Now they had a new partner to share the adventure with; Louis, a runaway, freed slave Bill had met on the death boat in the year 1825. Bill, Louis, and Rebecca had jumped ship together to escape certain death that was following them on the small paddleboat, the *Alice Mae*.

When Thabo, now called Louis, had tried to drown Bill, the runt stabbed him, leaving him to the mercy of the Mississippi River. But their trails had crossed in the months to follow. Bill had saved the Zulu several times since then. Now the tall black man was indebted to the runt for the rest of his life.

Bill sat on the same brown mare he had since the first days in Missouri. The same one Ann, Mary Beth, and Rebecca had bartered for in the early summer of 1825. In all those days he had never thought to name the creature that carried him from the flatlands of Missouri to the ragged mountains of Utah. Looking at the back of the animal's head, he watched her ears flick one at a time as flies and gnats would pester the lumbering creature.

He pondered aloud as they rode out, "Doggone we done seen beaucoup gettin' to that rony'viou, eh, girls? Been more fun if'n I hadn't got all cut up. Like to have got in a shootin' match." Bill continued to ramble though neither one of the girls were paying attention to him.

"Most likely a good thing 'cause I'd probably lost my ass. Now, Rebecca, you coulda cleaned up." he spoke without turning his head to the fiery redheaded woman that sat off to his side. She sat on her gelding with one leg hooked over the horn, exposing her red briar patch. She was naked except for her leggings and moccasins. Bill had been oblivious to her forwardness all morning. His mind seemed too occupied with the past events to even notice her advances.

"But the wrestlin' match was fun. I wonder if'n we'll bump inta Bridger or Jed Smith in some beaver pond. Damn, them streams is cold." Bill changed topics quicker than a bat plucking mosquitos out of the pitch black of night. White Moon sat straight in her saddle. She was dressed the same as Rebecca as she was watching the horizon when she could see it. She knew the land they were traveling to was no place to become comfortable with. The Utes didn't mind the white men roaming their land, but they disliked the Pawnee with the same hatred the Sioux had for the Shoshone. There were many dangers that couldn't be seen as she let Bill chatter away like a lark as they headed north to the land of the Blackfoot, Crow, Flatheads, and yes the slap tails they wanted so badly.

"They's good trappers. Clay reminded me a lot of our late friend Daniel." He looked over to the white girl that had been with him for nearly two years. No response. Then he noticed her red hair showing, smiling to her. Then he licked his lips thinking of the snack he could be having instead of moving north. Reality came back to him as a fly buzzed his ear. Swatting at it, he continued,

"Damn. That nigger was kilt a horrid death. Them rotten

Arapaho sumbitches! They can all rot in hell fer all I care. Ya know, I heard that they was the death of white folks all over. Accordin' to that there Billy Sublette, them Hudson Bay niggers have 'em in their pockets. They do all their killin fer 'em. Chasin' off us free trappers. We'll see how that goes this fall. We gotta get there yet."

A gloom quickly came over Bill. The young lad had fits of depression that would last a few minutes or a few days. Rebecca and White Moon had lost interest in cheering him up. They just left him to his own accord. He would perk up when he got ready, but it made traveling with him more entertaining. They would gamble when and what would set him in or take him out of the gloom that seemed to follow the small brigade.

Rebecca thought of the Pawnee beside her as they plodded along the edge of the red canyons. Her lover's skin was a tawny brown from being exposed to the sun continually. The shape of her breasts and her straight long coal-black hair reflected the morning sun. She loved this Pawnee woman like no other woman. Ann, the hell bitch, had taken her heart a year or so ago, but this Pawnee woman had revived her passion for women like no other.

Bill snapped out of the gloom in a few minutes.

"Be sharp, girls. It's prime ambushin' country. These here trees are thicker than ticks on a badger. It appears to me if'n we could hook up with some other free trappers, well, we might have a better chance of gettin' through the country. I do remember Two Sticks sayin' that the Flatheads were friends to us 'Mericans. Bridger was in tight with 'em. Glad we got a place to winter up." Bill spoke softly to the young girls that traveled at his side.

They were both excellent shots with the bow, and Rebecca could hold her own with a long rifle too. Lord, help the poor soul that pulls a knife on Rebecca. She was smoother than silk and as dangerous as a cornered wolverine.

The scenery was magnificent as they wove through the cedar and ponderosa pines. The sun's brightness reflected off the jagged cliffs dotted with mesquite and scrub oaks as the morning wore on. The thought of being ambushed brought him back to reality.

"I'm happier than a pecker in a pussy to know you got all schooled on shooting." he spoke as he looked at the Pawnee woman.

"Don't worry, she has taught me. Hope you don't mind. We had'to have something to do while you was a healin' up. I can shoot just fine, but that goddamned gun was too fuckin' heavy for me. One of the men that worked for Sublette made one of ours shorter for me so I can hold it up better. I traded him for the work." Then she giggled.

"You weren't supposed to tell him until later." scolded Rebecca. Then they both giggled.

"Oh, you traded him. Like back when you all traded fer these here horses?" young Bill asked with a tang of jealousy.

"Okay, Bill, we were gonna surprise you later. Here." Throwing her leg over the horn to sit correctly, she rummaged through an elk skin pouch hanging from her saddle. Then carefully she pulled out a beautiful French pistol, handing it across to the small trapper.

"Oh my god! This's too much fer words. It's so purty. This really shines. How in blue blazes of hell did you manage this?" Bill asked flabbergasted as he stroked the ornate hammer and sculpted wood stock. He looked at the hammer. It was a dragonhead; the flint was being held in its mouth. The lock had an impressive engraving on it of a boar and bear fighting. He turned it around, admiring the flintlock pistol, as the sun would reflect sporadically off the shiny metal. Rebecca lifted her leg back up once again, exposing the playground of her lover and husband.

"The smithy had heard of you. So when Moon said she wanted a gun shortened so she could shoot, well, he did all the work. You ain't gonna believe this. Champeau killed his friend. He was fixing to do in Champeau, but Sublette told him that he couldn't do it while he was collecting wages from him, or he'd let 'em go. Martin, that's the smithy's name, said he had to have the wages for his family, so he had to let it go or not be employed. It was a sticky situation to be truthful. Somehow, he had got that gun from a Frenchman. Now, he didn't say how he happened to get it, and I didn't ask either. Anyway he said you could have it for doing in that bastard. He got his pay for the work on White Moon's gun though." Then she winked at the bronze maiden as they giggled

"I suppose you had some fun with 'em?" Bill smiled through his blond beard.

"Yeppers, we did. Now, Bill, before you fly off the handle, let me tell you this. It was just work. It didn't mean nothin' to either one of us. It was a way to get the gun shortened so she could at least defend herself. The twenty bucks you had left wouldn't do us much anyway. So I spent it all buying some things for White Moon and me. We can trade the beads and such things later on when we get in to a pinch."

As she was talking, Bill thought of the bartering, *sex was a currency, yep, just a means of payment out here. Those men may be married, but they have needs.*

"Most likely, you minks screwed the hell outta him. Shit, he was probably happy to give the gun up after you forked him three ways to Sunday." Bill teased the girls, letting them think he was upset.

"Did ya show him some of yer tricks?" He smiled at her. He could see the relief on her face as he spoke.

"Only poked him straight out Bill. He was so fast I just touched his pod and he went off. Poor guy only had one squirt in him. Makes me glad we got you." She laughed, winking at White Moon.

"Bill, in my village, a woman will screw a shitload of men before she figures out which one will satisfy her in the robes and bring food to the lodge. In some tribes a man may have more than one wife, like you. But there are some that will not put up with such behavior. Then the man will cut off his wife's nose if she is not true to him. I met a goddamned Cheyenne with no nose. She was an old woman, but I could tell that she had been very beautiful.

I'm happy you didn't cut the redheaded slut of a whore's nose off." Then she turned her attention back to the trail ahead of them.

"Thank you very fucking much Moon." Rebecca called over her shoulder. Bill sat quietly, looking at the walls of red that shone through the trees.

"Well, the pistol's a very nice gift. Thank you both." he spoke softly to them as he tucked it under his wide belt. She quickly went on with information about the handsome pistol.

"It's a special fifty four caliber. Martin made it like that so as he could use the same molds as our rifles. We got the mold too. He showed me and White Moon things about making the balls so we wouldn't waste very much lead." She was still defending herself. She knew she was rambling now but felt the need to keep talking.

"Lookie here. I ain't mad at ya. Okay, I'm happy ya got to learn stuff. Shit, ya can show me sometime." Bill looked at her as he watched her expression. Her jaw unclenched as she relaxed.

"Honest? Ya ain't pissed?" she quizzed, looking directly into the deep-blue eyes of the small blond trapper.

"Nah, I was jus' hacking on ya." he confided as he watched again as the flies pestered his horse.

"You fucker." White Moon called to Bill's back.

"Yeppers. Let's look for a place to make camp fer the night."

After the subject had been dropped, they rode on in silence. Looking at the magnificent scenery around them, they plodded north toward the Yellowstone River.

They moved effortlessly through the escarpments of breathtaking scenery of plateau after plateau; butte after butte came and went from sight. The evening wind blew gently, causing White Moon's hair to flutter like the delicate feathers of a jay or swallow.

"Did ya talk to anybody 'bout us goin' north an' all?" he asked.

"I told Billy Sublette where we were going. He introduced me to Jed Smith. He told me all about Yellowstone. Says there was a man named Colter who found the whole place back in '17. Says they call it Colter's Hell 'cause it was bubbling with stink water and it's hot enough to boil a gopher. They figured he was smoking too much of tic-nick-nick until other trappers saw it. Then they believed him. There's water that comes shooting up through holes in the ground. Jed was telling me that we should get there just after the New Year if we trapped on the way. You know it's a huge area Bill. Not jus' a valley like we stayed in. There's buffalo, elk, grizzly bear, and deer. Shit! Just about everything we need to live out the winter. There's a catch. The Blackfoot live up there too, but we already knew that. I told Jed when we got to the Absaroka land we'd winter up with Iron Hand's tribe.

"The Crow I've met from the Absaroka's were good-enough people, but it was only one family. I don't know why they were so south, though, but that's where I met them." White Moon chimed in the conversation. The young Pawnee stretched, arching her back, jutting her chest out.

"Well, girls, looks like we're on our way." Bill called over his shoulder. "You reckon we'll have a good row of it up north?" No response from either girl.

"How about you, Louis?" Bill turned to ask the newest member of his brigade.

"I've only heard what Mr. Sublette had spoken about. I don't really know much more than that. He said that the north had good fur. Mr. Smith knew a great amount, but he never addressed me directly. Sounds about the same thing as Moon heard." the black man spoke eloquently.

"Goddamn, Louis, ya can sure talk good. Billy Sublette teach ya how to use all them words all smooth like?" White Moon turned in her saddle to address the man pulling the supply horses.

"Yes, he did. I'm mighty grateful too. He says folks will respect me more if I don't talk like a nigger slave. Seems to work because when guests would come to visit, they treated me fairly, not at like the others I've been associated with." Louis remembered the slave traders that had caught him back in the Missouri Territory and how Bill had killed them all then set him free.

Now here he was with the small man and his two fine wives. Quietness filled the air as the foursome settled into a rhythm heading to the Yellowstone Valley. Bill led with Rebecca and White Moon, bringing up next. They rode side by side when the trail was wide enough, leaving the black man to bring up the rear. *I think I like my real name better than Louis or the name the owner gave me back on the paddleboat. This Jonah of their Bible didn't fit me.* Thabo's mind raced thinking of the best way to approach Bill.

"Billy." he called.

"Yeah?" Bill answered the ex-slave without turning his head.

"Thabo. My name is Thabo." The man called up to Bill's back.

"Well, make up yer fucking mind nigger." Rebecca turned to see his reaction; she expected a scowl but saw a toothy smile.

"I just did. Thabo." He just kept smiling.

"All right then. Thabo." she continued to harass the man.

"Shit, nigger. I'll call ya whatever I want."

"Yes, I'm sure you will." he answered, looking at her long red hair cascading down her back as she lost interest in verbally abusing the man. The brigade rode north away from the white men they had fun with, the ones that had drunk themselves into stupors, vomited and fought other over nothing. Bill watched the scenery pass by.

About the Author

I've always been intrigued by the fur trappers of 1800's. The rough life of the mountain man appealed to me, as did the challenges that these frontiersman faced.

I come for a family of hunters and trappers. I dipped my foot into mountain man reenactment. I dressed as

Billy White. Yes, throwing tomahawks and knives, shooting muzzleloader long guns, pistols, and bow and arrows. In addition to fire starting with flint and steel, I have learned how to trap, field dress critters, and construct a lean-to for shelter. I made my own buckskins leggings to protect me while hunting.

I've always been an adventurous person. Upon discharge from the Navy, I stayed in San Diego. I used my frontier reenactment knowledge to plan off-road mountain bike adventures; leading groups of 5-10 riders on 30+ mile off-road adventures throughout California, Utah, Arizona and Baja Mexico.

About the Book

The story of young man's dream of being a mountain man. Billy White is struggling with an adventurous spirit, working hard on his parents' farm. But wanderlust gets the best of Billy, and he leaves his old life behind and heads west to fulfill his dreams.

Billy's travels take him through all means of adventures and romances. Billy's eye for women gets him in trouble more often than not.

He travels on a flat boat, steamship paddleboat, and horseback to get to the mountains while his lust for women never stops as he heads west. There's a new adventure at every turn of his journey.